YOUR SIGNAL IS CHARLEY

A NOVEL

BY

RON RYPEL

Your Signal Is Charley

ISBN: 1-934035-23-8
ISBN-13: 978-1-934035-23-8

Cover Layout & Design
Ashley Spears
AES Graphics

Published by
Trent's Prints & Publishing
Chumuckla, Florida
www.trentsprints.com

DEDICATION

TO THOSE WHO FLY

Pilot Officer Gillespie Magee met death in his Spitfire in the skies over England in December, 1941. Magee was a Canadian serving in the Royal Canadian Air Force. He was just nineteen years old when he died. A few months earlier, he wrote this beautiful and poignant poem about the wonder of flight. Jack Rooney might have said, "I am not fond of poems, but this one goes straight to my heart."

HIGH FLIGHT

Oh! I have slipped the surly bonds of earth
And danced the skies on laughter-silvered wings;
Sunward I've climbed, and joined the tumbling mirth
Of sun-split clouds -- and done a hundred things
You have not dreamed of -- wheeled and soared and swung
High in the sunlit silence. Hov'ring there
I've chased the shouting wind along, and flung
My eager craft through footless halls of air.
Up, up the long delirious, burning blue,
I've topped the windswept heights with easy grace
Where never lark, or even eagle flew --
And, while with silent lifting mind I've trod
The high untresspassed sanctity of space,
Put out my hand and touched the face of God

Pilot Officer Magee
No. 412 Squadron, RCAF
Killed December 11, 1941

This book is dedicated to Pilot Officer Magee and all those friends and fellow-airmen who have fallen while taking on the challenge of flight.

May they rest in peace.

Skyraider at sunset

The Rypels of Various Places

About the Author

Like Harry Ferguson, Ron Rypel was born and raised in Milwaukee. He holds, from Marquette University, a Civil Engineering degree which he never used. He joined the Navy in 1955. That led to a flying career, of which the first twelve years were as a Navy pilot. His Naval service included one year in Saigon, during which President Diem was assassinated, duty as a flight instructor at the Naval Air Station in Meridian, Mississippi, and seven months on the USS Kitty Hawk in the Tonkin Gulf, where he flew 94 combat missions. He left the Navy in 1967.

As an airline pilot, he flew for nine different companies (eleven, if you count two of them twice). All but two were abroad. He worked in Europe, the Middle East, and the Far East. He retired from Air Malta in 1993. He and his wife, Irene, live in Milwaukee during the summer, and spend the winter months in Malta.

Irene is a lovely Belgian lady from Antwerp. She and the author met during a flight to Rio de Janeiro from Brussels. Their son, Van, born in Antwerp, was commissioned from the U.S. Naval Academy in 1997. He, too, is a Navy pilot and he flew F14 Tomcats from the USS Constellation during Operation Iraqi Freedom in 2003.

Synopsis

Your Signal is Charley opens with a night combat mission from the USS Kitty Hawk in the Tonkin Gulf. The pilot is Harry Ferguson, who does his best to follow the Rules of Engagement, despite their absurdity. Difficulties in following them are described. The no-win policy promotes among pilots, including Harry, a goal of survival rather than victory. It leads to Harry's resignation from the Navy.

He finds a job in New York with an airline which goes bankrupt. A phone call leads to a start-up company in Oslo, Norway. He flies to Australia, from where he hauls a load of Merino sheep to Moscow. Labor unions, led by Robert Hawke, who later became Prime Minister, try to prevent the sheep from leaving because they are unique to Australia. Harry is castigated daily on the front pages of the Sydney Morning Herald, which labels him "The Norwegian Ram Runner." Harry falls in love with Astrid, a Norwegian flight attendant.

From Brussels, on a flight to Rio de Janeiro, he meets Irene, who later becomes his wife. Harry carries religious pilgrims to Jeddah from Africa. Brewing tea over an open fire in the airplane cabin is one of many unusual and interesting problems he faces.

Harry is sent to Saudi Arabian Airlines in Jeddah, where he learns the character of the Saudis and the difficulties in working with them. He flies to places such as Ouagadougou in Burkina Faso, and to Mogadishu, with the President of Somalia, who invites him to an unusual lunch in the jungle. Sent for several months to a Beirut-based company, he arrives as a civil war breaks out.

Caught in a Saudi Arabian financial downdraft, Harry's contract is ended and he finds a job in Malta. It becomes a home for his family. Their son, Van, becomes a Navy pilot and flies F14 Tomcats from the USS Constellation during Operation Iraqi Freedom.

Harry and Irene meet The Connie on her arrival in Pearl Harbor and, as Tigers, travel to San Diego on the ship as guests of the Navy. Harry returns to San Diego, where his Navy career began.

AUTHOR'S NOTES

This novel might best be described as autobiographical fiction. It is based on my experiences, first, as a Navy pilot, then, while flying airliners. Most of what follows involved me or someone I knew. The experiences are recalled as well as my memory -- reaching back, at times, five decades -- allows. Some of the flight events were handed down as part of the lore of Naval Aviation. They might have been embellished or altered as they were passed down, one pilot to another, across the years. As far as I know, they are true.

The evolution of Harry Ferguson as a person is basically my own; his thoughts and observations are mine, too. Some of the personal events have been re-shaped and re-arranged, in time or place, to fit the constraints of a book and the story it tells. They, too, are basically true. Invention and imagination have been used at times to make the book fit together. Most of the names are fictitious, but a few are real.

I wish you bon voyage on your flight through Harry's life and times.

Ron Rypel
Milwaukee
November, 2006

TABLE OF CONTENTS

BOOK TWO

1
PEARL

May 2003

The angled rays of the early morning sun slanted across the blue-green waters of Pearl Harbor, glinting off the ships of the fleet nestled there. One of those ships was making her way towards Pier Hotel, her movement barely perceptible. Harry Ferguson and his wife wound through the throng gathering at the foot of the pier. As they did, they kept glancing towards the giant ship silently gliding into her berth alongside the pier. The ship was the USS Constellation and she was returning from the Persian Gulf, where she had taken part in Operation Iraqi Freedom. Among the five thousand crewmen on board the Connie was their son, an F14 Tomcat pilot. They had not seen Van for many months and now they had come halfway around the world to see him step down onto the pier. Harry's wife could not hold back her tears and Harry himself had difficulty controlling his emotions.

As a Navy pilot, Harry had once flown from ships like this one. It had been many years since he had been on a carrier and he had forgotten how enormous were these great ships. The Connie loomed ever larger as she closed with the pier and settled into her berth. Harry watched as the ship's lines were thrown down to the pier and secured to large iron cleats there. Very soon, the brow would be put in place and the crew would begin to leave the ship. His pulse began to quicken.

Memories of Harry's own service on board the USS Kitty Hawk flooded across his mind. That service was thirty-seven years ago, but those memories were still vivid. He could still smell the jet fuel, still hear the catapults flinging airplanes into the sky, still feel the gentle roll of the ship as the sea tried to have its way with her. Those memories might fray around the edges, but they would always be there. They were the memories of a lifetime, experiences which could never be understood by someone who had not gone through them. You had to be there.

NIGHT LAUNCH
November 1965

There was a word, actually three words compressed into one, that Harry Ferguson didn't like and rarely used; never within earshot of others and seldom even to himself. He said it only in moments of stress or frustration. An errant shot on the golf course might provoke it, or perhaps dropping a drink he had just mixed. It seemed to capture certain feelings in just the right way, at just the right moment. Now, taxiing his A4 Skyhawk onto the Number 2 catapult seemed as good a time as any.

"Goddammit," he mumbled softly into his oxygen mask as he peered over the nose of the aircraft and followed the signals of the plane director. It was a moonless, overcast night, and he could see only the faint amber glow of his instrument panel and the illuminated wands of the director. *What am I doing here?*

"Here" was the flight deck of the USS Kitty Hawk, which was gently slicing through the South China Sea as she turned into the wind before flinging off the first of eighteen aircraft poised for this night launch. In the cockpit, Harry could feel the slight list of the deck as the ship turned; then he felt the great ship level herself as she settled onto the launch course.

The wands slowly guided his aircraft into position, straddling the cat track. He inched the plane ahead until he saw the wands cross in an X, then gently applied his brakes and smoothly stopped the aircraft. He felt the plane wobble ever so slightly and he knew that back there in the dark, someone was attaching a cable to the rear of the plane. This was the holdback cable which connected the plane to the flight deck and which would prevent the plane from moving forward until the moment was right.

Now, the wands began moving again, slowly, slowly, and he responded by releasing the brakes and cautiously adding power, moving his plane forward until he felt the tug of the hold-back cable. Now, he knew, a crew would fix cables from a point beneath each wing to a shuttle in the catapult track. The cables formed a slanted "V" and, in a few moments, the shuttle, connected to a powerful steam-driven piston beneath the track, would accelerate Ferguson and his aircraft from a standstill to 125 knots in a distance of just 250 feet. The sensation would be almost like that of an orgasm.

Earlier, before finding his airplane, Ferguson had stopped at Flight Deck Control. It was at flight-deck level in the forward part of the island superstructure. Atop a pedestal in the center of the space, a scale outline of the flight deck was etched into its metal top. On it were metal cutouts of each aircraft, cut to scale, showing its position as it was on the flight deck itself. This was the nerve center of the flight deck. All planes scheduled for tonight's launch were listed here on a large vertical sheet of plexiglass. Written next to each plane was its takeoff weight. The weight of the airplane determined the power at which the catapult would be set to provide the needed end-speed. It had to be right.

After checking the weight noted next to his airplane, Harry stepped out into the blackness that enveloped the flight deck and made his way to his plane. This was, some pilots thought, the most hazardous part of a night launch. That was because avoiding vehicles and aircraft tie-down cables was not easy in the dark. He had often suffered knocks and bruises just getting to his plane. He had learned to wear his flight helmet during his search.

The positions of the planes had been passed to the pilots before they left the Ready Room. Harry knew the location; it was getting there that was a problem. Tonight, he had been lucky; the plane was right where it was supposed to be and he got there unscathed. So far, so good, he thought. Now, he found his way to the nose gear. There, just above the strut on a panel that would close after the gear retracted, Harry found a rectangular outline. In it, using his flashlight for illumination, Harry wrote with a grease pencil the takeoff weight of his plane. This would vary with the fuel load and the amount of ordnance loaded beneath the aircraft. Tonight, he would carry a full fuel load and enough bombs to bring his total weight to 22,500 pounds, the maximum allowable takeoff weight for the Skyhawk.

Using his flashlight, Harry had then inspected the entire exterior of his airplane, checking movement of the flight surfaces as he did. The plane captain, an enlisted man assigned to check the plane and assist the pilot during the pre-start routine, had already done this. All was in order and Harry climbed the small ladder that fit neatly into the side of the airplane. It would be removed after Harry hoisted himself into the cockpit. With the help of the plane captain, Harry strapped himself in. Actually, he connected himself to the backpack parachute that was already in place. He attached his oxygen hose to the plane's system, plugged in his radio cord and went through his pre-start checklist. He waited for the announcement over the flight deck loudspeaker to start engines. It had been heard for decades and it was always the same. "Now check all chocks, tie-downs and loose gear about the deck. Stand by to start engines." When the command was given to "Start engines," Harry signaled by hand to his plane captain who, with an external air compressor, sent high-pressure air into the plane's engine and it began to rotate. At a certain rpm, Harry brought the throttle "around the horn" to provide fuel and ignition. The engine then "lit off" and became self-sustaining. He signaled the plane captain to remove the compressor air.

Next came the tricky part, and that was to taxi to the catapult. Harry had to place himself under the complete control of the taxi directors as they signaled with illuminated wands and slowly brought his airplane to the area just aft of the catapult. These signals were a "come ahead" motion with both wands, a single wand pointed at a wheel, which was a signal to touch that brake to make a turn, or wands crossed into an "X." That meant stop. Both wands pointed in the same direction meant that control was passed to another taxi director. Following these signals, Harry had carefully made his way forward to the catapult. He had watched intently as the airplane ahead of his moved onto the catapult track.

As it passed a certain point, as if by magic, a large rectangle had appeared behind it. This was the jet blast deflector. It was normally stowed flush with the flight deck and its purpose was to deflect the jet blast upward as the airplane turned up its engine to takeoff power. Jet blast was a constant hazard on the flight deck and it was not unusual for a careless sailor to be blown overboard. He had once seen a crewman blown under a spinning propeller, saved only because he was flat on his back as he slid beneath it. Now, fascinated, Harry watched as the airplane ahead was slung off the deck with a roar and was almost instantly swallowed by the night. The blast deflector disappeared back into the deck, allowing Harry to taxi over it. Following the wands, Harry slowly inched into position over the catapult track. Now, it was his turn.

As he set himself for the catapult shot, Harry glanced to his right and saw the plane of his flight leader, John Dawson, dimly outlined on the Number 1 catapult. John would go first. Harry turned his attention back to the plane director who indicated with his wands that Harry was now under the control of the catapult officer. For the tenth time, he checked his instruments. All were normal.

Next, with his left hand, he extended a small lever from the side of the cockpit. It had been held by a spring in the vertical position against the side of the cockpit wall. When its top was pulled down, it would align neatly with the throttle when it was at full power. Both would be grasped tightly with his left hand. This connection to the airplane would keep the throttle from moving aft out of the full power position when the plane was thrown forward into flight. A friction lock was supposed to prevent this, but you never knew.

Now, Harry heard John's engine as it wound up to full takeoff thrust. He could feel the vibrations. From the corner of his eye, he saw John's wing tip navigation lights suddenly illuminate. This was the ready signal. Until he saw these lights, the catapult officer, known as Shooter, would not initiate the catapult stroke. Seconds later, in a roaring flash, John's aircraft hurtled down the track, left the flight deck, and disappeared into the black. It happened so quickly that it seemed not to have happened at all.

In the daytime, the ready signal was a smart salute by the pilot. In either case, once the throttle was at full power, the pilot was committed to launch. Under no circumstances, would he retard his throttle once the ready signal was given. That was because he did not want to be launched unexpectedly with his power less than full. That would mean a very short flight, one that ended in the sea just ahead of the ship. But, now and then, it became necessary. This might happen if, for some reason, the catapult was not ready to shoot, or if the launch was suddenly cancelled. In these situations, the catapult officer would disable the catapult, then stand in front of the airplane and give the signal to throttle back. The pilot could then be sure that it was safe to bring his throttle to idle.

On Harry's first cruise, an Air Force exchange pilot had the habit of saluting and then lowering his helmet's sun visor. He did this one day to discover with alarm that he had forgotten to remove the felt liner from the visor. So there he was, unable to see, at full power with one hand on the throttle and the other on the control stick and terrified to remove either one as he thought he was about to be shot off the bow. The alert catapult officer noticed the predicament and disabled the catapult. Since the pilot could not see, the cat officer advised the Air Boss to inform the pilot by radio that it was safe to raise his visor. When he did, he saw the cat officer standing in front of his airplane, doubled over with laughter.

Now, glancing down to the port side of his plane, Harry saw a crewman holding an illuminated slate board on which was written the weight of his plane. He checked the figure and confirmed it by shining his flashlight on his raised left thumb. "Weight OK," it said. Now, with his wands, the plane director passed control of Harry's plane to the Cat Officer, who raised one wand into the air and made a circling motion. He was asking for full power. Harry slowly pushed his throttle forward and then grasped the lever so that he held both the lever and the throttle in his grip.

This was it. Harry made sure the engine was at full thrust, checked his instruments one last time and placed the back of his helmet firmly against the headrest. That would prevent his head from being thrown backwards as the airplane was thrust forward. He looked straight ahead, took a deep breath, then flicked a toggle switch that turned on his wing lights. The catapult officer saw the ready signal, took one step forward and dropped to one knee as he inscribed in the air a slow, sweeping arc of yellow, ending with his wand pointing towards the bow. The launch signal.

With a great *whoosh*, Harry was propelled down the track, his back compressed against the parachute pack behind it. He felt the plane leave the deck with a thump. At the same time, all visual references were lost. Now came the hard part. If everything had worked as advertised, Harry would leave the deck at 125 knots; plenty of flying speed, he knew. But the sudden acceleration left all the air pressure instruments useless for the first few seconds. The airspeed indicator and, more importantly, the vertical speed indicator, were fluctuating wildly. It was impossible to know for sure what the airplane was doing; so Harry did the only thing he could do: peering intently at the artificial horizon on his instrument panel, he eased the plane into a 12-degree nose-up attitude while holding his wings level. And he waited.

The flight deck was just 80 feet above the sea, so he did not have long to wait. If the plane did not hit the water in those first few seconds, the pressure instruments would start working and he would know what his plane was doing. In the daylight, the pilot could see what was happening. If something went wrong, a light cat shot for instance, and not enough flying speed, he could do something. But in those first few seconds, the only "something" was to eject. At night, he waited and he hoped for the best.

A week or so ago, squadron-mate Bud Johanson had gotten a light catapult shot and had almost instantly ejected. He was free of the aircraft almost before it was airborne. That had been in the daytime, and Harry had seen it on the closed-circuit TV in the Ready Room. Afterwards, during the replay, he had timed the interval between the launch of the plane and the splashdown. Three-and-a-half seconds. Not much time, but enough for Bud to realize his airplane would not fly that day and to pull the handle which blew the canopy up and away from the plane and blasted him out of the cockpit, still attached to his seat. Everything worked as it was supposed to. An inflated bladder separated Bud from the seat. The chute had opened seconds before Bud hit the water. The hovering helicopter, always airborne during flight operations, had plucked him out of the sea almost immediately and Bud had barely gotten wet. If that had happened during a night launch, he would be a dead man.

There is an old Navy adage called Murphy's Law. It says that if something can go wrong, it will go wrong. Just last week, an incredible coincidence occurred during the catapult launch of Andy Curley, one of Harry's squadron-mates. An airspeed indicator had been improperly secured during installation. During the cat stroke, it was thrown aft as the plane accelerated forward. In a one-in-a-million chance, the gauge struck a T-handle which ejected the canopy. In another one-in-a-million chance, the speed of the aircraft was such that the canopy smashed into the vertical stabilizer, shearing it from the fuselage. The plane was still controllable, so Andy dumped fuel to get below the maximum landing weight and brought his craft safely aboard.

One of many space problems on a carrier is that the launching aircraft are spotted throughout the landing area until they are airborne. Landing aircraft need to wait their turn. Another problem for Andy was that he had launched with a full fuel load. That meant he was too heavy for the landing. Because carrier airplanes are designed to land on a ship, landing above the design weight might, for example, rip the tail hook from the fuselage when it catches a cable. On a long airport runway, there would be no problem. It's that sudden stop that complicates landing on a ship.

Tonight, there was no problem. The catapult shot was normal, the critical few seconds passed and Harry's pressure instruments began giving him essential flight information. When a fully-laden Skyhawk was catapulted, it settled about 20 feet right off the bow, stabilized and very slowly began to gain airspeed and altitude. So, as a squadron-mate once put it, "No sweat. If you don't hear a big splash in the first couple of minutes, you're okay." There would be no splash on this flight, not yet anyway.

Harry had not been aware that he was holding his breath, but as the pressure instruments began to work and he saw his plane begin to climb slowly back up through 80 feet, he exhaled loudly into his mask. *Okay!* he thought, and reached forward to raise the landing gear lever which retracted the wheels. He heard the gear tuck in with a *thunk* and he kept his eyes riveted to the instrument panel, straining to scan them all as quickly as possible. Each one told a different story. Only after he passed 1,500 feet did he dare to lower the nose very slightly and begin to accelerate. Then he raised the flaps and, with a rush of excitement, was on his way.

John had briefed the flight to rendezvous at 20,000 feet and at 30 miles on a bearing of 030 from the ship. Now, Harry eased his craft into a right turn and took a heading which would intercept the 030 radial. To do this, he used his TACAN needle that pointed continuously towards the ship. At the same time, it provided distance information. Once he was on the radial, he flew outbound on it, checking his distance as he went. He cleared the clouds at 8,000 feet, and leveled at 20,000 feet, still glued to the radial.

He was always exhilarated to climb above the clouds at night and find himself in clear air with a sky full of stars. They were bright and shimmering, and they seemed to be everywhere. At sea, there was no other light, so the stars sparkled brilliantly. Harry gave himself only a few moments to enjoy the breathtaking view, then it was back to work, for now came the second hardest part of a night launch: joining in formation with his flight leader. Harry knew that John would be flying a circular pattern, making left turns. Harry looked out of the cockpit more often now, hoping to spot John's navigation lights. Because the port wingtip light was red and the starboard light was green, Harry would know whether John was flying inbound or outbound when he found the lights.

Join-ups at night are difficult, especially for inexperienced pilots. A new pilot, fresh out of the training command, was known as a "nugget." As a nugget on his very first night flight from a carrier, Harry had three vivid memories. One was the night catapult launch. In those days, the catapults were driven by hydraulic power and all of the force was applied instantaneously. Harry had been warned, but he was not prepared for the violent shock of the acceleration when he was fired off the bow. A few years later, thanks to the British, the catapults were steam driven and the acceleration was spread throughout the stroke, instead of all at once. This made life vastly more comfortable for carrier pilots.

The second memory was the rendezvous. He had been briefed to join on his flight leader, who happened to be his squadron skipper. As he neared the join-up point, he spotted his leader right where he was supposed to be and orbiting as briefed. But Harry, still somewhat disoriented from his nerve-jangling catapult experience, mistakenly read the CO's navigation lights as flying away from him while, actually, they were flying towards him. Harry passed directly beneath the skipper's plane flying in the opposite direction. Harry underwent a long and painful debrief after that flight.

Memory number three was the approach and landing. Harry lost his cockpit lighting system just as he entered the landing pattern. There were two instruments vital to a safe landing. One was the airspeed indicator and the other was the altimeter. Harry thought furiously for a minute or two, then pulled out his flashlight, turned it on, and stuck it between his thigh and the strap from the parachute pack that encircled it. By adjusting the position of his knee, he could shine enough light on these two instruments to allow him to monitor them and get aboard.

Tonight, the rendezvous worked out just right. As Harry neared the 30-mile mark, he saw John's lights flying outbound. It was tricky when the lead aircraft was headed towards the joining pilot. He clicked his mike button on the throttle and said, "Tally-ho." John replied with one word: "Roger." That meant he understood Harry's transmission. Harry checked his airspeed. It was essential to be right on the briefed speed of 360 knots so there would be minimum relative speed differential between the two planes. Harry measured John's turn, waited until the plane crossed in front of him, then banked to the left and turned until the other plane moved into a position about forty-five degrees to the right of Harry's nose. This was the rendezvous bearing. Now, by increasing or decreasing his bank angle, Harry kept John's plane on the same relative bearing. He was, in effect, turning away from John or towards him, as the distance between them slowly closed. Nearing John's plane, he was already on nearly the same heading, and he needed to make only small changes to align himself with John.

During the join-up, Harry had let his airspeed increase somewhat. As he approached within a few plane-lengths, he realized he had too much speed. He quickly pulled back his throttle and adjusted his bank to match John's. He added the power he had just taken off, and flew just aft and under John's airplane. As he did, he increased his bank to stop the lateral relative motion and there he was, neatly tucked beneath John's wing and headed for Cambodia. The cloud layer beneath them diminished, then ended, as they neared the coastline. It was, he thought, a fine night for bombing.

2
NEW YORK

June 1970

Harry Ferguson blinked and squinted as he walked out of his apartment building onto East 80ᵗ Street and into the sunlight. His apartment was a void sculpted from steel and concrete with almost no connection to the outside world. He always referred to it as, "my Big Apple cave." There was only one window and it looked out on more windows like his own. He never saw the sun unless he went outside and, even then, he had to be lucky. It had to be the right time of day and even, sometimes, the right time of the year before sunlight's shafts could reach into the caverns between the city's giant buildings and find the sidewalks of New York. That was a part of life in Manhattan that he would never get used to.

Harry nodded to the doorman and turned west along 80ᵗ Street. He was headed for Central Park and he was wearing jogging clothes, which, for Harry, meant a sweatshirt, old pants, and tennis shoes. Harry always went jogging when he needed to think and the Central Park reservoir was the only place in town for that. For Harry, New York offered the best and the worst of big-city life, and now Harry began enjoying part of the best. That was simply walking along the streets of Manhattan and looking at the people passing by. There was no place like New York for people-watching, thought Harry, and a bright June morning was the best time to do it.

Back home in Milwaukee, on a day such as this, Harry would be on the golf course with old friends. Here in New York, thinking about a golf course was like thinking about outer space. They were out there, but they were expensive and hard to get to. He did not miss them. Manhattan had its own attractions, especially in the summertime. The one Harry liked best was the people.

There was always a colorful array of people on New York's sidewalks; but on a glorious morning like this one, it was the pretty girls in summer dresses who reached out and caught his attention. Harry had an eye for pretty women and now his heart melted as he watched them pass. They looked -- how best to describe them? -- "delicious" was the best word he could come up with. A pilot he sometimes flew with had nicely captured the appeal of a pretty woman. He was from Yugoslavia and his English was basic. But he neatly summed up in a few words how he felt about a pretty woman. "Ah," he said one day, as an especially pretty one boarded the airplane, "How is nice." Harry sometimes wondered if a woman realized how "nice" she often looked and how a simple movement, a curve of her body, a glimpse of her cleavage, or even something as ordinary as a bra strap, could trigger a man's feelings.

At the age of thirty-four, Harry was still an unlikely bachelor. He thought of himself as a one-woman man, so he treaded softly and carefully in relationships with women. He never turned away when opportunities came along, but he always looked at them with a long-term view. He disliked that about himself but "What can I do?" he asked himself. "That's me." He envied men who never thought farther ahead than a night in the sack. It happened for Harry now and then, but it was never by plan. It just happened. "So, a confirmed bachelor?" they would ask. "No," he would answer, "unconfirmed and still looking."

Harry was no Robert Redford, but he had other qualities that some women found attractive: straightforward, an easy grin, and a wry sense of humor. He was not tall -- he thought of himself as having a low center of gravity -- and that slowed him down somewhat. That was because social correctness dictated that the man should be taller than the woman. That was nonsense, he tried to convince himself; but he had to admit that most women seemed to agree. It was hard to argue with convention, so he usually sought out short women. He regretted that so many women were automatically eliminated just because they were taller than he, but that was how it was. Anyway, there were plenty of women shorter than he was. He just had to find them.

Finding them was not always easy. It was, for example, hard to judge a woman's height when she was sitting down. Harry, now and then, found himself gauging their height by analyzing the rest of their bodies. Long legs usually belonged to a tall woman. When he got it wrong, he might end up dancing with a woman taller than he. Some saw that he was shorter than they were and simply declined to dance. Harry didn't mind, as he knew the woman might feel uncomfortable. Those few inches of height made a difference far out of proportion to their meaning. They could actually change a person's life. That, thought Harry, was just not right.

Harry was from Milwaukee. For many, that was a statement about who he was. It was true, he thought, that those from the midwest had well-defined characteristics. Most were honest, friendly, generous, and well-connected to the real world. They called a spade a spade. They avoided idealism, flamboyance, and pretense. That was for folks from Florida, say, or perhaps California. Harry fit the template; take it or leave it. It took him some hard experience to learn that some people preferred to leave it. He eventually realized that you can't get the whole world to like you, so why bother to try? He did not make close friends easily; but once friendship was struck, it was forever. A friend could count on Harry.

3
SAN DIEGO

1965

He'd had a near miss in the months before he went to Vietnam. His squadron was based near Fresno in California's San Joachim Valley. Lemoore had offered little social life for bachelors. The few eligible women were in strong demand, and Harry did not like the odds. So he often visited San Francisco and San Diego during weekends. He had friends in both places and standing offers to stay with them.

During a visit to San Diego, he met Jeanne over a punch bowl at a party in La Jolla and for Harry, it was love at first sight. Maybe it was love at first sight of her smile, which was dazzling. Either way, Harry was lost when she offered her hand, beamed that smile, looked into his eyes and said, "Hello, I'm Jeanne." She was easy to talk to and that was always important to Harry. She was bright and pretty, and she seemed to like Harry. That surprised him.

He was always surprised when a pretty woman was attracted to him. It wasn't because of low self-esteem; it was because meeting women sometimes made him nervous. That probably came from trying too hard. When that happened, he did not make a favorable first impression. He never experienced such feelings when meeting men, and he wondered why that was. Once past that awkward stage, his relationships with women usually improved as they came to know the real Harry.

Jeanne had been favored with rich auburn hair which, along with her luminous green eyes, gave her an exotic look. High cheekbones accentuated that look. Dressed casually, she had an elegant look. Some women could wear anything and look good. She was trim and fit and her handshake was firm. Harry's first thought on taking her hand was that she was out of his depth. That reaction happened now and then, and it turned out not to be true most of the time. This was one of those times.

"Milwaukee!" she exclaimed, when Harry told her where he was from. "I've never met anyone from Milwaukee. I don't even know where it is." Harry smiled. Milwaukee was not big on the map.

"Just up the road from Chicago. You heard of Chicago?"

She wrinkled her nose. "Yes, even in California, we've heard of Chicago. But what's there? In Milwaukee?"

"Depends when you go," he answered. "Great in the summer, cold and snow in the winter."

She frowned ever so slightly. "Oh, I could never live in a cold place. How cold does it get?"

Testing, he replied, "Blue balls cold. And that's cold."

She laughed, her green eyes sparkling. "Yes, it certainly does sound cold. You must like our California sunshine. Not too boring, I hope, sunshine every day."

"You kidding? This kind of boring, I like. I'm still thawing out from Milwaukee. Too many winters there. It'll take years."

She smiled again and touched his arm. "Let me know if I can help."

"When can you start?" Harry asked impulsively.

"What? Start what?" she asked with a bemused expression.

Harry smiled. "You know, helping me thaw out. How about dinner tomorrow night?"

The next evening, they had dined at an Italian restaurant owned by a retired opera singer. They started with martinis. A friend had once told Harry never to trust anyone who did not drink. He was not sure if that applied to women, but he liked a woman who enjoyed a drink. The pasta was excellent. Over coffee, they had the good luck to hear the owner sing, "Happy Birthday" to a diner at a nearby table. The lights were turned off as he entered, carrying a small cake with a candle. Okay, Harry thought, it's only "Happy Birthday," but he had never before heard an operatic tenor. He was enthralled and it was not only the singing. Jeanne had a lot to do with it.

Driving home, he felt the spark between them growing brighter. It had started to glow during "Happy Birthday," when Jeanne reached across the table and took his hand. Parking in front of her house, he wondered how to manage that important first kiss. He was never good at that. Jeanne solved his dilemma by falling into his arms almost before he had turned off the engine. No clumsy fumbling, and that was a relief. The steering wheel bothered her and she said so.

"Why don't we move to the back?" she asked. Without waiting for an answer, she slithered over the seatback and into the rear seat. Harry, smiling broadly, quickly followed. It was much better without the steering wheel.

Despite being born and raised in California, Jeanne was down-to-earth, both feet firmly on the ground. A Catholic, she went to church "not every Sunday, but now and then." Did she believe? "Well, it's pretty hard to believe all those things in the Bible, but you have to believe in something. And I like the rituals, the singing, the incense. I feel good when I go to church."

That was good enough for Harry. He did not think he needed to be concerned about Jeanne trying to save his soul.

She had an enthusiasm for life that Harry envied. She loved to dance, and that was not Harry's strong suit. She put up with his best efforts and even found ways to compliment him now and then.

"Harry, you will never be another Fred Astaire, but I like the way you hold me," she had whispered in his ear during a dance. Like Harry, she was a long-time Frank Sinatra fan and if he needed another omen, here it was. She was a free spirit and some of that rubbed off on Harry. You could not pretend to be a free spirit; you had to be born that way. But you could enjoy it in others. And Harry did, every chance he got.

It was a long-distance romance, but sometimes those work best. Some said that absence makes the heart grow fonder. Others thought that "out of sight" meant "out of mind." For Harry, it depended upon the size of the fire. He likened absence to wind. It made big fires bigger, but blew out the small ones. For Harry and Jeanne, the times apart seemed to make those together more special than they might otherwise have been. Harry began spending every weekend in San Diego. Jeanne visited Lemoore once, and to Harry's surprise, she liked it.

"Okay, it's not La Jolla," she said with great understatement. "Not many places are. But I like the people. These Navy pilots are okay."

Jeanne described La Jolla as the home of the newly wed and nearly dead. Lemoore, she had said generously, was not very glamorous; but the Navy pilot community had energy and she liked that. "It lives," she had said, something that La Jolla did not always do.

Their relationship matured in a steady and comfortable way, always deepening, almost never disappointing. In 1965, sex was not expected, even among serious couples. Harry would never have even thought of going farther than passionate kissing, even when his juices started to flow. He ached to touch her breasts, but did not dare. That was the Catholic in Harry. The Catholic church could make anyone feel guilty about anything, especially if it was even distantly related to sex. Anyway, Harry preferred it that way, just in case Jeanne ended up as Mrs. Harry Ferguson. As the months passed, Harry had begun thinking of Jeanne in that way. But if you asked him why he preferred it that way, he would have had difficulty answering. It was just the way it was, no reason needed.

The moment of truth came as Harry was about to leave on the Kitty Hawk for the waters off Vietnam. The ship would leave from the jetty at the North Island Naval Air Station at Coronado, a short ferry boat ride from downtown San Diego. Harry's squadron moved aboard a week or so before the ship's departure. He spent every evening with Jeanne. The last night came quickly and he wanted that night to be special. He was not sure what he would say, but he thought it should be something meaningful. He did not want to lose her, but six months was a long time to be apart.

Complicating his thoughts was the possibility that he might not come back. The Navy was already losing airplanes in the Tonkin Gulf. Two pilots Harry knew had already been brought down over North Vietnam.

"Doesn't that scare you?" Jeanne had asked as they sat outside her house late one night.

"I know it should," he answered after a few moments, "but somehow it doesn't. I can't explain why. Just a feeling, but I suppose all of us have it. Otherwise, we'd look for a different line of work."

He told her the tale, known to all Navy aviators, about one-hundred pilots being briefed for a mission. So dangerous was this mission, they were told, that only one would survive. Each pilot looked at all the others and thought, "I sure am going to miss all you guys." That confidence is important to a pilot. Without it, he could not be a good pilot.

Harry remembered a placard prominently displayed in the hangar at Whiting Field in Milton, Florida where he had started flying. Flying, it read, is not inherently dangerous. But, like the sea, it is mercilessly unforgiving of human error. Harry knew he was a solid pilot. Not the best, perhaps, but confident and competent. And cool. Harry never felt panic in an airplane. Frustration and exasperation at times, and, now and then, anger. But never panic. He wondered why. Ordinary experiences sometimes brought him anxiety: speaking before a group, for example, or approaching a pretty girl in a bar. Everyday events sometimes caused his breath to quicken and his heart to race. That was unreasonable, Harry knew, but there it was, beyond his control. But in the cockpit, no matter how dire the situation, he remained calm. Perhaps it flowed from confidence. In an airplane, Harry was truly the master of his fate.

He had sold his car a few days before, so he borrowed one from a friend. It was a 1956 Thunderbird, and it was perfect for their last night together. They decided to drive to Tijuana, where Jeanne knew of a restaurant named Angel's that served "out of this world" margaritas. There was music and they danced while waiting for their dinner. It was one of those evenings Harry wished would never end.

On the way home, Jeanne had suggested stopping atop Mount Soledad, more a hill than a mountain, but offering a grand view of San Diego at night. The margaritas, the dinner, and the splendid view all came together in a way that went straight to Harry's heart and he was overcome by emotion. Should he propose right then and there? That had not been in his plans, but it surely seemed like a good idea at that moment. But what if he did not make it back? What then? Well then, ask her to wait. He was not sure what that meant, but it would be something, and better than nothing. He wanted her to know that he cared deeply. In the end, he said nothing.

Sensing the moment, Jeanne offered to visit the Kitty Hawk in the morning before the ship left. Harry surprised himself when he said no. Better to say goodbye here, he thought, after a wonderful evening and in such a beautiful setting. A nice memory while they were apart. Jeanne seemed disappointed, but said nothing. Harry would re-live that moment many times over the next few years and always with great, sometimes painful, regret. It might have all turned out differently if he had agreed to say goodbye on the ship. What he would have given to relive that moment! Harry would love again, but not with that same head-over-heels, mind-numbing exhilaration. A great love, but a different kind of love.

The ship's first stop was at Pearl Harbor six days later. Those six days gave Harry plenty of time to think about Jeanne. Just before reaching Hawaii, Harry sat down and wrote a letter from his heart. He wrote on paper the things he had been unable to say on Mount Soledad. They seemed easier to write than to say. And although he did not ask Jeanne to marry him, he made clear his feelings for her and asked her to wait for him, still unsure what that meant. He dropped the letter into a metal mailbox attached to a passageway bulkhead, and he held it over the slot for a minute or two before he let it go. He knew it was a letter that might change his life. He would remember the "thunk" the letter made when it hit the bottom of the empty box. He smiled as he heard it. That smile meant he had done the right thing.

No one knew why, but that letter never found its way to Jeanne. Harry waited anxiously for a reply to a letter Jeanne had never received, a letter she longed to read. On such things does a life sometimes turn. He would see Jeanne only twice after that magic evening. The first was on his return from Vietnam, when she told him she was engaged to be married.

"You must have known I loved you," Harry had said with disbelief.

"You never told me, and you never asked me to wait," was her teary answer, "and I never saw any letter."

Harry's reply was feeble. "I didn't think it was fair," he said with anguish. He did not mention that he had in his pocket a diamond engagement ring he had bought in Hong Kong. She would never know about that ring.

The second time was thirty-eight years later, when Harry visited San Diego with his wife. Jeanne was still lovely and attractive. For Harry, the spark was still there, but the exhilaration was gone. It had taken a long time.

4
LOOKING FOR WORK

California 1967

Finding a job had not been easy. A year earlier, the airlines were hiring pilots who had very little experience; but when Harry started looking, things had changed. First, he was too old for many companies. Some would not even talk to pilots over the age of twenty-eight. That reduced the possibilities considerably. To increase his chances, he had signed up for a three-day course in San Diego. It was geared to help prospective airline pilots pass the Stanine Exam, administered by a testing organization, and used by most airlines as a way to screen candidates.

In his small group was a brash and bright young man named Mike Roamer. Mike was handsome and outgoing and it was hard not to like him. He was a used car salesman with a few hundred hours of flight time in light airplanes. He was, he told Harry, determined to become an airline pilot and he would do whatever it took. That turned out to be a lot.

He had been placed on the interview list at a major airline, but he was far down that list. So he began dating the secretary who handled the interviewing process. With her help, he had been moved up near the top of the list. At the interview, he actually sold to the interviewer a used car at a bargain price. Next up for him was the Stanine Exam. This course would help him with that; but, to tilt the odds even more, he had scheduled a visit to Miami where, for $400, he would buy a copy of the exam.

Harry had to admire Mike's enterprise. There was more. He'd had calling cards printed which identified him as an executive with an airline in Hawaii. All dressed up and armed with his fake card, he had presented himself to the offices of Pan Am in San Francisco, stating that his company was reorganizing their recruitment program and would Pan Am mind showing him how they did it? They did not, and Mike came away with the fifty-question test given to applicants at their interviews. He gave a copy to Harry, cautioning him that the Pan Am exec had told him that they did not want pilots who scored 100%.

"If Pan Am calls you for an interview, be sure to miss a few questions on purpose." Harry promised to do that if the chance came. Harry never saw Mike after that course, but he had little doubt that he would make it as an airline pilot. Such persistence and ingenuity were sure to be rewarded.

Harry sent hundreds of resumes to airlines around the world. Most were answered, usually with a form letter that thanked him for his interest, telling him that there were no openings right now, and that they would keep his application on file. He never lost heart, but his morale was dealt a hard blow when a cargo company in Miami answered with a mimeographed form, which told him of the disposition of his letter by checking boxes. The first boxes came after the words, "Your letter has been…," and the box checked read, "Destroyed". Now that was devastating. He was a U.S. Navy carrier pilot with combat experience, and he thought he deserved better. The airlines did not seem to agree.

"Better" finally came in a job with a charter company in New York. Harry had never heard of the company, but "any port in a storm." He quickly and gratefully accepted their offer and was soon off for the east coast. He quickly came to love both Manhattan, where he had a small apartment, and the company. It flew mainly to the Caribbean but, now and then, to Europe. Flying a Boeing 707 was not like landing on a carrier, but it had its compensations: great places to go and wonderful people to go with. As one of his colleagues put it, "I don't need the job. I just need the transportation between crew parties." Harry thoroughly enjoyed the life of an airline pilot. And, except for a few minor drawbacks, he liked living in Manhattan. It was both the best and the worst of big-city life and it was, after all, the center of the universe. At least New Yorkers said so, and Harry tended to agree.

Harry was one of the few company pilots who lived in Manhattan. Because of large blocks of off-days and because schedules could be easily rearranged to suit crew needs, pilots lived away, sometimes far away, from New York Free, or almost-free, staff travel airline tickets helped. They commuted to "crash pads." These were accommodations shared by several pilots and used as a place to stay for brief periods before and after working a flight. They came from all over the country, some from as far off as California. Harry had once talked with a Pan Am pilot who was based in Hong Kong and lived in Las Vegas. That was too much time on the road for Harry and, anyway, he liked Manhattan.

Timing was important in life. Harry had been hired as a First officer. A pilot might be the world's finest, have substantial experience and hold a degree in aeronautical engineering; but to find a job, someone had to need him. To be upgraded to the left seat, there had to be an opening. Harry had been lucky. After one year in the right seat and performing well, a slot opened for another captain. Harry was sent through a rigorous training program and emerged a captain.

Except for a very few, those in the aviation brotherhood were fine and decent men; but every now and then, Harry ran into one who could only be described as an asshole. Harry used that word sparingly, but it fit perfectly the captain who supervised much of his training. He made life miserable for Harry in many ways, usually ways that were meant to demean more than to instruct. Others shared Harry's opinion.

Retribution was sweet. It came during a training flight with several trainees doing touch-and-go landings at a nearby airport. Harry had finished his turn "in the barrel" and sat in the cockpit observer's seat as a colleague was put through the wringer. Tim Hutton was perspiring and grinding his teeth as he withstood one derogatory comment after another. They were delivered with withering scorn. Tim's face was flushed with exasperation when the asshole said to Tim, "I have just had a heart attack and died. What are you going to do?" Without a moment's pause, and without looking over his shoulder, Tim said, through clenched teeth, "Harry, get someone up here to help you drag this dead son-of-a-bitch out of the cockpit."

Harry loved sitting in the left seat. He was once more in charge of his own life. Nothing could happen on his airplane unless he said it could. Sitting in the captain's seat made him feel like the king of the world. Of course, along with the authority came responsibility. Harry didn't mind. The Navy had taught him the basics of leadership and they applied well to operations on an airliner. People often asked him how he could shoulder the life-and-death responsibility of all those passengers. He always answered, "It's my life, too. If I take care of mine, they'll be okay."

Then disaster struck. After three fabulous years, the company had gone "belly-up" and Harry found himself without a job. Like flicking a switch, he had no income, and, almost as bad, no flying. That had been a real bone-crusher for Harry because for him there could be no better job in the world. Flying to wonderful places with great people -- how could you beat that?

"It not only beats working," a friend once said, "it beats not working."

Harry could not agree more. As the weeks passed with no prospects for a job, Harry had become more and more discouraged.

5

LOVING AND LEAVING

1967

With great misgiving, Harry had left the Navy after his return from Vietnam. He once thought that life as a Navy pilot was life at the top of the world. Harry had been born to fly airplanes from aircraft carriers; but Vietnam had changed all that. It was not because of the danger; that went with the territory. No, it was because of the way that he had been ordered to face that danger. The conduct of that war was stupid and disgraceful. Harry would never have forgiven himself if he had ended up splattered across a hillside in Vietnam while destroying a pontoon bridge that would be put back in place the very next morning.

Harry figured that the Kitty Hawk, had she been turned loose, could have neutralized North Vietnam in one month. That one ship dropped about 100 tons of bombs every day, rain or shine. Most were wasted on meaningless targets, sometimes making deeper and bigger the bomb craters where targets once stood. The rest ended up on the bottom of the Gulf of Tonkin. That was because aircraft were not allowed to return to the ship with non-expended bombs. They might be thrown loose when the airplane was brought to an abrupt stop during the organized crash known as a carrier landing.

After a mission, any bombs still attached to the airplane were dropped into the sea. More than once on a bad weather day, Harry had been briefed to launch, drop his bombs in the sea, then orbit the ship until the recovery time. So, instead of turning Harry and his squadron-mates loose to win the damned war, lives and aircraft had been thrown at worthless targets at great risk with scant hope of inflicting serious damage. In so doing, Harry's Air Wing lost twenty-seven airplanes and twenty-nine aircrew during seven months in the Tonkin Gulf. All, Harry thought, for almost nothing. So, upon his return to Lemoore, as a kind of personal protest to the way the war was fought, Harry had left the Navy that he had truly loved. It had been the most agonizing decision of his life, but, once made, he had never looked back.

Harry had given himself one month to come to this decision. Near the end of those thirty days, he was stunned to learn that a very close friend had been lost in a fire that had broken out on the USS Oriskany in the Tonkin Gulf. Harry had once served on that ship. He did not learn the details until much later. At first, there was only a phone call. Harry knew well the parents

Ron Rypel

of his friend, but not their address or telephone number. He knew only that they lived in Miami. He tried to contact them. "Sorry," the operator said, "the number is unlisted." Harry hesitated for only a second, then told the operator the reason he wanted the number. He heard a catch in her voice as she said, "I'll call you right back." And she did, within minutes. He called the number.

His friend's parents had already been officially notified. Harry could hear the heartbreak in their voices as they spoke. He had been an only child. They asked a favor.

"Anything," said Harry.

"Would you please escort his body to his funeral?" they asked.

Of course, he would do that, he told them. And he did. That was the second time he had placed the body of a friend into the ground. Somehow, it made easier his decision to leave the Navy.

There were other reasons for his decision. For one, the captain of the Kitty Hawk, or perhaps someone higher up the chain, seemed determined to set a record for bomb tonnage dropped during a cruise. How else to explain launching fully-loaded aircraft when the weather precluded finding a target, never mind hitting it? Harry had once sat in his cockpit, ready to start his engine, and listened to a weather report from an airplane flying along the coast of North Vietnam. Reporting heavy rain and low clouds, the pilot recommended cancelling the launch. There was no chance to reach any targets, he said.

A few minutes later, Harry had been fired off the bow into the heavy rain. Anticipating this possibility, Harry had briefed the four-plane flight to split into two sections, each to operate in a different sector of the coast. Somehow, Harry's wingman had managed to find him and off they flew towards North Vietnam to see for themselves, knowing what they would find. The weather was as reported, and there was no way to fly inland without risking flying into rocks embedded in North Vietnamese hills.

Upon reaching the coast, Harry turned into his sector, searching hopefully for a break in the weather. A few minutes later, at 500 feet and in heavy rain, the other section suddenly appeared out of the mist and streaked directly over Harry in the opposite direction. They were no more than twenty-five feet above Harry and were past him before he had time to become scared. Instead, he became angry and screamed into his oxygen mask. The near-collision had caused a heated discussion back in the Ready Room. The section leader had not seen Harry's section and wondered loudly what all the fuss was about.

22

On another day with awful weather, Harry had been slotted as the section leader in a flight of four. So terrible was the weather, that the division leader had termed the brief "provisional." Surely, he said, they will not launch in weather like this. The brief was to the point: Launch, jettison all bombs, head for the holding point, then orbit until the recovery. Harry's airplane was spotted just aft of the number three catapult. Peering ahead through the driving rain, he could not see the bow. *Jesus,* he thought with concern, *this does not look good, not at all.* Will they really send us out in this? They did and Harry flew as briefed. He hoped the ship would find some good weather for the recovery but this was not to be their day. Radar brought Harry down to 500 feet aft of the ship and advised him to call the ship in sight. But there was no ship in sight. He continued, following the instructions of the Landing Signal Officer. The LSO stood on a platform on the port side of the flight deck, just aft of the touchdown area. By radio, he controlled all landings on the ship. Harry finally saw the "meatball" of the optical landing system, but he did not see the ship until a few moments before he touched down.

Pretty useless, thought Harry, as he climbed wearily down from the cockpit. But, on the bright side, his flight counted as one official combat mission; and his bombs, now resting on the bottom of the Tonkin Gulf, were part of the ship's ordnance expenditure total. And in the end, the Kitty Hawk did, indeed, set a record for bomb tonnage dropped during a deployment. The bombs Harry jettisoned that day were part of the record.

These two flights would become major reasons in his decision to leave the Navy, but there were others. When the ship arrived in the Gulf, all the flyers were enthusiastic about winning the war. This was, after all, what they had trained for; but they did not know that they would not be allowed to win this war. Harry, like most, had figured out, in just the first few weeks, that the U.S. was not serious about winning. And, like most, he had determined that the name of this game was survival.

"These piss-ant targets are for damn sure not worth the bombs we drop on them, never mind an airplane and a pilot," was how Harry's roommate, Bob Norton, had succinctly put it. Still, Harry was always conscious of his duty. Except for those few times when weather made it hopeless, he made a determined effort to complete every mission. All but one.

Of course, there were always those few who saw life differently. They wanted to win the war all by themselves and they took foolish risks to do it. In a way, they enjoyed the war. Harry just wanted to get back alive.

To help him do that, Harry adopted two of his own "rules of engagement." They stemmed from his very first mission over North Vietnam. On a clear day, he had led a two-plane flight just north of the Demilitarized Zone. He was after a small bridge and he found it. He was not in a good position for a bombing run but he rolled in anyway. Unable to line up the bridge, he had aborted the run and gone around again. When he rolled in a second time, the sky around him erupted into a storm of automatic weapons fire. He managed to drop his bombs somewhere near the bridge, stayed down low after his pull-out, and headed for the sea at a low level. From that day, Harry followed two basic rules: never roll in on a target unless you are well-positioned to make a run, and never make a second run, even if you were not able to release your bombs on the first one. Harry's Rules.

In the end, all of these reasons for leaving the Navy boiled down to one. Lyndon Johnson and Robert McNamara were trying to kill him. Not intentionally, perhaps, but that was the result of the way they fought that war.

6
FAREWELL, NEW YORK

June 1970

Today Harry felt better. After months of looking for a job, with not even a glimmer of an offer, something had finally turned up. Earlier this morning, he had received a phone call from Elliott Morton, a friend who flew for Pan Am and who had just been offered a job. It was for only three months with a start-up airline in Norway. Elliott was not interested and had thought of Harry. A few minutes after hanging up the phone, Harry called the number he had been given. From the area code, he knew it was in Miami. Harry asked for the captain who had called Elliott. Yes, he was told. Another pilot was needed, but needed right away.

"My bag is packed," Harry told him.

In a conversation lasting less three minutes, Harry had agreed to be at JFK Airport that evening, where a ticket would be waiting for him at the Lufthansa counter. That call would change Harry's life in ways he could never have imagined when he mounted the steps leading into Central Park on Fifth Avenue at 90ᵗʰ Street and began jogging around the reservoir. And thinking. There was a lot to think about.

Now, at the Lufthansa counter, Harry had a problem. An obtuse clerk with a German accent refused to give Harry his ticket.

"It's for Trans Polar Airlines and I have been told to pick it up here," said Harry wearily, for the third time.

"But I have no ticket with your name written on it," said the accent for the fourth time.

Just as Harry's pulse began to quicken in frustration, a fellow-pilot from the now-defunct company had checked in ahead of Harry. He turned from the counter and, seeing Harry, asked, "Are you part of the Trans Polar deal?"

"Supposed to be," said Harry, "but this gentleman won't give me my ticket."

Charley Dunlap paused a few seconds as he analyzed the situation, then turned to the clerk, furrowed his brow, and in a commanding voice said, "This man is with me. Give him his ticket!"

That was all the clerk needed and he quickly handed Harry a ticket.

"These Germans," said Charley with a chuckle as they left the counter. "They won't do anything unless they get a direct order."

25

Harry settled into his seat on the B747 with a sigh of appreciation. A first class-seat was not only a nice surprise, it was perhaps an omen. Harry believed in omens. Harry thought that as a kind of non-believer, he had to believe in something. Now, another omen, one that would not be recognized as such for a few weeks, sat down next to Harry. Figuring that it made sense for the Trans Polar seats to be grouped together, Harry asked his latest omen if he was also traveling for Trans Polar Airlines.

"Yeah," he said, "and I'm not sure I want to be."

It turned out that Joe Thomas had just retired from Eastern Airlines and very much preferred to be sitting on his boat in Miami instead of on an airplane bound for Oslo, which was where the crews were needed. For unexplained reasons, his wife wanted him to go to Oslo.

Joe Thomas did not look like an airline captain. He was short, stocky, bald, and he wore thick glasses; but he drank like one. After the takeoff, Harry had suggested a before-dinner drink in the upper-level bar.

"No, thanks," said Joe. "I used to have a problem with that stuff, so I never touch it anymore."

Harry murmured something pleasant and went up the spiral staircase for a drink. He returned to his seat just as a pretty flight attendant came along and asked if he would like another drink before the dinner service. Why not, thought Harry, the price is right. He ordered another Manhattan on ice. As the girl turned away, Joe reached out and took hold of her apron.

"Maybe I will have a drink after all," he said, as she glanced down at his fingers clutching her smock. "A little bourbon, please."

She quickly reappeared with a bottle of bourbon and a glass, and began to pour. And pour. And pour. She filled the glass.

"Mud in your eye," mumbled Joe, and drank down the entire glass without pausing for breath. With that running start, Joe would be in various stages of drunkenness for the next two weeks. They would be weeks to remember.

7
BACK TO VIETNAM

1965

Once you're alongside, flying formation is not difficult. What's hard is doing other things while focusing on keeping a proper position. Changing a radio frequency, for example, can lead to disaster if a wingman is not careful. Focus and concentration were essential. Much depended on the flight leader, and John Dawson was a good one. John, as Executive Officer, or X.O., was second in the squadron chain of command. An excellent pilot, he flew smoothly and he always let you know what he was up to. Night formation was more demanding because the reference points were more obscure. To fly formation, the wingman aligned his aircraft in a relative position determined by lining up reference points on the lead aircraft. If he was on that line, he had the right bearing.

Heading towards Cambodia now, Harry flew in a cruise position. That meant his aircraft was stepped down so there was vertical clearance between the two planes. During a turn, he was free to leave his formation bearing and turn inside or outside of John's radius of turn so that he could close or open the distance between the planes and, in that way, keep the gap between them about the same, despite the difference in their flight paths during turns. Otherwise, when flying tactical formation and holding the same relative bearing, Harry would have to add power when John turned away and take off power when the lead turned toward him. Flying in cruise formation allowed the wingman to stay in position by turning inside or outside of the lead plane's turns. This was easier and it saved fuel.

Tonight, John was carrying parachute flares and Harry had the bombs, 500-pounders. The plan was to drop flares at predetermined places and hope they would illuminate some of the trucks pouring through the Mugia pass. They were carrying supplies to the south. That part was hard enough. If they got lucky and actually found a few trucks, which almost never happened, the truly hard part came into play. That was Harry, rolling in at night, in mountainous country, partially blinded by a flare that seemed as brilliant as the sun, and trying to hit a very small moving target. Well, damn, thought Harry sardonically, why would anyone think a truck driver would keep on truckin' if he heard an airplane which meant to do him in? Harry figured it was just a harassment drill, but he was not sure who was more harassed, he or that truck driver down there.

No one had any real expectations of success on a mission like this one because flying over Cambodia at night was like flying over the dark side of the moon. You never saw anything, with or without the flares. One problem with a flight like this one was what to do with the bombs after the flares were gone. During the ship's Pacific crossing, all pilots had been carefully briefed on the official Rules of Engagement. One of those rules specified that on missions without a predetermined target, such as Harry's flight tonight, bombs could be dropped only on "mechanized vehicles within 200 yards of a motor-able road or trail." What horseshit, thought Harry, when he first heard the rules.

Other rules allowed ships to dock in Haiphong and unload their deadly cargos, including surface-to-air missiles. Once, Harry had actually seen this taking place. That had happened when Harry, coming back from a strike near Hanoi, had made a wrong turn and suddenly found himself looking down briefly on the port of Haiphong. As he did, the sky around him erupted in a firestorm. Ramming his throttle full forward, he had quickly headed for the safety of the open sea. In those few minutes, he saw several ships unloading cargo, including what appeared to be SAMs, onto trucks. There was no way to know, but it was certainly possible that one of those missiles might one day be fired at his airplane.

Much of North Vietnam's war materiel entered the country through Haiphong. Harry and his fellow-pilots often talked about the foolish and dangerous anomaly of allowing weapons to enter North Vietnam unimpeded, then, at great risk, trying to find and destroy them. A few years later President Nixon changed the rules of the game and mined Haiphong's harbor. This tactic had an immediate and dramatic effect on bringing the war to an end. Why, Harry wondered, had this not been implemented from the start. Done earlier, it might well have changed the course of the war.

Rules of engagement also prevented pilots from attacking missile sites while they were under construction. Before firing at North Vietnamese airplanes, fighter pilots were required to sight them visually. American missiles were designed for use at long range, so this restriction gave away a great advantage. Harry figured that such rules were meant to lessen the chance that Russia and China, who were providing assistance to North Vietnam, would somehow become involved militarily. That perhaps worked, but at what cost? Not counting helicopters, the U.S. lost some 1850 aircraft in combat during the war in Vietnam. Almost all were lost over North Vietnam.

Many losses resulted from following rules, made in Washington, which hamstrung our pilots. This, thought Harry, is no way to win a war.

Tonight, technically, since they had found no trucks, they were supposed to jettison their bombs into the sea; but that meant using precious fuel, just how precious the pilot never knew, to carry to the sea bombs that could not be brought back aboard the ship. This was a stupid war, thought Harry, but that rule has got to be the dumbest of them all. You would have to be a moron to follow such a rule, and no one did. The dilemma was neatly solved by spotting an imaginary truck while the last flare was still lit and then unloading all the bombs on it, or at least in its general vicinity. The certain result was the destruction of more enemy trees and the total number, by now, had to be astronomical.

All bombs and flares were away and not one round had been fired up at them. It was a happy mission; so much for the easy part. Now, for the hard part: getting back on board the ship.

A group of physiologists had recently wired selected pilots in Harry's Air Wing and measured their blood pressure, heartbeat and whatever else makes a man's adrenalin flow. They found that the subject pilots showed greater stress during the carrier-landing phase than during the combat mission itself. I can believe that, thought Harry, at the time. Night carrier landings were generally considered to separate the men from the boys. They were not easy under good conditions and the degree of difficulty went up exponentially on dark nights, especially when the weather deteriorated. Tonight, the weather would not be a factor, only the dark. Thank Christ for that, thought Harry, as he settled into position alongside John for the flight home.

8
OSLO

June 1970

After a long but pleasant trans-Atlantic flight, a plane change in Frankfort, and a very expensive taxi ride, Harry, Joe and Charley checked into the Norum Hotel in Olso. Harry and Charley were dead-tired. Joe was feeling no pain from some serious bourbon inhalation and, during the taxi ride, he had begun speaking in a strange language that the driver told Harry was some kind of Norwegian. He could barely understand, he said, but, "That is for sure Norwegian." When Harry, the next day, said, "Hey, Joe, I didn't know you could speak Norwegian," Joe answered with a blank stare.

"I can't," he said, "not one single word." When Harry recounted the taxi conversation, it struck a chord with Joe.

"Damn," he exclaimed, "my parents were from Norway and they spoke it at home. I must have learned some I don't even remember learning. I sure as hell can't speak any this morning." Joe, it would turn out, was full of surprises.

Later that day, the fourth member of the crew arrived at the hotel. He was also an ex-Navy pilot and his name was David Warner. Harry had not met him before. That afternoon, a meeting was arranged for the four of them with the president of the new company.

Thor Larsen turned out to be both pleasant and serious about his new airline. He was tall and rangy with a shock of blonde hair that sometimes fell over one eye. He seemed confident and capable. Let's hope he's as capable as he is confident, thought Harry. Thor had lived in the U.S. for a few years and it was obvious that he liked Americans. He spoke English fluently, but with an unusually strong accent. They would quickly learn that his accent got worse as his anger rose, and when his face reddened to full flush, he was almost incomprehensible.

He had bought an old Boeing 707 from Eastern Airlines at a bargain basement price. He named his new company Trans Polar.

"Why call it Trans Polar?" Harry asked.

Thor explained that he and a friend had once tried to circumnavigate the earth, over both poles, in a small, twin-engine airplane. Harry was pleased to learn that Thor was a pilot, and that he had the stuff to attempt such a remarkable feat. They had crash-landed somewhere in Canada, survived, and Thor had become something of a national hero. That name, and the company logo showing a plane flying over both poles, would look strangely out of place in the warm weather airports of the world his airplane would soon be in.

After a few minutes of introductions and polite conversation, Thor ordered coffee and snacks, saying, "I would order drinks but they are very expensive here, and we must be careful about our money." The four new employees smiled and nodded in agreement. Now the conversation turned serious. It was about money.

After some very low-key negotiating, Charley Dunlap tore a page from a spiral notebook in his flight bag and began to put down the terms of employment. It did not take long, as Joe Thomas did not need the money and the others badly needed a job. The going rates for crews in 1970 were well known and they settled for $25 per flight hour for captains and $15 per hour for First Officers and Flight Engineers. They would be provided with hotel rooms and $15 daily for expenses. For Harry, that was one room and $15 per day more than he was getting now. All agreed it was a fair contract.

To celebrate the signing, Thor ordered a bottle of wine, which quickly arrived. Thor filled their glasses.

"Well, gentlemen," -- he pronounced it 'yentlemen' -- "I believe we are off together on a great adventure," Thor announced as he stood and lifted his glass. After a first sip, he raised his glass once more. "To adventure. And to Trans Polar. Long may she fly."

Oslo in the summer was a fairy tale place. Beautiful countryside, friendly citizens, all of whom spoke English almost as well as Harry, great food, and, of course, plenty of pretty Norwegian girls to melt his heart. Oh, they looked even more delicious than those in New York. He would meet them soon enough, as the first flight of the new company would take place in just three days.

As far as Harry could see, Oslo's only fault was the high price of its beer. It was available with several different levels of alcohol content, including one version with almost none. Harry tried them all.

The pilots' first task was to get Norwegian licenses. That meant a written test and a medical examination. They were assigned a Norwegian pilot to teach them the national flight regulations and after one day of intensive cramming, they all passed through with flying colors. They knew most of the answers even before they saw the questions. They were issued not a license, but a validation; a temporary Norwegian license based on an American one.

Ron Rypel

That Thor was not very knowledgeable about running an airline would become painfully obvious as the days passed. But he seemed to know very well the ways around the rules that got in his way, and the people to help him do it. That ability would prove to be a lifesaver in the weeks ahead.

The first demonstration of Thor's talents came as they were preparing the first flight of the new airline. Thor had decided that the first few flights would operate with two captains, Joe being the captain in command. That would turn out to be less than a great decision as problems arose during the next few months.

The passengers were on board, and Joe and Harry were in the flight operations area, trying to figure out how to fill in the blanks on an international flight plan. Company staff had always filled them out for them and they had never even seen one before. After a long struggle, they finally had it filled in and Harry handed it to the agent behind the counter. He glanced at it and then very politely told them that he had been instructed not to accept their flight plan.

"Sorry, Captain," he said, almost apologetically, "but my orders are clear. I shall not accept your flight plan."

Just then, Thor came in, looking cross, and asked about the delay.

"The passengers are all on board and we are ready," he said. "What is the problem?"

Joe gestured to the agent behind the counter.

"He won't take our flight plan," Joe said. There followed a brief but intense discussion in Norwegian. Thor's face began to flush. He picked up the phone, dialed, spoke for a minute or two, then handed the phone to the agent. He said nothing, only listened, then hung up and asked for the flight plan.

"Captain," he announced with a smile, "I am most pleased now to accept your flight plan."

Trans Polar was about to launch its maiden flight carrying 155 tourists to Palma de Majorca in Spain.

Later, after getting airborne, Harry leaned back towards the jump seat behind the captain, where Thor had stationed himself. Over the next few weeks, he would almost never leave that seat.

"Thor, what was the problem back there?" Harry asked.

"No problem," he said, and explained that he did not yet have the authorization to land in Spain.

"Wow," Harry whistled, "how did you get around that one?"

"Easy," he replied with a grin. "I just told them it was not a commercial flight, that I was taking some of my friends to Spain for the weekend."

Harry was impressed. "They bought that? You're flying one-hundred-and-fifty-five of your friends to Spain for a weekend holiday?"

"Oh, sure," he said with a grin. "I am a very popular fellow."

As if to underline his statement, he picked up the microphone and made an announcement in Norwegian which brought down the house. Harry heard the cheering through the closed cockpit door.

"Now what?" Harry asked. "What was all that?"

Thor leaned back in his seat and winked. "I just told them it was a private flight," he said, "and they would all get their money back."

In the weeks ahead, that announcement would cost Thor dearly. But Harry was impressed. Here is a man who can get things done. He had to do them all over again when the Spanish authorities refused to let the flight depart from Palma; but Thor and his magic telephone came to the rescue again, this time by calling the Norwegian ambassador at his home on a Sunday afternoon.

9
BACK TO THE SHIP

1965

Daylight landings on an aircraft carrier are not as difficult as one might imagine. They required precision flying, of course, but they were practiced so often that they became almost routine. Almost. Just a few weeks ago, as the ship left Cubi Point in the Philippines after a four-day stay, a standard refresher landing session was held on the way back to Yankee Station. Harry had watched the show from Vultures' Row. That was a weather deck six levels above the flight deck which looked aft over the landing area, and was the best seat in the house. There were more bolters than arrested landings during each pilot's first few approaches.

Of course, four days of trying to make up for thirty-four days at sea might have been a factor. Most of the action had taken place at the Cubi Point Officers' Club. Letting off steam after a month of combat flying was the excuse, and Harry had to admit it was a good one; but it was not only the hangovers that caused the bolters. Another reason was that the time between times, the intervals between landings, made a pilot less sharp than he needed to be.

Bolter was a dirty word among carrier pilots. To land on a ship, a pilot needs to fly the right glide path at the right airspeed until his aircraft and the ship collide in what is loosely called a landing. There are four arresting cables strung across the landing area. If the approach is done right, the aircraft's tail hook will snag the number three wire, which is the target wire. If the speed or the flight path is not right, the plane might catch another wire, or it might not catch any. That's a bolter. The instant the plane touches the deck, the pilot rams the throttle forward to full power. That's in case the tail hook bounces over the wires or the aircraft lands forward of them. That way, the engine is at full power so the plane can bound back into the air to go around and try again. If the plane grabs a wire, its engine will still be at full power for those few seconds it takes the pilot to realize that he is on board and to pull the throttle back to idle.

Daytime bolters are easily handled. At night, it is a heart-stopping maneuver. That's because during a night bolter, all visual references are instantly lost, and all a pilot sees is the black. There are not many references, anyway. The ship's running lights are there and so are some runway lights on the flight deck to outline the touchdown area. It's not much, but better than nothing. Sometimes a plane would bolter after a perfect pass. That happens because even though the hook is held down by hydraulic pressure, it sometimes bounces right over a wire. It's not supposed to do that, but it happens. Harry had seen a hook skip over two wires after a perfect approach. Now, that is demoralizing. The pilot knows that if he flew a poor approach, he might expect a bolter and be ready for it; but after a good approach and a touchdown in the wires, a bolter comes as a great surprise, especially at night.

Daylight recoveries in good weather are done in visual flight conditions. The flight flies over the ship in the same direction and the individual planes break off at five-second intervals and come aboard using visual references and a circling approach. The leader of the first flight is given a "Charley Time." It is based on the ship's best guess for when the launching aircraft have cleared the landing area and the ship has a ready deck. The flight leader of the first flight must then plan his entry into the landing pattern, and his approach, so that he will be at the ramp and ready to land at Charley Time. He will be expected to be there not one minute before or one minute after, but right on time. This required good judgment and solid airmanship and was a point of pride among flight leaders. Arriving early at the ramp usually meant a wave-off because the deck was not ready. Arriving late was not only embarrassing; it usually resulted in barbed comments from the Air Boss. Flight leaders of following flights keyed their approach on the last airplane of the flight ahead so as to land at the proper interval. Precision flying was required.

For Harry, Charley Time was a term that applied well to life itself. The signal was usually given with a time appended: "Your signal is Charley Eight" might be the instruction radioed to the leader of the first flight scheduled for the recovery. It meant that exactly eight minutes later, he was expected to be at the ramp and ready to land. To get there on time, he had to consider many factors: his distance from the ship, the ship's course for recovery, the time needed to get to the break position over the ship, and the time to reach the ramp from the time he broke away from his flight. He was given an objective: Be at the ramp in eight minutes.

At times, when the deck was ready sooner than expected, the signal was given as "Your signal is Charley," with no time specified. That meant the flight leader was supposed to be at the ramp, ready to come aboard, as soon as possible. Whether or not a time was specified, the flight leader was on his own. How he got to the ramp was up to him, using his knowledge and experience. Get from here to there the best way he can, relying only on himself. It was like many problems of life.

The aircraft carrier counterpart of an airport traffic control tower is called Primary Flight and known as Pri-Fly. It stands six decks above the flight deck and commands a view of the entire deck, fore and aft. The officer in charge is the Air Operations Officer but no one ever used that title. He was known to all as the Air Boss, and, to some, just Boss. His responsibility was enormous. He coordinated all the launches and he controlled the daytime recoveries visually, using radio contact with the airplanes about to come aboard. At night he worked closely with the Combat Information Center, which controlled the airplanes with radar.

At night, the returning aircraft are held in orbit at 20,000 feet some 20 or 30 miles aft of the ship, and the individual aircraft are radar-controlled down to the "meatball" at 500 feet. From there, the approach becomes a visual straight-in landing. The "ball," as it is usually called, is a part of the optical landing system that guides a pilot down the glide slope. It appears to the pilot as a round orange light between two horizontal rows of green lights, and one row on each side of the meatball. If the pilot allows the plane to drop below the glide path, the orange ball dips beneath the rows of green lights. The meatball rises above the green lights when the airplane goes above the glide path. The pilot then corrects his flight path to center the ball.

There are two problems that make a pilot's life difficult during a carrier approach. One is line-up. The landing area of the flight deck is angled away from the ship's centerline by twelve degrees; so a pilot lined up with the angled deck sees the landing area steadily move to his right as the ship moves through the water. You will get the picture if you extend your hand flat, palm down, pointing straight ahead. Now rotate your hand so that it points slightly to your left. Next, move your hand straight ahead away from your body while holding that angle. That is what a pilot sees during a carrier approach. This is not a problem during daytime and is usually adjusted unconsciously; but at night, because of the absence of visual references, a large line-up correction is sometimes needed instead of the many small ones a pilot makes, almost automatically, during a daylight approach. The plane is lined up perfectly one moment, and left of the centerline the next. This can, at times, require a relatively steep turn close-in, and that can be dangerous.

The other problem is speed. An airliner landing at an airport has a target airspeed determined by the weight of the aircraft. This is corrected for wind conditions; but it's only a target and there is plenty of room for error. Being 20 or even 30 knots above the target speed is poor airmanship, but a landing can still be made safely if the runway is long enough. Precision is needed on an aircraft carrier. The landing area on a carrier is defined by four cables stretched across the deck and supported by metal arches to raise the wires slightly off the deck. The distance between them is about 20 feet. Each cable is about 2,200 feet long, and most of it is beneath the flight deck. Its ends are connected to hydraulic devices there. These are set with hydraulic resistance determined by the type, weight and speed of the landing aircraft. After a plane snags a cable, or wire, as they are usually called, its resistance brings the aircraft to a stop in a distance of about 250 feet.

Speed is critical. If the speed is too low, the airplane becomes difficult to handle and can even cause an aerodynamic stall. That happens when the airflow across the wings does not generate enough lift for flight. The airplane then becomes just another falling object. If the speed is too high, there is a risk of a tail hook being ripped off when it engages a wire. So the acceptable speed is a narrow band of just a few knots. There is another problem associated with speed. A landing aircraft descends by moving through the air with enough speed to generate lift, but not enough lift to hold level flight. A rate of descent results. This is how an airplane gets down to the ground. It flies at a speed that generates less lift than the airplane weighs, so it comes down until it lands. Simple.

And it would be simple, except for a few basic principles of physics. Theoretically, an airplane on the glide path at the proper airspeed and throttle setting should hold the right descent rate until touchdown. Theoretically. In real life, there are external forces, such as wind and air currents continuously working on the plane, so corrections are always needed during an approach. Suppose the pilot finds himself above the glide path. He can either lower the plane's nose or take off power to increase his descent rate until he is back on the glide path. Once there, he must adjust his correction to remain at the right airspeed and on the glide path. If he reduced power to increase descent, he must then add just enough power to stay on the glide path at the right speed. If he got there by lowering his nose, he must then readjust his nose attitude to establish the right rate of descent. What makes this hard is that the airspeed and the rate of descent are interrelated. When you correct one, you change the other. In this way, continuous corrections with power and attitude are made throughout an approach until the airplane slams onto the flight deck.

Of course, Harry Ferguson knew all this so well that he had forgotten most of it; but it was well engraved in his behavior patterns. He did not need to think about how and why he made these corrections during an approach; he just made them. That came from experience, and Harry had plenty. Now, slicing back through the night sky over the South China Sea, Harry began readying himself mentally for the landing. No matter how many you made, there was always that apprehension just before you started down towards the ship. Harry likened it to the nervous feeling he had felt playing on his high school football team. Just before the kick-off, the tension was palpable. Once the game started, he never noticed it at all.

That tension was once observed by Harry as he sipped a cup of coffee in the Ready Room as a flight of four pilots, briefed and ready, waited for the command, "Pilots, man your planes." That soon came via an oversized screen which displayed typed information from the ship's Flight Operations control center. This would be a night launch in bad weather and such launches caused the most apprehension. The dreaded words appeared and the pilots slowly made their way out of the Ready Room and headed up to the flight deck. But first, each made a stop in the nearby "head," or toilet, for a last-minute, nervous pee. This was standard before most flights, but especially for night flights, when tension was higher. Five minutes after the pilots left, the information screen clicked into action once more and typed, "Launch cancelled." A few minutes later, the four pilots reappeared in the Ready Room, all smiling broadly in obvious relief. One, Jack Rooney, who was a close friend of Harry, very nonchalantly strolled up to the teletype screen, hands clasped behind his back. Reaching the screen, he suddenly and enthusiastically kissed it. That said it all; almost all, anyway. A few weeks later, he added a postscript. After a safety lecture for the Air Wing pilots in the Officers' Wardroom, the speaker asked for suggestions to make carrier flying safer. Rooney quickly provided the solution.

"Eliminate night landings," he said. There was thunderous applause.

10
KARACHI

July 1970

Harry was nursing a drink and thinking about carrier landings when Joe Thomas punched his arm. They were at 35,000 feet in a Lufthansa 707 on the way to Karachi. The entire crew was being positioned there to operate the second half of a flight from London to Hong Kong. Joe had not had one single drink since they left Oslo. The rest of the crew, including four stewardesses, was enjoying a great flight. The plane was only half full, which left plenty of room to move about and have an impromptu crew party.

The flight engineer was a veteran named Gene Daily. Well, thought Harry, as he watched Gene drinking bourbon, if he can fly the engineer panel as well as he handles the bourbon, we'll be all right. Gene was from the old school, back in the days when flight engineers were flight engineers, not pilots. That change had come along as the unions at the major airlines had squeezed cockpit personnel into one organization for better leverage.

Short and stocky with black, wavy hair, Gene was outgoing and friendly. Rough socially, he had more than his share of common sense. He liked to start his day with what he called his Mexican Breakfast -- a cup of coffee and a cigarette. Gene had been an enlisted man in the military, but the only thing he held against officers was that they drank Scotch instead of bourbon. Snooty, he called that; but he said it with a smile. Harry would always remember a comment Gene made at breakfast one morning in Karachi.

"How can you eat those eggs?" he had asked.

Harry looked up from his plate and shrugged. "They're eggs." said Harry, somewhat puzzled, "You don't like them?"

"No, no," Gene had answered. "I like eggs. I just don't like *these* eggs. I just can't eat them when I think about where those Pakistani chickens have been."

Gene would do just fine, Harry decided.

The girls were Swedish and Norwegian. Harry had come to know them over the past couple of weeks and he was impressed. On his scale of ten, he rated each of them as eight or nine. What he liked about these European girls was their no-nonsense attitude towards life. No Hollywood, no girlish games, just straightforward acceptance of what life is all about. Harry liked them. He liked them all, but he liked one more than the others. Her name was

39

Astrid and she gave off some very friendly vibrations in Harry's direction. Harry had laid some solid groundwork in the last two weeks and he liked his chances.

Unlike the image of Scandinavian women, Astrid did not have blonde hair. It was jet black and it framed a pretty Norwegian face, somewhere between beautiful and attractive. Like most Scandinavians, her English was excellent, although she made their usual mistakes. She had difficulty with words beginning with the letter J, for example, and found it easier to use Y instead. She wore yeans, not jeans, and she might have ridden in a yeep. Harry never corrected her because he liked it.

Once, she used the word "onion," and Harry had tried to decode it. Did she mean "engine," or perhaps, "Indian.?"

"No, no," she said with exasperation. "Onion. You eat them and they make you cry when you peel them." Then, Harry understood; onion really meant onion.

She liked to laugh and she did it often. She even laughed at Harry's jokes and, more than that, she seemed to genuinely enjoy them. She was short, which was one reason Harry had zeroed in on her, but with a figure proportioned in a way that made her look taller. Lean and firm, she had the look of an athlete and she moved like one: with an easy grace that looked effortless. She was a good worker and, unlike most hostesses, almost never complained. She took the problems as they came and met them head-on and always with a smile.

It was almost exasperating, thought Harry, that she was always in good humor. No downs, just ups.

"How do you do that?" he asked her one day.

"Do what?" she asked, this time with a slight frown instead of her usual smile.

"Be in such a good mood all the time. How does that work?"

Her frown became a smile again. "Oh, it's easy. I just avoid people who are always complaining. I try to be with people who are always happy. Like you."

"Astrid, please. I am not always happy. You should see me in the morning when I get out of bed."

"One day," she said with an impish smile, "perhaps I will. Maybe you are not always happy, but you always seem happy to me. It's enough."

"Did you ever think that I'm happy when I'm you with you, because of you?" Harry asked.

She smiled. "I hope so."

Harry could only envy such a philosophy. Too bad more people didn't share her outlook. Too bad he didn't have it himself. He had mood swings, sometimes for no reason at all. He would try to adopt Astrid's outlook on life. An easy, friendly relationship evolved between them. Harry looked forward to a few days in Karachi where he hoped to raise it to another level.

Harry had noticed that Joe had not removed his jacket or left his seat since the flight began. Harry also noticed that Joe appeared to have a death grip on something in the inside pocket of his coat. "Harry," he said now, "I want you to do something for me."

"What do you need," Harry had responded. Joe removed a fat envelope from his pocket and held it out to Harry.

"What is it? "asked Harry.

"It's money," Joe said, "and lots of it. Thor gave it to me this morning. We need it to pay for landing fees, catering and I have no idea what else. I never heard of a ship's fund, but we got one. And I want you to take care of it for me."

"How much you got there, Joe?" asked Harry. Joe grimaced.

"Would you believe there is forty grand in here? Some of it is in English pounds. All together, forty grand."

"Wow," said Harry with raised eyebrows and a low whistle, "and you want me to hold it for you? Why, for Christ's sake?" asked Harry.

"Because," said Joe, "I trust you more than I trust me. Damn, I'm afraid even to even have a drink with all this money on me." Harry had to admit that Joe was not a man he would trust with forty thousand dollars in cash.

While moving about the town in Oslo, Joe had been incapable of figuring out the exchange rate of the Norwegian kroner. And it was easy. Four kroner to a dollar; anyone could do it. Joe could not do it. He just could not do it and he came to rely on Harry to change the kroner price into dollars. Harry thought hard for a few moments, then he decided that despite the responsibility, the money was far safer in his pocket than in Joe's. It might be a way to help them make it through the unknown that stretched ahead.

"Okay, Joe," said Harry, as he held out his hand. "I'll hold the cash as long as I don't have to sign for it."

"Hell," snorted Joe, "I didn't even sign for it myself."

As Harry reached down beneath his seat for his flight bag to put the money in, Joe pushed the call button to order a drink. That would be the first of many.

Arriving in Karachi, they taxied to the Intercontinental Hotel. Harry arranged a crew party in his room. It was really the continuation of the one held in the airplane. By then, Joe was well-lubricated and the alcohol not only loosened his tongue, it seemed to arouse his libido as well. He was sitting next to Margaretta, an earthy Swedish girl about a third of his age; but a few drinks can uncover hidden courage and, at one point, Harry saw Joe open his wallet, withdraw a one hundred dollar bill, and offer it to Margaretta. He asked her if she would let him kiss one of her breasts.

"Only one?" she teased with a grin. "What is your offer for both of them? Perhaps I will give a discount, an airline discount."

After the party, except for briefly joining the crew for dinner the next evening, Joe was not seen for three days. That was when Harry learned the departure time of their flight and decided to check up on Joe to see if he was still operational. Harry entered Joe's room in mid-afternoon to find the curtains drawn, the room dark and smelling foul, and Joe in bed, drink in hand. He did not need the drink. He was already drunk and looked like he had been drunk for the entire three days.

Harry said, with a hard edge in his voice, "Joe, you have got to straighten up. We leave tomorrow afternoon. You can't fly like this."

"Now, Harry," he said, "if it comes down to it, I fly better after a few drinks. No need to worry."

Harry drew in a deep breath and said, in what he hoped was a commanding voice, "No, Joe, you are not getting on that airplane tomorrow unless you are stone-cold sober. You got that?" Without waiting for an answer, Harry turned and left the room, slamming the door as he left. Had he gotten through to Joe? He hoped so

It was only three days, but it seemed as if they had been in Karachi forever. They came to know many of the hotel staff. Among them was the leader of the band that played in the hotel restaurant. They dined there every night and each time they entered the room, the band would stop the song they were playing and break into "Leaving on a Jet Plane," which was one of Harry's favorites.

"I call that a very special favor," Harry told Hasan, who was Pakistani, "and we appreciate it." The reason for that special favor, Harry knew, was that Hasan was infatuated with Margaretta. She had asked for that song.

"What about that, Margaretta?" Harry had teased her. "Looks to me like a very big love. I'm not sure Hasan could handle a woman like you, but he would for sure like to try. Swedish and Pakistani. That's a great combination. Just think of the beautiful babies you'd make."

They were eating dinner and Margaretta picked up her napkin and threw it at Harry. "Harry, that is not nice. I cannot imagine making babies with Hasan. Now, if you were to make an offer, then I might be interested. We will make beautiful babies. What do you think?" She was laughing as she said it.

"Sure," he answered, "your room or mine? But don't forget, I can't play a guitar."

"Never mind," she said, still laughing, "we do not need music for making babies."

Another song they heard often was "Spanish Eyes." Hasan played that song because Joe paid for it. It started when they were eating dinner on their first night there. Joe had reached into his pocket and pulled out the roll of one-hundred dollar bills he always carried. Peeling off one, he handed it to Harry and asked him to give it to the band because he wanted to hear "Spanish Eyes." Harry, evaluating the situation in a few seconds, agreed; but by time he got up to the bandstand, he had pocketed Joe's bill and replaced it with a five-dollar bill of his own. He would straighten it out with Joe later.

The bandleader, expecting more donations, broke into "Spanish Eyes" often when the crew was there, so Joe's five dollars went a long way. A few days later, Harry gave Joe his change. He seemed puzzled, but accepted the money, not wanting to appear that he did not know what it was for. Joe obviously loved that song, and he became emotional every time he heard it. Harry had once seen tears in Joe's eyes as he listened to the song. For the rest of his life, Harry would think about Joe every time he heard, "Spanish Eyes."

During their stay, the crew had toured the city and done some shopping. Not a shopper, Harry usually went along if Astrid was in the group. They spent some time together by the pool where they began to know each other. She introduced Harry to a concoction called compari and tonic. He liked them. One afternoon, Astrid told him about her broken engagement to a fiancée named Martin. He could see it bothered her very much. Who had broken it off, Harry had asked.

"I did," she answered, "because I wasn't sure, and I wanted to see more of the world, not only Oslo. Was this the right decision?"

"Sorry, Astrid," said Harry, "but I don't give advice to the lovelorn." Astrid's eyebrows rose.

"Lovelorn?" she asked, puzzled by that word.

"Never mind," he answered. "Let's just say that when it comes to love, no one is ever sure."

For their last night in Karachi Harry arranged a crew dinner where they not only dined well but heard "Spanish Eyes" several times. Joe was certainly getting his money's worth. It was a splendid evening. Harry sat next to Astrid, and they danced while waiting for their dinner. During one of those dances, with Astrid holding him closely, Harry gathered up his courage and asked if she would like to come to his room for a drink after dinner.

"Oh, yes," she said as Harry held his breath. "I would very much love to come to your room. But not to drink, to make love. I want to go to bed with you."

Harry struggled to control his surprise. Astrid was nothing if not straightforward. Then he exhaled slowly and nodded.

"I think I can help you with that," he said.

The next morning Harry was awakened by the pleasant sensation of Astrid's fingertips softly stroking his thigh. The next sensation, even more pleasant, was the tip of her tongue in his ear. His groin began to stir almost before he was awake.

"Now, that is a nice way to wake up," he said sleepily.

"Harry," she whispered, "this was a wonderful night. I very much enjoyed it. And I enjoyed meeting your beautiful friend."

"Friend? What friend?" asked Harry, not sure he had heard right.

"You know. Your friend! I don't know his name in English."

Then Harry understood. "Ah, that friend!" He chuckled. "Oh, he is called by many names," he said, "but I don't think beautiful is one of them." He smiled as the memories of last night flooded across his mind. "Yes," he said after a pause. "Last night was very 'bra' for me too. It was a wonderful night, wasn't it?"

Astrid kissed his cheek. "Yes, even more than wonderful, and I hope we can do it again soon. But now I think we need some 'frukost.'"

"Frukost?" asked Harry quizzically. "If that means breakfast, count me in. I'm starving."

She smiled. "Really? I wonder why." Still smiling, she said, "Harry, I am very pleased to discover that you are a happy person in the morning."

Now, it was Harry's turn to smile. "I wonder why," he said. "Let's go have some breakfast.

11
BACK FROM CAMBODIA

1965

"Pawtucket, Pawtucket, Battlecry three zero one. Over," John released the mike button on the throttle and glanced over his shoulder to assure himself that Harry was still there. They were "feet wet," meaning they had crossed the coastline and were now over the sea, headed back to the ship. Harry was relieved to be over the water again. There was no reply from the ship, but that was not unusual. John would try again when they were closer. Harry checked his fuel gauge and began calculating how much fuel he would have on arrival at the ship. Fuel was a never-ending concern for all pilots, but especially for carrier pilots.

Tonight there was little need to worry. The flight had been a smooth one and they had gotten rid of the bombs early. That meant less weight and less drag for the flight home. They would be overhead with plenty of fuel; but you never knew when a problem might arise during the recovery. A blown tire on a jet landing ahead of them, for example, might cause a fouled deck. You never knew how long it would take to clear the landing area when something like that happened. Fuel was a carrier pilot's best friend. He never had too much.

All the pilots flew with a small pad strapped to one thigh. The kneeboard carried all sorts of vital information on different cards that were clipped to the board in a stack. One of those cards told John how much fuel he would need to fly from the ship to the nearest airfield ashore. He could then calculate how long he could hold over the ship and still have enough fuel to make it to that airfield if that became necessary. The minimum fuel needed to reach that airfield was called "bingo" fuel. No one knew why. The bingo fuel number was an important one. Once the fuel dropped below that number, the pilot was committed to landing on the ship. Sometimes, with enough fuel for landing, but not enough to reach an airfield ashore, he might have to eject from a perfectly good airplane. That might happen if a fouled deck could not be cleared in time, and the pilot would run out of fuel before the ship was ready to bring him aboard. Ejection over the ship was far safer than landing on the sea.

Pawtucket had responded to John's next call, and he was directed to a position 30 miles astern of the ship at 20,000 feet. There, the flight held in a circular pattern awaiting instructions. There was a launch underway and the landing area on the deck would not be clear until the launch was completed. After fifteen minutes of making circles, Harry was switched to a Carrier-Controlled Approach radio frequency, known as CCA. As the wingman, he would be vectored in first. A few minutes later, John would follow.

Harry flicked his wing lights to tell John he was breaking off, then left them on. Next, by rotating a lever on the starboard bulkhead, he lowered his hook. His attention was inside the cockpit now as he turned to the heading given by CCA. John, whose running lights had been in the dim position to make it easier on his wingman, flicked a toggle switch to put his lights on bright so he could be more easily seen from the ship.

After Harry had broken off, he had been switched to a different radio frequency and John was no longer in contact with him. There was a lot of silence, but Harry didn't mind. He had plenty of fuel and it was a beautiful night. After a few minutes, he heard, "Battlecry three zero six, turn right to heading 345. Descend to and maintain angels ten." Angels ten meant ten thousand feet.

"Roger, Pawtucket, three zero six turning right to 345 and descending to angels ten."

Harry was given heading and altitude commands that eventually brought him inbound to the ship at 500 feet, on the ship's course. He lowered his landing gear and extended his flaps. His airplane was now configured to land. He was given continuous heading corrections and kept apprised of his distance from the ship. Finally, he heard, "Three zero six, you are at one-half mile, report the ball."

Now, for the first time since he had left 20,000 feet, Harry took his attention away from his flight instruments and looked outside the cockpit, and there she was. He could make out the masthead and running rights and a few seconds later, he found the meatball neatly squeezed between two rows of green lights.

"Battlecry three zero six has the ball, state one point eight," said Harry.

The "one point eight" was the amount of his remaining fuel, stated in thousands of pounds. That was part of the aircraft's total weight, and it was needed to set the resistance of the arresting gear.

"Roger, zero six, continue visually."

At that point, another voice came up and said, "Three zero six, Paddles. You are on the glide, slightly left of centerline." That was a familiar voice and it was music to Harry's ears. Paddles was the Landing Signal Officer and he now had control of Harry's approach. Harry was flying the airplane, but

Paddles was flying Harry. His commands were mandatory, whether Harry agreed with them or not.

Landing Signal Officers were legends in Naval aviation. All Navy pilots had heard about Walt McCall, an LSO in Harry's first squadron. "Mac" happily carried around a belly that he described as "185 pounds of ice cream and cookies." Some of those pounds came from drinking beer. "It's a beautiful day," he liked to say. "Let's go find a bar with a big picture window." He was affable and unassuming, except when he took up his post on the LSO platform. There, he became intense and focused. The pilots he brought aboard never heard his intensity over the radio. Always unruffled, he never raised his voice no matter how badly an approach was flown. Harry was always pleased to hear his reassuring voice when he switched his radio to LSO control during an approach.

The landing area and the four cables stretched across it were Mac's domain and he brooked no interference from anyone. This crusty LSO was once sharply criticized by the ship's captain during a recovery. Mac's reply was hard-edged.

"Captain," he said firmly, "with all due respect, you run the sharp end of the ship and let me run the blunt end until we get these birds aboard." That Mac felt such a retort was warranted said much about the authority of LSOs.

Before the optical landing system came along, the LSOs used flag-like devices, called paddles, to issue commands to aircraft landing on the ship. In a kind of semaphore system, they told a pilot what his airplane was doing and what they wanted the pilot to do. The LSO could see what was happening to the flight path of an airplane even before the pilot knew it. That came from undergoing rigorous training that included observing thousands of approaches, both on the field and at the ship. They held pilots' lives in those paddles and they made damned sure that a trainee knew what he was doing before he was deemed qualified. With a paddle in each hand and using various movements, the LSO would signal the pilot that his approach was okay and, if not, what to do to get it that way. If the aircraft was on the right speed and on the glide path, he would see the LSO extending both arms horizontally. If that position did not change throughout the approach, it was graded OK. No corrections had been needed. That was a Roger Pass and it was what every pilot wanted to hear when he was debriefed in the squadron Ready Room after his landing.

Each squadron posted a chart on its Ready Room bulkhead. It was called the Greenie Board. On it was a list of all the pilots, with a row of squares following each name. Each square represented a landing. In it were the comments of the LSO for that landing. This chart was a public display of a pilot's ability to get aboard the ship. If there were no comments, the approach was graded OK, and the box was colored green. "Greenies" were highly regarded and they were a strong incentive to fly well. Also noted was the number of the wire caught by the tail hook upon landing. The "four" wire was the most forward wire. There was nothing wrong with snagging this one, except that a miss meant a bolter. A "four" wire said the pilot had landed slightly long. The "three" wire was the target and it was the safest. The "two" wire was farther aft and meant less hook-to-ramp clearance. It was acceptable but raised LSO eyebrows. The "one" wire caused a sharp intake of his breath. Worst of all was T1. That meant "Taxi to the one wire." That sent out alarm signals because it meant the airplane had landed well short of the "one" wire, with minimum clearance between the airplane and the flight deck as it passed over the ramp. "OK 3" was what the pilot wanted to see in the squares next to his name.

LSOs used their own shorthand which they squeezed into the squares. HAR, for example, meant High at the Ramp. HS meant High Start, and so on. FAB, rarely used, meant Fast as a Bastard. One that Harry had heard about, but was not sure he believed, was FNKUA. That one stood for Fucking Near Killed Us All. It could well have been true, Harry knew, because the LSOs stood on their "platform" on the port side of the flight deck aft of the touchdown area. They were vulnerable. A net had been placed outboard of the platform for them to jump into if a badly-flown approach had them bore-sighted. The net was not often needed, but Harry knew for a fact that it had been used at least once. He had been one of those leaping into the net one day while observing landings with the LSOs. A late go-around by an airplane left of the centerline had caused it to fly right over the LSO platform and scatter all those standing on it. That pilot's debrief consisted almost entirely of four-letter words.

Each pilot was debriefed by the LSO after each landing. Those sessions took place in the pilot's Ready Room and were overheard by all those who cared to listen. Even though the LSO had God-like authority in the landing pattern, not every pilot agreed with the assessment of the approach he had just flown. Disagreements were frequent and sometimes sharp.

During one debrief, Harry had a disagreement with an LSO, who was a close friend.

"John," Harry had said, frowning with irritation, "are you sure that's my approach you're talking about?"

Apparently, John Allen had heard enough complaints that day. Without one word, but with a fierce glower, he had wheeled around and stomped out of the Ready Room; but his debrief ended up in a square after Harry's name. The LSO always had the final word and his comments were entered onto the bulkhead chart, whether the pilot liked them or not.

LSO Tom Exley once ran a Field Carrier Landing Practice session, known as FCLP, on the main runway at the Miramar Naval Air Station. Harry was in one of six Skyraiders in the landing pattern that day. The pilots were at one point instructed to discontinue their approaches and orbit the runway. That was unusual, and during the debrief, Harry had asked the reason for the interruption. Exley smiled thinly and shook his head.

"You won't believe this," he said, and went on to tell them how, in the midst of six Navy airplanes making practice carrier landings, a light airplane had touched down and made a landing. Not only that, the plane had lifted off, turned downwind and had come back around for another landing. This time, the LSO crew was ready. They piled into their Navy vehicle and pulled alongside the light plane as it was adding power to go around again. Using hand signals, they waved the airplane to the side of the runway.

The pilot was a middle-aged woman wearing a man's fedora hat and smoking a cigarette that dangled from a corner of her mouth. She was, of course, surprised and puzzled. What was the matter?

"Lady," Exley asked sarcastically, "what in the hell are you doing here?"

"Why, making practice landings, of course, and why are you asking?"

"Where do you think you are?" Exley asked, still fuming.

By now, she was beginning to suspect she was not where she thought she was. "Isn't this Montgomery Airport?" she asked tentatively.

That airport, a few miles away, had a small, narrow landing strip about one-fourth as long as the Miramar runway and was made of black-top. You had to work hard to make a mistake like that one, but somehow, she had managed to do it. With a few unkind words about "lousy women drivers," Exley sent on her way. First, he made her promise never to land at Miramar again.

Because the Landing Signal Officer used paddles to control carrier landings in the early days, the LSO himself was always, in all squadrons, called "Paddles." That name stuck even after the optical landing system made paddles obsolete. In those early days, with different movements of

49

his paddles, the LSO signaled the pilots and in this way controlled their approaches. If the pilot was on the glide path at the right speed, he saw the LSO standing with both arms extended straight out horizontally. This was a Roger signal and it meant "You're doing fine, keep it coming." If a correction was needed, the LSO would, with his paddles, tell the pilot what his airplane was doing. A pilot going above the glide path, for example, saw the paddles rise into a V, like the wings of a seagull. The paddles went down if he was too low. The paddles would return to the Roger position as the airplane came back onto the glide path. If the pilot needed power, he saw the paddles come together in front of the LSO in sweeping motions. That signal was known as a "Come-on." It said, "Come on, put on some power." Power was added according to the speed of the motions. If the LSO remained in the Roger position throughout the approach, no corrections were needed and the approach was graded a Roger Pass.

Harry's first squadron had once made a brief visit to Rio de Janeiro. The first sight they had seen upon entering the port was an enormous statue of Jesus Christ standing atop Mount Corcovado, grandly overlooking the harbor, arms outstretched. To Naval aviators, the statue resembled the LSO during a Roger Pass, and that's what they named him. That might be irreverent, thought Harry, but it was certainly apt.

The paddles signal pilots did not like to see was the Wave-Off. This was a rapid criss-crossing of the paddles above the LSO's head and it meant go around and try again. Either the airplane was not in a good position to land or the deck was fouled. A fouled deck meant the landing area was not clear of other aircraft. It also happened when the cable drawn out by the preceding airplane during an arrested landing had not yet been fully retracted.

As a flight student in Pensacola, Harry had qualified aboard the ship using the paddles system and it worked fine; but it had serious limitations. It required visual landing patterns at night and that could be frightening for an inexperienced pilot. At night, the LSO wore a special suit and used special paddles. He was lighted electrically so the pilots could see him. Landing on a ship at night was never easy, but it was much more difficult and dangerous using paddles. Compared to the optical landing system, the paddles were very primitive. Navy pilots were grateful, very grateful, when the optical system came along.

Now, Harry saw the meatball and squeezed his mike button. "Three zero six, ball, state one point four. "

"Roger, ball, continue approach," answered Paddles. Now the LSO knew that Harry had the ball visually and that he had 1,400 pounds of fuel remaining. So far, so good. Harry was in level flight at 500 feet when he first saw the meatball. A few seconds later, the ball began to rise ever so slightly. That meant Harry had intercepted the glide path and had to start his descent. With hook, gear and flaps already down, his airplane was set to land. To start descending, he eased back the throttle and held his airspeed. He would not look inside the cockpit again until he was on deck.

To enable him to monitor his speed without looking in the cockpit, Harry watched an indicator mounted on top of the left side of the glare shield above the instrument panel. Its red, green and yellow lights told him whether he was slow, fast, or on speed. A remote indicator of these signals was shown outside the airplane for the LSO. Now, it became a game of airspeed, rate of descent and line-up. Sometimes, if he caught it just right, he could come down the glide path barely moving the throttle. Usually, though, it was a continuous series of corrections. Going low? Add a bit of power, but not too much or the airspeed would get out of hand. Back on the glide? Complete the correction by taking off a bit of power.

It was instrument flying using the optical landing system as a primary reference; but there was a seat-of-the-pants element, too. That came from experience. The hard part came just as the plane crossed over the ship's fantail. At that moment, if the plane was on the glide path, there was a clearance of just twelve feet between the tail hook and the flight deck. A pilot had to be careful in-close for another reason. Often, especially in the daytime when the air was more unstable, the wind created by the ship's movement through the water augmented the actual wind, causing a strong downdraft just aft of the ship. He had to be ready to pour on some power to avoid going low as the plane closed with the ship.

Tonight, the air was calm and Harry's approach was on the money all the way down. Because other landing airplanes were on different radio frequencies, Harry heard only silence as he flew down the glide path. That meant the LSO was satisfied with his approach and no corrective commands were needed. Harry was aware of this, but, even so, that silence was eerie.

From habit, Harry added power as he crossed the fantail, then hit the deck. As he did, he rammed the throttle full forward in case he missed a wire. He retracted his speed brakes, too. They had been extended to create drag and allow the engine to operate at a higher power setting. Engine acceleration was better in higher power ranges. A split second later, Harry was thrown sharply forward against his shoulder straps as his hook caught a wire and brought him to a stop over a distance of about 250 feet.

Once, and only once, had Harry forgotten to lock his shoulder straps before landing. The arrested landing threw his body forward and the visor of his helmet had struck the gun sight above the instrument panel. An inertial device was supposed to prevent this, but it seemed to be off duty that day. A line of a Navy pilot drinking song recalled, "He wears a Mark 8 gun sight where he used to wear his face." Harry was thankful for that visor.

The arresting wire always recoiled slightly after roll-out, and it was then that the crewman on deck signaled Harry to raise his tail hook. Without looking down, Harry found the lever that raised the hook and rotated it. Now, the crewman, with a gesture of both wands pointing forward, passed control of Harry's plane to another crewman, who guided Harry to the parking area on the bow. It was essential to clear the landing area quickly for the next airplane. The target interval between landing airplanes during daylight operations was thirty seconds. At night, it was longer because taxiing on the flight deck was more hazardous and extra time was needed.

Harry very carefully followed the taxi commands until he saw the signal that the chocks were in place. When he saw the "cut engine" command, he pulled the throttle back to the cut-off position, released his shoulder straps, removed his oxygen mask, and exhaled a long sigh of relief.

12
OFF FOR KUALA LUMPUR

July 1970

The day began with Harry giving Joe a personal wake-up call. Joe's room still smelled like a distillery and Joe looked like death warmed over, but at least he was sober. Harry figured that Joe would be of little help in any condition, but sober made him legal and easier to control, and he was grateful for that. In the taxi to the airport, one of the stewardesses, in a discreet moment, asked Harry in a whisper, "Is it safe with him?"

"Sure," Harry had replied "just a little too late last night."

He would keep a close eye on Joe.

Thor had decided that even though both Harry and Joe were qualified to fly in command, Joe would be in charge of the airplane. That had seemed right back in Oslo, but it was looking less so as Harry came to know Joe. One of the things he had learned was that Joe had, for fifteen years with Eastern Airlines, flown the same Miami/Houston route. That meant he hadn't had to think very much in the air. Harry also found out that, until now, Joe had never in his life been outside the United States. Harry wasn't sure why, but that piece of news made him uneasy. He would soon find out why. Joe, it would turn out, was unable to read an airways chart or make a proper position report. During those fifteen years with Eastern, his mind had been on autopilot, along with his airplane.

The Trans Polar flight arrived from London and the Karachi crew was there on the ramp to meet it. Thor was on board, and before he said hello, he asked Joe Thomas for the ship's fund.

"Now that I'm here, I will take control of the money - - not that I don't trust you," he added with a smile.

He did not know, and Harry did not tell him, that Joe should not have been trusted with the money in the first place. He hoped Thor would not ask why Harry, and not Joe, held the cash.

"He's got it," Joe said, and pointed to Harry, who placed his flight bag on the deck, dipped into it and brought out a large envelope wrapped in a plastic sack. In it was the $40,000, less the expenses from the hotel in Karachi.

"The receipts are in there, too," said Harry, as he handed the sack to Thor, who, without looking inside, dropped it into a black satchel at his side. As he did, Harry saw that the satchel already held what appeared to be a substantial pile of money. Thor then took up a position in the jump seat behind the captain's seat and he would almost become a part of that seat in the hours ahead. He left it only to visit the toilet. The black satchel full of money might have been the reason.

Harry knew they were in trouble when he searched for the Hong Kong airport approach charts after settling into his seat in the 707 cockpit. The charts for the other airports were there, but not those for Hong Kong. The ramp at Karachi International Airport was not the place to look for replacements. Still, they couldn't leave without those charts. It was mid-July in Pakistan and Harry had been sweating since leaving the hotel. Now, his frustration began to rise, along with his body temperature. This was no way to run an airline.

It was no use; the charts were nowhere to be found. Harry picked up the mike and called Ground Control and asked if there was any chance of getting the needed charts at Airport Operations. Harry's request was met with silence. Then an amused voice said, "Say again." Harry repeated his request, but it was soon obvious that the charts would need to be found elsewhere. But where? Harry had an idea. Telling Joe he would be back soon, he left the airplane and began a tour of the airplanes in transit which were parked around the ramp. His third stop took him to a Cathay Pacific crew who had three sets of charts for Hong Kong.

"That's three more than we have," said Harry, with what he hoped was an engaging smile. "Any chance of borrowing one?"

The Captain was British, right down to wearing his cap in the cockpit. He offered a condescending smile and said, "Of course. You Yanks never could make it without us."

Harry thanked him and smiled back. "I won't mention saving your ass in the war," he said, as he left the cockpit and hurried off to his own airplane.

By this time the passengers, who had boarded the plane in London, had been in their seats for about twelve hours, the last two on a hot-as-hell ramp in Karachi in the summer. They were not happy travelers.

"Okay, Joe" said Harry, as he climbed back into his seat. "Call for start-up."

He picked up the mike and made a brief announcement that the plane would soon be on its way, and he was answered with a loud cheer.

The first stop was for fuel in Calcutta. Harry knew from the start that Trans Polar would be a do-it-yourself operation but, until now, he did not realize just how much there was to do. In other airlines there were other people to file flight plans, figure out fuel requirements, obtain landing and overflight rights, and do all the many tasks associated with running an airline.

The first clue that something might be amiss came when they approached India's air space and were asked for their overflight authorization number. Harry and Joe looked blankly at each other. What in the hell was he talking about, they wondered. Thor, who had come all the way from London, was fast asleep in the observer's seat behind the captain. Harry reached back and shook his leg. He stirred. Yes, he said sleepily, they had applied for all the necessary permissions but not all of the requests had been answered. This was all news to Harry, who, before now, had never even heard of an overflight authorization.

"So, what should we tell this guy? He wants a number."

Thor thought for a few seconds, then said, "Tell him that we have the number and we are looking for it. We will send it when we find it."

While pretending to search for the number, Harry heard a series of radio transmissions that could happen only over India. When an Indian pilot misunderstood a clearance, the controller tried to straighten him out by spelling a word. The pilot was still confused. Was that letter a B or a P?

"No, no" said the controller, "that is a 'B' like in Bombay."

Harry had noticed that Indians sometimes pronounced B like P and also the other way around.

This pilot thought about that for a moment, then asked, "Yes, but is that B like in Bombay, India or B like in Pompeii, Italy?"

Harry supposed you had to hear it to appreciate it, and he did, chuckling to himself as he shook his head.

There followed a radio cat-and-mouse game that bought them enough time to pass into another control zone and the number request did not resurface. Thank God for that, thought Harry; but he wondered what other problems lay ahead. They struggled through a transit stop in Calcutta and if Harry never saw that airport again, it would be too soon.

While the refueling was going on, a passenger wandered into the cockpit. He had once visited Calcutta.

"Oh?" said Harry, making polite conversation. "What's it like?"

The passenger frowned. "You don't want to spend any holidays here." Interested, Harry asked the reason. Poverty reigned supreme, the passenger responded. The city was filthy, and nothing worked. Worst of all, he said, was the daily sight of the local "meat wagon" collecting its morning round of dead bodies from the streets of the city. Harry nodded.

"Thanks," he said. "It sounds like there are better places to visit. I won't put Calcutta on the top of my list."

The next stop was in Kuala Lumpur and, for this part of the trip, the services of Savak Munchurchi would be needed. Harry did not need Savak, but the Norwegian air law said he had to be there for crossing the Bay of Bengal. Savak was a London-based Indian from Bombay, and he had been introduced on the ramp at Karachi as "our navigator." He was short and swarthy and his face was badly pockmarked. He tried so hard to be friendly that he was obsequious. Savak must have come cheap because he knew almost nothing about navigation. It takes only a few hours to cross the Bay, but in the summer it is usually packed with thunderstorms. That meant a lot of detours. There are few navigation aids in the area, so much of the flying was with dead reckoning, a technique which uses time and heading to establish the aircraft's position. It's old and basic, but if done right, it works. Savak had never heard of it.

Before long, they entered Burma airspace and they heard again that request for an overflight number. This time, the caller meant business. If you do not produce your number right now, we will launch our interceptors, said the voice on the radio. Harry raised his eyebrows. Burma has an Air Force? There seemed to be no sense in finding out, so Harry turned to the heading instructed by ATC. That took them out of Burma airspace.

In 1970, navigation, in general, was less than pinpoint perfect, especially in the backwaters of the world. So, here they were, dodging very menacing thunderstorms that looked to be well above Harry's altitude of 35,000 feet, and trying to figure out how to find their way to Kuala Lumpur. Harry grimaced as he looked over the monster storm cells that were all around them. He knew from experience the strong turbulence within them. He had seen cells like these cause loose objects to fly about the cockpit. He had often deviated far off-course to avoid such cells and he would do so now, if necessary. He had boasted, "My off-course deviation record is 130 miles." The many course changes made it hard to navigate but, for now, it was more important to stay clear of the thunderstorms.

Savak kept looking frantically out the window for landmarks that are hard to find over water.

"Anybody see any islands?" he kept asking.

The situation had even prompted Joe to rouse himself to see what all the fuss was about. He had a tendency to sleep in the cockpit. At first, that bothered Harry; but as he came to know Joe's airmanship abilities, he decided it did not make much difference if he was asleep or awake. Either way, he contributed very little. When it came to taking off or landing, no one flew better than Joe; but, except for that, he was basically useless. Gene Daily, the flight engineer, was an old-timer and he had been through it all. He could be counted on to do his job well.

For an hour or so, Harry was seriously concerned. Well, hell, he thought, we've got to hit land somewhere on this heading. Harry used a technique known as offset navigation that he had used in Vietnam. Instead of aiming directly for a coastal checkpoint, he headed to one side or the other. That way, he knew which way to turn when he reached land. It had served him well in Vietnam and it worked here, too. They finally picked up a low frequency radio beacon, and then a VOR from Kuala Lumpur, and that led them in. By now, the night had closed in around them, making a bad situation worse.

During most of this time, due mainly to weather interference with the radio, they had been out of contact with any airways control; so the Approach Control at Kuala Lumpur was somewhat surprised to hear them check in. Harry knew their bearing from the VOR station but because of the maneuvering to avoid thunderstorms, he could only guess at the distance. Then, through a break in the weather, Harry suddenly saw the shimmering lights of Kuala Lumpur, 35,000 feet directly beneath them. It was definitely time to start down.

The descent was somewhat harrowing because of the high rate necessitated by their nearness to the airport, and because they flew through numerous layers of cloud. The turbulence was nerve-jarring. There was almost nonstop lightning flashing all around them as they skirted several massive thunderstorms. This was no way to arrive at an airport, thought Harry, as he followed the instructions of the approach controller while he configured the aircraft for landing. This was always the uptight part of a flight, especially under difficult weather conditions.

The controller directed Harry to the radio beacon that served as a marker for the runway in use. There, he would start an instrument approach to the Kuala Lumpur airport. He was then cleared for an approach using the Instrument Landing System. Being cleared for an ILS meant Harry was now controlling himself and would follow the flight pattern depicted on the approach chart for runway 33. That chart showed the top view of the flight pattern, as well as the profile view. On reaching the beacon, he turned to a heading which took him away from the airport. As he did, he punched the clock on the instrument panel to start timing his outbound leg. He was now level at the altitude at which he would, in a few minutes, intercept the glide path to the runway.

After exactly one minute, Harry began a turn back to the beacon, leveled his wings and watched intently for his instruments to tell him he was intercepting the localizer. This was a radio beam that would provide guidance to keep him aligned with the runway. Another radio beam would give Harry electronic glide path information. The entire presentation was presented visually on Harry's instrument panel. All he had to do now was to hold the aircraft on both of these radio guidance beams, one indicating his position relative to the extended centerline of the runway, known as the landing line, and the other, his position relative to the glide path. To make all this easier than it might seem, Harry used an instrument known as a flight director.

This instrument displayed a miniature airplane and its position relative to both of the guidance beams. If the aircraft wandered off course, either vertically or horizontally, the flight director not only showed the pilot the picture, it computed a way to get back into position. All Harry had to do was to keep the miniature airplane centered on the crosshairs representing the intersection of the two radio beams, adjust his speed as necessary, and fly the airplane down to the decision height. This was the minimum height to which the airplane could descend without sighting the runway. Pilots have been known to "sneak a peek" below the minimum authorized altitude. Harry never did that. At the decision height, the pilot landed if he saw the runway and went around for another try if he did not. The go-around procedures were shown on the approach chart. They were not needed tonight, as the plane broke out of the clouds well above the decision height, and Harry made a good landing, despite gusty winds.

13
YANKEE STATION

December 1965

There was a place in the Tonkin Gulf known as Yankee Station. It did not appear on any map, but it was there all right. It was the focal point of a nucleus of aircraft carriers that carried out air strikes against North Vietnam, Cambodia, and Laos. In December 1965, the entire world knew about the operations in North Vietnam; but most of the world was unaware of those taking place in Laos and Cambodia. Harry figured that was part of a public relations campaign to make the war appear smaller than it really was. More horseshit, thought Harry, who believed in calling a spade a spade.

Life, however, did not work that way in the military mind, so Harry and his squadron-mates had been ordered not to disclose these operations to anyone. Not even, they were told, should they so much as mention those countries by name; so they came to be known as Those Other Countries, and you could almost hear the capital letters when they came up in conversation. There was another carrier focal point in the southern Tonkin Gulf. It was called Dixie Station, and it was from there that close air support missions were sent out over South Vietnam; but Yankee Station was where the action was.

As compensation for the danger the aircrews faced flying in the Tonkin Gulf, they were paid an extra $65 per month, called hazardous duty pay. That was not big money even in 1965, thought Harry. Why bother? To receive this money, a man had to be within a defined geographical area at least once during the month. The aircrews, of course, were in it almost daily. To qualify the rest of the ship's crew for this pay, the captain, once each month, took the ship into the designated area, then did a quick U-turn back to Yankee Station. Well, hell, thought Harry. Why not? It seemed a fitting commentary on this bizarre war.

The strikes of Yankee Station were of three kinds. First, there were the road reconnaissance flights that searched for those mechanized vehicles within 200 yards of a motor-able road or trail. Harry and his squadron-mates had scoured hundreds, perhaps thousands, of miles of those roads and trails and not once did Harry catch sight of a mechanized vehicle.

Then, there was a list of targets designated as JCS targets. These were targets authorized by the Joint Chiefs of Staff to be struck anytime. The list was not very long, so when you got to the bottom, you went back to the top and started all over again. Some of these targets had been hit a dozen or more times; so, in most cases, there was only an enormous hole in the ground where the target once stood.

On Harry's very last mission before heading home, he had been assigned a target in westernmost North Vietnam, near the border with Laos. The pilots shunned these targets because there was an awful lot of real estate to cover if they got hit during the strike and had to make it back to sea, where the chances of rescue were high. As Harry scowled at his assignment that day, his irritation was clearly visible. Tom Curry, the squadron Air Intelligence Officer, noticed the look on Harry's face. It was hard to miss.

"Problem?" asked Tom, as he slid into a chair next to Harry.

"My last one," said Harry painfully. "And look where they send me."

Tom glanced at the assignment, stood up and said, "I'll be right back. I just want to check something."

He returned a few minutes later to tell Harry that, believe it or not, Harry's strike would be the twelfth strike against that target. Harry thought he was by now inured to being incredulous but he managed to muster up some incredulity anyway.

"Goddamn!" he exploded. "This is supposed to be a suspected storage building and they send twelve strikes against it? This is horseshit, Tom. It's for damn sure there's no building there anymore, if there ever was one. You can tell the Admiral that I'm not going. I'll unload on the first target of opportunity."

Tom shrugged. "Be my guest, Harry. There's no need to bother the Admiral over this."

This little farce was the result of a shortage of authorized targets. Well, thought Harry angrily, I'll be damned if I'll end up getting shot down way over there on my last flight. This one, they can shove up their ass or asses, as the case may be. Until now, Harry had made a conscientious effort to carry out every mission, however absurd; but this one was over the line, especially on his very last mission. On that flight, for the first time, Harry had launched with no intention of going to the target; and somehow, that seemed right and felt good.

The third type of strike was called an Alpha Strike. Like everything else in this peculiar little war, no one knew why. Alpha Strikes were a one-time operation and they were controlled in great detail by the Pentagon, and, in some cases, Harry suspected, by the White House itself. Numbers and types of aircraft, bomb loads, time of strike, direction of strike, direction of pullout: all were specifically programmed by far-off bureaucrats and no discretion was left to the on-scene commander. This kind of planning would best be done here, where the action is, and by those who understood the situation. Still, there was no arguing with City Hall.

Many years later, at a squadron reunion, Harry would speak with an Air Intelligence Officer who had gone on to a career with the CIA. He told Harry about taking part in a three-way telephone conversation with his boss and, incredibly, President Johnson himself. The subject was a series of recent photos taken over North Vietnam. They showed a newly-erected building, its purpose unknown. The former AI and his superior were seeking guidance. They got it when LBJ, after a pause during which he was presumably examining the photos, ordered succinctly, "Bomb the fucker." There was no way to know for sure if that conversation had taken place as described; but Harry thought it probably had. It would have been in keeping with the conduct of the war as Harry saw it.

City Hall had decided that the day before Christmas 1965, would be a good day for an Alpha Strike. A sense of foreboding always came with an assignment to one of these strikes and Harry felt it as soon as he got the word. Not panic. Not even close to panic. It was just a vague feeling that, this time, he might not make it back. The strike was to be part of a pre-holiday barrage coordinated with the Air Force. Its aim was to make Ho Chi Minh sit up and take notice when President Johnson announced a Christmas bombing pause the next day. He was supposed to think that this might be his last chance for a peaceful settlement. Harry predicted that Uncle Ho would see this as a sign of weakness and, at its end, say, "No thanks, I am not interested." And that's exactly what happened, thirty-seven days later.

Harry was drinking coffee in the squadron Ready Room when the word was passed down about the next day's Alpha Strike. The Ready Room was, in a way, the family room of the squadron. It was the heart of squadron shipboard life, both socially and professionally. During periods of flight operations, it was all business. Although the pertinent target information was received in the Air Intelligence spaces, the flight briefings took place here. When there was no flying, the Ready Room became a social center. Movies were shown regularly on the ship's TV system. There was usually an Acey Deucy game in progress in one corner.

This board game was a sea-going version of backgammon, and every Navy man considered himself an expert. The games often drew large cheering sections that regularly offered unsolicited advice. Not only was such advice not asked for, it was usually disdainfully ignored, often to hoots and catcalls from the onlookers. Like much of life, Acey Deucy decisions were easier as a spectator than as a player. The games sometimes turned serious, and tournaments were held regularly. Harry recalled watching a championship match in which the finalist contenders showed up wearing robes and were accompanied by seconds with towels and water bottles, just like at Madison Square Garden.

As Harry sipped his coffee and watched an Acey Deucy game, the strike information began to come in. He quickly moved to the Duty Officer's desk. At first, the information was thin. Only the time and the target were disclosed.

"What are we carrying?" asked Harry. The type of ordnance dictated the tactics.

Bill Elliott paused while writing the strike pilots' names on the chalkboard. One was Harry's. He turned to give Harry a bemused look, and replied, "Come on, Harry, even if I knew, it'll change thirty-eight times between now and tomorrow morning. You know how it goes." Harry sighed. Yes, he thought, I know how it goes.

The target was the Haiphong bridge. It was known to be a hard target and well-defended. The Kitty Hawk's part of the strike would be made up of twenty-four airplanes, including four Skyhawks. The skipper would lead the flight, and Harry was assigned as Section Leader. That meant that he would fly the number three position as the leader of the two-plane second section. The mission would require in-flight refueling to top off the tanks after the launch and climb-out. Because of low ceilings in the target area, it was decided that the A4s would carry Snake-Eye bombs. Harry frowned when he heard that. These were bombs which, when released, deployed fins. They slowed the bomb after it was dropped. It was a low-level weapon and the fins made sure that the bomb, slowed by the fins, would not impact beneath the airplane that dropped it.

A few weeks earlier, an A4 pilot from another carrier had blown himself out of the sky with one of his own bombs. Unable to get to his target, and not allowed to bring them back to the ship, he had jettisoned them in low-level flight over Tiger Island, an island off the coast, near the Demilitarized Zone. It was a favorite repository for unwanted ordnance. The pilot had forgotten to de-arm the bombs, so, after they were released, they moved right along with the airplane and detonated almost beneath it. He managed to fly back to the ship. But, due to flight control problems caused by the explosions, he was forced to eject overhead and was hoisted out of the sea by the helo. After such a blunder, Harry would not have been surprised if the pilot had declined to be rescued.

The fins of the Snake-Eye bombs were supposed to prevent that sort of self-destruction. Harry had frowned because use of that bomb meant that low clouds were expected. That meant spending extra seconds at low levels, where aircraft vulnerability was sharply higher. Down near the ground, it seemed that all able-bodied citizens were shooting at him. Although the SAM missiles were effective, they were easily countered if you saw them coming. They could not turn with an A4. The 57mm and 85 mm anti-aircraft guns were not accurate.

But, down there, near the ground, the sky was filled with metal from all sorts of weapons, mainly automatic anti-aircraft guns. It was not a healthy place to be if you realized that the shrapnel did not have to hit the plane to bring it down. Sometimes the plane hit the shrapnel and it was everywhere. The sky was sometimes saturated with it. A standard tactic of the North Vietnamese was simply to fill the air over a target with metal and dare the pilots to fly through it. Other problems with the Snake-Eyes were that the fins made it less accurate and the slower impact speed of the bombs made them less effective. To Harry, using these bombs was an attempt to chalk up a mission, even if the chances for success were not good.

Like a mole coming out of its burrow, Harry squinted into the bright sunlight as he emerged from the bowels of the ship onto the flight deck. It was a glorious day for an Alpha Strike, he thought sardonically as he pre-flighted his aircraft, and then climbed into the cockpit. A bomb crew philosopher had painted "Joy to the World" on one of the bombs slung beneath his plane. Some Christmas, thought Harry, as he went through his pre-start checklist.

The flight had been well planned and it was well briefed by the skipper, but Harry knew what happened to plans once you were in the air. Plans are like golf balls, he had once heard someone say. They never go the way you want them to. "Plans are only for those unable to improvise," went another bromide, but you had to start somewhere. The flight path would take them north to a point east of Cam Pha, where the coast turns up towards China. There, they would turn west and fly overland to the target, hoping to catch the defense looking the other way.

The join-up after the launch went smoothly. That was a good omen, thought Harry. Sometimes, things went to hell before the airplanes ever got together. The Skyhawks positioned on the F4 Phantoms which would lead the strike and provide, hopefully, some quick punches against the missile sites they knew were waiting for them. They were also there as insurance against any North Vietnam pilots who felt lucky that day. The NVN air force had learned the hard way that they were no match for U.S. pilots and they had stopped trying; but you never knew.

About thirty minutes after the flight had rendezvoused and headed north, the skipper had led the four-plane flight into position behind the A3 tanker that had been trailing alongside. In-flight refueling was not difficult, but today the pressure was on. Any plane not able to take on fuel would have to turn back to the ship. The skipper had placed his section left and aft of the tanker, while Harry had put himself and his wingman to the right. On a prearranged signal, the tanker extended his hose. It trailed about thirty feet behind the tanker and drooped down below it. At its end was a drogue, called a basket, which was cone-shaped and reminded Harry of the shuttlecock used in badminton. The periphery of the cone had lights on each side, one at three o'clock and another at nine o'clock. Harry could see that both lights were amber, indicating that the drogue was fully extended and ready to refuel.

The refueling probe on the Skyhawk ran along the right side of the nose, stretching beyond it. That meant it was off center by a few feet and that sometimes made it difficult to line up with the drogue, especially at night. Detaching from his wingman, the skipper eased into position behind the drogue and slowly moved forward until his probe made contact with it. He could miss a little and the cone shape would still guide the probe into the nozzle. Once clicked in, he had only to stay in the same relative position, just as in flying formation. This was done with airmanship and small power adjustments to hold the relative position constant. The pilot could push forward on the drogue, and the hose would reel in to keep the probe connected. It disconnected if he drifted too far aft of the fully-extended hose. After engagement, the amber lights turned green, indicating that the fuel was flowing. It would stop flowing if the probe disconnected from the drogue or when the receiving tank was full. The skipper made it look easy. Funny, thought Harry, here I am at 20,000 feet over the Tonkin Gulf, cruising along at 360 knots, and watching an airplane refuel on our way to bomb a bridge in North Vietnam. And on the day before Christmas! *Damn,* he said quietly into his mask. *Can this really be me sitting here?*

Tanks full, the skipper eased back on the power, withdrew from the drogue and drifted aft of his wingman and into position on his left side. Now, it was his turn. Harry was next and although he had done it many times, this time, he missed the drogue on his first try. *Damn,* he thought fiercely, *this is no time to screw around!* He backed off slightly and lined up again, then added power until he felt the probe engage. Harry felt relieved as the lights ahead turned green. He would almost prefer to be shot down over Haiphong than to turn back now. The four planes were refueled in twenty minutes, then rejoined the main group, which was some 500 yards to starboard. The tanker separated and headed to an area seaward of the target area so fuel would be there, if needed, after the strike.

When flying in formation, hand signals were often used between aircraft. These might be needed to avoid using the radios for security reasons or, now and then, when a pilot had a radio failure. Just the other day, Bill Elliott, flying on Harry's wing, had lost his radio returning from a mission near Cape Mui Rahn. The weather at the ship was low clouds and light rain, so Harry had made a radar-controlled approach with Bill on his wing, using hand signals to tell Bill what he was doing. A wingman could more easily cope with power changes and configuration changes when he knew they were coming. Nearing the ship on the glide path, Harry broke away and Bill landed normally.

Hand signals were used routinely on the flight deck, as well. Most were standard; but one day, while taxiing, Harry had become confused. The hand signal he got next was one he had not seen before. The taxi director had covered one fist with the palm of his other hand, then sharply pulled his fist out of the closed palm.

"What was that?" Harry had asked after he got down from the cockpit.

The taxi director did not smile as he explained what it meant. "Get your Head out of your ass!" he said sharply.

Harry smiled ruefully. He had deserved that one.

Another non-standard signal Harry had once seen on the flight deck was an exasperated pilot throwing up one hand with the fingers spread.

"What's that?" he was asked.

"A fistful of these," he replied good-naturedly, extending his middle finger in the traditional salute known to all.

Approaching the descent point, the skipper gave a hand signal which simulated firing a pistol. That was the order to arm the bombs. Harry leaned forward slightly and clicked a switch on his panel. With that click, a solenoid beneath the aircraft closed and grasped a wire that led to a small propeller at the nose of each bomb, preventing it from spinning in the air stream. When the bombs were released, the wires, now attached to the aircraft, would be drawn from the propellers, allowing them to spin and arm the bombs.

Now, about 150 miles from the coast of North Vietnam, at a predetermined point, the skipper gave the signal that he was reducing power. He did this by thrusting his head backwards several times. He slowly pulled back his throttle and eased the nose over to descend. In so doing, the attack element of the strike force detached from the Phantom aircraft which would provide the anti-aircraft gun and missile suppression. They had their own targets. The show was about to begin. *Okay, said Harry to himself, let's get this over with.*

As the skipper gave the hand signal for level flight, he thrust his head forward several times as he added power. Harry glanced down at his altimeter. Three-hundred feet. They had descended through several layers of broken clouds and now they were just below scattered clouds. The visibility was good, and Harry shifted his view forward briefly and saw the coast of North Vietnam forming through the haze on the horizon. They crossed the coastline right on track, passing a well-defined bay. Now, the skipper turned to a pre-planned heading which took the flight parallel to the coast and several miles inland.

So far so good, thought Harry, as he examined, as best he could, the terrain they were flying over. Pretty country, he thought, hills and valleys and eye-catching colors. Coastal bays could be seen off to their left. The clouds became more widespread as they neared the turn that would take them over the ridge and into the coastal plain of Haiphong. The skipper turned south, added power, and began to climb along with the terrain ahead. The cloud cover rose, too, and just as they cleared the ridge, the clouds fell away and it was clear ahead.

Right then, Harry felt, rather than saw, the first fire from the ground. A 37mm shell went off somewhere beneath him and he felt his plane buffet. Within a few seconds, the air was filled with automatic weapons fire. It was unmistakable because of the bright orange streaks it left. To Harry, they looked like orange golf balls. They were deadly because there were so many of them. Suddenly, the shell bursts from more and more 37mm guns were all around them. *Holy shit!* thought Harry, his mind racing. *We need to find that bridge and get the hell out of here!*

The skipper had started bobbing and weaving and it was tough staying in position. Suddenly, there it was! The skipper had apparently missed it, so Harry called out "Skipper, target three o'clock!" He was later chastised for using that word "Skipper," which would indicate to those listening on the ground that a commanding officer was in one of the planes. By now, moving at high speed, the skipper was no longer in position to roll in. Harry, in a flash decision, detached and rolled in while he still had the target in sight.

"Battlecry three, rolling in," he called, as he made a hard right turn to put the bridge at his two o'clock position, rolled into a nearly inverted position, pulled his nose down through the horizon, rolled back upright, and flew right down the length of the bridge span in a shallow dive a few hundred feet above it, hitting the bomb release button on the control stick as he did. The golf balls were everywhere. He hoped fleetingly that his wingman, Jerry Greene, could keep up with all this quick and hard maneuvering. Jerry's a good stick, he thought, he'll be okay. Harry's decision to roll in first had put the skipper's section behind his own, in a good position to spot Harry's hits. They were on target, and so were Jerry's. Later photo reconnaissance would show that the four planes had scored seven direct hits on the bridge, but had not knocked out a span. Harry was not surprised.

Now to get the hell our of here! He made a hard turn towards the open sea, jammed the throttle full forward, and headed for the deck. He streaked out the bay, just above the waves, twisting and turning, and the golf balls diminished and then stopped. Harry, who had felt no panic during the attack, was now breathing heavily and was drenched in sweat. Only now, out of danger, did Harry remember Jerry on his wing. He looked out and there he was, right where he was supposed to be. Harry nodded, clicked his mike button, and said, "Check me, please." Jerry rogered the call and then slowly and carefully made a visual inspection of Harry's airplane, looking for battle damage. He gave a "thumbs up." Now Harry passed the lead to Jerry, eased back his throttle, slid aft, and checked his wingman's airplane. He drew in his breath sharply at what he saw.

Ron Rypel

14
HONG KONG

July 1970

The good news was that they had finally landed at the Kuala Lumpur airport. The bad news was that they might never leave. The first clue that trouble was in store was when the ramp agent told Thor that the transit passengers would not be able to leave the aircraft. Harry sniffed a problem, a big one.

"Sorry," said the agent, "but your flight seems to be out of order."

Well, thought Harry, he certainly got that part right; but why no disembarkation for those in transit? After the problems with the overflight authorizations in Burma air space, Harry suspected another such problem.

And, sure enough, there was one. The next stop was Hong Kong, and Thor was informed that, sorry, there was no permission to land there. Now what, Harry asked himself. This looks like a tough one; but once again, he had underestimated Thor's telephone magic. This time it took twelve hours, all of them on the airplane, before the flight was cleared to continue. So, off they went. Harry seemed to be the only one to realize that a worn-out crew, under the command of a captain who could barely read an airways chart, was headed for one of the most difficult airports in the world. He was not feeling cheerful.

The flight to Hong Kong was several hours, long enough for Harry to carefully study the approach chart for runway 13 at Kai Tak airport. Flying from a carrier was always demanding, but landing a 707 sometimes had its own special moments. This was one of those times. The instrument approach chart showed a top view of the area within 25 miles of the airport, along with a profile view of the airplane altitudes at key points of the approach. Most such approaches have a radio beacon that leads the pilot onto an instrument landing system. Often the radar control will vector the aircraft onto the final approach course and that makes it even easier. Once on the ILS, the pilot simply follows the glide path and the localizer right down to the runway. In Hong Kong, because the mountainous terrain precluded a straight-approach, this system was not feasible.

Runways are numbered to correspond with their compass headings. Runway 13 at Kai Tak airport had a magnetic heading of 130 degrees. It ran from the center of the city of Hong Kong out into harbor like a peninsula.

That end was clear; but instead of the open area usually found at the approach end of a runway, this one was packed with hills and buildings. There was no cleared space for an ILS. Another way was needed; so a radio beacon had been installed on the island of Cheung Chow in the harbor. A second beacon was placed on another island farther out in the harbor to lead the plane to the first one. After passing the first beacon, the plane descended to a lower level until it reached the second one. Here is where it got tricky. Passing the Cheung Chow beacon, the pilot punched his clock and descended to 500 feet. He then tracked outbound from the beacon for a number of seconds determined by his airspeed. Until now, the pilot was flying on instruments; but now he had to look outside and find a large billboard on a hillside dead ahead. This board was painted with red and white squares and was the Checkerboard. If the Checkerboard was not in sight after the specified number of seconds had passed, the pilot was required to execute a missed approach. They are often difficult but none was as complicated as this one. That was because the plane had to be maneuvered through the gaps in the hills and mountains surrounding the city until a safe altitude was reached. Harry hoped like hell that it would not be necessary.

Airlines require special training and an official qualification before a captain is allowed to fly into Hong Kong; but Trans Polar did not know about such rules, and even if they did, no one would have cared. Joe had wisely decided to let Harry do this one. Harry was apprehensive, but not worried. He would have been seriously concerned if Joe had tried to fly the approach. The weather was fine, with light, scattered clouds, so he was feeling pretty good when he called out the Checkerboard. He had configured the aircraft for landing and now all he had to do was find the airport and land. That was easier said than done. A few nervous seconds after spotting the Checkerboard, Harry saw the airport. It did not look easy. He quickly started a hard turn to the runway heading and pulled back the throttles to begin his final descent. The hard turn was needed because he had to turn through 45 degrees of heading change while, at the same time, using only his eyeballs for guidance, put himself on the glide path to the touchdown.

All of this, he was expecting. What he was not expecting was how close he came to the buildings he overflew as he neared the end of the runway. He seemed to be skimming the TV aerials. For the first since he could not remember when, Harry held his breath as he slipped over the rooftops and seemed to fly between a couple of tall apartment buildings as he made the last adjustments to his heading and rate of descent.

"Damn, that was almost like making a carrier landing," he joked after he touched down and taxied in for parking. He did not mention that he felt a lot more relieved at that moment than he ever had after landing on the ship.

Thor, sitting in the seat behind Harry, pounded Harry's back enthusiastically.

"Good," he said. "Very good." Good, thought Harry, was not a big enough word.

This was not Harry's first visit to Hong Kong. That had happened in 1959 during Harry's first trip to The Orient on the USS Ranger. The memory was still vivid. Along with other units, Harry's squadron had been part of Flight Deck Parade on that glorious morning. That was a formation of white-uniformed personnel covering the flight deck, and it was impressive to see. The giant ship was nosed carefully and gently by tugboats into its mooring position. From his first glimpse of Hong Kong Island on one side of the ship, and Kowloon on the other, Harry was captivated by the place. He could hardly wait to go ashore. En route, Harry had read *"The World of Suzy Wong."* He had been enthralled, and now he wanted to see it for himself.

Hong Kong harbor was a show all by itself. The view in every direction was fascinating. There were plenty of junks and sampans crisscrossing the water and then there were the Star Ferry boats, always a few in view, carrying people between Kowloon, on the mainland, and Hong Kong Island. Another type of boat was called a wallah-wallah. These were canoe-type vessels propelled by a single long oar resting on the stern and waggled in some strange pattern to drive the boat through the water. Like taxicabs, these boats were everywhere, and the ship's crew used them to go ashore.

Damn, thought Harry, a few hours later as he stepped out of one of those boats and onto the wharf in Hong Kong and looked around, I think I'm going to like this place.

And he did. One reason was a lovely young Chinese girl he met that afternoon at what Harry later described as a tea parlor. He had found the place by chance while wandering through the streets and alleys of this fascinating city. It was the menu posted outside that caught his eye. Instead of food, it showed photos of the girls inside who were, for a price, available as tea-drinking companions. This I've got to see, Harry said to himself as he entered a brightly lit room and looked around.

It was late afternoon and the room was almost empty. He was shown to a table and handed a menu. In it, were more photos of more women, all beautiful. The menu listed the price of their company. The rates were hourly. The menu also told Harry which language each girl spoke. Well, hell, thought Harry. I might as well go first class. He "ordered" a lovely girl, who, according to the menu anyway, spoke English. She appeared a few moments later and Harry congratulated himself on his judgment, blind though it was. She was gorgeous. Harry often described people by comparing them to movie stars. He thought of himself as a kind of a minor league, midwestern Steve McQueen; not handsome, but with a certain boyish appeal that attracted some women. This girl was an Oriental Ava Gardener. Her name, she said as she offered her hand, was Nancy Wong. Now, there's an omen, thought Harry, as he rose and took her hand. Her English was fluent and it came with a British accent on top of a Chinese accent. Harry loved it.

A few years before, Harry had been drinking Irish coffee in the Buena Vista in San Francisco. That was a favorite drinking place in a favorite city. He was with a long-time friend who lived there. Harry, surreptitiously admiring the women around him, as men do, noticed an unusually attractive girl approaching. She was tall and beautiful and she was headed his way; but it was his friend Joe whom she tapped on the shoulder as she said hello. Well, thought Harry, too tall for me anyway. Joe introduced the girl and, after a few minutes, she asked Joe, "Where is that friend you promised to line me up with?"

"Gerry, I haven't forgotten," said Joe, "I just want to be sure he's the right man for you. You are a very special lady."

"Look Joe, I'm not difficult," she replied, "just a nice guy, kind, good sense of humor and okay, reasonably attractive." Then, almost as an afterthought, she added, "And tall."

Joe was very quick and, without a pause, he asked, "How about a short guy who jumps high?"

They had all laughed, but that incident had started Harry thinking. Wasn't it strange how much importance was placed on the arrangement of our flesh and bones? Imagine if we all looked alike and, to know someone, you had to find out what a person was like on the inside. That usually took a while. Harry often had the experience of meeting an attractive woman who became less attractive as he came to know her. Sometimes, it worked the other way and a plain woman became more attractive as the relationship moved along. At times, looks could indeed be deceiving.

Now, in a Hong Kong tea parlor, Harry was not thinking about getting to know the lovely woman standing before him. He only knew he liked her instantly and that was enough. Using a technique stolen from *"Pal Joey,"*

Harry used his treat-a-tramp-like-a-lady approach. Harry was not sure Nancy was a tramp. She certainly did not look like one. But in this place, it seemed a reasonable assumption. And, anyway, it was hard for Harry to treat a woman badly. It just was not in him.

Harry had never before in his life drunk a cup of tea. That afternoon, he drank eight. It took that long to convince Nancy to spend the evening with him. In between the cups of tea and Harry's trips to the men's room, they danced to recorded music. A strange way to spend an afternoon, thought Harry, but he was enjoying it. More tea drinkers arrived as the afternoon wore on. Nancy seemed unused to being treated like a lady and she said so.

"You are a kind man," she said with a shy smile.

"Yes," she finally agreed. "We will have dinner together and we will see Hong Kong, but my hour rate will still have to be paid. If not paid, I cannot leave. Would you agree?"

Harry happily agreed. He was even happier when he learned the rate ended at midnight; there was no charge after that. That was one of the best agreements Harry had ever made, and one of the best nights he had ever had.

The memories of Nancy never left Harry. They had spent four days together, and they were among the most memorable days of his life. A woman like that in a place like this! They would never believe it in Milwaukee. Damn, he could hardly believe it himself. He might go years without thinking of those memories; but they were always there, close to the surface, and they broke into view every now and then. Now, as he stood on the tarmac alongside his 707 and looked across the water at the Hong Kong skyline, those memories returned with a rush.

One day, Nancy had taken Harry to see Aberdeen, on the far side of Hong Kong Island. It was famous for its floating restaurants. They had visited one for lunch in a wallah-wallah; and it was more than just a lunch, it was an experience. They selected their own meal from an assortment of live fish swimming in glass cases. The fish they chose were the ones they ate. Hard to find a restaurant like this in Milwaukee, Harry thought, as he looked around the restaurant at the exotic Chinese decor and viewed with delight the hills of Hong Kong Island across the water.

Returning to the pier, they witnessed a disagreement between a western couple and the old woman who paddled one of the wallah-wallahs there. Nancy stepped in as interpreter. The couple wanted to tour the Aberdeen harbor by boat because they were interested in buying a Chinese junk, a common type of sailing boat in The Orient, one with a square stern that sloped forward as it met the water. The man, tall, dark, and movie-star handsome, told them the junks that were for sale were marked with a large yellow "X" on the slanted part of the stern.

"Come along," he said. "We'll take a harbor cruise together."

Harry looked at Nancy who nodded her agreement, and off they went.

The harbor was full of boats of all kinds, including many junks; but only a few were for sale. At one of them, they stopped beneath the overhang of the stern as the prospective buyer inspected the hull. As he did, a large clump of excrement landed in their boat with a loud, wet thud, barely missing their fellow passenger.

He cried out in surprise and everyone looked up to see where the missile had come from. What they saw was someone's rear end protruding through a round hole that had been cut in the flat part of the stern. The backside quickly disappeared and was replaced by a very bewildered Oriental face.

"Who has interrupted my call of nature?" the face seemed to ask.

They laughed about it later when they ate lunch together.

"What do you do?" asked Harry as he sipped a beer.

The man was Australian and told them he planned to sail the boat to Australia and live on it there. His wife was a gorgeous American woman with striking good looks and long blonde hair.

"I'm in the movie business," he said.

"What part?" asked Harry with interest. He had always been fascinated by movies.

"Believe it or not," the Australian said, "I'm an actor. But you have probably never heard of me. I usually work in movies made here in Hong Kong."

"Well," said Harry, "You certainly look like a movie star. I'll keep my eyes peeled. You'll be hard to miss. What's your name? For the movies, I mean?"

His name did not ring a bell for Harry, but he would remember his classic good looks. He was friendly and pleasant and after lunch, he posed for pictures with Harry and Nancy.

"Just in case you become famous," Harry said with a laugh. "You never know."

A few years later, watching a movie in the Officers' Wardroom, Harry met his Hong Kong lunch companion again. There he was on the screen, playing the role of James Bond. Lazenby was his name, George Lazenby, and his image recalled pleasant memories of Nancy and Hong Kong.

One memory Harry especially cherished was the day he brought Nancy to the ship for lunch in the officers' wardroom. She wore a cheongsam that day and she looked sensational. Despite its high collar, this form-fitting dress with slits up the thighs had to be the sexiest dress Harry had ever seen; and Nancy had the figure for it, lean and firm, but not thin, as were many Chinese women. She created a stir everywhere she went, but she seemed not to notice. Funny, thought Harry, but I feel pleased to have this tea-parlor girl at my side. A tea-parlor girl she might be, but she has class.

She appeared unimpressed with the ship. Later, her only comment was, "I see that black men serve white men in the restaurant. Why is it like that?"

Harry started to smile. That was a complicated question.

"Damn," he said "you've just seen one of the great ships of the world and you're asking a question like that one? Can we discuss it later?" Harry looked curiously at her as he spoke. He tried to think of an answer that would make sense to a Chinese girl in Hong Kong, but she did not ask again.

The highlight of her visit to the ship had come when Harry showed her his stateroom after lunch. "Hmm," she murmured as she glanced around, "small but clean. May we lock the door, please?" she asked with a demure smile as she began to undo her collar. "I have never before made love on a boat."

Harry smiled back. "Neither have I," he said, as he reached for the door's lock. There was a first time for everything.

Harry was right there, the best part of his reverie, when he was startled to hear Gene Daily ask, "How much fuel we gonna take, Boss?"

To answer that question, many factors had to be considered. Harry had gone through them all. Of course, they needed enough fuel to fly from here to there, which, in this case, was back to Kuala Lumpur. But that amount depended on how much the aircraft weighed, how high it would fly, the winds aloft, which would influence their ground speed and thus the flight time, and how much fuel they wanted to arrive with at the destination. That was determined by the weather there, along with other needs. He did not want to land with fuel he did not need. That only burned fuel to carry fuel. All in all, it was a complicated calculation.

It was made more so by certain limitations. The maximum takeoff weight was determined by runway length, surrounding terrain, which dictated climb-out performance needs, and the temperature and wind at the time of departure. Contrary to common belief, an airplane wanted headwinds, not tailwinds, for a takeoff. That was because a headwind augmented the lift generated by the aircraft's speed as it made its takeoff run. Harry had once seen a light plane launched from a carrier by simply holding it down, turning the ship into the wind, and then releasing the plane. It had gone right straight up like a helicopter.

To make the fuel calculation even more complicated, the takeoff weight had to meet a requirement that the aircraft could lose an engine at a critical moment during its takeoff run and still continue the takeoff and climb-out safely. At that moment of engine failure, there also had to be enough runway ahead to stop the airplane, should the pilot decide to do so. The landing weight at the destination also had to be considered. That was restricted by factors such as temperature, wind, and runway length. Computers were just coming into use in aviation and they had done much to simplify this puzzle; but the captain still had to make the right basic inputs and punch the right buttons to make it work.

Harry smiled and shook his head gently as he recalled calculating the fuel load in Karachi as this odyssey began. *My God*, he thought, *was that only yesterday?* An important piece of information used to figure out the maximum takeoff weight, which decides how much fuel can be carried, is the temperature. It determines how much thrust the aircraft engines will develop. Hot air is less dense than cold air, so the energy of the fuel/air mixture is lower on hot days. The temperature is an especially important number in Karachi in July, so Harry and Joe had asked the meteorologist on duty for this very basic number: what is the temperature today?

In Pakistan, Harry was to learn, you did nothing that was not routine. That led to problems. The meteorologist frowned at the question.

"I am just now completing your weather folder, Captain, sir," he said "and that information will, of course, be included."

"No," said Joe "we need it now."

The clerk hesitated, unsure. This was a non-routine request.

"Please, Captain," he almost implored, "I will complete your folder in a few minutes. Please, sir." Joe had a low patience threshold. His fist came down on the man's desk like a thunderclap.

"I want it now," he roared, "right this goddamn minute. Is it asking too much to tell me the goddamn temperature?"

For an exclamation point, he snorted, "Jesus!" Jesus probably did not mean much to him, but that fist got the man's attention. Harry could almost hear the gears turning in his head. Finally, after a brief hesitation, he reluctantly decided that it was better to give the temperature in a non-routine verbal way than to risk another fist crashing down on his desk. He finally surrendered the number.

In Hong Kong, the temperature was not so zealously guarded. With that key piece of information, Harry was able to turn to Gene and give him a number. Curiously, that number was in pounds, not gallons. That was because the volume of fuel in the tanks varied with the temperature. Tanks full on a warm day would be less than full the next day, if the temperature went down. That change in volume and density had to be factored into the engine's performance. That was based on the mass of the fuel-air mixture burned by the engine. Gene thought for a moment, then turned away to begin refueling, satisfied with the number. Before pumping in the fuel, he would convert that number to gallons, after adjusting it for the temperature.

That there would be no passengers to Kuala Lumpur made one fewer complication in Harry's calculations. They would board passengers in Kuala Lumpur. If we ever get there, he thought sardonically. The way this trip was going, anything was possible.

Fatigue. That was another problem, and Harry had been hoping to stop in Kuala Lumpur for a few hours of sleep. He was unsure how that would play with Thor, who wanted to press on to Karachi, where the other crew was waiting. We'll play it by ear, he decided.

Looking idly across the water towards Hong Kong, Harry saw a large ship leaving the harbor. Could that be an aircraft carrier, he asked himself. He recalled being on the Ranger when she had been completely repainted during the few days of the ship's visit here. This feat was accomplished by Mary Soo and her all-girl crew of painters. The Navy provided the paint and Mary provided the means, which was a series of planks let down from the flight deck by lines. The girls, barefoot and wearing conical hats made of straw, swarmed over the ship like ants. They didn't paint so much as slosh. Using rags thrust into buckets up to their elbows, they smeared the paint over the ship's hull. Harry had watched in amazement as these women scrambled up and down, fore and aft, repositioning the planks when necessary, and all at a breakneck pace. To his astonishment, Harry had heard that for this entire enormous project, Mary Soo's pay was the ship's garbage. Of course, the leftovers from a U.S. Navy aircraft carrier probably looked pretty good to hungry people. But still....

Harry returned to the cockpit and once again his thoughts turned to that post-lunch session with Nancy in his stateroom. He smiled. A few years before his first visit to Hong Kong, Harry would have considered such behavior "sinful;" now he relished just thinking about it. Even though he had been raised as a strict Catholic, Harry had never been sure what sin was. All he knew was that it was someone's definition of evil and that committing one might cost him his place in heaven. He was taught --indoctrinated, he later decided -- that sex outside of marriage was the fast track to hell; and he had taken it very seriously. Faith can be a strong persuader, he decided; so strong that it could, at times, overcome reality.

15
THE MOMENT

1958

He could recall almost the exact moment he began to seriously doubt being a Catholic. While in his first squadron, Harry had gotten himself and his wingman, Gino Farrugia, into an unscheduled "hassle" with a couple of pilots from another squadron in his Air Wing. During the ensuing "dogfight," Harry was suddenly horror-stricken to see Gino headed straight down towards the southern California mountains.

"Zero six, zero six, pull up PULL UP!" he had screamed in shock. A moment later, Gino had struck the ground and was instantly engulfed in a huge fireball. Harry could never remember flying back to the base and landing. He did, of course, but he had no recall of it, such was his state of mind. Imagine, he thought, not being able to remember something like that; but all he could think of was that fireball.

Gino was what was then known as a "fallen-away Catholic." He and Harry had discussed that fall, and it was plain that Gino had no regrets. He had done what he thought was right. Harry had regretted Gino's decision, but it had not affected their friendship, which grew very close. Harry came to know that Gino was a fine human being, Catholic or not; so after his death, Harry had sought out the Navy chaplain and asked straight out. Gino was as good as they come, Harry told the chaplain. Would he qualify for heaven? The chaplain, a good-natured Irishman named O'Leary, sympathized with Harry. He made some high-sounding noises but in the end, he was sorry. Gino had renounced his faith and the door was closed. *How could an all-merciful God do that?* Harry had asked. In effect, the priest had replied, "Those are the rules."

That was the moment. Harry had continued going to mass but it was never the same. The doubts grew and the conviction that the church was wrong became stronger. All those tenets Harry had taken as gospel for so many years -- holy water, purgatory, angels, walking on water, rising from the dead -- became hard to accept. How could he have believed all that? It was as if he was now looking from the outside into a room in which he had once lived. The perspective was vastly different.

One Sunday morning, about a year after Gino's crash, Harry found himself at mass with a serious hangover. In fact, the hangover was just starting because he was not yet fully sober. That was because he had come straight from an all-night party. Suddenly, a question overcame him and it was loud and clear. *Why am I sitting here if I no longer believe? Is it only because of a rule of the church?* Until that moment, he was unaware that he was no longer a believer. I have questions, he admitted as he struggled, but he told himself that he still believed. That question, at that moment, seemed to overwhelm him and even though he was not completely sober, he understood clearly that he was wrong to be in church that morning; so he stood up and left. Like some find religion, Harry lost it. It seemed sudden; but it was only that final question that was sudden. It had been simmering for a year.

Along with that loss of faith came a sense of freedom he had never known existed. Included was the freedom of sex. That sex was a sin had never made sense to Harry. How could it be a sin, whatever that was, one time, and create a human being another? Harry believed in commitment. As a devout Catholic, he had kept his virginity. He had to admit that he did not have many opportunities to lose it. Life was different before the sexual revolution.

Well, thought Harry, *that's just the way life is.* So he accepted it. If Harry had known the word "libido," he would have said he had a strong one. He had a friend who used to claim that he had been born with a hard-on. Harry knew what he meant; so it wasn't easy. Although his future wife was nowhere in view, he had been steadfast in waiting for her. *Was it stupid,* he sometimes asked himself, *to wait for a woman he might never meet?* Losing his religion made it easy to give up his virginity. He lost it to a nightclub hostess in Japan, and he lost it with a clear conscience.

16

JAPAN

1959

For a young man from Milwaukee, Japan was pure enigma. Harry had read much about Japan and its truly horrific behavior when it invaded China and Manchuria in the 1930s; but Yokosuka, Harry's first-ever port of call, showed him none of that. His experience with the Japanese was positive. The country was well-organized, the beer was good, the people were friendly. And best of all, the women were shorter than Harry -- every single one of them.

Part of Harry's measure of Japan came after the ship's first few days in port. The Ranger was then the newest and biggest ship in the fleet and, as such, was often called upon to display its prowess. No one knew who Princess Chichibu was, but judging by the size of her retinue, she must have been important. She and her entourage came aboard early one morning, and the Ranger set out to sea to show the princess what a ship like this one could do. The air show was impressive, even to Harry, who did not take part.

The opening act of the show was the spectacular launch of four F8 Crusaders that were shot off the four catapults within a few seconds and immediately formed a diamond ahead of the ship. Because they launched in afterburner and carried a short fuel load to make them lighter, the planes climbed at a steep angle. That, added to the forward speed of the ship, made it appear that the F8s were going straight up. The show included fly-bys of various aircraft and the dive-bombing of smoke markers that were laid by one of Harry's squadron-mates in the sea near the ship. A highlight was a Crusader streaking alongside the ship at flight deck level, sharply raising its nose as it passed, and triggering a five-inch high-speed rocket. The firing of a sidewinder missile quickly followed that. This missile homed in on heat sources and, within a few seconds, flew up the tail of the rocket and destroyed it. It never missed. Harry had seen these missiles being checked after being loaded on an airplane on the flight deck. A crewman would stand across the flight deck, point a flashlight at the missile and slowly move it from side to side, watching the fins of the sidewinder follow the heat generated by the flashlight bulb.

A few months earlier, Harry had taken part in an air show off the coast of California. He was part of a two-plane flight that dropped bombs on the smoke marker that had been laid near the ship on its port side. Harry flew wing. Dive-bombing in formation is like all formation flying: the wingman simply follows the leader. He released his bombs when he saw those of his flight leader fall away. Normally, the leader would make a smooth pull-up after the bombs dropped so that his wingman could easily stay in position; but this time, the flight leader simply disappeared. That was because he pulled up so sharply that he appeared to vanish. One moment, he was there and the next, he was gone. Harry knew that could mean only one thing: he had pressed his dive too low and pulled up hard. Harry very quickly did the same and his nose came up through the horizon, he checked his altimeter to see that he was climbing through 800 feet. He did not like to think about how low he had been at the bottom of the dive, but it had to be very close to the sea. Back on the ship he exchanged sharp words with his flight leader, who had misread his altimeter while focusing on the target. Flying into the sea was not on the program that day, but it would certainly have stolen the show.

What most impressed Harry about the Chichibu Special, as it was called, was what happened afterward. A large contingent of reporters spilled out onto the flight deck to file their stories. Commercial communication with the shore was not available in those days, so the Japanese media came up with a brilliant substitute. They released a flock of pigeons that carried the news back to their offices. *Ingenious*, thought Harry. The Japanese were clever people, and Harry would see many examples of their ingenuity as he found his way among them.

On his very first night ashore in Japan, he and a few friends decided to visit the Kanko Hotel. You could not be a Navy pilot and not visit the Kanko Hotel. Leaving the ship, they had flagged a taxi just outside the base. "Kanko Hotel," they ordered, after piling in, and the taxi took off. Upon arrival, the driver refused payment. That was puzzling until they figured out that it was not a taxi, just an ordinary car with an inordinately friendly owner. In Japan, things like that seemed to happen all the time.

The nightclub of the Kanko Hotel was famous throughout the fleet, and with good reason. It was vast, had several bands that played American music, and was well-stocked with pretty girls, called hostesses. About once every hour, the band struck up a tune that all the girls knew as a call to duty. From all corners of the club, they descended upon the dance floor and preened for a few minutes. That was to display the club's goods.

Harry had fallen in love that very first night with a girl he noticed out there during the dance-o-rama, as Harry's companion called it. She smiled only for Harry, he thought, and was amenable to a drink, a few more drinks, and some dancing. Her drinks, of course, were only colored water camouflaged as drinks, but Harry did not mind. For him, there was little difference between buying colored water for Kyoko and buying real drinks for girls he dated back home. It was the price of their company.

He returned to the Kanko the next night and spent the entire evening with her. This time, he went home with her. There, in a small, spare room, warmed only by a charcoal brazier, she took his virginity. Harry gave it up happily. He was clumsy and awkward, but Kyoko pretended not to notice, and Harry was grateful for that. He was a quick learner. Next time would be better.

In this first sexual experience, the moment that stood out for Harry was not his orgasm. In his excitement, he almost didn't feel it. What he remembered most was the first sweet feel of a woman's nude body against his own. How could something so wonderful be wrong? That Kyoko was a nightclub hostess did not bother Harry at all. He liked her and enjoyed her company. In the years ahead, that would be the test. To the dismay of a few friends, he would, now and then, decline an unspoken offer of sex because he was not attracted to the woman. "That's not normal," one had said in exasperation.

With Kyoko, it had all been natural. Over the brazier she made a dinner of sukiyaki. It was delicious, especially with the hot sake that came with it. Afterwards, she had filled a wooden tub with very hot water. Before getting in the water, she had scrubbed Harry thoroughly. The tub held only one person. It was more a box than a tub and he sat on a small stool while he soaked himself. As he did, Kyoko washed herself. Then she helped Harry out of the tub and dried him gently with a large towel.

"Hai, dozo," she said, "please to go to the bed now."

Warm, clean and well-fed, he slipped into the bed, which was a thick mat on the floor, and waited for Kyoko. She came a few minutes later, smiled down at Harry, opened her robe and let it fall to the woven straw mats that covered the floor. Then she laid her body next to his.

"You want to climb Mount Fuji now?" she whispered. It was a singular moment in his sexual transformation.

The next day Harry and Kyoko went by train to a town near Mount Fuji. Traveling by train in Japan was fascinating. First, you could set your watch by them. They were always on time, almost to the second. They were crowded, so crowded that a special uniformed crew known as Train Pushers was used during peak hours to herd crowds on board. Sometimes, people were pressed into a train even if they did not want to go. That had happened to a friend while he was saying goodbye on the platform. An unusual aspect was that at every stop, vendors appeared outside the windows to sell a variety of food and drink, most of which Harry could not identify.

They spent the night in a hotel close to the famous mountain and viewed it by tour bus the next morning. The bus had a hostess, and, on the way, she led the passengers in song. One of those songs sounded familiar and it took Harry some minutes to realize the entire busload of Japanese was singing, in Japanese, "Old MacDonald." As the bus rounded a curve and Mt. Fuji burst into view, the passengers gasped and broke into spontaneous applause. Harry had to admit, in its near perfect symmetry, it looked truly majestic.

Upon returning to their hotel, Kyoko had suggested a visit to a famous bathhouse nearby.

"It is the very largest in all of the world," she said with pride.

"Let's go," said Harry, and she took him to a complex for which the word bathhouse was nowhere near adequate. It was immense, with a transparent roof, several levels of large pools, and more fountains than Harry could count. Foliage and flowers were abundant throughout and brought the outdoors inside. One feature that took some getting used to was that the bathers, both men and women and of all ages, children to very elderly, were nude. Well, why not, thought Harry; this is the way God, or whoever, has made us. He had never understood why nudity was considered by many to be wrong. Here in Japan, it seemed natural.

During a visit to Tokyo, Harry and a few friends decided they wanted to see a Kabuki show. They had no clue what a Kabuki show was, but they had to see one. Looking for directions, they were unable to find an English speaker, but did manage to find a sales clerk who knew one. Up the stairs she led them, then wound through a maze of counters until she found the man who could speak English.

"Ah, yes," he said after they explained their problem. "I will take you there. Come. Please to follow me."

He led them back down the stairs, out the door and to the theatre, which was several blocks away. That was not enough. He stood in the queue and bought their tickets for them, and that was not enough. He escorted them into the theatre and to their seats, bowed and disappeared. How could these kind and gentle people have acted with such cruelty? It was a question Harry could never answer. Another question he could not answer, was; what is a Kabuki show? Even after seeing one, he still had no clue.

In Yokosuka, Harry discovered one of the great joys of life. That was a hotsy bath. It started with a hot shower, followed by a thorough scrubbing by one of the young female attendants. She cleaned the entire body except for his groin. For that, she would hand the soap to Harry and discretely gesture towards his crotch. After a rinse with buckets of hot water, he sat in a steam room as long as he could stand it. Then, he was led to a small pool, filled with water so hot that immersing himself, even very slowly, was a test of courage. So hot was the water that it was actually painful to move, once he was in the water. Then came the climax, so to speak. That was a massage that did not omit one square inch of his body. This was done with great pressure applied with strong fingers, kneading, squeezing, rubbing.

Once, feeling especially heavy pressure on his back, Harry had glanced up over his shoulder to find the girl standing on his back and massaging with her toes. She was not only standing on his back, but pressing her hands against the ceiling. Harry could hardly breathe.

A rubdown with talcum powder finished the routine that usually lasted about ninety minutes. That hour-and-a-half could make a new man of almost anyone, even those who came in late at night with percolating hangovers. Harry wondered why they were not available back home.

Now, sitting in the cockpit on the ramp at Hong Kong's Kai Tak airport, Harry put aside his memories of Japan and reviewed the departure chart for runway one three. It was straight ahead with a few altitude requirements. *Well, that's a relief, and even Joe could handle this one.* The opening of the cockpit door interrupted his thoughts. Astrid came in, and, with a loud click, locked the door behind her. Harry glanced up. She looked wan, but she was still smiling. She slid into the jump seat behind Harry and slipped her arm over his shoulder and across his chest, nestling her breast against his shoulder as she did.

17
AFTER THE STRIKE

December 1965

To Harry, the Haiphong bridge strike had seemed a great success. He and Jerry had gotten in quickly, dropped their bombs on target, and were now over open water and headed back to the ship. He quickly changed his mind as he scanned the underside of his wingman's airplane. Jerry had been hit in his center fuel tank and fuel was gushing out in a thick and steady stream. Keeping his voice measured, Harry pressed his mike button.

"Zero three, you took a hit in the center tank and you're losing fuel. Keep the lead and turn to one three zero. Level at angels one five. Say your fuel state."

A heading of 130 would take them in the general direction of the tanker. Fifteen-thousand feet was the briefed altitude at which the tanker would be orbiting.

"Yeah, I have two point six but I can almost see it going down. How bad is it?" Jerry asked as calmly as though he were asking about the weather.

"Pretty bad, Jerry, and we need to find the tanker ASAP. Give them a call and see if they can paint us." Harry wanted to know if the tanker could see them on their radar.

The tanker responded on Jerry's second call. "Activate your squawk and stand by." That was a request for Jerry to turn on his IFF. This was an electronic gadget that sent out a signal that would show up on the tanker's radar screen.

"I got you, Battlecry. You would like to buy some fuel? We have a special price today. Come right about ten degrees. You have forty-three miles to run." That was about seven minutes, figured Harry. He should be make it okay, but judging from the rate Jerry was losing fuel, there was no way he could reach the ship. Thinking quickly, Harry called the tanker.

"Listen up, tanker. I'm on zero three's wing, and he's losing fuel fast. He might need to plug in and get dragged back to home plate. That gonna work for you?"

Serious now, the tanker replied that since Jerry was his only customer so far, that was feasible; but he would need to wait until he was sure no one else needed fuel.

85

"Zero three can plug in and we'll see how it all shakes down. He might need to unplug for a few minutes if we get someone else who needs a drink. We'll play it by ear. You should have us at your twelve in a minute or two. Call tally-ho."

Harry rogered the call, then told Jerry to resume control of the radio. Flying lead, the radios would be easier for him, and he was also better positioned to look out for the tanker.

"Tally-ho," Jerry called a minute later. "We'll join in a left turn. Go ahead and extend the drogue. This is looking serious."

"What state now, zero three?" asked Harry.

"It's going fast. Down to one point two already. You gonna stay with me or head back?"

Jerry was thinking ahead. There was no reason for Harry to remain with Jerry after he was plugged in.

Harry thought for a moment. "Nah, better stick together. My fuel is okay and I can borrow some from our tanker friend if I need it, and we need to think about ejecting. You might need some help if you have to punch out."

Jerry rogered, then called that he was in the cone for the join-up. With Harry on his wing, Jerry made a perfect rendezvous, drifted back to the drogue, and plugged in on his first try.

"Down to point eight," he called as he did. "I'm very thirsty."

What we need to know, thought Harry, is whether he can tank fuel faster than he's losing it.

"How does it look, Jerry?"

"I have the green light," he replied, "but the gauge is not going up. Looks like a wash."

Harry had been afraid of that.

"Tanker, looks like we'll need you to drag us home, and maybe all the way home. You might need to make the approach with zero three plugged in, then go around close-in. That sound feasible?"

There was a very slight pause before the reply. "Whatever it takes," he said.

"Roger that," said Harry with a mental grin.

Just then, another airplane showed up needing fuel. Harry was reluctant in such a tight situation to ask Jerry to unplug, wait for the second airplane to tank, and then re-plug in. Jerry had no fuel to spare. The newcomer, an F4, agreed to wait his turn, fly back with the tanker, then take fuel after the tanker brought Jerry into the groove. He had not been hit, he explained, just burned more than he should have.

"Very kind," said Harry. "We owe you a big one."

"My pleasure," said the Phantom pilot. "I might not need to tank after all. We'll see how it goes."

The tanker turned and headed for the ship. "I've cleared all this with Pawtucket," he announced. "They'll have all emergency crews standing by. We have priority and we'll take your bird up close and then go around. What kind of approach speed we talking about?"

Good point, Harry thought. Different airplanes flew approaches at different speeds. He gave the tanker a number.

"That'll work," he said. "Let's go home."

Normally, in-flight refueling is carried out in straight and level flight. This time, Jerry would have to stay plugged in throughout the entire descent and approach. That included speed and configuration changes, and it would not be easy. Harry decided to fly loosely on Jerry's wing during the initial approach phase so that he could provide cockpit information. That would be hard for Jerry to do for himself. He would need to focus all his attention on staying plugged in. Harry wondered if this had ever been done before.

Jerry reported that his fuel was decreasing slightly. That was bad news. From the numbers Jerry was reporting, Harry figured he would arrive at the ramp with about 500 pounds. That was enough to get aboard and maybe enough for one go-around, if it became necessary. After Jerry unplugged, the tanker would orbit at a low level just ahead of the ship, in case it was possible to plug in again; but that was a fuel-consuming maneuver. Better get aboard on the first try. The weather was good, and it was daytime. Harry did not even want to think about doing all this in the dark.

Harry had once read a quote which said that, of ten problems coming down the road, nine will fall into the ditch before they reach you. He was not sure that included problems like this one, but he hoped this landing was one of the nine. There was something else to think about: with such a big fuel leak, there was the possibility of a fire after landing. The ship had reported that all emergency equipment was standing by.

Jerry managed to stay glued to the tanker right up to a quarter-mile out. There, the tanker retracted its hose and broke off to the left. Jerry, concentrating on staying connected, had just a few moments to shift his attention forward, assimilate the situation, and land his airplane. He caught a three wire; but when the airplane abruptly stopped, some of that loose fuel sloshed into the engine's hot section and the airplane burst into flames. Jerry thought about ejecting, he said later, but he knew the fire crew was there and would be all over the plane within seconds. He decided to stay with the airplane, keep the canopy closed, and watch as the fire crew put out the fire. It was the right decision. The fire was out quickly and Jerry opened his canopy and climbed down unscathed -- not only unscathed, but grinning hugely.

Harry had broken off as the tanker, with Jerry still in tow, neared the ship. He was abeam of the ship on his downwind leg in the landing pattern when he saw Jerry's plane erupt in flames. *Jesus*! he thought, *I hope it doesn't explode!* That was a possibility, even with the fire crew on the scene. He extended his downwind leg, hoping to give the flight deck crew more time to move Jerry's airplane out of the landing area. He asked Pri Fly to give him a heads-up when it was safe to turn in. The burned-out airplane was quickly repositioned, and Harry was advised to turn in and continue his approach. Despite his fatigue, his approach and landing had been near perfect. The adrenalin always seemed to kick in when he got near the ship.

Damn, he thought, after landing and taxiing forward to clear the wires. *This has been one hell of a day.* Despite all the excitement, he felt no emotion. He did notice a slight trembling of his legs when he touched his brakes as he taxied into his parking position. He shut down the engine, opened the canopy, paused for a deep breath, then climbed down to the flight deck. There, with one foot still on the ladder, he lowered his other foot to the deck. Feeling the contact, he lowered his foot from the ladder to the deck. Both knees buckled when he put his full weight on them and down he went, collapsing in a tangle of arms, legs, helmet and kneeboard.

"Okay, sir?" asked his plane captain as he leaned over to help him up. Harry mumbled something, brushed him away and found his footing. *What the hell?* he asked himself. Apparently his legs knew enough to be scared even if he did not.

Somewhat unsteady, he made his way down the ladder leading to the deck-edge catwalk, then to the hatch that led to the ship's interior. Despite the maze of passageways, Harry could have found his way to the Ready Room blindfolded.

I think I need a drink, he thought, as he waddled along in his flight gear. Entering the Ready Room, he fell like a lump into the seat with his name on the headrest. Just then, the squawk box on the Duty Officer's desk boomed out. "You got Ferguson down there? He's supposed to be up here in A.I."

Jesus, thought Harry, he had forgotten to go to the Air Intelligence spaces for his debrief. "I'm on my way," he said tiredly as he heaved himself out of his seat, dragged himself out of the Ready Room, and headed up to his debrief. He was not eager to go. The debriefs were more fancy than fact.

Everyone up the chain of command wanted to look good, so the debriefs were usually exaggerated and distorted to suit that purpose.

If Harry told the AI that he had missed a bridge, for example, it was usually recorded as "cratered bridge approaches." That annoyed Harry. Once, in a moment of frustration, he had instructed the debriefer to write down, "missed bridge and approaches completely."

"Shit!" said Tom "I can't write that down."

"Put it down," said Harry, "and I'll sign it." He did, and he never heard a word about it.

Today's debrief would be an easy one. They had actually hit the target. Jerry had seen two bombs land directly on a span. He was already there when Harry arrived. Harry shook his hand.

"Jerry, that was some good airmanship out there today."

Jerry smiled a big smile. "Thanks for your help."

He listened as Harry told Tom what he had seen. The debrief went well until Jerry interrupted, describing a missile which had barely missed them.

"Missile?" asked Harry with surprise. "What missile?"

Jerry was incredulous. "You didn't see it? Christ, it nearly took your wing off. It must not have been armed."

The missiles armed at 3,200 feet, and they had been well below that altitude. Harry looked at his wingman and furrowed his brow.

"Jerry," he said, "I wish you hadn't told me that."

That night, Harry and Jerry made a trip to the tanker's Ready Room, where the tanker pilot was drinking a cup of coffee and reading the "Stars and Stripes."

"We forgot to get our Green Stamps," explained Harry as they all shook hands. "And nobody cleaned our windshield. But we'll overlook it this time. Thanks for the help."

"Any time, Battlecry, any time," he said with a smile. "We appreciate your business."

18
MEDALS

1966

This delusion during debriefs extended to other aspects of the war as well. Another part of the war that was sometimes more fancy than fact was the system of awarding medals. Different pilots regarded medals in different ways. Some saw them as nice-to-have but no more than that. Others considered them to be important career credentials. Although the first group could live without them, they disliked awarding undeserved medals. It was a situation with built-in friction. Harry had always believed that politics were unavoidable in life. It went by other names, such as personal relations, compatibility, compromise, and others; but it was all politics, in one form or another. If he needed proof, he found it at the Awards Board meetings.

Because Harry had some writing ability, he had been designated by the skipper as the squadron's "awards writer-upper." That meant Harry had to talk to pilots who had taken part in noteworthy missions, write a description, and forward it up the chain of command. At first, Harry had tackled this task in a straightforward manner. Talk with the pilots, get the facts, write them down in a reasonable way, and then push the paperwork along. How little he knew. His first clue came when he attended his first meeting of the Awards Board. Politics showed up, uninvited.

Each squadron had an officer there who was Harry's counterpart. The board's purpose was to evaluate the recommendations. Although the board could not block a recommendation, it could, with its endorsement, go a long way towards deciding whether the Air Wing Commander would approve it. After that, approval farther up the chain was more or less automatic. Now and then, the medal might be downgraded a notch, and a Distinguished Flying Cross, for example, might become an Air Medal; but that was unusual. Most of the time, once the recommendation got past the board, it was all downhill.

Usually, the process worked in an honest way; but Harry quickly learned that the straightforward approach would not always do. What was sometimes needed, he saw, were a few minor facts and some major embellishment. Part of this problem stemmed from the differences in missions between different squadrons. Different missions translated into different levels of danger and difficulty.

At that first meeting, the first proposed award was for a photo pilot. Harry knew that these pilots flew in the teeth of danger on every mission. First, the intelligence spooks always wanted the battle damage assessment right away. The North Vietnamese were not stupid, and it did not take long for them to figure out that thirty minutes after a major strike, they could expect a photo airplane. Why not wait a day or two, thought Harry; but he knew that was too logical. Because of this absurd policy, the Air Wing had lost three photo airplanes in the first three weeks on Yankee Station. The NVN tactic was simple: fill the sky over the target area with metal and wait for an airplane to fly into it.

Second, in order to take their pictures, the photo pilots had to fly straight and level over the target area. Evasive maneuvering would negate their mission. That was a problem for their awards writer. It was hard to describe straight and level flight in prose dramatic enough to merit an award. That was where embellishment came into play. The photo squadron's writer was a master at the game. He made straight and level flight seem daring, dynamic, and difficult almost beyond description; but describe it he did and in marvelous fashion. Harry had actually applauded when Lt. Watson finished reading his recommendation. There was no way Harry's work could measure up. He had the goods: a very difficult strike in bad weather against a heavily-defended target. There had actually been some damage inflicted; but after listening to Lt. Watson's artistry with words, Harry quickly decided that his recommendation needed to go back to the drawing board. His re-write passed muster a few weeks later and then Harry had a handle on how it worked.

He passed the word at a squadron All Pilots Meeting. I need a few basics, he told them, a lucrative target – "lucrative" was the buzz word of the day, especially among Air Intelligence officers -- and some enemy fire, the more the better. Surface-to-air missiles were best. Bad weather was a plus, but not required. It helped if the target was destroyed, but Harry learned this was not essential. That part could be adjusted.

With these guidelines, Harry was eventually able to win a Distinguished Flying Cross for each of his squadron-mates. The skipper had set that goal when he gave Harry the job.

"For what these guys are going through out here," said the C.O. in the Ready Room one night after the movie, "I want them all to have a DFC. Do it any way you can; just do it. Let me know if you need help."

Harry had great respect for his skipper. Cdr. Dueffel was a good officer, an excellent pilot, and a fine commanding officer. Short, lean and hard, the skipper had great common sense and led by example. He took his share of the hard flights and made sure that each squadron pilot did the same. If Harry ever became a squadron commanding officer, he would try to emulate Hank Dueffel. Harry agreed with his judgment that all the pilots deserved a DFC. He thought of it as a cumulative DFC. So, he told himself, if a pilot does not fly a DFC mission, I'll embellish his best one up to the DFC level. Harry, of course, would be writing own citation. But what the hell, someone had to do it. And by now, he knew how it was done.

Other squadrons played by their own rules, and that meant that some medals would slip through the cracks. Well, that was life. The most egregious example was an F4 senior pilot who was recommended for a DFC for firing his rockets at a fishing village that was some twenty-five miles from the assigned target. Harry had been part of that strike against the Cam Pha harbor and, with one exception, it had been very successful.

That exception was an errant bombing run by Bill Elliott, who flew number four in Harry's flight. Bill had gotten disoriented during his roll-in; that was easy to do. As the flight leader, Harry had had a few moments to identify the target before rolling in. Bill, as tail-end Charley, had to focus on flying formation. That meant he saw the target for the first time as he rolled in.

A bombing run on a practice target was easy. Harry had made hundreds. All the parameters that went into a bomb run, such as roll-in altitude, speed, dive angle, and release altitude, were easily controlled. It was very different when you had bad weather and enemy fire to contend with. Then, the bombing run, which was basically an eyeball maneuver anyway, had to be adjusted. Experience made a big difference. The dive angle and the release altitude were determined from charts back on the ship; but when things got tight, those numbers went out the window. If clouds dictated a low dive angle, for instance, the pilot had to compensate by releasing a bit lower. But how much lower? A hunch and a guess lower was all the pilot could do. Harry had seen some outstanding bombing under extreme conditions. On the other hand, he had seen some bombs impact a quarter-mile from the target.

Bill had not been able to sort it all out that day and had planted his bombs very near a Polish ship that was taking on coal in the Cam Pha harbor. That looked to some like the seeds of an international incident. After the strike photos had come in, Harry had been invited for a personal chat with the Admiral who was the Task Force Commander. What could he say? He accepted his berating as best he could, all the while thinking, *What horseshit!*.

I wish Bill had hit that goddamned ship -- then maybe someone would take us seriously!

The Rules of Engagement meant that pilots had to ignore ships in Haiphong's harbor, which were loaded with trucks, then try to find those trucks after they were on the road and headed south. They were then legal targets as long as they were "within 200 yards of a motor-able road or trail." So far, Harry had not seen one single truck on a road, not one.

Also untouchable in Haiphong's harbor were ships unloading surface-to-air missiles, known as SAMs. Instead of destroying them when it would have been easy, the pilots would have to evade these missiles while their airplanes were being tracked by them. *How stupid is that?* Harry had often asked himself. How many pilots were lost because of this inane policy would never be known; but rules were rules, and that they were stupid seemed not to make any difference to anyone. It was a strange way to fight a war if you wanted to win.

Except for Bill splashing seawater on that Polish ship, the Cam Pha strike had been very effective. It was so effective that those higher up the chain of command had bypassed the Medals Board and made recommendations by decree. All flight leaders, those who led four plane elements, would be put up for a DFC. Here was where one of those medals slipped through the cracks.

That medal was intended for the F4 pilot who had mistakenly fired his rockets at a fishing village far from the target. Not only far from the target, but on an island located some distance from the mainland. Harry was there and had seen it. It was a combined strike on the Cam Pha coal dock facility along the coast east of Hai Phong. The F4s were carrying rockets and were supposed to provide flak suppression for the bomb-carrying A4s. Harry's flight of four was right behind the Phantoms. The strike approached from the east and even before reaching the mainland, the F4 leader called, "Target in sight at three o'clock. I'm rolling in," as he banked steeply and dove for the "target." His wingman, who knew where he was, refused to follow.

"Black Jack One," he cried, "that's not the target!"

Oblivious, Black Jack One pressed his run, firing all his rockets at the village.

As a flight leader, he was part of the cadre recommended for DFCs. That was too much even for his own squadron-mates. In a medal mutiny, they very respectfully told him to remove his name from the list. Or else. Harry never learned what "or else" meant, but whatever it was, it persuaded Black Jack One to reconsider.

"Never mind," he reportedly said. "I already have a DFC. I'll take an Air Medal instead."

And he did. That Air Medal, thought Harry, diminished every medal honestly won.

DFCs are fourth on the medals list. At the top was the Congressional Medal of Honor. There was no way to win that one with politics. The right stuff was needed, courage almost beyond belief. Until Vietnam, only 659 of these medals had been awarded since its inception in 1862. Harry had once read the citation for one of these medals won during World War II and he had almost wept reading it. The right stuff was strong stuff, and no one played politics with it. For those who understood courage, Medals of Honor inspired awe and commanded respect.

A month before Cam Pha, Harry had almost been involved in a small role in an action in which a Medal of Honor was later awarded. That had taken place in a God-forsaken valley in northern South Vietnam called A Shau, where a small contingent of U.S. soldiers had come under intense attack from both hillsides. Their cry for help found its way to the Kitty Hawk. There, flight operations turned on a dime so that A4s, the most suitable airplane, could be diverted from their scheduled missions and sent to the rescue. Harry was slated to lead a two-plane section there late in the day. His flight was scrubbed when his wingman's bird was unable to launch because of an engine problem.

The airplanes sent to A Shau were re-armed with rockets instead of bombs because the rockets were better for the weather conditions in the valley. They are more accurate than bombs, as well. Harry's roommate was one of those who went, and he described his experience later in their stateroom. Bob had map-navigated to the area beneath low clouds, found the target, and managed to put a few rockets into the North Vietnamese positions. Because of the low clouds, his dive was shallow and his pullout was very low. He had actually flown through the mud thrown up by his own rockets.

"Bob," Harry said, after hearing his tale, "you might be the only Navy pilot ever to bring a piece of Vietnam back to the ship."

Bob smiled and shook his head. "That," he said, "is collecting souvenirs the hard way."

Only later, did Harry learn of the heroic action that had taken place there. An Air Force pilot, flying a propeller-driven Skyraider of the type Harry had flown in his first squadron, had landed in the valley on a very short, very narrow runway, leapt out of his airplane, with the engine still running, picked up a wounded soldier, and hauled him back to his airplane. He somehow managed to climb up on the wing and get both him and his passenger into the cockpit. As Harry well knew, that was difficult enough to do alone. He whirled his plane around, and took off in the opposite direction. All of this took place under heavy fire. Now, that is courage.

A few days after the Cam Pha strike, the squadron had some good news. Bob often said, "There is no good news around here. It's just that some news is not as bad as other news." This, however, was genuine good news. Because of maintenance needs, the ship would head for Cubi Point three days ahead of schedule. Harry started feeling better immediately. Cubi Point was not San Francisco, but it would do.

19
CUBI POINT

1966

Harry stood in Vultures' Row and grimaced into the early morning sun. The Kitty Hawk had raised its brow at 0800, eased gently away from the Cubi Point jetty, and slowly made her way out of Subic Bay. She steamed around the Bataan Peninsula and out into the South China Sea, headed for the Tonkin Gulf. After a couple of hours heading west, the great ship swung around to the east and into the wind. An F4 was fired off the number one catapult on the bow and flight operations were underway.

Each of the Air Wing pilots would make four refresher landings to sharpen the skills that had eroded while they were in port. Harry's turn would come tomorrow, so, today, he could enjoy the circus that was sure to start soon on the flight deck he was now overlooking.

Vultures' Row provided the best seat in the house for watching these landings. It stood six decks above the flight deck and had an unobstructed view of aircraft approaches and landings -- or bolters, as was often the case after an in-port period. Harry had a slight hangover, so he was pleased that he was not on today's flight schedule. That made him feel somewhat better, but not much. *Why do I do this to myself?* he asked himself. *I know better.*

The ship had been in Cubi Point for just four days, but the social action was intense and nonstop as the crew made up for lost time. Along with Dixie and Yankee Stations, a major focal point of the war was the bar at the Officers' Club at the Cubi Point Naval Air Station.

"I won't try to describe it," a friend had written, "because those of you who have been there know what I mean, and those who haven't would never believe it."

Thirty days on Yankee Station and two days en route to Cubi Point created a powerful thirst. The Cubi Point Officers' Club was where it was slaked.

A day in port usually began with a visit to the club; and no matter what time Harry got there, sometimes as early as 1000, someone had gotten there earlier and was already fully-gassed and flying high. It was not a large club, not by Air Force standards, but it was cozy, and it was home for the pilots of the Tonkin Gulf.

Although a coat and tie were required, that rule was easily avoided by wearing a barong-tagalog. This was a local shirt with long sleeves, and it was made partly of lace. It was worn outside the trousers. The shirts were elegant and beautiful. What made them more beautiful was that they could be worn instead of a coat and tie. They could be rented at the entrance and that made life easy; but they were not often laundered, so a rented shirt might still hold last night's residue, deposited there by whomever wore it the night before. Still, they were convenient and comfortable, and, after a few drinks, no one seemed to notice the stains of the previous evening.

The alcohol started to flow well before noon, and the pace gained speed as the day wore on. By late afternoon, the club began to resemble Times Square on New Year's Eve. Many never got past the club, spending entire days there, eating, drinking, and exchanging war stories. If a pilot waited at the bar long enough, he was likely to meet friends he had not seen in years. The Cubi Point O Club was, for Navy pilots in those years, the crossroads of the Pacific.

At some point during the evening, a few well-lubricated pilots would try their luck with the club's very own carrier landing system, installed by several inventive pilots. This was a sled-like contraption that was pulled along a track towards a giant tub of water at the bottom of a few steps leading to a lower level. Its "pilot" controlled a hook which, when dropped at the right moment, would catch a wire stretched across the track. That would stop the sled, and its passenger would avoid a plunge into the tub. Not many could do it, and almost none after drinking a few San Miguels. Most landings ended up in a big splash, to loud applause.

On one visit to the club, Harry had met a newly-minted Naval aviator on his way to join his first squadron. He was wholesome and fresh, an All-American young man whom any parents would be proud to have as a son. His squadron was on Yankee Station and he was eager to get there. They had met at the bar over a couple of San Miguels, then had dinner together. The nugget had asked Harry for advice that might be useful over Vietnam. Harry had given him an earful, emphasizing that staying alive was the main goal.

"Nothing you can do can make any difference in this war," Harry told him earnestly, "so don't be a hero." Winning the war was in distant second place, he had said, far behind basic survival. He had passed along tactical information that might help him do that. The young pilot was fascinated but not intimidated. Harry wished him luck. It had been a pleasant encounter, one that might have taken place at any of many Officers' Clubs around the world.

"Good luck and fly safe. I mean that," Harry said, as they shook hands in parting.

One week later, Harry learned that his dinner companion had been killed by a SAM over Haiphong on his second mission. His flight had been alerted to an imminent missile launch, and he had rolled inverted and pulled for the deck to get below the arming altitude of the missile. This tactic was known as a "split S" and was often used over the north. Harry had talked about it that night over dinner. Just as the young pilot had rolled inverted, his cockpit had taken a direct hit from a 37mm shell.

In the Tonkin Gulf, every pilot heard heartbreakers like this one almost every day. This one hit Harry harder than most, even though he had barely known the eager young man. What might have he achieved in life, Harry wondered. No one would ever know. Harry had become inured to such news. It was how things were. But this time, it touched his heart in a place he never knew he had.

Sometimes, when you experience them often enough, abnormal events become normal. So it was in the Tonkin Gulf. Harry recalled one morning when he sat down to breakfast to learn that the Air Wing had lost three airplanes during the night. He did not ask the names, only the squadrons. He was relieved to learn that none were from his squadron nor from any squadron in which he had close friends. *Damn,* he thought, *I ought to be just as concerned with pilots I don't know. They have friends, relatives, and squadron-mates, too.* But Harry's first reaction was to ask someone to pass the salt. That surprised him, but there it was, and it bothered him greatly. Losing pilots was becoming normal.

Many years later, Harry would attend a squadron reunion at the Pensacola Naval Air Station. There, in the Naval Air Museum, Harry would once again drink a San Miguel at the Cubi Point Officers' Club bar. The entire original bar room had been taken apart, brought to Pensacola, and re-assembled. The San Miguel there tasted even better than those he had drunk in the Philippines during the "Tonkin Gulf Time-Outs," as Jack Rooney had dubbed them. He wasn't sure, but he thought he found the very same dent Jack had made in the bar with his head one night after drinking one San Miguel too many.

20
OLONGAPO

1966

For those seeking a more daring evening, the Cubi Point Officers' Club was only a starting point. It was a place to gather a cadre of adventurers, soften their judgment and inhibitions with a few San Miguel beers, then strike out for the town of Olongapo, just outside the base. Its center was only a few hundred yards from the gate, but Harry always hired a jeepney to get there. That was to reduce the "squalor exposure rate," as a squadron-mate neatly put it. You smelled Olongapo before you saw it.

Jeepneys were jeeps left over from the war. They had been converted into taxis in colorful and artful ways, and they were the heart of the public transport system. Some were used as buses along regular routes. Others freelanced and could be flagged down anywhere. Passengers jumped in, then alighted where they pleased -- a great system and it cost almost nothing. You usually had to share your jeepney with others, but no one minded. Although they offered protection from the sun, passengers were at the mercy of the wind and the rain. In the Philippines, rain could be serious. Sometimes you could not see the other side of the street; but that was a small price to pay for the economy and the convenience. Some pilots refused to use them, but Harry liked them and rode them often.

Olongapo's mission in life was to provide nightlife for the U.S. Navy, and it did this with flamboyant enthusiasm. Harry had visited several clubs and bars on its brightly-lit main street and finally settled on two he liked best. The first was New Pauline's, where it was said that girls hung from the chandeliers. That turned out to be an exaggeration, but not a big one. It was an enormous place with several bands and although the girls were not swinging from the ceiling, there were certainly enough to make anyone forget Yankee Station. New Pauline's was adjoined to a hotel, so there was always the option of taking your dancing partner to the next level.

The girls of the Philippines were delightful. They were pretty, personable, and they liked to laugh and dance. Best of all, they spoke English, some better than Harry. Another favorite drinking place was one which had been adopted by the Air Wing as the unofficial Officers' Club Annex. You could always find someone you knew at The Willows. It was cozy and charming and well stocked with pretty girls. Harry had found one he especially liked,

Connie, and he visited her whenever he ventured into town. The Willows was usually worth a few pleasant hours.

All the bar girls took American names, which were displayed on their name tags, along with a number. You could order by name, or by number, if you forgot the name. There was an honor code among bar girls. When a relationship was established, such as Harry's with Connie, the other girls would not so much as glance in his direction. He was "taken" and they would risk losing their friends or even their jobs if they appeared to be interested in him. Harry appreciated that kind of loyalty. It meant finding another girl in another bar if the relationship ended, but that was the unwritten rule. It was a rule that was easy to live with.

Harry had once seen Olongapo in the daylight and could not believe how different it looked without the filter of the night. The glamour was gone, and the town was not at all what it had appeared to be the night before. A delicacy of Olongapo, which Harry thought captured that difference, was a balut. It, too, was not what it appeared to be. A balut was a chicken egg that looked normal until it was opened. It had been partially matured in a pile of manure. When the time was right, the egg was cooked to stop further growth. Cracked open before eating, the egg contained a recognizable chicken embryo with beak, claws and tiny bones. After drinking enough San Miguels, eating a balut became a test of courage. Usually adventurous enough to try anything once, Harry had never been drunk enough to eat a balut.

21
GOODBYE, HONG KONG

July 1970

"Er du tret?" asked Harry, using a few of the Norwegian words Astrid had taught him.

"Your Norwegian is perfect," she remarked.

"I had a good teacher," said Harry, with a smile. "And not only for Norwegian."

"Yes, I am tired. And what about you?" she asked. "Are you 'tret?'"

"I am beat," he said, "but still going strong."

"Beat?" she queried. "Beat meaning what? Tired?"

He nodded, as she stroked his chest with her palm, then began kissing his ear.

"Does this help?" she whispered. Despite his fatigue, Harry was almost instantly aroused. A woman's tongue in his ear always seemed to do that.

"It helps," he said "but maybe not the way you think."

"Harry," she cooed softly, "I think I know the way you mean. Like in Karachi? I enjoyed that very much. I hope we can do it again. Where will we sleep tonight? The girls are asking."

"I wish I knew," said Harry. "Kuala Lumpur, I hope. I think we'll have to wait until we're in a hotel room somewhere before we can continue our Norwegian lessons. And maybe sleep first. We want to be rested. And ready, right?"

She smiled sweetly. "Oh, we can sleep when we are old. Now is the time for excitement. I am always ready."

Harry grinned. "I noticed that in Karachi."

He didn't know if it was her tongue in his ear, her hand on his chest, or the soft pressure of her breast on his shoulder, but Harry felt a burst of energy coursing through his body. Who needs sleep, he asked himself.

On the way back to Kuala Lumpur, Harry brought up Astrid's question. Turning to Thor, seated half-asleep in the jump seat, as usual, he asked about a hotel stop.

"Thor, goddammit, we've been on duty for more than 24 hours. It's not only illegal, it's unsafe. We ought to night-stop in KL." Harry did not mention that he had discussed the situation with Joe and Gene. Both had adamantly declared that KL was as far as they would go.

"Okay," said Thor, "we will talk about it on the ground."

Harry took that as less than a commitment, but it was a foot in the door. The problem was that the on-coming crew was in Karachi, not Kuala Lumpur, so the aircraft would stand idle during any night-stop; and the waiting passengers would have to be taken care of. Harry saw that Thor was counting on using his magic personality to have his way. Well, he thought, we'll see.

22
FLYING AROUND INDIA

The terminal in KL was an open one. The terminal itself was open to the weather, and so were its fingers, spreading out in different directions. The aircraft nosed alongside one of those fingers and Harry shut down the engines. He wondered what would happen next. The first piece of news was that the passengers were already at the airport. They had been there many hours and would not appreciate waiting ten more hours while the crew went off to a hotel.

The Astrid Effect had worn off during the flight and Harry was feeling fatigue right down to his toes. He was willing to discuss it because he knew the stakes; but his body desperately needed sleep.

"Okay, Thor, what about it?" asked Harry, using a direct approach.

"Come," said Thor genially. "Let us go out on the grass and talk about this."

Harry noticed that Joe and Gene made serious furrows in their brows, and looked expectantly at Harry. He quickly evaluated the situation.

"Well," he said politely, "it never hurts to talk."

The four of them left the aircraft, descended the stairs, and looked around. Where to sit? Harry noticed that the finger the aircraft was nosed up against had a luxurious layer of green grass beneath the elevated ramp.

"Here," he pointed. "What about right here?"

After sitting down awkwardly, Thor took up the challenge. He explained that because the relief crew was in Karachi, and because of hotel expenses associated with extending the stay for the passengers, a night-stop would probably mean the end of the company. Was that true, Harry asked himself, or was this an exaggeration to persuade them to continue? Well, he answered himself, it certainly could be true. This was a shoe-string operation if ever there was one. It would not take much to snap that string. Joe was still unconvinced, but Gene was wavering.

Another problem was the passengers waiting here in Kuala Lumpur. They had already been at the airport for many hours, Thor said; how many, no one knew. They would wait ten more hours if the crew went to a hotel. Harry knew that should not be a factor in his decision, but, after all, he wanted Trans Polar to succeed as much as Thor did.

Then, Thor sweetened the pot. He offered double pay if they carried on to Karachi. That brought Gene on board. Joe, however, had more money than he could ever spend, even the way he spent it. He always carried a couple of thousand dollars in cash because, "you never know." The momentum was slowly swinging towards pressing on, and it soon became three against one. Finally, realizing he was out-manned and out-maneuvered, Joe agreed, but under one condition: they would have to make it nonstop.

Thor looked at Harry, who shrugged ever so slightly. They would have to look at the charts, he said. Thor saw that this was the best deal he could make, and they all agreed. Jack, of course, knew nothing about reading charts. That left it in Harry's hands. After an hour of flipping through the charts, and using assumed numbers when he couldn't find the real ones, Harry finally announced that they would land in Karachi with 6,000 pounds of fuel. That was much less than the amount officially required, but Harry knew they would pass over Bombay en route; so if they ran short of fuel, they could drop in there.

Thor gave Harry a broad smile when they made the final decision to continue. He stood up and walked back up the stairs leading to the airplane to tell the ramp agent to begin boarding the passengers. Harry, however, was not smiling. Starting in Karachi, they had soldiered on to Calcutta, Kuala Lumpur, Hong Kong and now back to Kuala Lumpur. Counting the ground time, they had now been on duty for some forty-five hours, all of it in the airplane and all of it without sleep. Stretching ahead was another flight of six hours -- if nothing went wrong.

Back in his jump seat, Thor fell asleep as soon as the wheels were up. Their route took them across the Bay of Bengal to Madras, then overland to Karachi. They were approaching Madras when things started going wrong. Because they planned to fly through Indian airspace without stopping, they were asked to provide an over-flight authorization number. The ruse used successfully when outbound from Karachi did not impress the man on the radio below. He wanted the number and he wanted it now. Harry thought for a moment, then reached back and shook Thor's leg, waking him.

"Thor, this guy wants our over-flight number. We got one?" Harry knew the answer before he asked the question. The look on Thor's face confirmed it. Thor screwed up his face in thought.

"Tell him," he finally said, "that we will not fly over India. We will fly around it."

Was he serious, Harry asked himself. A glance at his face told Harry he was.

"Listen, Thor," Harry explained tiredly, "we might be able to fly around part of India; but not all of it. There is just no way to do that." By now they were almost over the Indian coast.

The controller had heard enough. "Trans Polar," he said in a commanding voice, "you are ordered to land at Madras so that your flight papers can be inspected. Please advise your intentions."

Harry knew the game was up. "Roger, Madras, Trans Polar requesting descent. Over." They were given immediate descent clearance.

By now, they were too close to the coast for a straight-in descent, so Harry made a couple of 360-degree turns to lose altitude. Turning the controls over to Joe, he switched over to the airport's ground control frequency. He explained the unscheduled landing and asked if they were able to service a 707. "Oh, yes, sir," a voice answered. "Air India comes once each week with a 707. No problem, sir."

Harry felt better and asked the ground control to advise the ramp agent that only fuel would be needed, no other services. He got a roger, then switched back to the air traffic control frequency. There was no other traffic, and the approach and landing were routine.

As they were about to shut down, Gene Daily had a thought. "Boss, are we sure they got external power and an air starter here?"

That had not occurred to Harry, and it was a good question.

"We'll keep Number 3 running until we know how the wind blows," he announced. That way, the airplane could provide its own electric power and, if necessary, provide its own air pressure to restart the other three engines.

The first clue that they were in serious trouble came when the cockpit door burst open and an American, of all people, practically bounded inside.

"Jesus H. Christ!" he exploded. "What in the hell are you doing here? You might never get out of this place."

"Why?" asked Harry, puzzled at the outburst. "What's the big deal?"

"Well," he answered sharply, "just for starters, I hope you don't need any fuel."

Harry told him they did, in fact, require fuel. "But," he added, "we have cash, plenty of it."

By now, Thor's hand had dived into his black satchel, withdrawn a fistfull of U.S. dollars, and thrust them in the face of the American.

"Sorry, guys, they don't accept dollars. There are currency restrictions."

Thor shoved his fist back into the bag and it reappeared full of English pounds. "We have pounds," he said somewhat triumphantly, "plenty of them."

"Sorry," the American said, "pounds won't work either."

By this time, Harry was beginning to feel irritated at this man who would not accept their money. Who refuses money?

"Well, for Christ's sake," he asked in exasperation. "What does work? What will they take?"

"Guys, I hate to ask, but by any chance, do you have an Indian Oil credit card?" he asked hopefully. "That's the only thing they take here. You're not in Chicago now. And that's not all. The fuel crew needs 24 hours' notice before they will even start refueling. Can you make it to Bombay? You can get fuel there."

Harry was becoming seriously annoyed. With the unscheduled stop and an engine running during their transit stop, there was now no hope of reaching Karachi with the fuel remaining. They had to have fuel. Unless, he thought, they stopped in Bombay. Wouldn't that do it? Harry quickly went over the airways charts, made some fast calculations, and decided they could; but they could not waste much more fuel here on the ground and still have enough to reach Bombay. Harry and Joe headed for Flight Operations to file a new flight plan. Thor went off on his own to try, in his own way, to find a way to buy fuel in Madras, but Harry had heard enough. Get out while we can, he thought, or we might never get out. They found Thor on the telephone in the Air India Station Manager's office. Strangely, he was speaking in Norwegian.

Later, after their departure, Harry learned he was talking to a Norwegian Counsel, somewhere in India, trying to arrange the purchase of fuel. Harry had quickly explained the change of plans, and they all hurried out to the aircraft, still running its Number 3 engine, several hours after landing. Harry turned to Gene as the pre-start checklist was completed.

"Gene, I owe you one for thinking about keeping Number 3 running. You might have saved our ass."

"No sweat, Boss," he answered with a grin. "You can buy me a beer in Karachi, if we ever get there."

They launched for Bombay, an hour-and-a-half away, with only 22,000 pounds of fuel in the tanks, not much for an airplane that burns 12,000 pounds per hour. Thor stayed awake for this sector, and Harry soon knew why. He wanted to overfly Bombay and go straight to Karachi.

Harry asked Gene to update their fuel situation every few minutes to see how feasible this was. It looked like the best number Gene could come up with was about 5,000 pounds remaining on arrival there. Thor made a determined effort to persuade them to continue to Karachi. He thought in terms of money, not fuel. At one point in a somewhat heated discussion, Joe, who had not said one word since they left Madras, finally spoke out.

"Now, goddammit, we are going to land in Bombay and that is the end of it. Thor, I want to hear not one goddamn word from you until we're on the ground."

Harry could not suppress a smile. Joe was right, of course. He had taken the direct approach, while Harry had been trying the tactful route.

Joe was at the controls on this sector, and during the approach to the Bombay airport, in the landing configuration, the stillness of fatigue in the cockpit was suddenly pierced by an excited call from Gene Daily.

"Airspeed!" he almost shrieked.

Harry, in the right seat, had not noticed that Joe had let the airspeed fall well below the Reference Speed. That speed, known as V-ref, is determined by the aircraft's landing weight. It is adjusted for wind. Usually, a pilot will err on the safe side of that number. It never hurts to add a few knots to V-ref for the wife and kids; but a speed below V-ref can lead to a stall. When that happens, the airspeed across the wings no longer follows the curved surface of the wing and creates a turbulence resulting in the loss of lift. The airplane then becomes a falling object.

Harry quickly covered Joe's hand with his own and pushed the throttles smartly forward. In those few seconds, the plane had dropped below the glide path, and that is no place to be when close to the ground. Low and slow is a dangerous combination; but a burst of power did the trick, and Joe made a perfect landing. He did not know much about the many and various aspects of getting an airplane from one place to another, but his landings were always perfect. What disturbed Harry about these few seconds was that he had not been aware that the airspeed was in the danger zone until Gene had cried out. There was no excuse for that.

They taxied to the ramp and shut down the engines. Joe was half-asleep, even before the checklist was completed. Savak had sprawled out across the navigator's desk, head on his arms, fast asleep. He had obviously been trained to call out the time of landing, which he did without fail in a loud and clear voice. He had done so this time; but in the few minutes between the landing and the shutdown, he was out like a light and snoring loudly.

Harry had to admit that this had been a long and difficult flight. Just how long was it, he wondered. He turned and looked back at Gene. He looked haggard and worn, even worse than Harry felt.

"Gene," he said with a tired voice, "this has, for sure, been a long one. How many hours have we been on duty, anyway?"

Gene answered with a croak, "Boss, you don't want to know."

Harry tried to smile. "Humor me. Just for the hell of it."

Gene flipped a few pages in his maintenance logbook, then looked up with some disbelief. "Would you believe we've been on duty for fifty-seven hours? Without leaving the damn airplane? No goddam wonder I feel like a bucket of warm vomit."

Wow, thought Harry. Fifty-seven hours was not only illegal by a long way, it was unsafe as well. Let's hope no one finds out about this.

"Maybe not a record," he said finally, "but close enough for the kind of girls we hang around with. What about a nice cold beer?"

A wide smile creased Gene's crusty features.

"Boss," he smiled through his beard, "you just said the magic word. Even this lousy Indian beer will taste good right now."

After shutting down the engines, Thor informed the crew that they would spend a day in Bombay, then fly to Beirut, where the other crew, now in Karachi, would meet them. Well, Harry had often said that planning is only for those who are not able to improvise. There were several reasons for this decision, but the main one was that, for political reasons, the crew in Karachi was not allowed to travel to Bombay. Suits me, thought Harry. Bombay was never on my list, but now that I'm here, let's give it a shot.

For the passengers -- there were only fifty -- it meant a surprise visit to a city they had never expected to see. Some complained, but most were pleased with a free hotel room in exotic Bombay.

Getting through customs and immigration took three hours. They were told later that three hours through Bombay customs was faster than normal. Harry was afraid to ask what "normal" was. The ordeal might have been shorter, but at the first sign of harassment, Savak, who was from Bombay, decided to impress the crew with his influence in his hometown. To look forceful, he had placed one foot on the custom agent's stand and was about to complain. Harry, next in line, could not miss the look of contempt, then anger, that came over the agent's face as he looked down on Savak's shoe intruding into his personal domain. Savak had not said even one word before the agent exploded. Harry had not a clue what he said, but Savak certainly did. He removed his shoe with lightning speed, almost falling over backwards as he did. He began apologizing, then grovelling, as he realized his mistake. Each crew bag was then examined slowly and minutely down to its smallest crease and fold. The agent was an expert at exasperating travelers, and he reveled in it now. Scowling furiously, he seemed to take forever, but, eventually, he passed them through the airport terminal and into the world beyond. It would be an interesting world.

23
BOMBAY

The next morning Harry and Astrid rented a taxi and made a tour of this fascinating city.

Harry had seen many cities as he had crisscrossed the world; but Bombay was a new experience. "Kaleidoscope" did not begin to describe the colorful maze of vehicles, people, and assorted creatures that made up the streets of Bombay. Just walking down the street, any street, was an adventure.

First, there were the beggars. They were everywhere, and they were usually children. They were often intentionally maimed or disfigured, Harry was told, to evoke sympathy from passersby. Harry was struck by their perfect teeth, which they often displayed in wide smiles to encourage contributions. Even a few rupees, almost nothing, resulted in great manifestations of gratitude and even wider smiles. Unfortunately, it also resulted in a lightning-quick doubling of the crowd of beggars as the word spread, as if by magic, that here was someone willing to part with a bit of money.

Some of the beggars were older, and these were usually crippled or were, in some other way, abnormal. Harry was impressed with their cheerful nature. They were a pathetic lot, but they always seemed to be in good spirits, even when no rupees were forthcoming. Here, thought Harry, was a great lesson for some people he knew who had plenty, but who always seemed to whine and complain about the petty problems of life. Let them come to Bombay for a few days. Hell, he thought, let them come and stay.

The traffic in Bombay was nothing, if not spectacular. There were the ubiquitous little yellow-and-blue taxis. They were all identical, and there was always one available when needed. They cost almost nothing. For someone used to riding taxis in Manhattan, it was almost a pleasure to hire a taxi in Bombay; almost a pleasure because the cabs were bare-bones vehicles, even compared to New York taxis. The ride itself was usually a death-defying experience. There were not only other cabs to avoid, which was thrilling enough, there were all manner of other obstacles to deal with. The streets were thronged with pedestrians all the time, even throughout the night.

The rush hour was permanent here. People. They were the main problem. They jammed the roads as well as the sidewalks, and although they were often fascinating to look at, they made movement very difficult. Animals. They were another problem. They had seen water buffaloes, monkeys, a camel, horses and many cows. In amongst the cows, people carried birds, monkeys, various reptiles and creatures Harry had never before seen. They had even watched a snake charmer playing his flute while a cobra arose in a basket, just as in an old movie. For religion reasons, cows were allowed to wander freely throughout the city. Curious, Harry asked why.

The Hindu religion, he learned, believed in reincarnation. People came back in the next life at a level that depended upon their behavior in this one. Holy men came back as cows, someone said. Although Harry could not understand how that was a step up, he thought the philosophy was brilliant. What a great way to motivate people! And it took the grief out of dying. No need to feel sad for someone who was coming back to the world better than when he left it. No need to feel bitter towards a mean and hateful person. He would come back as a cockroach or whatever else he deserved. Wonderful!

As long as religion is all about concepts which cannot be proven, thought Harry, as he reviewed their day, you might as well choose one that provides some incentive to live a decent life. It seems light years ahead of our concept of heaven and hell, thought Harry, and Astrid agreed.

"Maybe I will become a Hindu," she said later, over a gin and tonic in the hotel bar.

They were staying at the Farrias Hotel, nondescript, but cheap, and well located near the famous Gateway to India. Gene rated it "minus one-and-a-half stars," but it was clean and quiet, and those were Harry's basic requirements.

"I like very much the idea of coming back as a sacred cow," Astrid said. "Maybe then people will think I am important."

"Astrid," said Harry gently, "you are important, and especially to me. I can find cows anywhere. Where could I find another Astrid?"

Astrid smiled and raised her glass. "I will certainly drink to that," she said happily.

In Bombay, alcohol was rationed. To buy the gin and tonics, Harry had first gone to a government office near the hotel and obtained ration cards. These cards were then presented to a man sitting behind a desk at the back of the bar. He carefully recorded the drinks Harry had just bought. Before ordering the gin, Harry had tried the Indian beer. He liked to sample local beer wherever he went; but, here, it was like liquid yeast and he could not drink it. The gin and tonic, on the other hand, tasted great. That was one of the more useful remnants of British colonialism.

Drinking gin and tonics, they laughed as they talked about their do-it-yourself tour of the city. What wonders they had seen! One of the memorable places they had driven past just outside the city was a mound of corpses awaiting cremation. The driver told them it was the Tower of the Dead. A cloud of vultures circling overhead marked it. They were told that many of the bodies were unidentified and unclaimed corpses picked up from the streets every morning.

Harry and Astrid had witnessed a corpse being burned in a pyre. They had actually heard his head explode. By coincidence, they met his relatives. There was no sadness, only joy. That was because whoever had died was a good person and would come back better than before. They had been invited to a celebration at his home to celebrate the death. The family was disappointed when they declined.

An unforgettable visit was to the Street of the Cages, a low-class prostitution center. It was a street a few blocks long, lined on each side with dilapidated, two-story buildings. Instead of glass, the windows were filled with young girls for rent. Some were young, indeed, not more than twelve or thirteen, thought Harry. Many other girls mobbed the street, and some crowded around the taxi and tried to open the doors. Thanks to the driver, they were locked; but Harry would never forget the faces of all those girls crushed against the taxi windows, beseeching, even begging, for business.

That Astrid was in the taxi seemed not to matter. The driver explained that homosexuals often visited the cages and that not all of the girls were girls. Some only looked that way. There was something for everyone. The experience was unsettling, even frightening, and Astrid was anxious to leave.

"Harry," she said between clenched teeth, "I am feeling very nervous. Can we please go elsewhere?"

They left as quickly as they could but, because of the throngs of girls and transvestites, the taxi could not move faster than a slow walk. As they moved through the crowd, Harry asked the driver how much these girls, or whatever they were, charged for their services, whatever they were. He gave a number in rupees that worked out to half a U.S. dollar.

"Well," said Harry, "the price is certainly right. Any extra charge for the gonorrhoea?"

A man would need to be drunk or desperate to even leave the car on that street, but many did. Harry was reminded of a friend who had once told him that he had gone places with a hard-on that he would be afraid to go with a gun. The need for sex can make a man sometimes do outrageous things, and the cages certainly qualified as outrageous, even dangerous. I hope I never need it that badly, thought Harry, as they finally cleared the crowds.

111

Heading back to the hotel, they passed a completely nude man walking nonchalantly along a busy street with a bear on a leash. No one seemed to think that was unusual. Here in Bombay, thought Harry, it wasn't.

Those small spaces not occupied by people, animals and taxis were taken up by bicycles, some looking like World War I vintage. The streets of Bombay were a circus, and Harry never knew where to look next. He tried to look everywhere at once so he would not miss anything.

"We really saw very much," said Astrid in the hotel bar later.

"Yes," agreed Harry, "but just think of what we must have missed."

Well, he thought, you can't see it all; but she was right. They'd had a great day and now, thought Harry, there was still tonight to look forward to. He raised his glass and nodded towards Astrid.

"To Bombay," he said cheerfully, "and to us in it."

Astrid clinked her glass gently against Harry's and smiled.

"What shall we do tonight?" she asked.

He grinned and said, "Try to guess."

24
DIXIE STATION

1966

Dixie Station was the southern version of Yankee Station. Like its counterpart in the northern Tonkin Gulf, it was a moving focal point for the carriers stationed there. It was the launch pad for missions flown in support of the forces trying to hold back the takeover of South Vietnam by the Viet Cong and the Army of North Vietnam. For the pilots, life on Dixie Station was a relative holiday. Harry usually referred to it as a Gentleman's War; compared with those up north, a mission in the south was like a walk in the park. The difference between Dixie Station and Yankee Station, he often said, was like the difference between a beautiful day and a shitty night.

On Dixie Station, it was daytime-only flight operations. That alone was an enormous difference. The pilots returned to the ship after "a day at the office," as Harry's roommate put it, and enjoyed an evening as close to normal as shipboard life can be. A shower before dinner, perhaps a martini, helped make life seem almost pleasant. A fine dinner in the Officers' Wardroom, wearing his khaki uniform and not a dirty flight suit, contributed to an aura of normalcy. After dinner, a movie was usually an option. The movies were always old, and one of Harry's Laws of the Sea was that the film would break at least three times during the showing. Still, it was a diversion and was much appreciated. For Harry, the most entertaining features of watching a movie -- they were shown in the Officers' Wardroom -- were the viewers' nonstop comments. They were crude, ribald, and hilarious.

The martini was mixed with ingredients securely locked in his stateroom safe. Drinking alcohol was technically not permitted on Navy ships; but what the hell, this was war and no one seemed to care, as long as discretion was used. That meant sneaking the stuff on board and keeping it stored in a private safe. Each officer had one in his room; it was supposed to be used for private papers and such. A bottle of Beefeaters fit nicely inside. Before leaving San Diego, Harry had bought a small refrigerator and squeezed it into his room. It held a jar of olives and it provided a small supply of ice for the occasional cocktail hours Harry enjoyed behind his locked door. There was no need to advertise.

Up north on Yankee Station, Harry also took a drink now and then; but these were serious drinks. They might be taken at any hour and were usually drunk not for relaxation and reflection, but to help get his pulse rate back to normal after a particularly unnerving mission. Almost any night mission qualified. For Harry, drinking was not about getting drunk but for soothing his mind. He seemed to feel better with a drink in his hand, even to think better. Here on Dixie Station, a drink before dinner was more of a social event and made life seem almost livable. Now and then Bob, or one of their neighbors, would join the party. The discussions always ended up about how this nasty little war should be fought. The more the gin flowed, the better the suggestions. They had plenty.

There were two main reasons why life on Dixie Station was a different world from that on Yankee Station. First, the flying was almost exclusively done in the daytime. The second reason was almost as important. Although there were people in the south who wanted to shoot Harry down, they had nowhere near the means to bring down a plane as did those in the north. You did not need to fly with your heart in your throat. Yes, there was shrapnel falling through the sky in the south, too; but it was mainly small arms and automatic weapons fire. No big guns and, most important, no SAMs to worry about.

In the north, most flights were monitored by Overpass, the Kitty Hawk's flying electronic eyes and ears. The area over North Vietnam was divided into sectors, each with a label. It was essential that pilots keep track of which sector they were in. When Overpass detected a SAM search radar signal, it broadcast the codeword of the day, followed by the area emitting the signal. A pilot might, for example, hear, "Garden Gate Alpha November Yellow." "Garden Gate" was the code word of the day. "Yellow" meant a search radar signal had been detected in sector Alpha November. "Red" meant Overpass had detected a fire-control radar and a launch was imminent. If a pilot was in sector Alpha November and he heard the word "Red," he had to do something quickly.

SAMs armed at 3,200 feet. Below that, they were flying objects and did not explode. During the Kitty Hawk's first week on Yankee Station, she had lost a low-flying A5 Vigilante when an unarmed SAM had knocked off its wing. For a pilot in the sector who was above 3,200 feet and hearing the word Red, the quickest and safest action was to roll inverted and pull back hard on the stick to head lower. That placed the airplane in a different environment, one of automatic weapons and small arms; but it was a case of first things first. The transmissions from Overpass that a SAM launch was imminent got Harry's attention like nothing he had ever heard. Those heart-stopping calls were not heard in the south.

Forcing airplanes lower and into a high-intensity fire zone was the main threat of the SAMs. They could not turn with a Skyhawk, so if the pilot saw it coming, he could make a hard turn which the SAM could not follow. That was the trick. The pilot had to see it coming. Overpass saved many airplanes by calling out imminent SAM launches. That gave the pilots a few seconds to duck below its arming altitude or to help him see the missile and out-turn it.

Most of the work in the south was at low altitudes. Napalm runs, especially low, were made at treetop levels. Pulling out of one such run one day, Harry had glanced down to see a man, who looked to be an ordinary peasant, shooting a pistol at him. Occasionally, small arms would bring down an airplane, or so claimed the North Vietnamese. Harry had seen a photo from a Hanoi newspaper depicting a lovely North Vietnamese woman aiming a rifle with which she claimed to have shot down an F4 Phantom. Did it happen? Who knew? Could it happen? Hell, yes, thought Harry. A direct hit was not necessary to shoot down an airplane. A plane could be brought down by flying into a piece of falling metal. Zigging instead of zagging might make all the difference. You have to be lucky in life, Harry had often said, and especially when flying over North Vietnam.

Harry had read an article by a French journalist who had been in Hanoi during several bombing raids. After the all clear had been sounded, he had been cautioned not to leave the shelter even though the raid was over. Puzzled, he heeded the order, then understood the reason. For more than five minutes, shrapnel could be heard hitting the streets after its long fall from the high altitudes at which it had exploded.

Dixie Station was a daytime-only operation because of the nature of the war there. The missions were of two types. The first was with a pre-assigned target, much like in the north. These targets, unlike in the north, were not hard targets, but were designed to help ground forces who were involved in actual combat operations. The second type was controlled by a Forward Air Controller, known as a "fack," for FAC. He flew close to the ground in a small, slow, propeller-driven aircraft and directed the fire of the ordnance-carrying airplanes, such as Harry's.

FACs commanded great respect, for theirs was one of the most dangerous jobs in the war. Farther down the road, Harry would meet a FAC in a Saigon bar who said he carried a rifle with him on all his flights. Interesting, thought Harry. Then the FAC told him that he had seven notches on the piece, one for each Viet Cong he had killed while carrying out a mission. Now, that was more than interesting: it was incredible. Harry could not imagine firing a rifle out of the window of a low-flying airplane, never mind hitting a moving target. It was so incredible that Harry could not at first believe it. But after a few beers together, Harry not only believed him, he marveled at how he had done it.

"Well, shit," the FAC had said that night. "Those sumbitches were trying to shoot me down!" FACs, Harry decided that night, were a different breed.

A rendezvous with a FAC was pre-arranged. The pilots got the necessary information in their pre-flight brief before leaving the ship. All they needed to know was the FAC's position, radio frequency and call sign, and the time of the rendezvous. Usually, the FAC was not spotted visually, and this did not matter. The bomb-carrying airplanes just had to be sure they were talking to the right man in the right place. Once this was established, the FAC would designate a target by description, if possible, but most often by firing a marking rocket that was very easily seen from higher altitudes. The rockets made a vivid and highly-visible mark on the ground. It was unmistakable.

He would then denote the target by calling a range and distance from the mark. "From the mark, target is two o'clock at 150 yards," he might call. The system worked well. It needed to be responsive and it needed to be quick, and it was. Later, Harry would learn that a request from a ground unit could be filled in as little as two hours. That was amazing when he considered all the information needed to coordinate such an evolution. Imagine, thought Harry, delivering a bomb on a target just 120 minutes from the time the need was determined. That was astounding, and it was an impressive measure of what cooperation between different units could achieve.

Today, Harry and his wingman, Bill Bowlen, were assigned to connect with a FAC northeast of Saigon, where a ground engagement was in progress. After the briefing, the two pilots headed for "the roof" to man their airplanes. Harry was almost blinded by the bright morning sun as he stepped out of the ship's bowels and onto the flight deck. He was always surprised to leave the dark and cavernous interior of the ship and find himself in the daylight. Sometimes, several days went by without seeing the outside world. During these periods, it was easy to lose track of what time it was or even what day it was. Now and then, Harry would look at his watch and ask himself, "Now, is that morning or evening?"

For those not involved in flight ops, life was routine. Meals, for example, were served at scheduled times; but once caught up in the war machine, the strings were pulled from above. Flight crews flew at all hours, and ate and slept when they could. Often Harry would see the ship's crew asleep in nooks and crannies throughout the ship. During around-the-clock flight ops, one of the officers' wardrooms served breakfast twenty-four hours daily, to match the flight ops. That rankled the aircrews who soon became fed up, so to speak, with eating eggs three times a day. The ship's company, meanwhile, lived a 9-to-5 life, with scheduled meals and movies every night. Harry might go for days within the Great Gray Iron Cavern, as Bob called it, without seeing the sun or the sky, or breathing fresh air. Life became surreal, and it was easy to forget there was another world out there.

Harry's first sensation, as he walked across the flight deck to his airplane, was that something was not right. The ship was making good speed through the water, but there was no wind across the deck. It took him a moment to realize that the ship was steaming downwind at the same speed as the wind blowing across the water. The result was no relative wind. He glanced up at the ship's stack and, sure enough, the smoke was rising straight up as though there was no wind at all; and on the flight deck, there wasn't. It was dead calm.

Strange, thought Harry. Even stranger was what he heard next. As he approached his aircraft to begin his pre-flight routine, Harry heard the ship's loudspeaker announce that Sunday mass would begin on the hangar deck in five minutes. Harry wondered if anyone else was aware of the anomaly of preparing to launch a strike, the purpose of which was death and destruction, while at almost the very same moment, a religious service was about to begin. Here on the Kitty Hawk, some of the crew were praying for love and peace while others were about to carry war to people who were also praying for love and peace. Well, hell, thought Harry, nothing has made any sense since we got here, so why should it start now?

During flight operations, the flight deck was always a precarious place. It was much more so at night. Darkness brought its own special problems. High winds made ordinary tasks hazardous. With the ship headed into a strong wind, work on the deck became a test of strength, a primal struggle between man and nature. Men and equipment were sometimes blown overboard. "Man Overboard" drills were held regularly.

Other drills were held regularly, too. One was "Prepare to Abandon Ship." After the alarm for General Quarters was sounded, the ship's crew headed for designated areas to receive life vests. During the drill, the ship's loudspeaker helpfully pointed out the location of the closest landfall.

"Now hear this," the loudspeaker might intone, with the ship in the middle of the ocean, "The nearest point of land bears 278 degrees, and one-thousand, one-hundred-and-forty-three miles." That always made Harry smile. He was a good swimmer, but not that good.

Today, the bright sun and calm wind made the flight deck seem almost unreal. Crewmen went about their duties in an almost nonchalant manner, joking and laughing as they did. The duty of each man could be determined by the color of his jersey. Those who fueled the airplanes wore purple jerseys; plane captains wore brown. Maintenance men wore green shirts, and those who loaded the bombs and rockets wore, appropriately, red. The plane directors, those who guided the airplanes about the flight deck, wore yellow jerseys. As Harry went to his plane, he saw the scene around him as an actor might view a stage. What appeared casual was, in fact, highly coordinated. The planes were the stars of this flight deck show; but a large supporting cast had to be well-choreographed for the operation to work.

His pre-flight inspection done, Harry climbed up into the cockpit of Skyhawk number 504 -- a lucky number, he hoped. Today, Harry and his wingman would carry twenty-millimeter cannon shells, known as twenty mike-mike, for the guns mounted in the wings. A 300-gallon external fuel tank was attached to the center main station. Beneath the wings, one on each side, were Cluster Bomb Units, which were anti-personnel weapons. Known as CBU, or Charley Bravo Uniform, these were canisters that contained hundreds of tiny "bomblets." When Harry activated the canister, its nose would fall away and allow ram air to rush in and drive the bomblets out the rear end. They dispersed while falling and detonated on impact, covering a wide area with fine shrapnel. They were very effective in the right situation, and Harry would not like to be on the receiving end.

The start-up and taxi were normal, and within a few minutes of lighting up his engine, Harry was perched on the number one catapult. Unlike night cat shots, which made Christians out of most carrier pilots, daytime cat shots were almost enjoyable. The pilot could actually see what was happening and, most important, could take instant action to deal with any emergency. Starting at an altitude of just eighty feet, there was not much time to sort out problems when things went wrong. Keeping focused during the launch was essential to a long and happy life. Someday, although Harry was not sure when that might be, he hoped to have such a life. It did not seem in the cards right now.

Because his load was relatively light, Harry noticed a definite decrease in the power of the catapult. Less power was needed to reach flying speed at the end of the stroke. There was another difference: As the airplane cleared the deck, there was almost no loss of altitude, and Harry was able to climb straight out to the rendezvous point. There was no settling off the bow, as when the aircraft was fully loaded.

The join-up was routine and within ten minutes after being shot off the bow, Harry had Bill neatly tucked beneath his wing. He turned gently and headed for South Vietnam. As usual, the ship had not been where she said she was, so Harry missed his pre-planned coastal-in point by a few miles. It was a fine day with good visibility and he had no problem with fixing his position and heading inland. Soon, he picked up the TACAN signal from the Tan Son Nhut airport. That was another advantage to flying in the south. Up north, most of the flying was by map navigation. That became difficult when evasive action was necessary and a pilot could not continuously track his position.

As he approached the assigned area, and using hand signals, Harry instructed Bill to switch to the tactical frequency on which he would contact the FAC. He pressed his mike button. "Fencepost, Fencepost, Battlecry One, over."

The FAC responded on the first call. Well, that's a good omen, thought Harry. Establishing communications was sometimes a problem.

"Battlecry One, good morning to you and welcome to our Sunday morning service. Say your position and your ordnance."

"Fencepost," answered Harry, "we are a flight of two Alpha 4, each with twenty mike-mike and two Charley Bravo Uniform. We are on Tan Son Nhut radial 035 at 23 miles. Angels three."

"My goodness," replied the FAC. "What are you doing way up there? I need some help down here near the ground. I hold you at my 12 o'clock. Check your 9 low. I am at 300 feet moving west to east."

A few days earlier Harry had checked in with a FAC just ahead of a flight of A6 Intruders. They were new in the fleet, and this was their first deployment on a carrier. What they could do was impressive. Especially impressive was what they could carry.

"What you got, Battlecry?" the FAC had asked.

"Four Alpha Fours, each with two five-hundred pounders, total eight five-hundred pounders."

"Roger that," answered the FAC. He then called the Intruders, asking their ordnance.

"Flight of two Alpha Sixes," was the reply "each with twelve five-hundred pound bombs, total twenty-four five-hundred pounders." There was a pause. Then the FAC: "Did I hear that right? Twenty-four bombs? On two airplanes? Battlecry, you will need to make a few more trips today."

Today, there were no A6s to embarrass him.

"Stand by," Harry answered and began peering intently in the direction the FAC had indicated.

"Sorry, Fencepost, no joy," said Harry after a few minutes of looking so hard he could feel the strain in his eyeballs.

"Hey, no sweat. I'll give a mark and no extra charge. What we have here this morning is a ridge running east and west. Plenty VC parked along it on the north side. I'll mark and direct."

"Roger," answered Harry. "Standing by for your mark."

"Okay, here it comes. I think it's purple today."

As he spoke, Harry picked up a brilliant plume of purple smoke that ended in a great splash of color as the marking rocket hit the ground.

"Got it," said Harry. "Do you still hold us?"

"Yeah, still got you up there. Come on down."

Harry had already begun a gradual descent. He did not want to get too low too quickly, as that would make it more difficult to keep the mark in sight.

"Now listen up, Battlecry. I need you to make a run from east to west. That'll keep you out of the sun. The ridge I'm talking about is from my mark 040, about two-hundred yards. Got it?"

"I think so," said Harry. "Is that the ridge with the stand of trees north of the middle of it?"

"Good man. Now, listen. I'm orbiting just south of the ridge. Do not, I say again, do not, fly south of the ridge. Confirm."

"Roger that," said Harry. "We have the picture and we'll roll in from the north, drop heading west. We'll drop one cluster bomb per run, then, if you want, we'll give you some twenty mike-mike. We'll pull out to the north. That sound okay?"

Harry could almost hear the FAC smile. "Better than okay. Commence when ready and I'll spot."

Harry adjusted his descending turn so that he would intercept the bomb line at about 1,000 feet, with plenty of room to go lower before he got to the ridge. To be effective, cluster bombs had to be dropped low. At just the right moment, with the ridge off his right wing tip, Harry signaled Bill to arm his ordnance, then broke away and headed lower. He adjusted his flight path to fly along the ridgeline.

Back at the ship, Harry had briefed Bill that the runs would be individual with twenty-second intervals. That would give ample time for the lead airplane to clear the area before Bill made his run. Glancing down into the cockpit, Harry clicked the switch that armed his ordnance and accelerated down towards the ridge. As he closed, he saw lots of yellow flashes along the ground. That was automatic weapons fire coming up at him. Harry ignored it and pressed on. He depressed the bomb release button on his control stick just as he came over the target, pulled up hard and began a sharp right turn. Glancing back, he saw Bill in his run, then saw him pull up and head for Harry's airplane. They would rejoin before the next run. That would lessen the possibility of a mid-air collision if things got confused, as sometimes happened.

As Bill pulled off the target, Harry clicked his mike button.

"Any bullseyes?"

"Not bad, Battlecry, but the next time around, pickle just a hair later. Part of your drop hit short." Harry tried to remember exactly where he had pressed his bomb release button.

"Roger, Fencepost. I'll be rolling in from the east in about one minute."

Gauging his turn by looking at the ridge, Harry began a descending turn, signaled Bill, who was now alongside, broke away and headed in for his second run. This time, the orange flashes were more intense. Getting their act together, thought Harry. As he dropped his bombs, the FAC called, "On the money, Battlecry. You can choose anything from the top shelf."

Harry smiled. "Is there a bottle of Beefeaters up there?"

"Now don't be difficult, Battlecry. Take a teddy bear for now and I'll owe you the bottle."

"Battlecry Two," the FAC called as Bill dropped, "you are on target. Now, if you guys can spare some twenty mike-mike, I sure would appreciate it. I'm getting some automatic stuff over here. Oh, shit!"

That "Oh, shit" was an octave or two higher than the rest of his transmission, and Harry sensed a problem.

"Fencepost, okay down there?" asked Harry urgently.

"Well, damn," came the answer, his voice back to a normal. Pilots prided themselves in staying calm in tight situations. Fencepost had just had a very temporary loss of that control, but had recovered quickly. "I'm going to excuse myself, gentlemen. I got a rough runner here and I'm heading home. Thanks for all your fine work."

Harry's heart skipped a beat. An engine failure here, in the midst of all the Viet Cong, would be catastrophic.

"Fencepost, can we help? Anything? How is the engine right now?" But Harry knew there was not much he could do.

With complete calm, the FAC replied, "Nothing you can do, my man. It's cutting in and out, but still running. I just need about ten more minutes of flying out of this bird. You guys might as well go home, too."

Harry checked his fuel and the time. He could spare another ten minutes. He might be able to call for help if the FAC went down.

"Just for the hell of it," Harry said, "we'll wait until you're down. Keep us posted."

"Very kind, Battlecry, and thanks for your offer. I'll call when I get home."

A few minutes and several transmissions later Fencepost called, "Runway in sight and it's looking good." Then: "I am back on good old Mama Earth, and thanks again. Catch you next time. And hear this. I'll knee-cap the next guy who says something bad about Navy pilots."

Harry smiled and said only, "Roger, Fencepost. See you next time."

With Bill in cruise formation behind him, Harry began climbing, turned east, and headed for the Kitty Hawk. That, he said to himself with a grin, was one hell of a Sunday morning service. Back at the ship, after the post-flight debrief, Harry found his way to his stateroom. It was only 0930 here on Dixie Station, but Harry was exhausted. Bob was still in his sack. Well, never mind, thought Harry, with a twinge of irritation. His turn will come.

"Welcome back," said Bob. "How was your day at the office?"

An hour later, with Bob gone, Harry mixed a Sunday-morning martini. Sunday morning meant it was a serious martini, but that seemed in order. Bob's off-hand query had triggered the idea. Funny, thought Harry, as he took his first sip, but a few hours ago, I probably killed human beings. Sure, I was following orders, he reassured himself, but he wondered how he would feel about following those orders up close and personal. With a pistol, perhaps, and one victim at a time? Dealing death from a cockpit was easy because it was not connected to the place where the deaths took place; but the result was the same. Ah, he finally told himself, I'm too tired to think such complicated thoughts right now. Later, maybe, after I've had some sleep. He downed the last drops of his drink and slipped into his bunk. Despite his complicated thoughts, he fell asleep almost instantly.

25
GOODBYE, BOMBAY

1970

Leaving Bombay was not easy. The most frightening part of the entire departure was the taxi ride to the airport. If there was a more dangerous city for traffic, Harry had not seen it.

"I think it was safer over North Vietnam," said Harry as they missed by inches, for the third time, another taxi carrying several of the crew. They had left the hotel in a gaggle of three cabs, and each driver tried to be more daring than the others. They were trying to impress the pilots with their skill and courage, thought Harry. His stern warnings to slow down were ignored and, in exasperation, he had finally leaned forward and dealt a sharp jab to the driver's shoulder. The driver thought that was hilarious and drove even faster. Harry hung on and hoped for the best. To his surprise and relief, they arrived at the airport alive -- terrified, but alive. So far, so good, he thought.

There was the usual bureaucratic nonsense to put up with; but by now, Harry had learned how to read which way the wind was blowing and he managed to coordinate a relatively painless departure. Starting the engines was unusual. The old-timer manning the fire bottle looked to be straight out of a rice paddy. He was barefoot and shirtless. Instead of holding up three fingers to indicate that engine number three was clear for start-up, he held up two fingers on one hand and one on the other. It took Harry a few moments to decode that one. Even that, he thought, is different here. The start, taxi, and takeoff were as normal as might be expected, and they were off for Beirut. As usual, Thor was asleep in the jump seat as soon as the wheels were up.

In Beirut, hopefully, another crew would be in place to take the airplane onward. Harry counted on at least two days there, maybe more, before the plane returned for another trip to the Far East. That it might not return did not occur to him. Harry had never been to Beirut and he was excited at the prospect of visiting such an exotic city. "The Paris of the Orient" was how it had been labeled in the travel book, so it must be special. The flight, to Harry's great relief, was routine. That was how he liked them.

The approach to the airport brought them along the coast, landing to the south. The weather was clear, and Harry had plenty of time to sightsee along the way. The mountains surprised him. Who expected mountains in Lebanon? Some were snow-capped, and on a glorious day such as this, the view was magnificent: mountains on one side and the blue Mediterranean Sea on the other. It was an exhilarating moment, and he enjoyed it immensely. Not many years ago, Harry had been a college student and his life had revolved around grades and girls. Today, he was landing a 707 in Beirut and his blood tingled just thinking about it.

Harry recalled a placard posted in the hangar where he had started flying. Flying, it read, is not inherently dangerous; but, like the sea, it is mercilessly unforgiving of human error. There is another adage that says flying consists of hours and hours of sheer boredom interrupted only by occasional moments of stark terror. Harry had made his share of errors and he had experienced a few of those moments of stark terror; but there were other moments, moments of surpassing awe and beauty, moments when a pilot could become so captivated by a breathtaking view that he stopped minding the store. That could be dangerous.

Harry had never forgotten one such experience during an exercise at sea. He had been assigned to deliver a rocket-propelled nuclear weapon on an island target near Okinawa. The rocket was needed to fling the bomb forward so that the delivery aircraft would not be caught in its blast. The aircraft was the old propeller-driven Skyraider. Old it was, but classic, too, as anyone who had ever flown it would testify. Harry had made many training runs with practice bombs. This weapon was a real one, missing only the fissionable nuclear material. Atomic bombs work by detonating high explosives that line the inside of a sphere. That compresses the plutonium in the center of the sphere, which then achieves the critical mass that causes a nuclear explosion.

In an actual mission, after leaving the ship, Harry would have used a switch to insert the plutonium into the sphere mechanically. Unless the plutonium is in place, it is just another bomb. That day, there was no plutonium, only the high explosive. The weapon was launched in a maneuver known as loft bombing. There are several variations, but that day Harry used a high-speed, low-level run-in for a pre-selected distance. Then, he pulled up sharply with wings level. At a preset angle, the bomb was thrown away from the airplane by a 20mm canon shell. That was to be sure the bomb was clear of the propeller's arc when its rocket lit off and blasted towards the target.

After the bomb's release, Harry rolled into a 135-degree bank -- nearly inverted -- then pulled hard aft to get the plane headed away from the bomb's impact. It was at that precise moment, almost upside down, that Harry looked up to see the bomb just a few yards away and flying right along with him.

An instant later, the booster ignited with a blinding orange flash and the weapon was on its way. Harry was mesmerized. He could not take his eyes off the rocket as it streaked to its target. Finally, he did, and what he saw was terrifying.

Because he had not completed his recovery, he had put his airplane in a position that had it diving straight for the sea. At such moments, there is no time for thought, only for reaction. Instinct takes over. Following those instincts, Harry began to roll the plane upright and at the same time pulled back on the control stick. Because the plane had been nearly inverted, he could not pull back too hard or too soon. That would have accelerated the dive. He was not sure how he did what he did, and he was not sure he could do it again. As he got the plane upright and the nose coming up, a glance at the altimeter showed him climbing through 300 feet. He had very nearly made an enormous splash in the Pacific Ocean with himself in the middle of it.

One moment of sheer fascination, one of stark terror; Harry had experienced both at almost the same time. Those moments were unforgettable.

26
HELLO, BEIRUT

Harry had learned that he could tell a lot about a country from its airport. Some were safe, efficient, and looked like an airport should. Almost as soon as he touched down at the airport in Beirut, Harry had begun to form an opinion about Lebanon. The air control during the arrival had been adequate, but not more. That was for a starter. Taxiing into the ramp was simple because the airport was basic. The main runway ran north and south and it had only one taxiway. There was no way to get lost, but the Ground Control almost did it for him when he told Harry to turn right instead of left after the roll-out. The sea was on the right, so the mistake was obvious, and Harry did not bother to correct him.

Taxiing to the terminal, he could not miss seeing the litter that was everywhere. There were several goats peacefully grazing in the grass that separated the ramp from the runway.

"No sense wasting good grass," Harry replied when Joe pointed out the goats.

They had not yet parked and already Harry was wondering why Beirut was called the Paris of the Orient. Harry had been to Paris, and this airport was more like Sheboygan, Wisconsin, which Harry had also seen. The Sheboygan airport was cleaner and neater. So far, Beirut was not impressive. Still, there much more to see and Harry kept an open mind. Things were not always as they seemed.

The oncoming crew was waving enthusiastically from the ramp as Harry taxied into his parking slot. That's a relief, he thought. He was half-expecting to be told, "Sorry, but the other crew couldn't make it to Beirut. Would you mind continuing on to London?"

Harry signed the aircraft log book, and he and his crew said their goodbyes to the crew continuing on to London. They left the plane and descended the staircase to see what Beirut had to offer. Astrid was at his side. "What about the crew party?" she asked.

Harry only smiled. "You have a one-track mind. I think this crew party will be a small one. Just you and me."

He'd had a few words with Thor before deplaning and was told that the plane would be back within twenty-four hours for another trip to the east, probably Singapore.

"Fine. Please keep me informed. Thor," he had almost implored, "no more monkey business. Let me know what's happening."

"Monkey business?" replied Thor. "What monkey business?"

"Never mind," said Harry. "Just keep me informed. See you soon, I hope?"

"Yes, of course. Soon. Perhaps tomorrow. Enjoy Beirut."

"Thanks, we'll do what we can. See you later." Harry had no idea then how much later that would be, and he could not have imagined where their next meeting would take place.

Customs was relatively easy. Hell, thought Harry, after Bombay, there was no way to go but up. Customs in the Middle East could be exasperating. Harry had once flown with an English captain who had it all figured out. They were part of a cockpit crew scheduled to fly as passengers from Cairo to Amman with Mid-Eastern Airlines. They would spend the night there and operate eastbound the next day.

Checking in at the airport ticket counter, they were told, "Sorry, Captain, but the flight is fully booked and you will need to take a later flight."

Without even one second's pause, the captain replied, "Oh, that's a shame because we're supposed to operate a charter flight for Mid-Eastern on arrival in Amman, but I am sure they'll find another crew."

With that, he turned to leave the counter. As he did, the agent reached out, took his shoulder, turned him around and said, "Sorry, Captain, my mistake. You are booked and here are your boarding cards. Gate number 17, please."

Arriving in Amman, the captain had placed his suitcase on the customs stand. On its top, in plain view, he placed a few packs of cigarettes. In the wink of an eye, the cigarettes disappeared and an "X" was chalked on his bag. Cleared by customs. Harry was next and he spent a frustrating twenty minutes watching the customs man check every nook and cranny of his bag. Once through the terminal, the captain looked quizzically at Harry.

"Have you not been any place before?" It was a comment, not a question. Such behavior was normal in the Middle East, but Harry never got used to it.

He got another lesson the next morning as they called for start-up clearance. Despite many requests, the reply was, "Please stand by." Finally, the Captain had enough. He called for the purser and asked for a half-bottle of whiskey. He tucked it into his belt behind his back, donned his jacket, and left the aircraft. He returned twenty minutes later and, as he entered the cockpit, he removed his jacket and said, "Call for start, Harry." He did and they were immediately cleared to start. Harry turned toward the Captain and grinned.

"The whiskey was well-received, Captain?"

The captain smiled. "Sometimes," he said, "it helps to know the territory."

The best advice Harry ever heard in the cockpit was when this same captain tried to bend a regulation in flight.

"Excuse me, Captain, but that's against the rules," said Harry, trying to be helpful.

The captain thought for a moment, then half-turned to Harry, paused to be sure he had it right, and said, "Harry, rules are made for the guidance of wise men and for the blind obedience of all others. Remember that."

Harry carried those words through the rest of his life.

The Beirut airport was far enough from the city that the crew had a good look at Lebanon during the taxi ride to the hotel. The countryside was somewhat bare, but the distant mountains gave an illusion of beauty. That was Lebanon, Harry would learn, more illusion than substance.

They were booked into the Intercontinental Hotel, and it was perfect. It stood in the heart of the city, with a view of the mountains on one side and the sea on the other. Harry had finally relented to Astrid's pleas for a crew party. It took place in Harry's room and, because it was a daytime flight, everyone had energy to spare. Harry wondered how he had ever gotten along in the Navy without crew parties.

Later, when hunger struck, the concierge directed them to a restaurant in the hills overlooking the city. Harry was always suspicious of hotel recommendations, but this one was on the mark and exactly what they were looking for. They sat outside on a large terrace that offered a splendid view of the city below. It took some time, but, eventually, they enjoyed a typical Lebanese dinner know as mezzeh. Instead of one main course, it was an endless parade of small dishes. Harry could not identify the food they were eating; he just knew it was delicious. The Lebanese kitchen, he would learn, rivaled that of the Chinese for flavor and variety. Along with the food, they had ordered local wine.

"Excuse me, sir" said the waiter, "but are you sure you would not prefer arrack? It's what we drink with mezzeh. Would you like to try it? Please, one moment."

He was quickly gone and reappeared a few minutes later with a bottle of arrack, poured a small amount into a glass, added water, and offered it to Harry. He took a sip, then a mouthful. It had a liquorice flavor, and was similar to ouzo, which he had drunk before, but stronger.

"I like it," announced Harry. "You can leave the bottle. And cancel the wine. We'll go native tonight."

When the last small dish was brought several hours later and the dinner had finally ended, the dishes were stacked in layers on the table. Harry counted them. Fifty-five in all, and every one was delicious. Of course, the arrak had helped, and Harry had to admit the waiter was right. It went well with the food, whatever it was. It was powerful stuff, and Joe had taken an instant liking to it. He was drunk before the first dish arrived. Gene Daily and the others were enjoying its glow.

Astrid, sitting next to Harry, was becoming very affectionate. Ah, the magic of alcohol, thought Harry. He felt the magic, too, but he was not sure it was all from the arrack. It was hard not to feel enchanted sitting under a starry sky, overlooking the city lights of Beirut, and eating exotic delicacies. The arrack contributed, of course, but there was more than alcohol to the glow Harry felt at that moment. Another evening to remember, thought Harry. When he whispered that thought into Astrid's ear, she smiled happily, squeezed his thigh gently, then replied, "And it's not over yet. I think there is more to come." And there was, later, in Harry's room.

Beirut was already starting to look better. It appeared to be a lower-class Paris. Not lower, perhaps, just different. But it had much to offer: Great food, beautiful scenery, good wine and a nightlife that did not stop. Like Paris, French was often heard. That was because France had governed Lebanon since the end of World War I. Harry could not speak French, but he loved the sound of it. If he could learn one foreign language, it would be French.

The next day, Astrid, Harry and two others rented a taxi and went to Balbeck, a very old city east of Beirut and which held ancient ruins. On the way, Harry had asked the driver about the hashish he had heard so much about. The driver slowed and stopped the car.

"Come," he ordered as he left the car. Come where, wondered Harry. Fields of agriculture surrounded them. The driver walked a few feet off the road into the field, squatted and drew an arc with his outstretched arm.

"All hashish," he announced proudly. "Would you like to buy some? It's not costly."

They had not bought any, but the picture of the driver surrounded by a sea of hashish would stay with Harry. He would forget what Balbeck looked like. It was, according to Gene, "just another pile of old rocks;" but he never forgot that image of their driver amongst those fields of hashish.

A few nights later, the crew had gone to dinner at a nearby restaurant. They dined outside in a garden surrounded by high walls. The Lebanese took their food seriously, as did the French who had governed them for so long. Harry liked that. Back in Milwaukee, most ate just to keep body and soul together, without much thought of how the food tasted or how it was served. On his first trip to Europe, he had been impressed by the importance given to eating even simple dishes. For Europeans, eating seemed to be more pleasure, less obligation. The crew was enjoying a fine dinner with plenty of laughter and good local wine. Harry was surprised to find good wine in Lebanon.

Midway through the meal, just as Joe had raised his glass to propose a toast, they heard a shot ring out, then a series of shouts, then the alarming sound of angry voices -- many angry voices. They did not sound far off. Before Harry had time to become concerned, the waiter appeared at his side.

"Sir," he said in low, urgent tones, "there is a problem."

"Yes," Harry replied, "I figured that out for myself. What is it? What's happening?"

By now, the gunshots were more frequent, the voices nearer.

"There is bad news. Nasser has just been assassinated. An American, they say. It might not be safe for you to stay here."

Nasser, Harry thought, who the hell is Nasser? The name rang a bell, but faintly.

The waiter, noticing Harry's brow wrinkle in thought, said, "The president of Egypt. The hotel might be safer, perhaps?" There was a question mark at the end, but it was a statement, not a question.

"Your hotel, it's near?"

This time, it was a question, and it reinforced the statement.

"The Intercon," said Harry, thinking furiously. "Not far."

"Good. Leave now. Come again at a better time." Harry reached for his billfold. The waiter put out his upraised palm. "We will discuss the payment when you return. Leave quickly, please."

The crew had heard the exchange and began pushing back their chairs and standing up.

"Harry," asked Astrid, her eyes widening with alarm. "Is there danger?"

Harry smiled, reassuringly, he hoped, and replied that there was no way to know, but "we'll go back to the hotel. Better safe than sorry." He headed out the door leading to the street.

It was not well lit, and that heightened his anxiety. The voices were near and growing louder, but the street was empty. The voices sounded like they were just around the corner. They are close, thought Harry, as he felt the first tiny knot of fear in the pit of his stomach.

As they neared the hotel, they saw the source of the noise. A large crowd, all men, was approaching from the opposite direction. They sounded very angry and they were firing guns, including automatic weapons, into the air.

"Run," ordered Harry, as he broke into a brisk trot. The others followed. They reached the hotel just before the angry crowd got there. They dashed up the stairs leading to the reception area.

Feeling safer now that they were in the hotel, Harry saw signs of panic in the crowd pressing against the reception counter, pushing, shouting, pounding and demanding their room keys. The man behind the counter was frozen in fear. Harry quickly realized that the only way he would get his key was to take it himself. He darted around the counter, found his room key, and snatched it from its hook.

"Come with me," he shouted, hoping the crew could hear him above the bedlam.

He looked quickly towards the elevators, and saw with some relief, that one was waiting, doors open. But the terrified crowd was pushing and shoving, fighting to get in. That's not going to work, he thought, as shouts and shots rang out from below the steps they had just come up. He heard from the lower level the frightening sound of glass shattering and women screaming. The hotel shops were down there.

Breathing hard, he pushed clear of the mob, moved to the next elevator and pressed its button. Like a miracle, its doors opened and it was empty! Harry counted heads as he ushered the crew inside. All present and accounted for, he noted, as he pressed the button for his floor. As the doors closed, Harry suddenly became aware that his heart was pounding and he was drenched with sweat. He looked at Astrid, standing next to him. She looked cool and calm and, sensing Harry's alarm, smiled sweetly.

"I am fine, Harry, but you look like you need a drink."

"A big one," he answered. "I have a bottle of whiskey in my room. I think we could all use a drink." He marveled at her nonchalant demeanor.

"Maybe in the next life," he said, managing a smile, "you should come back as a fighter pilot."

Harry's room overlooked the street they had rushed along just minutes before. Harry picked up his bottle of Ballantine whiskey and poured drinks for everyone. The tension slowly subsided and was replaced by excitement.

From the balcony, they looked with disbelief at the scene just a few floors below them. The crowd had grown larger and angrier, the gun shots more frequent.

"Better than New Year's Eve on Times Square," said Gene, and everyone laughed. They felt safe here. Over the next few hours, the clamor and the gunfire slowly diminished and eventually died.

The next morning was quiet except for an occasional car passing by with its riders shouting and shooting mindlessly into the air.

"What's happening?" Harry asked the concierge when he went down for breakfast. "Is it true? Was Nasser killed last night?"

Harry was told that Nasser was dead all right, but not from an American assassin. It had been an ordinary heart attack. "Well, that's a relief," said Harry.

"Sir?" queried the concierge. Harry realized his mistake.

"Never mind," he said, as he turned and headed for the coffee shop. He had missed dinner and he was ravenous.

Harry did not hear from Thor the next day, and not on the day after that. Two weeks passed and there was no word from Oslo. Harry had sent a few telexes and had even tried to call; but there was nothing, and he was becoming concerned. Beirut had turned out to be a wonderful city, and it got more wonderful each day. With concern gnawing at him, however, the pleasures of Beirut were beginning to dim. *Damn*, he thought, *we might never get out of here.* Thor's fund had left with the airplane, and the crew was rapidly running out of money.

Just before leaving the plane, Thor had dipped a hand into his black satchel containing the ship's fund. He had withdrawn a fistful of one-hundred-dollar bills. Without counting them, he handed the wad to Harry.

"This is for expenses tonight," he'd said. "Have a fine time."

There had been seven of those bills, and they were long since spent. The hotel was pressing Harry for partial payment of their charges, and no one had much money. They had been signing for meals in the hotel restaurant. He wished he had asked for more money, but they were supposed to be in Beirut for only one day. How could he have known? Next time, he thought, I'll do it differently. If there is a next time. But, for now, the situation was looking bleak. *Was it possible*, Harry asked himself darkly, *that the company had gone belly-up and that no one had bothered to tell him?* Yes, he had to admit, it was not only possible but becoming more likely by the day. He had to start thinking about the worst-case scenario: They might have been abandoned in Beirut.

27
AUSTRALIA BOUND

September 1970

Harry could not believe his good luck. Instead of being an unemployed passenger on a flight to New York, he was sitting in the captain's seat on a 707 somewhere over the Pacific Ocean, bound for Australia. Australia! Harry had always wanted to go there, but for no particular reason. Something about the place appealed to him. He had never even met an Australian.

There was plenty of time to think on flights like this one. Harry found his thoughts going back to his latest Trans Polar adventure. That had started in Beirut when, after reviewing the situation in a realistic way, he had decided that the company had gone down the drain and that his next problem was somehow to get the crew home, wherever that might be. There had been two weeks of unanswered telephone calls and telexes to Oslo. Most of the crew had run out of cash. The hotel had twice asked Harry for a partial payment of the mounting bill.

Socially, Harry was enjoying the hell out of Beirut. Financially, he began to sniff disaster. He had even heard that, under Lebanese law, non-payment of their hotel bill might put them in prison! He did not really believe that, but the outlook was not bright. If only he'd had some information from Oslo. Any news would do, just to let them know that they had not been abandoned.

The moment of truth came when he returned to the hotel one evening after a fine Lebanese dinner to find a note from one of the stewardesses. The Head Office had called, the note read, and had instructed the crew to return to Oslo immediately. "Head Office" was a term that usually made Harry smile, but not this time. He tried to call Oslo, but there was no answer. He called the stewardess, but she could provide no further information. It turned out later that there had been no call. She feared the crew had been left in Beirut forever and she wanted to go home; but Harry had already been thinking about bailing out of Beirut. There had been no word from Oslo in nearly three weeks. The crew was now living on the credit cards of Harry and Joe, charging everything to the hotel and a few restaurants. That could not go on indefinitely.

Putting it all together, Harry decided it was time to pull the curtain. He called Mid-Eastern Airlines, the passenger airline of Lebanon, and arranged for discounted staff travel tickets. MEA was Trans Polar's handling agent at the airport. Harry had expected a problem, but no, there was none, as long as they got their money. Harry once more volunteered his credit card. Next was the problem of paying the hotel bill, which was, by now, substantial. He decided that the crew would pretend it was leaving on a normal flight.

To make it look that way, he asked the girls to report for the pick-up wearing their uniforms. That was the best the crew could do because the cockpit crew had not yet been issued uniforms. Their uniform was whatever they were wearing that day. The crew met the next morning in the lobby, and, to Harry anyway, if you didn't look too closely, they did resemble a regular crew about to leave on a flight. Harry held his breath as he went up to the concierge to sign the bill.

"The incoming crew will pay our bill," Harry said, somewhat nervously, as he went up to the counter. He was surprised to realize that he was holding his breath. That would not do for someone who had flown all those combat missions in Vietnam; so he exhaled and smiled, hoping to appear normal. By now, of course, Harry knew almost every employee of the hotel. He knew the bartender especially well, but that would not help here.

"Ah, bien sur, Capitain," said the concierge pleasantly. "Bon voyage a vous et votre equipage."

Harry loved that French! He had understood only the word "voyage," but the meaning was clear, and he nodded his thanks. Many Lebanese spoke both French and Arabic; the country was about evenly split between Christians and Muslims. The problems caused by this division would turn out, in the years ahead, to be great and insoluble. Harry would one day end up right in the middle of this awful conflict.

Harry signed the bill and ushered the crew to three waiting taxis, pre-positioned to ensure a quick departure. Or "getaway," as Joe described it.

"Goddammit," he fumed, "this is no way to leave a hotel."

Against the odds, Harry managed to shepherd his flock out of the hotel, out to the airport, and, finally, out of Lebanon. Mid-Eastern did not operate to Oslo, so Harry had bought tickets to Copenhagen. Close enough, he thought.

The problem of how to continue to Oslo became moot, or, as the English might say, "overtaken by events." As the crew got off the airplane at Kastrup Airport, they saw, parked right next to their MEA airplane, like a miraculous apparition, a 707. It was freshly painted in Trans Polar colors. Harry could not believe his eyes, but there it was, resplendent in all its glory in the late afternoon sun. There was more to this miracle. Standing beside the plane, part of a small group, stood Thor and the Chief Pilot, Tomas Wilman. Harry almost exploded. By chance, Harry and Joe were just passing a door, with steps leading down to the tarmac.

"Come on, Joe," said Harry, with rising blood pressure. "Let's go down there and see what the hell is going on."

Joe looked confused until Harry pointed down to the group on the tarmac. Harry saw the anger rising as Joe's cheeks became crimson. He asked Gene Daily and Astrid to tell the girls to wait while he and Joe went down the steps.

"Tell you later," said Harry tensely when Astrid asked what was happening. Thor did not see them until they were near, then reacted with a frown, which grew fiercer as they came closer.

"What are you doing here?" Thor asked sharply. "I thought you were supposed to be in Beirut."

Before Harry could speak, a torrent of words gushed from Joe. Please, Joe, thought Harry, don't make it worse; but he did. Joe had done some serious drinking during the flight and it showed. Within one minute, Joe, normally a man of very few words, let Thor have it with both barrels.

"Christalmighty," he began and, in colorful and well-chosen words, summed up the situation in Beirut, ending with, "we thought we would end up in the goddamned jail!"

Thor listened without a word, his frown becoming a glower, his face reddening. Finally, when Joe had let loose with all he had been holding back for the past few weeks, Thor pointed to Harry, turned to the Chief Pilot and said, "This crew is fired."

Wilman quietly slipped behind Harry and, speaking softly into his ear, told Harry to take the crew to the bar of the Dan Hotel and wait.

Well, thought Harry, as he sipped a Carlsberg beer at the hotel, this was great fun while it lasted. He fully expected to be on his way back to New York very soon. About halfway through his second beer, Wilman and Thor entered the bar. They saw the crew, but took a table across the room. There was serious discussion for about twenty minutes. Then, Wilman stood and made his way through the crowded bar to the table where Harry, Gene, and the girls were sitting and waiting -- waiting to learn their future.

Without sitting down, he said, "The crew is back on the payroll -- all except Harry and Joe. But I am working on it. Have another beer. Do not go away."

Harry had first met Wilman in Shannon, Ireland, when both were undergoing flight training in the 707. Harry had to be certified by the Norwegian Director of Civil Aviation. Wilman was a former fighter pilot in the Norwegian Air Force. He had lived in the U.S. during his pilot training and he spoke near-perfect English. Unlike Harry, he had no experience in large airplanes, so he had been hired as a co-pilot.

Then, an unusual series of events had taken place that resulted in Wilman's promotion, first to captain, then to Chief Pilot. That happened within one week and while he was not yet officially qualified to fly the 707! It came about when the company's second crew was fired. That crew included the Chief Pilot whom Wilman replaced. Damn, thought Harry, that is some kind of career advancement. Harry learned later why the crew had been fired.

During the time Harry was waiting in Beirut, the second crew had operated a flight that had ended up in Basle, Switzerland. While there, Thor had learned that the airplane was about to be impounded for failure to pay landing fees in England. Also after him was the Norwegian government, which was trying to reclaim the money Thor had promised to refund to the passengers when he flew 155 of his "friends" to Palma. His solution to these problems was to call the captain in Basle and ask him to fly the airplane "out of Europe."

The captain thought about this request very briefly.

"Out of Europe? Where, out of Europe?"

Thor had not thought that far ahead. "Anywhere," Thor had said. "What about Africa? That's close. And could you leave tonight? The situation is urgent."

"Ah, I understand," said the captain, not understanding at all. "Okay, then, where in Africa?"

"Anywhere," was Thor's answer. "We just need to get the plane out of Europe. Temporarily, until I can fix a problem. One more thing," he added. "The crew you are with has been fired, so you will need to operate alone."

Now the captain had the picture. "Let me see if I have this right," he summed up. "You want me to take this airplane to anywhere in Africa, without a crew, and you want me to leave tonight."

"Yes," answered Thor, "and the sooner the better."

The captain, whom Harry met later, considered this proposal for all of three microseconds, then politely declined, so he was fired, too.

Thor quickly found a replacement First officer and Flight engineer. He had hired them just a week before. Captains were harder to find. By remarkable coincidence, Captain Larry Owens, a 707 captain with Northwest Orient Airlines, was sitting out a ticket agent strike in Minneapolis when he heard about Trans Polar. The strike looked like it might be long and bitter.

Owens somehow found Thor's telephone number and called him in Oslo at almost the same moment that Thor was wondering where to find a captain.

Yes, Thor told him, he needed a captain.

"I'm your man, "Owens had replied.

"Could you," Thor asked after a few minutes of conversation, "operate a flight from Basle tomorrow?"

He could, and he would, but how about getting there? "Anyway you can," Thor told him. "I will pay you back later. Call me when you get there."

Thor never bothered to ask about his experience or even whether he held the proper license. He did not bother with such details. For all he knew, Owens might have been a tugboat captain. He also did not bother to tell Owens that he was hired to fly a 707 alone to "somewhere in Africa."

Owens agreed to make his way to Basle and got there only to be fired for refusing to fly the airplane to Africa without a crew, just like the captain he was replacing.

"That was a short career," Harry said, laughing, when he talked with Owns later.

But then, with another wave of his magic wand, Thor somehow avoided the seizure of his airplane and Owens was quickly rehired. A First officer and a Flight engineer were sent to Basle, and Thor's airplane was rescued.

Harry met Owens several weeks later at the Head Office in Oslo, where he was trying to get reimbursed for his trip to Basle.

"Any luck?" Harry had asked.

"Still working on it," he answered.

"Good luck," said Harry. "I'm still waiting for my first payday." Owens, who looked to be an old-timer, winced. Harry smiled an encouraging smile.

"You won't get rich with Trans Polar, but the excitement will more than compensate. It's a thrill a minute around here."

Owens did not smile back. "I already have more thrills than I need. I'd rather have the money, or should I say, my ex-wife would rather have the money?"

"Wouldn't we all?" Harry had replied. "Wouldn't we all?"

Now, in the bar of the Dan Hotel, the crew waited for Wilman to return to their table. Harry knew Wilman to be straightforward and honest. In fact, every Scandinavian Harry had met seemed to be like that. All except the company president, who said what needed to be said to keep his airplane moving. You could always tell when he was lying, said Joe, because his lips were moving. Still, the world needs movers and shakers, thought Harry, and Thor certainly qualified.

Wilman appeared at their table thirty minutes later.

"Okay," he said with a smile, "you are all rehired. You can unpack."

Harry laughed out loud. "You're joking, right? I haven't unpacked since I got over here, but I'm getting used to living out of a suitcase."

"I am pleased to hear you say that, Harry," said Wilman, "because you and your suitcase are going on a long one."

"Hey," said Harry. "I just got back from a long one. Not back to Beirut, I hope. I hear the police are looking for me there."

Wilman smiled broadly. "What would you think about going to Australia?" he asked.

"In what?" asked Harry. "I heard our airplane is missing. And, by the way, what about that airplane you were standing next to when we got here? It looked like a new one. And who were you talking to anyway? Thor seemed very pissed off back there. Hell, we thought the company had gone down the drain. Not one damned word in three weeks. What was that all about?"

Wilman picked up a chair from a nearby table, set it down next to Harry and sat down.

"Just a few small financial problems. Our phone line was cut because we did not pay the bill. It's okay now." Harry looked skeptical. No telephone for three weeks? There had to be more to that story. "The new plane," Wilman continued, "is one we just bought from Air Lingus, so Trans Polar has just doubled its fleet -- from one to two."

Wilman ordered a bottle of Carlsberg beer, then leaned across the table towards Harry. "Thor was talking to Simon Borgman when you came down onto the ramp. He is only the biggest travel agent in all of Scandinavia, and he and Thor were closing a very big deal when you came along and nearly shot down the whole damned thing. It's no wonder he was pissed off."

Harry figured discretion was the better part of this conversation. "Well, goddammit," he said, lowering the irritation level in his tone. "How in hell were we supposed to know? Someone should have told us."

"How?" asked Wilman. "You never gave us a chance. Anyway, it's all okay now, as long as you are okay for Australia. That's part of the deal. About getting your job back."

Harry began to feel uneasy. "So," he said finally. "A new airplane and a trip to Australia. It sounds like a lot has been happening while we were stranded there in Beirut."

"Not stranded, Harry," said Wilman with a smile. "Just overlooked, maybe. Now, about Australia. You are going to Sydney to haul out some sheep. A whole airplane full. They are going to Moscow. How does that sound?"

Harry thought for a long moment. "Complicated," he said. "It sounds very complicated. Before I agree to anything, we need to talk about money. You know, none of us has gotten one single paycheck since we started flying. We've been living from our per diem and, in Beirut, we didn't even have that. We need some money."

The per diem had been agreed at $15 per day. Trans Polar would pay all hotel bills. As the months passed, Harry learned that some of the hotels in Oslo would not extend credit because their bills were not being paid. It was embarrassing to check into a hotel and be asked, "Who is paying, you or the company?" There was no way Harry could pay, so he would slink off to find a hotel that would bill the company. He had stayed at five or six different hotels in Oslo. Although there had been no paydays, Harry could survive nicely on a free hotel room and $15 per day. That was a lot better than nothing, which is what he had been getting before he joined Trans Polar.

Although there had been no regular paydays, per diem money had been doled out at crew parties along the way. That money was paid from the ship's fund, and it was on the honor system. Somewhere around the third drink, Harry would break out the fund and ask each crew member how much per diem was owed. He carefully counted it out, then asked the recipient to sign for it. He paid himself, too, and dutifully signed those receipts, as well. These were hotel napkins, coasters and whatever else was at hand. He had stuffed all these receipts into a plastic sack that he carried around in his flight bag, looking for a place to unload them. Here, in the bar of the Dan Hotel, seemed a suitable place.

After some discussion, Wilman agreed to accept the sack of receipts, but that was as far as he would go. "I will be sure these will reach the office," he promised. "And we will try to give you one month's salary before you go. Now, what about Australia? Are you okay for the trip?"

"Who is the crew, when do we leave, and how in the hell do we carry sheep on a passenger airplane?" Harry asked.

Wilman frowned as he thought how best to tell Harry the plan. "The airplane will go empty. The seats will be removed. The only problem is that the flight leaves day after tomorrow and there is no time to pre-position a crew. We are sending two crews, so one can rest while the other operates. You are resting as far as Singapore, then operating to Sydney and back to Singapore. There will be plenty of room to rest in the plane and plenty of time to do it," Wilman said, with a note of hope in his voice. "Joe is heading home. His wife is already here from Oslo. She took one look at Joe and said, 'Come on, Joe, get your bag. We're going home before it's too late.'"

Harry was about to ask, "Too late for what?" when he realized he already knew the answer. Joe's wife was trying to save Joe from himself. One look at Joe and she knew she was doing the right thing. He looked awful.

"Rolf Bandel will be your first officer. Gene Daily has already agreed to go."

While Wilman had been speaking, Harry had been thinking -- thinking about how far Singapore and Sydney were from the bar of the Dan Hotel in Copenhagen.

"Jesus!" he exclaimed. "Did I hear that right? We're going to deadhead all the way to Singapore, then operate to Sydney? Without a night stop? Is that legal? And a load of sheep? To Moscow?"

The very idea of such a trip seemed preposterous; but he saw that Wilman was not smiling, not at all. He ordered another round of drinks for the group. Except for Joe, who had gotten a room at his own expense, and had been hauled up there by his wife to "freshen up," the Beirut crew was still at the table, waiting to learn their fate. They had been relieved to hear they still had a job, but they wanted to know more.

Astrid had been sitting next to Harry during the conversation. She had not said much, but she let Harry know her feelings by squeezing his thigh with varying intensities every time Wilman spoke. At least, that's what he thought she was doing. Harry was not sure what all that leg massage meant, but he enjoyed it, anyway. He would ask her about it later.

"Listen, Harry," Wilman said with a lowered voice. "It's maybe not completely legal, but it is necessary if the company is going to make it through these next few months. The trip is very well-paid, and I know a few people at the DCA. I promise I will take care of any problems about crew legality. There are ways. The seats are being taken out tomorrow and the plane is set to go the next day. What do you think?"

Harry knew that if he thought about it too long, he might never persuade himself to do something as foreboding as this trip promised to be. There was plenty of potential for things to go wrong.

Still, he was getting used to the idea, and he could almost feel Australia tugging at his sleeve. And it was a whole lot better than going back to New York without a job. He did not think Thor would fire him. He needed Harry. Still, you never knew. So, almost without thinking, he said, "Yes, of course, I'll go. I just hope the FAA never hears about all this. Who's the other crew?"

Harry thought he saw Wilman exhale a quiet sigh of relief. "You don't know them, but you will meet them in the morning. We have hired some new pilots. I will call you later with more information. Now you and the others can take a room and get some rest."

Harry smiled. "Just to be sure, the company is paying, right?"

Now it was Wilman's turn to smile. "Yes, Harry," he said with a sigh, "the company is paying."

"Just one more question," said Harry as he rose to leave. "You didn't know we were coming back until you saw us at the airport. Who in hell was going to do this flight if Gene and I hadn't shown up?"

Wilman grimaced. "I have no idea," he said. "I would have gone myself if Thor didn't need me to shovel all this horseshit he keeps piling up. See you in the morning."

28
THE LITTLE MERMAID

The next morning at breakfast, Astrid suggested a tour of Copenhagen. She had been there before and said, "We do have a free day. Come, let me show you this city, a wonderful city. You will like it, believe me." That seemed a fine idea to Harry.

"Sure," he said, as he sipped his coffee. "Let's see Copenhagen. Who knows if we'll ever be back here again?"

They took a bus to the center of the city. There, they found a large square with a church on one side. Next to the church, a street led away from the square. This was the Stroget, the famous walking street of Copenhagen. Its long, cobbled surface took walkers down a long lane of shops, bars and restaurants. One large shop of several floors was Illums Boligus. Harry had never heard the name.

"You must see what's inside this shop, Harry, it's just beautiful," said Astrid excitedly, as she took his hand and pulled him through the door. Harry, not fond of shopping, allowed himself to be taken inside this shop and was instantly pleased he had. Illums Boligus was on the leading edge of design for household furnishings such as dishes, lamps, paintings, and even furniture. Harry had never seen such elegant, artful goods. Too bad, Harry thought, I have no place to put these things, even if I had the money to buy them. They were ordinary products made special by imagination.

They stopped in a bakery shop to sample the renowned Danish pastries. It took them several minutes to choose because every piece looked delicious. The pretty young girl behind the counter was fresh and wholesome. She spoke perfect English.

"You will enjoy them, guaranteed. We say, 'Two minutes in the mouth, two hours in the stomach, and a lifetime around the waist.'"

Harry tasted his tart with obvious pleasure. "A lifetime around the waist?" he asked. "It's worth it." Her mouth full, Astrid nodded in agreement.

The far end of the lane met a garden square. There, they turned right, walked one short block, and went down three steps into a bar that had been serving beer since before Columbus came to America! Now that, thought Harry, is tradition. They enjoyed a typical Danish lunch of open-faced sandwiches. These were sandwiches in name only, and they were the culinary counterparts of the beautiful things they had seen at Illums. They were almost too beautiful to eat. They tasted even better than they looked.

Not far from the Stroget was the Little Mermaid of Copenhagen. Astrid insisted Harry see it. He had heard of it, of course. It was a world-famous landmark, the Washington Monument of Copenhagen. Astrid knew about the mermaid. Based on a character in a children's tale by Hans Christian Andersen, it had been sculpted "very long ago, before the first war." She meant World War I. Harry was disappointed in the mermaid's size, only about three feet tall, but not in her grace or elegance. She sat serenely on a large rock near the shore and overlooked the harbor. For Harry, it was love at his first sight of this lovely lady with the tail of a fish.

They took a bus back to the hotel. "Astrid, this has been a long day," Harry said as they entered the lobby. "I think I need a little rest. What do you think? Er du tret?"

She smiled at Harry's Norwegian. "Rest? What kind of rest? Rest meaning 'sleep' or rest meaning 'something else'?" Harry smiled back and took her hand. "First," he said, "we'll go to bed. Then we'll decide." She wrinkled her nose. "It sounds to me," she said with amusement, "that you have already decided. But I do feel a bit tired."

"I think I can help you with that," Harry said as he led her to the elevator "We'll have a nap before dinner."

29
SAIGON

April 1966

Harry had sometimes found himself in places he had never expected to be. He had long held a mental list of places he would like to visit one day. The list was made up of exotic, fanciful, and even romantic places. He knew he would never see most of them; but he enjoyed fanaticizing about them and, who knew, maybe one day he would end up in one or another. He had already seen a few of them. Saigon was not on the list; but here he was, jauntily strolling down Tu Do Street in the heart of that city. He knew he should not feel jaunty, but he could not help himself.

What a wonderful street! Tu Do Street was the Champs Elysee of Saigon. It did not have the elegance of that famous avenue in Paris, but it compensated for the lack of charm with high-voltage energy. Harry could feel that energy in the air as he made his way past the Caravelle Hotel and headed for the Capricio Bar, just a few blocks from his room in the Brinks Hotel. He was going there to meet the Billeting Officer for lunch. Harry had met Lt. Riddle when he checked into the housing office to get a room for his two-week stay in Saigon. Harry and Riddle had connected almost instantly when they met in Riddle's office.

Funny how that happened sometimes, thought Harry. Almost like a dog sniffing another dog's rear end to decide whether friendship was in the offing. There had to be some kind of chemistry at work when you took an almost instant liking to someone you did not know. It happened rarely, but, when it did, that first instinct was usually right. Harry and Riddle had agreed to meet for lunch at Riddle's favorite "rest stop," as he called it. "I'll tell you everything you need to know about Saigon," said Riddle, "whether I know it or not, and even some things you don't need to know."

Riddle was a happy-go-lucky young man from a small town in Minnesota.

"A long way from Saigon, in more ways than one," he told Harry later. He could not remember not wanting to be a Navy pilot. "And now look at me, pushing hotel rooms instead of airplane throttles." He looked like a young man from Minnesota should look: wholesome, fresh and alert. Tall, crew-cut black hair and an easy way of moving suggested that he had been a star athlete in high school. An avid golfer, he played every Sunday morning, "drunk or sober," at the Saigon Country Club.

"We'll fit you in next Sunday," he told Harry, after asking if he played. "We work six-day-weeks here, so Sunday is our only day off. We tee off early, so try to hold down your hangover level," he said with a grin. "They're easy to come by around here."

New bars in new cities were always interesting to a bar researcher like Harry, and he looked forward to spending an hour or two with a fellow Naval officer, especially one who knew the city.

To a young man from Milwaukee, the streets of Saigon were fascinating and even exotic. They were jammed with all kinds of vehicles, including some powered by animals. But most were cyclos, small Renault taxis, and, most abundant, motor scooters. They filled the streets of Saigon in swarms.

A cyclo was a hybrid that combined rickshaws and bicycles. The front half of a bicycle was attached to a kind of bench with wheels. It was a simple, efficient and pollution-free way to get about town. Not that the pollution-free cyclos made any difference on a street already choked with it. Taxis were everywhere, in case you wanted to travel first-class. Harry had not yet tried either one, but this was just his first day.

A few minutes ago, Harry had spotted a motor scooter with six people on board. The driver's entire family appeared to be with him: his wife and their four small children. His wife was nonchalantly riding sidesaddle on the seat behind the driver, the skirts of her ao dzai whirling in the scooter's slipstream. Two of the children were crammed between the driver's legs, the other two on the seat between their mother and their father. Now, that, thought Harry, is economical transportation.

The ao dzai was a form-fitting, full-length gown with slits on each side from the waist to the bottom. It was worn over tight slacks with narrow bottoms. Despite its high collar, similar to those Harry had seen in Hong Kong, it was, to Harry, a very sexy dress. Of course, for Harry, almost any dress qualified as sexy. A conical tropical hat completed the ensemble. Very fetching, thought Harry. Saigon had a large adjacent sister-city of about the same size named Cholon. It was comprised mainly of Chinese, so there were plenty of cheongsams on view as well.

Vietnam, as a part of Indochina, had, for many years, been a colony of France. Its influence was everywhere, most remarkably in those women who had some French blood. Some took Harry's breath away. This is a girl-watcher's paradise, thought Harry as he ambled along Tu Do, his head on a swivel, trying not to miss any. He looked forward to meeting a few. He hoped Riddle could arrange it.

Just two days ago, Harry had returned to the ship after an early-morning flight into the delta area south of Saigon. It had been a routine flight and, after his debrief, Harry had flopped into his seat in the Ready Room and was enjoying a cup of coffee as he eavesdropped on the brief of a flight heading out on the next launch. He felt someone drop into the seat next to his and was surprised to see it was the skipper. He usually sat in his own chair. Something was up. After a few pleasantries, the CO got to the point.

"Harry," he said, between sips of coffee, "we need to send a rep into Saigon for a couple of weeks of TAD at the Target Coordinating Center. You're a few missions ahead of the others, so I plan to tap you for this one. What do you think?"

Harry's first thought was, *Damn! That would mean more Yankee Station flights and fewer down here on Dixie*! You never knew. One flight too many up there on Yankee Station might be your last one. Aloud, he said, "Target coordination? Could that have anything to do with liaison between the FACs and us? I was working with one just a couple of hours ago in the delta. Sounds interesting, Skipper, and anyway, I'm guessing that I don't really have a choice here. What's the deal?" He figured the skipper had already made a decision, so he might as well look eager.

"It's no big deal," the skipper answered. "The billet is rotated among the squadrons on Dixie and it's our turn in the barrel. You'll be involved with matching airplanes with targets, and that's about all I know. Basically, a connection between the guys in the trenches and the bomb loads they call for. The office is at Ton Son Nhut. You'll go in by COD tomorrow morning and report to a Marine colonel who runs the office. Your orders are being run off right now, so I hope you say yes." He grinned as he said it.

COD stood for Carrier On-board Delivery, and it was pronounced as one word. It was a twin-engine propeller aircraft used to transport people, mail, and supplies between ship and shore.

"Yes, sir," said Harry. "Since you put it that way, I would like to volunteer for the duty. Just don't go home without me."

The Skipper smiled. "Harry," he said lightly, "would I do that to a nice guy like you?"

Twenty-four hours later, Harry stepped down from the COD at the Saigon's Tan Son Nhut airport. It was, he learned, now the busiest in the world.

Following Riddle's directions, Harry walked for a few blocks along Tu Do, then turned left and, there, just a half block down the street, stood Capriccio's. Harry pushed aside the curtain covering the door and stepped inside. He had been in many bars just like this one, dimly lit, no windows, American music. So far, nothing special.

Among a group of pretty bar-girls, Riddle was perched on a stool near the back. He waved as Harry entered.

"Have a beer, Harry, it'll help make the place look better."

The local beer was Bami Ba. That was 33 in Vietnamese. After his first bottle, Harry decided it would make any place look better. It was strong stuff.

"What's in this beer, anyway?" asked Harry, with his nose crinkled to indicate his distaste. "It doesn't taste like beer, but it for sure has got some alcohol in it. I can feel it already."

"Have another one," said Riddle, as he waved the bar maid over. "The more you drink, the better they taste. But you're right. It's strong stuff. According to a friend who should know, this brew is about 15% alcohol, so treat it with respect. Just needs a little getting used to. Grab your beer. We'll eat at a table."

Riddle had reserved his "regular" table for lunch. As Harry glanced at the menu, he realized Riddle was right. The second beer really did taste better. Or could it be that the first one had numbed his taste buds? A middle-aged Chinese woman shuffled to their table to take their order. She was plump and smiling, her hair drawn back in a bun.

"Harry, meet Olga. Olga is the brains of the operation here. Her husband owns the place. You'll meet him tonight." Olga looked Chinese, but her English was perfect. She had been born in San Francisco and had lived for many years in the United States. "You'll enjoy meeting him. He's something else. Used to be a delegate to the League of Nations, speaks English better than I do, even better than Olga here. He never uses words with less than four syllables. He claims to drink his weight in Johnny Walker every week. Of course, that's not saying much. He's just a skinny little runt."

Olga's antennae rose. "Hey, Dick Tracy," she said, "who you calling a skinny little runt? You want me to tell Wan? He will break your knees for you."

"You mean he'll have someone else break my knees for me. Okay, I retract the comment. Now what about some lunch? I'll have my usual."

Harry hated reading menus. "I'll have the same," he said, as he handed the menu back to Olga. "What is it, by the way?"

"Cheeseburger," she said, "with French fries."

Harry chuckled. "Cheeseburger? In Saigon? What about all that famous French cuisine? How about some of that?"

Riddle put down his beer and leaned over the table. "Harry, these are not only the best cheeseburgers in town, they're the best in any town. Hands down better than any French food you ever heard of. The French just disguise bad food with good sauce, anyway. Try a cheeseburger, guaranteed good."

"Okay, sold," said Harry. "One cheeseburger with fries. It better be good."

Olga picked up the menus. "Two cheeseburgers. No likee, no payee," she said as she winked and turned away.

"I get the feeling you've been in here before," said Harry.

"Oh, not more than two or three times a day. It's user-friendly. Good food. They let me run a tab. Pretty girls, but they don't bother you unless you want them to. This is the daytime staff. Tonight, the A-Team will be here. You might find something you like."

"So, tell me," asked Harry "how did a nice guy like you wind up in a place like this? There has got to be a story there somewhere. And why did she call you Dick Tracy?"

"Private joke," answered Riddle. "I sign my tabs with different names. This week I'm Dick Tracy."

Riddle made a long one short. His previous assignment had been as a flight instructor at a Navy base near a backwater called Meridian, Mississippi. He enjoyed the flying and he liked instructing. But Meridian! He felt like life was passing him by.

One weekend, he and a friend flew to Washington in a squadron airplane on a "training" flight. One of the perks of the job was being allowed to fly all around the country on weekend training flights, either with a student or with a squadron-mate. Riddle wanted to talk to his assignment officer at the Pentagon to see if he could arrange a change of duty, ahead of schedule. No way, he was told. You are stuck in Meridian for two more years, like it or not.

By this part of the story, Riddle was into his third beer, and his story was becoming interesting. On the return flight to Meridian, they had run into unexpected head winds and a fuel stop was needed. As a training aircraft, it did not have long range. Something else it did not have was a way to urinate in flight, and his colleague in the back seat was becoming desperate to pee. Finally, as a last resort, he had removed his flight boot, laced it up, and emptied his bladder into it.

Riddle had chosen an Air Force base near Nashville for a pit stop. It was one of those airports with the military on one side and the civilians on the other. It was Sunday night and it was snowing all across the east. As Riddle, flying the airplane from the front seat, was approaching the runway, he heard his back seat say, somewhat plaintively, "Now for Christ's sake, Riddle, don't bounce it in." Riddle was puzzled by that until he remembered that John was sitting in the rear seat, holding in his hand a flight boot full of urine.

"I thought about making a hard landing on purpose, but I just couldn't do it to poor old John in the back," said Riddle, as though that qualified him for some kind of Nice Guy award. After landing, Riddle had been directed to a parking area; but there was no one there to guide him into a parking space. They notified the tower several times, but no one appeared. Riddle decided to de-plane and look for help.

He got down to the ramp first and, as he described it, "There was John, holding a bootful of piss in one hand and trying to climb down with the other. When I broke out laughing, he paused and tuned his head to scowl down at me and threw his bootful right at me, almost falling on his ass as he did. The wind blew most of the piss right back in his face; his own piss! He was not happy." Riddle laughed out loud just talking about it.

No help had yet arrived, so Riddle decided they would split, one to search in each direction. "I can still see John limping across the ramp through the snow with one boot on and one boot off," Riddle howled with laughter. After some minutes, Riddle found himself in front of the Flight Operations building. He entered to find a room that had all that a Flight Ops should have -- except people. There was no one there. The lights were on, a radio was playing, the weather machine was whirring away, but there was no one there.

As he pondered his situation, a telephone on a desk just behind a counter rang. Riddle picked it up and, in his best military voice, said, "Lieutenant Riddle speaking."

He heard a voice say, "Yeah, there is someone there." There was a pause, then John's voice began to state their problem.

"John, it's me," Riddle interrupted. "Where the hell are you?"

"Hey, no shit! I'm here with the crash crew. Where the hell are you?"

"Flight Ops, but the place is empty. Put someone on who knows what's going on around here."

A new voice spoke. "What do you need?" it asked.

Riddle explained they needed to refuel and file a flight plan to Meridian.

"Where you standing?" the voice asked. Riddle told the voice where he stood in the room. "Okay," said the voice. "Lean over that counter and tell me if you see a red phone."

Riddle leaned. "Got it," he announced, as he felt the first faint hope of getting out of there.

"That phone," said the voice "is a direct line to the FAA. They will take your flight plan. What else do you need?"

"Fuel," said Riddle. "We need fuel."

The voice solved that problem, too. "The fuel truck is on the way to your bird and will be there in a few minutes. What else?"

Riddle thought hard. "We need someone to stand by as we start up and taxi out."

"Done," said the voice. "He'll be with your co-pilot here. We'll run them out to airplane right now. Can you find your way back there?"

Damn, thought Riddle, does he think I'm stupid or what? "Yes," said Riddle, "I'll follow my footprints back to the plane. See you there." I hope so, anyway, he thought, as he hung up the phone.

Riddle dug into the zippered pocket on his flight suit and took out the copy of the DD175. This was the military flight plan he had filed in Washington. Very carefully, he went over it and, where needed, inserted new information for the flight to Meridian. Then he picked up the red phone and, sure enough, a voice from the FAA was on the line. Riddle told the voice he wanted to file a flight plan, then recited all the information he had just written down. That took a few minutes. There was a pause. "Well," said the voice, "we really don't need all that. What color is your airplane?"

"Civilians," snorted Riddle, as he thumped the table with his beer bottle. "Ain't they something?"

Eventually, it all happened and Riddle made it back to Meridian early in the morning. A few hours of sleep and he was back at work. He was interrupted while briefing a student when someone handed him a note to immediately call a number at the Pentagon. When he did, he found himself talking to the assignment officer.

"You still want to get out of Meridian?" he was asked.

"I do," he replied.

"Got a spot just opened up with Headquarters Support Activity in Saigon. That's in Vietnam. How does that sound?"

What kind of duty?

"No idea," he was told. "But I have to know right now. You want it?"

Without thinking, Riddle had said yes, and that was how he came to be the Billeting Officer for the entire city of Saigon and how he came to be sitting and drinking Bami Ba beer in Capriccio's with a fellow-pilot from Milwaukee.

"You know," said Riddle, "when that guy called, I was tired, I hadn't eaten in a while and I felt miserable. If that call had come on another morning, I might have thought about it for a while before I agreed. But what the hell, here I am. Let's have another beer. I told my office I was taking a VIP on a tour of the town, which, depending on how you define VIP, is true. They're not expecting me back."

Riddle had arrived in Saigon before the war had escalated. There were some 15,000 U.S. military in Vietnam then. That number would eventually grow to more than half-a-million and the death toll would reach 58,000. The names of every single man who died there would one day be etched into a granite memorial wall in Washington known as The Wall. One of the most mystical experiences of Harry's life would be a visit to that wall, where he read the names of friends who had been killed in Vietnam. He could not describe the emotions which overcame him as he stood there, reading those names on that black granite wall. He took a photo of one name, that of Norman Levy. Harry had been close to Norm and knew his parents well. He would send them a photo of Norm's name.

Before the war had mushroomed into a vast military adventure, Saigon was a city like others in the Orient, said Riddle. Most of the excitement was political. Bombings were not unusual. The Buddhists became involved in major ways and tried to make their point by regularly immolating themselves on the streets of Saigon. Buddhist cookouts, they were irreverently called. *Damn*, thought Harry, as he listened intently and tightened his grip on his bottle of Bami Ba. *That is a hard way to make a point.*

Riddle had been there during the coup d'etat when Ngo Din Diem had been flushed out and assassinated. There were several days when Saigon came to a dead stop, except for bands of soldiers and police. There had been plenty of excitement and almost no news. No one knew what was happening. Part of the excitement included gunfire and even a few bombs going off here and there around the city. They had all hunkered down until the smoke cleared; but, after that, it was pretty much business as usual.

One exception was that dancing again became legal. Madam Nhu, wife of Diem's right-hand man, had declared dancing to be wicked and she had prohibited all such evil behavior. As a result of the ban, back-room dance halls sprang up all over Saigon. You had to know someone to get into one of these dens of the depraved, and Riddle did. He called them dance-easies, and, he said, he had never enjoyed dancing so much as when it was illegal.

A Navy enlisted man who worked for Riddle returned from lunch one day. When he came into the office, Riddle saw that he was ashen-white, trembling violently, and unable to speak. His mouth was moving, but no words came out. Finally, he spoke, haltingly, and what a story! He had been a passenger in one of the gray Navy buses used for transporting personnel around town. He was sitting on the seat that ran along the side, right behind the driver. At a stop, just as a man stepped off the bus, a motor scooter zipped past and its driver heaved a bomb through the open door. Caught in the ensuing panic, Riddle's clerk had been crushed into the space between a vertical metal pole and the seat he had been sitting in. Unable to move, his head on the floor, he saw, just a few inches from his face, the bomb that had just been thrown onto the bus. It failed to explode, but, for several excruciating minutes, thinking it was timed, he expected it to go off any second. No wonder he was speechless, thought Harry.

Life is strange, thought Harry. He did not realize how strange until two beers and a cheeseburger later, when Riddle told him about his experiences as a Billeting Officer. Harry could not believe his ears. They were adventures more than experiences. Riddle oversaw some fifty hotels in Saigon and Cholon. They had been leased for military use and they held thousands of rooms. No two were alike and therein lay the source of Riddle's conundrum.

There was no way to please everybody, although nearly everybody demanded to be pleased. There was the Army colonel, staying in Riddle's flagship Rex Hotel, who complained bitterly because the smoke from the Sunday night barbecue drifted past his window. Even worse, an officer junior to him had a room closer to the elevator. There was the Army major who threatened one of Riddle's desk clerks with bodily harm if did not allow entry to the major's Vietnamese girlfriend. The clerks were local men who were easily intimidated. They often faced the problem of bar girls coming into the hotels. The girls were not allowed in the hotels for security reasons; but a few drinks and a pretty girl often made the rules seem made for breaking. Although these scenes were frequent, they did not often involve Army majors. The desk clerks called Riddle at all hours when such situations arose and the problem was usually resolved tactfully, depending on how drunk the girl's companion was.

Then, there was the Army major who coveted the room of a Navy Lieutenant Commander. He waited until the officer was up-country for several days, bribed the maid to gain entry to the room, piled all of the occupant's belongings into the corridor and moved himself in. They were the biggest headaches, said Riddle, those damned Army majors.

"Tell me this," thundered this one while pounding on Riddle's desk during his dispute with the Navy officer. "Does a Lieutenant Commander have scrambled eggs on his visor?"

Riddle had to admit they did not.

"Well, by god," said the Army man fiercely, "an Army major does," as if no more proof was needed to establish his right to the Navy officer's room.

Riddle had politely informed the major that Navy Lieutenant Commanders, even without the gold braid on their visors, sometimes commanded destroyers and nuclear submarines. The major was not impressed. It took three weeks of administrative battle, said Riddle, to evict the Army major. It was one of his few victories in an endless series of daily battles.

Instead of a name plate on his desk, Riddle's, etched in brass, read "Break it to Me Gently." That was a reference to a popular song of the day. It elicited sympathy and smiles, he told Harry, but not much cooperation. "The worst job in Vietnam," was how one of his "tenants" put it. He spent hours every day fielding complaints and listening to pleas about quarters. He had tried to institute a program using self-interest to determine room assignments. Anyone could place himself on a waiting list for any hotel --first come, first served. The brass had a better idea. A Navy captain was assigned the tedious task of establishing a grading system for all of Riddle's rooms. It awarded points for features such as size, number of windows, location of the hotel and other details that make a hotel room desirable.

Riddle predicted disaster for the plan because it left out one essential ingredient: personal preference. Barbecue smoke and distance from elevators could not be factored into any such plan. The one advantage of the plan was that it took Riddle out of the loop; but it collapsed of its own bureaucratic weight, and soon the game was back to square one.

Harry sympathized. Even Yankee Station was better duty than handing out rooms in Saigon. But some upscale perks helped make the duty bearable. One of Riddle's responsibilities was providing services for all his rooms. That involved regular contact with local tradesmen, and that made Riddle the target of nonstop offers of bribery in one form or another. Women had been offered early and often but Riddle, tempted though he might be, declined. Despite their allure, he knew better.

He did, after checking with his boss, accept offers of free dinners, and they came along about once each week. By good luck, this week's dinner was tonight and Harry was, of course, invited. It was an ostentatious affair held at one of Saigon's leading Chinese restaurants. There were thirteen diners sitting around a circular table. A few of them were pretty girls who had been rented for the evening. The host was Mr. Wan Wai Nam himself, one of Riddle's contractors. Each person was given a small printed menu that listed the eleven courses to be served. A tiny, elegantly-shaped whiskey glass stood at each place. One waitress had the sole duty of keeping those glasses full. That was all she did the entire evening, and she did it well. She held in each hand a silver teapot, one filled with Scotch and one with bourbon.

The toasts began as soon as the last guest arrived, and they continued almost nonstop throughout the evening. Anyone could make a toast about anything, and everybody arose when a toast was proposed. The empty glasses were refilled almost before they hit the table. In-flight refueling, Riddle called it. Mr. Wan, said Riddle, was a drinking dynamo. Harry enjoyed a memorable evening -- the part he could remember, anyway.

"Any extra charge for the hangover?" he had asked Riddle the following evening.

Riddle had seated Harry next to Wan Wai Nam. He was called Mr. Wan, as the Chinese put their last name first. As promised, he was a fascinating dinner companion. He was fifty-five, short and thin, with jet black hair slicked straight back from his forehead. His English was flawless and, at one point in their conversation, he had paused to ask if Harry understood the word, "labyrinth." He owned several of the hotels managed by Riddle and, of course he knew Saigon like the back of his hand, as Harry would see over the next two weeks. His French sounded flawless, but, to Harry, any French sounded flawless. He had, indeed, been a delegate to the League of Nations, but now he was just another entrepreneur becoming rich from the war. Wan drank Scotch whiskey drink-for-drink with Harry and the others, and he was often on his feet toasting something or other. No one seemed to care what it was.

Along with investigating Saigon by night, Harry had his assigned duties at the Target Coordination Center. The job was not demanding, and Harry quickly fell in with the routine. Requests came in from field officers, and they were filled by an assortment of aircraft, including those from the Kitty Hawk.

During his second week, a Kitty Hawk F4 had been shot down just a few miles south of Saigon. Harry knew the pilot and visited him in an Army hospital in Saigon. He had been working with a FAC when he took a hit from small arms fire that caused complete loss of the hydraulically-powered flight controls. Almost before he knew he was hit, he found himself inverted at a very low altitude. His aircraft was uncontrollable and he realized his only option was to eject. The ejection rocket normally propels the seat and pilot upward. But with the aircraft inverted, upward meant downward, and the pilot found himself looking at a large rice paddy, which was getting larger very quickly. His chute opened a few seconds before he was about to smash into that paddy, but his only injury was a sprained back. "Not too painful," he told Harry with a smile, "and it's a ticket home." Harry was almost envious.

Even in a war-like environment, Saigon was a fascinating, almost enchanting, place. There were broad, tree-lined boulevards with bicycle paths alongside. The French influence was in view everywhere. Also ubiquitous was the GI. He was hard to miss; he stood a head taller than the local people and often carried a weapon. Most were in town for a few days of Rest and Recreation, known as "R and R," away from "up-country," as the rest of South Vietnam was called. R and R was known to some as "I and I," for Intercourse and Intoxication. Barbed wire and military posts were on every corner, but no one seemed to notice them. They were part of the landscape.

Even the Saigon Country Club, where Harry played golf one morning with an awful hangover, had military revetments throughout. The course was unique for other reasons. The caddies were barefoot and, by skillful use of their toes, Harry's ball always had a perfect lie when he reached it. They spoke no English, but communicated in other ways. When Harry chose a club, for example, his selection was sometimes met with a hissing sound. It did not take Harry long to figure out that the hiss meant, "No, no, not that club." When he chose another club, the right one, the hiss became an "Ahhhh." Every little bit helps.

Stopping for lunch after nine holes was mandatory, and that suited Harry just fine. That too, was the French influence. A couple of gin and tonics, along with some local food, did not do much for his game, but he enjoyed them thoroughly. Riddle had a standing game every Sunday morning and Harry had filled in for a friend who had canceled. One of the foursome was an American civilian who, obviously still somewhat inebriated from the night before, emerged from his fog on the fifth tee.

"Where am I?" he asked, scowling.

"Just about to hit off on the fifth," Harry told him.

The American squinted, frowned, then asked, "How am I doing?" He was a fine golfer and, even half-drunk, was hitting the ball well.

One distinctive feature of the golf course was that, at one point, a small agricultural plot lay behind a corrugated enclosure between two fairways. It was reachable from the tee, and Harry had the unusual experience of buying back his own golf ball after he had hit it into the plot.

To earn his flight pay, Riddle flew an old C45 airplane around South Vietnam. This was an ancient tail-wheeled craft with two propeller-driven engines and space for eight passengers. It was known as a Bug Smasher and it was used for logistics and transport of personnel. Riddle managed to arrange an overnight flight to Nha Trang on the coast and took Harry along.

"What about the hostile fire?" Harry had asked.

"Well, what about it?" Riddle had replied with a shrug. "Part of the package."

The beach at Nha Trang was as beautiful as a beach can be. Wide, with rolling dunes and a strong surf; it took Harry's breath away.

"Imagine," he said, on the flight back to Saigon, "what the Miami mafia could do with that beach."

Riddle only smiled. "Not in our lifetime," he said.

The flight had become interesting even before the wheels were up. That happened when Riddle got a weather briefing at the U.S. Air Force weather office. Staffed by three officers, it had all the bells and whistles and might have been a weather office at a major base in the U.S. -- machines clicked and buzzed as the officer on duty gave Riddle his weather folder. It was several sheets thick.

The next stop was across the hall at the Vietnamese weather office.

"I always check in here, too. These guys have the local knowledge."

And indeed they did. It was just one man, old, with thick glasses, and smoking a cigarette.

"Ah, Mr. Riddle," he greeted them pleasantly. "Please to have a seat. To where do you fly today?" he asked through the cigarette smoke. "Ah, Nha Trang," he said when Riddle told him. "One of our most beautiful destinations." He had no machines, only telexes from other stations. He looked at a few briefly, then looked out the window for a long minute. Then he wrote down a forecast that turned out to be remarkably accurate. The old-fashioned way, thought Harry, sometimes works best.

Harry's first night had started at Capriccio's and it started right. One of the A-Team members was a lovely Chinese girl from Cholon. Her bar button said her name was Terry and her number was 33.

"Any connection to the beer?" Harry had asked when they met.

Her real name was Lo Mei, and she was delightful. Harry was booked for the weekly dinner that night, but there were two weeks to get to know Lo Mei better. She proved to be a fine guide to the nightlife in Saigon. One of the bars she had taken Harry to was the Phoenix Café. Harry had heard interesting stories about it and, over some protest, persuaded Lo Mei to take him there.

What made it interesting was that the face of the bar had holes that facilitated oral sex from someone, no one knew whom, on the other side. Harry passed on that one. Some decisions were easy. In one of Saigon's bars, Harry was not sure just where, he met a Forward Air Controller, a very drunk Forward Air Controller. Harry had worked with them, coordinated with them, and now he was drinking beer with one of them. He heard stories that night that were beyond belief; but he believed them, every single one of them. No one could have invented stories like those. Life on Yankee Station was hard, thought Harry, but nowhere near as hard or as dangerous as flying low and slow over people who would slit your throat if they had the chance.

Between his days at the office, the hours at Capriccio's, the night tours of Saigon with Riddle, Mr. Wan, and Lo Mei, the two weeks passed more quickly than Harry liked. When they were over, he almost wished he could stay longer.

Harry's Saigon adventure had begun at Capriccio's. It ended at a historic happy hour atop the Brink's Hotel, where Harry was billeted. Navy happy hours are more than a tradition; they are an institution. One tradition says that caps may not be worn at happy hours. A bell rung by the first man within its reach announced breaking this rule. The offender must buy drinks for the house. During happy hour, with a full house, this can be expensive. Harry recalled one such happy hour when the club was packed with thirsty officers. The wife of Harry's friend entered, carrying an armful of packages, found her husband, and sat down to enjoy a drink. Later, rising to leave, her husband reached down and scooped up her packages from the chair where she had placed them.

"Don't forget your cap," she said as he bent down, placing the cap on his head. He tried desperately to avoid the cap, but, with an armload of packages, it was difficult. The cap went on, the bell was rung within seconds, and he bought drinks for some 125 happy drinkers.

Even in war-torn Saigon, happy hours were a regular Friday feature at various locations. The main one was on the roof of the Brink's, some eight or ten floors above Tu Do Street. The roof was adorned with beach umbrellas, colored lights, and other reminders of stateside happy hours. A live band played American popular music. Hamburgers and hot dogs were featured at ten cents each. Drinks also cost only a dime. That made it more palatable when Harry lost at liar's dice and had to buy a round for nineteen players. Harry had played many times at Navy clubs around the world, but never with more than five or six players.

The game uses five dice, a leather dice cup, and psychology. To lose with nineteen players was extraordinary, especially as Harry considered himself a good player. To lose a second time was disconcerting, even at ten cents a drink. But when he lost a third consecutive time, he also lost, for a moment, his self control and, in a moment of exasperation, pitched the cup and dice off the roof and onto Tu Do Street. To jeers and hisses, he held up a hand.

"Sorry guys, I lost it. Have another round on me." The jeers quickly became cheers. To lose three times with nineteen players had to be some kind of record. Did the *Guinness Book of World Records* keep track of such things? He wondered.

30
RAM RUNNERS

September 1970

The flight to Australia had changed since that night at the Dan Hotel. The sheep mission was still in place, but Thor had made a last-minute deal to take a load of passengers from Athens to Sydney. At Sydney, the seats would be removed from the cabin and stowed in the cargo compartments. As Harry had foreseen, complications arose early and often. The two crews left with almost no funds.

"No problem," said Thor, "you will collect money from the travel agent in Athens. Plenty of money."

He was right; but he forgot to say that the money was Greek drachmas that were basically worthless once they left Greece.

They had enough real money to get them through Bombay; but to get past Singapore, something had to be done. Many plans were discussed and discarded. There seemed to be no way around the drachma dilemma. No one wanted them. Wait a minute, thought Harry, finally. These passengers will need Greek money when they return to Athens. Why don't we sell them our Greek stuff for whatever they have in their pockets? It's worth a try, was the consensus. Harry was elected to pry the money loose; and it worked, but only after the passengers were told they were up against the wall and that they would not reach Australia if they did not cooperate. An astonishing amount of real money was collected and that got them almost, but not quite, through Singapore.

The operating captain as far as Singapore was a Swede named Eric Danielson. On paper, Harry and his crew were resting on this part of the flight. In real life, there was no way to rest and no place to do it. The cabin was jammed with passengers, so Harry often found himself on the jump seat in the cockpit. It was neither spacious nor comfortable, but it was quiet. Astrid was working the flight and she came up front now and then to offer food, coffee, or, sometimes, a gentle look or a soft touch. Too bad, thought Harry, she would have to stay in Singapore while he pressed on to Sydney. They would make up for lost time when Harry and his sheep got back to Singapore.

Harry and Danielson discussed the financial problem. Eric would take his crew to the hotel and, from there, he would call the Head Office, wherever that was these days, and try to sort it out. There did not seem much hope for a money miracle from that quarter. Harry did not learn the outcome of this phone call until he saw Eric on the plane after Harry had landed in Singapore with his planeload of sheep. From the hotel, Eric had called Oslo collect. Incredibly, Thor refused to accept the charges. Eric cursed in Swedish and told the operator that he would pay for the call.

"What are you doing in Singapore?" was Thor's hello, apparently unaware of the location of his only operational airplane.

Some hard Scandinavian language had followed. Harry was surprised to learn that although Swedish and Norwegian were different languages, they seemed to communicate easily. The bottom line was that there was no money. Harry had figured out as much when Eric did not return to the airport; and he knew better than to count on money coming to Singapore from a far-off place, where there was probably none to begin with. There were still those leftover drachmas, but the airport services would not touch them. What to do?

Gene Daily had been in Singapore before, and he had a suggestion. There was a place he knew called Change Alley, near the financial center. There, any money from any place could be changed. Of course, the exchange rate might be less than great, he said, but they will, for sure, take those drachmas off our hands.

"It's worth a try," said Harry, so he and Gene went through customs, hailed a taxi and were soon in the modern and beautiful center of Singapore.

Along the way, Harry marveled at the tropical greenery that seemed to be everywhere. Singapore was known as The Garden City, and the reasons were everywhere. Beautiful flowers and lush green vegetation were all around them. When the taxi stopped, the driver gestured towards what looked to be an opening between two large buildings. There, nestled amongst the gleaming skyscrapers of this great financial hub, was Change Alley, a narrow, dark passageway lined with moneychangers.

At first, Harry thought they were in the wrong place. Where were all the fancy offices, the well-dressed businessmen? He saw only scruffy Orientals wearing sandals and pajama-like trousers. Some had no office at all, only a desk and an abacus. That was a small rectangle of stringed beads used as a calculator. *Now, why in hell would any of these characters be interested in buying our drachmas?* Harry asked himself.

They approached the first one, an ancient Chinese with a wispy beard and fingers stained dark brown from nicotine. He looked at the money as Harry removed it from the bag.

"Ah, Greece money," he said, even before he had it in his hands. He took a few bills at random and scrutinized them through a magnifying glass. He coughed through his cigarette smoke as he examined the money.

"Yes," he said, after a close examination. "Money good. Exchange rate not good." He had already started the negotiations. Harry was not good at haggling, and the changer seemed to sense that.

The moneychanger began to deftly flick the beads on his abacus. His fingers flew across the rows of beads and he offered a price. Harry had never seen an abacus before, and he could not believe that such a gadget could calculate such large numbers so quickly. Harry was clearly out of his depth, and he knew it. He offered only token resistance by threatening to take his drachmas elsewhere. Quickly, a deal was struck and the moneychanger had certainly got it right that the exchange rate was not good. Harry sold the drachmas for about one-quarter of their value in Greece. A large part of the value of any asset is determined by where it is, Harry knew, and these drachmas were definitely in the wrong place. Harry had not had much bargaining power and had not put up much resistance. But twenty-five percent? Astrid would be disappointed. Still, what could he do? He had to unload the damned drachmas and move on.

Harry and Gene were soon on the way back to the airport with an ordinary brown paper bag holding two bundles of English sterling – enough, thought Harry, to pay the bills at Changi Airport and continue onward to their rendezvous with destiny and the Australian sheep. Eric had not yet called from the hotel.

Before Eric left the plane with his crew, Harry had tugged Astrid's elbow as she cleaned the forward galley. She glanced up and raised her eyebrows. Harry nodded towards the cockpit, then turned and went in. He knew it was empty because he had, a minute ago, chased a mechanic out of it. Astrid followed after a few minutes. Harry reached around her and locked the cockpit door. Astrid looked puzzled.

"Harry," she said, drawing in her breath, "we are not going to -- not here. Are we?"

"No, no," replied Harry quickly. "That'll have to wait until I get back, whenever that is. I just want to say goodbye in private."

He pulled her close and nuzzled her cheek, kissing her ear. The warm feel of her body aroused Harry and, for a fleeting moment, he thought about making love right there in the cockpit.

"Oh Harry, I am going to miss you."

Harry could not resist, and he whispered into her ear. "You mean me, or my friend? He's beautiful, you know."

She smiled through a tiny tear. "I know," she said softly. "I can feel him becoming more beautiful right now." She tilted her head back and stopped smiling. "I will miss you. Come back soon."

Just then, Eric knocked on the cockpit door. "Astrid," he called sharply. "Come. We are all waiting."

Now, high above the sea, Harry smiled as he thought about doing business in Change Alley. How different life could be in different places. The memory works in strange ways, and he found himself thinking about a man he had once met at a glitzy cocktail party in Dallas, Texas. No one there had ever been concerned with changing Greek drachmas or even knew what they were. Harry was with a pilot from Austria with whom he had flown a few times.

"Ah," said the well-dressed Texan, upon being introduced to Werner Stockel, "Austria, the country with all those kangaroos. How interesting."

Werner looked puzzled. "Ve haf not kangaroos in Austria," he said with a slight frown. Now, it was the other fellow's turn to look puzzled.

"So tell me," he asked after a pause, during which he had obviously been thinking very hard. "What have you done with all those kangaroos?"

Geography, thought Harry, did not seem a strong suit for most Americans.

Harry had once flown with Werner into an airport in Algeria. The night was dark and the weather was awful. Werner asked for the wind. His accent was more than strong, and even when he spoke English, it sounded like German. The poor fellow in the tower could not understand one word.

"The vindt, the vindt. I vant to know the vindt."

"Sorry, say again, sir," said the man in the control tower, for the third time.

Werner exploded, thinking that turning up the volume might help. "The vindt, the vindt, you dumbkopf. Tell me ze movement of ze air mass across ze ground." That got through and they finally got the wind.

Well, Harry thought, as he looked out over the endless blue Pacific Ocean and reviewed the past few days, I hope Australia is ready for Trans Polar. He knew there was plenty of potential for things to go awry.

The first thing that went wrong happened right after arriving in Sydney. There was no external power after the aircraft was parked. Night had already reached Australia, and power was needed for aircraft lighting.

In flight, an airplane uses electrical power from its own engine-driven generators. On the ground, with the engines shut down, external power is provided from an electric cart which is brought alongside and plugged into the aircraft's electrical system. This time, there was no power cart. After a long wait, the engines were shut down, and the passengers were off-loaded in the dark. The lack of light was inconvenient but manageable.

Next, the crew was told that fuel would not be available for them. No fuel! How could that be? Harry began to smell a pattern. Then, as he exited the forward cabin door at the top of the staircase, someone stuck a microphone in his face. A bright light blinded him. A disembodied voice began asking questions, and it took Harry some seconds to realize he was being interviewed.

"What the hell is going on here?" he demanded in an irritated tone.

"You don't know?" asked the voice. Harry's expression obviously said "Hell no, I do not."

"The sheep," said the voice. "They are Merinos."

"So?" responded Harry, pretending to know what a Merino was, even though he had not the slightest idea. In the next few minutes, Harry learned that they were a special breed of sheep, unique to Australia, the export of which, until now, had been prohibited by law. Although it was now legal to export them, the people of Australia protested. Chief among the protestors was Robert Hawke, who headed the Australian workers' union.

He had laid down the rules of engagement for the battle he was expecting. No services for the Trans Polar, neither airplane nor crew, until further notice. The next morning, Harry almost dropped his coffee cup when he saw his picture on the front page of the *Sydney Morning Herald*. The headline was: "Norwegian Ram Runners Take Our Sheep." Later, he had the strange sensation of watching himself being interviewed on television. He had blinked and stammered and seemed confused, but there was good reason for that. He was confused, totally confused. If the Australians did not want their sheep exported, then why in hell was he here?

A political issue, he was told. No fuel and no service until it was cleared up. No service included the hotel. The chambermaids refused to make up the rooms of the crew. It could have been worse, Harry consoled himself, they could have refused to even give us rooms.

Now that he knew all the aspects of the problem, he could begin to work on it. He started with the agent who had contracted for the export of the sheep. Harry had his telephone number somewhere in his grab bag of flight documents. He rummaged around, found it, and called the agent. He half expected his room telephone to be cut off, but it worked normally. The agent was in Harry's hotel room thirty minutes later.

"It's all one hundred percent legal," Harry was told, just some political problems.

"But big ones," replied Harry. "How in the hell are we going to get these sheep out of here?"

Harry did not know what a typical Australian was like; but if he imagined one, this agent would have been it. He was a tall, heavyset man, gruff, honest and straightforward.

"This service problem is huge, very huge," Harry was told, "and we need to think about other options."

"Like what? We can't go anywhere without fuel. And that's just for starters. What about loading the sheep. What about flight planning services. What about airplane service. What about all that?" Harry demanded.

The agent calmly went about addressing the problems, one by one.

"I have spoken to the Prime Minister," he said, "and he is with us. He will allow you to refuel at Richmond Air Force Base just outside of Sydney. The sheep can be loaded there, as well. The military people will help. The first question is: can you make your way there without assistance?"

Harry had to think. That the PM was helping was good news. It meant that weather information, flight-planning, and airways service would be available. That was a start.

The flight would be a short one and the fuel they had landed with would be enough. Normally, the engines were started with an external air compressor. That, Harry was told, would not be available; but the airplane carried a steel sphere of compressed air in the wheel well. For situations like this, its air could be used to start one engine, then the air compressor on that engine, normally used to pressurize the airplane during flight, could be used to start the others. He would need to check the numbers for the Air Force base runways to see how much load, including fuel and cargo, they could get airborne with. Mainly, the runway length would determine that. Harry began to see some daylight at the end of this tunnel.

"Okay," he said, "I think we can do this. Where do we start?"

About an hour later Harry found himself in a telephone conversation with the head of the Royal Australian Air Force. At the same time, in Gene

Daily's adjacent room, the travel agent, as Gene called the sheep broker, was talking to the Prime Minister. Every now and then, Harry or the agent would dash next door and break into the other's conversation to find an answer to a question that had come up. Gradually, a plan evolved.

The Norwegian Ram Runners were about to strike. The plan needed a few days to implement, and Harry and the crew used them to investigate Sydney. They were celebrities now, as they were front-page news every morning. That opened some doors and they were invited to parties all over Sydney. Harry liked Sydney and he liked Australians. They were rough-and-tumble in some ways, but open, friendly, and straightforward.

They liked their grog, as Gene put it, and would have drunk beer nonstop if not for laws regulating open hours for pubs. They had to close early in the evening, at what Gene called an "obscene and ridiculous" time. That was a foolish attempt to cut back the drinking. But instead of decreasing, the pace of the drinking rose steadily as closing time neared, and people began drinking with both hands. The Law of Unintended Consequences strikes again, Harry thought one night as he watched a bout of high- intensity drinking just before pub closing time.

Before dawn, a few days later, Harry, Rolf, and Gene threw their bags into a taxi and headed for the airport. There, they were met by an officer of the RAAF who would help them escape to Richmond Air Force Base. He had lined up an airport service car, and the four of them drove out to the Trans Polar airplane. On the way, Harry was briefed on his departure from Sydney. No flight plan was needed, but he would need to call for clearance to taxi and take off. As there would be no electrical power on the aircraft until an engine was running, he would be unable to call for start-up clearance. Tower operators had been fully briefed, Harry was told. No service personnel would be available, and the RAAF officer would man a fire bottle during start-up.

Also unavailable were stairs to enter the airplane. The 707 has a kind of trap door on its belly just behind the nose wheel. It leads into a compartment in which most of the airplane's electronic equipment is installed. From there, another hatch led into the cockpit. This hatch allowed in-flight entry into the electronic compartment to check electronic boxes, for one reason or another. It was hard negotiating the two hatches and the passageway between them but, except for some thudding and scraping and a loud curse when someone bumped into something, all three managed, with difficulty, to reach the cockpit.

Now came the vital part. The bottle of compressed air was a one-shot attempt. If the engine did not start on the first try, that was it. Harry had never done it before, and neither had Rolf or Gene. It was finger-crossing time. Harry, using his flashlight, broke out the 707 flight manual from his flight bag. Using the index, he found the abnormal procedures section, then the one that would tell him how to start an engine using an air bottle. It had to be done right. The three of them settled into their seats and Harry went over the start procedure very carefully. Then, he went over it a second time, also very carefully.

When Harry was satisfied that they were ready, he told Rolf to alert the RAAF, standing next to the Number 3 engine, that he would start Number 3.

"Ready down here," he heard the officer call back. Funny, thought Harry, we're breaking dozens of rules here tonight but at least we have someone manning the fire bottle during start-up. As Rolf read the checklist, Harry moved the switches. When he called out, "Air Bottle Switch ON," Harry sucked in his breath, held it, and flicked the switch, intently watching the N2 gauge for the first sign of engine rotation. They heard a *whoosh* of air, and the engine began to turn. At the predetermined rpm, Harry moved the start lever to START, switching his scan to the EGT gauge that indicated engine temperature. With the start lever in the START position, fuel and ignition were provided to the engine. When the engine lit off, he would see it there first.

The start was normal and Harry exhaled loudly.

"Goddamn, Boss," said Gene triumphantly, "we did it!"

As the engine whined up to idle speed, its compressor took over the task of providing air and the engine became self-sustaining. Using the checklist, they started the other three engines. This required Harry to turn up Number 3 to a power that provided enough air pressure to turn the other engines. The engine's roar, in the stillness of the night, was thunderous. He started Number 4, then 2 and 1, and all started normally.

Harry throttled back Number 3 and began to relax. Now, the RAAF officer climbed up through the equipment compartment and into the cockpit, closing the hatch as he came through. Grinning, he flashed "thumbs up." The After Start checklist was done and Rolf called the tower for taxi instructions. Harry was not familiar with the airport and although he had taxi charts, it was not easy at night to find his way around a strange airport. The RAAF pilot knew it well and he guided Harry to the takeoff position.

This would be a brief flight and, in some ways, short flights were more difficult than long ones. All the action was compressed into a few minutes instead of being drawn out over several hours. The communications, the checklists, operating landing gear and wing flaps, the airplane control: It all happened very quickly. The RAAF officer was very helpful. The wheels touched down at Richmond Air Force Base just seven minutes after leaving the runway in Sydney. When Rolf called for landing instructions, Harry was relieved to be under normal air traffic control again. There had been none since they had left Sydney, and that silence was deafening. Harry taxied in and parked, following the signals made by the lighted wands of the linesman. He smiled when he saw a staircase being wheeled up to the main cabin door. Even stairs! The external power was plugged in and Harry shut down the engines. After completing the checklist, he hurriedly made his way out of the cockpit and down the stairs.

He was anxious to know what would happen next. He was met by a slight, short man with an unusual accent. He turned out to be from Malta, wherever that was, and his name was James. Although Harry had heard of Malta, he was not sure where it was. Wherever it was, it was not on the list of places he wanted to visit. Curious, Harry asked James how he had found his way to Australia. Oh, there are more Maltese here than there are in Malta, he was told, and explained the reasons. Harry knew that Australia had been partly populated with convicts from the British Isles.

"Did some come from Malta, too?" he asked James.

"No, no," James said quickly, "the reasons were economic."

James was the direct representative of the Prime Minister. He briefed Harry about the sheep. The fuel truck was on the way. The sheep were standing by, loaded in individual crates, and Air Force personnel were on hand to load them. These people seem to know what they're doing, thought Harry.

Aloud he said, "Tell your troops they can start by moving the seats into the cargo compartments. Our engineer here," he nodded in Gene's direction, "will show them how to remove them. Gene, would you shotgun stowing the seats in the cargo holds? Thanks."

Harry looked towards James and asked, "How many sheep are we talking about and do we know how much they weigh? And we are going to need the runway performance charts for the airport."

Among the ship's library of manuals and documents were a couple of binders containing runway performance charts for those airports for that part of the world in which the airplane was planned to operate. They did not include RAAF bases.

James reached into his coat pocket and withdrew a folded paper. "The sheep numbers," he said, as he handed it to Harry. "I don't know about those runway charts. Are they essential?"

Harry grimaced. The runway data charts made life easy. There was one for each runway. Entering the charts with the temperature, the wind, and a few other variables, and the maximum allowable takeoff weight could easily be found. There was another way, but it was laborious. It involved doing the entire process from the basic manual. It had graphs that could be used for any runway. Harry had not done it since his ground school days. He knew it could be done, but he knew it was a complicated calculation.

"No, not essential," he answered, "but see if you can find one somewhere. Now, let's have a look at these numbers." He scanned them quickly. There were one-hundred-and-twenty-five sheep, each weighing about 135 pounds. That seemed reasonable; so far, so good.

This information was needed to fill out the load sheet. This was a form which determined the airplane's center of gravity after it was loaded. The center of gravity of the empty airplane was a fixed number. It had to be within a range that ensured airplane stability in flight. This number changed as weight was added, and it changed according to where the weight was placed. A weight placed farther from the ship's center of gravity changed this number more than the same weight placed closer. It was a kind of teeter-totter effect.

The location of the center of gravity had to be known so that the horizontal stabilizer could be properly set for takeoff. During flight, the up and down movement of the aircraft's tail was controlled by the elevators. These were small wing-like surfaces hinged to the horizontal stabilizer at the airplane's tail. They were moved by a link to the control wheel in the cockpit. When the wheel was repositioned forward or aft, the elevators moved up or down. This changed the aerodynamic shape of the assembly in a way that created lift to move the tail either up or down. The airplane nose moved in the opposite direction, causing the plane to climb or descend.

The elevators were useless until they had high-speed air flowing across them; so the position of the horizontal stabilizer did this job during the takeoff run. Its setting had to be right. Ground staff usually filled out the load sheet; but in a do-it-yourself airline such as Trans Polar, it sometimes had to be done by the cockpit crew. Harry had done it before. Now, if he could just remember how he did it. He sighed. If all else fails, follow the instructions. There were plenty in the airplane manual.

James had returned with a runway performance chart for the runway in use. That would save time. Harry quickly calculated the maximum allowable takeoff weight. He added the weight of the sheep to the empty weight of the airplane, then subtracted this total from the maximum allowable takeoff weight. That number was the amount of fuel the airplane could lift off with. Using the performance charts in the manual, Harry and Rolf next calculated the amount of fuel they would need to reach Singapore. To do this, they used the total which was found by adding the weights of the airplane, the sheep, and the fuel.

The pieces of the puzzle were beginning to fall into place. The runway was long enough to get airborne with enough fuel to reach Singapore. He and Rolf next began working on the load sheet. Just about the time they had it figured out, Gene entered the cockpit with bad news. Even with all the seats removed from the cabin, there was not enough space for all the crates of sheep.

"Let's have a look," said Harry as he left the cockpit. Now, for the first time, Harry saw the crates of sheep neatly arranged in the cabin. Gene had loaded them through the rear entry door and placed the first ones, the First-Class Sheep, he called them, in the forward part of the cabin, then loaded from forward to aft. All those crates made a strange sight, and Harry had the uneasy feeling that something here was against the regulations. Well, he said to himself, what's one more broken rule? And anyway, we're a long way from Oslo. The cabin floor had been covered with sheets of plastic, and the sheep had not been given food or water for three days. That would cut down on the waste they produced. But, despite these precautions, this airplane came to be known as the sheep wagon, and the smell of sheep urine never left it. Standing at the top of the stairs, Harry could see the problem. Too many crates, not enough cabin.

He left the airplane and found James in the Flight Ops center. He passed along the news: not all the sheep would fit on the plane. What did he want to do? James put down his coffee and lifted a finger.

"Just one moment, please. I will make a telephone call." His coffee was still hot when he returned a few minutes later. "I have just spoken with the Prime Minister, and his instructions are that all these sheep will leave Australia tonight, on this airplane, one way or another."

As a former Naval officer, Harry had always appreciated an order clearly given. This one was certainly clear enough. He returned to the plane, where he and Gene discussed the problem. They agreed there was only one solution. Some of the sheep had to be removed from their crates and jammed into the cabin, along with those in the crates. How many, was the question. Another lesson Harry had learned as a Naval officer was delegation of responsibility. He remembered a training course in which the stated problem was raising a flagpole without using heavy equipment. The solution was to take aside the Chief Petty Officer, show him the pole and issue the order. "Chief, raise this pole right here. Let me know when it's up."

Now he said to Gene, "Gene, old buddy, you need to bird-dog this loading evolution. Keep an eye on how much space is left and when it looks like the right time, take the last ones out of those crates and load them any way you can."

Harry expected an argument but Gene simply said, "Okay, Boss. Keep you posted."

Using a judicious eye, Gene had taken the last thirty-seven sheep out of their crates and filled up the remaining space in the aft cabin with sheep. They were wall-to-wall and shoulder-to-shoulder back there. Gene had read this one right on the money and not one of those sheep could move.

"Got 'em all in, Boss," reported Gene cheerfully about an hour later.

Damn, thought Harry. I wonder how this will affect the load sheet. He looked dismally at the sheet he had completed just minutes before. How would this change affect his numbers? He thought quickly. He finally decided that the missing crates did not weigh enough to make a difference. He would just tweak the stab trim one bleep aft to compensate for the difference. Sometimes, thought Harry, a captain had to improvise, and this seemed one of those times. Using the fuel consumption figures from the airplane performance charts and adding the reserves, the required fuel was determined and pumped on board. The project was shaping up. They might get these sheep out of Australia after all.

James came into the cockpit and asked how much longer Harry would need. The urgency in his voice caused Harry to raise his eyebrows.

"Problem?" he asked. James said that the news media had figured out the ram-runner plan.

"They cannot enter the base," said James, "but the PM asks that you depart as soon as you can. 'Expeditiously,' he said."

Harry grinned. There was nothing he wanted to do more. He'd had enough of Australia.

"You tell your boss we'll be on our way just as soon as we can fire up and taxi out."

Rolf had filed a flight plan long ago. Harry looked at Gene. "How are our passengers doing?"

Gene replied that they were strapped in and ready to go.

"Okay," said Harry. "Let's do it. Rolf, call for start-up."

Flying across Australia at night was like flying across the dark side of the moon, and Harry was reminded of flying over Cambodia. There had been nothing down there either, just a vast, dark void. But now, instead of flying on adrenalin, he was casually sipping a cup of coffee. There was, Harry saw, a lot of empty space in Australia.

Some years before, Harry had flown into Darwin with a captain who had been a fighter pilot during the war. As they taxied to the hotel, the captain asked the driver a few questions that suggested he had been there before.

"Been here before?" asked Harry.

The captain smiled. Yes, he had been there before. He had been shot down near Darwin and had spent some weeks there near the end of the war.

"It's a small world, isn't it?" remarked Harry, "and welcome back. Was there anything here?"

"Not then," the captain replied. "But maybe now."

Harry asked the driver the population of Darwin, which, of course, he had heard of. The number was surprisingly low.

"Not many people," said Harry. "What's the nearest big city?" Alice Springs was closest.

"How far is that?" asked Harry.

"Oh, about 800 miles," replied the driver. The nearest big city was a place that Harry had never heard of, and it was 800 miles away! That gave some dimension to this continent that was, Harry knew, about the size of the U.S. As big, perhaps, but nowhere near as full. There were almost as many people living in New York City as were living in all of Australia.

It took them five hours to reach the west coast, then it was another three hours to Singapore. The contrast was striking. Singapore was brightly lit and, from the air, looked like a giant pinball machine. It would be nice to be back among friendly natives, thought Harry, and wouldn't Astrid feel great against him again! He was not sure Astrid and the other girls would still be there. The sheep did not need them for their trip to Moscow. He was not sure how the crew would return to Oslo, but one thing was sure: It would not be on this airplane. There was no place to sit. Harry had sent a telex to the Ming Court Hotel advising Eric of their arrival time. As soon as the cabin door opened, Eric boarded the plane and came into the cockpit. Astrid and the other girls were right behind. Astrid pushed into the cockpit behind Eric and reached around him to take Harry's hand. She smiled lovingly and she looked even better than he remembered. Harry's heart skipped a beat.

31
SINGAPORE

"What's happening?" Harry asked, when the buzz of the greetings had died down.

"Harry," said Eric, "Your crew is supposed to extra-crew back to Oslo with me. And my girls, too; but I see the sheep have left not much space. I think we have a problem. It seems no one thought to leave some seats in the cabin. Do you think we could put some seats back in there? We need only six."

Harry thought about that for a few milliseconds. "No way, Eric. Just take a look at how those sheep are jammed in back there. The only way you can put some seats there is to take out some sheep. You want to do that? Why can't we go back as passengers? On a real airline?"

Eric had been on the phone with Thor, he said, and those were the orders.

"Well, Thor will just have to change his orders. We have the two jump seats in the cockpit. Gene and Rolf could sit there, if they agree, but that's it. I'll go to the hotel with the girls and we'll start over from there."

His layover had not yet started, but he was already enjoying the idea of a day or two in Singapore with Astrid.

"But, Harry," asked Eric, "what about the orders?"

"I'll get some new ones at the hotel," said Harry as he squirmed out of his seat. But Eric was determined to follow instructions. He had noticed that the sheep in the rear were not in crates.

"Look," he said earnestly, "Can we not remove more of the sheep from the boxes in the front and make more space that way?"

Harry had thought of that, too, but he decided that was not a good idea for several reasons, one of which was that it would cancel his stay in Singapore before it started.

Duty, however, raised its ugly head and Harry sighed. He and Eric went over what would need to be done. After much discussion, with suggestions from the entire crew and even a few from the ground engineer, a plan evolved. The sheep were removed from the crates just behind the ones that were farthest forward in the cabin. Those forward crates were then pushed back just far enough to allow six seats to be installed, three on each side. The released sheep would be loose, but boxed in between the crates. Harry did not expect them to complain. They were not, after all, paying passengers.

Several hours and a lot of grunting, groaning, and an occasional Swedish curse were needed, but finally it was done. The sheep did not seem to care whether they were in the crates or out.

"Too bad all passengers are not so easy. They do not smell so nice," said Astrid, as she wrinkled her nose, "but at least they will not press the call button every five minutes."

During the re-arrangement of the sheep, Harry had only a few minutes alone with Astrid. Now he flopped into one of the newly-installed passenger seats and patted the one beside him.

"Have a seat, Astrid, and tell me about Singapore." Astrid quickly sat down and snuggled close to Harry. She took one of his hands in both of hers.

"Oh, it's a wonderful city, more wonderful if you were with me, but now we will have a nice flight together. I think our passengers will need not much service, so I will take good care of you."

Harry was not sure exactly what that meant, but with a plane full of sheep and crew, taking good care of him could only go so far.

"Very good," said Harry with a smile. "You can start right now by serving me a kiss, a big one. I need it."

Astrid smiled back. "Only one? I have many more for you. Here is the first one." She tilted his head down and kissed his cheek. "They will get better later," she said, "when the lights are out and the sheeps are not watching."

Harry had already forgotten his disappointment in missing a few days in Singapore. Looking forward was always better than looking back. You already knew what had gone before. Ahead was experience still to be tasted.

32
XO GOES DOWN

1966

Harry was watching a movie in the Officers' Wardroom when Karl Laney entered the room and slipped into the chair next to his. He was the Squadron Duty Officer, and Harry was instantly alarmed. Laney would be there only for an important reason.

"Harry," Karl whispered urgently, "we've lost a bird. Better get back to the Ready Room."

He rose and left the wardroom in measured haste, with Harry close behind. Harry had quickly asked, "Who is it?" but Karl was already on his way.

The Ready Room was nearby and they were there in a few minutes. When something like this happened, you could almost feel it before you heard about it. Harry felt it as soon as he entered the room. There was an unmistakable sense of foreboding. In the front of the room, near the Duty Officer's desk, was a group of several pilots, some in flight gear and some in khakis. Paul Arnett, still perspiring in his flight suit, had just landed and was talking in a subdued and earnest way about the flight from which he had just returned. Alongside Paul was one of the other three pilots of the four-plane division.

Only two had landed. One pilot had come back the hard way, ejecting over the ship at ten-thousand feet. He had come back aboard on the rescue chopper after being plucked from the sea. The fourth pilot, the division leader and the Executive Officer of the squadron, had not come back. He was last seen by his wingman, Arnett, as he ejected from his burning aircraft over North Vietnam.

Just before going to the movie, Harry had listened in when the XO had briefed his flight a few hours before. The briefing item Harry remembered most clearly was this: If you take a hit and need to punch out, head for the sea. Help is waiting there. Harry knew the basics of the mission. It was flak-suppression for a flight of A6s. Their target was a bridge west of Than Hoa in an area known to the Air Wing pilots as Happy Valley. It was so named because, although the pilots could always count on being shot at there, they could also count on being missed, and usually by a wide margin. The gunners in Happy Valley were not very accurate, so the pilots called them "Happy."

Harry quietly approached the front row of chairs, where Paul was speaking -- and gesturing. Pilots could not talk without using their hands to show what the airplanes were doing.

"It was late afternoon," he said, "and looking into the sun made it hard to pick out the target. The XO had called tally-ho a minute or so before he rolled in, and I was able to pick up the target just before that. It looked just like the photos from the brief. I rolled in a few seconds after the XO, and there was a thin undercast, so with the setting sun and that thin layer of clouds, it was hard to keep the target in sight. I lost it for a few seconds, then picked it up again as I was heading down. Just about then, I heard the XO call 'I'm hit. Battlecry One is hit.' He said it in such a calm way that, at first, I didn't take it seriously. Someone else called out, 'Battlecry One, you're hit! You're hit!' I pulled out of my run heading east and started looking around, then I saw a trail of smoke above me and off to my eleven o'clock. I headed over that way, then I could make out the plane. It was making a descending arc and I followed it until it hit the ground, almost straight in. There was a huge fireball and I figured that was it. The next thing I know, I see Jack coming across my nose and, just behind him, I saw a chute. I followed the chute, but I couldn't tell if the XO was okay or not. I saw the chute hit the ground and was trying to figure out how to mark the spot in case a chopper could get in there. I picked up Jack again and decided to join on him in loose wing. Just as I came up, I saw a bright orange flash right at his starboard wing root. I actually saw some pieces flying off his plane.

"Jesus, Jack, you just took a big one," I called.

"No shit," he said, "I noticed it, too."

"The fuel must have caught fire because there was a humongous sheet of flame going back about two or three plane-lengths. I mean, it was a helluva fire."

"Jack," I told him, "you better punch out."

"Hell, no," he said. "This thing is still flying. I'm heading for the water."

"I stayed with him until he crossed the coast, still on fire, but not so big now, then turned back to see if I could help with the XO. Number four had caught up to us by then, so I figured Jack would be okay. By this time, there were a lot of people trying to help. I heard the Spads asking for a steer, but I wasn't sure where I was. I did find the place where the chute had landed because there was a big empty area there with some big trees along the edge of it. Pretty easy to mark. I keyed my mike for five-second intervals, in case they could take a DF steer on me, but the chute wasn't there. I was pretty sure I had the right place, so they must have moved the chute. I remember thinking about that chute those guys spread out on Tiger Island that time a couple of months ago, when they used it to lure in a Spad. They shot him down when he checked out the chute, remember that? So, I didn't want to hang around too long. I never did see the XO, only his chute, so there was no way to tell if he landed okay or what. I was getting low on fuel so I asked for the position of the tanker. It wasn't that far away so I stayed another five minutes, then I had to head back. I never did see the chute again. I joined up with the tanker and took some fuel. I contacted the ship while I was plugged in and told them I had enough fuel to go back and help look for the XO, but they told me to go back to the ship for the recovery."

As Harry listened, he suddenly thought about the other player in this drama.

"What about Jack Rooney?" he broke in. "What happened to Jack?"

Someone in the knot of pilots surrounding Paul, he was not sure who, said that he had punched out over the ship and was picked up by the chopper and was okay. He was in sickbay for evaluation.

33
JACK AND HARRY

1956

Jack and Harry had started out in flight training together in Pensacola. Jack was from New Jersey and saw the world differently than Harry did. Milwaukee and New Jersey did not fit together on the drawing board, perhaps; but in real life they worked well. As sometimes happens, they had connected from the first moments of their meeting. Harry had learned to trust those instincts, and he would be proven right about his instant feelings of friendship towards Jack.

In some ways, Harry envied Jack. He was, in those ways, what Harry could never be: tall, with sandy hair, an engaging smile and a casual charm. He was outgoing and made friends easily. He attracted women easily, too. Harry had to work at it, and, now and then, Jack would jokingly offer Harry one of his "rejects." Jack liked them all, the pretty ones and those not so pretty. That was perhaps one of the secrets of his success.

"Just my type," he liked to say. "Legs all the way up to her ass and double-breasted." He sometimes promised to share his secrets by one day writing a book he would title, "How to Attract Women Even If You Are Not a Jet Pilot."

He had a quick wit that became quicker as he drank, but he was never crude or vulgar. He was good-natured and generous. One night, in the late stages of a boisterous party, he had removed his shirt and presented it to someone who had admired it.

"The shirt off my back," he said with a grin as he proffered the shirt. "Please, be my guest."

After a few drinks, he liked to talk about how Navy pilots were caring and loving people. "The only problem," he would end with a grin, "is that these feelings usually don't involve anyone else."

His one big flaw, Harry thought, was that he enjoyed being drunk.

"Let's get drunk and be somebody," was his happy hour battle cry. He was good-humored and entertaining when he drank too much, but it sometimes got him into trouble. One night, after a party at a friend's home, Jack, drunker than usual, insisted on driving home. Fearful for his friend, Harry had offered to drive him, which, in those days, was a serious insult. Despite

Harry's persistent efforts to dissuade him, Jack just smiled confidently and said, "I drive better drunk."

He fell backwards off the porch as he fished in a pocket for his car keys. Unable to get up, he was soon fast asleep in the bushes into which he had fallen. Harry decided the wise course was to let him lie there. He awoke in the morning, embarrassed and apologetic.

"Never again," he said, a promise he broke at the very next party.

Jack had a strong New Jersey accent. Harry sometimes mimicked it when Jack became excited and his accent got even stronger. He usually retaliated by calling Harry by the nickname he had given him: The World's Tallest Midget; but Harry had heard worse and he just smiled when Jack used that name. That usually made Jack's accent even stronger and Harry's smile even broader.

That Jack was a quick thinker had been firmly established during pre-flight training when he had crept out of his room one night after Taps had sounded. That was against the rules, and he had done it to empty his wastebasket into the dumpster to be ready for room inspection the next morning. As he lifted the lid of the dumpster, he spotted the Duty Officer on his nightly rounds. He quickly scrambled into the dumpster, closing the lid as he did; but the officer saw Jack disappear, went to the dumpster and lifted its lid. Jack sprang to attention, saluted smartly, and reported, "Dumpster all secure, sir." The officer struggled to keep a straight face.

"Yes, the dumpster certainly seems very secure. Keep up the good work," he said, as he turned and walked away, hiding a smile as he did.

Harry had once heard flight training described as a one-hundred-thousand dollar education rammed up your ass, one nickel at a time. Pretty apt, thought Harry at the time. It was a grind that never seemed to let up. One-third of those who started would not finish. And these were America's finest: dedicated young men of character and intelligence; but the grind wore them down.

Perseverance: that was the key. Many who were smarter and quicker than Jack did not make it through. Intelligence was important, but not key. Needed to win those precious wings of gold were motivation, common sense, and judgment; and above all, the ability to perform under pressure. Jack was not exceptionally smart, but he had the rest. He could not remember not wanting to be a pilot, he told Harry. He described how, as a boy, he would sit on a toilet and pretend to fly an airplane, using a plumbing plunger as a control stick.

Nothing ever seemed to bother him, and he exuded self-confidence.

"Well," he once announced, a few years later at a happy hour. "I might not be the best pilot in the world, but I must be third or fourth -- or somewhere around there."

Harry thought he probably was. That confidence was once expressed in an unusual way when the Navy issued a directive that forbade pilots from flying cross-country flights to their hometowns.

"Why do they make such a stupid rule?" Jack asked irritably when he read it.

"They do it," said Harry, "to stop guys like you from flying inverted at fifty feet down the main street of your hometown."

Jack grinned over his irritation. ""Damn," he exclaimed, "that's exactly what I want to do. How do you think they knew?"

Harry was usually tense before one of the many periodic check flights. Check flights did not bother Jack. Do your best, he counseled Harry, and the pieces will fall into place. Still, you could not order a tooth not to ache, and you could not order yourself to be calm before a check flight. Like golf balls, the body and the mind did what they wanted to do, and to hell with what you told them to do. Harry was a slow learner, but once he got the picture, he performed well.

Pensacola, in those days, was where the basic training took place. The various stages of training were at different bases in the area. Primary flight, instruments, formation, gunnery, and, finally, the jewel in the crown, carrier qualification, or cq, in the jargon of the training command. Harry had his ups and downs along the way, but finally made it to Barin Field, looking forward with great anticipation to landing on an aircraft carrier. That was, after all, what "The Program" was all about. Flight training was never referred to as such; it was always, "The Program."

If a neophyte pilot wanted to talk to someone about his problems in The Program, he could always find him at Trader Jon's. This legendary bar in downtown Pensacola was, for decades, the unofficial headquarters for student pilots. If he was searching for a friend, Trader's was the first place he looked. If he badly needed a beer after a rough day in The Program, he headed for Trader's. If he had guests from out of town, Trader's was the first place he took them. A few local girls could always be found there, hoping to meet a future Naval aviator. Trader's was the social center of the pilot basic training universe. It was also a center for sorting out flying problems. A common sight there was that of two students earnestly discussing a flight maneuver, describing it with their hands, as they usually did when they talked about flying.

Trader's was not only for student pilots. Fleet pilots stopped by often to revisit their past. With luck, a visitor might meet one of the Blue Angels there. Pensacola was their home base. This famous flight team demonstrated precision flying at its exciting best. Harry would see them often over the years and, each time, he was awed and thrilled by their flawless flying. They made it look easy; but every pilot who had ever flown in formation knew how difficult their maneuvers were. Every Navy pilot aspired to be a Blue, but only the very best were selected. They were the rock stars of Naval aviation.

Now and then, a Commanding Officer would bring his entire squadron to Trader's to celebrate a special occasion, or to instill spirit and foster camaraderie. The unwritten rule was that no one could leave before the skipper did. No one minded that rule.

You did not need to be a Navy pilot to drink at Trader's. It was a Pensacola landmark, and tourists liked to drink there, too. Even celebrities stopped in now and then. Elizabeth Taylor, John Wayne, and Bob Hope were among those who had lifted a glass with Trader. He treated them all the same, famous or not. They were welcome, but his focus stayed fixed on Navy pilots, and especially Navy student pilots. He somehow knew they needed him.

Trader's was a hybrid. Part bar, part aviation museum, part tropical island, it was a place that quickly became a home-away-from-home for many Naval aviator hopefuls. The main reason was Jon himself. He was always there and always wearing his trademarks: a tropical shirt, short pants, sandals, and a welcoming smile. Short and paunchy, with thinning hair, he had a big heart and a beautiful soul. He was more than the owner of a famous bar; he was a friend to those who drank there. Trader allowed student pilots to run tabs, and he freely lent money to those who needed it. He never kept a record of the loans, and always told the borrower, "Just pay me back when you can." Trader Jon's was as much a part of Pensacola and The Program as were the planes and the pilots who flew them.

At Barin Field, Harry learned to fly the SNJ. It was in this airplane, old and worn, that Harry would land on a carrier for the first time. The SNJ was not easy to fly. It was hard to handle on the ground, as well. It had a tail wheel, and that meant the upraised nose of the aircraft obstructed the forward view during taxi. The airplane had to be taxied using S-turns, making movement difficult.

Practice landings, scores of them, were made on a runway which had the outline of a carrier flight deck painted on it. The flight pattern for the landings was at 125 feet, 58 knots, with the canopy open. The air thrown back by the propeller, known as prop wash, impinged on the vertical stabilizer and caused it to yaw the airplane. The prop wash moved the tail one way, which moved the aircraft's nose the other. To avoid that, the pilot had to compensate with the rudder for every power adjustment. If it was not done right, the nose would swing across the pilot's field of view and the Landing Signal Officer would disappear. That meant the pilot had to add power, fly down the runway and re-enter the pattern to try again. Just thinking about "hitting the boat" created apprehension. To student Naval aviators, it was like crossing the Rubicon. Those who had done it were hailed as heroes and were questioned endlessly about it.

One of Harry's most vivid memories was flying out to the ship, usually referred to as "The Boat." This was no outline painted on a runway. This was the real thing, an actual aircraft carrier, on which he had to make his qualification landings. He needed six. The instructor led them out, and Harry flew on his wing. Focusing on flying formation, he did not look around until the instructor called the ship in sight. Then, Harry ventured a quick look down and saw what appeared to be a floating cigarette box. Oh, it looked small! He gritted his teeth as he felt the tension rise. *Damn*, he told himself fiercely, *if others can do it, I can, too.* The six landings took only thirty minutes and he could not remember much about them. It was a blur, and Harry was caught up in the overwhelming thrill of the moment.

After one of his landings, he looked out to see that he was being given the signal to cut his engine. That, he thought disconsolately, had to be a bad sign. He had not yet made his six landings.

"What is it?" he asked anxiously, as he climbed down onto the flight deck.

"You've finished your six, sir," he was told.

"No, no," Harry said quickly. "I've made only four. I was counting."

The crewman smiled. "No, sir," he said. "You've made six landings. Now, you need to get below and let someone else have your airplane."

Later, in his first squadron, Harry had an XO who had once been an LSO in Pensacola. He told of an incident that captured the intensity of landing for the first time on a carrier. On his first attempt, a student had made an awful landing. He caught a wire, careened to the deck edge of the flight deck and straddled it, one wheel in the catwalk and the other on the deck. His propeller was furiously chopping the edge of the flight deck into splinters.

The deck crew frantically signaled the student to cut his engine; but his head was down, looking inside the cockpit. A long minute passed. When he finally looked up and saw all the commotion, he quickly cut the engine.

"Goddammit," said a vexed crewman. "What in the hell were you doing up there?"

"Going over my before-takeoff checklist," he replied.

He got a dumbfounded glare from the crewman. "Jesus, you didn't realize something was wrong?" he asked incredulously.

"Well," said the student sheepishly, "I did think that if all the landings were as rough as this one, it would be a long afternoon."

Along with landing on a carrier, Barin Field introduced students to air-to-air gunnery and night flying. Unusual about gunnery was that the gun was mounted on the center of the fuselage, in line with the engine. A timing mechanism was supposed to prevent the rounds from hitting the propeller; but it never seemed to work right, and all the propellers had bullet holes in them. When a hole appeared, the problem of unbalance was solved by drilling an identical hole on the opposite propeller blade. Not the best solution, Harry thought, but certainly the quickest.

Harry's first night flight was a session of touch-and-go landings. Getting airborne after his first one, he followed the airplane ahead to stay in the proper pattern. After a few minutes, Harry realized that the pilot ahead had forgotten to turn back onto his downwind leg. After a few more minutes, he realized he was following not an airplane, but a truck, headed for New Orleans. Night flying was difficult for beginners.

Harry and Jack had gone on to advanced training together at Cabanis Field in Corpus Christi. There, they flew Skyraiders, aircraft still in use in the fleet. They were in the same six-man flight and they shared a room in the BOQ. They enjoyed being temporary Texans. Jack especially liked it because his New Jersey accent delighted the young ladies of Corpus Christi. They all liked Jack. As usual, Harry got the overflow, but he didn't mind.

Padre Island was just off the Texas coast and, in 1957, it had no man-made structures, only sand and cactus, so the Navy put its bombing targets there. The pilots flew a racetrack pattern, and Jack was usually just ahead of Harry. Each pilot called, "Rolling in," "Off Target," and "Turning downwind," so they could keep track of each other. One day Jack made his calls but Harry could not see him. The practice bombs made a small puff of white smoke upon impact. The instructor, orbiting the target to spot the hits, called "No spot" after each of Jack's runs. Finally, suspecting something awry, the instructor called, "Three zero four, what target are you on?"

After his first run, Jack had gotten disoriented and had ended up on a target several miles away. He was following his own personal bombing pattern on the wrong target. It was embarrassing, but not dangerous. It meant a "down" for Jack, and the flight had to be re-flown.

Because they flew old, propeller-driven airplanes, the Navy decided student Skyraider pilots did not need g-suits. They were reserved for fleet pilots. These suits were cutouts made of nylon and they were zipped into place over the regular flight suits. They were connected to the airplane with a hose. They held bladders that filled with compressed air when the airplane sensed increased gravity forces. The pressure of the inflated bladders against key body areas prevented blood from leaving the head, lessening the chance of blackouts.

Lack of g-suits made no sense because these old birds pulled plenty of g's, especially during recovery from dive-bombing runs, some of which were as steep as forty-five degrees. Five or six g's were normal during such pullouts. During one bombing session, Harry saw Jack make two or three aileron rolls as he pulled off target.

"Jack," Harry told him seriously when they were back on the ground, "better knock off that hot dog stuff. I saw those rolls after one of your runs."

Jack was genuinely puzzled.

"Rolls? What rolls?" he asked, brow furrowed.

Jack had then revealed that he sometimes blacked out for a second or two during his pullouts. "Those rolls must have happened then."

Harry looked at Jack intently, unsure if he was coloring the truth.

"Okay," he finally said, "but for Christ's sake, don't do it again. You could be busted out of the program for that."

The flight's final training session was a cross-country flight to Dallas, where they would spend the night. It was their reward for making it through The Program. The flight instructor was a Marine captain who had friends there and he arranged a party for the flight. Near its end, the captain told Harry, who was the senior student in the flight, to round up the others. They would head back to the base because they had an early-morning departure. Harry looked everywhere, but Jack was nowhere to be found.

"Okay," said the captain, frowning. "He'll have to find his own way back to the base."

They had rented a convertible that they parked in the driveway leading to the house. Harry suspected that the captain had been turned down by one of the young ladies, as he seemed in a foul mood. As he backed out at high speed, there, on the lawn, was Jack, lying in a hammock, one arm around a beautiful girl, the other holding a can of beer and a cigarette. The captain screeched to a stop.

"Rooney," he thundered. "Get in. We're going back to the base."

Jack thought about that for a long moment, inhaled deeply from his cigarette, flicked it in an arc across the lawn, exhaled slowly and said, "I don't think so, Cap."

The tires screeched again as the captain stomped on the accelerator and rocketed down the driveway. The next morning, a taxi pulled up to the BOQ just as the pilots were leaving for the flightline to fly back to Corpus Christi. Out stepped Jack, scowling into the morning sun, face covered with lipstick and still, at eight in the morning, drunk. He went home as a passenger in one of the other airplanes which had an extra seat. There could have been hell to pay, but Jack had a knack for slipping out of tight places, and he somehow managed to wiggle out of this one, too.

34
LEMOORE

1964

After winning their wings, Harry and Jack had gone to the same Skyraider squadron at the Miramar Naval Air Station in San Diego. It was often said that a pilot's first squadron would be his best squadron. For Harry, that would turn out to be true. Every squadron pilot was a fine officer and an excellent aviator. The squadron would win many awards, both individual and collective, during the years Jack and Harry served there.

For a group to function well as a unit, there has to be not only strong individual performance, there has to be respect, understanding, and cooperation based on mutual goals. This squadron had that to spare and it had more: the bonds of friendship. These were most visible on Friday afternoons at the weekly happy hour held at the Officers' Club. All the pilots came for the first drink. Some, usually those with families, began leaving after one or two drinks. Others, like Harry and Jack, were still there when the bar closed. They were part of the "hard core," and it was not unusual for them to miss dinner on Friday night. Survival training, Jack called it.

These hours were indeed happy. Rolling dice determined who paid for the drinks. Along with the drinking, there was often singing and sometimes squadron chants aimed at rival squadrons. One of the pilots in Harry's squadron had a hard-to-pronounce Polish name that, after a few beers, came out as "Wazoola." That, somehow, became the squadron battle cry, and it often reverberated off the Officers' Club walls on Friday nights. It usually started when a pilot would jump up, rotate his arm with a forefinger extended, and start the cry with a low growl that quickly became a roar as the others joined in. "Wazoola!" became its signature whenever the squadron gathered in a bar or club.

Happy hours sometimes featured unusual drinks. One was a Flaming Hooker. This was a shot-glass full to the brim with whiskey with its surface fumes ignited. The whiskey had to be drunk down in one gulp, and the glass returned to the bartop with the flame still burning in the empty glass. It wasn't easy, especially after a few drinks, and facial burns sometimes resulted. Another drink was a Snifter. This was an upturned wine glass with its slightly-hollow base filled with vodka. It had to be ingested through one nostril, while the other nostril was held closed with a forefinger. The drinkers,

185

who were usually losers in dice games, seldom enjoyed these drinks, but the onlookers took great delight in them.

Harry and Jack separated when they left the squadron, but they kept in touch. A few years later, both were assigned to the same Skyhawk squadron in Lemoore, California. Before checking into the squadron, Harry had been invited to a house party. There, he saw Jack for the first time in several years. Their reunion was joyful and exuberant. Separations, even long ones, seem not to affect true friendships. Jack was obviously enamored of the lovely young lady at his side. After being introduced, she excused herself, saying, "Jack has told me all about you, and I know you two have a lot to talk about."

Jack seemed different somehow, not as boisterous, not as carefree. Harry realized that not only was Jack not drunk, he was not even drinking. Now that was a major change. When the moment was right, Harry mentioned his abstinence.

"Jack," he asked somewhat incredulously, "is this really you? What gives?"

Jack sipped his Coke. "Harry," he said seriously, "you're not going to believe this, but I've found religion."

Harry smiled in a way that said, "Sure, and the moon is made of green cheese."

"I'm serious," Jack said in a serious tone. "I'm in love, Harry, and it's the real thing. Seriously."

Then, Harry understood. A woman can change a man, Harry knew, even a man like Jack.

"Well, congratulations, old buddy. It looks like you've found a good one. I'm pleased to see you on the straight and narrow."

Jack smiled a happy smile. "Janet is a wonderful girl, and not only have I stopped drinking, I've started going to church. Can you believe it? Me, going to church?"

Jack became serious again. "Maybe you should think about it, Harry. I'd like to talk to you about this. It's changed my life."

Harry began to feel uneasy. Jack had not only stopped drinking; he had apparently started saving souls. Harry decided to head this one off at the pass.

"Jack, I'm happy for you, but just in case you're trying to save my soul, you can forget it. My soul does not need saving. And, even if it did, you would not be my first choice to save it."

Jack frowned ever so slightly. "Who said anything about saving your soul? But I might be able to help you find inner peace. Janet has taught me all about it and it's wonderful. I'm not the same Jack you knew. Let's talk."

"Sure," Harry replied. "And I do appreciate your concern. But, first, I need another drink."

Why, Harry wondered, were so many people trying to save his soul? Did he give off vibrations that said, "This Soul Needs Saving?" From tearing down screen doors to saving souls was a huge transition. How had all that happened? Never mind, he answered himself, I really don't want to know how it happened. There was one thing he did want to know, however; and he asked with a smile as he turned away. "Jack, do they still call you Shipwreck?"

Jack grinned and put a forefinger in front of his lips. "No, and you'd better not do it, either. Not in front of Janet, anyway. Those days are gone forever." A pause, then, "But they sure were fun while they lasted."

Did Harry detect a wistful note as he said it? Saving souls was a worthwhile mission in life, Harry supposed, for some, anyway. But was it fun? Somehow, he doubted it.

A few weeks later, Jack stopped at the Officers' Club for a beer at the weekly happy hour. Harry arrived late because he'd had to fly that afternoon. He heard Jack even before he entered the bar. It was the old Jack, very loud and very drunk and enjoying himself immensely. Harry smiled. Jack's romance, he learned, had ended, and, with it, his zeal for saving souls. Harry knew he should not feel good about that, but he just couldn't help it.

"Jack," he said after hearing the news, "should I offer my condolences?"

In answer, Jack put his arm around Harry's shoulder and led him to the bar. "Hell, no, he said happily "I'm celebrating, and now I want to buy you a beer for not trying to talk me out of all that nonsense."

Jack ordered two beers, handed one to Harry, clinked his bottle against Harry's and raised it in a toast.

"To the old Jack," he said with a grin. "He's back."

The base was at Lemoore, in the San Joaquin Valley, and no one had ever figured out why it was there. Brutally hot in the summer, it was, at times, too hot to get airborne with a fully-loaded airplane. The engine simply could not develop enough thrust. The winters were cold and, at times, the fog was so thick that a driver had to stick his head out of his car window to follow the dashes on the road's centerline. The number of dashes that could be seen ahead graded the density of the fog. Worst of all, from Harry's point of view, was that the social scene was dismal, so he spent many of his weekends in San Francisco, a city he came to love dearly, and in San Diego. At Lemoore, Harry and Jack picked up where they had left off, as though their years apart had never happened.

Now, hearing about Jack's latest adventure over North Vietnam, he became alarmed and decided to go to sickbay and talk to his good friend. I want to hear his version of all this, Harry thought, as he left the Ready Room and tried to remember how to get to sickbay.

35
MY NAME IS SHIRLEY

September 1970

Harry was sitting in the cockpit as Eric went through the pre-flight checklist. Everything was normal until he directed the first officer to "turn three." Then, Murphy's Law struck. The starter valve, which allowed compressed air from the mobile ground unit to turn the engine, refused to open. After several tries, Eric accepted Murphy's verdict and called the tower to cancel the start-up. This would need looking into, and a ground mechanic was called.

"Sorry, sir," he said after a quick check, "but you need to change the start valve and I'm not sure we have one on hand."

Harry began to sense a night in Singapore, after all. There was much discussion between Eric and the maintenance crew and, finally, Eric was told the airplane would have to remain overnight while a valve was brought from Kuala Lumpur. Bad luck for the sheep, thought Harry, but good luck for me. Astrid and the other girls were delighted.

The handling agent quickly arranged rooms at the Ming Court Hotel in the center of the city. Harry wondered how they would pay the hotel bill, then thought, Ah, the hell with it. We'll worry about that later.

Harry had felt exhausted after his long flight from Sydney, but a shower and the prospect of seeing Singapore by night, with Astrid at his side, left him fresh and ready for whatever the city might offer. He spoke with the concierge, explaining they had only one night, and asked how best to spend it.

"Ah," he said, "you must have dinner at Fatty's and then you must see the girls at Bugi Street."

"But I already have a girl," said Harry, gesturing towards Astrid at his side.

"Not like these," replied the concierge. "Go and see them. You will enjoy."

It did not take long to see that, in Singapore, everything worked. The taxis were cheap and plentiful. A man Harry had spoken with at the hotel told him that he had once called for a taxi and was told it would arrive in four-and-a-half minutes. Four-and-a-half minutes? Really? Yes, sir, he was told, the taxi is on its way. And, sure enough, four and a half minutes later, there it was. The traffic was orderly and the streets were clean. One reason, Harry had been told, was that gum chewing was illegal and the fine for littering the streets, even with a cigarette or a match, was large. Hard rules, but they worked and the streets of Singapore looked as though you could eat from them. Tropical foliage and beautiful flowers were everywhere. It was not for nothing that Singapore called itself The Garden City.

The word "restaurant" was too elegant to describe Fatty's. It was more like a sidewalk café that spilled over onto Albert Street in a local part of town. There were some tourists, but also many Singaporeans. These were mainly Chinese, Harry learned, but also Indians and Malaysians. Nice, thought Harry, that these very different ethic groups, with very different religions, could get along so well. Harry had long believed that a major disruptive force in the world was religion. If only people could learn not to press their own views on others, how much more peaceful the world would be; but the world did not seem to work that way. Faith, the belief in the unknowable, could not be instilled by force; yet many tried over many centuries, with horrific results. In Bombay, Harry had learned something about the Hindu religion, and this one seemed to make the most sense. The concept of reincarnation provided motivation to live honorably in this life so that you would come back at a higher level the next time around. This seemed to him far better than the reward of heaven and the punishment of hell promised by Christianity.

There was no menu at Fatty's, and no kitchen. The waiter, wearing shorts, a tee shirt, and sandals, recited the list of dishes. The food was prepared right there in front of them, and one astonishing sight was that of an old lady chopping vegetables with a large cleaver. Her strokes were almost a blur as she very rapidly brought down her cleaver just millimeters from the hand holding the vegetables. Wow, thought Harry, that is a precision operation. I just hope her thumb doesn't end up in our soup. Harry and Astrid watched with great interest as the food was cooked in woks over an open fire. A wok is a large semi-spherical pot that seemed to be a Chinese version of a frying pan. They ordered a large bottle of Anchor beer and that was perfect with the Chinese food. Unlike the surroundings, the food was exquisite, and Harry could not believe that such delicious food could come from such a basic beginning. Eating at Fatty's on a soft and pleasant evening was a dining adventure, and Harry and Astrid enjoyed it immensely.

Bugi Street was a short walk away, and it was their next stop. There, Harry and Astrid could not believe their eyes. Bugi Street was an intersection with metal tables and folding chairs strewn about. They found an empty table and sat down. From somewhere, Harry could not say where, a waiter appeared. "Waiter," was not exactly the right word. He was a shirtless lad of about ten in shorts and sandals. They ordered another bottle of Anchor beer and watched the show around them.

Bugi Sreet's claim to fame was the pack of transvestites that camped on it; but these were no ordinary transvestites. Most were stunningly beautiful, well-groomed, well-dressed and, thanks to hormones, well-endowed. Harry had never before seen so many great bosoms in one place. As a breast man, Harry was impressed, even though the breasts were not supposed to be where they were. Most of the women were very attractive, even though they were not women at all. They circulated among the tables and soon, one joined Harry and Astrid.

"Hello," he said in a raspy baritone, "my name is Shirley."

He knew, of course, that he would not be able to offer his body for rent at their table, but he was very pleasant, accepted a drink, and brought out some photos of "herself" and others. They all looked like movie stars and Harry bought a few. Like a movie star, Shirley signed his. The price was three-for-a-dollar, he said. Harry tested Shirley's negotiating skills by countering with two-for-a-dollar. Shirley automatically refused.

"No, no," he said firmly "the price is three-for-one-dollar. Ask anybody." Smiling, Harry turned over the dollar. "Listen better next time," he said as Shirley left, "and you might save a few photos." A mindset is hard to change, thought Harry.

Near the intersection, there was a squat, square building that served as a community toilet. Just as Harry and Astrid were finishing their beers, one of the British sailors from a boisterous group at a nearby table climbed onto the roof of the toilet. As they watched, the drunken man lowered his trousers and his underpants. Nude from the waist down, he rolled a newspaper into a cone and, to Harry's and Astrid's astonishment, shoved the small end into his ass and lit the other end with a match. As the cone flamed behind him, he stomped about as his friends below shouted what sounded like a tribal chant. Some sort of test of manhood for the British Navy, thought Harry, incredulously. Harry had done some wild things after a night of drinking, but nothing that could even approach this dance, or whatever it was, on top of the toilet.

Once, leaving a squadron party at an Officers' Club in San Diego, Harry had turned north onto the southbound lane of one of the busiest highways in California. Worse, he was unaware he had done so until the oncoming traffic, blinking lights and blowing horns, made him think dimly that something was amiss. Gino Farruggia, riding shotgun and as drunk as Harry, had finally realized the problem and said, "You know, I think we're on the wrong side of the road."

Harry could barely hear him over the blaring of the horns, but, yes, he agreed, something was not right. Without further thought, Harry had made a hard right turn, bounced over the median strip and onto the northbound lane, where he narrowly missed a collision on that side.

In those days, you never had enough, and he and Gino had continued to the home of a squadron-mate for a nightcap. Somehow they found the house and, after some difficulty in maneuvering the car into a tight space, Harry looked back to see that he had parked the car right in the middle of the street. Harry never again drove after drinking. That was an awful experience; but not as awful as dancing on the roof of a toilet with a flaming newspaper jammed up your ass. That had to be the epitome of something or other; Harry was not sure what. Bugi Street had certainly lived up to its reputation.

36
GOODBYE, SINGAPORE

The departure from Singapore the next morning was routine, and Murphy did not intervene. After the flight from Sydney, and a night on Albert Street, Harry had fallen asleep the moment his head touched the pillow. Astrid, who had for days been looking forward to making love with Harry, tried to wake him; but it was hopeless. Harry usually fell asleep easily and slept intensely. He did not need much sleep. He awoke around dawn and now it was his turn to wake Astrid.

Sleepy at first, she soon roused herself, especially when Harry kissed her ear as he whispered, "Astrid, good morning. This is your wake-up call."

"Already? she asked, her voice muffled with sleep. "Is it time for 'frukost?'"

Harry smiled into her ear. "Breakfast can wait. We have more important things to do. I hope you are ready."

She turned to him, stifled a tiny yawn, and grinned. "I told you in Hong Kong, Harry, I am always ready. Remember? What do you have in mind?"

"Try to guess," he said, as he drew her close and began caressing her back.

"Ah," she had murmured as she began to stir, "how I have missed you."

Now, at 35,000 feet on the way to Moscow, she turned to Harry, sitting beside her.

"Harry," she said with a serious tone, "I enjoyed our morning very much, especially waking up. I would like to wake up like that every morning. And last night! It was wonderful even if you did fall asleep so soon. I will always remember Singapore. It is a very special place. There is no place in Oslo like Fatty's. Do you remember what I told you there?"

Harry had been dozing with his head on Astrid's shoulder. Now, he sat up, rested his forearm there, and nodded. "I do," he answered, "how could I forget? And what about that sailor on the toilet?" he asked. "Can you see that in Oslo?"

She wrinkled her nose. "I have already forgotten that disgusting person. Now I am looking forward to a nice rest and some good Norwegian food. I would like to cook some for you."

Now wide awake, and with the scent and the nearness of Astrid, Harry's pulse began to quicken. As he looked at her, a shaft of sunlight caught her hair for a moment, almost like a frame around a picture. She never looked lovelier. As Harry thought about their morning together, and looked at her face outlined in the soft glow of the sun's rays, he was suddenly taken by an urgent need to hold her; to kiss her.

He quickly looked around. The sheep were awake, of course, but the off-duty crew was sleeping after a night exploring Singapore. The girl sitting next to Astrid had gone into the cockpit an hour ago, so her seat was empty. No one was watching, only the sheep.

Harry turned to Astrid. Looking at his face, she somehow sensed the meaning of the moment. Her eyes widened and her eyebrows rose, questioning.

"What are you.....Harry, this is not the proper place to....."

"Never mind about proper places," he whispered as he put his arm around her and gently pulled her towards him. "This place will do just fine."

Loving and tender at first, Harry's kiss quickly became ardent and -- as Astrid responded -- passionate. It seemed to last forever. When Harry finally drew back, she let out a deep sigh. "Oh, my goodness!" she breathed, her eyes still closed.

She opened her eyes, looked into his face, and slowly smiled. "This was a most wonderful kiss, Harry," she said with some emotion. "I felt it even down in my toes. I hope no one was watching."

Harry smiled affectionately. "Only the sheep," he said, "and they won't tell anyone."

37
SICK BAY

March 1966

Jack looked up from the Playboy magazine he was reading when Harry entered sick bay. There were thirty beds and, except for Jack's, only one other bed was in use, its occupant asleep. Jack smiled broadly when he saw Harry and let the magazine drop to his chest.

"Harry," he boomed, "how the hell are you? Nice of you to stop by, but where are the flowers?"

Harry chuckled, pleased to find Jack in good spirits. "I'm fine. And flowers are for funerals. I'll try to sneak a martini up here later, but how the hell are you? You're the one who's just been shot down."

"Yeah," Jack said. "Ain't that a kick in the ass? Still alive, though, for what that's worth. I don't recommend it, Harry. Try to avoid it if you can."

"Thanks a lot for the good advice. I'll try to remember it. So what's the skinny? I got part of the story from Paul. Sounds pretty hairy."

"Well, you know how it goes," he said. "There was no time to be scared, just to react. Is there any news about the XO?"

"No, nothing, but, for sure, he won't be back anytime soon. It doesn't look good. So, tell me, how does it feel to be a hero?"

"Hey, listen. It's no big deal to punch out of an airplane, especially if everything works, and it did. Thank Christ for Martin-Baker," he said, referring to the company that made the ejection seats.

Harry sat down in a chair next to Jack's bed and listened intently as he drew the details from Jack, one by one. Jack knew he had been hit badly, and he had to be uptight when Paul told him about the flames trailing his airplane and advised him to eject. No way, he had replied, not while this thing is still flying.

"Never jump out of an airplane that's still working, remember?" He was determined to make it to the sea, where the chance of rescue was high. He feared the airplane might explode, but it was a risk he had to take. He had already dropped his bombs, but there was all that fuel. The fuel cell had obviously been ruptured and the streaming fuel had been ignited and had become a plume of flame streaming behind him. It was several plane-lengths long, according to Paul. Still, better to take a chance, ride it as far as he could, and hope for the best. The situation looked grim, and Jack was ready to pull the curtain at any moment.

Miraculously, the fire went out as he crossed the coast and became "feet wet." Things were looking up and Jack's morale improved instantly. It was then that Paul had left Jack and headed back to try to locate the XO. Jack was still losing fuel, but, with the fire out, there was still a chance to land on the ship. His problem now was having enough fuel to reach her. A glance at his fuel gauge told him he was losing fuel rapidly. Better to head for the tanker, and then review the situation. If he had to eject over the sea, well, that would probably end up okay. The tanker, normally orbiting in the vicinity of the ship, headed for a quickly calculated rendezvous point, and gave Jack a vector and an altitude. Shit, thought Jack, this might work, after all. Luckily, the weather was clear and he spotted the tanker from a few miles away and began to maneuver into the refueling position behind it. Incredibly, his airplane was still flying normally, and Jack was able to plug in on his first try. He was almost flying on fumes by then, so it was with great relief that he saw the fuel gauge begin to increase slowly.

With Jack plugged in, the tanker turned gently and headed for the ship, still about 100 miles away. Jack was gaining fuel faster than he was losing it, but not by much. Better to stay connected to the tanker until he was near the ship. Once overhead, he eased back on the throttle, disconnected from the drogue, and tentatively began to check his airplane. He had to know if the airplane was controllable in the landing configuration. That meant with gear and flaps down and flying at normal approach airspeed; but the damned landing gear refused to come down. He recycled the lever several times but the gear seemed determined to stay up. Then, with the gear lever in the down position, Jack applied a sharp, positive "g" force, hoping to lower the gear that way. Still no luck.

Now, the handwriting was on the wall. There would be no way to avoid getting wet. Coordinating with the ship, Jack flew overhead at 10,000 feet, held his breath, reached up and, with a sharp tug, pulled the curtain down over his face. The next few seconds, Jack said, were just a blur and a roar. The canopy was blown away and a split second later, the seat fired out of the cockpit with Jack in it. He had ejected at a relatively low airspeed to lessen the force of the air stream as he exploded into it. A timing device inflated a bladder that separated Jack from the seat. As he was within the altitude envelope of the barometric actuator, his chute opened at almost the same time and jolted Jack hard into his harness.

"I really don't remember much at all about the ejection," Jack said. "It was only after the chute opened that I finally figured out I was okay. A lot was going through my mind, but, somehow, I did remember to get the life raft out from the pack as I came down. I almost forgot to unhook my chute straps, which might have ruined my whole day; but I remembered it at the last minute and let the chute go as I hit the water.

"I watched my airplane all the way down until it hit the water. I even saw the canopy falling away from me. I had a great view of the ship, and I spotted the chopper waiting to pick me up. Shit, I actually enjoyed it. The only hard part was that goddamn down-blast from the chopper. Man, that thing makes some breeze! And now they tell me I'm going to get a Purple Heart because somehow, in all that mess, I got a cut on my leg. Ain't that something? A Purple Heart for getting shot down?"

Harry did not say it, but he thought: that was pretty much in character for just about everything Jack did. Why should getting shot down be different? Harry later learned from the tanker pilot that once Jack had decided to eject, he had nonchalantly asked, "You guys got a camera? I'd like to get this on film." The tanker did not have a camera and Jack's ejection was lost to posterity. "You really ought to carry one," was his disappointed reply.

Harry had once witnessed a similar controlled ejection from an F8 Crusader. He had been out on the LSO platform, watching a recovery, when the pilot was unable to lower his landing gear. He, too, had ejected at 10,000 feet over the ship. After Harry saw the chute open, he looked at the airplane, now an unguided missile. The plane began a descending turn and, Harry could not believe his eyes, headed back towards the ship. *No, it just couldn't happen*, he thought. A few minutes later, the F8 hit the sea, less than half-a-mile from the ship. Jack, at least, had the good sense not to target the ship with his airplane after he left it.

Watching from the LSO platform as the airplanes came aboard fascinated Harry. He often went there just to observe and he never grew tired of it. One time, he was there when an F8 had been unable to lower its hook. While the aircraft orbited, the ship quickly raised its barricade. This was a large net-like mesh which was hung between two posts which had been raised to a vertical position from their stowed position on the flight deck The mesh was made of nylon strips and was connected to an arresting gear cable. The hook-less F8 landed normally and ran into the mesh, which collapsed around the plane and brought it to a stop, much like a routine landing. The airplane was almost undamaged.

Another day, Harry was on the platform when an F8 had landed in the wires; but instead of snaring one wire, the hook grabbed two. Because of a design flaw, the two wires caused the tail hook to snap, and an ordinary arrested landing instantly became a bolter. Following normal practice, the pilot had gone to full power as he touched down in case he missed all the wires; but the brief engagement of the two wires reduced his speed significantly. Thinking quickly, the pilot went into afterburner as he left the angled deck and slowly began to sink. Afterburner adds large quantities of fuel to the exhaust gases and this provides a great increase in thrust.

The plane dropped out of sight of the LSO platform and Harry held his breath, expecting to see an enormous splash. A few seconds passed and there was no splash. A few more seconds passed and the F8 slowly came into view, a few feet above the water. The exhaust from its engine was actually in the sea. Since the pilot could not lower his nose to gain speed, he could only wait and hope the engine, still at full thrust, would provide the few extra knots he needed to begin a climb. It seemed like forever, as the plane skimmed the wave-tops, before Harry saw it gain a few feet of altitude, then a few more, then saw the pilot lower his nose enough to accelerate and climb very slowly. The barricade was quickly put into place, and the pilot brought his airplane safely aboard.

The F8 Crusader was then on the leading edge of Naval aviation. It looked more like a missile than an airplane. Its fuselage was long and sleek, with a cockpit near its nose. It incorporated a unique feature: Its wing, made in one piece and resting on top of its fuselage, went up and down. Whether it was the wing or the fuselage that went up and down was the subject of many happy hour debates. The moveable wing enabled the supersonic airplane to fly at slower speeds to facilitate landing on the carrier; but those speeds were relatively high. The F8 needed an abnormally high wind across the deck to fly from a ship.

Its high approach speed, combined with a sensitive pitch control, made the Crusader tricky to bring aboard. These pilots had to be good. Although pilots of other airplanes would never admit it, they envied Crusader pilots. The difficulties of getting aboard, however, caused the F8 to have more than its share of go-arounds and bolters. In light of these problems, it was decreed that, for a time, the Crusaders would fly only in daylight and only under optimal wind conditions. That invited derision from other pilots. One day, Harry picked up the ship's daily newspaper and, among its genuine news items, he read this:

Johnstown PA 5 Feb 1959 (API) The U.S. Navy announced here today at its experimental research facility that work on its Wind and Sun Machine has been discontinued. The revolutionary device would have enabled the F8 Crusader to fly at night and in periods of little or no wind. "The cost of the Wind and Sun Machine was enormous," a spokesman said, "and it has been determined that it would be cheaper to lose the war."

The F8 pilots did not think it was funny. All the others thought it was hilarious.

The Anti-Crusader struck again a few days later when readers of the ship's newspaper found this amusing attack:

THE CRUSADER PILOT'S CREED

I am a United States Navy Crusader pilot. My life is dedicated to protecting the skies of America between sunrise and sunset. Nothing shall deter me from performing my duty except clouds, darkness, or lack of wind. My country has invested in me the faith of its people, by training me to fly faster while doing less than any other pilot in the world. I shall always do my utmost, provided the weather is clear, to ensure that this sacred trust has not been placed in vain. I shall never forget, nor allow anyone in my general area to forget, that:

* I can fly 1,000 miles per hour.
* I can carry a Sidewinder missile.
* My wing goes up and down.

I do hereby solemnly swear to observe faithfully the ensuing code of professional ethics:

1. Whenever Naval Aviators congregate in drinking establishments, I shall conduct myself in a loud and obnoxious manner, especially if less fortunate, low-performance pilots are present.

2. While deployed (and not yet off-loaded), I shall strive to maintain the long-cherished tradition of daylight fighter pilots by attending every nightly movie, regardless of whether I can follow the plot.

3. I shall not permit interruptions of occasional flights to prevent me from maintaining my proficiency in Acey Deucy at fighter pilot standards.

4. I shall never go ashore without my F8 lapel pin and my F8 baseball cap.

5. I will not bolter.

6. If I should bolter, I will have readily available an assorted variety of colorful excuses.

7. I will wear my space suit and helmet for all airshows, Dependents' Day cruises, and those operational flights which do not require any movement in the cockpit (providing someone helps me in and out of the airplane.)

This is my creed and these are my ideals. With the help of God and my afterburner, I shall do my best to justify the confidence that has been placed in me, even if I have to fly during lunch time.

This time, even the Crusader pilots chuckled at this parody of their limitations. In later years, its problems overcome, the Crusader became a classic fighter plane and the heart of carrier air defenses. It served for many years with distinction, and its pilots were regarded with admiration by other Naval aviators.

One interesting aspect of viewing landings from the platform was the problem of a pitching deck. Normally, such a large ship was not affected by the sea state, and the flight deck remained level; but when the sea became heavy, the deck began to move up and down. The optical landing system used by the pilot for glide path guidance was gyro- stabilized up to a point; but with more than eight degrees of deck pitch, the system began to move with the ship and the pilot had to average out the movement of the meatball as it moved above and below the green reference lights. This complicated the approach problem and it got worse as the sea state became heavier. The landing itself was affected because an airplane did not want to touch down as the deck was coming up. Harry had once seen a hard landing onto a rising deck. The landing gear had punched right through the wings.

To overcome the problem of a pitching deck, an LSO devised a "mechanical meatball." By moving a lever manually, he could position the meatball where he thought it should be, giving the pilot what appeared to be a normal view of his position on the glide path. This simple device was a great help in heavy seas.

The Landing Signal Officer, looking aft from near the ship's stern, could not easily tell what the deck was doing because he saw only a short section of the ship's length. As a result, in heavy seas, an enlisted man was posted in the catwalk just aft of the LSO and looking forward. His only job was to tell the LSO what the deck was doing so that a landing airplane would not land into a rising deck. He did this with a running commentary that went like this: "The deck is coming up; the deck is coming up; the deck is coming up. The deck has stopped coming up. The deck is coming down; the deck is coming down." Of course, he was looking at the bow, so he saw most of the flight deck. The LSO had to reverse the "up" and the "down" because the landing area was aft and it went up as the bow went down. Any airplane about to touch down into a rising deck was sent around to try again. This was a primitive, but effective, technique.

Once, somewhere in the South China Sea, Harry had landed his Skyraider on a ship caught in a typhoon. The sea was so heavy that the forward part of the flight deck, some eighty feet above the water, was actually digging into the sea. That had been a memorable landing. An old-timer Navy pilot once told Harry that boats and airplanes were basically incompatible, and he probably had that right.

Somewhere in the middle of Jack's description of his ejection, the sick bay's only other patient had awakened. He appeared to be an old-timer, and Harry could see him listening with great interest. He was part of the ship's company, and he had a few interesting experiences to add to the conversation. He had flown carrier airplanes in World War II. There were still a few pilots around from those days and, every now and then, Harry ran into one. They always had fascinating stories to tell.

This one had just joined the Navy when Pearl Harbor was attacked, and the need for Navy pilots rose sharply; but there was no time for proper training. They were needed right then. He had completed his primary training in Pensacola in an SNJ, the same airplane Harry would fly years later for his first carrier landings. He and his fellow trainees were shipped immediately to Pearl Harbor. There, they were quickly trained in operational airplanes and field-qualified for carrier landings at Ford Island's small airfield. They were then sent to a ship in the far reaches of the Pacific. They island-hopped to get there. When they finally found their ship, none of them had ever before seen an aircraft carrier. Of the fourteen airplanes in his group, he said, only nine made it aboard. The others, after numerous tries at landing, finally ditched into the sea and were picked up unharmed.

His very first flight from a carrier, he told them, had been a pre-dawn launch on a combat mission. He joined his flight as it headed for its target, an island, the name of which he could not recall. When the sun came up, he realized he was in the wrong flight, one with a different mission. Well, hell, he thought, now that I'm here I might as well do what I can. Armed only with 20mm guns, he joined in the bombing pattern and managed to destroy a Japanese airplane parked on the ramp.

Later, based at an airfield on one of those islands, he had seen an F4U Corsair land with its wheels up. The plane skidded down the runway, then flipped onto its back and came to a stop off to the side of the runway. As the crash truck approached the plane, its crew saw a curious sight. The wheels of the airplane were slowly coming down. Or up, in this case, as the airplane was inverted. In the cockpit, the pilot was furiously turning the crank that lowered the wheels. He was, of course, trying to hide the fact that he had neglected to lower the wheels before landing. It did not sell. You are supposed to lower the wheels before you land, not afterwards, he was told.

Later that night, Harry sneaked into sick bay not one martini, but three. There were more great memories from the old-timer, and the martinis made them even more fascinating than they might have seemed without the gin.

He had also flown in Korea and related this interesting conversation overheard while airborne there. It was between two British pilots, one in a helicopter and the other overhead in an airplane. The helicopter had made two attempts to rescue a downed British pilot, but had been driven off both times by ground fire. Finally, he gave up.

"I just can't get in there," he said.

"Why not?" asked the second voice.

"Because if I try again, I will for sure be killed."

There was a pause.

"Well," said the second voice, now with a hard edge, "get it one way or the other. Isn't it better to get it from the other side whilst doing your duty?"

Somewhere along the way Harry had met, in a bar in some far-off place he could not remember, another WWII old-timer, this one from the Army Air Force, as it was then known. After a few drinks, Harry listened in rapt attention to one exciting war story after another about the war in Europe. The one that stuck in his memory was of a flight over Germany in a B24 bomber. The aircraft had been struck by anti-aircraft fire after releasing its load of bombs. Both engines on the starboard side had been hit and neither could develop full power. The aircraft began to lose altitude, and it soon became obvious that, while the plane might reach the English Channel, there was no way it could climb over the cliffs on the other side. The sea was calm that day and the pilot decided to ditch in the channel. A water landing was hazardous, but safer than a collision with a cliff.

When an aircraft descends near the sea or land, it creates a phenomenon known as ground effect. The air beneath the wings cannot be forced downward as at higher levels, and instead creates lift from the layer of air compressed between the wings and the earth's surface. Ground effect came to the rescue, and the plane was able to maintain level flight just a few feet above the water. The pilot called ahead, asking for boats to stand by as the aircraft landed in the sea. Scanning the aircraft manual, he carefully briefed the crew about leaving the airplane after it came to a stop, but before it began to sink. He cautioned them that the plane could sink quickly and haste was essential. He made a textbook landing, smoother than some of his landings on a runway, he said.

The entire crew left the airplane safely, clambered onto the wing, and stepped into one of the waiting boats. "Would you goddamn believe it?" he said. "No one even got wet."

Harry thought that was the end of the tale, but there was more. As the boat headed for England, the pilot looked back and was surprised to see his airplane still afloat. "Goddamn," he said then. "Look at that."

The skipper of the boat looked back and asked, "Look at what?"

"The goddamn airplane," the astonished pilot said. "It's still floating."

The boat skipper squinted, and replied, "Oh, it will be there like that for quite some time."

"You don't understand," said the pilot. "According to the manual, the airplane should sink in less than three minutes."

"Maybe," came the answer, "but the water is only three feet deep here."

It was probably the martinis, but the two listeners in sickbay roared with laughter as Harry finished the story.

The old-timer had told Harry that some 18,000 B24 Liberator bombers were built during the war and about one-third were shot down over Europe. A few made it back to England, but most were lost. Each aircraft carried a crew of ten. "Do the math," he'd said.

The old-timer told them he had once had a conversation with an even older old-timer, one who had flown one of those B24s. That pilot, old and frail, but still with a twinkle in his eye, asked about the pilot-cooling machines now in use.

"You mean air-conditioning?" he asked.

"No, I mean pilot-cooling machines," he had replied. "That's what we called propellers. It was amazing how a pilot began to sweat when one of them stopped turning."

38
PULLING THE CURTAIN

The ejection seat that saved Jack's life had saved the lives of hundreds of Navy pilots. Before its advent, getting out of a disabled aircraft was difficult and cumbersome. In the Skyraider, for example, the pilot had to open the canopy manually. He then had to somehow climb on his seat and throw himself over the side while attached to an awkward parachute pack dangling beneath his backside. Once free of the cockpit, he had to hope the horizontal stabilizer did not strike him as it went by. And he had better not forget to open his parachute on his way down! The ejection seat had done away with all that.

An ingenious device, it followed a sequence of events and it could be activated by either of two handles. The first was over, and behind, the pilot's helmet. This was a rectangular loop that was pulled down in front of the pilot's face. This movement brought a small fabric over the pilot's face to protect it from the jet stream when the pilot left the aircraft. This was known as "pulling the curtain," and was used by carrier pilots in various social situations. It meant "Let's get the hell out of here!"

The second activation handle was a similar loop between the pilot's legs. It was placed there in case the pilot was unable to raise his arms to the primary loop. That might happen if the aircraft's flight path was such that it created high gravity-type forces that pinned the pilot's body to the seat. That might be compared to the way a rapidly-rising elevator compresses the body of its passengers as it starts its ascent.

These forces might prevent the pilot from raising his arms to the primary loop. They are the result of sudden and sustained aircraft directional changes. They might be likened to the tension felt by a by a rope when it is rotated in a circular pattern with a weight at its end. The faster the weight is rotated, the more force it will feel. These forces are measured in units of gravity known as "g." Resting in a chair, a man's weight is determined by the mutual attraction of the mass of his body and the mass of the earth. In a way, this attraction is what keeps us from flying off the earth. We are stuck here by gravity. In terms of physics, we weigh one "g." In an aircraft, gravity forces resulting from directional changes might be six or seven times the force of gravity. Under such conditions, raising an arm against this force would be impossible.

In a normal ejection sequence, the seat is powered away from the aircraft by a rocket that is triggered a split second after the canopy is blown off. In earlier days, the propulsion was from a 20mm cannon shell, and all the power was imparted to the seat instantaneously. That sometimes caused a pilot's backbone to compress. Harry had once served with a pilot who had ejected three times with earlier seats and he claimed to have lost an inch-and-a-half in height. Harry could easily believe it. Now, with a rocket, the acceleration was spread over a longer time.

The new seat was known as a "zero-zero" seat. That meant that even with the airplane motionless on the ground, the rocket powered the pilot high enough for the chute to open before he hit the ground. Any speed and altitude were gravy. Once, a pilot in Harry's Air Wing had an emergency that forced him to eject while still on the flight deck. The seat worked fine, but bad luck had placed the "cherry picker," a mobile heavy crane, directly in his trajectory. He died from a broken neck.

Once the seat, pilot still attached, is clear of the airplane, a timer separates the pilot from the seat by inflating a bladder. Now, if the pilot is below 14,000 feet, an aerobic device opens the chute to complete the sequence. If the pilot is above that altitude, he will free-fall until he gets there. A tiny bottle provides oxygen during the fall. From high altitudes, that can last several minutes. The earlier chutes were set to open at 10,000 feet, which cleared almost all the terrain in the U.S. Almost. No one had thought about the Sierra Nevada Mountains that reach well above that level.

A pilot from Harry's base in Lemoore, California, had once ejected over these mountains with a 10,000-foot chute. He landed in a deep snow bank, chute unopened, about 11,000 feet up. He suffered a broken back, but survived. As he and his chute were being hauled back to the base, the chute opened as programmed when the vehicle passed 10,000 feet. So, it was back to the drawing board.

That canopy-releasing T handle also needed some redesign when a pilot Harry knew mistook it for a similar handle that deployed a Ram Air Turbine into the jet stream for emergency electrical power. He had just entered the landing pattern when he remembered that he had not checked the RAT. Because the system had been miss-rigged during a maintenance check, he inadvertently fired the ejection sequence. As the squadron Safety Officer was driving home that afternoon, he was astonished to see a Skyhawk crash a few hundred yards from the road.

Stopping and looking up, he saw a parachute, its pilot dangling beneath, about to land nearby. He ran to the scene.

"What happened?" he asked excitedly as the pilot touched down.

"Damned if I know," was the reply. "I looked around, and all of a sudden, my airplane was gone."

Harry had later spoken with this pilot. After he unhooked himself from the chute, he had looked up to see his pilot-less airplane heading straight for the airfield control tower. It soon veered away but, for a few heart-stopping moments, it had that tower in its crosshairs. Naval aviation can be full of surprises; "all of a sudden, my airplane was gone," was a big one.

39
FORNABU

October 1970

It was mid-morning when Harry walked into what passed for a Head Office at Fornabu Airport, outside of Oslo. The flight from Singapore had been a pleasant one, thanks mainly to Astrid. The plane had stopped in Moscow just long enough to off-load the sheep. As far as Harry could see, they all survived the trip, if not in good spirits, at least in good condition. One of the girls praised the sheep as ideal passengers. They never rang the call button, never asked for a drink, and never complained about anything. Perfect, she said.

The people who serviced the airplane in Moscow looked just as Harry expected them to look -- like peasants and cleaning women. They spoke almost no English, but they were pleasant and helpful. Everything looked old and tired. Harry had tried to buy a bottle of vodka, but finally gave up after meeting some inflexible bureaucracy in the liquor shop. He had heard that nothing worked in Russia, and now he could see why. On arrival, the airport air traffic control had been awful, and Eric had needed to make a sudden, evasive turn to avoid another airplane. How could these people ever hope to make it to the moon, Harry wondered. Compared to the Moscow airport, Oslo looked modern and marvelous.

The office was bare bones. Nothing hung on any wall, and the room looked to be an old military barracks. Bare bones, thought Harry as he walked in, was a good description of the entire Trans Polar operation; but it was certainly interesting, even though he was spending more than he was earning. That was partly because he had been paying some of the company's bills along the way. In Singapore, he had used his own credit card to pay for the rooms of the crew. That was why he was here now. He wanted his money back. As he said good morning to Thor's secretary, he heard Thor call out from his office, "Is that Captain Harry out there? Come in please, Captain Harry."

Harry went in, sat down, and accepted a cup of coffee.

"So, how was it, the flight? All the sheep, did they arrive safely in Moscow? All were alive?"

Harry sipped his coffee and said, "Yes, as far as I could see, all of the sheep made it, but I don't think they enjoyed the flight. And that airplane will never smell the same again."

Thor chuckled. "Never mind," he said, "Those sheep paid a lot of money for their trip, so some little smell is not so bad."

Harry saw an opening. "Speaking of money," he began …. "

"Who is speaking of money?" Thor interrupted when he saw what was coming.

"You were. Just now. I'm running low. I paid for the rooms in Singapore with my credit card and here's the receipt. Also, is there some possibility of getting my salary one of these days? It's late and I need it."

Thor frowned. "Always money," he said. "I thought pilots worked because they like to fly. No? Okay, now you will be repaid for the hotel bill, but the salary will have to wait a bit. Can you manage? I have a nice job for you now."

Harry was almost afraid to ask. "What is it this time, a load of pigs to Timbuktu?"

Thor smiled. "No. Not pigs. People. Some Belgians want to go to Rio de Janeiro and you will do the flight. It's from Brussels in a few days. It's a charter for a new company just starting up -- Trans European Airways, I think. Their airplane is not yet ready, so they will hire ours, and the cockpit crew, too. They will provide the cabin crew. All very pretty Belgian girls, I am told. How does this sound to you, Captain Harry?"

Harry tried not to sound eager, but it sounded great. Brussels, Rio de Janeiro, and pretty Belgian girls! It sounded like a wonderful package. He had been thinking about telling Thor that he would not fly again until he was paid his salary, already several months late; but Brussels, Rio, and those pretty Belgian girls were too enticing to even think about passing up. He did not want Thor to give the flight to Eric, so, almost without thinking, he said "Okay, Thor, as a personal favor to you, I'll do the flight and get paid later -- but not too much later, I hope."

Thor leaned back in his chair and beamed. "Captain Harry," he said, with a broad smile, "you are first on the list."

Harry was in Oslo for just a few days and he had seen Astrid only once. Busy, she said, seeing family and friends. Harry wondered if one of those friends was her former fiancé. They'd had dinner together and it was a pleasant evening; but somehow it was not quite the same as eating at Fatty's in Singapore. A change of scenery could do that, Harry knew, and he did not think much about it. He would be back from Brussels in a week or two and then, he was sure, their relationship would be back on track, even without Fatty's.

40
BRUSSELS

October 1970

The Metropole Hotel overlooked the Place de Brouckere in the heart of Brussels. It was an Old World hotel, and that suited Harry just fine. He much preferred them to the modern glass and chrome hotels that seemed to be everywhere these days. Its wood-panelled bar, just off the lobby, was one of the best Harry had ever seen. He, Rolf, and Gene had ferried the empty airplane to Zaventem airport on the edge of Brussels, checked into the hotel in late afternoon, and were now ready to explore Brussels. The flight to Rio was set for a late morning departure the next day. The Chief Pilot, who had met them on the aircraft after they had parked, had given Harry a packet of information about the flight. Also on the flight would be a navigator whom Harry would meet the next day. He was a very special kind of navigator, the Chief Pilot said. He would tell them more in the morning; but that was tomorrow. Right now, Brussels awaited.

For Harry, it was always a special thrill to see a city for the first time. He had taken a walk after checking into his room, and he found the city center to be an interesting and vital place. He had stopped at a bar for a beer and learned that there were hundreds of different beers in Belgium, each with its own special glass. Each beer was served only in that glass. Belgium was a nation of beer drinkers and one of the world's leaders in per capita consumption. He was surprised to learn that the Belgians outdrank even the Germans. He had asked for something special, and the lady behind the bar had poured a Kriek beer, which, she said, was made from cherries. They would never believe that in Milwaukee, thought Harry, as he drank his beer. Different, but delicious, he decided.

He would learn much about Belgium over the next week or two. It seemed to be two countries squeezed into one. The Flemish Belgians lived in the north. They spoke Dutch with a different accent. The Walloons lived in the south. They spoke French. Their cultures were very different and there were serious differences between them. The street signs, Harry noticed, were in both languages, so at least they had gotten together about that -- but not about much else, he was told. Brussels was in the center of the country.

Both Flemish and French were spoken there, but the influence seemed to be mainly French.

The trio met at the hotel reception to have dinner and to see those parts of Brussels that were near the hotel. After questioning the concierge, they were directed to the Grand Place, which was within walking distance of the hotel. They came there about dusk, and it was impressive. It was a large square with a surface of cobblestone surrounded by very old, very elegant buildings. The faces of most of the buildings were decorated in gold leaf and were illuminated. The Grand Place was aptly named, thought Harry, and it was breathtaking. They would never believe this in Milwaukee, either.

They strolled about the square and, following the suggestion of the concierge, they went a few steps up one of the streets leading out of the square and viewed the Manneken Pis.

"It's world-famous," the concierge had said, "you must see it."

Despite its fame, none of them had ever heard of it. Hell, Harry had barely heard of Belgium! The manneken was a small statue in a niche about shoulder-high. It depicted a small boy urinating.

"Okay, we've seen it," said Gene after a few seconds. "Let's have a beer."

Harry made a mental note to find out why the statue was famous. And why was that boy peeing?

What he learned the next day from one of the hostesses was that the statue of the boy was commissioned by the boy's father after his son had been lost, then found, while taking a pee. The father wanted that moment preserved. True story, she said, but Harry had his doubts. True or not, it made a nice tale. She also told Harry that the statue had many changes of clothes, some for the seasons and others for various holidays. In later years, he would see replicas of this little statue in many places, some as far from Belgium as Singapore and Bangkok

They stopped at one of the terraces for a drink. Not bad for a guy from Milwaukee, he thought, as he looked around the square, enjoying a very special moment. Sipping a beer, Harry noticed that the façade across the square had a tower in middle, but that the door that served the tower was not centered. That was odd, he thought. Such a magnificent building with such an obvious mistake. Or was it a mistake? Indeed it was, said their waiter, and the architect had killed himself because of it. Well, thought Harry, the mistake was not *that* big, but some took their work seriously.

The area surrounding the Grand Place was the restaurant quarter, and there were dozens nestled among its narrow streets. It was hard to choose because they all looked inviting. They were standing before several of them, trying to decide where to have dinner, when a man came out of one, saw their indecision and asked, in a strong New York accent, "Looking for a good restaurant?"

When they nodded, the man, obviously pleased, said, "You have just got to eat here in this one. Fabulous! Trust me."

He gestured towards the La Cotelette, facing them. Unable to contain his enthusiasm, he had to tell someone about the great meal he had just enjoyed. Harry was reluctant to trust those who said, "trust me," especially one with a New York accent; but he had rarely seen a New Yorker so enthusiastic.

"Okay, sold!" he said. "Where can we find you if we don't like it?"

The New Yorker smiled. "You won't need to find me. This place is guaranteed good, personally, by me."

It was a family restaurant, small and charming. The New Yorker was right. The food, the service, and the ambience were first-class. And the wine! A carafe of ordinary house wine was perfect. Of course, Harry had long believed that taste was somehow connected to mood. When the mood was right, things tasted better. Beer, for example, never tasted so good as it did after a round of golf; so it was now with the wine. The surroundings made the wine taste better. Food, Harry would learn, was near the top of the list for Belgians. He liked Belgium already. World-class beer drinkers and fine food. Two of the basic ingredients of life, thought Harry, and who could ask for more?

41
FALLEN FRIENDS

To Navy pilots, losing friends and squadron-mates became a way of life. The first time Harry had seen a fatal crash was as a control tower observer at Barin Field. Students were sometimes given such duties to fill in the empty hours when they were not scheduled to fly. Several SNJs were in the landing pattern, practicing carrier landings. Both traffic controllers were focused on the airplanes landing and taking off. Harry had turned away from the field to watch the airplanes in their downwind legs. As he did, he saw two airplanes approaching the turn-in point abeam the end of the runway. The altitude in the pattern was 125 feet and the lead airplane looked right. Then, Harry went instantly from boredom to shock as the second airplane closed the gap between the planes, climbed slightly, and flew into the belly of the first one. Harry, for a split second unable to cry out, raised his arm and pointed to the collision. As he found his voice, the planes flipped in opposite directions and crashed into the ground just outside the airfield. Both students were killed.

Since then, many pilots whom Harry had known had been killed in flying accidents. Of course, every pilot figured it could not happen to him. That feeling of invincibility was common among pilots and, Harry believed, that was a necessary trait -- but only up to a point; it could lead to risk-taking and that sometimes led to disaster. Disasters, most pilots believed, happened only to others, not to them.

Two bizarre accidents occurred in Harry's first squadron. The first was when the pilot who lived next to Harry on the ship was killed while coming aboard in an aircraft with side number 506. Both the pilot and the airplane were replaced. The new airplane was given the same number, and the new pilot was berthed with the same roommate. The second accident was one week later, when the new roommate, flying the new 506, crashed at sea and was never found. Somehow or other, Navy pilots got used to stories like this one.

Harry often thought about Gino Farrugia. After watching his close friend disappear in a fireball, Harry had been assigned to escort his body, or what was left of it, to his hometown, Fresno. It was a depressing task, a night journey on a train. Harry had been assigned a sleeping berth, but there was no way he could sleep; so he made his way to the club car. There, well into his third Scotch, he fell into conversation with a fellow traveler.

He was on his way to Reno, he told Harry, to earn a living. He was, he said, a professional gambler. He was not only a professional gambler, but a famous one.

"Ever seen 'Gilda?'" he asked. Of course, everyone had seen this popular movie.

"Yes, I have," replied Harry. "Rita Hayworth and Glenn Ford; but wasn't that in Argentina? That's a long way from Reno." This was beginning to sound like a barroom fable.

"Remember the name of Glenn Ford? In the movie?"

Harry, a movie buff, did remember. "Sure. Johnny Farrell. Don't tell me you know him."

"I know him very well," he said. "I'm him, and I was an advisor on the movie."

Harry looked into his eyes and believed him. Why would anyone invent a story like that one?

Except for the hours the casket was in the baggage car, Harry had to be with it. He was with it during the church service, the short trip to the cemetery and when it was lowered into the ground. When the first shovelful of dirt hit the casket, the honor guard fired a salute, and then a bugler sounded the time-honored notes for the dead: "Taps." When the first clear note rang out, the entire crowd let loose a cry of grief that went straight through Harry's heart and that he would carry with him forever. This was the first time, but not the last, that he would take the body of a shipmate to its final resting place.

Norm Levy was an unlikely Naval aviator. Short, plump and Jewish, he was far from the Hollywood version of a Navy pilot. Religiously, he was as Jewish as Harry was Catholic. Maybe that was why Harry liked him. They had quickly become fast friends, then like brothers. When Vietnam broke out, Norm was flying F8 Crusaders from the Oriskany, a ship Harry had once called home. A week or so before his ship was to head for the Tonkin Gulf, Norm's airplane had a complete hydraulic failure in the "groove" off San Diego. The groove is that last piece of straight-ahead flying as the airplane approached the ship's ramp, seconds before touchdown. His only option was to eject. He was picked up by the ship's chopper uninjured and was pronounced fit for the trip to the Gulf.

There, after surviving six months of combat flying, and in the last weeks of his cruise, he was shot down over North Vietnam. He managed to reach the sea, where he ejected. Again, he was picked up, this time by a rescue helo, and brought back to his ship. Surely, he must have thought, the Gods of Naval Aviation are with me.

A few days later, Norm was sleeping in his bunk forward of the hangar deck and on the same level. Because so much ordnance was being dropped in those days, it was stacked everywhere on the ship, including places where it was not supposed to be. One of those places was an ordinary storage area just aft of Norm's stateroom. While Norm slept nearby, a sailor was moving parachute flares from that storage space to the forward elevator for further transport to the flight deck. He accidentally triggered a flare he was carrying. He could have run to the nearby elevator, which was down at the hangar deck level, and pitched the flare into the sea; but he didn't. He heaved it back into the storage area where all the other flares were stacked, then closed the hatch that led into the space.

Flares are made mainly of magnesium. They burn with a fierce intensity. All the flares in the storeroom torched off with such searing heat that they burned straight through five steel decks. In so doing, they sucked up all the air in the vicinity, including that in Norm's stateroom. He suffocated in his bunk.

At the request of his parents, Harry had been given the duty of meeting Norm's body in San Francisco, and escorting it to San Diego, chosen by his parents for interment. Norm was an only child and Harry knew his mother and father well. That made the service especially heartbreaking. He could still hear Norm's mother's anguished cry of, "Goodbye, Norman," as the earth hit his coffin.

A few weeks after the funeral, a letter which Harry had sent to Norm was sent back to him. "Return to Sender. Recipient Deceased" was stamped on the envelope. A few months after that, Harry ran into Norm's roommate from the Oriskany. Incredibly, Harry learned that Norm had died in the very same bunk that Harry had slept in when he was based on that ship.

Another memory burned forever into his mind was that of a memorial service on a hangar deck a few days after one of Harry's squadron-mates was lost at sea. Harry was flying that night and they were doing practice landings. The weather was awful, and Harry learned later that his CO had tried to get the session canceled. They launched and it was somewhat frightful for Harry as he was new at the game of night carrier landings. As he took off after his second landing, he was directed by the ship to join with his flight leader.

A rendezvous at night is difficult, at best. But that night, with low ceilings, mist, and intermittent showers, it approached one of those occasional moments of stark terror that pilots sometimes talk about. After some confusion, Harry found his flight leader and began to join. This was done visually, looking out of the cockpit, straining to stay in the correct relative position -- or what he thought was the correct relative position. As he did, he noticed that he was taking off more and more power to stay in the cone. Some sixth sense told him that something was wrong, very wrong. Glancing quickly into the cockpit, he discovered he was passing through 100 feet of altitude. To hell with this join-up, he thought quickly, I'm getting out of here. As he added power and began to climb, he was terrified to see that he had been trying to rendezvous on the masthead light of a ship.

Lights at night can be deceptive. Once, his student pilot class had been put into a windowless room, all lights were turned off, then one single light appeared on the opposite wall. Each student was asked to describe the direction of the light's movement. All gave an answer, each different from the others. None realized that the light was not moving at all. Night does strange tricks to visual perception. Harry had almost become a victim of one of those tricks.

Harry and the other pilots who were airborne eventually managed to join on the leader and headed to a nearby Naval air station, where they spent the night. The next day, they returned to the ship and spent an entire day searching for the lost pilot. He had disappeared after what appeared to be a routine launch. He was never found.

The chilling moment Harry would never forget happened during the eulogy. It was a humid, hot day, even more so on the hangar deck, where the ceremony was held. One of the marines in the honor guard suddenly fainted and pitched face forward onto the deck. His rifle made a nerve-shattering clatter as it hit the deck next to the fallen marine. None of the other marines in the honor guard even flinched, never mind tending to their prostrate comrade. He lay there, unmoving, through the rest of the service. Harry admired and respected marines, but not that day.

42
AFTERMATH

March 1966

Now, Harry was involved in the aftermath of the XO's shoot-down. Alive or dead, no one knew, but matters had to be attended to, and Harry had volunteered to help.

The XO's stateroom was on the second deck. That was one deck below the hangar deck, which was the Main Deck. Going up from there, the decks became 01, 02, -- until the uppermost part of the island superstructure was reached; that was the 09 level. Although the flight deck was officially the 04 level, it was always called the flight deck, just as the hangar deck was always called the hangar deck, and not a numbered deck. The flight deck had a nickname: The Roof. Many of the squadron's officers, including Harry, lived in the XO's vicinity. The junior officers shared a large compartment on the 03 level known as the JO bunkroom. There might be six pilots sharing one berthing space. The skipper and the XO each had rooms of their own, while the other officers were berthed in two-man rooms.

Two days had passed since the XO went down, and there was no longer any hope that he might be rescued. It would be a long time before he came back, thought Harry, and maybe never. That was a dreary thought. Harry and Jack Rooney were in the XO's stateroom to inventory his belongings and to prepare suitable items for shipment home. It was a depressing task. There, but for the grace of God, go I, was never more relevant than when flying on Yankee Station. A zig instead of a zag might mean a pilot's demise. Whether he was on any given flight was out of his control and in the hands of the junior officer assigned to make up the daily flight schedule. That, too, could determine his fate. It was, of course, approved by others; but that was usually a formality.

Jack had brought along a bottle of Ballentine Scotch, but Harry was not sure whether that helped to dispel the gloom. Jack drank Ballentine's because its square bottle fit so neatly into a corner of his safe. They talked of many things, but it always came back to the war. Harry was already beginning to have serious doubts about the way the war was conducted, and whether he wanted to be a part of it.

"Hell," he said, as he shuffled through some papers and magazines, "the way they're making us do this thing, it could go on forever. For sure, they're not trying very hard to win it."

Harry had often wondered who "they" were. There had to be some real people running this operation, but it was hard to put faces on them. The Big Picture. That was another term that made Harry wonder. Why did "they" have it, and he did not? Set free to do their best, Harry figured the USS Kitty Hawk, all by herself, could neutralize North Vietnam in just thirty days. Why won't they let us do it?

"Look at this way," said Jack, as he went through the XO's drawer, the large one beneath the bunk. "It all counts on twenty, so what does it matter how you do it?"

That was an old bromide that was heard in many discussions. It worked for Jack, who loved to fly and did not care about anything else. He was one of those few who actually enjoyed this war. He sometimes volunteered for extra missions because, for him, there could be no flying as exciting as this flying. Harry, on the other hand, always did his fair share of the hard flights, but did not ask for more. Enthusiasm for one's work was admirable; but in this profession, it sometimes led to recklessness, just for the thrill.

Harry had heard that Jack sometimes bent the rules of engagement. One of those rules, for example, prohibited firing within the stone walls surrounding a village, even when the village was shooting at our airplanes. The North Vietnamese had quickly learned this rule and often placed firepower within village walls.

"Screw the rules," Jack often said. "What's fair for them is fair for me."

"What about the children and civilians in there?" Harry had asked.

"They are the enemy," said Jack, in his typically straight-ahead thinking. There was never a detour in Jack's mind and, in some ways, Harry envied that.

They were about half way through the Ballentine by now and Harry's mood began to lighten.

"Well, damn," he said, "I just hope you're not going through my room one of these days."

"Breaks of the game," answered Jack without looking up from the box he was filling. "Any special instructions?"

"Yeah," said Harry. "Be sure to give my Beefeaters to someone who appreciates a good martini. And that's for sure not you."

"Hey, no big deal. I don't know how you can drink that stuff anyway. Tastes like jet fuel to me. I drink it only when there's nothing else around."

"Jack," said Harry only half-joking, "one of your problems is that you never get your mind off flying long enough to enjoy the good things of life."

"Good things? What good things? What can be better than flying from a carrier? And in a war, too! Sometimes I think about women, really, but they're too damned demanding. They always want something. I had a bad experience once. And women, they're not very exciting; at least, not compared to flying an A4."

"Ah," said Harry in another bromide, "you just haven't met the right one. What ever happened to your Bible-thumping girlfriend back in Lemoore?"

Jack made a disagreeable face and ignored the question. "Maybe I have met the right one. I almost got married once. Can you believe that? But I haven't met anyone since then that makes me stop thinking about airplanes. I know you won't believe this, Harry, but I am looking for that special one. She'll show up one of these days, but not out here, that's for sure. Let's have one for her, whoever she is." They raised their glasses.

"But first," said Harry seriously, "let's have one for the XO. I sure hope we'll see him again one day." They clinked their glasses together.

"I'll drink to that," said Jack, solemnly.

43
FINDING BRAZIL

November 1970

Harry and the TEA Chief Pilot were standing at the top of the stairs just outside the forward entry door. They were discussing the flight's departure. Judging from his accent, Eddie LeBlanc was from the French side of Belgium. He had introduced Harry, Rolf and Gene to the cabin staff, and Thor had been right. They were, indeed, pretty girls and all spoke English well, some with a French accent and some with a Flemish one. Another gold star for Belgium, thought Harry, when he met them. Belgium was looking better all the time. Harry and Eddie were reviewing the flight's departure from Zaventem airport.

There were well-defined departure routes for every runway and each was depicted on the departure charts for the airport. The airport was using runway 26 today and that was the chart they were looking at. These charts were sometimes very complicated, as airports drew up routes to avoid residential areas, other airports, and sometimes, obstacles to low-flying aircraft, such as terrain and man-made structures. Along with routes, the charts also listed altitude restrictions and often denoted points at which power reductions had to be made to satisfy noise requirements. There were listening devices placed along the route, and if a pilot "rang the bells," he would hear about it later. The departure for 26 was straightforward.

As he finished, Eddie looked up and said, "Ah, here comes our navigator."

Harry could not believe his eyes as Savak Muncherchi crossed the ramp. "Damn," said Harry. "Can that be Savak?"

Eddie turned to Harry, raised his eyebrows and said, "Savak, yes. Do you know him?"

Just then, Savak put his foot on the first step, looked up at Harry and Eddie, missed the step, fell to the pavement and dropped his flight bag, which opened and spilled its contents onto the ramp. He banged the metal case holding his sextant into the second step. Some navigator, thought Harry, he can't even find the step. He hoped this was not an omen for the flight, but suspected it was.

"Yes," said Harry, "we've worked together before."

Although Savak had been born in Bombay, he now lived in London. As with Trans Polar, he had been hired for just one flight.

Now, he picked up his bag, retrieved its contents, and made his way carefully up the stairs, smiling a very embarrassed smile. Eddie greeted Savak, who was his usual friendly self. Well, thought Harry, let's hope he can navigate better than he climbs stairs. Savak spoke with them for a few minutes, then passed Harry and Eddie and went into the cockpit.

"So, you know him. And what do you know of him"? asked Eddie.

"Well," said Harry, "I've worked with better navigators, but he'll do. He'll have to, won't he?"

Eddie chuckled softly. He told Harry about his first experience with Savak. That was a few days before, when they had made a training flight to Dusseldorf, about twenty-five minutes away, where several hours of practice landings were made. A refueling break was taken after they finished.

Savak had come up to Eddie and asked, "Where are we, Captain?" Dusseldorf, he was told. With a puzzled look, Savak replied "My goodness, I never thought Dusseldorf was so far from Brussels."

Harry did not smile. "Well," he said, "I hope he can find Brazil."

Just then, Gene came bounding up the stairs after completing his aircraft pre-flight. "All okay, Boss," he said as slipped past the group at the top of the stairs and disappeared into the cabin. The fueling had been completed and the catering was being loaded into the galleys. An airliner becomes a very hectic place as its departure time nears. There were times when all that simultaneous activity -- fueling, catering, maintenance, flight planning --made it seem impossible to leave on time; but it all came together in the end.

Harry glanced at his watch. "Looks about that time," he said and turned to go to the cockpit. Rolf was already in his seat going through the pre-flight checklist. Gene was busy confirming the fuel load. Just as Harry slid into his seat, the cabin chief came into the cockpit to announce that the catering was all on board and that she was ready for the passengers. Harry turned to look at Eddie, who had taken the jump seat just behind the captain.

"Okay for passengers, Eddie?"

"But of course," the Chief Pilot answered. "You are in charge, Captain, I am just here to learn how to do it. I will depart from the aircraft after the passengers have boarded, if that suits you."

Harry nodded and smiled, first to Eddie, then to the cabin chief. Her name was Michelle, and Harry had already noticed that she wore no wedding ring, that she was very friendly, and that she had a fetching smile.

"Gene, okay?"

"Ready here, Boss," he announced.

"Ready when you are, Michelle. Send them out."

Harry had already arranged his charts and now asked Gene for the pre-start checklist. As the passengers boarded, the three crewmembers went through the list, item by item. The cockpit was ready to start engines; but, first, Harry needed an "All Secure" report from Michelle. That would tell him that all passengers were on board, seated, and that the cabin was ready for departure. Just then, Michelle stuck her pretty head into the cockpit and said, very officially, "Cabin ready for departure, Captain."

Harry nodded his thanks, turned to Rolf and said, "Call for start-up."

Hearing those words, Captain LeBlanc slipped out of his seat and offered his hand, first to Harry, then to Rolf and Gene.

"Gentlemen, I wish you bon voyage and a safe flight. I look forward to your return." He left the cockpit and, a few minutes later Harry saw him wave goodbye from the ramp, then turn and walk towards the terminal.

The route to Rio would be in three sectors. The first stop was in Tenerife in the Canary Islands. Although Savak's navigational skills were not needed on this leg, he seemed inordinately busy at his navigator table, just behind the jump seat. It had its own chair. Okay, thought Harry, at least he's industrious. The weather was fine and the flight to Tenerife was routine, just the way Harry liked them.

The airplane was refueled and soon they were on the way to Recife on the northern coast of Brazil. It was for this sector, where there were no navigational aids on the surface, that Savak had been hired. The sun had gone down ahead of them and it had been a splendid sunset. What's more, because the airplane was flying towards it, the sunset lasted much longer than if they had been standing still on the earth below.

Harry had often marveled at sunsets viewed from aloft. They were often stunning. Unusual things happened while flying airplanes, and one of them was watching the sun rise in the west. That happened on east-to-west polar flights when the path across the arctic allowed an airplane to catch up with the sun and see it rise in the west. It could do that because, at high latitudes, it covered the earth's surface at a rate faster than that of the sun. The east-to-west lines circling a globe, known as lines of latitude, become shorter as they get nearer to the pole.

It was full dark when Savak opened his metal case, took out his sextant, and went to work. Harry watched with curiosity. He had first begun to question Savak's knowledge when he referred to the two needles on the radio magnetic indicator as "the thin one and the thick one." They indicated the bearing to the radio aid that was tuned in, and they were the Number One needle and the Number Two needle to anyone who had ever flown an airplane. His next clue came when he had asked Harry to make a heading change to intercept a VOR radial. He asked for a left turn when a right turn was needed. So, thought Harry, he does not understand bearing. How is it possible for a navigator not to understand the simple concept of bearing? There was more to come.

The opening for the sextant was in the overhead, just forward of the cockpit door. Savak was too short to reach the sextant opening, so he stood on his sextant case, removed the cover of the opening, and attached his sextant. After some minutes, during which Savak began to perspire heavily, he was finally ready to take a celestial fix.

"Stand by for a celestial fix," he announced in a loud and, he hoped, authoritarian voice.

"Ready when you are, Savak," said Harry. Then, as if launching a moon rocket, Savak began counting down. Ten, nine -- and when he got to zero, he announced, even louder, "Commencing celestial fix! Hold the wings level! Hold the wings level!"

The three other cockpit occupants looked at each other and frowned quizzically. What the hell is he saying, the frowns asked. Does he not know we're flying on autopilot?

The distance between Tenerife and Recife is not great, and the winds over the south Atlantic are usually light; so Harry was not concerned about finding Recife. Dead reckoning would do the job. That meant flying a pre-planned heading across the sea to Brazil. There were radio beacons on the other side, and the weather radar could be used for navigation, too, when they neared the coast.

The next thirty minutes were frantic as Savak took frequent readings and plotted the results. After several position fixes, he began to sweat the sweat of fear. Soon, the chart on which he plotted his positions was drenched with his sweat. Harry began to feel sorry for Savak, who was obviously near panic. To give him a break, Harry called, "Well, Savak, you've been navigating for a while now. Could you show me our position, please?"

The dreaded moment of truth had come. He picked up his chart, and carried it forward. As he placed it on Harry's lap, parts of it fell away because the map was soaked with perspiration. "Well, Captain," -- he pronounced it 'Cap-ee-tane' -- "according to my latest fix, we are right here," and he indicated a point with his pencil which went right through a wet spot on the chart. "But if I were you, I wouldn't believe it."

Despite the shortcomings of Prince Savak the Navigator, as Gene began to refer to him, they would find Brazil, which is, after all, a very large country and hard to miss.

The airplane was not full so Harry decided to invite the passengers into the cockpit, one or two at a time. He picked up the cabin mike and made the announcement. Soon, the passengers began streaming through his "office," as he liked to call it. Passengers always found cockpits fascinating and usually said so. Most of these Belgians spoke English. Well, thought Harry, this sure beats the hell out of hauling sheep. These passengers were obviously people of quality, well-dressed and well-spoken -- especially one.

She caught Harry's eye the moment she entered the cockpit. Most of the visitors seemed to be with someone, but this very attractive woman appeared to be alone. She had long blonde hair that fell over Harry's shoulder when she leaned over to look out the window. She smelled delicious. She spoke only briefly, but in almost perfect English, as she asked a few questions about the airplane. Harry made a mental note. They would stay in the same hotel in Rio as did the passengers. This lady might be worth looking into.

Well before approaching the Brazilian coast, Harry had set the Recife VOR frequency into his receiver. Then he had turned its course selector, located on his instrument panel, to the inbound course. When the signal was eventually received, the instrument would depict the position of the airplane, shown in miniature, with respect to the selected course. Of course, after a long sector with only Savak's navigation to guide him, Harry did not expect to be on course when the signal came in; but close enough for government work, as he used to say in his Navy days. Savak became even tenser as the clock told him that they were nearing the coast. Suddenly, the VOR needle, which had been rotating aimlessly, vibrated gently a few times, then pointed to the station in Recife. Incredibly, the instrument showed that the airplane was precisely on course! That was pure luck, Harry knew; but he turned to Savak, who was about to burst with pride, and congratulated him. Savak, smiling broadly, climbed back up onto his metal box and kissed his sextant. Savak had found Brazil!

44
A RIVER CROSSING

1966

It was, in a way, a typical day on Yankee Station. Harry and his wingman, Bill Bowlen, had launched in mid-afternoon for a road reconnaissance mission in "that other country." The rules of engagement for such flights were the same in Cambodia as in North Vietnam. The target was any mechanized vehicle within 200 yards of a motor-able road or trail. That meant trucks. They operated only at night and only when no airplanes were in the neighborhood; so Harry knew, even before leaving the ship, that no trucks would be seen that day. So, what else is new, he asked himself. On such flights, a provisional target was assigned in case no targets of opportunity were found. These were bare-bones targets, as Harry called them, and were taken from an authorized list. When the bottom of the list was reached, they went back to the top again. Other squadrons shared this list so that what was once, maybe, a real target, soon became a hole in the ground, one that got larger as the days passed.

Today's provisional target was, believe it or not, a river crossing. A river crossing! Even Harry, by now used to the strange ways of this strange war, was disgusted. With each aircraft carrying four bombs of five-hundred pounds, the flight crossed the northern part of South Vietnam, then descended into Cambodia. One bright spot was that surface-to-air missiles did not exist there. That made life easier in different ways. They might expect some medium and heavy anti-aircraft fire and, of course, the automatic weapons guns were everywhere. It could be worse.

From the air, Cambodia had an unreal, almost artificial look about it. It was not solid jungle, as was South Vietnam, nor did it have the plains and walled-in villages of North Vietnam. Instead, it was a land of escarpments, sheer gray cliffs that broke through the jungle which surrounded them. There were no signs of life anywhere. Harry began his usual pattern of weaving his flight through continuous heading changes while climbing and descending between three-and five-thousand feet. If there were any guns down there, that would make it harder for them to track the airplanes.

Even the roads were hard to find, never mind a truck. Still, Harry managed to find one that he tracked as best he could. It was not easy because the road sometimes disappeared into the jungle canopy and it was hard to see where it came out. Hopeless, thought Harry, as he crisscrossed the vast expanse of trees and escarpments.

Harry would not like to go down in such territory. A pilot he knew had ejected over Cambodia and he did not enjoy it, even though he was rescued within twelve hours. They were very unpleasant hours, he said, and he had advised Harry to, "avoid it if you can." His plane had been brought down at night and he had gotten safely out of his airplane; but as he dropped near the ground, his parachute had become entangled in the jungle canopy, suspending him in mid-air. It was a dark night and he could not see the ground. Jungle canopies can be as high as fifty feet, he knew, so, instead of releasing himself from his chute, he waited for daybreak.

That, he said, was the longest night of his life. The sounds of the nighttime jungle were loud, varied, and nonstop. He could not identify most. As the first rays of dawn began to penetrate the mass of foliage around him, he saw, with great relief, that his feet were dangling a mere two feet above the floor of the jungle. He slipped out of his harness and looked for high ground with some sky above it. There, he began transmitting on his emergency radio. Two helicopters were on the scene within a few hours and two days later, he was back on his ship. One day after that, he was back over Cambodia. This time he carried a homemade gadget he called a "jungle penetrater," which was a pointed weight on a long string. The next time he was hung up in a jungle canopy, the penetrater would tell him how far above the jungle floor he was. He hoped he would not need it.

A tricky part of flights such as today's was to keep track of fuel and time. They had to be back over the ship in time for the recovery, and they had to have enough fuel to get there. Once overhead, the tanker was usually available for in-flight refueling before entering the landing pattern. Even before the launch, Harry had given up hope of finding a mechanized vehicle. He now did so officially and headed for his provisional target. He had planned the flight to arrive there just before heading for home. They would unload their bombs somewhere near the target, then it would be a quick flight back to the Kitty Hawk, a landing, a debrief, which was more invented than real, then a shower, a martini, dinner and perhaps even a movie. It would be a gentleman's mission today.

Harry map-navigated his way to the river crossing. Reading a map while hand-flying a Skyhawk was not easy, especially when the aircraft's heading and altitude were continuously changing. As he approached the crossing, Harry directed Bill, by hand signals, to switch to the common tactical frequency used by all aircraft, not just the aircraft of his squadron. He then depressed the mike button and announced to no one in particular that he was nearing the target and would commence a bombing run within a few minutes. He did not expect a reply and was startled to hear another aircraft say, "Hey, Battlecry, you're late to this party and you need to get at the end of the line."

Harry paused, then said, "Sorry, guys. I didn't know there was a line. Where's the end?"

Harry was told that his flight was number three in this particular bombing pattern, and that flights one and two were orbiting the target and waiting for yet a fourth flight to clear the area, so they could unload their ordnance before heading for home. Harry actually sighed into his mask. Imagine waiting in line to drop bombs on a river crossing! And how does anyone know that it really is a river crossing, he asked himself. What difference does it make, he answered himself. If not dropped here, the bombs would be let go somewhere in the Gulf of Tonkin. There, they would find plenty of company with the thousands of other bombs resting on its bottom.

He coordinated his altitude with the other flights, kept a close eye on his fuel gauge, and waited for his turn to attack the crossing. He had predetermined the time at which he would say to hell with the target and start back to the ship. In that case, they would drop their bombs into the sea. Their turn finally came with a few minutes to spare and both Harry and Bill managed to drop all their bombs. There was always the chance that a bomb would not drop when it was supposed to, and that could cause serious problems.

Airplanes were not allowed to land on the ship with unreleased bombs. One might come loose when the airplane was brought to an abrupt stop during an arrested landing. All undropped bombs had to be jettisoned before the recovery. At times, it became necessary to do this at a low level. It was crucial to release such bombs in an unarmed mode. This was because a released bomb fell away with the same forward speed as the airplane that dropped it. At higher altitudes, this was not a problem because the airplane was well above the exploding bomb. Even then, in some cases, the percussion of the exploding bombs could be felt in the airplane that dropped them. The airplane might buffet, sometimes severely, if the bomb was a big one, despite being several thousand feet above it and even though the aircraft was climbing away from the explosion.

But at altitudes of a few hundred feet, the bomb would hit the ground while it was still beneath the releasing airplane. Just a few weeks ago, a Kitty Hawk A6 Intruder was lost when it dropped an armed bomb at a low level and blew itself out of the sky. The pilot had armed the bomb, expecting to drop it on a target. For some reason, he had been unable to get to the target, then forgot to disarm the bomb before he jettisoned it. Sometimes, as a comic strip character used to say, "the enemy is us." The airplane, flyable but just barely, managed to reach the sea and the two crewmen ejected safely. A chopper soon picked them up, very wet and very embarrassed.

When an airplane had a hung bomb, it was sent to an airport ashore to have the bomb removed. Usually, they went to Da Nang for their bomb-removal service. As Harry and Bill climbed off target and headed back to the ship, they inspected each other to ensure their bomb racks were clean. Then it was back to the ship. Harry was beginning to taste his pre-dinner martini.

Squadron-mate Andy Curley, had, just a few days before, been sent to Da Nang to offload a bomb that had refused to drop. Too late to return to the ship, he spent the night there. He returned the next morning and Harry was in the Ready Room when Andy came down from the flight deck. Incredibly, he was not completely sober. He had brought back an injured finger and a wild tale of an all-night drinking session with Air Force pilots at the Officers' Club in Da Nang.

Andy had been told that he would not be sent back to the ship until late afternoon, but had been roused out of bed at 0600 and given instructions to launch for the ship as soon as possible. Part of his tale involved taking part in a game of drunken courage that involved stopping an overhead fan with his finger.

"Shit," he said as he sipped a coffee, "I was not going to let these Air Force guys make me look like I was scared."

"So," replied Harry, "you decided to make yourself look stupid, instead. How did that play?"

Andy stared at Harry for a moment. Then, without answering, he finished his coffee, stood up, and left the Ready Room. Jesus, thought Harry. I know he's a good pilot but this is a new one. He wondered if there were any regulations against landing on a carrier under the influence of alcohol.

Later that day, struggling with a hangover, Andy came to the Ready Room and told the rest of his story to a small group gathered there watching an acey deucy game. In the middle of his drinking session at Da Nang, he had fallen into a conversation with an Air Force colonel, who was somewhat drunk. Asked what he did when he was not drinking, he replied that he was charged with tracking the number of Navy airplanes that diverted to Da Nang for removal of the bombs the planes were unable to drop. Why in the world would anyone want to know that, Andy had asked. The colonel smiled indulgently.

"Try to figure it out," he said, still smiling.

The answer to Andy's question could only be surmised. Harry thought a good guess would be that the numbers the colonel collected were used as ammunition to illustrate a major weakness in the Navy's operations. Why give more money to the Navy, the numbers might ask, if they must use an Air Force base to clean up their problems? That might explain why the Kitty Hawk sent out missions in hopeless conditions with no chance of striking a target. Those sorties and those bombs, whether on target or not, counted in the Navy's statistics.

Harry's return from Cambodia was routine. Some ninety minutes after releasing his bombs on the river crossing there, Harry was alone in his room, drinking his pre-dinner martini. The flight had been a waste of fuel and bombs. Still, he asked himself as he sipped, wouldn't it be nice if all our missions were like this one? Daytime, good weather, no enemy fire, and a martini before dinner. Better enjoy it while you can, he answered himself. There are darker days ahead.

45
HELLO, RIO

November 1970

The transit through Recife was routine, and soon the airplane was on its way to Rio de Janeiro. Harry had been in Rio during his Navy days when his ship had once spent a few days there. He remembered three things: Beautiful women, wonderful food, and great beer. He looked forward to renewing his friendship with all three. There were other attractions, of course, especially when you were staying in the Miramar Hotel on Copacabana Beach.

After checking in, Harry had gone out onto his balcony to look around. One thing he had forgotten was that skin color seemed to play no part in life on the beach. It was a splendid beach, he remembered, and it had been filled with skin hues of every shade; yet no one seemed to care about color, and people gathered and played in groups made up of all shades. There was plenty of activity on the beach and many beachgoers took part in them. Volleyball and soccer seemed nonstop everywhere he looked.

From the balcony, off to the left, Harry could see famous Sugar Loaf Mountain. The water was clean and the surf looked just right for Harry, who liked to body surf. That first day was needed for the body to catch its breath. The trip across had been long and tiring. The crew and the passengers were staying at the same hotel, and Harry hoped he might run into the lovely blonde woman he had met briefly in the cockpit. They would be there for one full week, so he kept his eyes open when he was around the hotel, alert for the right opportunity.

That first evening, Harry, Gene, and Rolf met in the reception area, then set out on the famed mosaic walk along Copacabana Beach as they looked for a restaurant. It was another of those moments that Harry tried to inscribe in his memory. The list of such memories was becoming very long. The beautiful beach, the famous mosaic sidewalk, a soft seaside evening with the smell of the salt spray. It was certainly a moment that deserved to be on his list.

Harry preferred restaurants that served local food. Soon, just around a corner, off the beach walk, they found one that looked as local as local can be. It was small, with an outside dining area under a thatched roof. It looked just right. Harry had long ago figured out that choosing the right restaurant in a strange town was very important. It could determine, in large measure, one's view of the town. Harry recalled that a famous dish in Rio was barbecued pork, served with a huge fresh salad and a plate of steaming black beans.

The fruits and vegetables of Brazil were wonderful, and they included several that Harry had never seen before. Along with the meal, they enjoyed a couple of bottles of Brahma Shoppe beer. Harry always drank local beer, and this was a good one. He remembered it well. It came in large bottles with a top held in place by a wire hinge.

"What the hell kind of a beer bottle is this?" asked Gene as he poured beer into his glass.

"Never mind," said Harry. "Just shut up and drink your beer. This one is as good as it gets."

Gene took a long drink and smiled. It was a smile that said, "Hey, this is one helluva beer."

Their dinner arrived just as they finished the first bottle of beer. The food looked great and tasted even better than it looked. So far, so good, Harry thought as they paid the bill. Portuguese was the language of Brazil and not many people spoke English. Their waiter was one who did and Harry decided to ask him to suggest a nightclub.

"Ah, yes," he said. "There are many. What kind of club do you wish to visit?"

Harry smiled. "One with pretty girls and good music. Just the basics."

The waiter raised his eyebrows. "Basics?" he repeated. "How do you mean 'basics?'" Then he smiled back at Harry. "Ah yes, the basics. I believe you will find them here." He quickly wrote a name on his pad, tore off the page and handed it to Harry. "The taxi, he will know."

It was more than a nightclub, more like a ballroom. It was vast and it was crowded with people drinking, laughing and dancing. It was not carnival time, but carnival was in the air. They were shown to a small table at the edge of the dance floor and ordered drinks as they looked out on it. It was enormous and it was packed with beautiful bodies dancing exuberantly to Latin music. Now, this, thought Harry, is real music, not just someone in tattered clothes, needing a haircut, and pounding on an electric guitar. This music had rhythm, not just a beat. He liked it.

The band was perched on what appeared to be a large cylinder. When the music ended, to a roar of approval, the cylinder dropped slowly into the floor as another arose with another band, and the music continued almost without a pause. Later, a third band would appear, almost like magic, on another giant piston at the far end of the floor.

"Hey Boss," said Gene, as he leaned across the table with a grin. "They got any bars like this in Milwaukee?"

Just then, the band began to play what Harry guessed was carnival music. Those few who were not already there, quickly joined the throng of bodies gyrating enthusiastically on the dance floor. Within a minute or two, the three of them were the only ones in the entire place who were not dancing; but not for long, as three lovely young ladies who were dancing past swooped down upon their table, grasped their hands, and pulled them out onto the floor, laughing as they did. Dancing seemed to be in the Brazilian blood, but it was not in Harry's. What the hell, he thought, just do the best you can. After a few minutes, his partner shouted something into Harry's ear, then danced away from him. Everybody seemed to be dancing with everybody else. Suddenly the music stopped and the crowd cheered and whistled. Harry found his way back to their table. He needed to catch his breath and a beer might help. Gene soon appeared with his shirt soaked in sweat, grinning broadly.

"You ever seen anything like this?" he asked, as he wiped his forehead with his forearm.

Harry had once been in a cavernous nightclub in Japan that had been staffed with 800 hostesses. Harry had been dubious about that number posted outside the club -- 800 girls? Be serious, he said to his companions. His doubts were erased once he was inside. Girls were everywhere. They had lined the stairs and the halls leading to the club, bowing as the customers passed. Inside, the girls were available for dancing, pouring your beer, or playing the silly games that all Japanese bargirls seemed to know. All this happened as instructions blared out nonstop from a loudspeaker. The orders were in Japanese, of course, so it was impossible to figure out what was going on. Girls would appear, disappear, dance, pour beer, play games, and tell Harry how handsome he was.

Of course, all of this ended up on the bill, which was astronomical. The atmosphere there had been commercial; here it was emotional. These people loved to dance. They did it with great passion and obvious pleasure.

"No, never," he answered Gene. "This place is something else. Maybe after I hang up my scarf and goggles, I'll open a bar like this in some exotic place. What do you think?"

"Count me in, Boss, just be sure to serve some of this Brazilian beer."

Rolf returned a few minutes later, sweaty and gasping for breath. They decided they'd had enough for one night and agreed to head back to the hotel.

"Goddamn," said Gene as they left. "This is one helluva bar. And this was one helluva night."

The week in Rio flew past. Several of the crew spent time at the beach every day. Harry was one of those. He, Rolf, Gene, and Savak watched a soccer match one afternoon at an enormous stadium outside the city. It looked to Harry as though an artist, not an engineer, had designed it. It held more than one-hundred-thousand spectators, and all of them seemed to shout and scream nonstop. Rolf chided Harry for calling it a soccer match.

"Can't you Americans get it through your heads that this is football. Football!" He repeated it for emphasis.

"Nah, it's soccer," replied Harry. "Football is what they play in Green Bay on Sundays."

After their return to the hotel, they decided to have a drink on the terrace overlooking the beach. As they sat sipping their beer, Harry could not help but notice that Savak was becoming more and more uncomfortable, squirming and wiggling in his chair.

"Savak," asked Harry, "is something wrong? You seem to be having a problem."

Savak decided to admit his problem. "Captain," he asked in his usual deferential way, "would you mind if I went to the toilet?"

Harry controlled his urge to smile. "Savak," he said courteously, "you can go to the toilet anytime you want to. You don't even have to ask."

Savak smiled a smile of relief, leapt out of his chair, and darted off in the direction of the men's room.

One day, Harry organized a trip to Mount Corcovado to view up-close the famed statue of Christ with His arms outstretched towards the city and the sea beyond. He was "Roger Pass" to any Navy pilot who had ever seen him, but Harry decided not to try to explain that one to the crew. The view from there was a splendid panorama and included much of Rio, Sugar Loaf Mountain, Copacabana, and Ipanema Beach, with its musical image of girls who were tall and tan, young and lovely.

Harry and Rolf had spent one afternoon there and although there was an abundance of beautiful female bodies in scanty swimsuits there, they seemed to be everywhere, and not only on the beaches. The view stretched north across the bay and along the coast until it blended into the horizon. Harry would remember this view as the most magnificent he had ever seen with his feet on the earth. He tried to etch this one in his memory too, alongside that of the stroll along Copacabana on their first night in Rio.

On the way back to the hotel, the group was shown the slums of Rio. They are built into the hillsides and they are known as favelas. The living conditions were wretched, but Harry was struck by the happy nature of the people living there. They smiled and waved as the group passed through, sometimes calling out in Portuguese. Imagine being happy living here, thought Harry. He knew many people who were unhappy with vastly more. The difference was relative, he thought. Those who have much, want more. These people seemed satisfied with what they had because "more" was beyond their reach.

Harry tracked down Michelle with the lovely smile. "What about dinner? he asked. She hesitated and Harry quickly added, "No strings. Just dinner." She looked puzzled and Harry realized that "No Strings" had no meaning for her.

He explained and then added, "After all, you're not married," he said, glancing at her hand to reassure himself it had no wedding ring.

"Ah, no," she replied "Not officially. But here." She tapped her temple with a forefinger to indicate she was married mentally.

"Since two years," she added, to make sure Harry got the point. She then smiled her lovely smile and thrust out her hand. "But merci for asking," she said courteously.

Well, thought Harry, no harm in trying. They shook hands as if they had just concluded a secret agreement.

On their last night in town, Harry had arranged dinner for the entire crew. They met on the hotel terrace and enjoyed a drink as they waited for the group to gather. As they did, who should appear but the blonde woman with the delicious scent who had visited the cockpit. She took a seat at a table near Harry's, nodded towards him, and ordered a coffee. She had a suntan now and, along with her blonde hair, it gave her a look both ravishing and wholesome. She smiled at Harry as she sipped her coffee. A nice smile, a friendly smile.

Harry had hoped to see her during the visit and had kept a watchful eye for her. Their paths had not crossed, but it was better late than never. He invited her to join their table and they were soon discussing their week in Rio. Yes, a wonderful city, she agreed. She still had that delicious scent, and Harry was pleased when she accepted his offer to join them for dinner. They went to the same restaurant they had discovered on that first night. Harry maneuvered himself into the chair next to hers and enjoyed her company as much as he did the dinner. She was from Antwerp, she said, and she worked at the Chase Manhattan Bank there.

"Antwerp," said Harry, "I haven't been to Antwerp. Maybe you might show me around one day?"

"Yes, of course," she said with a smile. "You must see our beautiful Antwerp."

She gave Harry her telephone number and he wrote it down on a corner of his menu, tore it off , and slipped into his pocket. They agreed to have another dinner together after they returned to Belgium.

So far, so good, Harry thought after dinner as he ordered Brazilian brandy for the entire table. She was pretty and vivacious. Her name was Irene and she accepted a brandy and raised her glass as Harry toasted the good life in Rio de Janeiro. He didn't know why, but he took that as a good omen; and Harry believed in omens. When the bill came, Irene took a cursory look at it and quickly calculated each person's share. Smart, thought Harry. Unlike many men, Harry favored intelligent women. Another good omen, he thought, as he sipped his brandy.

46
CAM RAHN BAY

1966

It was the only war Harry had ever seen, but he knew a strange war when he saw one; and in strange wars, strange things were bound to happen. One such event took place one night on Dixie Station. Harry had not taken part but he talked with those who had. A recovery of eight airplanes started normally just about dusk. Night carrier landings were recorded in the pilot's logbook in red ink. These would be night landings officially and logged in red ink; but a dusk landing was almost a daytime landing. These were known as "pinkies." There were always plenty of volunteers for missions which ended up with pinky landings. There was a great difference between a pinky landing and a serious night landing, although they counted the same in the logbook.

There was no night flying in the south, and this was the last recovery of the day. The second airplane to come aboard was an F4 Phantom that came down hard and partially collapsed a main gear strut. The six airplanes still aloft were directed to orbit the ship until the deck was cleared. Only a brief delay was expected; but on aircraft carriers life did not always go as expected. The F4 had swiveled toward the deck edge in a way that made it very difficult for the tow vehicle to line up its tow bars.

When it became obvious that clearing the deck would take longer than foreseen, the airborne aircraft were directed to head for the airfield at Cam Rahn Bay. This was a new airfield recently completed but not yet operational. It had long concrete runways, and no problems were expected. Wrong again. The six airplanes arrived over the airfield to find that the tower was not manned and that there were no runway lights. By now, it was full dark and these birds were low on fuel and getting lower. First to land was Sam Brunet, a squadron-mate of Harry's. He had flown over the field during daytime a few days before and could make out the runways in the light of a moon that was nearly full that night. After landing, he taxied to the end of the runway, made a sharp turn and pointed his airplane so that his taxi light illuminated part of the runway.

Without coordination from the tower, it was every man for himself. Amidst the chaos, there was one very near mid-air collision and another close call when an almost-dry F4 overtook an A4 Skyhawk that was about to touch down. The pilot of the F4, who later said he did not have enough fuel for a go-around, pulled sharply back on his stick, arced over the A4 and landed barely ahead of it with enough extra speed to pull away from it on the roll-out.

"Too quick to be scared," said the A4 pilot, when asked the next day about his near demise. The F4 pilot was right about not having enough fuel to go around. He flamed out as he rolled down the runway after landing. There was a skeleton ground crew at the airfield and fuel was available. The six airplanes appeared over the Kitty Hawk early the next morning and two of the pilots were launched on missions that same afternoon. There was no rest for the weary.

Another time, on another ship, a similar incident had a different ending. That time, an A3 Skywarrior had landed, and as it taxied forward to clear the landing area, its nose wheel got stuck in the track of a catapult. That fouled the deck, and the aircraft about to land was waved off and told to hold overhead until the deck was cleared. The aircraft, an A4 Skyhawk, was the last one in the recovery. Only a brief delay was expected; but the nose wheel of the A3 was well stuck and would not budge.

This was the largest and heaviest airplane in the carrier fleet, and it covered a large area of the flight deck. It was not for nothing that the A3 had been dubbed "The Whale." So large was the A3 that if it landed more than six feet to the right of the centerline, its starboard wingtip would rip through those aircraft parked just aft of the island superstructure, as they routinely were. The A3 was a difficult airplane to bring aboard, and Harry had much respect for the Whale drivers. The crew on deck cursed and grunted, but the A3 refused to budge. This whale was beached.

As the time stretched out, the lone Skyhawk still airborne went below bingo fuel state. That meant no airfield ashore was within reach, and the pilot was committed to landing on the ship. The ship's captain considered taking the Skyhawk on the fouled deck; but, first, he had to know how far it would roll out after landing. Would it collide with the stranded A3? The Catapult and Arresting Gear Officer, under pressure, raced through his manuals. Nowhere could he find any information regarding the distance an airplane would roll out after snagging a wire.

Each arresting gear cable was 2,200 feet long and most of it was beneath the flight deck, attached to machinery that controlled its pull-out. The resistance set into the hydraulic devices that controlled the cable pull-out was determined by the weight and speed of the landing aircraft. That the wire would safely stop an aircraft was well-documented but the distance in which it would do that was not. By now, the pilot overhead was beginning to sound nervous. He wanted to come aboard, and the sooner, the better. A decision had to be made, but before he made it, the Captain asked his Cat and Arresting Gear Officer for his best guess. The odds favored a safe landing, he said, but no guarantees.

"Okay," said the Captain. "Let's bring him aboard."

The pilot overhead was apprised of the situation. Would he prefer to eject?

"Hell no," he said, somewhat unprofessionally. "I'm goddamn coming aboard. And the sooner, the better. I'm flying on fumes up here." That decision was one of self-confidence. He knew he had to make a near-perfect approach because catching a number four wire lowered his odds. That was because his roll-out would start farther forward on the deck and closer to the stranded A3. Normally, the target wire was number three. It provided optimum clearance between hook and flight deck as the aircraft passed over the ship's ramp. This was known as the "hook-to-ramp" clearance and on the larger carriers this distance was about twelve feet, and on the smaller carriers it was about half that.

Harry's first cruise had been on the USS Ranger, a large carrier and one with maximum hook-to-ramp clearance. Harry's second cruise had been on a smaller carrier, the USS Oriskany, which was in the Essex class. He flew the propeller-driven Skyraider then. Its landing technique was much different than that of a jet. Instead of staying on the glide path until it collided with the flight deck, the Skyraider used the SNJ landing technique used in student training.

At a certain point, as it closed with the ship, the Skyraider pilot would receive a "cut" signal from the Landing Signal Officer. This command was mandatory and required the pilot to pull his throttled back to idle, then make a flared landing. He did this by slightly lowering the nose to increase the descent rate slightly, then raising it so that the aircraft would land tail wheel first. That ensured that the tail hook would grab one of the wires and not float above them. On the Ranger, the cut signal came after the aircraft had passed over the ship's ramp.

Months later, on his very first approach to the Oriskany, Harry was more than surprised to get the cut signal while still over the sea! No one had warned him about that, and he was startled by what appeared to be an early cut. Still, discipline kicked in. Harry brought his throttle to idle and landed the airplane neatly onto the number three wire. That extra six feet of clearance on the large carriers let pilots breathe much easier during a landing. When an airplane was not on the glide path or not at the correct speed, the "cut" technique allowed the LSO to give the cut signal early or late and so control the point of the airplane's touchdown.

The "cut" technique would not work for the Skyhawk. Jets flew on the glide path all the way to touchdown; but a modified version might help. The pilot and the Landing Signal Officer discussed the approach. Both agreed the pilot would fly a normal approach and aim for the number three wire, which was the usual target wire. Then, as he passed over the ramp, he would pull his power to idle, "dive for the deck" and try to catch number two. This meant pushing forward on the stick to increase the descent just before touchdown and landing farther aft than he would by leaving his descent rate unchanged as he closed with the deck.

Under pressure, the pilot flew a good approach, and as he crossed over the ramp, he lowered his nose slightly and, at the same time, sharply pulled back his power. There was no need to follow the normal procedure of pushing the throttle full forward at touchdown so that the engine would be at maximum power in case of a bolter. There would be no bolter this time. Many collective breaths were held as the aircraft came down the glide path, caught a two wire, rolled out, then came to a stop with its fuel probe, the most forward part of the airplane, gently kissing the tail section of the A3. A thunderous cheer erupted across the flight deck as the arresting cable released its tension at the end of its pull-out and dragged the aircraft back a few yards and clear of danger.

In another time, in another place, on a different ship, another such incident had a tragic ending. This time, an F4 Phantom was unable to lower his hook for a night recovery. This was another low-fuel situation with no airfield within range, and finally it was decided to raise the barricade, a net-like device suspended across the landing area from two stanchions raised from their stowed position on the flight deck. The net was attached to an arresting gear cable. The aircraft simply made a normal approach, but instead of catching a wire, flew into the net, which then collapsed around the aircraft and brought it to stop with the attached cable. Usually, such a landing caused almost no damage to the airplane; but this time, the pilot, probably feeling a sense of panic, flew into the net at very high speed, tore it from the cable, and continued off the angled deck and into the sea. Both the pilot and his backseater were lost. Flight operations from aircraft carriers were never easy, especially at night. Harry sometimes wondered why men did it. Probably, he guessed, because every one of them thought, "It'll never happen to me."

Someone had once told Harry that boats and airplanes are basically incompatible. Harry had seen many examples of this conflict between airplanes and ships. Long runways made dangerous situations much less dangerous. On Harry's first cruise -- that word usually brought up images of luxury liners, but that was how they were known -- a pilot from the Air Wing had flamed out just aft of the ship as he was about to land. At an airport, he might have made the runway, if he had some extra speed; or he might have landed in the area short of the runway, which is usually clear of obstructions.

At sea, he had two choices: eject or ditch. Ditch meant landing in the sea, which was not recommended for high-speed carrier jets. They were built for performance, not for strength. The landing gear was built to withstand the shock of a carrier landing. The rest of the airplane was somewhat fragile in order to save weight, and it usually broke into pieces when ditching. The pilot had scant seconds to decide. He opted to ditch, and came down in the ship's wake with his airplane still in one piece. The ship's "angel," a helicopter that was airborne during all flight operations, was over the aircraft within seconds. The crew later reported that the pilot, still alive, was desperately beating at the canopy with both fists, as his plane slowly sank beneath the ship's wake. Canopies are designed to be blasted away in an emergency. Either this one had malfunctioned or the pilot did not think of it. An awful way to go, thought Harry, as he tried to imagine sitting in the cockpit of an airplane sinking slowly into the sea.

Harry personally knew two pilots who had gone into the sea ahead of the ship because of underpowered catapult shots. These were known as "cold cat shots." They happened when the catapult pressure was less than needed to provide enough power at the end of the stroke. That meant not enough speed to fly. Both of these pilots had kept their heads, landed in the water, and waited. They waited for the ship to pass over them before they somehow managed to exit the cockpit. One of them told Harry that he had actually seen the ship's propellers turning as it went over his airplane. Standard procedure required pilots to be on oxygen for all launches, and that allowed them to keep breathing as they waited for the right moment to leave their airplanes, figure out which way was up, then swim frantically in that direction. Staying cool in tight situations went a long way towards getting through them.

Harry had not spoken with the F8 Crusader pilot involved in another heart-stopper, but he had heard it so many times, it had to be true. Like countless others before him, he was positioned on one of the bow catapults, expecting a normal launch. It quickly became spectacularly abnormal. At full power, he gave the ready salute; but, instead of being powered down the track by the shuttle, his aircraft began moving ahead, very slowly, towards the bow. The catapult had malfunctioned. The pilot slammed on his brakes, shut down his engine and watched in shock as his airplane slowed, then stopped, with its forward section hanging well over the edge of the flight deck, teetering precariously as the ship pitched gently with the sea. The Crusader's cockpit is at the very front of its sleek, long fuselage. As the airplane oscillated slowly, the pilot saw nothing but sea and sky, first one then the other. Still in radio contact with the ship, the Air Boss instructed him to remain in the cockpit while a tug was attached to his airplane. It would drag him backwards to safety; but then, the ship took a heavy swell and over he went.

As he fell, the aircraft turned on its side as it hit the water. The pilot saw the ship's bow slicing through the sea towards him, then felt the impact as the aircraft was snapped in two. The break was aft of the cockpit and the pilot was sealed inside. Now underwater, he saw clearly the ship's hull, and felt the shocks as the cockpit bounced and skidded against it as the ship passed by. As he neared the stern, he heard the ship's giant propellers and was drawn into their vortex. Miraculously, he passed right through the turning blades. Then, he suddenly saw sunlight and realized that his cockpit, with himself still inside, had bobbed to the surface. He pulled the handle that blasted away the canopy, then found the cockpit filling with seawater and sinking fast. By the time he fired the ejection seat, he was some thirty feet below the surface. He swam frantically towards the daylight, broke the surface and found the ship's rescue chopper directly above him. He was pulled from the sea unharmed and badly in need of a drink.

High on Harry's list of brave and skilful pilots was one he met at an Officers' Club bar at the Norfolk Naval Air Station. They enjoyed a few drinks together, then agreed to have dinner. His fellow diner was a Crusader pilot. During their meal, he told Harry one of the most harrowing sea tales he would ever hear. It had taken place in the North Atlantic when his ship noted a radar blip which might be a Russian airplane.

"I was assigned Fighter Alert that day," he began, "even though the sea conditions were extremely rough. Flight operations had been canceled, but not the Fighter Alert. I knew that there was no way they would launch me, because the flight deck was actually digging into the sea. The North Atlantic can be nasty, and that day it was as bad as it gets. I was feeling major 'g's just sitting in the cockpit. There was a thin sheet of clear ice covering the flight deck, and taxiing was almost impossible. It had taken ten sailors on each side of my aircraft just to get me on the catapult. My airplane kept sliding sideways every time the ship rolled. That was a helpless feeling.

"Finally, with heavy chains, my bird was tied to the cat. The ship was bucking and heaving something awful. The worst is over, I told myself. They will never send me up in weather like this. Just then the bull horn sounded. LAUNCH THE DUTY FIGHTER! *Holy Shit*, I thought, are these guys serious?

"My engine wasn't running, so I had no power for my radio. But the launch crew was already removing my tie-downs and putting a ground starter in place. A crewman gave me a two-finger 'turn up' and pointed to his headset, telling me to call Pri-Fly. Before I could transmit, I heard, 'We have an unidentified target approaching the 250 mile circle. You will be launched as soon as the ship is turned into the wind.' These guys were not joking.

"The ship was pitching so much that the shooter would need to time my launch with the movement of the ship's bow. He would have to shoot me off with the bow pointed up very steeply and in a bank of maybe fifteen degrees. It would be a very hairy launch, but I was a U.S. Navy pilot, right?

"I cranked up my engine and checked all my engine instruments. I was half hoping for a problem so I wouldn't have to launch, but all systems were go. I pushed the throttle up, saluted Shooter and braced for the shot. It came just as the bow started up. I was airborne at 180 knots in two seconds. There was no way I could keep my feet on the rudders during the catapult run, and it felt like I was going straight up! As I was recovering from the shot, Combat Information Center gave me vectors to the incoming target, ordering maximum speed. That meant afterburner. Even while climbing five miles high in less than sixty seconds, my airplane was accelerating supersonic. Ninety seconds later, I was at 30,000 feet and heading for the target.

"Then I got a call from CIC. 'Silverstep,' they said. 'Your bogie now appears to be a false target, possibly caused by the rough sea.' *Goddamn!*, I thought. They send me up in this for a false target? They gave me a vector back to the ship. Now I had to think about getting back on board a ship bouncing around like a cork. 'Your signal is Charley, on arrival,' the ship told

241

me. It got more interesting when they told me there was no tanker airborne. I would get back with enough fuel for five or six approaches but with that sea, it might not be enough.

"On my first approach, I saw the ship was pitching and rolling like I had never seen before. The pitch was more than the lens gyro could handle, so the LSO used the mechanical meatball. Ever done that? He uses a lever to put the meatball where he thinks it should be. His comments helped a lot. The pitch was so bad that, at times, I could see the whole damn flight deck! Sometimes I actually saw the ship's screws, completely out of the water! The roll was bad, too, and I knew I was in deep trouble. On the first couple of passes, the LSO got me in close enough to land, but the ship's movement wouldn't let him bring me aboard. He had to time it with a pitching ship, and couldn't let me land on a rising deck. The ship's roll was a problem, too, because I might roll out into parked airplanes.

"I got even closer the next three times but still got those wave-off lights. I was down to the fumes now, just enough fuel for one more try. Somehow, don't ask me how, I got down on my last pass. If I'd missed that one, it would have meant punching out, and, for damn sure, I would never have been seen again, not in that sea. Ah, the thrills of Naval aviation! Taxiing out of the wires on that sheet of ice was thrilling, too, but at least I was down. And, man, did that feel good!"

47
GOODBYE, RIO

November 1970

The departure from Rio was in late evening. The route back to Brussels took them via Freetown in Sierra Leone. Not only was Freetown not on Harry's dream list of cities he wanted to see, he had never even heard of it. The first leg of the crossing was towards the northeast and paralleled the coastline of Brazil. That meant Harry could use his weather radar to track their position; so he was surprised when Savak asked him to make a heading change to the left of twenty degrees to "return to course, Captain."

This presented a small problem in diplomacy which Harry solved by making the heading change, then imperceptibly returning to the original heading and hoping that Savak would not notice. When he glanced back over his shoulder to see whether Savak had seen through his little subterfuge, Harry saw he was fast asleep, his head on an arm thrown across the navigator's table. Without Savak's continuous "suggestions," as he called them, the crossing went smoothly. No star fixes, no commands to "Hold the wings level." Harry still could not believe that one.

He simply put the autopilot on heading control and hoped for the best. The winds in the south Atlantic are usually light; and Africa, like Brazil, would be hard to miss. Still, if anyone could do it, Savak was the one. He awoke as the sun was rising and realizing he had been somewhat negligent, began working furiously; but by the time he had broken out his sextant the stars were no longer visible and he was at a loss as to what to do next. He began searching for islands which appeared on his map, but which were impossible to see in the early-morning haze.

"Anybody see any islands?" he kept asking.

"Relax, Savak," smiled Harry. "The ADF has just been turned on at the airport and we're on course. And I have the coast on radar. I believe we've found Africa. You can put your sextant away. Thanks for your help."

Freetown looked like a lot of other places Harry had seen: A strip of concrete about 250 feet wide and two miles long. That was as much as he ever saw of many of his "destinations." The next stop was in Malaga, Spain and there was a grand view of the Rock of Gibraltar just before they began the descent. There, Harry felt safe in leaving the airplane to visit the duty-free shop, where he bought a bottle of Spanish brandy. Who should he see but Irene, there on a similar mission. Another good omen. She looked just as fetching in the daylight as she had in the restaurant. They exchanged a few words and Harry promised to call her in Antwerp.

"Don't forget," she said as Harry headed back to the airplane. Things always seemed to go wrong when he left it; but not this time. This time, they went just right.

48
SPADS

1957

In late 1957, when Harry reported to his first squadron, there were no ballistic missiles, and satellite technology was just getting off the ground, so to speak. He would long remember the near panic caused by Sputnik that year, but who would have imagined that this grapefruit-sized satellite would evolve into the extensive system of navigation, communication, and intelligence gathering that it later became? The Soviet threat had to be countered in other ways.

An integrated strategic plan was conceived and it included assets of the Navy and the Air Force. That meant aircraft carriers and long-range bombers. The goal was to provide mutually-assured destruction to deter Russian attack. This meant that the plan had to contend with numerous targets throughout the Soviet sphere that then included China. Some important targets were assigned to multiple assets to ensure their destruction. Some targets might be targeted by both B52 bombers, for example, and strike aircraft based on carriers. Only certain long-range aircraft could reach other targets, especially those deep within China.

That was where Harry's squadron came in. Despite its age, the propeller-driven Skyraider fit the bill perfectly. When its external tanks were full, it could fly up to sixteen hours and would run out of oil before it ran out of fuel; and it could perform these Herculean flights just fifty feet off the ground, where it was hard to spot on radar. That was a great advantage over jet aircraft. Their fuel consumption increased greatly at low altitudes and severely limited their range. Many important targets were assigned to the venerable Skyraider simply because no other airplane could reach them.

It was known throughout the fleet as the Able Dog. That came from using the phonetic alphabet of those times to pronounce the letters A and D, which was its official nomenclature. The airplane and those who flew it commanded respect among aviators who knew airplanes. Because it called to mind airplanes of an earlier era, it was often called a Spad, after the famous airplanes used in World War One, and its pilots were known as Spad Drivers. This was a badge its pilots wore with pride.

Although an anomaly in the jet age, the Skyraider was a classic aircraft, and with good reason. It could carry more than its own weight, the only military aircraft with that capability. Harry had once escorted several Air Force officers throughout the ship when she was at anchor off Okinawa. Looking down on the flight deck from Vulture's Row, one of them had spotted a Skyraider, its wings folded and looking more like a crane than an airplane.

"What is it?" he had asked.

"A Skyraider," Harry had replied proudly. "It can carry more ordnance than the old B17." "C'mon," said the visitor. "A B17 could carry several one-thousand pound bombs."

"This airplane," Harry told him, "can carry three of them, along with six 250-pound bombs on it wing racks, and six rocket pods between the bombs." The Air Force was impressed.

The Skyraider had been designed to deliver conventional bombs and rockets and had served with honor in Korea. It did yeoman service in Vietnam, too, but because of its slow speed, it was vulnerable. Despite their vintage, Skyraiders had managed to shoot down two Russian-built jets over North Vietnam. Harry had talked with Ned Greathaus, who had brought down one of those airplanes.

"Talk about being in the right place at the right time," he told Harry one night at the Flying Spinnaker. The North Vietnamese pilot had attacked his section of two airplanes, he said, thinking he had found easy targets. The Spads split into a defensive tactic. First, they separated, taking up positions several hundred yards apart, flying parallel to each other. Then, they began weaving in a crisscross pattern. The jet, after firing at Ned's wingman, had flown right in front of Ned's airplane.

"All I had to do was press the button and shoot," he said. "Pretty lucky." He grinned, as he drank his beer.

Outlines of both jets were painted on the Skyraiders' Lemoore hangar. They were depicted with red X's slashed across their profiles, much in the way pilots had painted their victims on the sides of their airplanes in earlier wars.

To be effective in the war of deterrence, the Skyraider had to have a nuclear capability. There was just one problem. Because of its low speed, a way had to be found to enable the delivery aircraft to escape the nuclear blast of its own weapon. The first idea was to drop the weapon from a high altitude. That meant a long and slow climb to some 20,000 feet, then rolling over and diving for the target, releasing the weapon at 14,000 feet. The dive was made with speed brakes extended. These were enormous panels known as "barn doors." When retracted, they were contoured around the aft fuselage, one on each side. Extended hydraulically, they provided stability during the dive and allowed a few extra seconds to line up the target. To the pilot, the airplane seemed to be in a vertical dive as it corkscrewed towards the earth. The brakes slowed the aircraft in a way that the pilot was actually suspended by his shoulder straps.

During this maneuver, the airplane was vulnerable to enemy fire. That was one problem. Another was that it was highly inaccurate. Hits one-or-two thousand feet from the target were not unusual.

Over a beer one night after a practice session, Jack said with disgust, "There has to be a better way. Up there today, going down through fifteen-thousand, I was still wrestling that bastard, trying to line up the target. You know, you have to be lucky just to hit the ground with that kind of horseshit bomb run."

Of course, accuracy was not essential. Like horseshoes, nuclear bombs had only to be close.

A third problem was survival. Harry had read the manual and looked at the charts and, despite their claims of a safe escape, he concluded he would not get out alive; so he was very pleased when other methods were conceived.

Several other types of bomb delivery were found to be safer and more accurate, at least in theory. Harry and his squadron-mates had attended a special course related to delivering nuclear weapons using these new deliveries. There were two effects of the bomb to be avoided. The first, radiation, would not be a problem, they were told. But, just in case, the pilot would wear a dosimeter. This was a small card clipped to his flight suit that would record the amount of radiation it absorbed. It would not prevent radiation, only measure it. This did not inspire confidence in the pilots.

The second effect, shock wave, could destroy an aircraft in a heartbeat. To avoid that, a special type of bomb was developed, and a different method of delivery was used. The bomb was propelled by a rocket which threw the bomb far ahead of the airplane. The method of delivery was a high-speed, low-level run into the target area. The speed was increased significantly by adding water to the fuel-air mixture to increase its density and, thus, its power.

This type of delivery was called loft bombing, and a wing-under maneuver was the kind used with the rocket-propelled weapon.

This delivery was started with a sharp pull-up until the weapon was released, followed by a 135-degree bank, then a hard pull-back on the control stick with the airplane almost inverted. That meant pulling the aircraft towards the ground and pointing it in a direction opposite to the run-in. Going away from the target, the airplane was returned to the upright position. That was supposed to provide what was known, hopefully, as escape distance. Harry had studied these charts too, and he had serious doubts about surviving one of these blasts. Still, it was hard to imagine launching one of these bombs in real life, so it was, for most, "interesting, but it will never happen."

The mechanics of the delivery were straightforward: As the pilot flew over a pre-selected point on the ground, known as an Initial Point, he depressed a button on his control stick. That started a timer, into which had been set a number of seconds which translated into the distance the airplane would fly to reach the pull-up point. There, a tone sounded and a light illuminated. That was the signal to initiate the pull-up. During this phase, the pilot followed instruments that kept the wings level and helped him to apply the proper amount of "g" force needed for the aircraft to follow the programmed profile. As the airplane reached a pre-set angle, which depended upon the distance to the target, and was usually about forty degrees nose-up, the bomb was automatically released. This was done by firing a 20mm cartridge that threw the bomb away from the airplane so that it was clear of the propeller when it ignited. The rocket and the bomb would then be on their way as the airplane headed in the opposite direction.

The pilots often practiced wing-unders at an instrumented bombing range. The profile of each maneuver was tracked by ground instruments and traced on paper so the pilots could later see how close to the desired pattern they had flown. They used practice bombs that made a tiny puff of smoke upon impact. After each release, Harry banked his plane sharply to see his bomb hit. It seemed nervously close. He thought about that escape distance. It looked to him like there was no way to escape that nuclear blast. A pilot had to pay close attention to his airplane during a wing-under because it was started just fifty feet above the ground. Harry's squadron had lost a pilot on the practice range when he flew straight into the ground recovering from one of these maneuvers.

The instrumented range was at China Lake, a Navy facility in central California, near the Sierra Nevada Mountains. The complex was manned by civilians, and the pilots developed good rapport with them. Back at Miramar, after two weeks on the range, the skipper decided to show his appreciation by inviting them to a squadron party.

Transportation was provided by a version of the Skyraider which carried two pilots side-by-side, with one control stick. Several passengers could be carried in a cut-out section of the fuselage. Harry and Jack offered to fly them home the morning after the party. After a coin flip, Harry took the left seat and flew the airplane, with Jack sitting alongside.

The Navy taught its pilots to fly instruments expertly. What it failed to teach them was how to fly the airways which crisscross the country. That requires special knowledge. So Harry and Jack, as did most Navy pilots in those days, avoided the airways and flew to China Lake under visual flight rules. That meant they were, themselves, responsible for keeping clear of clouds and other airplanes.

They left under scattered clouds. Going north, the sky slowly became overcast and the clouds got lower as they flew, forcing them down to remain in clear air. Soon, they were down to just a few hundred feet above the ground, where navigation was difficult. Harry became apprehensive, decided discretion was in order, and turned back to Miramar. By now, the lowering clouds made visual navigation impossible and they were lost. Finding a road leading south, Harry followed it, hoping for the best. After a few minutes, the road split, one section leading up into the clouds and the other into a valley.

Harry turned into the valley, and Jack said tersely, "I wouldn't go in there if I were you."

"You got a better idea?" asked Harry, looking intently ahead and beginning to feel nervous.

The valley quickly narrowed and it was soon obvious that Harry had made a mistake. He decided to turn back.

"Hang on!" he said as he rolled into a steep turn and pulled the airplane around hard, sucking in his breath. Harry was not sure they could turn around without plowing into a hillside. Somehow, they made it and, somehow, they found their way back to Miramar, hugging the ground as they flew. The clouds rose as they neared the airport.

After shutting down the engine and climbing down to the tarmac, Harry opened the hatch leading to the passenger compartment. Those inside had no windows and no idea where they were. They scrambled down, thinking they were at China Lake, and Harry had to tell them they were right back where they had started a couple of hours ago. Never mind, they all said in high spirit, they had enjoyed the flight. They would have enjoyed it less, thought Harry, if they knew how close they had come to flying into a hillside.

Returning to the Ready Room, Harry poured a cup of coffee and raised it to his lips with a slightly trembling hand. As he did, he saw a safety poster on the wall depicting an airplane under low clouds about to fly into a hillside. Its caption: Do not fly under the weather or you might end up under the sod. Harry almost dropped his coffee mug. Jack, unfazed, as always, patted Harry on the back.

"That was one helluva U-turn you made back there, my friend," he said, with a grin.

Planning a nuclear strike was hard work. Photos of target areas were provided and only some years later, did Harry figure out that it was a U2 aircraft that had taken them. Now and then, when the ship came into port at Yokosuka, the Air Wing would be temporarily based at the nearby Atsugi Naval Air Station for training flights. After one such flight, Harry had just left his airplane when he noticed a flurry of activity near the end of the runway on which he had just landed. Curious, he stopped to look. What he saw was an unusual airplane with an extremely long wing-span, which touched down at a very low speed, ran a short distance, then was literally taken in hand by crewmen who grabbed its wingtips before it came to a stop, and hauled it into a hangar. That was a U2, but Harry did not know it at the time.

Each target had six or eight Initial Points, and the pilot could select one that correlated with his approach to the target. The IPs were prominent landmarks, and each one denoted the exact course and distance to the target.

Of course, none of this mattered if the plane did not reach the target. That was the hard part. Much of the planning went into navigation. Some targets were easy to find. One of Harry's, for example, was a submarine base at Petropavlosk on the Kamchatka Peninsula; but others were deep inland. One such target was some 800 miles deep into China. When Harry finished his planning for that one, he saw with concern, that he would not have enough fuel to return to the ship. Even Skyraiders ran out of fuel eventually. He informed the Air Intelligence Officer of his problem.

"Let me talk to the Admiral," he said. "I'll be right back." And he was, with the Admiral's message. "The Admiral says he wishes you good luck." The Admiral did not share Harry's concern.

With a pilot's optimism, Harry had complete confidence in his ability to deliver a weapon once he got to the target. But getting there: that was a different problem. First, he had to find his coastal-in point. That depended on the ship being where it said it was at the launch. That could not be counted on, so most pilots aimed for a point well left or right of the desired landmark. That way, crossing the coast, the pilot knew which way to turn to find his starting point for the overland part of the mission. Once found, he was faced with the difficult problem of map-navigating over unfamiliar terrain, flying only fifty feet above the ground.

A concept of vertical envelopment evolved. It used prominent landmarks that stood out against the terrain during low-level flight. Heavy dependence was placed on a very old and tested navigation technique: time and distance. The pilot simply flew from one landmark to the next, using only his compass and his clock. He also needed to hold the programmed airspeed, as the sector timing depended on it. Strict discipline was needed to maintain heading. This was difficult because of the need to focus attention outside the cockpit to keep track of the airplane's position. This was flying at its most demanding.

Arriving at a checkpoint, the pilot made a sharp turn to the new heading, then reset his clock for the next leg. Charts had the route drawn on them, with prominent features marked. It was a strip map and the strip was just ten miles wide. It was folded into segments like an accordion so that it would fit onto the pilot's kneeboard: a small pad strapped around one of his thighs. The pilot was in serious trouble if he wandered off the strip.

These flights, known as sand-blowers, followed the terrain, rising and falling to stay fifty feet above it. That was another problem, and it was a big one. Besides navigating, which, at such a low level was hard enough, the pilot had to think far enough ahead of the aircraft to avoid flying into obstructions. He had to add power soon enough to climb over them, then reduce power, sliding back down to fifty feet and, all the while, holding a target airspeed. Harry and his squadron-mates were well trained for this kind of mission. From their base at the Miramar Naval Air Station in San Diego, they flew at fifty feet all across southern California, Nevada and Arizona, map-navigating all the way. On one such flight Harry, had experienced the thrill of doing an aileron roll inside the Grand Canyon, well below its rim.

These flights could last up to ten hours or more. That was a long time to sit strapped into a cockpit. Bladders were emptied through a funnel connected to a hose that vented urine into the slipstream.

"Talk about pissing into the wind!" was Jack Rooney's comment.

This was one of the most challenging aspects of such flights. Unzipping, finding a well-covered penis, extracting it, urinating, returning it to its original position, and zipping up, all while manually flying an airplane close to the ground, was daunting work.

A friend of Harry's had once flown as a passenger in the old Bug Smasher. This ancient twin-engine, propeller-driven aircraft had a relief tube, too, back in its passenger cabin. On this particular airplane someone had forgotten to connect the funnel to the tube. As a result, when its user began to pee, he was surprised to see his urine splashing across the deck of the airplane -- not only on the deck, but also on the uniform jacket of his boss, who was flying the airplane. It had been tossed there from the cockpit during the flight. It was with great embarrassment that the urine-soaked jacket was handed to its owner after landing. The officer, a commander, threw his jacket to the ramp in disgust and stomped off.

Low-level flying was even more daunting while using an external fuel tank. Each of these tanks held 300 gallons but it had no fuel-quantity gauge in the cockpit. The pilot could not know how much fuel was remaining, and he had to guess when it was time to switch to the internal fuel tank. Sometimes a tank ran dry before the pilot expected it. If that happened, the engine quit and that sudden silence caught the pilot's attention very quickly; but if the pilot switched to the internal tank within a few seconds, the engine would sputter and backfire a time or two, then continue running. That was no problem when there was some space between the airplane and the ground; but it was a major concern when the airplane was flying at fifty feet, as they usually were during sand-blower missions. Flying near the ground and running on an external tank, a pilot had to pay very close attention to his work.

The next best thing to a fuel gauge for an external fuel tank was a passenger who kept an eye on the fuel pressure gauge. A sudden loss in pressure meant the tank was empty. Such a passenger was with Harry one day when he ran a tank dry. It happened in the squadron's one multi-seat version of the Skyraider. The occasion was a flight to an abandoned airport at Douglas, Arizona, which was just across the border from the Mexican town of Agua Prieta. The flight's mission was to buy inexpensive Mexican rum; and the passenger, an enlisted man named Filomeno Escobar, was there as an extra body to buy an extra bottle. This version of the Skyraider was designed for anti-submarine missions and could carry two pilots and four men in a compartment carved out of the fuselage just aft of the cockpit. On this trip, all seats were occupied to maximize the purchase of alcohol for an upcoming squadron party.

The airport had a row of five or six cars parked near the terminal. They belonged to the owner of a liquor shop on the Mexican side. The key was in the ignition and on the seat was a map marked with directions to his shop. It was not unusual to see several military airplanes standing on the ramp, all on missions similar to Harry's. After landing, the six men drove across the border, found the shop, loaded up on party supplies, then headed back to the airplane for the trip home.

They were at 8,000 feet and in the clear when suddenly Escobar began screaming, Sweetch! Sweetch!

Harry and his fellow pilot exchanged glances that asked, "What the hell is he shouting about?"

Just then the engine sputtered and stopped, and they knew. Escobar had been intently monitoring the fuel-pressure gauge and when he saw it drop, he very loudly told Harry to switch tanks from external to internal. "Sweetch!" was not Mexican; it was English with a Mexican accent. Harry turned the grip-style handle to the internal tank position and, within a few seconds, the engine coughed, then resumed its steady beat, and Escobar smiled, sat back, and relaxed. No one had ordered him to act as an external fuel tank gauge, he said later, he just did not like the sound of silence in an airborne airplane.

The party was held at a house near the sea in Solana Beach and was a huge success. The house was a "Snake Ranch," which was one occupied by a group of bachelors. The party theme was grunion. Someone had explained to Harry that grunion were small fish which, at certain times of the year, lay and fertilize eggs on the beach between successive waves. He thought it was an ingenious hoax but, what the hell, any excuse for a party was a good one. The Mexican rum was thrown into a new metal garbage can along with "no-one-was-sure-what-else," and a vicious brew was concocted, recipe unknown. A few drinks were enough to encourage most of the grunion hunters to head for the beach, armed with buckets and nets. Harry was one, and the sight that he recalled most vividly was that of his squadron skipper, at the surf's edge, holding a lantern and searching diligently for grunion. A sudden, unexpected large wave inundated him, and all Harry could see above the water was the lantern and the hand that grasped it. Against all odds, a few grunion were found and grilled. That was catering at its most basic level.

All Navy pilots had heard the tale of the squadron based in Jacksonville that had modified an external fuel tank to carry Cuban rum. That rum could be bought for just ten cents a gallon at Guantanamo Bay in the pre-Castro days. On his way home from a rum-run, the pilot had made a fuel stop at another military airport along the way.

"All topped up?" he asked as he returned from flight ops where he had filed his flight plan.

"Yes, sir," was the reply, "but I could get only a few gallons into your external tank."

On sand-blower flights, the catering was provided by the Navy in a white cardboard box containing enough basic food to get the pilot back to his starting point. To eat lunch, the box was placed on a flat, plastic plotting board which was used for navigating at sea and which was neatly stowed beneath the instrument panel. Drawn from its storage slot, it made a flying picnic table. The box lunch always included a couple of hard-boiled eggs. On his very first sand-blower flight, Harry learned the hard way that egg shells cannot be thrown from an airplane in flight. He nearly flew into the ground as a blizzard of airborne eggshells was blown back inside the cockpit. Someone should have warned him about that.

"Hell," said one of Harry's squadron-mates over a cup of coffee when Harry told him about the flying eggshells. "I can top that."

He went on to relate a story about the death of a friend who had stipulated in his will that he be cremated and his ashes scattered over the sea. He had enlisted the help of a mutual friend and they had rented a small propeller-driven airplane to accommodate their friend's wishes. No one had warned them, either. When they opened the sliding window and tried to throw out what was left of their dead friend, his ashes were blown back into their faces and, instead of being scattered over the sea, they were spread in a fine coat of dust throughout the cockpit.

"Those ashes are probably still there," he said, "flying all over the place. But what the hell, isn't that better than floating on the ocean?"

Harry agreed that it probably was.

Despite their problems, sand-blowers worked fine in theory and that was good enough for Harry. If the bell rang, well, he would just do his best and hope it all worked in the real world as well as it did in the practice world; but somehow, he had his doubts.

49
SKYHAWK SAND-BLOWERS

1964

A few years later, Harry would be flying sand-blowers in an A4 Skyhawk. Now, that was exciting. The Skyhawks flew 200 feet off the ground, higher than the old Spads; but the airspeed was more than double at 360 knots, more than 400 miles per hour. It became crucial to stay on course. Precise navigation was required. One advantage of the jets was that their higher airspeed allowed them to "zoom climb," in case of trouble ahead. Harry could still hear the urgent cry of "CLIMB!" from his wingman during a Spad sand-blower in southern California. When a pilot hears a call like that one, he doesn't think; he reacts. Harry had instantly pulled back hard on the control stick just in time to see power lines flash beneath him. A squadron-mate had once blacked out half of Phoenix when he flew into its power lines. Another advantage of the jets was that the flights were of much shorter duration. Still, it was intense flying, and Harry always felt drained when he returned from one of them.

Because a jet consumes much more fuel at lower altitudes, its strike profile was different from those of the Skyraider. The Skyhawk climbed to a high altitude after launching, then descended to 200 feet for the overland part of the mission. That was to avoid radar. To simulate these profiles, training flights from Lemoore climbed high, flew westward over the Pacific for some distance, then turned back toward the coast, dropped down low, crossed the coast, and flew to the target. The overland parts of these flights took Harry over parts of northern California, Oregon, and Nevada. The scenery, even close to the ground at 360 knots, was often stunning.

The Skyhawk was developed, from concept to first flight, in less than one year during the early fifties, to take over the nuclear mission of the Skyraider. It was a single-seat, sub-sonic airplane designed to deliver a nuclear weapon on a low-level mission. It could do that, but it could do more. The war in Vietnam pressed it into a role it was not meant to fill, that of an air-to-ground attack airplane. Because of its original mission, the airplane was small and lacked excess thrust; so, when the Navy began hanging iron bombs on the Skyhawk, its performance suffered. Insufficient power and its small size combined to limit its load, but it performed valiantly in the Tonkin Gulf.

Its reduced size made it the smallest airplane ever to operate from a carrier deck. Among its nicknames were "Scooter" and "Tinker Toy." With its high nose gear strut and a delta-shaped wing, it somewhat resembled a gnat. Its small wings did not take up much deck space, so they did not fold, as did every other carrier airplane ever built. Folding wings saved enormous deck space, and one of the important items on the takeoff checklist was to ensure the wings were down and locked. Harry knew of two pilots who had ignored their checklists and had made airfield takeoffs with folded wings. Both managed to get airborne, but not for long. Checklists were only as good as the pilot who used them.

Because of their high speed, a different delivery method could be used in a jet. Instead of lobbing a rocket-assisted bomb from a distance, a jet could simply fly over the target and begin a loop. When the aircraft was nearly vertical, the bomb was automatically released and kept going straight up as the aircraft continued its loop until it was about two-thirds of the way around. It then rolled upright and streaked away in the opposite direction. By the time the bomb reached zero speed at its maximum height and dropped back to earth, the delivery aircraft was long gone. This type of delivery was known as toss bombing, and this particular method was called over-the-shoulder. The run-in was at 500 knots, about 575 miles per hour, and just 200 feet above the ground. If a pilot did not get a thrill from the earth rushing beneath him at that speed, he was missing his full ration of adrenalin.

50
BACK TO BRUSSELS

November 1970

Chief Pilot Eddie LeBlanc was the first person to board the airplane after Harry shut down the engines in Brussels. He was all smiles as he burst into the cockpit and enthusiastically shook Harry's hand as he and Gene were completing the shutdown checklist. He was positively beaming with pleasure that the first flight had gone well.

"Well done, Harry," he said several times. As soon as the last passenger left the airplane, he went into the cabin.

"Come, join us. We will make a party," he said over his shoulder as he left the cockpit.

They did, and within minutes, the party was underway. The cabin crew, a few mechanics, fuelers, and finally, even the youthful president of the fledgling company joined the celebration. Bottles of champagne appeared and plastic cups were passed around. Now, this is the way to end a trip, thought Harry.

Along about his third drink, Harry tapped Eddie on the shoulder. "Eddie, I was expecting some news from Oslo. Have you heard anything about when we're going back?"

Eddie's eyebrows went up. "Ah, mon Dieu, j'ai oublie. Yes, here. I have a telex for you."

He handed a yellow sheet of paper to Harry. "You are not going back so soon, it seems. We need your help and I hope you do not mind."

Harry read the telex quickly. It directed Harry, along with his crew and the airplane, to remain in Brussels until further notice. They would be on a "wet" lease to the new Belgian company for "some months." "Wet" meant the lease of the airplane included the crew. More information would follow. Harry folded the telex and slipped it into his pocket.

The course of Harry's life had often been abruptly changed by a slip of paper or a telephone call. He was, at this moment, drinking champagne on an airplane at Zaventem Airport in Brussels because of a call from a friend a few months ago. That call had certainly been a life-changer. This telex might be another. You never knew.

Thoughts of Astrid came into his head. He missed her and hoped she missed him. He made a mental note to call her soon. He sipped his champagne, then smiled at Eddie and said, "No, of course, we don't mind. I just hope all the flights are as pleasant as this one. How does it look for you now? When do you expect to be flying your own airplane?"

Eddie shrugged and said, "Difficult to know. We have one crew ready now; two are almost ready; and we have just purchased another airplane. We are searching for crew, so if you are interested in working here, for us . . . ." He did not finish that sentence and he did not need to.

"Is that a job offer I just heard?" asked Harry.

"Most certainly," Eddie replied pleasantly. "How do you think about it? We do need you. Your crew, too."

"Well, thanks for the offer; but I need to think about it first. There is my contract with Trans Polar."

"Eh, bien," Eddie said. "We hope you will join us."

Contract, Harry thought with a mental smile. A few words scratched on a page torn out of a spiral notebook; but Thor had insisted that some of those words held both sides to a three-month notice of termination. Fair enough, thought Harry, at the time.

Just then he caught Michelle's eye. Their frequent close contact during the trip had generated a spark, tiny but definite. She smiled, raised her glass towards Harry and nodded. Was that an invitation, Harry asked himself. Should he try again? He was reluctant. Harry admired men for whom rejection was no reason not to try. They were straightforward in their chase. If it worked, fine. If not, well, there were other women and no harm done. Harry, on the other hand, was fearful of rejection. At times, he thought he would rather make a night carrier landing than approach a woman he did not know. Irrational, he knew, but there it was. It was a trait that Harry seriously disliked about himself. In other pursuits, he was persistent almost to a fault. But with women, one rejection was usually enough. And, at times, he was unsure if the rebuff was real or imagined. Sometimes, he knew, a relationship reached a point where it became physical. If that moment was lost, it was usually lost forever.

Now, emboldened by the champagne, Harry, using most of his French vocabulary, said "Excusez moi" to Eddie, then edged his way to Michelle's side. He nudged his plastic cup up against hers and said, "Michelle, I enjoyed working with you. If ever you decide to get unmarried, will you let me know?"

She leaned over and kissed his cheek lightly. "Ah, oui, Harry, you shall be the first I shall tell. Promise."

Harry smiled back, bowed ever so slightly, and lifted his glass in a small salute. That was a rejection he could live with.

258

51
JACOBOWITZ

November 1970

TEA arranged accommodations for Harry, Rolf, and Gene. It was not five stars, but it was certainly colorful, which was, for Harry, even better. Each had a room in what was once an elegant mansion, now a rooming house run by an elderly Jewish man named Jacobowitz. Harry called him Mr. Jacob and he seemed to like that. He was short and plump with a body that resembled a bowling pin. What hair he had left was white and thin. He looked old until you talked to him. Then, his bright blue eyes twinkled as he fixed you with an intelligent gaze. He was Old Europe personified: courteous, friendly, and helpful.

He seemed to enjoy their company, and Harry liked talking to him. That was not easy at first because he spoke English with an accent that was half-French and half-Jewish; but after a while, Harry learned to decode him quite easily, and he sometimes translated for Rolf and Gene.

"Harry," asked Rolf, after one of these conversations, "do you realize you are translating English into English?" Harry grinned as he thought about it.

"No, I didn't. But whatever works, right?"

Their rooms faced an interior court that was used as a kitchen and dining area. Mr. Jacobowitz cooked and served breakfast, and it was a good one. Eggs to order, Belgian waffles, good, strong coffee and, of course, pistolets. These were rolls, crisp on the outside, soft on the inside and delicious all over, especially when filled with French cheese or Belgian salami. In the afternoons, their host provided tea and in the evenings, on request, chilled bottles of beer.

The old house was within walking distance of the TEA office. They had been given three days off and directions to the office. It was a fine day and they enjoyed a stroll through a commercial area and found the office easily. There, they learned what would happen next. They would operate a series of flights to Palma de Majorca.

The flights would be turn-arounds, meaning returning to Brussels after refueling. Palma de Majorca had an exotic ring and Harry looked forward to seeing it, even if only from the air; but where the hell was it? Someone pointed it out on wall map in the office. A Spanish island in the Mediterranean? Okay, thought Harry, let's go to Palma! He glanced at the map.

"Hey, wait a minute!" he exclaimed. "I've been there! One of my first flights with Trans Polar; but we never left the airport. Maybe now I can see the rest of it."

On their way home, the trio stopped at a local café and drank a few good Belgian beers on an outside terrace. Belgians seemed to enjoy drinking outside, and terraces were everywhere. The late afternoon sun warmed Harry inside and out. Life was good. Tonight, he would call Astrid. He smiled just to think of her.

52
TRIPOLI

1971

Harry could not imagine why anyone would want to visit Libya, but there were always people who wanted to see unusual places. Before his first flight to Palma, Harry was assigned to carry a plane filled with such curiosity seekers to Tripoli and then return with an empty airplane. Harry had never been there, and it was with some misgiving that he landed in Colonel Kadaffi's backyard. The Colonel was known to harbor anti-American sentiments. The first sign of trouble came after parking, when Harry handed the fueler the credit card. This card, stowed in the cockpit, was the usual way to pay for fuel.

"Sorry," he was told in a courteous but firm voice by the driver of the fuel truck, "no credit card. Cash only, please."

A 707 could safely fly without many components, but fuel was not on that list. Harry's first action was to call Brussels. There, the problem could be resolved; but making a telephone call from Tripoli proved to be an exercise in futility. The telephone system in Libya was hopeless.

"Good luck, Captain," the agent in flight operations had said as he handed Harry the telephone; but Harry had no luck at all. He then tried sending a telex, but who knew if the message was received or even sent? Or when it would be read if it got through to Brussels? He did not hold out much hope.

Back at the airplane, he tried to persuade the fueler to accept his personal credit card, but he knew what the answer would be.

"Sorry, Captain, but my orders, they are cash only," he said several times, somewhat apologetically. Harry went back into the cockpit and began thinking. He pulled out his billfold and counted his cash. He always carried a few hundred dollars for emergencies, but who would expect one like this?

He turned to the first officer and the flight engineer. "Either of you have any cash?" he asked hopefully.

The first officer shook his head without bothering to look in his billfold. "A few francs, Captain."

The flight engineer furrowed his brow in thought. After a few moments, he replied, "Oui, Harry, I cashed my paycheck just before we left. I am just considering if I shall have it returned to me if we use it for fuel."

Harry's face broke out in a grin as he saw a glimmer of hope.

He extended his palm. "Let's have it, Michel, or we might be here forever. I promise you *will* get it back."

A hectic few minutes followed as Harry and the first officer dove into the aircraft manual to determine the minimum quantity of fuel needed to reach Brussels. Harry used methods that bent the charts in favor of a smaller number. The number was surprisingly small and, at first, Harry questioned his own answer; but Tripoli was not as far from Belgium as it might seem at first glance. It was another world in many ways, but its location was on the south shore of the Mediterranean Sea, almost part of Europe. The weather was clear over the entire route. An empty airplane meant they could fly at a high altitude, where fuel consumption was lower, and direct routing more likely.

Next, they counted their cash, translated the amount into fuel and found that, although it was close, they could legally launch for Brussels. Of course, the flight might not be assigned a high altitude or direct routing, but that was in the hands of the airways gods. As long as the departure was legal, they could legally land with less fuel than the charts promised. Leaving Libya was looking better.

The fuel had to be paid in U.S. dollars, so Harry took Michel's francs to the airport bank and exchanged them for dollars. He added them to his own and handed the total to the fueler, who took it with a huge smile and quickly counted it. Harry stood by the truck as the fuel was pumped, to ensure they got their money's worth.

It was with a large sigh of relief that Harry saw the runway fall away as they climbed for home. Nothing seemed to work in Tripoli, and he would be happy if he never came back. It was not only the telephones that did not work. The navigation radios serving the airport were unserviceable. The communications radios were almost incomprehensible due to strong static. Harry had learned to judge a country by its airport. This one was at the bottom of the list, and it did not speak well for Libya.

In the midst of all this inefficiency an obnoxious man in a uniform entered the cockpit just as they were preparing to start their engines. He asked to see Harry's pilot license. That was, of course, his right; but Harry could barely suppress his indignation as reached into his flight bag and withdrew his license. From his English, Harry suspected the man could not read it. It would be the only time that Harry would ever be asked to show his license; and it had to happen in Tripoli where almost nothing worked the way it was supposed to. Harry hoped that the airport in Palma was more user-friendly. It could hardly be worse.

53
VIKKI CARR

1966

Even during a war, life on an aircraft carrier could sometimes become boring. The tedium on Dixie Station was one day unexpectedly broken by a visit from a courageous group of Hollywood luminaries. They had flown to the ship on the COD, and that was reason enough to admire them. Undergoing a carrier landing to boost shipboard morale was surely beyond the call of duty. The troupe included Danny Kaye, Vikki Carr, Ann Margret, and a golfer named Billy Casper. They were instantly taken into the hearts of all who saw them. They performed on the hangar deck at hours that had to fit into the ship's operating schedule. That meant some shows early in the morning and others late at night. The makeshift stage and the equipment must have seemed prehistoric to them, but no one complained. The shows were stopped often by enthusiastic applause and loud shouts, but the performers seemed to love it. If Harry's reaction was typical, everyone who watched these shows would remember them fondly for the rest of their lives; and the artists would always hold that special place in their hearts.

While they were aboard, the ship recorded a landmark landing. Harry wondered who kept track of such things, but someone knew that a junior pilot that day had made the ten-thousandth landing of the Kitty Hawk's career. Traditionally, this was an important event. An enormous cake was baked with the number 10,000 written across its frosted top It was presented to the pilot after dinner that night in the officers' wardroom. Vikki Carr did the honors, and when she gave the pilot the first piece, she gave him, along with the cake, a friendly kiss on the cheek. The pilot, seizing the moment, answered Miss Carr's kiss with a serious kiss. She responded in the same way, and the dining room erupted with whistles and prolonged applause. Danny Kaye separated them with the comment, "A lot of people are watching here." Harry, along with dozens of other Navy pilots, fell in love with Vikki Carr that night. How could you not be in love with a woman like her?

Harry became a lifelong fan of Vikki Carr. Many years later, Harry happened to be in Las Vegas while she was performing. He bought tickets and sent a note to her hotel, reminding her of her visit to the Kitty Hawk long ago. Did she remember? A reply came quickly and it invited Harry and his wife to join her backstage after the show. She did, indeed, remember.

Those shows, she told Harry, with some emotion, were the most memorable of her career. Miss Carr was warm, kind, and gracious. She was a lady with class. Harry and his wife liked her immediately and they very much enjoyed a drink together. Harry had been right to be a little in love with her for all those years.

54
GOODBYE, ASTRID

1971

After some difficulty, Harry managed to get through to Astrid on the telephone. When using telephones abroad, Harry was always reminded of the wonder of efficiency that was the American telephone system. Finally, with the help of Mr. Jacobowitz, he heard Astrid's voice and it was good to hear. There was a minute or two of hello, how are you. Harry thought, "Oh, oh, she does not sound like the same Astrid." She was pleasant and friendly, but somehow diffident. He had expected more enthusiasm. Something is different, thought Harry. He went straight to the point.

"Astrid, I miss you here in Brussels. Now, it looks like we'll be here for a few weeks, maybe longer. So I'm thinking about coming to Oslo for a few days. Or maybe you could come here. What do you think?"

There was a pause, a long one. Then: "Harry, please do not come to Oslo. Not for me, anyway."

Harry was stunned. "What do you mean, do not come to Oslo?"

"What I said. I mean do not come. My life is changed very much since we were together. And I am feeling very," she paused to find the right word, "uncomfortable if you come."

"Changed? Changed how? "

There was another pause, even longer. Harry could actually hear her breathing, all the way from Oslo. "Harry, I am going to be married."

Now, Harry was more than stunned, he was shocked. He felt a tiny jolt of electricity shooting through his body, as if he had run into a wall. He had been starting to think that Astrid might be the one, his life partner. He had never said so, and now he wished he had.

"Married? How can you be married? You said you loved me. In Singapore. Remember? How can you be married?" He wasn't sure, but he thought he heard a faint catch in her voice.

"Harry, I told you about Martin, remember?"

Damn said Harry softly to himself, sensing bad news.

"What? What did you say?"

"Nothing. I'm thinking," said Harry. Martin, Martin. Who the hell was Martin, and how did he get into this conversation? A memory flickered.

"Martin? Your old boyfriend? Is he the one? You told me that was over."
He heard her inhale sharply.

"We were engaged to be married. Now, we are again engaged to be
married. I do love you, Harry, but my life is here, not in Singapore, and God
knows where else. You will always be in my heart. Believe me, please. I did
mean it when I said I loved you. I did, and perhaps I still do; but I do not
want for you to come here. It would be too difficult for me. Later, perhaps,
but not now. Please?"

Then, *Click!* and her voice was gone. Harry thought about calling back,
but what was the use? No, he would go to Oslo and talk to Astrid. But she
had just told him not to come! Harry was confused. More than confused, he
was bewildered. He needed a drink and some time to think. He handed the
phone to Mr. Jacobowitz, who was standing next to Harry, timing the call.

Harry said, "You won't believe this, but I've just been dumped."

Mr. Jacobowitz smiled pleasantly and replied. "Dumped. Yes, I am
happy for you. I will add this call to your bill. Would you care for a beer?"

55
PALMA

1971

From the air, Palma de Majorca did, indeed, look exotic. On the ground, it looked less so. That was because so many airplanes came to Palma that the traffic around the airport, and on it as well, was chaotic. Everybody, it seemed, wanted to come to Palma; and Harry had trouble understanding the Spanish controllers. They sometimes spoke to other airplanes in Spanish, which they were not supposed to do. English. It was supposed to be English. There was always a holding pattern for arriving airplanes, so Harry had plenty of time to look at the island. Once on the ground, he had to call for a place in the takeoff sequence even before they parked the airplane. Delays were several hours and, at times, Harry was number forty or fifty in the queue for departure. But, what the hell, the weather was good, it was exotic Palma and even the airport held a certain mystique for Harry. He usually spent an hour or so in the duty-free shop. There was plenty to look at and, even though he had not been paid his salary in several months, there was always enough to buy a bottle of Spanish brandy. Since becoming a regular on the Majorca Metro, as one stewardess called it, Harry had tried different kinds of brandy and had finally settled on Magno as his favorite. He already had an impressive collection of Spanish bottles in his room. The price was certainly right, usually about one U.S. dollar for a bottle.

Harry had argued with himself for a week after his conversation with Astrid. Should he call back? Should he go to Oslo? He wished he were one who would not take no for an answer, but he often did, when it was a woman who was saying no. It was an old failing, and one he regretted. But, somehow, he could not persuade himself to call Astrid back. If it was meant to be, he told himself, it will sort itself out; but he was not sure he believed himself. In the end, Harry had done nothing, and he never saw Astrid again. He would often wonder, in the years ahead, what might have happened had he pursued Astrid. There had been many "what ifs" in Harry's life and this was one more. This was a big one.

56
HELLO, IRENE

1971

Harry dug out the corner of his menu from the Rio restaurant with Irene's telephone number, held his breath, and called. He could still remember the tension he had felt in his youth when he called a girl for an ordinary date. Usually, he procrastinated until it was too late. At other times he felt his heart race as she answered the phone. Stupid, he thought to himself, but it's still there. The girls of Europe seemed more natural, more straightforward, more -- what? -- uncomplicated -- he decided that was the right word. Irene was certainly in that category. Yes, of course, she remembered Harry. How could she forget the man who had taken her all the way to Rio de Janeiro? She would very much like to see him again.

"I am free on Saturday," she said. "Perhaps we might have lunch." She said it with a question mark on the end, letting Harry make the decision. That was a nice touch. Irene had a car. A rendezvous was agreed upon. She would stop in front of his building to pick him up at noon on Saturday.

"Nice," said Harry as he slipped into the seat beside her and glanced around the car. "Looks like a cockpit." It was not just a car. It was a dark green Alfa Romeo with leather bucket seats. Irene smiled as she thrust her left hand across her chest to Harry.

"Yes, but not as fast as your airplane."

Harry took her left hand in his right one and gave it a polite squeeze. "Sure? It looks like mach one just standing still."

"Mach one? Is that airplane language?"

"The speed of sound," replied Harry, as he studied the instrument panel. "Nice to see you again," he said. "Are you hungry? I remember you had a very good fork there in Rio."

She smiled again. "I will accept that as a compliment. I am always hungry. And you?"

"Almost always. Depends what's on the menu."

"Ah, of course. Today the menu will please you. I do hope so, anyway. As Americans are famous for their fine steaks, today I offer you one from Belgium. We have good ones, too. And of course we will have some of our famous Belgian pommes frittes. You call them French fries. Does it suit you?"

"A Belgian steak sounds just fine. And I like French fries, too. But why are yours famous?"

She smiled. "First we shall see if you like them, then I will explain."

Harry smiled back. "Fair enough. And what about some wine? Can we add wine to our menu?"

"Most certainly," she said, looking back over her shoulder at the road behind. "But the wine will be French," she said, as she eased away from the curb. "The cognac, too. I remember you like it."

Harry grinned and said "Yes, I'm always ready for a drink in good company."

He was starting to like her already, and that was a good sign. After just a few minutes, he could sense that tiny tug of chemistry that told him that this girl would be a pleasure to be around. Another sign was that he immediately felt comfortable with her; and she looked great; even better than he remembered. She smelled great, too. Astrid was beginning to fade away ever so slightly.

Irene deftly guided the car through the midday traffic to a small restaurant just outside Brussels, chatting as she drove. It was a fine day and there was an outside terrace. Perfect! thought Harry as they were seated beneath a large umbrella. The steaks were perfect, too, as was the wine. It was a wonderful lunch and Harry would remember this one for a long time. It marked the beginning.

Along with learning about pommes frittes, Harry learned much about Irene during their lunch. Her father played the first violin in the Antwerp symphony orchestra. He was sixteen when World War I broke out. Almost all of Belgium, including his family, prepared to flee the advancing German Army; but her father, learning that his violin professor would remain behind, decided to stay in Antwerp. He lived alone throughout the war, learning music and practicing on his violin. That, thought Harry, was dedication. The Germans came to Belgium in the war's early days and left before it was over. They would be back a quarter-of-a-century later.

Harry knew almost nothing about classical music and even less about the instruments used to play it. The violin, Irene told him, was the instrument around which much of the music turned. It was always the violin, she said, that was heard during the most touching, most poignant, and most moving parts of the performance. She talked about how the first violin, often playing solo, was under great pressure to play well. One false note could not only ruin the performance, but set tongues wagging the next day. "Think of it," she said, "always alive"-- she meant 'live' -- "and always before a very critical audience with never a chance to correct mistakes. There are no second chances." With recorded music, she went on, a bad note could be replayed. Not on the stage. It had to be right the first time.

Opera singers, unlike rock stars, sang without microphones. They also had to sing from memory an entire score that might last several hours. They had to be actors, too. "Take away the microphone," she said, "and most rock stars would have to find employment elsewhere. Not many would listen to them."

Harry, who did not like rock music, even *with* a microphone, thought she probably had that right. They would have an even harder time finding an audience, he thought, if their drums and electric guitars were taken away. Rhythm and melody were not important. For them, the beat was everything.

Harry had never been to an opera or a symphony; but her point was well made. Classical music performers needed far more talent and substance than rock stars, yet they were almost unknown outside their orbit. Rock stars found fame and fortunes based on beat and volume, and they performed wearing clothes Harry would not have even given to the poor; but the masses of youth ignored the classics and threw large amounts of money and adulation at rock stars. There was no explaining taste.

When she met her father, Irene's mother was a pianist, studying at the Antwerp Conservatorium of Music. Her father, also studying there, was preparing for a recital before a panel of expert musicians who would decide whether he merited the King's Medal. This award was the highest honor a Belgian musician could win. Her mother, just seventeen years old, provided his accompaniment. In the world of Old Europe, although they practiced together daily, they addressed each other by their surnames. One sunny, but cold, morning, during a respite from their practice, they strolled together in a garden.

"Oh, my hands are so cold," said Irene's mother as they began to walk. Without speaking, the violinist took her hand in his. "Mr. Van Doren," her mother said in surprise. "Do you know what this means?" In the innocence of those times, it meant very much. Walking a few more steps, her father stopped abruptly and turned to her mother.

"Miss Verhaegen," the violinist asked, "will you marry me?"

Her mother was stunned.

"But Mr. Van Doren," she asked, "do you love me?"

"To be honest," he answered, "no. But that will come." And it did come. Irene was the proof. The King's Medal also came, distinguishing her father as one of the finest violinists in Belgium. Harry's expressed surprise that two people working together would use formal surnames. "It's different in the States," he said.

"I know," Irene said, "I work with Americans."

She went on to relate an incident that took place in the home of a colleague. For some reason, Irene had to spend a night with a woman with whom she had worked for years. There was only one bed and they shared it. Before turning out the lights, they said goodnight to each other using their surnames.

"Wow," said Harry, "that is for sure formal. She really said, 'Goodnight Miss Van Doren' to a girl sleeping in the same bed with her?"

Irene laughed. "That's Europe," she said.

Because she was raised in a musical family, Irene knew music, especially classical music and, among the classics, especially the operas. She attended the theater regularly when her father played. She met and collected signatures of many noted performers of the time. Later, she would often astound Harry when, hearing three or four notes, she identified the aria and singer. She would sometimes sing the words or hum the notes a moment or two before they were heard.

"After all," she would say. "I grew up with them."

As a child, she had lived in Antwerp during its occupation by the Germans and had experienced horrific sights. Jewish neighbors were hauled off to death camps. Friends were taken away to work in factories outside of Belgium.

The Gestapo, feared by all, wore around their necks a chain connected to a curved metal plate that hung across their breasts. In central Antwerp, Irene had once seen this plate used to cruelly beat a German soldier. As the soldier lay on the street, motionless, the officer had stomped violently on his stomach. After the beating he had been dragged off by other soldiers, his body lifeless. Irene had no idea what the soldier had done or whether he survived.

"This," she said with some bitterness, "it says much about these Germans. The way they think. The way they act. Imagine! One of their own! So, perhaps, you can understand why some Belgians will always hate the Germans."

Despite the war, the Germans managed to enjoy their classic entertainment. Operas and symphonies were regular features of wartime Antwerp. Wagner, their favorite, was often heard. Because of her father, Irene was at some of these performances. She talked about how, in a city that had not seen an orange in many months, the audience saw one peeled and slowly eaten during a scene from Carmen. The scent of that orange filled the theater, reminding the Belgians that something so ordinary could smell so special.

"I was there that night," Irene said, with a trace of sadness, "and sometimes, even now, I can smell that orange."

Her eyes misted as she reached back to recall that bittersweet memory. Horses were seen on stage in Wagner's "Rienzi." The Germans loved their opera. Unfortunately for Belgium, they liked oppression, too, and they sometimes applied it in a brutal fashion.

After the Americans drove the Germans out of Antwerp, German V bombs targeted the port. Irene remembered the awful silence when the V1 ran out of fuel. That marked the start of its descent. The later V2 bombs were precursors of ballistic missiles. Some of the V1 bombs were shot down, but it was not possible to bring down a V2. The bombs were aimed at the port, but many struck the city. People she knew were lost under some of them. Several landed within a block or two of her home. The blast from one had actually blown her off the street and through an open doorway. Another hit a nearby café on New Year's Eve. It was filled with her neighbors and English soldiers, dancing and celebrating. Most were killed, and some of these were later found still holding each other in a dance of death.

Irene's father came near death while practicing his music at home. A bomb explosion shattered a large window and sent pieces of glass crashing about the room. One of those shards, the size of a carving knife, narrowly missed his throat and imbedded itself in the wall like a dagger, scant inches from where he stood playing his violin.

One Sunday afternoon, a V-bomb struck the Rex cinema on Antwerp's main avenue. The theater was full, and some 550 Belgians lost their lives while watching "Buffalo Bill," an American movie starring Joel McCrea. One of the survivors was a friend of Irene's, spared because he sat beneath the balcony.

Even today, Irene said, many Belgians would have nothing to do with Germans or anything German. They remembered. What they remembered so painfully was what made them so grateful to the Americans for driving the Germans from Belgium. Americans, Harry told her, could not relate to such experiences. They had never had to undergo them. For them, the war was far off, in another world.

As they sipped a cognac after the meal, Harry sensed that this might be the start of an important relationship. This girl had it all. Irene was the personal assistant to the manager of a large bank. She was from Antwerp in the Flemish part of Belgium, so that was her first language. French was her second, and English was number three on her list.

Later, when Harry would now and then correct some small mistake, she reminded him that, "After all, English is only my third language." She also spoke Spanish and German. She could type and take shorthand in three of them. She was pretty, smart and vivacious; and incredibly, she seemed to like Harry. As always, Harry was surprised that such a woman could be attracted to him. He vaguely wondered why. Someday, he would ask one of them, perhaps this one.

It was late afternoon when they finally made their way back to what Harry called the Jacobowitz Chateau. Irene came alongside the curb to let Harry out.

On an impulse, Harry said, "It's too early to go home. How about a nightcap?"

"A nightcap? And what is that?"

"A nightcap. The last drink of the evening," replied Harry.

Without pause, Irene smiled and said, "Yes, why not? I am always interested in trying something new; but perhaps at this hour we might call it a daycap?"

Clever, too, Harry thought, as he smiled back. "Trying something new. Does that apply to people, too?"

Irene smiled her delightful smile. "Sometimes. It depends upon the people."

Irene parked nearby and they entered the building. Mr. Jacobowitz was there, drinking tea. Harry introduced them and they spoke a few words in French. Harry politely declined an offer of tea and cakes and, in a few minutes, they were in Harry's room. It was clean and spacious, and Harry was pleased he had tidied the room before he left. There was a balcony that had a view of the street below, but not much more. As Irene stood on the balcony, Harry found a bottle of Magno and poured the drinks.

As they touched their glasses together, Irene said, "Harry, you are going to think I am an alcoholic."

"Hey," chided Harry, "some of my best friends are alcoholics. Sante."
He raised his glass and sipped. Irene's sip was tiny, even for a sip.

"Would you believe me," she said as she set her glass down, "the brandy
after our dinner in Rio was my very first one?"

Harry smiled. "You could have fooled me. You looked like you did it all
the time."

"No, no, I was just wanting to look like that. To make a good impression.
I can still feel the alcohol from our lunch. I am not used to it. Feel my
cheek." Harry placed his fingertips on her cheek and looked into her eyes.
She returned the look with one that said, "I would like you to kiss me." Harry
hesitated, wondering. Irene's eyebrows lifted slightly. What are you waiting
for, they asked. Harry drew her close and, oh, she smelled nice. She returned
his embrace. Harry nuzzled her neck and her response told him that it was
time for their first kiss. That physical moment so important to a relationship
had come very early, but Harry knew it had come.

He kissed her lightly on her cheek.

"Yes, it does feel warm," he murmured, as he drew his lips over it and
found her lips. It was not only the "when" that made the first kiss important;
it was also the "how." This one was a great kiss, at the right moment. Harry
had learned that there were many ways to kiss, and Irene seemed to know
them all. Almost without knowing how it happened, they were in bed together
and it was wonderful. There were also many ways to be wonderful in bed,
and Irene seemed to know all those, too.

Later, she would tell Harry, "After all, you are not my first. But you are
my most"-- she searched for the right word -- "enthusiastic."

"I will take that as a compliment," he had replied, grinning.

The memory of Astrid faded a bit more.

Harry awoke just as the sun was setting. Beside him, Irene stirred. She
turned to Harry and smiled.

"That was a wonderful nightcap, Harry. I enjoyed it very much."

"Well," said Harry, "I'm not sure how all that happened, but I'm glad it
did. I enjoyed it, too."

"It happened," she said, "because it was meant to happen. I could see
this from the beginning. I was sure it would happen, but I was not sure when.
It's better sooner, isn't it? We can enjoy it more."

Harry grinned and thought, there is no pretense in this lady, that's for
sure. Aloud, he said, "What about another nightcap? That first one seemed
to do magic."

"So early in the evening? No, merci, I can still feel the first one. The magic will still be there, even without the nightcap," she said, as she put her arm across his chest and kissed his cheek. "You will see."

Just then came a knock on the door. They heard Mr. Jacobowitz say, "Captain, a telephone call for you. They say urgent." Damn, thought Harry, this is no time for urgent telephone calls. He thought briefly about asking Mr. Jacobowitz to tell the caller he was not there; but there was something about a telephone call that Harry could not ignore. They had been important in his life, and he could not ignore them, no matter how he tried.

Harry quickly put on his trousers and padded in his bare feet down to the telephone. It was Eddie LeBlanc. "Captain Harry," he said, although the way he said it sounded like Captain 'Arry. When speaking English, the French seemed confused about when to pronounce the letter H. A few days ago a stewardess had referred to herself as a "hair 'ostess."

"You are needed for a flight to Athens tonight," said LeBlanc with an urgent tone. "Please, can you come to the airport immediately? Sorry, but it is an emergency. Can you come?"

Harry paused a few seconds before he answered. He had, just a few hours ago, drunk half a bottle of wine and a couple of cognacs. There was Irene in his room to think about. TEA now had its own airplane and one or two crews. Another captain should be available.

"Is there no one else?" he asked, but he knew Eddie would not have called unless he was desperate.

"No. No one. You are the only one. Can you come, please. I will compensate another time." How could he say no?

"Okay, I'll come as soon as I can." He heard relief in Eddie's voice. "Merci beaucoup, Harry. I am grateful. The taxi will collect you in ten minutes. It is already en route."

Harry smiled into the telephone. LeBlanc knew Harry would come even before Harry knew it.

Harry explained the situation to Irene, who was understanding. Another good sign. "Do you mind if I stay a bit longer?" she asked. "I still feel a bit the alcohol. I promise not to steal anything."

"You still feel it? You are certainly a cheap date. Of course, stay as long as you like. I will be back early in the morning Stay the night if you like. We can have breakfast together."

"Ah, that sounds nice. Perhaps I shall. Sure you do not mind?"

"Mind?" he replied, "Not at all. I look forward to it." He had been getting dressed as they talked. Now he picked up his flight bag and turned to leave. "See you later? I hope so."

Irene smiled, fell back into bed, and pulled up the bed cover. "Yes, see you later. Bon voyage. What is a cheap date?"

"Tell you later," he said over his shoulder as he walked through the door.

Irene awakened as Harry returned from Athens. The eastern sky had begun to lighten and the first thin shafts of sunlight were filtering into the room.

"Still asleep? I'll go downstairs for a coffee and come back later."

Irene answered by throwing back the corner of the bedcover and patting the bed beside her.

"Come," she said. "I am no longer sleepy. But you! No sleep! You must be 'tres fatigue,' no?"

"What? Oh, am I tired? Yes, well, I was tired until I saw you lying there," Harry replied with a grin that grew wider as he spoke, "but now I'm wide awake."

Irene smiled an impish smile. "Awake? How much awake?"

"Very much," he said as he began to unbutton his shirt. "Would you like to see how much?"

"I am waiting eagerly. Tell me, how is it in Athens?"

As Harry quickly undressed, he said, "Everything in Athens is okay. At least the runway is okay. I didn't see much more. I brought you something."

As he slipped into bed beside her, he took her hand and pressed into it an inexpensive, locally-made ring he had bought at the airport.

"Here is a little piece of Greece for you," he whispered into her ear. Irene sat upright.

"Oh, Harry, it's beautiful and I love it," she exclaimed, as she put it on her finger and looked at it.

"Come on. It's nothing. Only $3.00"

"The cost is not important," she said, as she turned and bent her head down to kiss him lightly on his lips. Harry was not sure, but he thought he saw tears glisten in her eyes.

"The ring, it is important," she said with a trace of emotion. "The cost is not important."

That, thought Harry, as Irene began to work her magic, is the best $3.00 I ever spent.

57
RADIO FAILURE

1966

Some night flights from a carrier were better than others; but they were never easy. The outlook for this one looked low on the adrenalin scale; but you never knew. He and Bud Johanson were thrown off into the black at 0200. The mission was road reconnaissance over Cambodia. The weather was clear, and that was the only good thing to be said about a night flight. The mission was basically hopeless: try to find the trucks heading down to South Vietnam along the Ho Chi Minh trail. That was almost impossible. Then, if you found any, destroy them, which was even harder. Harry carried the flares and Bud had the bombs. The plan was to drop the flares and hope to get lucky. The flares were made of magnesium and they could turn night into day. In some way that Harry never understood, these flares created their own oxygen, which made them burn like the sun. Harry had once seen one of these flares burning brilliantly while it was underwater.

Tonight, over Cambodia, Harry flew randomly across some known truck routes, but it was like flying over the far side of the moon. There was nothing. Finally, it was time to head back to the ship. Harry clicked his mike button and told Bud that he would roll in, drop his flares, and then head for home.

"Try to find some enemy trees," he said.

Bud knew that meant to unload his bombs, whether he saw a truck or not. Harry dropped the flares one at a time. He was always stunned when the flares ignited. How could such a small flare create such brilliant light? Soon the flares were away, the bombs had leveled a few more enemy trees, and Harry pointed his plane east, Bud close on his wing.

As they crossed the coastline, Harry clicked his mike and said, "Battlecry 2, say your fuel state." A wingman always used more fuel than his leader because he had to maneuver more to stay in position. No answer. He tried again, and still no answer. Harry began to suspect radio failure. He tried a third time, and still no luck. Hand signals were difficult at night, but there was no other way. Harry trimmed the airplane as best he could for hands-off flight. Then, with his flashlight, he illuminated his right hand. He tapped his ear with his forefinger, then held up three fingers to indicate that Bud should be on channel three.

There was no reason he should not be on channel three, but this was the procedure. Bud replied with his own flashlight. He shined it on his left ear, tapped it with his forefinger, then, with his right hand, showed a thumbs-down signal. That meant his radio was inoperative. *Damn*, thought Harry. Still, it was not a serious problem. He would follow standard operating procedures. That meant keeping the lead until the final approach, then passing the lead to Bud, who would be on his own for the landing.

He advised the ship of the situation. They were cleared down to 500 feet, which was the altitude at which the optical glide path -- the meatball -- was normally intercepted. But, first, the airplanes had to be in the landing configuration. That meant gear and flaps down at the intercept, ready to land; and it was important for Harry to be at the right airspeed because Bud would not have much time to make corrections. The hand signal for lowering the gear was a rotating motion with his fist. That meant get ready. The execute signal was a vigorous nod of his head. The landing gear of both airplanes had to come down at the same moment so that Bud could stay in position on Harry's wing. The drag created by the gear coming down slowed the airplane suddenly. That had to happen to both airplanes at the same time. If Bud's gear came down after Harry's, he would fly right past Harry. To lower the flaps, the signal was both palms placed together, then opened and closed a few times in a V-like motion. Harry nodded his head again as he put down his flaps. These signals were easy in daytime, but at night and using a flashlight, they became very difficult.

Bud stayed in perfect position as they "dirtied up" the airplanes for the landing. The ship's radar brought them down to 500 feet and vectored them onto the glide path. They would intercept from beneath. That meant they would be under the glide path until the meatball was centered, then follow it down to the flight deck. Harry drew upon his best airmanship to make the approach easier for Bud. Coming onto the glide path from below meant that Harry first saw the meatball below the green reference lights; a "you are low" position. He held level flight as the meatball slowly came into the center of the green lights, then eased off power to start the airplanes down the glide path.

When they were well established, on glide path, on airspeed, and with the meatball centered, Harry shined his flashlight on his right hand, tapped the top of his helmet, then pointed to Bud. This signal said, "You have the lead." Bud acknowledged by flicking his running lights off and on. Harry then added power, raised his gear and flaps, broke to his left and re-entered the landing pattern, still under radar control. Bud, who had been focusing all his energy and attention on staying in position on Harry's wing, for the first time, looked ahead, saw the ship and the meatball. Until that moment, he was unsure of just where he was. He knew, of course, that he was in the landing pattern because his wheels and flaps were down; but where in the landing pattern? Seeing the ship and the meatball answered that question. That put him in a familiar position, and he flew his aircraft down the glide path for a normal landing -- as normal as a night landing can be, anyway.

Harry came aboard and made his way to the Air Intelligence Center for his debrief. As he left the black of the flight deck and entered the vast, brightly-lit interior of the ship, he was enthralled by the lights flooding the passageway around him. How great to go from a world of dark to a world of light! He felt his tension drain away. Most people would never know the feeling, not like this. He found Bud calmly drinking a cup of coffee and smoking a cigarette.

"Hey, Bud, you done good. Nice work."

Bud smiled a very big smile and said simply, "Thanks for the help, Harry."

Just then the Air Intelligence Officer joined them, clipboard in hand, and sat down. "You guys get any enemy trees tonight?"

58
BELGIUM

1971

Thanks to Irene, Belgium was good to Harry. He had seen much of Europe and, although he had heard of Belgium, he knew nothing about it. Irene and her Alfa Romeo changed all that. She showed him all the places the tourists go and some where they do not. It is a beautiful and beguiling little country in many ways, and the more he saw, the more he liked it.

Their first tour was to Brugge, known as the Venice of the north. It is an old and enchanting town with canals running through it. It looked, to Harry, as if it was right out of Grimm's Fairy Tales. A tour on a canal boat was a pleasant way to see much of the town. They visited the coast of the North Sea, where the Belgians spent their holidays in the summer. There were fine beaches, broad and long, with a promenade along most of them. The walkway was lined with restaurants, bars, and cafes. Most had outside terraces. Harry began to understand the appeal of these terraces and wondered why they were not more popular back home. Enjoying a drink or a meal outside on a fine day made Harry feel like the King of France, as Irene sometimes said. Of course, having Irene alongside contributed greatly to his sense of grandeur. Harry could not miss the glances of admiration directed at Irene wherever they went. It was she they were looking at, but it was Harry who felt good about them.

Knokke was the center of this area. It had a large casino and a residential area of villas that might have rivaled Beverly Hills. Of course, these were Old World villas and they were very different from those he was used to seeing; but they were large and impressive. In a nod to the past, some had thatched roofs. Harry wondered what they were like inside.

They spent a few days in Antwerp, which was Irene's hometown. Antwerp is somewhat off the tourist track and does not usually attract those who follow the London, Paris, Rome circuit; but Harry found Antwerp to be right up there near the top of the list. All major cities in Europe boast cathedrals, and the one in Antwerp, dating back to the 13th century, is splendid. It overlooks one of several plazas in the center of the city. The plazas are filled with cafes and restaurants, almost all with outside terraces. They enjoyed drinking beer in one of them, Den Engel, which dispensed beer from a building dating from 1750 according to the date inscribed above its door. The Angel had been pouring beers -- it served many different ones -- since 1912; and, as Harry looked about, he thought that probably nothing in the place had changed since then. Those ancient wooden tables with the marble tops had likely been there from the beginning. It was, he decided, a bar with character.

Harry had noticed that in Belgium, almost no one drank hard spirits. Everyone, young and old, men and women, drank beer almost exclusively. With such a variety of great tasting beers, why not? With its several hundred different beers, there was sure to be one for every taste. Harry tried many and liked them all. Some were better than others, but all tasted great.

In its center, was Antwerp's old quarter, and it was colorful, filled with shops of every kind. A few of these shops sold only pommes frittes. These are known elsewhere as French fries, but, in Belgium, they are much more than that. Almost a national dish, they are sometimes sold on street corners, like ice cream. They are served in a large paper cone with a large dollop of mayonnaise plopped on top. Harry could not understand how something so ordinary could taste so good.

"They are made a special way," Irene told him, "and we like them."

Harry liked them, too, and he ate plenty of them. They were a perfect complement to a glass of good Belgian beer. Belgium, Harry thought, as he munched his pomme frittes, is underrated.

There was another feature of Antwerp which surprised Harry. Everyone spoke English. He could speak to anyone and be answered in English. This was different from Brussels, where most spoke French. He asked Irene why. Here in Flanders, she told him, all students study English and French, along with Flemish. The Walloons in the south learned only French in school. Many Flamands study German, as well. Irene was one of those and, although she had studied German only one year, she was fluent enough to converse easily in German.

The people of Antwerp seemed different from those in Brussels, more open, friendlier. In Antwerp, strangers spoke easily to each other. Often, while sitting in a café or on a terrace, Irene would strike up a conversation with people she did not know.

"It happens all the time," she said. Harry had not seen that in Brussels. The citizens of Antwerp seemed drawn to the center of the city, not only for commerce, but also for entertainment. During weekends, Irene explained, the terraces of Antwerp overflowed.

How different from Milwaukee, Harry thought, where, during the weekend, the downtown area was nearly deserted. In Europe, people seemed to gravitate to the city centers. In America, as the U.S was usually called in Europe, the flow seemed to go the other way.

There was something else about Antwerp that was different. Americans were held in high esteem there. That was because the good folks of Antwerp remember that it was the Americans who liberated their city in September 1944. The city had been occupied by the German Army for several years, and Irene had spoken of some of the awful incidents she had seen there as a child. Many of Antwerp's Jewish citizens ended up at Auschwitz and other death camps. The liberation of the city by the Americans is now an official holiday in Antwerp. Hearing that made Harry warm with pride.

Irene later told Harry that her father, who usually shared a beer because one bottle was too much for him, had gotten exuberantly drunk that day. It was the only time she had ever seen him that way.

One of Irene's longtime friends had fought alongside Americans in Korea. He owned a small café and, one night, Harry and Irene visited him there. Harry was not allowed to pay for anything.

"Your money is no good here," Viktor told him, using an American expression. As they walked out the door to leave, late in the evening, they were suddenly blasted with a crashing recording of the Star-Spangled Banner. Harry turned around to see Viktor, wearing his old Army cap and standing at attention, saluting goodbye.

It was not for nothing that Belgium, Holland, and Luxembourg were known as the Low Countries. Not only low, they were flat, too. Amsterdam's Schipol Airport was the only airport Harry had ever seen where, parked on the ramp, the altimeter on his airplane displayed a minus number. The airport could be built eleven feet below sea level because the Dutch held back the sea with an ingenious system of dykes.

Belgium was mostly flat; but the Ardennes Forrest in the south rose to 2300 feet. Low compared with the Alps, the hills were high enough for skiing. Winter first came to Belgium in those hills. It was there that the famed Battle of Bastogne took place during the Second World War. Harry and Irene visited the site of this pivotal battle. They went in the summer, when it was hard to imagine this scenic countryside held in the frozen grasp of winter

There, around Christmas of 1944, during the harshest winter any Belgian could remember, the Americans turned back a major German counter offensive which took place after the invasion of Normandy. If successful, this drive by the Germans might well have changed the outcome of the war. In a splendid display of courage under pressure, the Americans stood fast.

Early in that battle, when it seemed the Americans would be over-run, the Germans sent in a message under a white flag; surrender, it demanded. The response of General McCauliffe is now classic.

"Nuts," was his one-word reply. The Germans, it was later learned, needed to have that word explained to them. Bastogne came to be known as "The Battle of the Bulge." It was American resolve at its finest. The cost was high; some 19,000 Americans were killed during this key battle.

After their tour, Harry and Irene walked along Nuts Street and enjoyed a coffee at Place McCauliffe in the town of Bastogne.

Their most memorable tour was not in Belgium, but in France. That was a trip to the beaches of Normandy, where the D-Day assault had taken place in 1944. They passed through a few picture postcard villages along the way and had lunch in one of them; the fairy tale town of Hon Fleur. Harry had always wanted to visit those famous beaches, but he was not ready for the emotion that overcame him there. Some of those craft, ships that became piers, and were known as mulberries, were still there where they beached so many years ago. There was a museum with films that were interesting. The sight of the cemetery brought tears to Harry's eyes and, for a few minutes, he could not speak. The resting place of those brave men was crisscrossed with plain white crosses arranged with great precision across a vast expanse of perfectly-tended grass. That sight and those emotions would stay with him always.

When not touring Belgium on the ground by Alfa Romeo, Harry went by air to other countries of Europe. Besides the many flights to Palma, he flew to cities in Spain and Italy, mainly holiday destinations. The flights were all turn-arounds, so Harry saw little more than airports. Later, when someone would ask, "Have you ever been to Barcelona?" Harry would reply, "Yes, and it looks like many other places I've been; a strip of concrete about 250 feet wide and two miles long."

Irene came along on a few of the weekend flights and, once, she was there in the jump seat for a double turn-around to Palma. That made a long day, but she enjoyed the flights and an hour or two browsing through the airport shops. Although there were problems with working for a company that was just getting off the ground, there were advantages, too. One was that Harry could bring Irene along on a flight any time he chose -- no forms to fill, no one to ask -- just bring her along and settle her in the jump seat.

They got lucky when Harry was given a flight to Tunis with a four-day layover. The city was not impressive, but there were some interesting places nearby. One was City Bou Said, a charming village in which every house was painted white with blue-trimmed windows and doors. Another was Carthage, the site that held the remnants of a time centuries ago when the Romans held forth in this part of the world.

Harry was not so lucky when he reported one morning for a flight to Malaga, in southern Spain. The route went straight through the heart of France. Today, there was a problem, he was told, and France was closed for the day. At first, Harry smiled. "You're joking, right? How can a country be closed?" It was easy, he was told. All that was needed was for the air controllers to go on strike. There would be no flights over France until further notice.

"So, are we cancelled, or what?" Harry asked. No, they would turn to plan B. That routed the flight along the English Channel, then down the coast of France to Spain. They would fly around France. Of course, that meant extra time and fuel. Imagine, thought Harry: flying *around* France! Harry was reminded of Thor, who had wanted to fly around India to avoid landing in Madras. That had been impossible; flying around France seemed merely ridiculous.

Because of the strike, there were long delays on the ground for departing aircraft. Upon arrival, Harry's flight was given a slot time for departure that was some five hours later. This, he decided, was a slot time that must not be missed, or they might never leave Spain. Planning ahead, he brought the passengers out early; but, as it turned out, not early enough. Glancing out the cockpit window as the passengers came on board, Harry saw that one of the last to come up the stairs was an elegant lady with a large dog on a leash. Somehow, the dog had been allowed by the ramp agent to board the airplane; but the plane was full and there was no seat for the dog. Confusion followed as Harry tried to figure out a way to put the dog in the cargo compartment; but that meant finding a kennel and none was available. He could have restricted the woman and her dog from coming on board, but her bags were already on the airplane and would need to be off-loaded. The slot time was rapidly nearing and something had to be done quickly.

Harry asked the cabin chief to bring the lady and her dog into the cockpit. The dog's owner was a friendly, middle-aged woman who spoke English with a French accent.

"This might sound strange," Harry said, "but your dog is a problem. Could we trust him to sit here in the cockpit for this flight? You, too. You could sit there," he pointed to the navigator's seat, "and take care of your dog. Otherwise, we might have to leave you behind. What do you think?"

The woman smiled a charming smile. "Captain, mais oui, we would most enjoy to travel here with you. The dog will not move, I promise."

Harry paused, thinking. Mostly, he was thinking of what missing their slot time would mean.

"Okay," he said quickly, "you and your dog are now part of the cockpit crew." He nodded to the cabin chief and told her to close the cabin entry door, then turned to the first officer. "Call for start-up."

For the long trip home, again *around* France, the dog behaved better than most passengers.

"Too bad," said the cabin chief after their arrival in Brussels, "that we do not have more passengers like this one. He asked for nothing and complained about nothing."

France reopened a few days later. For those airlines flying *around* France, they were very expensive days.

59
A TELEX FROM OSLO

1971

Harry enjoyed it all immensely. One day, as he reported for a flight to Palma, he was handed a telex from Oslo. He had been calling Thor now and then to find out how long he would stay in Belgium. He could not get a straight answer. We are working on it, he was told. He was starting to feel as though he had found a home. Except for the weather, which could be dreary, he liked his life in Belgium. The telex informed him that arrangements had been made for him, Rolf, and Gene to stay with TEA until further notice. The airplane would stay too. By now, TEA had enough crews so that they too would fly the airplane. It would, in effect, be part of the TEA fleet.

"We are renting you to TEA," Thor had told him. TEA would pay their salaries, including their back pay. More Belgium and money to enjoy it! Harry felt good about that.

Harry had once had a squadron skipper who insisted that "my boys" look sharp around the ship. During daytime recoveries, that meant flying tight formation and landing aboard with precise intervals between each airplane. The goal was thirty seconds. The skipper's policy included posting a squadron pilot in Primary Flight, the ship's control tower, who timed each interval with a stopwatch. This was, to Harry, somewhat unreasonable because every now and then an aircraft about to touch down would be waved off because the landing area was not clear. A 35-second interval would prevent most of these go-arounds. Still, he understood the skipper's psychology. Demanding higher standards usually spurred improved performance; but it could be tricky. Not only did the preceding airplane need to taxi forward and out of the landing area, but the arresting gear cable had to be pulled back into the ready position. Sometimes a plane in good position to land was sent around because that cable was not yet in place. That was a judgment call, especially when the cable was very nearly in position as the landing aircraft reached the wave-off point.

"You got to bet on the come," said the skipper, when the decision looked close. Harry was not sure how the expression applied, but he knew what it meant: Favor the likely outcome.

Harry now decided to bet on the come. Guessing he would be in Brussels for some months, he rented a small studio apartment near the Cinquantenaire, a well-known museum in the central part of the city. It overlooked a small park in which Harry introduced Irene to jogging.

"I don't enjoy it," she said after her first run.

"Neither do I," answered Harry, "but I like the way I feel when I finish."

Irene thought about that for a moment. "Yes," she said. "You are right. I like it, too."

The apartment was a short walk from an English pub, the Drum, which became Harry's favorite watering hole. He called it his home away from his home away from home. Harry even learned to throw darts there and became "not that bad for a bloody Yank," according to one of his regular opponents. The English had discovered a great pastime in combining beer and darts. Unlike golf, Harry's dart throwing skills seemed to get better as he drank more beer. "Must be the Belgian beer," Harry said, when he threw a winning dart. He spent many happy hours there and, because it was a gathering place for ex-pats, as non-Belgians living in Brussels were known, he made new friends there. Now and then, he would put one in the cockpit and take him to Palma and back, all expenses paid. There is no better life than a good one, Irene sometimes said, and Harry's good life had just gotten better.

Mr. Jacobowitz had been sad to see him leave, and Harry was surprised to feel some emotion too; but life moves on. Harry came back "home" regularly to enjoy a cup of tea with him. His eyes lit with pleasure every time he saw Harry come through the door. Harry liked the old man and enjoyed his company; and, by now, Harry could understand his English perfectly.

Harry began to feel less a vagabond, more a part of a community. He liked that feeling. He met some of Irene's friends and relatives, and that meant more roots planted in Belgian soil.

The arrangement Thor made with TEA included Harry and his crew flying TEA airplanes when the need arose. Sometimes they flew together, but not always. Harry, Rolf and Gene had some unusual experiences in those early days of the new company. One day, Rolf showed up at Harry's apartment in an irate state. He had just returned from Palma with a Belgian crew and the story he told was incredulous. In a start-up company, anything could happen because financial pressure could make or break a company early in the game. Safety was often a casualty. Rolf's captain had cut some big corners on this flight and Rolf did not like it.

60
SHATTERED WINDSHIELD

Rolf was a typical Swede in that he was straight, honest, and reliable -- and handsome. Women's admiring glances followed him everywhere. He was medium height and solidly built, and he had bright blue eyes and blonde hair that he kept closely cut. He had an easy, friendly manner and seemed to always be in a good mood; so Harry was surprised early one evening to find him at his door with a scowl creasing his usually pleasant countenance. Harry gestured into his apartment.

"Rolf, come on in, have a seat. You don't look happy. How about a nice cold beer?"

After sitting down, Rolf exhaled a loud snort and said, "Harry, I am for sure very pissed off and a cold beer will be welcome. You will not believe what happened in Palma today."

Rolf sat down as Harry handed him a cold bottle of Stella Artois, and he began to calm down. After a long drink, he began explaining why he was "pissed off." That was an American expression, and Harry had been surprised to hear Rolf use it, so he knew Rolf was seriously upset.

On landing in Palma, he said, the windshield on the Captain's side had shattered. These windshields were designed to withstand the pressure differentials at high altitudes where the atmospheric pressure was very low, too low to provide enough oxygen for the passengers; so outside air was compressed and pumped into the cabin and the cockpit to compensate for this shortage of oxygen. In this way, the cabin of the airplane could be kept at sea-level pressure until 22,000 feet was reached. After that, the cabin began to climb with the airplane while holding a constant differential between inside and outside air pressures.

Usually, the air pressure of the interior of an aircraft at 35,000 feet was like that at an altitude of 6,000 feet on the ground. This "thin" air held less oxygen than air on the earth's surface. This was the reason that passengers felt fatigue, dehydration, and other adverse symptoms on long flights at high altitudes. The difference in pressures inside and outside the airplane could be substantial; so the windshields were made to bend, but not break, at extraordinarily high pressure differentials.

One of the pilot emergencies reviewed in the flight simulator during each semi-annual flight check was an "explosive" decompression. That might happen when, for some reason, there was a sudden loss of cabin pressure. A blown-out window or a hole in the fuselage could do that. If that happened, the altitude of the cabin would rise to meet the altitude of the airplane itself. The passenger oxygen masks would be automatically released. That supply was limited, so quick action had to be taken to bring the airplane down to a level where there was enough oxygen in the air to sustain life, usually below 10,000 feet. For the pilots, this meant donning oxygen masks, lowering the landing gear and extending the air brakes, then diving the airplane. It almost never happened in real life but the possibility was always there, so the maneuver was practiced regularly. The windshield would not break even under these unusual conditions. But now and then one might shatter and that was what had happened in Palma. It remained whole and in place, but had become opaque.

A shattered windshield was a major problem even at home base. In Palma, it was a catastrophe. It might take days, and perhaps weeks, to locate, ship and install a new one. That meant lost revenue and lots of it. The captain was Eddie LeBlanc, and he realized immediately what was at stake. Such a situation could easily imperil the future of a new company that was financially weak. That it might bring the company down was not unthinkable. He had to prevent a disaster. On the other hand, he did not want to invite an accident. The windshield was not supposed to break; but in its shattered condition, it certainly looked like it might. Must he take that risk? He considered the situation carefully. His first goal, he decided, was to get the airplane home as best he could. His solution was, first, not to log the windscreen problem in the aircraft maintenance logbook. That could be done after the plane returned to Belgium, where it could be grounded with better prospects of quick repair. Once an item listed as "Unsafe to fly" was logged, the airplane could not legally fly until it was corrected. It was a fairly common practice to fly with less serious maintenance items, those that did not affect aircraft safety. Second, he would let Rolf fly the airplane home while he himself sat in the cabin.

The control used to turn the nose wheel and steer the airplane during taxi was on the Captain's side of the cockpit. Only the Captain could taxi the airplane; so LeBlanc taxied the airplane to the takeoff position on the runway, then went into the cabin where he remained throughout the flight. Harry could not help but wonder what the passengers thought about that. Rolf, sitting on the right side of the cockpit, made the takeoff using brakes, then the rudder, to steer the airplane along the centerline. He flew the airplane to Brusssels. To reduce pressure on the windshield, the flight was flown at a relatively low level and at a reduced airspeed. This minimized the potential damage from differential air pressure and also from the pressure resulting from ram air against the windshield. Rolf landed, stopped the airplane on the runway after landing, then waited for LeBlanc to resume his cockpit seat and taxi the airplane into its parking spot. The windshield had not broken during the flight.

Listening to all this, Harry kept asking himself what he would have done. This was surely asking for trouble in several ways, including the possible loss of the pilots' licenses. Still, he knew the powerful pressure on a captain to get an airplane home. Much depended on it. He had cut corners himself, but none so large as this one. Still, you had to be in a situation to know how you would deal with it. It was easy to second-guess such a decision while drinking a beer later. It was another matter to be there, to feel the pressure, to make the decision. What LeBlanc had done was certainly illegal; but, Harry asked himself, was it unsafe? Suppose the future of the company hung on this decision? That was certainly possible.

"Rolf," asked Harry, "did you think about refusing to operate the flight? No one could have blamed you."

"Yeah, I did," he answered as he accepted another beer. "I even spoke up about how serious this was and how it might go wrong. We looked in the manual and read about it. The windshield should not break; but flying alone back to Brussels, well, shit, that was wrong and I said so. But it might break the company, he said; so I said okay, but I for sure did not like it."

Harry told Rolf, "Look on the bright side. You might have saved the company from going belly up."

Rolf just shrugged and drank his beer, looking glum. Harry could not blame him.

These situations arose in all companies, but they were less critical in companies with money and resources. During the next few months, Harry would fly an airplane for two days in which the only way to trim the elevator was with the autopilot engaged -- not even the manual controls would move it. These used cables running from small wheels alongside the pilots' pedestal all the way back to the elevators at the rear of the plane. Handles could be extended from their stowed position so that the wheels could be cranked by hand. They were designed for use as a back-up when the normal system failed. They would not budge. Now, that, according to the manual, was not supposed to happen. Engaging the autopilot immediately after takeoff solved this problem -- not a happy solution -- but it worked.

Harry reported for a flight one day to find a notice posted informing him that, until further notice, the number two engine on his assigned airplane was restricted to 90% power. That was because a bird had struck the inlet of the engine and distorted it in a way that reduced the airflow into the engine. Harry could live with that, legal or not; but he found it less than smart to post it on the notice board, where the whole world could read it. There was no need to advertise.

61
WHERE IS MY COFFEE?

Not all the flights were maintenance nightmares. Boeing built their airplanes tough, and most of the flights went smoothly despite problems cropping up here and there. On one flight to Palma, the cabin chief advised the cockpit crew that one of the flight attendants was making her very first flight. Gene decided to have some fun. On the return trip, he pressed the service call button. The new girl was serving the cockpit and answered the call immediately. Gene ordered a cup of coffee to "get my heart started." She raised her eyebrow at that, but left to fetch the coffee. When she did, Gene slid back the observer's chair, behind the captain's seat, opened the grill door which led into the electronic compartment below, and carefully lowered himself down, closing the grill as he did. When the girl returned with the coffee, Gene was no longer in the cockpit.

"Just put it on his table," said Harry. "He's probably back in the cabin, maybe in the toilet."

After some minutes had passed, Harry called the girl back up front and told her that the flight was nearing Brussels and ready to descend. "Please get Gene and tell him to get back here right away."

Obviously confused, she nodded and went out to look for Gene, returning very distraught a few minutes later to say that he was nowhere to be found.

Harry pretended to be annoyed. "He has to be back there somewhere. Well, never mind. It's too late now. We'll have to land without him and find him later. Keep looking."

Gene, with a mischievous smile, reappeared from the lower compartment and took his seat at the panel. After the airplane was parked, Gene once again disappeared into the lower compartment. This time, he opened the access panel that allowed him to leave the airplane just aft of the nose wheel. The stairs were already in place, and Gene went up the steps and stood before the forward entry door. It was opened by the new girl, astounded to find Gene standing there with a scowl of irritation.

"Where the hell is my coffee?" he demanded.

62
WHERE THE HELL IS HASSI MESSAOUD?

"Hassi Messaoud! Where the hell is Hassi Messaoud?" Harry asked no one in particular one afternoon in the company office. He had just learned that two crews, including him, were about to be based there for a few weeks hauling Muslim pilgrims to Jeddah for the Haj. Two other crews would be based in Lagos. That was, according to Gene, "somewhere in Nigeria." Harry was puzzled.

"Why Nigeria? What has Nigeria got to do with the Haj, whatever that is?"

"For your information," someone answered, "Nigeria is full of Muslims. They all go to Mecca sooner or later."

Harry was thinking hard. Nigerians are Negroes, right? How could they be Muslims? Never mind, he told himself, try not to look stupid. I'll figure it out later.

"Oh sure, I think I knew that. But what the hell is the Haj?" was his next question.

There were a few embarrassed smiles in response. In the next few weeks, Harry would get more answers to these questions than he really needed.

Hassi Messaoud was deep in the outback of Algeria. It was a small town that was to be used as a staging point for the gathering of Muslims for transport to Jeddah, which was in Saudi Arabia. Before they die, he was told, all Muslims are supposed to visit the holy places in Mecca and Medina. These were the bedrock of Islam. This voyage cleanses their souls of a lifetime of wrongdoing and entitles them to paradise after death. Those who make the pilgrimage are held in high regard and are entitled to add "Haj" to their name. It was a mark of honor.

"Sounds like a mass confession to me," Harry remarked, when someone told him about this plan for the salvation of Muslim souls. "Seems like a good idea. Do it all at once instead every few weeks. And if you get the timing right, once should be enough."

There was, of course, much more to the Haj than this simple description, and Harry was interested to learn more. The big surprise, still to come, was the common thread running through both Islam and Christianity. Jesus, for example, was a prophet in the Koran. Gabriel was in there too, and so was Mary. From these common elements, and many others, how had these two religions grown so far apart? Interpretation, thought Harry; it probably came down to that. As beauty was in the eye of the beholder, belief was often in the mind of the reader.

63
KEEPING THE FAITH

Religion had fascinated Harry ever since he had decided to leave the Catholic Church. He had more interest in it now than when he was a churchgoer. He didn't fall away, he sometimes said, it was more like a leap from a burning building. That had happened very suddenly after he had been thinking about it for a very long time. You will be back, his friends said. There are no atheists in foxholes; but Harry had once been in a foxhole, a mental foxhole.

That was on the flight deck of the Kitty Hawk just before launching on a bright, sunny day. He was scheduled for a high-risk mission in the north. That was not unusual but his reaction on this particular day was most unusual. He felt uneasy about this flight and he could not explain why. It gnawed at him throughout the brief, and his unease grew stronger as he went up the escalator to the flight deck. There, it became a feeling of dread and it was strong, powerful. It was almost physical, and somehow he knew, he just knew, that he would not come back from this one.

So, he asked himself as he strapped himself into the cockpit, are you going to change your mind and be a believer again? It can't hurt and, who knows, it might help. Why take the risk? No, he answered himself; I'll take what comes. What came was nothing. The mission turned out to be routine and Harry lived to fly another day. That pall of dread never came over him again. Still, he thought, I've passed a test.

He never told anyone about this fear, but the next day someone asked, "Harry, you looked awful grim up there on the flight deck yesterday. What was that all about?"

Harry just smiled. "Me? Grim? You must have me mixed up with someone else." It felt good to be alive, even on Yankee Station.

Once he stepped outside the church, his view of those inside became very different. It changed his life in unforeseen ways. Relationships with men did not change. But with women he found himself asking innocuous questions which were meant to sound out a girl's religious beliefs. Religion had such a stranglehold on some people that he did not want to get too deep into a relationship with a woman who had strong beliefs. That would almost guarantee a land mine somewhere down the road.

He knew that faith played a big role, perhaps the only role, in believing all the church taught. Faith was difficult to counter. In discussions with those who had it, their final argument always came down to faith. In the Navy, Harry had often been told, "there is no reason, it's just policy." In religion, it was just faith. Well, thought Harry, either you had it or you didn't. If you didn't, there was no use pretending that you did, although some seemed to do that. So Harry left it at that. He avoided discussions about religion because they always ended up at that impasse of faith. Reason could not budge it. Harry did not have the answer, but he did not invent one. He just accepted that he did not know the answer and that satisfied him. That religion relied so heavily on faith to sell its programs said much about its product. It would be interesting to learn how Islam handled this question.

No one could deny that life, for many, was pain, misery, and heartache. Yet no one seemed to hold God responsible. When good things happened, it was always "Thank God!" A man whose house had just been blown away might say, "Thank God it wasn't worse," and not, "Why did God do this to me?" He always got the credit but never the blame. Such was the hold of faith.

Imagine, thought Harry, usually after a few drinks, how much better the world might be if all those vast resources spent on instilling religion were directed instead to teaching people how to live in a decent and honorable way. The Golden Rule would be a good start. Teaching the value of respecting, instead of violating, the rights of others would come next. Logic, for example, could make a good case against taking something belonging to another. Harry believed that a few such concepts, taught with the same fervor as was religion, and from an early age, would benefit the world far more than did religion. Religion, after all, had been a great cause of death and disaster through the ages.

How about this? he asked himself. There are minimum ages for smoking, drinking alcohol, and voting. How about a minimum age for choosing a religion? Instead of being based on circumstance of birth, religion would be selected intelligently after reaching an age of understanding; but Harry was not holding his breath waiting for change. Human nature was against it. People needed to believe. They wanted to believe. Worse, they wanted him to believe, too. That was the problem.

64
HASSI MESSAOUD

1971

Two crews in one airplane flew to the small airport serving Hassi Messaoud. In Harry's crew were Rolf, Gene, and four girls. The airport was basic. Its single runway was short, and its only navigational aid was a low-power radio beacon. An Algerian who spoke English with a strong French accent met them. The French had been all over this part of North Africa for many years. The crews would not be quartered in Hassi Messaoud, he told them, but in the nearby town of Ouargla, about thirty minutes away.

"Better, 'plus grande.' More cafes and restaurants," he explained. "Here, there is nothing."

Their hotel was interesting. If ever a building could be described as consisting entirely of arches, this was the one. They were everywhere, and even the rooms had arched ceilings. Arabs, he would learn, liked arches. Nothing hung on any wall. The furniture was basic, too: one bed and a chair that looked like an oversized beanbag. Harry plopped down in one, and pronounced it, "comfortable, but can someone help me get out of this thing?" The restaurant had no bar, of course, as the Muslims did not believe in such amenities. They seemed to miss many of the good parts of life.

The Algerian made sure that everyone was accommodated, and Harry could not but notice how he could not take his eyes off the girls. It was as if he had never seen one before. His lust was plain to see and he made little effort to hide it.

The Algerian asked the crew to gather in the restaurant, where he briefly went over the plan. Two crews and one airplane would operate nonstop between here and Jeddah. The first flight would leave at 0600 in the morning. Crew rest would be as long as it took for the plane to fly to Jeddah and back. How long was that? He didn't know. Harry asked about crew transport to the airport. All arranged, he was told. A large bus was assigned to the crews. Crew pick-up would be two hours before the flight. Any more questions? No one could think of one. The Algerian left with effusive farewells, especially for the girls, kissing the hand of each. Probably, he had learned that from the French. They suppressed giggles, but they obviously liked it. The two crews agreed to meet in the restaurant for dinner. No cocktails, please.

Harry and his crew arrived at the airport early the next morning. It was bedlam. The terminal was very small, so a large tent, raised alongside, augmented it. If it had walls, it would have been packed wall-to-wall with passengers. Without walls, they spilled out of the tent on all sides. All looked to be very old, and that made sense to Harry. If this trip would wipe the slate clean, then later in life was better. It was their version of a deathbed confession. For nearly all, he was told, this would be their first flight. That would lead to some interesting in-flight passenger behavior.

Soldiers controlled the crowd. The control was by force, sometimes brutal. Harry could not believe how some of these old folks, setting out on the soul-saving adventure of a lifetime, were handled like cattle. They were pushed, pulled, struck with rifle butts and, in some cases, thrown roughly to the ground. This, thought Harry, is no way to treat religious pilgrims; but no one in authority seemed to notice the abuse. Not my problem, thought Harry, as he passed through the terminal area, but this is terrible. Even the Catholics did not abuse their followers in this way, not these days anyway.

To Harry's surprise, there were few problems in departing. One came when the crew arrived at the airplane and the stairs were not in place. After a few minutes a staircase was pushed across the tarmac by a gaggle of workers. Apparently, motorized stairs had not yet found their way to Hassi Messaoud. The problem was that the pushers did not seem to understand that when one end was pushed one way, the other end went the opposite way. It was only on the fourth try that they managed to line up the stairs close enough to the entry door so that the crew could board.

Once in his seat, Harry had a close view of the passengers embarking. All looked to be ancient. They were very docile and followed very carefully the instructions of the group leader, a much younger man who spoke broken English. The takeoff was routine, and soon Harry and his pilgrims were on their way to Jeddah.

The route took them across eastern Algeria to Monastir, on the east coast of Tunisia. Next was an over-water sector across the Gulf of Sidra north of Lybia. At Matru, on the Egyptian coast west of Cairo, the route turned south to New Valley. There the plane turned east again, passed over the Nile River, then to the western shore of the Red Sea, where the route turned southeast to Jeddah. It was a long flight, with almost no radio contact along the way. The sparse ground contact was with high frequency radios that are like short wave radios: poor quality and plenty of static. The strong accents of the controllers made ground communication even more difficult.

The first surprise came shortly after takeoff, when the cabin chief came to the cockpit and told Harry that all the passengers were undressing! Harry had been warned about this, and he explained to the flustered girl that they were not undressing, just changing to the garb they would wear throughout the ceremonies in Saudi Arabia. These were loose- fitting sheets and, in some cases, only a strip of cloth covered their upper body with a kind of loincloth below the waist.

The next surprise came a few minutes later when she excitedly returned to the cockpit to report that a small group in the rear of the plane had lit a gas burner in the aisle and was preparing to brew a kettle of tea. This was serious. Harry quickly left his seat, found the group leader, and hurried to the back of the cabin. To get there, he had to push and jostle many of those standing in the aisle, changing their clothes. They were very deferential as soon as they saw his uniform. Sure enough, a burner was lit and water was heating. Several partially-clad men were happily passing out cups and sugar. Through the group leader, Harry quickly had the fire put out and, in a very angry tone, instructed the leader that there would be no more campfires on his airplane. They were disappointed but complied quickly.

What next? Harry asked himself as he made his way back to the cockpit. The answer came quickly. One of the stewardesses had discovered footprints on the seat of one of the toilets. Obviously not used to toilets, passengers had climbed onto the toilet, squatted, and did their business in their usual way. Apparently, they had not been introduced to toilet flushing and there was an awful stench in the compartment. Harry told the leader to make a loudspeaker announcement which briefed the passengers on the proper use of a toilet. That had to be a first, thought Harry: teaching passengers how to use a toilet. On subsequent flights, he inserted the toilet-training instructions, and the restriction on brewing tea, into the standard pre-flight safety briefing made by the group leader.

Flights like Harry's were converging on Jeddah from around the world. Some pilgrims came from as far away as Indonesia, the Philippines and other far-off places. Harry admired their dedication. Many of his friends would not make the effort to go a few blocks to church on Sunday. Arriving in the Jeddah area, Harry was instructed to orbit in a holding pattern to wait for his turn to land. That made a long flight even longer. Finally on the ground, Harry was directed to a parking spot among a vast assortment of airplanes. Their vertical tail sections created a colorful man-made forest that stretched as far as he could see.

After the passengers had left the plane, smiling and happy, Harry asked Rolf to request a departure time. You are on the list, was the answer.

"How about an estimate?" asked Rolf.

Not less than four hours, was the reply. The plane would leave without passengers. Those brought today would be collected some weeks later, their hearts and souls cleansed. The delay was for refueling -- there were many ahead of Harry -- then for waiting until their takeoff time came up.

That would be a long four hours. With some difficulty, Harry arranged for the crew to pass through the airport and visit the shops outside the terminal. First, half the crew would go, then, when they returned, the rest would go. Passing through immigration was difficult. The Arabs were arrogant and condescending, thought Harry. Unimportant people often behave that way when they are given uniforms. Forms had to be filled out and passports had to be left behind. Still, four hours! Harry decided it was worth the effort. He cautioned the crew not to leave the area.

Harry went with the second group and found many shops on the other side of the terminal. He decided he needed a souvenir. After looking in several shops, his eye fell on a handsome handmade carpet. Harry had never learned to haggle and the shopkeepers always seemed to sense this. He bought the carpet without negotiating, probably disappointing the seller, and took it back to the plane.

"Goddamn," said Gene "you are supposed to bargain with these guys. You probably paid way too much."

Harry shrugged. "I know. I just can't do it. Must be the Milwaukee in me."

Where to store it? He finally settled on the electronic compartment beneath the cockpit. No one ever looked in it, and his carpet would be safely hidden among the equipment there. The more he had looked at the carpet in the shop, the more he had liked it. Carpet love at first sight, he thought later. On the next trip, he bought another, then another and, before he knew it, he had a collection of five carpets traveling almost nonstop between Hassi Messaoud and Jeddah. They would not leave their hiding place until the plane returned to Brussels a few weeks later.

"Those goddamn carpets," growled Gene, after Harry had bought another one, "have got more flight time than I have."

The return flights were easy because there were no passengers. The girls were often in the cockpit because they were bored. That made the flight more pleasant for the cockpit crew. There was only one area of concern. After passing Monastir and heading southwest towards Hassi Messaoud, there were no navigation aids until they picked up the low frequency radio beacon at the Hassi Messaoud airport. Because of its low power, it could not be received beyond thirty miles; so there was a stretch of flying where Harry had to rely on the compass and the clock. There was one more aid. This was oil country and the burning gas released from the wells made enormous torches. After the first nighttime return, Harry had fixed in his mind the relative location of the brightest of these fires. By pointing his airplane ten degrees to the left of that very bright one on the horizon, he would find the airport. There was always a way.

The flights quickly became routine. Nothing was special once you got used to it, thought Harry, not even flights between two such unusual places. One round-trip took some sixteen hours. During that time, the off-duty crew had to sleep and eat, then find a way to relax. That was not easy in Ouargla. That it was bigger and better than Hassi Messaoud said much about that town.

Ouargla was comprised of low buildings made mostly of stone blocks and arches. No one spoke English. There were two things Harry had always found in off-track places: Coca Cola, and someone who could speak English. Here there was only Coke. Harry sometimes organized a tour of one or two of the local cafes. As these tour groups included pretty European girls in western clothes, they were a sensation wherever they went. After entering an empty café and ordering mint tea or Coke, the place was usually packed within minutes with wide-eyed spectators, all of them men with hairy faces and dark, intense eyes. They came and stared, and *Oh! How they could stare!* There was no pretense. They did not even bother to order tea, just stood and ogled the girls. As the minutes passed, they became less serious. None spoke English, so they began to smile, laugh, and gesture, in ways that said: "We are friendly."

In once such café, one of the girls took a Polaroid camera out of its case. That caused a stir of excitement. Could it be they had never before seen a camera? Using sign language to arrange some of those spectators for a group photo was not easy. There was a lot of laughing and talking, all of it in Arabic. Finally, they were lined up. They were not sure what was coming, but they were willing. The photo was taken and Harry motioned them to gather around as the picture came out of the camera. They were amazed. Harry thought there would be shouting and laughing, but there was only stunned silence. For these simple folk, this was a miracle. A girl had pointed a black box at them and a few minutes later, they were looking at themselves. Miracles, thought Harry. Could they, like much of life, be relative, too?

While Harry was off duty, his carpet collection continued to accrue flight time. Back and forth it went, or, forth and back, as the English more sensibly put it. As it worked out, the second crew operated the final flight. The captain was a Belgian named Rene, whom Harry barely knew. They met only when one crew took over from the other, and sometimes not even then. On this last flight, Harry's crew would travel as passengers, then fly the airplane to Brussels with the second crew on board. Eventually, the last pilgrim was deposited in Jeddah, and Harry and his carpets were finally on the way home. Harry looked forward to showing his collection to Irene.

Persian-style carpets were also made in Belgium, but these were made by machine. They could not compare with hand-made carpets from the middle east. A few weeks before leaving for Hassi Messaoud, Harry and his crew had spent a couple of days in Baghdad. There, one of the girls asked Harry to accompany her to a carpet shop, one where she could buy "a real Persian carpet." Harry went along and, after changing taxis several times to drive though different taxi zones, they finally found a carpet shop. On entering, they saw piles of carpets. The girl excitedly ran to the nearest stack, threw back the corner of the top carpet, and found a label that read, "Made in Belgium." Harry's carpets had no such labels. They were the real thing.

65
BRUSSELS, THE HARD WAY

The route took them across the Red Sea, north to Cairo, where they enjoyed a spectacular view of the Pyramids, which could be clearly seen from their high altitude, then north and west over Cypress, Malta, Sardinia, Corsica and on into Europe. As there were no passengers, only the cockpit crew was working.

Before leaving Brussels, someone with great foresight had hidden a bottle of Johnny Walker Scotch whiskey in a secret recess in the cabin. Along with Harry's carpets, it, too, had been making regular round-trips between Algeria and Saudi Arabia. As soon as the wheels were raised after takeoff, the bottle was retrieved from its niche and opened. A boisterous "Farewell to Jeddah" party was soon under way. The flight and the celebration went well until just after passing Crete; then, their old friend Murphy made an appearance.

When a flight engineer checked one of his gauges he often flicked it with a forefinger. That was to make sure the needle was not stuck. It was said that a flight engineer would never tell you the time without first flicking the face of his watch with his forefinger. Now, Gene had flicked the oil quantity gauge of number three engine a dozen times, so he knew the needle was not stuck.

"Boss," he said, "I think we might have a problem here."

Harry knew Gene would not bring it up unless it was serious or about to become so.

"Like what?" Harry asked, as he half-turned in his seat to face Gene and the flight engineer panel.

The panel was a maze of gauges, lights, and switches that was incomprehensible to anyone but an engineer.

"Been checking this number three oil quantity for a while now, and it looks like we're losing oil. About one quart per hour looks like, near as I can tell."

Damn, said Harry softly to himself. This was not good news.

"Sure?" he asked but he knew the answer. Gene frowned at the query that questioned his proficiency, but he understood it.

"About as sure as it gets," he said.

By the time Gene answered, Harry had already started reviewing his options. The engine would run out of oil long before reaching Brussels. To prevent engine damage, it would have to be shut down before that happened.

There was no problem flying on three engines. The aircraft performance would suffer somewhat, but not seriously. There was no problem unless a second engine was lost. That would present a huge problem. The 707 could fly on two engines, just not very well, especially in adverse conditions. Two-engine landings were practiced regularly in the simulator, and they were not easy, especially if the two engines were both on the same side of the airplane. That creates asymmetrical power, which is difficult to control. Landing with two engines would constitute an emergency. The company policy in a three-engine situation was to land at the nearest suitable airport.

That word, "suitable," had many meanings. The runway had to be long enough, the weather had to be favorable, and the airport had to be able to service a 707. The next airport along the way was at Malta. Harry knew that Air Malta operated one or two 707s so it could handle this one. That meant the runway was also suitable but, just to be sure, he asked Rolf to check the manual to confirm that the runway was usable. It was. He then asked Rolf to get the latest Malta weather. This could be heard on aviation weather broadcasts that reported the weather at all the airports in the region on a continuous basis. The Malta weather was fine. Harry had all the information he needed to make a decision.

Before he made it, he asked Rene to come up to the cockpit. He did not look like an airline captain. Slender, with a large nose, his thinning hair made him appear old. He had a timid demeanor that was unusual for a pilot. Harry apprised him of the situation and asked, "What do you think?" Rene listened carefully, looking at the oil quantity gauge as he did. By this time the needle was almost off the gauge.

"But, Harry," he said in heavily-accented English, "the airplane flies well on three engines, does it not? I see no need to go down before Brussels. And there is the maintenance, if we need it. I believe we should continue." Harry's eyes narrowed. Ah, there it was. The classic case of "get home-itis." It often overruled common sense, and Harry was determined not to let that happen. Yes, he was as eager to get to Brussels as the others, but without unnecessary risk.

Risk is a concept difficult to grasp. Some think that a risk that did not materialize had never been there. That was hindsight. Now, at 35,000 feet between Crete and Malta, the risk was still there and had to be faced. Harry briefly looked out at the huge, towering cumulus clouds ahead and made his decision.

"Rene, thanks for your help on this one but it's my call and we will land in Malta. Any problem for you?"

Rene replied quickly. "No, no. No problem at all. You are in command and it is for you to decide."

Harry instructed Rolf to advise air traffic control of the situation, and to request a change of destination. Then, he asked Gene to break out the three-engine landing checklist. They would review it before descent. From 140 miles away, Rolf was able to contact Malta. Yes, they had been advised of the change and asked the reason. Harry motioned to Rolf that he would answer this one.

"We need to make a precautionary three-engine landing, and we do not declare an emergency; but we do request priority in the traffic pattern."

Air control replied simply, "Roger, you will have priority. There is no other inbound traffic. Expect radar vectors for runway 24. Call for descent."

Some captains made all the landings. They were, after all, the most interesting parts of every flight. Harry was not one of those. He shared them evenly with the first officers. This sector was supposed to be flown by Rolf and he had made the takeoff in Jeddah. But, now, Harry decided he himself would do the landing in Malta.

"Sorry, Rolf," he said, "but if anyone messes this one up, it should be me. I'll make it up later."

There was a flicker of relief in Rolf's eyes as he turned to Harry, smiled and said "Please, Harry, be my guest."

Harry and Rolf had already gotten out their approach charts and reviewed the airport. Runway 24 meant they would be landing to the southwest. He noted that it was much shorter than the other runway. That was runway 32. That was unusual so he asked Rolf to request the latest weather. Rolf wrote it down and passed it to Harry. The wind was from the southwest at 25 knots and that explained the use of runway 24. That meant the landing would be into the wind. Crosswind landings in the 707 were difficult, even with four engines. A shorter runway into the wind is often preferable to a longer runway that has a strong crosswind. Without passengers, the aircraft would be relatively light for the landing, so a longer runway was less important. Aircraft weight determined the approach speed, which was lower for lighter weights. That meant less rollout after touchdown, and less momentum to brake against. Harry briefed Rolf for the landing on runway 24.

Harry had been glancing back frequently at the oil pressure gauge. Now it was time to shut down the engine. He asked for the engine shutdown checklist. Gene already had it in his hand and began to recite the items. One by one, they were called and executed. It was a strange sensation to shut down an engine in flight. That was normally done only after landing.

Flying on three engines meant that the thrust was asymmetrical. To compensate, Harry pulled back the number two throttle to a lower setting. That lessened the thrust differential. He called for the descent check list, then asked Rolf to request descent. Three engine landings were also practiced regularly in the simulator, so there was little concern in the cockpit.

Because of the difference in thrust between one side of the airplane and the other, Harry would keep number two engine at a low power setting, and make power changes with numbers one and four in unison. With engine number three shut down, it would provide no thrust. The low power used on number two would cause the airplane to yaw, meaning it would tend to fly in a crabwise fashion because of the power differential. Harry compensated for that by introducing rudder trim, which was a small tab on the rudder. It was connected by a cable to a small wheel in the cockpit. The tab moved the rudder aerodynamically in a way that counter-acted the tendency of the airplane to crab. Once set, he would make power changes symmetrically with engines one and four.

Passing 10,000 feet, air control called. "Be advised that your radar vectors will now be for runway 32. Confirm."

Harry did not like that. "Ask him why," he told Rolf.

"Sorry sir, but we have just had a disabled vehicle on runway 24 and it will be closed indefinitely. Confirm runway 32 is acceptable."

Damn, thought Harry, when things go wrong, they really go wrong. His old friend, Murphy, was back on the job. Quickly, he reviewed his options. Too late to go somewhere else and 25 knots was manageable.

Harry nodded to Rolf who replied. "Roger, and we do accept runway 32."

There were two ways to make a crosswind landing. The 707 used the crab method. The airplane followed the landing line to the runway by heading a few degrees into the wind, just enough to offset the drift it caused. From the cockpit, because of the crab angle, it appeared the airplane was pointed to the windward side of the runway, and seemed to be flying slightly sideways. Actually, the airplane was flying a straight line over the ground, even though it was not aligned with the runway. Harry had once landed a 707 in a crosswind of 45 knots and, with such a strong wind, the crab angle was higher, and the appearance of being misaligned with the runway was very strong. That had been a tense situation.

Radar guided them onto the final approach. Harry told Rolf to ask for a long final so that he would have plenty of time to lower the gear and flaps and to establish the crab angle. Of course, as the wind changed, the crab angle would have to be changed; but these would be minor adjustments.

As the aircraft was about to touch down, the crab angle had to be taken out so the airplane was aligned with the runway for the landing. This was done by pushing in with his foot just enough rudder to swing the nose so as to line up the airplane with the runway. This movement increased slightly the speed of the upwind wing and that tended to increase its lift. Harry countered that by putting in just enough aileron to keep the wings level. The airplane was now cross-controlled: aileron one way and rudder the other.

As he neared the touchdown, Harry made sure that the airplane was stabilized with wings level, and aligned with the runway. He broke the rate of descent by gently lifting the nose, then slowly brought back the power to idle. As the airplane met the concrete, he quickly pulled back the lever that activated the speed brakes. These were panels flush with the top of the wings which, when raised, would increase the airplane's drag and reduce its speed. In almost the same motion he pushed the control column full forward to keep the nose wheel down, and turned full aileron into the wind to prevent the wing on that side from gusting up from the higher wind acting on it. Then he grasped the reverser thrust levers, which were positioned on top of the throttles, and pulled them sharply aft. This reversed the direction of the engines thrust and would greatly aid in decelerating the aircraft. His right hand a blur, Harry did all this in just two or three seconds. It was a tricky maneuver and it required good hand/eye coordination; and foot coordination, too. That was also important. More than one 707 pilot had scraped an outboard engine on the runway during a crosswind landing. Just twelve degrees of wing-down would do that.

66
MALTA

As Harry turned off the runway, he began thinking about whether he had made the right decision by landing in Malta. It could turn out to be a very expensive landing. There were many places Harry had never expected to visit, he thought, as he taxied into his assigned parking spot. Malta was one of them. Still, any port in a storm, although this was a very small storm and Malta was a very unusual port.

A tiny bell tinkled every time the name Malta was mentioned. Now, he remembered why. Malta was the home of -- what was his name? -- James, the man who had helped them escape from Sydney with a plane-load of contraband sheep. Harry smiled as he thought of that adventure. No one would believe him, but he had the newspaper clippings to prove it, plenty of them. They had been on page one for days, and Harry had photos of himself with captions which usually began "Captain Harry Ferguson of the Norwegian Ram Runners" . . . and went on to quote him making statements he had never made -- not in the way they were written, anyway. He was in no hurry to return to Australia. How would he list Malta? Would it be on the Runway-Only list or would he be able to say "Yes, I've been to Malta. I enjoyed it there?" He would know the answer soon.

After shutdown, the stairs were put in place, the entry door was opened and a mechanic was inside the cockpit almost before the shutdown checks were completed. Harry hoped he would be as efficient as he was quick. The first surprise was that the mechanic, although Maltese, spoke flawless English. That always made life easier. Harry described the problem in a few words. There was not much to tell. He then made an entry into the aircraft maintenance logbook. That made it official. The airplane would not leave Malta until someone in authority signed the log that the problem had been fixed and the airplane was again airworthy.

Next into the cockpit was the ramp agent from Air Malta. He would act as their handling agent and would be their liaison for all matters related to the airplane and the crew.

His first question was, "Captain, do you require hotel accommodations for tonight?"

Harry smiled. "Damn," he answered wryly. "I've only been here ten minutes and I don't know any more than you do. When I know, you'll know.

Let's see what the mechanics come up with; but I think we will need hotel rooms."

With that, he introduced the agent to the cabin chief and asked them to work it out as they went along. Harry had still not left his seat. Now, he leaned across the cockpit and looked out the window on that side to see if anything was happening. He was pleased to see that the cowl of the number three engine had already been opened and that several men were looking into the problem.

Of course all the girls, as eager as they were to return home, were excited at the prospect of spending a night or two in Malta.

"Imagine," one said, "they have cafes and restaurants here. And wine! And discos! After those terrible weeks in Ouargla, we have decided we would like to stay, Harry, so please arrange it if you can."

"If we stay," answered Harry with a smile, "it'll be arranged by the mechanics, and not by me; but right now, Malta by night seems to be a good possibility."

The girl beamed and hurried off to tell the others the good news.

By now the mechanics had looked at the engine and one came into the cockpit to report the findings.

"Captain," he said. "First, some good news. There is no engine damage. One of the seals on the main bearing has been torn. That was where you were losing oil."

Harry pretended to know what he was talking about. "And the bad news? What about the bad news?"

The mechanic was not sure they had a replacement seal on hand, one that was not marked as a spare for Air Malta. "And if you find one, how long will it take?"

It was hard to say, but certainly twenty-four hours, perhaps longer. "It all depends," he said, with a shrug.

"On what?" asked Harry. "It all depends on what?"

There was a long list, starting with a shift change for mechanics in half an hour. Harry had heard enough. He would send a telex to Brussels explaining the situation, then the crew would go to a hotel and await developments.

"Already arranged, Captain," said the ramp agent after Harry had sent the telex. "I have booked you into the Phoenicia Hotel -- one of our best -- and very near to Valletta."

Harry did not say that he had never heard of Valletta. The ramp agent gave Harry his telephone number, and promised to keep him apprised of the situation. He had arranged for a couple of vans to take the crews to the hotel and soon they were on their way. An unexpected adventure, but one Harry intended to take advantage of.

His first impression of Malta was that it was beige. Every building, he was told, was made of blocks of limestone cut from the bedrock of Malta.

"So," he said to the driver, "you're digging it out of one end and piling it up on the other. I hope you don't tip the island over one day."

The driver laughed. "So far, no problem, Captain. And the blocks, they are very strong. You can cut through them with a knife, but you cannot crush them, especially when they are old."

That explained beige. Now, what about the English that everyone spoke so well? The driver explained that too.

"The British," he said, "they were here for many years. Before them, we had others, Arabs and many others. In 1565, there were the Turks who came and tried to drive us off our island. But the Knights of Malta were here then. You know them? The Knights and the Maltese drove off the Turks instead -- a big story in our history. For the British, we were a colony until just a few years ago. We became independent in 1964."

Malta's location in the center of the Mediterranean had made it, for centuries, a very strategic island. During the war, the driver said, the British had airplanes based here to bomb the ships carrying supplies to the Germans in North Africa. In response, Malta had undergone heavy bombing from the Germans and the Italians. They had bases in Sicily. That was just forty or fifty miles north of Gozo, one of Malta's three islands. "When you go into Valletta," the driver said, "you will see what is left of our opera house. It was hit by German bombs and was never rebuilt. It is just inside the city gate on your right."

A gate to a city? What was that? The next day, he would see the City Gate and what used to be an opera house, now a broken monument to war.

The Phoenicia Hotel was just a few minutes' walk from the City Gate, which could be seen from the hotel entrance. It was a huge stone arch with a flat top. The hotel was old European, large and comfortable -- no glass, no chrome -- just the way Harry liked them. His phone rang as he was taking a badly-needed shower. Damn, he thought, as he reached for a towel, I hope the news is good. As often happens, the news depended upon your perspective. They would not leave, he was told, before the day after tomorrow.

"In the morning, we hope. There is a telex from Brussels here for you. I will send it by car and it will arrive in ten minutes. Okay?"

This news was, for Harry, neither good nor bad, just news. He would decide if it was good or bad after he read the telex. For the girls, it would be great news.

The telex arrived as Harry stepped out of the shower. It directed Rene and his crew to return to Brussels as soon as possible by commercial transport. They were needed there. Air Malta had regular flights there and they would leave in the morning. Harry called Rene with the news.

Well, might as well make the best of it, Harry thought. He had written down the room numbers of the crew when they checked in. Now he called them, one by one, and arranged a rendezvous in the lobby in one hour. Malta by night would start with a good dinner, something they had not had in some weeks.

"Captain," said the concierge with obvious pride, "there are so many restaurants. I will send you to the Manhattan. It has a wonderful view of Valletta. It looks across the harbor and you will see the bastions of the city. At night, they are lighted. Beautiful!" A restaurant named Manhattan? Now, that was an omen. But bastions? Harry's eyebrows lifted. "Yes, Captain, Valletta is on a peninsula and after the Great Siege of 1565" --Harry could almost hear the capital letters as the concierge said, 'Great Siege' -- "a moat was made by the entrance. The walls, if you prefer to call them that, were built all around the city. You must see them. Tonight, by night, and, tomorrow, by day, if you have the time. They are very special and we are very proud of them. To construct such bastions in those days! Miraculous!"

The Maltese believed in miracles; they had to. Ninety nine per cent were Catholic, and there were several hundred churches on this small island. That, thought Harry, ought to be enough, even if all of them went to church at the same time. One of those churches, St. John's Cathedral in Valletta, was one of the great churches of Europe.

"Even Napoleon has been there," said the concierge. They would look at churches tomorrow.

Now, they set out to find the Manhattan restaurant. That had to be an omen. It had been a long day and everyone was hungry. And, thought Harry, a drink would not hurt. By taxi, it was a short ride. The restaurant was on a jetty near a yacht marina. It did not look like much from the street side; but as they passed through it and came out on a deck on the harbor side, they were struck by the splendid view across the harbor. The bastions, fully illuminated, were spectacular. They were enormous and followed the contour of the peninsula on which Valletta stood. The buildings and steeples of Valletta rose behind them. Awesome, thought Harry, somewhat stunned.

"Some view," said Gene as they took their seats at a couple of tables pushed together. The dinner was a pleasant affair and included Maltese wine. Not as good as the French wine, they agreed, but not bad. And the price was right.

"It's almost free," said one of the girls.

Usually, at such crew dinners, each paid a share. This time, when the check arrived, Harry paid it and held up a palm of refusal when the others offered to pay.

"This one's on me," he said, "as a small thank you for your fine work during the Haj. You can buy me a beer when we get back to Belgium."

There was a loud protest and, in the end, they compromised. The crew would pay for the wine, and everyone seemed satisfied.

After dinner, Harry and a few others returned to the hotel. Another group, following the suggestion of the concierge, took a taxi to the nightlife center of Malta but Harry was fading fast, and tomorrow was another day. He suggested a tour of the island in the morning and there were several who agreed.

"But no shopping," decreed Harry. "Sightseeing only. I'll arrange the transport. Those interested will meet in the lobby at ten in the morning."

Malta was so far, so good. Tomorrow, they would see the daytime side of the island.

Their morning began with a walking tour of Valletta, just a few minutes' walk from the hotel. There, they they crossed a moat that was wide and deep; then they passed through the arches of the City Gate and, sure enough, just beyond were the remnants of the walls of the bombed-out opera house. The peninsula on which the city was built was an elongated hump with a backbone running down the middle. That was Republic Street. The cross streets fell away towards the water on both sides of the backbone like vertebrae carved of stone. Near the site of the opera house was a garden offering a view of the Grand Harbor. It was said to be one of the best natural harbors in the world, and it was a breathtaking sight. On its far side, stood a collection of villages that looked like a travel brochure. Adding to Valletta's charm were horse-drawn carriages used to carry tourists. The people were friendly and helpful. The Maltese, Harry noticed, as they walked about the city, were low-altitude people, especially the elderly. Harry had a proclivity for short people. Where has Malta been all my life, Harry asked himself.

They had a simple lunch in a local café, where Harry and Gene tested the local beer, then went back to the hotel, where Harry had reserved a minibus for the afternoon. He had also reserved a driver, and thank God for that. The drivers of Malta were fearless, and the passengers found themselves flinching often as they narrowly avoided one collision after another. Harry noticed that, in Malta, the steering wheel was on the right and driving was on the left. Perhaps that explained his high flow rate of adrenalin. The buses were old Bedford buses from England, and they were surely old. "From before the war," the driver told them. Most of the cars looked to be of the same vintage. Harry had never before seen so many old and battered cars. He could not identify most of them.

The first stop was at Saint Mary's church in Mosta. It was, said the driver, the third largest dome in the entire world. In Valletta, they had visited St John's Cathedral and it was, indeed, very special. Its floor was comprised of crypts, some of which went back hundreds of years. Each crypt was etched with the name of the person interred there and the date of his death. Looking down at one point, Harry discovered that he was standing on top of the final resting place of one Mr. Bertrandus, who had been laid there in 1647. Harry thought it strange to walk over people entombed there, but there was no other way. They were told that when Napoleon visited Malta, the church had painted all its silver artifacts black so that he would not confiscate them. Harry wondered about Mr. Bonaparte's reputation.

Saint Mary's was special in a different way. Instead of a heavy, dark interior and walls covered with old paintings of cherubs, angels, and saints, this church was light and airy. Instead of paintings, it had murals, and they were beautiful. Its chief claim to fame was an incident during the war. During a mass, a German bomb had pierced the dome. The driver showed them the exact place it had come through. It had ricocheted off the other side of the dome, then hit the floor without exploding, skidding and bumping right through the entire congregation without touching a single worshipper. Of course, that became the Miracle of Mosta, and Harry could understand that. The bomb was on display.

"Looks like a 500-pounder," said Harry, to no one in particular.

They were then taken to the city of Medina, known as the Silent City. It stood majestically on a hilltop, completely walled and looking formidable. It, too, had a moat, one that encircled the entire city. This city had also played an important role during the Great Siege of 1565. The narrow streets were traffic-free. Nice to visit, thought Harry, but I wouldn't like to live here. He felt confined just walking through those narrow streets surrounded by stone blocks. They stopped for coffee at a café on a rampart that overlooked the entire island of Malta. In the distance could be seen St Paul's Bay, where it was claimed that the apostle Paul had been shipwrecked in the year 61. Aha, thought Harry. That accounts for all these Catholics around here.

"How do you know? Do you have that on videotape?" Harry asked the driver, who looked blankly at him. "Never mind," said Harry. "A little joke. And not a very funny one."

The drive back to the hotel was another death-defying experience and they were grateful to reach it alive. There was a second telex waiting for Harry. The first had simply said, more or less, good luck with your problem. This one wanted details. The airplane was desperately needed back in Brussels. When would it get there? Harry called his liaison in Air Malta.

"Sorry, Captain, but the news is bad. It will require another day. After tomorrow, for sure."

Harry dictated a reply. They were faced with another day in Malta, and they had already seen most of it.

He had an idea and called the desk. "Is there a golf course here?" he asked.

"Of course, Captain, a very fine one and one of the oldest of Europe."

Everything in Malta seemed to be one of the oldest in Europe. The opera house in Valetta, which they had viewed the day before, was *the* very oldest in Europe. It looked it, thought Harry as he had looked around. It was old and small, but somehow charming.

"Just how old is this old golf course?" he asked.

"Oh, very old, sir. In the beginning the bastions were used, but now it's a regular golf course. The British made it sir, and it's very special. Very near the hotel."

Everything seems to be very near the hotel, thought Harry. Well, it's a small island, he thought, so how far apart can anything be? He understood that. What he did not understand was how in the hell even the British had played golf on the bastions of Valletta. From what he had seen there, those bastions did not look to be golfer-friendly. That needed looking into. He would investigate tomorrow.

He called Gene. "Gene, old buddy. How long has it been since you played a round of golf?"

There was silence. Then: "Say again." Gene was not sure he had heard that right. "Golf," said Harry. "How would you like to play a round of golf tomorrow? And you better say you can hardly wait because I've already booked a tee time for ten o'clock."

"Boss," said Gene wearily, "I haven't played golf in ten years, maybe longer. And I couldn't play for shit even then. I don't even like to think about how I'd play now. But it sounds like I don't have a choice."

"How perceptive you are," said Harry. "And don't worry, skill is not required, only enthusiasm. We'll discuss it at dinner. I'll call you later."

67
GOLF? IN MALTA?

Only a handful of golf courses around the world are allowed to include "Royal" in their name, and The Royal Malta Golf Club was one of them. It was, indeed, special, but perhaps not in the way the desk clerk meant. The clubhouse, made of limestone blocks, of course, looked more like a bomb shelter than a clubhouse. They rented clubs that were old and rusted. Like the buses, they looked like they were made before the war. The trolleys also looked ancient. They asked to rent a couple. Sorry, they were told, no trolleys for rent right now. Harry raised his eyebrows.

"Didn't we see some trolleys just outside the club?"

"Yes," he was told, "but those trolleys are hired out by Tony Galea and he is not here today."

"Okay," said Harry with a wry smile, "we'll carry our clubs. We can use the exercise."

The course had no other players, and Harry soon understood why. The fairways looked like the rough is supposed to look, and the rough was impossible. Harry and Gene each lost three or four balls on just the first few holes and all were in the fairway. Harry had never before lost a ball in the fairway, but these were fairways in name only. Despite the long grass on parts of the fairways, there were bare areas everywhere, some like concrete. A lucky bounce there could turn a mediocre drive into a winner. Like life, thought Harry, as he watched a mis-hit ball bound far up the fairway when it hit just right on one of those bare spots.

This course, Harry decided, was more like an obstacle course than a golf course. In a way it was like Malta itself: out-of-date and not well-kept. Still, it was interesting. One reason was that the course was not restricted to golfers. Anyone could walk there, and many did. They learned later that the course was on government land, so all of Malta could use it, not only golfers. As Harry and Gene approached the green on one hole, a car drove up and parked just before it. Its doors opened and out popped a man with his wife and three children. A blanket was spread on the green, a wicker basket was placed on it, and a family picnic was soon underway.

Harry had once played golf at the Willingdon Country Club in Bombay and there was a night-and-day difference between that golf course and this one. That course was beautifully tended, manicured almost, and it was hard to find a blade of grass that was longer than the others. That had been one of the few times he had played with a caddy -- not only one -- but two. The second was a fore-caddy, who positioned himself in the area where Harry's shot was supposed to land. That was to avoid having to look for errant golf balls and Harry usually hit many. Once, when he started into the dense foliage to look for one, he was stopped by the caddy because of "perhaps snakes, sir." He played badly, and the best part of his round was the gin and tonic he enjoyed afterward on the terrace of the clubhouse. It was a weekday and he was the only customer in an enormous, magnificent, colonial structure that seemed to be made mostly of marble and, with three men waiting on him, he felt like the King of England. He felt even better when he was presented with the bill. The total, including green fees, clubs, caddies, and the gin and tonic, came to less than $4.00!

Harry had played at another special golf course during his "Tonkin Gulf Timeouts" at Cubi Point in the Philippines. That course, tough and compact, was nestled in the mountains near Baguio, north of Manila. This up-and-down course had few level places and one of the holes there was named, appropriately, "Heart Attack Hill." The hill loomed directly ahead of the golfer as he stood on the tee. To prevent the tee-shot from rolling back down to the tee after striking the slope, several terraces had been dug into the hillside. To prevent heart attacks, a ski-tow helped pull the golfer up to the terrace where his ball had come to rest. The green was on the peak of the hill, so a misplayed shot rolled down the hill on the other side. It was one of the most challenging holes Harry had ever played.

Harry and Gene bypassed the picnic green and went along their way. On the next tee, just as Gene was about to play, two horses with riders trotted right across the fairway, just ten yards in front of them. Along with picnics, horse-back riding seemed a regular feature of the course. An equestrian track ran all around the course, and, here and there, it went right through it. That accounted for the hoofprints Harry had noticed on one of the greens.

Harry and Gene gave it their best, but they ran out of balls after ten holes. Their last ball was more stolen than lost. A dog had darted out of the bushes near where Harry had hit his drive, snatched the ball, and disappeared back into the bushes. *Was that a trained dog?* Harry wondered. By that time, they had had enough golf. Harry's game was less than brilliant but still better than Gene's, who seemed to hit the ground behind the ball as often as he hit the ball. A few times, he missed it completely.

316

"Ain't that something?" he asked in exasperation. "The goddamn ball ain't even moving, and I still can't hit it."

Harry, like most golfers, had been there now and then. He commiserated with Gene, then said, "Let's go check the bar and see if there's any beer there."

The bar room was almost as interesting as the course. Harry looked around as they drank their Cisk beers. The club champions were listed on placards, and the first one went all the way back to 1891. The club champion that year was Surgeon Moor, from Her Majesty's Ship, "Surprise," of the Royal Navy. Until recent years, nearly all were British military.

"What about playing golf on the bastions at Valletta," Harry asked the barman. "Was that true?"

"Oh, yes, sir. The first few years were there," he said, and he pointed to a wall near the bar.

Harry could not be sure if they were old photos or fine sketches, but they depicted golfers on the ramparts of Valletta's bastions. Talk about golf addicts, thought Harry. It took courage to play on a golf course like this one. How brave did a golfer need to be to play on the bastions?

Drinking his beer, Gene looked around the room and his glance fell on the crest of the Royal Malta Golf Course hanging above the bar.

"Royal Malta Golf Course, my ass," he said disdainfully. "More like the Royal Malta Cow Pasture."

Harry had to agree.

Golf was a funny game, and there was no way to explain the zeal of golfers. They loved the game and all that was needed was a place to play; never mind what the place was like. Harry liked golf, and one reason was the people who played. It seemed to attract a certain type of person, a type that Harry liked. He had never met an obnoxious golfer. Sure, some were so caught up in the game that they suffered no distractions from those around them. That was intensity. All were genuine people.

Golf was like life, thought Harry. Good shots end up badly; bad shots take lucky bounces. Golf was, in a way, a test of character. He had heard that the Japanese often transacted business on golf courses and that made sense to Harry. You could tell much about a man's character by playing golf with him. The game measured his responses to triumph and disaster. Opportunities to cheat abounded. Even on good days, frustration always lurked just around the next dogleg. It was a mysterious game.

In golf, the players play against the golf course, then compare their scores to see who won. That was possible because of the game's handicap system. Based on scores over many rounds of golf, each player established a number known as a handicap. A golf course was supposed to be played in an assigned number of strokes. That was par. Only the best players could hope to match it. For the rest, the handicap was the number of strokes more than par that the golfer would usually take on a round of golf. By comparing handicaps, players could compare ability and, by adjusting scores according to individual handicaps, a close competition could be held between players of very different abilities.

"What's your handicap?" was a common question among golfers, both on and off the course. It was an instant measure of a golfer's skill.

Too bad, Harry thought, that life itself did not have a handicap system. By knowing someone's handicap in the various categories of life, a comparison of "abilities" would help people know how compatible they might be. Take religion, for example. If the baseline was set at a known value, deeply religious, say, or mildly agnostic, then a handicap of plus or minus from the baseline would provide a grasp of a person's beliefs. Think of the time saved!

Yes, "mysterious" was the best word to describe golf. One day, Harry would play well; the next as if he had never played before. There was no explaining it. He recalled drinking a beer with a good golfer who had just suffered a horrendous round.

"You know," he said, as he drank his beer, "I played my first round of golf with my father when I was ten. I played better that day than I did today."

Still, despite golf's exasperations, it was hard to match the glow of satisfaction Harry felt as he followed the arc of a well-struck golf ball.

He recalled a moment during his flight training. He had just left the officers' mess after dinner and had paused a moment to enjoy the view of a full moon. Another student came out in his flight suit, on his way to a night flight. Unaware of Harry, he too, looked up at the moon, then raised one fist towards it and pleaded, "Oh, magic power. Be there tonight!"

And that, in a way, was how Harry viewed golf. He had tried his hand at many sports, and he was a good athlete; but he had never mastered golf nor even came close. Not many did. Maybe in the next life, he thought, the magic power would always be there, and not come and go as it does in this one. In learning to fly, experience and confidence eventually overcame the need for magic power. Such was not the case in the great game of golf.

318

Golf was not popular among the Maltese, the barman told them. It was mostly tourists and foreign residents who played there. Most of the ex-pats were English, as was the club, so English traditions were honored. One was the ceremony of installing a new captain. That had happened just a few weeks earlier, the barman said. The tradition included a change of command at the first tee where the new captain would hit the symbolic first drive of his captaincy. This was followed by champagne served at a makeshift bar near the tee. This time, the new captain had arrived in a horse-drawn carriage. There were many in Malta and Harry had seen them about the island. The driver had deposited the new captain at the first tee where he hit his traditional first shot. As he did, a loud roar erupted from the throng as the driver of the carriage, after off-loading his charge, had made a turn which took him right across the middle of a nearby green. From the commotion, he knew he had done something wrong, the barman said, but he had no ideas what it was.

"Not his fault," said Harry, as he guffawed loudly. "Someone should have told him."

This time, Air Malta got it right and they left the following morning for Brussels. At last, Harry's carpets were on their way to their new home. Malta had been a pleasant experience. What Harry had expected to be a vexing delay had turned out to be a rewarding visit. It was, for Harry, a kind of time warp, as life in Malta reminded him of his childhood in Milwaukee. Then, milkmen delivered fresh milk right to your door every day. In the summer, an ice truck delivered large blocks of ice to your icebox, as refrigerators were rare. In the winter, the back porch became an icebox. He remembered a man in a horse-drawn wagon who bought rags and old newspapers. In Malta, Harry had seen ancient trucks which sold bread, fruit, vegetables and who knew what else. Malta was a window to Harry's past.

The modern world had not yet reached this island, and life seemed simple. Harry liked that. Funny, he thought, how Malta could be so different from the great countries of Europe. It was just a few hours away, but those hours were a time machine that bridged two very different worlds. He was not sure he would like to live there, but it had certainly been a wonderful place to visit. He decided he would take Irene there one day. He would like another crack at that golf course.

319

68
BACK IN BRUSSELS

In Brussels, the carpets brightened Harry's apartment considerably. The five carpets more than covered his floor and the overflow went up the walls. "Too much carpet," Harry said, "not enough floor." He was pleased to see that Irene liked them, too. She had arrived right after work, carefully scrutinized all five and pronounced them, "exquisite. I love them all."

"Choose one," said Harry, "but not that one." He pointed at his first purchase. "That one has sentimental value."

"Harry, you are very kind but why would you give such an expensive 'cadeau'?"

"Hey," said Harry, "are you the same lady who told me that the cost of a present was not important?"

"Yes," replied Irene, smiling, "but I meant for small presents, not like this."

Then Harry grinned. "Well," he said, "when I think of the magic after I gave you that $3.00 ring...." For a moment, Irene thought he was serious.

Then, she smiled. "For the magic, there is no need for a present. But I do accept with a 'grand merci.'" She kissed his cheek in thanks.

Harry grinned more broadly. "Fair enough. Go ahead. Choose one. We'll call it part payment for all the gasoline you've been burning up, driving me around Belgium. Besides, as you can see, I've run out of floor space."

Irene took his hand and nodded toward the bed. "Must I choose now, or may I wait until after the magic?"

That first carpet became very dear to him, and he became an admirer of Persian carpets, buying one here, one there, and, over the years, he would collect many. They became good friends and he admired them all. Once he became used to a certain carpet in a certain place, nothing else would do. Irene bought a book about them and became somewhat of an expert. There was a lot to know, and even Harry became interested in the histories of the various types and qualities of the carpets. No one in Milwaukee would ever believe that Harry Ferguson had become a collector of Persian carpets. Who there had ever seen one? Or even heard of one? Harry was not only seeing the world, he was acquiring part of it.

Harry flew often to various places in the south of Europe. By car, he and Irene toured Belgium, and made a few excursions to Holland and France.

Interspersed were visits to The Drum, where Harry honed his dart-throwing skills. One night, he had teamed up with another American, and challenged a couple of Brits to a match. The Brits, condescendingly, agreed. Harry and his partner had drunk just enough beer to put them in the zone between very relaxed and slightly drunk. Incredibly, to the Brits anyway, it came down to the very last dart. It was thrown by Harry's partner in a nonchalant way and it drove straight into the heart of the double 8 needed to win the match. The entire bar watched that last dart, and now, broke into enthusiastic applause. Never had a beer tasted as good as the one that dart won for Harry and his friend.

One weekend in Amsterdam was enough to convince Harry that this was a first-class city. They visited the Rijksmuseum, where many of Rembrandt's works are displayed. One, titled "Night Watch," took his breath away. Even Harry could see that this was a master. He was awed by these paintings created so long ago. They would never believe this in Milwaukee, either. A canal trip in a launch showed them much of the city; and, in the evening, they enjoyed an Indonesian dinner in a local restaurant. The Dutch empire was at one time vast and included much of the Far East. Much of that influence could be seen in Amsterdam. It was a fascinating city.

69
JFK

A few months earlier, Harry had received a letter from old friend and former squadron-mate, Joe Schaedel. Harry and Joe had gone through much together, and they had kept in touch over the years. Harry had decided long ago that there were no friends like Navy friends, and Joe was near the top of that list. He had stayed in the Navy and was now the Air Operations Officer on the USS John F. Kennedy. As such, he controlled all flight operations around the ship. He did this from the ship's counterpart of an airport control tower. It was Primary Flight, known as Pri-Fly. It offered a view of the entire flight deck and was the nerve center of all operations there and in the air around the ship. It was a position of great responsibility. The letter said that the JFK would soon be in Palma for a few days. Was there a chance for a reunion? Harry had replied that, one way or another, he would be there when the ship came in.

Life sometimes works in wondrous ways. When Harry mentioned to Irene that he would visit Palma to meet an old friend on a certain date, she was dumbfounded.

"But, Harry!" she exclaimed excitedly. "I have long ago booked a holiday to Palma during this same time. Is that not extraordinary?"

Harry was not sure he would have used that word to describe this remarkable coincidence, but it would surely do. He arranged for five days off to coincide with Irene's package tour, and they flew to Palma on the same airplane, Irene in the cabin and Harry in the cockpit jump-seat.

The flight arrived in late afternoon. At Irene's hotel, Harry managed to arrange a double room with a view of the harbor. He was becoming expert at such "persuasions." A pleasant manner and a few banknotes usually did the job. After checking in, they spent a couple of hours at the beach, then had dinner in the hotel restaurant. Irene's package included breakfast and dinner, and Harry had negotiated an extra charge for a double room and his meals. After dinner, they took a short walk, then went to bed early. It was supposed to be an early night to be ready for a big day to follow, and they were in bed early; but as Harry reached for Irene to kiss her goodnight, the sweet feel of her skin pushed away the thought of sleep. He drew her close.

"I thought we went to bed early to sleep, to be ready for tomorrow," whispered Irene into his ear.

"We can sleep when we're old," said Harry softly as he began to stroke her back and nibble her ear. He remembered Astrid saying those very same words. Was that Freudian? Who cares, he thought. "And anyway, I'm not sleepy yet."

Later, as Harry was falling asleep, Irene turned off the bed lamp.

"Being a tourist can be tiring, can't it?" she teased, as she gently kissed Harry goodnight; but Harry was already asleep.

He awoke early and slipped out of bed. He padded over to the window, drew back the edge of the drape and peered out over the harbor. There, in all her glory, was the USS John F. Kennedy, gently washed in the early morning sun. The ship was anchored about a half-mile from the pier, and the sight of the great ship made Harry's heart skip a beat. He pulled the drapes open, flooding the room with sunlight and waking Irene.

"Irene, come and see. The ship is here!"

She held her forearm across her face against the light and frowned. Then she saw Harry's excitement and quickly joined him at the window. How could he be so excited at the sight of a ship? Still, she had to admit the ship had a majestic look about it. She had never before seen an aircraft carrier, and it was an impressive sight. So enormous, she thought, how could anyone build such a ship?

By letter, Harry and Joe had agreed to meet at the landing at noon. Harry had not seen a carrier since he had left the Kitty Hawk after his duty in Vietnam. He had seldom even thought about them because of the hard memories they held for him. Now, Harry was surprised to feel his blood begin to stir as he thought about visiting the JFK. He looked forward to seeing Joe and to showing Irene around the ship. Impressive from the hotel, it would be even more so once on board.

Last night's "physical stuff," as Irene sometimes called it, had generated a huge appetite, and Harry ate a breakfast which Irene described as, "How can you eat so much?"

Then she smiled. "I think I know the reason. Making love makes you hungry."

Harry smiled back. "Ah, how clever you are. What about going up to our room after breakfast to work on my appetite for lunch?"

She laughed. "Do you never have enough?"

"Enough? Making love with you? I can't imagine it."

Irene stopped laughing and was suddenly serious. A long moment passed. Then, she leaned forward and asked softly, "Shall we go up to our room for a few minutes? I just remembered I have forgotten something."

Harry rented a car and asked directions to the ship's landing. Harry knew about ships' landings. As a junior officer, he had sometimes served as Boat Officer in charge of the small boats the carrier stowed in the aft section of the hangar deck. These were known as liberty boats. When the ship was anchored away from a pier, they were used to carry the ship's crew, about 60 or 70 at a time, between the ship and the shore. This was dreaded duty, especially late at night. That was when the boats returned to the ship filled with sailors who had been carousing the entire evening. Most showed signs of drinking, some were drunk. A few were very drunk and looking for trouble. Arguments erupted and fights broke out.

Once, Harry had to intervene when a group of thoroughly inebriated sailors struggled to throw one of their shipmates overboard. Harry had ordered the coxswain to stop the boat and turn off the engine. The ensuing silence gave added volume to what he sincerely hoped were firm commands to "Put that man down and sit down or we will stay out here all night." Calm returned after several tense moments and Harry was relieved. He had no idea what he might have done next if something more had to be done.

Another time, he had barely managed to prevent a drunken sailor from leaving the boat by stepping away from the ship and into the sea instead of up the ladder leading to the ship. Boat Officer duty was not popular.

Jack Rooney, who was known as "Shipwreck Rooney," had once returned to the landing in Okinawa after the liberty boats had stopped running. He was seriously drunk, but he knew he had to return to the ship, and a liberty boat was the only way to do that. This time, however, the liberty boats were shore-based old personnel landing craft left over from the war. They were much larger than regular liberty boats.

Jack somehow got one started, then drove it out to the ship. He announced his arrival by caroming off the accommodation ladder with a thunderous crash, then turned back for another try at coming alongside. By then, the Officer of the Deck had thrown a searchlight on Jack and, with his megaphone, ordered Jack not to come aboard.

"No," shouted Jack. "I have to be back on board tonight. Stand by for landing."

There was another crunching collision with the ladder and another ricochet seaward. This time, Jack kept going and headed back to shore where he spent the night sleeping on the boat.

Jack managed to avoid a court-martial, but stood a Captain's Mast, in which the Commanding Officer metes out non-judicial punishment for transgressions within the unit. Jack was "awarded" two weeks in "hack," which meant he was confined to his stateroom for that period. He could leave only to go to the toilet. Meals were brought in.

"Room service," he called it, when Harry visited him the next day.

"Are you crazy?" he demanded.

Jack, with a rueful smile, said, "Temporarily, yes. Pretty dumb, huh?"

This drunken caper might have ruined his career but, thanks to a judicious CO, it did not. The accommodation ladder, however, was so badly mangled that it spent the rest of the cruise in the "junkyard" in the aft hangar deck, and was never used again.

Harry and Irene stood on the jetty as the JFK's boat slipped gently alongside and Joe jumped onto the pier with a huge smile. He and Harry had not seen each other in some years. They embraced warmly and pummelled each other's back enthusiastically. You look great, each told the other, and "not a day older," said Joe.

"You mean," asked Harry "that I looked this old five years ago?"

Joe laughed and took Irene's hand as Harry introduced them.

"You better be careful with this guy," said Joe. "And I know what I'm talking about. We used to live together. Separate bedrooms, of course."

Irene smiled at Joe. She liked him right away.

"Oh, I am always careful, especially with pilots." She said. "Are we going to visit your ship today? Harry told me you are one of the biggest shots on the entire ship."

Joe smiled at being called a big shot. "Don't believe everything he tells you. He never tells the truth, especially to women. Yes, we're going back with this same boat. Ever been on a carrier before?"

Irene replied that she had not, although she sometimes felt she had, just from listening to Harry talk about them. "I don't know how he lives without them."

The boat bumped up lightly alongside the ship and they scrambled up the accommodation ladder. Reaching the quarterdeck, Joe turned toward Old Glory, not visible, but flying from the stern, and saluted. Harry simply stopped, faced aft, and briefly placed his hand over his heart. Harry was surprised to feel an emotion he had not felt in a long time. They entered the vast reaches of the hangar deck and Harry stopped to look about. It felt good, very good, to be back on board an aircraft carrier, and he wanted to enjoy the moment.

Harry still knew his way around, but let Joe act as tour guide. Without seeing one, it's hard to imagine how awesome a carrier can be. As they moved through the ship, Harry noticed Irene's reaction.

"But it is incredible," she said at one point. "How could anyone build such a vessel?"

Joe provided statistics. The ship was 1,080 feet long and had seventeen decks from the keel to the top of the superstructure. At its widest point, the flight deck measured 250 feet. At flank speed, four giant propellers could drive this eighty-thousand-ton ship through the sea at 55 miles per hour. Harry translated that into kilometres-per-hour for Irene. Impressive, no matter how you said it, and Irene's expression said she was, indeed, impressed. Harry had once been on board the USS Ranger during part of her sea trials after construction. The ship had been taken to 48 knots and she had shuddered and shaken with such force that Harry thought she might come unglued. There was seldom a need for such speed, but it was there if needed.

The flight deck offered a fine view of Palma. The entire deck was lined with airplanes, including Skyhawks, like those Harry had flown from the Kitty Hawk.

"Ah, A4 Skyhawks," said Irene when she first saw them.

Joe could not believe his ears and said, "Hey, I'm impressed with your aircraft recognition. Did Harry teach you that?"

"Among other things, yes," Irene replied, with a coy smile.

With some difficulty, Harry and Joe managed to boost Irene into a Skyhawk cockpit for a photo. It would become one of Harry's favorite pictures of Irene.

Joe showed them the waist catapults on the angled deck. Those on the bow were covered with parked airplanes, each held down by tie-down cables connecting the airplanes to pad-eyes in the deck. The number of cables depended upon the expected movement of the deck. Here in port there, might be six cables on one airplane while at sea, in bad weather, there could be as many as twenty cables per airplane.

The catapult track was about 250 feet long. On the Kitty Hawk, Harry told Irene and Joe, a brass plaque was set flush into the flight deck near the midpoint of the number one catapult. The distance from this plaque to the bow, it read, is the total distance of the Wright brothers' first flight in Kitty Hawk, North Carolina, in 1903. Now, in just twice that distance, one of these powerful catapults could accelerate a 35-ton airplane from a standstill to 160 miles per hours!

They visited Primary Flight, which was Joe's duty station as Air Boss. It was the ship's control tower, and it looked down on the entire length of the flight deck and on all the airplanes parked there. How she would love to see this ship at sea, Irene thought, and flying its airplanes. Perhaps one day, you never knew. Joe took them to the bridge that was the ship's command center. Irene sat in the Captain's chair, looking very important. The caverns of the Combat Information Center, deep in the ship's bowels, were also on the tour. This was the heart of the ship's various electronic systems, including its radar. Dark and mysterious, thought Irene, as she looked at the various screens blinking in semi-darkness. I don't think I would like to work here, she thought.

The tour ended with coffee in the officers' wardroom.

"What do you think?" Joe asked Irene. "How do you like our ship?"

Irene paused before answering. "Only Americans could build such a ship. It is simply marvelous. I would like to make a voyage on your beautiful ship one day."

Harry and Joe exchanged glances. They liked her answer, although neither would have used the word "beautiful" to describe the great ship.

"You never know," said Joe, echoing Irene's own thoughts during the tour. "Maybe one day you will."

They agreed to meet the next morning at the ship's landing where they would begin to explore the island.

"This time," said Harry, "I'll be the tour guide. I've bought a guide book and I'll lead the way."

Joe smiled and said, "Harry, as I recall, you could never find your ass with both hands. How will you find your way around Palma? Never mind, don't answer. It might be more fun this way. I look forward to our tour."

It was not until Harry was back in Brussels that he realized how great had been his holiday in Palma. Life was sometimes like that for Harry. Some experiences were enjoyed more in the remembering than in the making. He was always cognizant of that and tried to enjoy the moment to the maximum; but it did not always work. There were too many distractions; too many annoyances. These were usually filtered out when remembering, leaving only the heart of the experience; so it was with Palma. The ship, renewing his friendship with Joe, Irene at his side, and the wonderful Mediterranean island of Palma; they all came together to make those few days very special. He often enjoyed recalling them, and Irene described it as a "truly wonderful holiday. I would like to have more like that one."

Harry was taken with the Spanish life style. Its reputation was "manana" but it did not mean the Spanish were lazy, only that they placed a high priority on enjoying life -- eating, drinking, dancing and all those parts of life that added pleasure: Those seemed important in Spain. Some discos did not open until midnight and did not close until dawn. Now that, thought Harry, was serious pleasure. They had gone to a restaurant at 2230 intending to have dinner. Sorry, they were told, but we do not open for another thirty minutes; but would they like a sandwich?

He especially liked the idea of siesta, during which commercial life stopped for three hours at midday, and the people gave themselves over to dining and drinking in the countless cafes that were everywhere. Instead of sitting at a table, most stood at the bar, sipping wine or beer and munching on snacks known as tapas. They were many, varied, and delicious. It was a delightful way to dine. Harry would return to Spain many times, and always with pleasure. The tapas and the cafes that served them were part of the reason why.

70

LOURDES

From Brussels, Harry was seeing places he had never heard of before. One such place was Lourdes, in France. Of course, he had heard of this famous place, but, for him, it was more an old movie than a real place. It was very real, as Harry learned when he was assigned a charter flight there. It was an early departure, a late return, and the entire time in between at Lourdes was spent waiting for the passengers. Most of them went, not for religious reasons, but for physical ones. Many were in wheelchairs or otherwise handicapped. The curative powers of this place were legend among Catholics, and many hoped for a miracle to rescue them.

Harry looked forward to seeing this renowned place, where a young girl had once seen the Virgin Mary. He did not know what to expect, but he certainly did not expect what he saw when he got there. This was religion at its most commercial. The town center was jammed wall-to-wall with shops selling religious artifacts. Among them, to Harry's astonishment, were plastic bottles containing authentic holy water from the grotto of Lourdes. Harry understood the hope of the afflicted. There was, after all, nothing to lose and everything to gain; but it was, for Harry, somehow pathetic to see crowds of people hoping against hope that God would make them whole again. It was, in a way, symbolic of religion itself. Why take the risk of going to hell if you can perhaps avoid it by following a few simple rules? What is there to lose? Fear of the unknown is a powerful emotion. Hope for the unknown is equally powerful. It was on full display at the grotto of Lourdes. Many charlatans profitted greatly.

Harry held nothing against people with strong religious beliefs. As long as they did not try to save his soul, Harry respected them. Harry's soul, if there was one, did not need saving. He lived by his own rules. They were built over many years around honesty, reliability, and respecting the rights of others. It was important to be true to yourself; and Harry stuck to his principles, even when it hurt. When he left the planet, he wanted those he left behind to be able to say: He was a good and decent man and never mind that he was not religious. He would be satisfied with such a legacy. But what about the next life, someone would always ask. Despite the absence of proof, Harry was willing to concede that an afterlife was a possibility. If it did exist, Harry was sure a just God would not turn away a good man just because he did not go to church.

In a way, he envied those who believed. They had an answer to a question which could not be answered, and that gave them a secure place to hold on to when life got hard. God bless them, he thought, somewhat paradoxically, and he wished them well as they faced the hardships of life. Just leave my soul alone.

The day in Lourdes strengthened Harry's convictions that religion satisfied the human need to answer life's basic question: Who made me and the world around me? It did little to answer this question.

71
DUBLIN

Airliners, by law, need regular maintenance inspections. Small companies, such as TEA, could not do such complex procedures, so they paid large companies to do them. Although Sabena, the Belgian airline based in Brussels, flew 707s and had such a facility, it was expensive. Aer Lingus in Dublin did the same work for far less money. That meant regular flights to Ireland for each airplane, and a three-day holiday for the crew that flew it there, waiting to fly it back after its inspection. These flights were hard to get, but, finally, Harry had one.

Harry found a home in Dublin. The crew stayed at Jury's Hotel in the heart of the city, and Harry felt he had been there all his life. The Irish were friendly, voluble, and outgoing. They all enjoyed a "jar," as a pint of beer was called, and it took only a few jars before one of them broke into song. The Irish loved to sing, and Harry enjoyed listening to them. There were no televisions in the pubs and Harry liked that. The patrons, not the "telly," provided entertainment. The publican behind the bar introduced strangers to other strangers; the regulars introduced themselves to strangers; and the atmosphere was pure conviviality, the way a pub should be. In Milwaukee, every tavern had a television, some had several, and they were always on. Instead of engaging in conversation, the drinkers watched television, and it made no difference what was playing. They watched anything. How much better without the tube! People acted like people: drinking, talking, laughing and enjoying each other's company.

Harry wandered into the hotel lounge early one afternoon and fell into conversation with a couple of American tourists at the bar. They were from Chicago. How did they like Ireland? Fabulous, they said, we love it, and especially this bar. How long have you been here, Harry wondered. Two weeks, they said, and every day was better than the one before. Two weeks? So what have you seen, where have you been?

The man put down his glass and pointed to a window. "See that car there? We parked it there when we came from the airport two weeks ago and we haven't moved it yet."

Harry was puzzled. The man, his wife nodding in agreement, said, "We've been having such a good time in this bar that we never left, not once. Every night is New Year's Eve. We love it. Besides, we nearly got killed driving here from the airport. Driving on the wrong side of the road and with the steering wheel on the wrong side of the car -- pretty scary. Much nicer in here. And safer."

Harry could only smile.

"Well, sure," he said, "whatever makes you happy."

Harry added Dublin to the list of places he would one day like to bring Irene. He missed her and wished she were with him. Was he starting to think of her as his life partner, a wife? Better not answer that question just yet. Guinness, the best tasting brew Harry had ever drunk, was reason enough to return to Dublin. Smooth and creamy, it was not only the best; it was far ahead of whatever was in second place. Real Irish coffee was another good reason. Why did it taste so much better in Dublin? Pubs, Guinness, Irish coffee: they would call Harry back to Ireland in the years ahead.

A footnote was added to Harry's Dublin visit when, the day before he left, he visited a nine-hole golf course near the hotel. He arrived in mid-morning to find no one there. Puzzled, he noticed a sign with an arrow pointing to a box with a slot. "Playing today?" the notice asked. "Put five pounds in the box. Enjoy your round." That, thought Harry, as he read the notice, is Ireland.

72
LAGOS

Lagos, Nigeria was a long way from Dublin in more ways than one. There was no Guinness, just for starters, and the list of differences kept on growing. Harry had his first clue when he and his crew checked into the Airport Hotel. No room at the inn, he was told. He asked to see the manager. He had brought the telex the hotel had sent to Brussels confirming the rooms, and now he handed it to the hotel manager. With the telex in his hand, the manager, who was fat, black, condescending, and obnoxious, said, "Ah, sorry, Captain. Some mistake. I do not know about this message. I wonder if we can find a way to fix this small misunderstanding?" That question mark on the end of his comment and his raised eyebrows were more clues. Harry sighed and understood. This man wanted money.

Harry thought quickly. He despised this pandering creature and loathed the thought of giving him bribe money; but was this worth making an issue? No, he decided, probably not. This is one of those arguments that cannot be won, and he desperately needed those rooms. Harry stooped, dipped a hand into his flight bag and withdrew a $100 bill, discretely hidden under a piece of paper. That discretion, he later learned, was not only unnecessary, it was unexpected. Bribery was the norm in Nigeria.

"Maybe you should read the telex again. Maybe you missed something," he said, with a tight smile. The manager inspected the bill openly, and then thrust it into a pocket.

"Yes, I do believe we have some rooms after all," he replied, without bothering to look at the telex. He nodded to the desk clerk. "Give the captain his rooms, please. Thank you, Captain, and welcome to the Airport Hotel."

Harry had seen this metamorphosis before. It was the one in which an ordinary person became supercilious and overbearing because he had been given authority. This manager was a classic example. Harry had seen many such people, usually at airports, and often working at customs and immigration. An official cap, one with golden braid on its visor, or perhaps an official rank on the shoulder of a shirt, gave some a feeling of superiority they could not resist displaying. Harry well remembered customs agents in Bombay and Karachi who abused their authority for money or other valuables, but often it was done so that a nobody could appear to be a somebody.

Passing through customs in these places was an adventure. Harry had once carried a bottle of whiskey through customs in Karachi. It was legal, but that did not stop the agent from fondling the bottle lovingly for a few moments. Then he looked across his customs stand to Harry.

"I need a bottle of whiskey," he said in a tone which said he would have that bottle one way or another. Harry explained that it was not his bottle, that he was carrying it for the entire crew. The agent refused to return the bottle. A potential whiskey crisis was averted when Gene dug into his flight bag and came out with a half-bottle of whiskey. Offering it to the agent, he asked in a tone both contemptuous and courteous, "Will this do, sir?" The man snatched the bottle from Gene's hand, stuffed it into his coat pocket, and handed Harry his bottle. That bottle tasted better than most, thought Harry, as they drank it later at a crew party.

In Bombay, especially, Harry had seen customs agents treat their countrymen with disdain and even contempt as they confiscated mountains of personal items as a way to seem important, especially to themselves. Harry had, now and then, seen this attitude in the Navy, but such officers never went far. Self-aggrandizement was easily seen through. In Saigon, Riddle had described many such officers, usually in the Army, where rank seemed more important. Harry recalled Riddle describing an Army major who had asked him if a Navy lieutenant commander, the counterpart of a major, wore gold braid on his cap. No, Riddle told him. Why did he ask?

"Because, by God, an Army major does!" To this major, the gold braid was meaningful. Some of the Army officers, Riddle had told him, often tried to bulldoze him into breaking rules to obtain a room which measured up to their self-image. This problem was everywhere, but it seemed worse in the Middle East. There, Harry guessed, opportunity to look important was scarce; it had to be seized when it could.

Lagos was not a rerun of Hassi Messaoud. It was Part Two, or, as Gene put it, The Jeddah Rewind. Harry and his crew would bring back from Jeddah those pilgrims who had started out in Lagos. They had done their religious duty, cleansed their souls, and were ready to meet their maker. On their return, Harry was told, they would be given a high order of respect. The pilgrimage to Mecca was the high point of any Muslim's life, and won them honor and esteem for the rest of their lives. It gave them the right to add the word "Haj" to their names.

Harry had seen Muslims in various places and, to his surprise, they did not always look the same. In Belgrade, he had met white Muslims. In Kartoum, the Muslims were chocolate skinned and the women were beautiful, the men handsome. They had fine, western features. He would like to know the reason. Even in different Arab countries, Arabs looked different from each other. He had once been in Teheran and was told not to call the Iranians "Arabs." They called themselves "Pharsees," and they did not speak Arabic, as was spoken in nearby Iraq and Saudi Arabia. Language and appearance changed as the belt of Islam moved east. Here, in Lagos, the Muslims were black.

These pilgrims looked very different from those of Algeria. Those were Arabs, and they had looked like Arabs. These were black, and looked like Africans were supposed to look. What they did not look like was Muslims. How, Harry wondered, had Islam found its way down here? When he thought about it, he realized that Islam covered a swath of territory that started in Morocco, swept across North Africa, dipped into dark Africa, wound through the Middle East, continued across the Persian Gulf, and went through Malaysia and Indonesia to the Philippines. Except for India, which was Hindu, but held large numbers of Muslims, the only island in this religious sea, which covered half the world, was the tiny country of Israel. No wonder the Muslims wanted to destroy it.

The airplane would fly empty to Jeddah and return full. These passengers would give new meaning to that word, "full." The first trip went smoothly until the passengers began boarding the airplane in Jeddah. Then, Gene roared into the cockpit after his pre-flight inspection.

"Goddamn, Boss, you gotta check this out. You won't believe the hand baggage back there."

Already in his seat, Harry turned and looked back at Gene. "So what is it about the hand baggage. What's the big deal?"

Gene's face was flushed and he was obviously upset. "These guys are bringing up everything except the kitchen sink, and there might even be one or two of those. Get back there and take a look."

Harry disliked leaving his seat once he was strapped in, but there seemed no choice. He unstrapped, climbed out of his seat, over the Flight Engineer's chair, which was not in its stowed position, and opened the cockpit door. He was met by a queue of Nigerians carrying hand baggage like Harry had never seen before. At first glance, he saw stereos, several television sets, bicycles, and even a small refrigerator. Looking farther aft, Harry saw those who had boarded earlier trying to stuff all manner of large objects into the overhead bins. Some, for lack of an alternative, had placed them on their seats and were sitting on top of them, smiling and ready for takeoff. The cabin looked like a garage sale. Harry took one look and called for the ramp agent. Hard to find, he was finally tracked down.

The agent seemed surprised by Harry's anger. All this was very normal, he explained. These poor people save much money by buying here in Jeddah. And, in many cases, he added, they are buying things they cannot find at home.

"No," sputtered Harry. "This is not normal, not in my airplane. Now, get all those people off the airplane. Remove all that" -- he could not think of the right word -- "equipment" -- he found the word and used it derisively, "and stow it all in the cargo compartments."

There was a loud objection. "But, Captain," he said plaintively, "that will take hours. You will miss your slot time."

This was a reference to their assigned takeoff time. "Never mind about our slot time," Harry said, his anger rising, "just get it off. And the sooner you start, the sooner we can leave. Now, get moving."

The agent glowered fiercely, turned and stomped off. He was not happy.

The next couple of hours were spent re-locating the hand baggage. There was no way to cram all of it into the cargo compartments. They would have to leave some behind, and Harry stood firm on this. No more "equipment" in the cabin. During boarding on later flights, Harry positioned Gene at the bottom of the forward stairs and the purser at the aft stairs. He gave them strict instructions. No more "equipment" in the cabin. Even in the cargo holds, it presented a problem. For aircraft weight and balance reasons, each passenger bag is weighed at check-in. Handbags are assigned an assumed weight; but how do you assume a weight for television sets and refrigerators? And who knew what else? There was no way, except to make a ballpark estimate. Harry did that very judiciously the first time, then used those same numbers for subsequent flights. That he had made a good guess would be known when he pulled back the control column at the rotation speed during the takeoff. If his numbers were right, the horizontal stabilizer was set correctly, and the aircraft would lift off without needing excessive control pressure. Not perfect, perhaps; but, as a friend used to say, close enough for the kind of girls we go around with. The aircraft rotated normally and Harry was pleased.

Someone had told Harry once that nothing is wonderful after you get used to it. That made sense and these flights bore it out. They were not wonderful, of course, but they should have been at least interesting. Despite the inevitable problems during boarding in Jeddah, they quickly became routine. The two crews quickly settled into a pattern of flying, sleeping, and eating.

The Airport Hotel offered few amenities. The restaurant was awful, "a minus two stars," according to Gene, but it was the only game in town. Not only was the food a disaster, but the service was almost as bad. The waiters never got it right. There was always something missing, the order was wrong or was brought to the wrong table; always something. One morning at breakfast, just to make a point, Harry kept track of the number of mistakes at their table. There were four diners and Harry counted twelve mistakes before they finished their meals. He gave up counting. Ah, well, what can you expect, thought Harry. They did not seem very bright to begin with: they had obviously not been well trained, and they had zero interest in their jobs.

"They would never make it at McDonald's" said Gene that morning as he sent back his eggs for the second time.

Not only would they not make it at McDonald's, they could not make it in the cockpit either. Harry heard, from an inside source, one who flew for Air Nigeria, that the country did not trust its own pilots. The pilot was an Englishman Harry met at the hotel bar late one evening. The Nigerians, who boarded the airplane in uniforms and carrying flight bags, were only window-dressing. They sat in the cabin while the foreigners, who had boarded long before, flew the airplane.

"False advertising, perhaps," said the Englishman, with a chuckle, "but it provides nice work for the rest of us. I fly to London twice each month. The money is very good and I really don't need the glamor."

The only unexpected event in Harry's routine came one morning after a late arrival. He decided to skip breakfast and instead went to the pool for a swim. He had, a few days ago, walked through the area near the hotel, searching for a suitable place to jog. The neighborhood consisted of ramshackle huts, open-air markets, and fierce-looking people. Harry did not feel comfortable and decided that this was not jogging country. So he exercised regularly in the hotel pool.

Usually, he was the only one in the water. On this morning, however, there was another person. It was a fully-dressed dead body, floating face down against the side of the pool. At first, Harry could not believe his eyes. He went closer, bent over, and peered down intently. No doubt about it. That was definitely a body, and it certainly was dead. He notified the hotel immediately, but there was almost no reaction. Could this be a regular event? Harry did not swim that day, or any other day. He had gone poolside once or twice in the evening and found that it was a gathering place for prostitutes and those looking for one. That did not bother him. Dead bodies did.

The first time Harry had flown into Lagos at night, he had been astonished to see the lights of an entire fleet of ships anchored in its harbor. How many are there, he asked someone the next day, and why are there so many? There are some 400, he was told, and each one was filled with cement. Some had been there as long as twelve months, waiting to off-load their cargo. Harry was intrigued. This needed explaining.

The cement, he learned, had been ordered and delivered before it was realized that the port did not have the means to unload it. They were working on it, he was told. It must be some of those ex-waiters from the hotel restaurant who were running the cement project, thought Harry. He would ask someone how long cement could last on the shelf. Those ships might be waiting all those months to off-load cement which had turned into concrete. It would serve them right, he thought with a mental grin. Hats off to the cement salesman, thought Harry. Whoever he was, he certainly could sell cement.

The city of Lagos was some fifteen miles from the hotel. One evening, Harry, Gene and two girls gathered up their courage and ventured into the city. Judging by the way the hotel, its restaurant, and the national cement programs were organized, Lagos had to be worth a visit. As Gene put it, "There has got to be some negative entertainment there."

"And," added one of the girls "we are here. So near. We must see it."

Getting there was a disaster. The roads were under construction, and barricades were everywhere. Probably waiting for more cement, thought Harry, and he wished them luck in getting it. The traffic was chaotic. It took two hours to go just ten miles. Eventually, they did find a restaurant at the edge of the city and had a reasonable dinner, with reasonable service, and that was all they could hope for. Harry ate an all-vegetable meal. He could not even think about eating meat in Nigeria. The trip back to the hotel was mercifully shorter, but Lagos would never see Harry again. Once was enough. He looked forward to going home to Brussels. He would be happy to see Irene again. He missed her. And his carpets; he missed those, too. He had bought one more, a beautiful Bokhara, to add to his collection. He would not miss Lagos.

73
ROONEY

Nicknames are handed out for different reasons. Some might play on a name. Others might relate to physical features, or a unique personal trait; but most are related to behavior. Such was the case with Jack Rooney. "Shipwreck" was how he was known throughout the fleet and with good reason. Jack had a great appetite for life in all its various aspects. He did not merely live life, he consumed it, and with great gusto. Drinking was one of those appetites, but it was only one of many. Cars and women were also on his list; but it was perhaps drinking that defined him best.

Jack loved to drink and when he had a few drinks, he always took center stage. Alcohol made him boisterous but not obnoxious, funny but not ridiculous, personal but not offensive. The more he drank, the funnier he got and in a witty and clever way. Even among Navy pilots, most of whom drank their share, Jack was a living legend, and Harry believed every word of the legend. After all, he and Jack had been squadron-mates in their first squadron. Harry had been there when most of the legends were made. Usually, Jack was a happy drunk; but not always. Every now and then, he went over the edge and did outrageous things. That bothered Harry. One day, he would talk seriously to Jack about it.

One night, Harry was driving a friend home from a squadron party. Jack had passed out in the back seat. The front seat passenger was telling a tale of a night spent in a jail in Mobile, Alabama, many years ago. What made the story funny was that his breakfast had been a plate of oatmeal that had been turned vertical so that it could be passed through the cell bars. Not a grain was lost or even moved.

That word --Mobile --was an alarm for Jack. He came awake, struggled to sit up, leaned on the back of the front seat, and said, "Mobile? That's the worst goddamn jail I've ever been in."

Harry and his passenger looked at each other and smiled.

"Damn, Jack," said Harry, glancing over his shoulder, "you sound like a connoisseur of fine jails. How many have you been in, anyway?"

Jack leaned back and considered his answer. Seven, he announced, after some ticking of his fingers.

One of those jails, he recounted, was in Mexicali. That was on the Mexican side of the border, near Yuma. The Navy often based squadrons at an air base there for a week or two while it used its nearby ranges for bombing practice.

Jack had gone there with a few friends and drunk plenty of Mexican beer. Feeling an urgent need to urinate, and not trusting the sanitation of Mexican toilets, he decided to empty his bladder in the street outside the cantina. As he did, he felt a firm hand grasp his shoulder. Looking around, he saw that the hand was attached to an arm that belonged to a policeman who was staring fiercely down at his own shoe. Jack followed his gaze and saw that he was pissing on the policeman's shoe. There was a scuffle, and Jack ended up in jail, where he spent three days eating beans and tortillas. He did not recommend the accommodations.

Harry had been there when Jack had been hauled off to one of the jails on his list. The party had been in Jack's apartment, one in a complex that housed several other Navy pilots, including Harry. One of those apartments was occupied by a lovely young lady whose husband was off in the Pacific on a carrier. As was often the case in such situations, both Harry and Jack looked in on her now and then to see if she needed anything. Looking after a friend's wife during his absence was friendship, nothing more.

With the party in high gear, and Jack feeling neighborly, he decided she should join the festivities, by now gaining momentum rapidly. The apartment doors were of different colors and Jack could not remember the color of her door. He knocked on two wrong doors before finding the right one. One glance at Jack, and one whiff of his breath were enough. Speaking through a locked screen door, she politely declined the invitation. Jack insisted and, in the good cause of a great party, began ripping the screen door right off its hinges. He meant no harm. In his good-hearted way, he wanted her to join the fun. She did not know about Jack's good intentions. She only knew that a drunk was tearing down her door. She very sensibly called the police, and they arrived within minutes. Jack flailed at one of them, was promptly subdued and taken away to jail. The squadron CO had to rescue him this time, and the next day, he presented Jack with an undated and unsigned copy of a formal letter of reprimand. Such a letter usually meant the end of a career. Jack finally began to see the light.

Nicknames were common among Navy pilots. Two were notable in Harry's first Air Wing. One was FUBAR, which stood for Fucked Up Beyond All Recognition. No need to wonder where that one sprang from. Another was WEFT. That came from Wrong Every Fucking Time. This one was also easy to figure out. Jack's nickname probably started that night in Okinawa when he crashed the LCM into the side of the ship while trying to return from liberty ashore; and by itself, that famous event justified his colorful label. But there were other reasons why it suited Jack.

He had once managed to drive his car off the Coronado ferry and into the water as the ferry neared the San Diego side. This was not supposed to be possible but Jack had found a way. Even in his inebriated state he had been able to exit the car and struggle to the surface. Probably, the cold seawater rushing into the car had something to do with it.

On a camping trip in the mountains, he was awakened in his sleeping bag by the sounds of a huge bear licking tobacco juice from the side of his car. Jack chewed while driving and streamed the juice against the side of the car when he spit out the window. Who knew that bears liked tobacco? This one lapped up the last flecks, then began sniffing for more. More was in Jack's pocket, inside the sleeping bag. Jack saw the bear point his nose in his direction and begin to lumber towards him. Thinking quickly, Jack found the tobacco and pitched it away from the bag. The bear, in hot pursuit, placed one giant paw on Jack's stomach as he went after the tobacco. A few seconds later, Jack was in his car, the camping canceled, and he never chewed tobacco again.

Then there was the Saturday morning that Harry was awakened from deep sleep by gunshots just outside his door in the BOQ. The evening before had been a heavy social one, but those reports would have awakened the dead. He stumbled out of bed and opened his door. The rooms opened onto an open walkway, and there sat Jack Rooney, rifle in hand, firing out across an open area of grass that led to the parking lot beyond.

"Jack!" screamed Harry. "What the hell are you doing?"

Jack fired off another round, then calmly turned to Harry. "Target practice," he said, as he readied for another shot.

Harry realized that Jack was still drunk. Before Harry could speak again, Jack let off another round, and Harry saw that Jack was shooting at his own car, parked across the grass and facing the building.

Jack turned back to Harry. This time he grinned. "I never did like that car," he said.

Apart from his personal life, his flying career also had a few near-shipwrecks along the way. Jack was an excellent pilot. Harry had flown with him many times and there was none better. And he was far from stupid. Still, he seemed to have a proclivity for turning normal events into crises. Harry put down this peculiar knack to a lack of focus. Flying an airplane came easily to Jack, and he did not need to concentrate. A less skillful pilot had to work harder to fly well. As in all professions, an expert pilot flew effortlessly. That was Jack. He flew an airplane in the same easy way that a good golfer hits a ball 300 yards without apparent effort. That allowed his mind to wander when it should have been on flying the airplane. That sometimes led to "special events," as he called them.

The Skyraider that Harry and Jack flew in their first squadron did not need a catapult to launch from a carrier deck. Its powerful engine generated 2,800 horsepower, which translated into plenty of thrust. The engine drove a huge four-bladed propeller with a diameter of almost fourteen feet. Its prop-wash added some lift as it flowed across the wings. Under most conditions of weight and wind, the Spad could get airborne by making a rolling takeoff down the center of the flight deck, just as it might do on an airport runway. It did, however, need the entire length of the axial flight deck.

During practice landing sessions, airplanes were trapped, taxied clear of the arresting cables, then deck-launched for another landing. It was straightforward, but somehow Jack, after landing and taxiing clear, lined up with the angled deck instead of the axial one.

"Shit," he said later. "Everything looked okay to me."

The angled deck was less than half the length of the axial deck, but Jack did not notice that he was pointed down the wrong deck. And no one else, including the Flight Deck Officer who launched him, noticed, either. So off he went. A very short takeoff roll and not enough speed at the end of it caused Jack to sink beneath the deck edge as he left the ship. He had eighty feet of altitude to trade for a few knots of speed, and he had plenty of power from that massive engine. The airplane dropped to within what looked like inches from the sea, stabilized, then slowly began to climb.

"No sweat," he said later in the Ready Room, laughing. "I had at least three feet of altitude to play with."

Maybe Jack wasn't sweating, but there was plenty of sweat on the flight deck as he very nearly flew into the sea. He was so close to the water, one flight deck sailor said, that his propeller made a small trail of mist as it spun furiously just above its surface.

It was not always Jack's fault. Sometimes, he was simply in the wrong place at the wrong time. During a launch from a bow catapult one day, one of the two cables which connected the airplane to the shuttle had snapped. One cable instead of two meant that the airplane was pulled partly sideways as it rode down the catapult track, and that meant a loss of speed at its end. Jack had already saluted and was on his way when the cable broke. He had one second, perhaps two, to make a decision. He could try to stop, which would have been very difficult because of that one cable still pulling him down the track, or, he could continue and hope for the best after leaving the deck.

In such situations, decisions are made instinctively. Jack kept going and, thinking quickly, lowered his flaps to full from the normal half-flap setting used for a catapult launch. That probably saved his life. The full flaps provided more lift -- more drag, too -- but the extra lift more than counteracted that. Due to his partly-sideways catapult shot, the airplane left the deck in a yaw, its nose skewed a few degrees to one side of its flight path. Jack instantly straightened his airplane with his rudder as it became airborne, then expertly guided it down to the sea without flying into it. That won him a few knots of airspeed. It was another close call for Jack; his second near kiss of death with the sea.

Typically, he laughed about it later.

"Who can I sue about that cable?" he asked those gathered around him in the Ready Room after landing.

A few days later, Harry sat next to the Catapult Officer at dinner. "Has one of those cables ever snapped before?" he asked.

"Never," was the firm reply. "Never saw one, and never heard of one. It can't happen."

But it did happen. And of course it had to happen to Jack.

Now and then, the ship, using uncommon common sense, would launch a weather airplane to survey the conditions around the ship. One very rainy and windy morning, Jack was assigned this task. He showed up on the flight deck to man his airplane, carrying an open umbrella. He launched into some awful weather and began climbing through it, announcing his altitude as he did. The ship made frequent requests for weather reports, but Jack did not reply. Finally, an exasperated ship asked angrily, "I say again, what weather?"

There was a long pause then Jack clicked his mike button and said just one word: "Shitty."

The launch was canceled.

Harry and Jack had flown Skyraiders together in that first squadron. They went separate ways after that and came together a few years later when both were assigned to the same Skyhawk squadron at the Naval Air Station in Lemoore, California. When Harry heard that he and Jack would again be squadron-mates, he was filled with a warm glow of anticipation. It would be great to serve together again. Although they had kept in touch, Harry had not seen Jack in a few years; but he had little doubt that they would come together as if they had never been apart. That was a mark of true friendship. He wondered if Jack was still the same happy warrior, the first to arrive at the weekly happy hour, the last to leave, and the one who drank the most in between.

74
BACK TO LEMOORE

1964

Lemoore was a small town in the San Joaquin Valley, not far from Fresno. Why a Naval air station had been built there was a question no one could answer. Unbearably hot in summer and with frequent dense fog in the winter, it was the wrong place to fly airplanes. The summer heat sometimes precluded flying because hot air, less dense than cold air, did not allow an engine to generate enough thrust to get airborne. Although there was plenty of runway, there was not enough power to reach flying speed. The winter fog was often so thick that Harry sometimes drove with his head sticking out the window so he could follow the dashes in the middle of the road. The fog was graded by the number of dashes visible. Luminous tape was pasted on lampposts and driveways so drivers could find their houses.

It was soon after Harry joined the squadron that the Tonkin Gulf incident occurred -- or didn't occur -- depending on whom you believed. Harry followed the action closely over the next months, and it became more and more apparent that his squadron would sooner or later be involved. One serious sign that the problem was worsening was the number of airplanes lost. Before long, they were being shot down with alarming frequency. One result was the black limousine often seen driving through the streets of Lemoore and nearby Hanford, where many Navy families lived. When Harry saw a black limo, with two uniformed officers in the back seat, he knew that someone was about to get terrible news.

It was a hard time for those who stayed behind, and especially for the families of those who would not come home. Women whose husbands were away were known as cruise widows. Some became real widows. Most were young with small children. Some were pregnant. In a great tradition of the Navy, those still waiting to go looked after these families as best they could. Harry became close to a woman who lived in his apartment complex. Her husband, whom Harry knew, had been shot down over North Vietnam. No one knew if he was alive or dead. She was seven months pregnant and had nowhere to go, no one to turn to. Harry stopped by often to see her, to help her. One night, as he left, she came to the door with him, as she usually did. As Harry bent to kiss her cheek, she suddenly took him in a desperate embrace. He felt her sob on his shoulder. She pulled back and smiled through tears.

"Sorry, Harry, it's just that I feel so lost."

Harry drew her close again. "It's not easy, I know, but you have got to hang in there," he said as he kissed her cheek. That was a dumb thing to say, but he could not think of anything better. She stepped back, looked at him for a moment or two.

"You're a good man, Harry. Your wife is a lucky girl, whoever she is."

There were others like her. It was not a good time to be married to a Navy pilot.

Despite the war, or perhaps because of it, social gatherings still took place. No one called them parties. That would sound insensitive in such a sensitive time; but the need to release tension was manifested frequently. Harry held one such "relief valve," as Jack Rooney called them, at his apartment. Among those he invited was a cruise widow named Sue Woodley. Asking her to join them was a hard decision; was it the right thing to do? Finally, he called, saying he would understand if she chose not to come. She said she would be there and thanks for thinking of her.

"I need some company," she said.

Harry knew her husband and knew that he had been hit over North Vietnam, made it to the sea, and ejected. He was not found and was officially listed as missing in action. Until a man was confirmed dead, the Navy listed him as missing. That way, his pay to his family continued. Sue had two young daughters, and she did not know if their father was alive or dead. She was a feisty young lady and she had determined that her husband was alive and would one day return to his family.

"I know in my heart that he will come home," she told Harry. "I just know it."

Harry hoped his name would not come up at his party. It did, and in a heart-wrenching way.

By chance, one of those at the party had been in the area where Walt Woodley had gone down. Like others in the vicinity, he quickly flew to the site and took part in the search for the downed pilot. Now, at Harry's party, his tongue loosened by bourbon, he told Sue what he had seen. As she listened, her face becoming ashen, the pilot described seeing Walt, face down in the water and lifeless.

"He's for sure dead," said the pilot to the suddenly silent group. Jack Rooney heard it coming and tried to intervene, but he was too late.

"Asshole!" he hissed to the pilot. "What were you thinking?"

The pilot looked confused. He did not understand that he had done something wrong. "I just thought she should know," he said lamely.

"Sure," said Jack, "one day, but not here and not now -- and not like this."

Harry never saw Sue again after that night. Some years later, he was gratified to learn that she had married again, this time to a dentist, and was living in Ohio. He felt happy for her.

If a pilot wanted to know the latest news from the Tonkin Gulf, he went to the Flying Spinnaker. This bar and restaurant, midway between the base and the town, became the unofficial source for the latest information about the war. Harry stopped in often and never failed to find friends there. He could usually count on meeting Jack there. The time of day did not seem to matter. Even pilots' wives stopped by to hear the latest news that somehow seemed to come there first, even before the base or the news media reported it. Single women were in great demand in Lemoore and they, too, could often be found at the Spinnaker. Harry met one who had come all the way from San Francisco. But mainly, it was a gathering place for pilots to drink and talk about flying, their hands describing aerial tactics as they did. The Flying Spinnaker became, for some, a home away from home. Harry always looked forward to stopping there even though its news was sometimes grim.

Harry and Jack became fast friends from the first minute of their first meeting. That friendship deepened over the years. Jack had qualities Harry wished he himself had. Jack was an extrovert who loved life. He was personable, quick, and generous to a fault. He was handsome in a rough sort of way, and he attracted women easily. When the occasional rebuff came, he took it in stride, as he did most of life itself. Still, Harry wondered. With all that going for him, why did he often get so roaring drunk? To Harry, he sometimes seemed desperate, determined to get drunk. Even among Navy pilots, for whom drinking was a badge of honor, Jack stood out from the pack. Was it the prospect of going to Vietnam? Harry didn't think so. It was just that Jack was no different than he had always been.

Harry had long thought, in the back of his mind, that he would one day talk seriously to Jack about his bouts of heavy drinking. He would wait for the right time. That turned out to be a long wait. The moment finally seemed right one night when their ship was in the middle of the South China Sea. There were no flight operations that night, and Jack and Harry had gone out on the flight deck for a moonlight stroll. The ship was steaming with the wind, and the air on the flight deck was still. That always surprised Harry.

75
A NIGHT AT SEA

April 1966

Without seeing one, it's hard to imagine how starry a night sky at sea can be. The complete absence of any artificial light creates an awesome sky, covered by a brilliant weave of glimmering, twinkling stars. There are almost more stars than sky. The first time Harry had seen such a sky, he had wondered why such a vast cosmos had been created for the handful of people living on the speck of dust that was the earth, lost in its unimaginable reaches. He had always been fascinated by the cosmos. Who could understand a light-year? Who could begin to comprehend a universe containing hundreds of billions of galaxies, each with billions of stars? Our own galaxy, the Milky Way, is just one of them. It is so vast that light, piercing space at one-hundred-eighty-six-thousand miles every second, needs one-hundred-thousand years to cross it! Harry had once read that a handful of sand held about ten-thousand grains and that the cosmos held more stars than were grains of sand on all the beaches of the earth. It was probably on a night like this that early mankind first asked themselves where it all came from, why they were here. The beginnings of religious beliefs might well have had their start on a night like this.

To better view the sky, Harry and Jack lowered themselves into a huge net that ran across the bow and just below its edge. It dropped down like an enormous scoop and was large enough to lie in comfortably. Hands clasped behind his head, Harry looked up in stunned silence. Neither spoke for a few minutes. Harry broke the silence.

"Wouldn't a little Scotch on the rocks taste great right now?"

"Sure would," replied Jack. "But I'm on the wagon right now. Maybe you heard?"

A few nights earlier Jack had gotten drunk in his room and tried to call a former girlfriend, who lived in Seattle. Instead, he found himself talking to the Executive Officer of the ship. Mercifully, the XO did not ask Jack how he expected to call Seattle from the stateroom of an aircraft carrier in the middle of the Tonkin Gulf. One of Jack's nine lives had kicked in, and the XO had handled it as a joke.

Harry had heard about the incident and brought it up now. It was perhaps that spectacular sky and the sound of the sea rushing past the ship that prompted Jack to respond. He began telling Harry about a lost love. A faint bell sounded in Harry's memory. Was that the girl he had almost married? He remembered Jack talking about her as they had gone through the XO's belongings after he had been shot down.

"What can I say?" Harry asked after Jack had opened his soul. This was the first time Jack had spoken from his heart about any girl. Harry was not surprised. There had to be something, someone. Jack spoke with great feeling, in a way Harry had not heard before. Harry felt sorry that he could help only by listening. He made what he hoped were sympathetic responses; he knew some women were hard to forget.

He tried to explain that everyone had problems like that. They went with the territory called life. Jack knew, of course, that drinking never solved problems, only camouflaged them for a while. But did he know, Harry asked, what it was doing to his career?

"This is serious stuff, Jack, and I hope you realize what you're doing to yourself."

After a pause, Jack, still looking up at the night sky, said only, "Is it that bad?"

Harry turned to Jack. "I'm talking from the heart here, Jack. Get a grip before it's too late."

Jack sat up and said nothing. Then he turned and stuck out his hand. As Harry grasped it, Jack covered it with his left hand. This was more than a handshake; it was a bond.

"Thank you, my friend," was all he said.

76
JACK'S LAST FLIGHT

The next day, Jack flew two missions, both in the north. The weather had turned bad in the morning and gotten steadily worse. Jack had managed to find his target on the first mission, and dropped his bombs in a very shallow dive angle beneath low clouds. That not only made the bomb run dangerous, it pretty much precluded hitting anywhere near the target. When a bomb was dropped at a low altitude, the pilot might feel his airplane buffet from the blast of the explosion. It was an uncomfortable feeling.

"A waste of fuel, bombs, and energy," Jack remarked caustically, back in the Ready Room.

"Not to mention adrenalin," added Harry, who was there drinking a cup of coffee. He was scheduled to fly early the next day. That was known as the Dawn Patrol, and it went out just before sunrise.

On Jack's second flight, there was heavy rain around the ship, but the launch went on schedule. Low clouds and rain made flying over the coastline impossible, even for Jack. He had jettisoned his bombs in the sea and returned to the ship. Because of the weather, the recovery took much longer than usual. Jack took some fuel from the tanker, which was above the clouds, as he waited for his slot in the landing sequence. The radar crew in Combat Information Center controlled that.

"This," said Jack, as he squirmed out of his g-suit, "was a long and shitty day."

In his debrief in Air Intelligence, Jack had said, "You guys are crazy to send out more airplanes in weather like this. There's no hope of getting over land. None. Zero. And even if you could, there is no way to find a target, never mind dropping on it. Start over tomorrow. It should be only A6s in crap like this. The A4s can't get in."

That advice was unlikely to be taken because it would mean fewer strikes flown and fewer bombs dropped. Keeping those numbers climbing seemed, for some, to be a key objective of this war. Then someone had a bright idea. Let's send out the A6s with A4s on their wings. That way, the all-weather A6s could lead the A4s to the target and the A4s could drop their bombs on a signal from the A6s. "Buddy Bombing," he called it.

A test flight was quickly set up -- one A4 and one A6. The airplanes were rounded up, but finding pilots was a problem. For Harry's squadron, the schedule was set and a spare pilot was nowhere to be found. Incredibly, Jack volunteered.

"Jack, are you nuts?" Harry asked urgently when he heard the news. "You've already flown two, take a break. Let them find someone else."

Jack grinned, supremely confident, as always. "There isn't anyone else. No one who wants to go, anyway. And this looks pretty interesting. Something different."

Harry saw there was no way he was going to talk Jack out of this one. "Be careful," he said with intensity, "and don't be a hero."

Jack grinned again. "I'm always careful. You know that. Almost always, anyway. You can have my Ballentine's if I don't make it back."

Harry glanced up at the PLAT screen just as an F4 was shot off the number two catapult. The airplane disappeared into the weather halfway down the track. Its red ball of exhaust was visible a few seconds longer, then nothing.

He turned back to Jack. "Be careful, buddy. I mean it."

These kinds of last-minute, pasted-together flights are always a bad idea, and this one was no exception. Too many things could go wrong. By launch time, it was dark; so they started out with a night catapult in heavy weather, and then a night rendezvous. A night cat shot always got the adrenaline flowing, and Jack, despite his long day, felt alert and ready as he neared the rendezvous point above the weather. He scanned the sky intently for his A6 flight leader. The A6 had a second flight officer who sat alongside the pilot and operated the radar and the weapons systems. Jack got some help from him, and joining the A6 was easier than expected. The two airplanes turned west and headed towards North Vietnam.

As a trial flight, the plan was to be in and out very quickly. The rain and low ceilings did not bother the A6. They did it all on instruments. It was Jack who had the hard work of flying close wing at night and in bad weather. The planes were in and out of the clouds. Jack did not even know what the target was. Drop on my command, he was briefed. They were above the automatic weapons, but could expect some 37mm as they neared the target. It materialized on schedule, but was sporadic and inaccurate. Still, it was somewhat unnerving to see those bursts light up the clouds in fuzzy brilliance. Eerie, thought Jack, and he was starting to regret raising his hand for this one. He clicked his master arm switch on. He was ready to unload on signal. That came a few minutes later, and Jack let go his bombs.

The A6 said calmly, as though announcing a train station, "Hang on for a hard left turn and let's get the hell out of here."

Back over the sea, Jack felt the tension begin to drain away and he noticed, for the first time, how tired he felt. It had, indeed, been a long and shitty day, and now he was feeling every minute of it. Cheer up, he told himself, one more landing to go, and then a good long drink of Ballentine's. He would need it, he thought, and he could almost taste it already. Usually, once the pilot was "feet wet" over the sea, the flight was as good as over and the pilot began to relax. This time, however, despite the lessening of tension, Jack felt nervous. Why was that, he asked himself. It was just another night landing and he had made many. Still, there was that vague unease and it would not go away. Jack was not used to that feeling and it gnawed at him. Just tired, he reminded himself.

The ship was neatly tucked beneath a patch of bad weather. When the A6 made initial radio contact, the news was unsettling. Although the airplanes were in the clear above the weather, the ship reported poor visibility in heavy rain. The sea was heavy and the deck had begun to pitch. Shit, thought Jack as he heard the weather report, is nothing ever easy around here? He exhaled a long sigh into his oxygen mask as the two planes were vectored to a position thirty miles aft of the ship. Following radar instructions, Jack broke away from the A6 and turned his airplane to his assigned heading. Flying wing at night is never easy, and Jack felt better on his own. He throttled back to idle power and began to descend. As he entered the clouds, he left the clear, smooth air and began to buffet in light turbulence, then he hit the rain and it made an awful noise against his plane. He was flying solely on instruments now, and following radar's directions. For the first time he could remember, Jack began to perspire in the cockpit.

Radar took him down to 500 feet and headed him towards the glide slope. He could see nothing, and the rain got worse. This, thought Jack grimly, is not a great night to come aboard.

"Call the ball," he heard radar say.

"Roger, call the ball," Jack replied, without thinking. That meant he was now expected to see the ship visually, find the meatball, and descend along the glide path. He looked up from his gauges and saw only black. He lowered his tail hook, flaps and landing gear, slowed to approach speed, and flew on instruments, looking outside the airplane every few seconds for the ship. Finally, her lights came into view and a few moments later, he could make out the meatball. He started his final descent; but flying through the rain made it hard to gain perspective. That the angled deck was apparently moving sidewise relative to his flight path did not help. Jack was flying on instinct now, without conscious thought; adjusting power, heading,

351

and airspeed to stay on the glide path. Usually, Jack flew OK passes. That meant they were graded as needing no correction; but now he grew alarmed, as the meatball seemed to move erratically above and below the rows of green lights. He found himself overcorrecting his pitch and bank control. *Goddamn,* he thought fiercely, *what am I doing!*

Paddles, who could see Jack much better than Jack could see the ship, was trying to stay calm, but Jack could hear the first faint tone of concern as he issued instructions.

"The deck is pitching." he said, "Try to average out the meatball."

That was easier said than done, thought Jack, with irritation. As he neared the ramp he was in a left-wing-down attitude and saw the meatball suddenly disappear off the bottom of the lens. His port wing struck the ramp and was sheared off. That caused his port landing gear to slam into the deck at an angle, collapsing it and flipping the airplane upside down. It burst into flames and skidded, inverted, down the length of the angled deck, arced off the forward edge and into the sea. In that moment just before impact with the ramp, inexplicably, Jack had pressed his mike button and transmitted one word: "Shit." That was the last word anyone ever heard Jack say.

77
ANGOLA

April 1972

Every now and then, Harry dropped into the TEA office just to check the news.

"Bonjour," he said cheerfully to no one in particular, as he entered late one morning. "Quelle nouvelle?" he asked Monique, who was Mr. Gettleman's secretary.

"Nice French, Captain," she smiled. "I understood every word."

Harry smiled back. "You're the only one. How is my accent?"

Monique pretended to consider his question seriously, then nodded and said, "American, I think, very American. It could use perhaps a bit of practice. But congratulations for your effort."

"So," asked Harry, "what's happening? Anything special?"

"Eh, bien," she replied, "did you know you are going to Angola?"

The only thing Harry knew about Angola was that it was somewhere in Africa. To hear he was going there was like hearing he was going to the moon. Angola? Was she serious?

"Mais oui, serious, Captain. Decided just this morning. You are pleased?"

There had to more to this story, Harry thought. "Maybe when I find out more about it. Is Captain LeBlanc here?"

"Oui, in his office. Entrez, s'il vous plait.

"Merci," said Harry, "your French is nice too."

She nodded and smiled. "Merci, Captain. You are very kind."

Eddie looked up from a telex as Harry entered. "Ah, Captain, I can see by your face that you have heard the news. I have more information, if you are interested. Please." He gestured to a chair and Harry sat down.

"It's true about Angola?" he asked.

"Yes, true. One airplane and two crews. You will take one crew. You will be based in Lisbon, and take passengers from a place called Nova Lisboa, to Lisbon. You have been to Angola?"

Harry laughed. "Heard of it, but I have no idea where it is. Isn't there a war going on there? What's this about?"

Eddie explained that Angola had, for years, been an enclave of Portugal and, yes, a civil war had been going on there for some years. Now the situation in Angola dictated that the Portuguese people there, many of them natives, needed to be relocated to Portugal. The flights would be continuous and would take place over one month.

"Well," said Harry, "not only have I not been to Angola, I haven't been to Lisbon, either. A wonderful city, from what I hear. Two questions: Will I need a bulletproof vest, and when do we go?"

Eddie smiled. "I am pleased you are satisfied to go. Others are not so eager. In about one week. It suits you?"

Harry stood to leave. "I see you're busy. Yes, that suits me right down to the ground, as my English friends would say. Now I need to find a map, and see where Angola is."

Ah, thought Captain LeBlanc, if only all my pilots were so agreeable. As Harry left he called out, "Captain, you will not need your vest. I am informed the natives you will meet are very friendly, especially the women."

Harry turned and grinned over his shoulder. "That," he said, "is the best news I've had all day."

Lisbon was, indeed, a wonderful city. Although the crews were based on its outskirts, a subway took them to the center in just a few minutes. And what a center! A wide avenida ran through its heart, lined with trees, flowers, and outdoor cafes. A bus connected with a superb beach on the Atlantic Ocean, and Harry went there now and then for a jog, a swim, and a delicious lunch of fresh fish. Harry fell instantly in love with Lisbon.

The flights were another story. They were long and tedious. Nova Lisboa was a high-altitude airport with a short runway, and that made the arrivals and departures more difficult. Because the airplane carried no passengers going there, it could take enough fuel to fly nonstop. The route took them across the Mediterranean Sea and cut through Morocco, Algeria, and several other countries Harry had never heard of. It was a tedious eight hours to a place some 600 miles on the other side of the equator. There were few radio aids along the way, so most of the navigation was dead reckoning. The radio communications were on the high frequency-band and were almost incomprehensible.

The return flight was with an airplane full of passengers. That load, along with a high-altitude, short-runway airport, sharply reduced the amount of fuel that could be taken; so the airplane stopped in Luanda, just an hour away and with a long runway at sea level. From there, the plane could easily take off with enough fuel to reach Lisbon.

Boarding the passengers in Nova Lisboa always took a few hours. Including ground time, the round-trip was about twenty-two hours; so the pattern was twenty-two hours on and twenty-two off. It was during those off-hours that Harry explored Lisbon and its beaches. That was enough time to sleep and to enjoy the good life of Portugal. Harry organized visits by car to Cashcai, a seaside resort with a famous casino, and to the town of Sintra, nestled in the hills and boasting a fascinating castle. Harry had never heard of either one, and he wondered why. The crew investigated the restaurants and a few bars near the hotel. Everyone gave a solid "thumbs up" to Lisbon.

The 707 is a reliable airplane. It flew between Nova Lisboa and Lisbon continuously for a full month without a serious maintenance malfunction. Problems sometimes cropped up on the ground. On one nighttime arrival in Nova Lisboa, the crew was unable to make radio contact with the airport. That was a problem for two reasons. First, because it was a high-altitude airport, it was important to know the current altimeter setting. This adjusted the airplane's altimeter for variations in local barometric pressure. The second reason was the need for current weather, especially the wind. Harry was not concerned about other traffic, as there seemed never to be any.

After many futile tries, a voice finally responded. The voice spoke very basic English and, after some difficulty, told the crew that the regular tower operator was not there. "Boss not here," was how he put it.

"Weather, meteo, we need the weather. What weather do you have?" asked the first officer. It was soon obvious that the voice knew nothing about weather.

"Ask him to look outside to see if it's raining," Harry said. At first puzzled, the first officer understood. Rain would let them know the visibility, as well as the weather. "No," the voice said, "no rain."

"Ask him to look up," said Harry. "Ask if can see any stars."

The first officer grinned and complied. Yes, he could see stars.

"Okay," said Harry "we'll use the latest Luanda altimeter and hope for the best. We'll land in the usual direction. That runway is usually into the wind."

Like many problems, this one melted away as they came in for a landing in clear, dry weather with almost no wind. They should all end that way, thought Harry as he taxied in and parked.

Flying fatigue is cumulative. Even with plenty of rest, it catches up with the flyer. Harry believed that all those hours in a low-oxygen environment had something to do with it. By the end of the month, Harry was feeling that fatigue. He needed a rest, a prolonged rest. Harry loved Lisbon, and he would miss it. He would not miss Angola. In one month, all he had seen was two airports. Nova Lisboa and Luanda went onto his "Airport Only" list, not that of places he had visited. He was happy to return to Brussels.

78
TRANSIT TORONTO

Harry frowned as he read the telex. It had been handed to him when he checked in for a flight to Toronto. His frown became a scowl as he took in its message. It came from Oslo, and it told Harry that his days in Brussels had come to an end and that he had been leased to Saudi Arabian Airlines for an indefinite period. Harry's life had often been changed by a telex or a telephone call, but this was more than a change; it was a transformation. Thoughts and images rushed through his mind in a torrent of confusion. Saudi Arabian Airlines? Its unofficial name was Saudia. He had heard of it, of course. Everyone had; but he had heard of it in the way that he had heard of Mount Everest or Timbuktu: more imaginary than real. He knew that it was based in Jeddah, and he had seen its airplanes at different airports, so he knew it was real. But to work there? In Saudi Arabia? No, something was amiss and he would call Thor to straighten this out. First, though, he had to go to Toronto.

It was a charter flight that had been sub-chartered by TEA in a last-minute arrangement. The charter company had been shut down, for unknown reasons, as its plane was about to depart from Manchester. The flight was simple on paper, but Murphy and the real world had other ideas. Because Savak had not reported for the flight, Harry would not be able to fly a normal north-Atlantic track. Those required a navigator. Although Harry thought of Savak more as comic relief than as a navigator, he met the legal requirement, so Harry would need to find another way. That meant taking an airways route across the sea, not a great circle route.

If a plane is passed through a sphere in a way that it goes through the center of the sphere, the plane will inscribe an arc along the surface of the sphere. The distance between any two points on that arc is the shortest way to go from one point to the other. In navigation, the earth is the sphere, and the arc is known as a great circle route. In flying, shorter is always better because it saves time and fuel. It might seem strange that an airplane flying from Brussels to Toronto would be routed over the north Atlantic, for example, but that is how the great circle would take it. It is the reason that an airplane going from London to Los Angeles flies near the North Pole. It's shorter that way.

Harry had flown several times near the pole, and these flights were interesting for several reasons. One was that the lines of longitude, those imaginary vertical lines that separate the globe into equal wedge-like sections, converge at an increasing rate as they near the pole and finally meet there. Those lines determine true north. Magnetic north, on the other hand, is determined by magnetic lines of force. The earth is a giant magnet, and lines of magnetic force flow from one pole to the other. It is these lines of force that tell a compass to point towards the north. Magnetic north is different from true north, and the difference is important. That difference is called variation, and it must be taken into account when a pilot reads his compass. Variation can be as little as zero in some locations. In the northern latitudes, however, this difference can be as much as 50 degrees.

Heading is the direction an airplane flies. This can be thought of as the angle with which the airplane crosses the lines of longitude. Near the poles, these lines converge and they are crossed much more rapidly than at lower latitudes. The result seen by the pilot in polar regions is that the heading of the airplane changes continuously, even though the wings are level and the airplane is not turning. Although the airplane is flying straight and level, the angles of the longitude lines, which the airplane is passing, are changing as they meet at the poles. That took some getting used to.

Another strange aspect of polar flights was that the great circle route took the airplane around the globe at a rate faster than that of the sun. Leaving from Amsterdam or Copenhagen in late afternoon, Harry had seen the sun set soon after taking off. Then, after a short night, he had actually seen the sun rise in the west. That was because he had overtaken the sun because of his shorter route over the earth's surface near the pole.

Without a navigator, there would be no great circle route today. There was another way, and that was to follow airways across Iceland and Greenland to Gander in Newfoundland. These routes were longer but they did not require a navigator because of the shorter distances between navigational aids and airports.

The first stop was Manchester, where they would rescue the stranded passengers who, Harry would learn, had already boarded the airplane when the company was shut down. The flight there was routine, and it would be the first of many that day. Next was a refueling stop at Shannon, on Ireland's west coast. Then they set out for Reykjavik. Harry' first visit to Iceland lasted just an hour. Then it was on to Gander on Canada's east coast. On the way, they passed over southern Greenland and, in the brilliant sunlight, the snow-covered mountains were a breathtaking sight. Finally, after a quick stop in Gander, they were on the way to Toronto. So far, so good, thought Harry.

It was a busy flight, but the telex was never far from his thoughts. Saudi Arabia! He could not believe it. What about his niche in Brussels, which he had come to enjoy more and more? And what about Irene? Their relationship was serious now, and Jeddah might mean the end of it. Harry did not want that. He did not want to leave Brussels. There had to be another way. By the time he reached Gander, he had devised a plan. First, he would talk with Thor and try to change his mind. Next, he would talk to Eddie LeBlanc about joining TEA. Months had gone by since Eddie had offered him a job and many Belgians had been hired since then. He was not optimistic. Still, there had to be a way. The problem was to find it.

The arrival in Toronto was normal and, looking back later, Harry wondered why. They were given taxi instructions to a remote part of the parking ramp. That was not unusual for a charter flight, Harry knew. But, after twenty minutes, when neither the external power unit nor the stairs appeared, Harry began to feel uneasy. Something did not feel right. He picked up the mike and called Ground Control.

"We're still standing by for the external power and the stairs," he said. "Is there a problem?"

After a pause, a Canadian accent replied, "Yes, some administrative problem. Please stand by and we will advise."

After fifteen minutes of hearing nothing on his radio, Harry was growing impatient. He clicked his mike.

"Ground, we need to shut down our engines and open the doors. What's going on here?" Ground Control asked Harry to call on another, less-used frequency. There, he was given the bad news. The charter company had neglected to obtain landing rights and they would not be allowed to discharge the passengers. Harry was dumbstruck!

"What do you mean?" he asked irritably. "We've already landed. Please send out the stairs and I'll come in and we can discuss the problem. And what about our passengers? They live here, and they want to go home."

"Sorry," came the reply, "but our orders are not to let anyone off the aircraft, not even the captain."

Harry could not believe his ears. "Then what the hell are we supposed to do, sit here with our engines running until we're out of fuel? Please let the passengers into the transit lounge until we sort this out."

Another "sorry," but they were not even allowed to open the aircraft doors.

And fuel would not be available.

This was starting to look serious, and Harry began to feel the first faint signs of frustration. His irritation was turning into anger. How was this possible?

"Look," he said, "we have a serious problem here and we need some help. You guys have any ideas? We can't just sit here forever."

The reply was unexpected. "Listen, you might think of going to Niagara Falls. It's not far, and you do not need a landing authorization. It's an open airport."

That idea seemed questionable, but it was at least a step towards resolving what looked like an impasse. Harry asked his first officer to check the charts to see whether the one for Niagara Falls was there. He would be surprised if it was. Sure enough, no chart. The airways chart would get them there, but without an airport chart Harry was reluctant to go. Still, it was a way out. Then he had an idea. Clicking his mike, he asked Ground Control if they could provide essential data from the Niagara Falls approach chart. Like what, they asked. Well, Harry told them, thinking quickly, they would need the elevation of the airport, the direction and the frequency of the Instrument Landing System for the runway in use. And what else? Tower and ground control frequencies. And the weather. How was the weather? The information was quickly provided. The weather was fine, just like here. It's just across water, they said.

"One more thing," Harry said. "After takeoff, we request a radar vector to the final approach there. We're getting low on fuel." Thanks to you, he thought, but he did not say it.

Just then Michelle came into the cockpit.

"Harry," she said with some concern, "the passengers, they are becoming very angry. Can you please tell them something?"

Jesus! Harry thought, he had forgotten completely about those poor people in the back. They had been through a lot today. He nodded and grabbed his mike, switched to the cabin address, and depressed the button. He gave them the bad news, but not the part about perhaps going to Niagara Falls. He heard a loud reaction, loud even through the closed cockpit door. Damn, he thought, what will they do when they hear they might have to take a bus home from Niagara Falls?

Okay, Harry thought, Niagara Falls seems to be the only way out of this mess. They went through the start-up and after-start-up checklists even though the engines were running. Better safe than sorry.

"Call for taxi," he told the first officer. Looking back over his shoulder, he looked at the fuel gauges. The flight engineer, a Belgian, answered before Harry asked. "About sixteen thousand pounds," he said.

Damn, thought Harry, that was a good number for landing, but not for takeoff. Still, it would be a short flight, and the weather was good. And, most persuasive of all, there were no other options.

Harry could hear loud rumbles of complaint from the passengers as the plane began to taxi. Might as well tell them now, Harry thought. When he did, a roar went up in the cabin. Well, Harry told himself, we don't like it, either.

After the takeoff, Harry switched to Ground Control and asked, "Just out of curiosity, why in hell did you let us land?"

After a pause, a quiet voice said, "We wish we knew. Have a safe flight."

"Thanks," said Harry with all the sarcasm he could muster. "And thanks for your hospitality. At least you didn't let the air out of our tires." His answer was a loud click.

79
NIAGARA FALLS

The flight was just seventeen minutes and, despite Harry's concerns, all went well and they landed safely in Niagara Falls. He explained that they had no airport charts and would need taxi directions. Harry remembered a comment he had once heard while waiting for start-up clearance in Frankfort. A British Airways captain, obviously confused about finding his way to his assigned parking spot, was sarcastically asked by an irritated ground controller "Have you never been to Frankfort before?"

"Yes," the captain replied. "In 1944, but we didn't stop."

Well, shut my mouth, thought Harry, with a grin, as he heard the reply. He grinned again now as he recalled the comment.

Another comment Harry heard over the radio had made him laugh out loud. That also happened in Frankfort, when a Lufthansa captain made a wrong turn on a taxiway, causing gridlock for a dozen airplanes. The ground controller, a shrill woman with a stong accent and with the mentality of a U-boat commander, criticized the captain with withering scorn, ending with the question, "How did you ever get to be an airline captain?" After such a blistering attack, no one felt courageous enough to speak. Finally, after a long moment of silence, someone did. "Didn't you used to be my wife?" he asked.

Lining up in their parking space, Harry noted, with satisfaction, that the stairs and external power unit were already waiting. It was great to be back in the U.S., he thought, where the natives are friendly and there is some common sense.

As Harry shut down the engines, the ramp agent pushed into the cockpit. He waited until the crew completed the shutdown checklist.

"They did not want you in Toronto, Captain? Never mind, we'll take good care of you here. We know about the problem and we already have buses standing by to take the passengers back to Toronto."

Harry was relieved to talk to someone who knew what he was doing. "That's the best news I've had all day. I just hope those folks in Toronto will let them off the bus."

The agent smiled sympathetically. "It's not the first time. What about you and your crew? I've made hotel reservations for you and we just need to know when you are leaving, and your fuel load."

Harry smiled back, a very tired smile. "I'm too tired to think right now. Can I call you from the hotel? It's been a long day and I need a shower and a cold beer to get my brain in gear."

"Of course, of course" he said as he quickly wrote down a telephone number and handed it to Harry. "Someone will be there all night. Just call anytime."

Harry tucked the slip of paper into his pocket. "Thanks. What happens next?"

The agent explained that the crew would need to pass through customs to a crew van on the other side. The hotel was close, he said and "it's a good one."

Harry's first sensation as he emerged from the terminal was the sound. It was a distant and steady rumble. He and Michelle looked at each other, puzzled. Then it struck him. Of course, it was the sound of the Falls. He did not know how far away were the world-famous Niagara Falls, but there could be no other explanation. The faint mist that permeated the air confirmed that first sensation. No, more like a spray, Harry thought. He turned to Michelle, explaining the phenomenon. She was instantly excited.

"Oh, Harry, we must see these wonderful Falls. I have read about them and I have seen them in the cinema. Oh, we must see them, we must."

Harry had already decided that one way or another they would visit the Falls. Who knew when he might have another chance?

"No promises, Michelle, but I'll do my best."

But first, they needed sleep. Before going to his room, Harry sent a telex to Brussels. It had been a tiring flight, he wrote, and unless otherwise instructed, they would take twenty-four hours of crew rest before returning to Belgium. Michelle had thoughtfully stuffed a handful of mini-bottles into an airsick sack, and now she showed them to Harry as the crew checked into the hotel.

"A small crew party before we sleep," she said. "I think we have earned a 'petite' celebration."

Harry grinned and nodded. If she could muster up the energy for a few drinks, who was he to object?

"My room in thirty minutes," he announced to the crew. "We're going to celebrate our survival before we go to bed." Then he turned to the desk clerk. "No calls for twelve hours, please."

The crew party was brief, but helped to ease the strain of a long and difficult day. It was magic how a shower and a drink could rejuvenate him, thought Harry. But the glow was short-lived and soon, one by one, they began falling asleep where they sat. Before leaving Harry's room, the crew agreed to meet in the morning for a quick tour of the famous Falls.

The rumble became a roar as they approached the viewing area in the morning. The mist was almost a shower. The view of the falls was breathtaking. And the sound! Taken together, they made one of the most spectacular sights he had ever seen. Michelle could not believe her eyes.

"So much water," she said breathlessly as she stared at the falls, wide-eyed. "Incredible! From where does it all arrive?"

Harry pointed across the vast expanse of water roiling before them. "Over there," he said. "From Canada. You know, all that water is making me thirsty. I think it's time for a beer and some lunch."

A telex from Captain LeBlanc had said okay, take a day off, so a beer or two would be legal. They would leave early the next morning.

The Belgians wanted to see the city of Niagara Falls, so they found a restaurant there. The city was disappointing. It was wall-to-wall souvenir shops, and it reminded Harry of Lourdes: all commerce, no class. The lunch was amiable and the portions were large. The Belgians were impressed more with the quantity of food than its quality. "It's the American way," Harry explained. But the beer was no match for the beer he had become used to in Belgium. After Belgian beer, the American beer seemed flat. In Belgium, every drink left a ring of foam around the inside of the glass. American beer seemed to have no foam. Who could he talk to about that? Because of the uneaten food on their plates, they were asked if they wanted "doggie" bags. The Belgians could not believe their ears when Harry explained what that meant.

The flight to Brussels was easy, with clear weather all the way. Because there were no passengers, they could take more fuel. And because the jet stream blows from west to east, they would have a welcome push from the wind. Harry was anxious to get back so he could begin to deal with the prospect of being sent to Saudi Arabia. He would resist, but he had to consider the possibility. His first thoughts were of Irene. As their relationship had gone along, Harry more and more thought of her as a partner, not just a girlfriend. He did not like the thought of leaving Belgium without her. He had, somewhere along the way, begun thinking of marriage. It was more an evolution than a decision, and it seemed to happen in a natural and unconscious way. Would she agree to leave Belgium? She had an important job that she liked. She would have to leave that, too. By the time they passed over Land's End, on the southern tip of England, Harry had decided to visit Oslo to talk to Thor.

80
LEAVING THE GULF

May 1966

All cruises end and, eventually, the last day in the Tonkin Gulf came for the USS Kitty Hawk and her crew. For most of the flyers, it had long ago become an exercise in staying alive to see this great day. For Harry, his last mission was one that would have taken him to the westernmost part of North Vietnam, deep into the bulge where it meets Laos. When he learned that this final flight would be the twelfth strike against a "suspected storage area," he had finally had enough. After informing the Air Intelligence Officer that he had no intention of going to the target, he launched with wingman Andy Curley, found a couple of barges just off the coast, dropped his bombs in the general vicinity, and, with an exultant *whoop!* sharply wheeled his airplane back towards the ship.

The day did not end as well for Harry's roommate. Bob Norton, on his final flight of the cruise and his 106ᵗʰ mission, did not come back. His wingman, Jerry Greene, came home alone. Bob had been hit with automatic weapons a few miles inland, turned for the sea, but lost control of his airplane before he got there. Jerry saw the ejection and orbited Bob's position after he reached the ground, less than one mile from the coast. Each flyer carried a small radio strapped to his chest. It was meant for situations like this one. After touching down, Bob broke out his radio and reported to Jerry that he was okay: there was no one around, send in the chopper.

During all flight operations in the north, two helicopters were airborne, on station near the coast, ready to respond when the need arose. Jerry called numerous times on the rescue frequency, but there was no reply. After forty-five minutes of anxious waiting, Jerry reported that Bob had said, "They're coming now. I'm going to destroy my radio. See you later." That was the last anyone heard of Bob Norton for six long years. Those years were spent by Bob in the infamous Hanoi Hilton where, eventually, some 470 pilots became "guests" before the war was over. Unofficially, Harry found out that because of an administrative foul-up, no chopper was on station when Bob's plane was shot down.

Jerry Greene had his own brush with fate just a few weeks earlier. That happened after he had flown an airplane to Cubi Point in the Philippines for the installation of a SAM warning device. Scheduled to return to the ship on

364

an A3, he was displaced by a higher-priority passenger. The airplane was shot down near the island of Hainan in the Tonkin Gulf. There were indications that it had been lured there by a false radio beacon which replicated the signal of the Kitty Hawk's beacon. All on board were lost. That was a "lucky bump," as he put it when he learned what had almost happened to him. Jerry had more than his share of good luck that day.

Another weapon in the Tonkin Gulf rescue armory was the P5M Marlin. This was an ancient seaplane that found new glory by retrieving from the sea pilots who had been shot down. A few months ago, one had landed near the shore to pick up a couple of very wet aviators. The airplane was close to the coast and it came under fire from shore-based mortars. A helicopter also appeared and reported that several North Vietnamese boats could be seen racing for the downed pilots. Just as the seaplane was pulling the pilots from the sea, it was struck by a mortar shell and destroyed. That put its five-man crew into the water, and now there were seven. As the boats neared them, the chopper lowered its hoisting cable, but seven bodies were more than the chopper could lift; so a couple of them grabbed the rescue collar at the end of the cable and clung to it tenaciously. The others took hold of the first two as best they could and the chopper headed away from the approaching boats, dragging the unlucky seven through the water and away from danger. A second chopper was called in, and all pilots were soon safely back on the carrier. The seaplane could not have helped Bob; but it might have been able to help direct a chopper to where he had come down -- if there had been a chopper airborne.

After the last airplane of the last mission had been taken aboard, the captain of the ship authorized the issue of medicinal bourbon to all flight crews, and there was boisterous celebration throughout the quarters where the flight crews were berthed. Bottles appeared like magic from safes throughout the area; but for Harry, it was anti-climactic, and the news about Bob saddened him greatly. He had one drink of bourbon and it did not help. Feeling depressed instead of elated, he went quietly to his room, passing through joyous knots of exhilarated pilots as he did. He wanted to be alone.

His first thought on entering his room was of Bob. How strange to think that his roomie would not walk in the door any minute to complain about the way the war was being fought. Without Bob, the trip home would be long and lonely.

Harry opened his safe and withdrew Jack's bottle of Ballentine Scotch. After Jack had been killed, Harry had offered to sort out his belongings for shipment home. He had kept the bottle for himself, as Jack had told him to do before he launched on his last flight. He had not touched it since then because he was saving it to celebrate the end of the cruise. He thought Jack would agree with that. He thought about Jack as he leaned back in his chair and took a first sip.

When we are young, we think we are indestructible and that we will live forever. Common sense denies this; but Harry was sure that if, at this very moment, he asked every pilot in the Air Wing if he had even once thought he might be killed while flying in the Tonkin Gulf, each would say no, not me. And this was despite the loss of friends and shipmates who would not make the trip home. Harry lifted his glass and drank to all those who would not return. Again he thought of Bob. Somehow, he would make it through, Harry was sure. Then, he lifted the glass several more times, finishing the bottle. Those were for Jack. Harry would miss him for the rest of his life.

The prisoners of the Hanoi Hilton were released while Harry was living in Brussels. He watched the television intently as the POWs came down the airplane ramp at Clarke Air Force Base in the Philippines. It was mid-morning in Brussels, and he was alone. He mixed a very large Scotch and soda as he watched the men disembark, and raised his glass to the television set. He watched carefully, but he did not see Bob among those emerging from the airplane in an atmosphere charged with joy and high emotion. But he knew he was there. He could not feel the same emotion Bob was feeling at that moment, he knew, but he thought it had to be very close.

Some thirty-five years after Bob was shot down, Harry was at a reunion of those who flew in the Tonkin Gulf. There, Bob Norton and his wingman Jerry Greene met for the first time since that day so long ago. Harry knew his old roomie well. He was from Iowa, the Heartland, he called it, and he had all the strengths of character usually associated with people of that region. Harry had often said that if anyone could survive the Hanoi Hilton, Bob was the one.

Later, over a few quiet drinks after the gathering had broken up, Bob spoke easily and without emotion of his years in prison. Much of what he said was hard to believe and even harder to listen to. Harry listened raptly for several hours as Bob talked about the horrific treatment he and others had suffered. The prisoners communicated by tapping on their walls, using a simple code they had devised. Leaving out the letter K, the remaining twenty-five letters of the alphabet were arranged into five lines, each with five letters. The letter C was also used as a K. The number of taps, separated by a pause, indicated a letter. The letter D, for example, was one tap, a pause, then four taps; first line, fourth letter.

Along with the painful memories he recalled that night, Bob mentioned two aspects that were surprising. First, Cubans, not the North Vietnamese, inflicted much of the torture. Second, and Harry was not sure why this surprised him, was that one of the hardest parts of his readjustment to normal life was making ordinary decisions. He had made very few for six years. Now, he said, it might take him several minutes to decide which socks to wear or when to shave. Harry could only think "There, but for the grace of God, go I."

Harry had made it back to the ship on that last day, and Bob had not. The difference was the luck of life.

BOOK TWO

81

BOUND FOR JEDDAH

November 1973

The flight to Jeddah was long and made longer by the absence of alcohol. That was Harry's first hint of what lay ahead in Saudi Arabia. He was not just changing companies, he would learn; he was changing worlds. The visit to Oslo had been pleasant but fruitless. The deal had already been signed, Thor told him, and there would be no other way.

"You will enjoy living in Saudi Arabia," Thor said, "especially the money. You will receive more, much more. And no place to spend it. You will become rich!"

He said that with a broad smile which said he did not really mean it. Harry did not consider himself to be an intelligent man; but he was smart enough to read the handwriting on the wall, and he knew he had to brace himself for Saudi Arabia

Harry had looked up a few of his former colleagues. That included Astrid. She spoke with him on the telephone, but adamantly refused to meet with him. No need to stir up those old feelings, she told him. She would be married soon and that, she said, with just a trace of those old feelings, was that. Harry seldom thought of Astrid since Irene had come into his life. He thought he had finally gotten her out of his system; but he felt a rush of those old feelings when he first heard her voice, so he knew something was still there. Well, he thought, as he hung up, his feelings for Astrid would always stay with him in a corner of his heart. That was just how he was, and there was nothing to be done about it. You can't order an emotion to go away; but then he thought of Irene in Belgium and he knew he had to look ahead, not back. He smiled mentally as he did.

The first thing Harry did on returning to Brussels was to arrange a meeting with Eddie LeBlanc. It took place in the TEA office on Rue d'Argen, not far from the Jacobowitz Chateau.

"Eddie," said Harry, after a few pleasantries and the first sip of a cup of coffee, "I hope you remember that you once offered me a job with TEA. I know this is late but if that offer is still open, I'd like to take you up on it."

Eddie frowned slightly. "Take me up? Of course I do remember that. When you returned from Rio de Janeiro, correct?" His frown deepened. "Take me up," he repeated. "I am assuming you are asking if the position is still available. Also correct?"

Harry nodded. He did not hold high hopes that TEA would offer him a permanent position. He knew that the company had been hiring Belgian pilots and that its goal, like airlines everywhere, was to have an airline comprised of its own nationals. Still, there was no harm in asking.

Eddie inhaled deeply and exhaled slowly. "Captain Harry, you know I have great regard for you and all you have done for us." Harry began feeling that sinking sensation that his analysis was right. "And if it's only me to decide, then, of course, I would, this moment, sign your contract. But, alas, it is not only me. And Mr.Gettelman has decided that we need no more foreign pilots. We can use you for a few more months, but after that . . . . Eh, bien, if we should need another pilot, you can be assured that you are the first."

This was beginning to sound like a reply to all those resumes he had sent around the world when he was searching for a job. But he understood.

"Yes, of course, and I had my opportunity. Still, no harm asking," he said, saying aloud what he had been thinking earlier.

Eddie smiled somewhat sadly. "I wish I could help, but I cannot. Not now. I do hope that you understand."

Harry did, he said, and told Eddie about his assignment to Saudia in Jeddah.

Eddie winced very slightly, then smiled, thinly. "So you are going to become rich in Saudi Arabia. I offer my congratulations and my best wishes for a successful position. Please keep me informed about your situation. Perhaps later, something?"

Now it was Harry's turn to smile sadly. There was no more to say. They shook hands warmly.

"Eddie," said Harry as he turned to leave, "thank you for everything. I mean that."

Eddie shrugged as if to say "What can I do?" Then Harry, for the last time, walked out of the office that had changed the direction of his life.

82
THE WEDDING

November 3, 1973

They were married in a civil ceremony in the Antwerp City Hall. Going to Jeddah meant a major change for Harry, but for Irene, too. The plan was for her to join him in the months ahead, and that meant leaving a job she loved. Harry had asked her if she was ready for that.

"First things first," she said in her usual straightforward and enthusiastic way. "And first for me is you and perhaps, one day, a family. Everything else comes after that. Until I met you, I was expecting to work in the bank until forever. Saudi Arabia will be an adventure. And anyway, I have always wanted to see it."

Harry knew she didn't mean that last part, but he loved her for saying it. Who wanted to see Saudi Arabia? Who had even heard of Saudi Arabia or knew where it was? But if Saudi Arabia was in their future, then that was how it would be. She was a woman of substance.

The wedding ceremony, small but pleasant, was held in a beautiful room which overlooked the city's main square. Irene's parents were the first to arrive. Harry had met them before and, although not fluent, they spoke English well enough for Harry to enjoy their company. Her father was stout, without much hair, but he had a classically handsome face.

"The girls," her mother once told Harry, "they were all pursuing him."

She had not even tried, which was, perhaps, why he had chosen her. They had come through much together, including a war, since that long ago day in the garden. Her mother was short and thin and seemed always happy. They were plainly people of quality, and Harry liked them very much.

Gene Daily was, of course, there. He was the best man. And Rolf had come, too. Irene's friend Vik, whose café Harry had visited, was there wearing a big smile and an American flag lapel pin. Also there was a long-time friend of Irene's who was openly homosexual. He had brought his "partner" who was, like himself, handsome, pleasant and charming. Two of Harry's dart-throwing English friends from The Drum were there, too. It was an unusual assortment of guests, Harry thought, and one that would be hard to describe in Milwaukee.

370

Also there, smiling nonstop, was Mr. Jacobowitz. His eyes had filled with tears when Harry invited him, and he took Harry's hand with both of his and pressed it warmly.

"It is a very long time since I have been asked to attend such an important event," he said happily, "and I do accept with the greatest of pleasure."

A few days later he was invited, he called Harry to offer his boardinghouse for wine and hors d'oeuvres after the ceremony. "Please allow me to make this very small contribution to my good friend."

How could Harry say no? So after the wedding, which was simple, dignified and accented with fresh flowers and soft music, a small celebration was held at the Jacobowitz Chateau. It was a grand success.

A brief honeymoon in Palma de Majorca was all that time allowed. That place seemed right, as that was where their relationship had become serious. Irene often mentioned their visit there and especially the tour of the USS John F. Kennedy. That had been one of the most exciting days of her life, she said, and that holiday was at the top of her list.

"What about Rio?" Harry had teased. Rio had been wonderful she said, but it was in Palma that she had fallen in love. It was also the place, they would learn, where she became pregnant. To Irene, that was destiny at work. A Saudi would have said it was the will of Allah.

83
CHANGING WORLDS

Harry gazed out the window of the Saudia B747 as the Swiss Alps slid past far below. He had seen this spectacular view many times, and it always awed him. He would have enjoyed the view even more with a drink in his hand, but alcohol, along with many other customs and habits of the western world, was not allowed on Saudia's airplanes. Well, hell, he thought, I can certainly live without alcohol -- not as enjoyably, perhaps, but it was surely not a question of survival. Some, he would learn, defined survival differently. Had he known how different was the world he was about to enter, he might not this moment be looking down on the Alps on his way to Jeddah.

Harry's contract was with Saudi Arabian Airlines. It had been signed in London two days earlier. Trans Polar would collect a fee from Saudia while he worked there. His contract was for three years, but they were not western years. In Saudi Arabia, the Hegira calendar was used. As the western calendar began with the birth of Christ, their's began with Mohammed's birth. So, in Saudi Arabia, the year was 1401. Also different about those years was that they were based on the lunar cycle. Each Hegira year was eleven days shorter than the solar year used in the west. Retirement for a Saudia pilot, Harry would learn, was at age 60, as it was in most countries; but those years came to only 58.2 years using the solar system. Harry could not imagine himself retiring in Jeddah.

While in London for an interview and a medical examination, Harry had stayed at the Park Lane Hotel, which was the Saudia crew hotel. It would be a good idea, he thought, to talk to a Saudia pilot. He was curious to know what he had let himself in for; so he checked the crew list at the reception desk and wrote down a couple of room numbers belonging to non-Arabic names. He called the first one and found himself talking to an American who had been flying with Saudia for two years.

"Sure," a friendly voice said, "come on up and I'll fill you in with all the gory details."

Harry hoped that was a joke.

The American had left his door ajar.

"Come on in," said the voice, this time from the bathroom. A tall, lanky, light-haired man with a moustache and a Texas accent came into the room, drying his hands with a towel. His first words were not, "Hello, how are you?" They were, "I make a lot of money working for Saudia. I wouldn't do it again for twice as much. Sit down and we'll talk."

Harry felt the first twinge of regret. "Ouch!" was all he said. The pilot, a 707 captain, ordered coffee from room service and, in the next half-hour, confirmed Harry's regret that he had signed a contract.

"But never mind," he said. "You'll get used to it. You'll be brain dead after the first few weeks but everybody's in the same boat. You can get used to anything, even working in Saudi Arabia. Once you do, it's not so bad. There are plenty of ex-pats there, and you'll meet some great people."

He said that last part with a smile, and Harry's spirit lifted a little. Well, he thought, somewhat disconsolately, there is nothing to do about it now. I've burned my bridges behind me.

"Yes," said Harry, "I know there are quite a few ex-pats there. They're okay, I'm sure, but what about the Saudis? How is it working with them?"

The captain frowned, put down his cup and looked at Harry. "Sure you want to know? Might be better to find out for yourself."

Harry nodded. "Go ahead. Forewarned is forearmed. Fire away. I can take it."

"Okay, here's a story for you. It's not true; but it could be true, which is almost the same thing."

There were, he began, some work-related problems the Saudi pilots were unhappy about; so the Chief Pilot had called them all together to dispel their concerns.

"First," he said, "we know you do not like to fly at night. So from now on, the foreigners will do all the night flying." A big cheer erupted. "Second," he continued, "we know you do not like to fly in bad weather, so the ex-pats will operate all the flights when bad weather is expected." That triggered an even bigger cheer from the Saudi pilots. "Next," he went on, "we know you don't like to fly on weekends because you like to be with your families then. The quadjis will do all the weekend flying." The cheers rattled the windows. "So," he concluded, "let me review. No more night flying, no more flights in bad weather, and no flying on weekends. To make it even easier, you will fly only one day each week. That's Tuesday. Everybody got that? Any questions?"

A hand rose in the back of the hall.

"Does that mean," the Saudi pilot asked, "*every* Tuesday?"

Harry smiled, but it was a tight smile. The lift in his spirits was quickly gone.

"I think I got the message," he said, "and thanks for the heads-up. It sounds like the Saudis don't carry their share of the load."

"That," said the captain, "might be the understatement of the year."

He spoke for some time about what Harry might expect working for Saudia. His final piece of advice was sound: you must let all the horseshit bounce off; otherwise you'll never make it. Those who don't, do not last very long. The captain gave Harry his telephone number in Saudi City and they agreed to keep in touch. Saudi City, Harry already knew, was the complex that housed all the foreigners working for Saudi Arabian Airlines.

Leaving the Alps behind, the airplane flew down the length of Italy. Lunch was served as the 747 passed over Rome. Dates stuffed with almonds were the starters. The food was superb, even without a glass of wine. But the coffee, oh, that coffee! Served in tiny cups without handles, it was Arabic, it was dark green, and it had a mud-like layer of coffee bean curd at the bottom of the cup. Harry had little doubt that it would have made a great heart-starter for Gene Daily's Mexican breakfast. Harry's first cup would be his last.

At one point along the way, several passengers had left their seats, unrolled small carpets in the aisle, and kneeled down to pray. Prayers had to be offered towards Mecca, the birthplace of Mohammed. To help worshippers know the right direction, Saudia had installed on each airplane's ceiling an arrow, connected to the airplane's navigation system. It pointed continuously towards this holy city, the most holy of Islam. It is revered not only as Mohammed's birthplace, but as the first place created on earth. It is the site of the Kaaba, an enormous rectangular block made of stone. This structure is draped with a black cloth exquisitely embroidered with sayings from the Koran. It is the focal point of all pilgrimages to Jeddah, such as those undertaken by the pilgrims Harry had earlier carried there. The sight of those in prayer during flight was a harbinger, although a very small one, of the life he would find in Saudi Arabia.

Harry would learn that this was a common sight on Saudia flights. He would fly with crewmembers who regularly carried these handmade prayer carpets. Harry would now and then see his first officer or his flight engineer unroll a carpet on the tarmac under the airplane's wing, and pray during a transit stop in "The Kingdom," as Saudi Arabia was usually called, and even, at times, while in the cockpit during flight. That, thought Harry, was dedication.

The B747 crossed the Mediterranean Sea, flew over Cairo southeast-bound to the Red Sea, then descended into Jeddah. The captain, obviously

English, made a standard announcement to the passengers as he started his descent. Later, Harry would hear of a non-standard announcement that had cost a captain his job.

"To be on local time," he had informed the passengers, "set your watch ahead three hours and your mind back one-thousand years."

In the next few months, Harry would learn that this captain had been on target with his advice. He would, in those months, learn of other such firings. The Saudis took such things seriously.

In two such cases, Harry had personally known the captains involved. The first had made the egregious request during a transit stop in The Kingdom to "turn off that goddamn music." That "goddamn music" was played over the cabin address system during all transit stops. It was Arabic and it bore little resemblance to real music. It had an abrasive, nerve-jangling sound, which was monotonous and aggravating; but the quality of the music was not the reason for the request. That was because it happened during Ramadan, a month-long period of religious fast lasting from dawn to dusk. During the fast, many Saudi pilots simply refused to fly. The "quajis," as the ex-pats were known, had to take up the slack. That meant extra hours under unique circumstance that led easily to fatigue and frustration. The harsh sound of nonstop Arabic music did not help.

The second captain, a Swede, made a similar remark, also during Ramadan, when his Saudi first officer decided to eat his dinner just as they were cleared for takeoff. After fasting all day, the first officer was famished as dusk approached and their B737 was waiting in the queue to take the runway. The captain noticed him checking his watch every few minutes, but that was not unusual. The Saudis knew, to the minute, the official time of sunset. After fasting all day, they began gorging themselves the instant that time arrived.

It came just as they were cleared for takeoff. The first officer acknowledged the clearance, checked his watch one last time, then pressed the call button to summon a hostess. She appeared immediately, and the pilot ordered his dinner.

"Excuse me," said the captain "but what in the hell are you doing? We have just been cleared for takeoff."

The first officer replied that he was "just going to eat my dinner. I am very hungry."

Swedes seldom got angry, but this one did.

"You could not wait five minutes until after the takeoff? You have to eat right now, this very minute?"

The first officer did not bother to reply, and he began eating the food from the tray that had just been placed on his lap. Of course, the captain had to relinquish his place in the queue, taxi to a holding area, and wait for his first officer to finish his dinner. That was when he slowly shook his head in frustration and said, under his breath, "This goddamn Ramadan." That was all he said, but that was enough. The first officer reported his comment, and he was soon on his way home to Sweden.

The question of the exact time of sunset was more difficult while airborne. When the sun touches the horizon, as seen on the ground, it is still shining brightly at higher altitudes. Flying during Ramadan, the cabin chief was often in the cockpit, asking for the time of sunset. The passengers were hungry and they wanted to eat. There was no way to know the exact time of sunset because it depended upon the altitude and the position of the airplane. Harry would later solve this little dilemma by making an official "Harry Guesstimate," then passing it on as hard information. Who could contradict him? And what difference did it make?

For their Ramadan comments, the two captains were fired and were on their way home within twenty-four hours. Their friends had to look after the departure of their families and the sale and shipment of their belongings. The Park Lane captain had cautioned him about this. Be very careful, he said, not to make disparaging remarks within earshot of Saudis. He himself had adopted the habit of always checking the immediate area before talking to a fellow ex-pat. He noticed that others did the same.

"They're like the KGB," he warned, "so be damned sure they're not listening. Do not discuss religion in the cockpit. That can lead to trouble."

The captain had told him that a friend, also a captain, had returned from a flight one day with an Arabic newspaper in his flight bag. Why do you carry this newspaper, he was asked, if you cannot read Arabic? The captain made the mistake of assuming the customs man had a sense of humor.

"I use it to line my birdcage," he said, lightly. Not only was it not funny to the customs agent, he reported the remark, and the captain was severely reprimanded by his superior. He was threatened with termination if it happened again. That word "termination" would be heard often in the months ahead. Harry always flinched when he heard it. It sounded to him more like a firing squad than a firing.

84
HELLO, JEDDAH

Harry's first taste of Saudi Arabia came as he passed through customs. A London newspaper had been discovered in the briefcase of the man just ahead of him.

"No newspapers," growled the customs agent with a fierce scowl as he threw the paper into a large bin behind him. The bin, Harry saw, was full to the brim with confiscated items. Somewhere in that bin, Harry would learn from another pilot joining the company that day, was a Bible. It had been not only taken away, but torn to shreds before it was tossed into the rubbish. Bibles were not welcome.

Later, Harry would learn that only newspapers that had been censored could be brought into "The Kingdom." They were censored with a marker pen, and, sometimes for strange reasons. Later, Harry would often read newspapers with an entire section blacked out. At other times, it might be just a word or two. One such word that never saw the light of day was "Israel." One day, Harry saw a travel ad in the International Herald Tribune. The travel was obviously to Israel and that one word was deleted in the two or three places it appeared. Once, Harry came across row upon row of packets of sauces on which had been written the types of food it complemented. "Pork" did not survive the censor's marker pen, and that one word was deleted from every one of scores of packets on the shelf. Harry tried to visualize the unlucky man who sat at a desk all day and struck the word "pork" from all those packets.

Newspapers and magazines, he would find, were regularly sold with entire pages cut out. In one newspaper, he saw a photo of a female Olympic skater with her bare thighs covered with marker ink. Movie reviews, if they referred to sex, were also excised. Harry could never have imagined the vast array of subjects which the Saudis found necessary to censor. Most dealt with women, sex, Israel and, of course, the word "pork."

Despite all these precautions, much uncensored material found its way into Saudi Arabia. Most of this was pornographic, and the Saudis paid a handsome price for it. A copy of *Playboy* magazine, for example, fetched fifteen or twenty times its newsstand price outside Saudi Arabia. Sex videos cost a fortune. A friend of Harry's would later observe, "If you have never held a woman, or even touched one, then sex magazines and videos can be very important." Alcohol was also prohibited, but a bottle of whiskey could easily be found for about $150 per bottle. Most ex-pats, eventually including Harry, made their own wine. It was surprisingly easy, but the quality varied greatly from one batch to the next, even when using the same formula. Some tasted like the real stuff, but others could be drunk only when mixed with juice or soft drinks. Still, it was better than nothing.

85
THE SAUDIA SHERATON

Of course, Harry knew little of all this as he and the former Bible-owner were driven into town in a new Mercedes. His fellow passenger was a former Air Force pilot. They met while being directed into the car by the driver who had been assigned to meet them. Mercedes and BMWs were everywhere, Harry noticed, as they made their way to the Sheraton Hotel, near the center of Jeddah. The entire hotel had been taken over by Saudia, and it was where the new-hires, as they were called, lived until they finished their initial training and moved to Saudi City. Many did not make it past the Sheraton.

The hotel was full, and one reason was the high rate of turnover among the flight crews. In the Park Lane Hotel, the captain had told Harry that in the preceding year about sixty-five per cent of the foreigners had left Saudia, many before the end of their contracts. Some left after only two or three weeks. It was not easy to leave the country, he said, and some departed by donning their uniforms and pretending to operate a flight. To stop that, Saudia instituted a policy whereby the operating crew was given a pass that was handed to a guard stationed at the door leading to the ramp.

"When you arrive in Jeddah," he had said, "you start with a bucket in each hand, one for money and one for shit. When one bucket is full, it's time to leave."

There had to be a reason for all that, Harry had thought, and now he was about to discover it.

There was, of course, no bar in the Sheraton Hotel; but there was a large lounge area and every night at five o'clock the hotel served snacks and drinks at what was known as the Five O'clock Follies. The drinks were coffee, tea, and soft drinks. There was no Coca-Cola, as Coke was forbidden in Saudi Arabia, as were all products sold in Israel. There was not much to do in Jeddah, so the Follies were well-attended. There, the pilots exchanged the news of the day, and it was often discouraging.

One reason, but only one, for the high turnover rate was the way in which the airline conducted its training. For the most part, Saudi nationals were placed in training positions, and they were often young and inexperienced. All Saudis, Harry heard, knew, by memory, most of the Koran. They learned religion by memory, and they trained pilots the same way. They knew the manuals verbatim, but they were missing the common sense that should have gone along with it.

One question Harry was later asked during his line training was, "How many times does the windshield wiper cycle per minute?" Well, damn, thought Harry, who cares? These kinds of questions were asked, he thought, to impress ex-pats with the Saudi pilots' technical knowledge, and to demean them if they did not know the answers.

This technique said much about the Saudi mindset. They had to demonstrate their superiority in various ways, and this was one of them. Western pilots were not used to this philosophy. They had learned to fly the airplane first and look at the manuals second. In Saudia, it was the other way around. The checklists, for example, had to be recited precisely as written. Nothing wrong with that, Harry thought, but getting it wrong should not be a firing offense. In Saudia, it could be. You could not respond to a checklist item with "Checked and Set" if the checklist asked for "Set and Checked." Harry could not figure out why, but different responses were written both ways.

Each of the pilots in the Sheraton had thousands of flight hours and extensive worldwide experience. Still, they had to sit there and listen to a 25-year-old training captain tell them the right way to read a checklist. Procedures were followed in an automatic way with no room for the common sense so important to flying an airplane. One captain at the Follies was fired because, during a check flight with a Saudi captain, he had turned off the seat belt sign at 10,500 feet instead of at 10,000 feet, as outlined by standard procedures. Harry had spoken with him a few days later.

"I did that," he told Harry, "because there were some cumulus clouds around and I just wanted to be sure we were clear before I turned off the sign."

Turning off that sign was the signal for the cabin crew to unbuckle and begin their service. Switching it off late, said the check captain, had denied service to the passengers for that minute or two, and he told him, "We don't do things like that in Saudia." Of course, there might have been more to this story; you never knew. But Harry heard so many tales like this one that they had to hold some truth.

This captain later worked for a different Middle Eastern airline and, by chance, Harry once flew with him as a passenger. He could not help but notice that soldiers, armed with automatic weapons, provided cabin security.

"Yes," the captain said when Harry mentioned the guards, "and they can be a problem."

He went on to relate an airborne incident involving a difficult passenger.

"One of these guards actually asked me for permission to shoot the passenger. 'Captain,' he said, 'I want to shoot this man and I need your permission.' He had his finger on the trigger, ready to shoot. Thank God, I managed to talk him out of it." Flying for Saudia had its problems, thought Harry, but shooting passengers was not one of them.

A Belgian captain had an unusual experience when he was scheduled for a base check with a young Saudi captain. A base check followed the cockpit trainer and the simulator. It was a session in the landing pattern making touch-and-go landings. After the cockpit trainer and the simulator, the company wanted to be sure a pilot could fly a real airplane. The Belgian had not even gotten strapped in when the first question came. It was a "windshield wiper" question, one whose answer was insignificant; but not to the Saudi.

"Don't bother to strap yourself in," he said acidly after the Belgian could not answer the question, "you have just failed your check flight."

The Belgian was incredulous. Failed? For not knowing the answer to one stupid question?

The Saudi brought the Belgian before their Equipment Manager and explained why he had failed him. Even the manager could see that the check captain's decision was absurd. He overruled him in a way the Belgian described as a father talking to his child. He scheduled the flight with a different captain, and the Belgian went through without a problem. He had spent the entire night before the flight rounding up "windshield wiper" questions from other pilots, but he was not asked any.

He talked with an English first officer who had quit right in the middle of a simulator session. The Saudi training captain overloaded him with minor problems and technical questions while he was trying to land the airplane with a failed engine. This had gone on for two hours and finally the first officer had enough. He told the training captain to stop the simulator.

"I was so pissed off," he said, still angry just talking about it, "that I couldn't see straight. This had been going on for three days. I grabbed the takeoff data card and wrote my resignation right on the back of it. 'I hereby quit,' I wrote. They tried to stop me from leaving the sim but, by then, my mind was made up. Enough is enough."

The takeoff data card is a circular card that fits onto the radar screen. On it is written all the data for a takeoff under conditions existing at the time of takeoff. The back is blank, but not this time.

Every evening, it seemed, there was news of another "termination." Eventually, Harry found the Follies too depressing and went only now and then, just for some company. All those horror stories did not do much for his peace of mind. Instead, he worked out in the fitness room or swam in the hotel pool. He did not miss hearing the stories.

86
CYA

Harry's ground school course began five days after his arrival. One of his classmates was George Bingham, the Air Force pilot he had met riding in from the airport. George was big and burly with frizzy hair that was not quite curly. He seemed to know all there was to know about the 707, every little nut and bolt. George was from California, where life was free and good, so he had a harder time than most in adjusting to Saudi ways.

"I don't think I'm going to fit in here," he told Harry, more than once.

He and Harry had quickly become fast friends. The class was small, four captains and one flight engineer. The flight engineer was Sudanese and he was, of course, a Muslim. He was tall, thin, very black and, Harry had to admit, very ugly. Until he smiled. Then, his whole face changed from ugly to friendly, as if a switch had been clicked.

During breaks, Harry spoke with him, once about religion, taking care not to sound intrusive. What about having four wives, Harry had asked. "How many wives do you have?"

The engineer smiled indulgently, as though he was answering a stupid question from a child.

"Yes, I can have four," he said, "but I cannot afford it. Not many can, so, for most, one is enough."

Sometimes, thought Harry, one is more than enough. They talked about the Koran and Harry was surprised to learn that people from the Bible were also found in the Koran. There must be a message there, Harry thought, but he was damned if he could figure out what it was.

One of the other two captains was German, the other was Lebanese. The purpose of the course was to review the B707 airplane and to learn the checklists and procedures Saudia used in operating them. The instructor was a Pakistani named Billy. He was short, thin, bald, and wore thick glasses. His accent was pure Pakistani with the singsong characteristic of that accent. His head nodded, not up and down as he spoke, but from side to side.

At the start of their first class of the first day, without saying a word, Billy wrote on the blackboard, with long strokes of his chalk, the letters "CYA." Then he stepped back, turned around and said in a somber tone, "Gentlemen, the most important words you will learn here are these: Cover Your Ass."

Harry and George exchanged glances. The message was clear but it was surprising to receive it in such a direct way.

"Never, ever, do anything here unless someone has ordered it. If you have an engine failure at V1, call flight operations for instructions before you do anything. That's how it is here, gentlemen. Remember it."

V1 is the pre-calculated takeoff speed that is sometimes called the decision speed. If an engine fails before reaching it, there is enough runway ahead to stop the airplane safely. If the engine failure happens after V1, the airplane has enough speed to become airborne and climb out safely on three engines, avoiding ground obstacles in its path. If the engine failure happens right at V1 speed, the pilot can elect to stop or to continue the takeoff. After passing V1 speed, the airplane is committed to the takeoff. That speed is the critical point in the takeoff. Calling flight ops then would, of course, be absurd but Billy's point was well taken: watch your back.

Engine failure at V1 was practiced regularly in the simulator but it almost never happened in real life. Harry knew of only one such case, and as Murphy usually works, it happened not only at V1, but at the worst possible V1. It was in Jeddah and Harry had some months later talked about it with the captain, who was Australian. It was a B747 departing from Jeddah on a hot night. Because the airplane was bound for New York, it had a full load of both fuel and passengers.

"The engine quit," he said, "precisely at V1, and I mean precisely. I decided to continue the takeoff."

Some checklists must be memorized to save precious seconds in emergencies. An engine failure was one of those. The engine failure is announced, and then the captain calls out the actions to be taken, step-by-step. The actions include shutting down the failed engine. It is essential that no action be taken without the command of the captain.

"The bloody engineer panicked," said the captain, his voice rising and his face flush with anger, "and on his own, without one word from me, he shut down the engine. *The wrong bloody engine!* " He became excited just talking about it.

"*Jesus!*" was all Harry could think of to say.

A direr situation could hardly be imagined. The airplane was skimming the ground, very heavy, with low airspeed, and flying on two engines instead of four. Theoretically, the airplane should have crashed. The captain raised the gear immediately and kept the airplane low, trying to gain a few knots of airspeed. At the same time, he ordered dumping fuel to lower the airplane's weight. As soon as he could, he climbed a few hundred feet, came back to the airport, and somehow managed to land the airplane. Since he had not yet completed dumping fuel, the airplane landed above the maximum allowed landing weight, and a hard landing resulted. He deserved a medal.

Instead, Saudi Arabian Airlines placed a letter of reprimand in his file for the overweight landing.

"And would you goddamn believe it," the captain sputtered, "the flight engineer got bloody nothing, not even a bloody slap on his bloody wrist."

The flight engineer was, of course, a Saudi.

87
BARROUM

One night, on one of his occasional visits to the Follies, Harry fell into conversation with an American first officer who had an interesting story to tell. Bill Ernie had completed his training and was flying the line. Flying with a Saudi captain named Barroum and taxiing at the Riyadh airport, the captain became confused and tried to taxi down a service road. Bill warned him several times, almost shouting in the end.

"Damn," he said, "there was just no way to get through there and I told him -- many times -- and louder and louder. But sure as hell, he put a wing tip through the nose of a Tri-Star parked there on the ramp. I was screaming at him."

There was an investigation into this incident and Barroum was demoted to first officer. Bill was given an official letter of reprimand, despite all he had done to try to prevent it. As far as Harry would know, Barroum was the only Saudi ever disciplined by the company. And their transgressions were famous. Six Saudi captains, Harry was told, were restricted by the FAA from flying to New York because of their near disasters there. Ex-pats, on the other hand, were often "terminated" for minor mistakes. The seat belt sign was an example.

By Harry's own unofficial count, some forty-five captains with experience comparable to his own were fired during the few months he lived in the Sheraton. Almost all of these came during the line-training phase. They had gotten through the hard part; learning the airplane, which, for many, was an airplane new to them, the simulator flights, and the check flights needed to qualify to fly the airplane. All that was behind them. Line training was supposed to be route familiarization. Unfortunately, many Saudi training pilots used these flights as opportunities to demean the foreign pilots. A way to do that could always be found. It was all about superiority complex, thought Harry.

Harry would later fly often with Barroum. He was what Harry called a non-Arab Arab. He looked like one and he talked like one, but he certainly did not behave like one. Ostentatious, he continued to wear his captain's shoulder boards while flying in the right seat. Harry had no problem with that, or with the solid gold Rolex he wore; but he did not like the gold bars on his shoulder boards being made of real gold and the star made with gems of some kind.

Many Saudis carried what were known to ex-pats as "worry beads." They resembled a rosary and they were frequently worked with their fingers. Harry was never sure whether they prayed while their fingers went around and around the beads, or simply used them like chewing gum. Barroum's beads were made with diamonds. Harry would later have some interesting experiences with Barroum while flying the line.

88
JEDDAH AND ISLAM

During the few weeks of ground school, Harry and George toured by foot the neighborhood around the hotel. Every evening, they went for a stroll, then ate dinner at one of several restaurants they had discovered. These were local places and usually they were the only non-Arabs there. Along with the Saudis, Jeddah was home to Arabs from around the Arab world. The Saudis themselves would take only managerial positions. "Oh, we could never do manual labor," one of them would later tell Harry. Jobs involving such work were given to Arabs from abroad. Some went to non-Arabs from places such as the Philippines and Thailand.

Harry had been cautioned against discussing religion with the Saudis, so he never brought it up; but and now and then the subject arose and he was curious. From different conversations, he learned much about Islam. The Prophet Mohammed was born in Mecca in 570 AD. At about age 40, he went off into the desert to meditate, saying he had revelations from God. These were written down with great care by his followers because Mohammed himself was unable to read or write. These revelations became the Koran.

The religion has three elements. The heart is the Koran. Second is the Sunna, a record of Mohammed's words and deeds. These two elements were incorporated into a body of law known as Sharia. The third element of Islam is the Hadith. This is a written record of the Prophet's pronouncements.

Combining these three elements, Islam incorporates laws and rules of social activity into a way of life. As such, it is much more than a religion. It controls all aspects of everyday behavior, such as how often to pray and how to wash after having sexual intercourse. He had noticed a variety of letters in the newspaper asking for guidance on such questions as whether using shaving lotion constitutes a violation of the rules of fasting. It even became part of their airways communications. Harry would often hear a Saudi pilot end an in-flight position report, including the estimated arrival time over the next position, with the words "Insha Allah": If God wills. Allah, not the pilot, was in control. The lines between religion, government, and social behavior are blurred into one system.

In Saudi Arabia, the Committee for the Protection of Virtue and the Prevention of Vice sets the rules of religion and morals. They are enforced by a religious police organization called the Matawain. This unit, in effect, controls the people's morality. It could, for example, arrest those who broke the fast during Ramadan. Punishment was severe. Non-Muslims are forbidden from eating or drinking in the presence of a fasting Muslim. Theoretically, they might be flogged with a camel whip or be subject to other punishment. Harry had never talked with anyone with direct knowledge of such treatment, but you never knew. It was judicious to be careful. The Koran allowed non-fasting during Ramadan for those traveling or working, provided they made it up another day; but Harry never saw this.

The Matawain is an important and powerful part of the political support for the royal family and, in return, receives strong support from the government. There is not much freedom from the religious police, but many prefer that to what they see as the decadence of the west.

In the beginning, Islam was an Arab religion. Successors to Mohammed were chosen by religious leaders and were known as caliphs. Under these men, Islam spread outward from the Arabian Peninsula, from southern Spain to Persia, which is now Iran, in the east. It would eventually form a swath from the Atlantic Ocean, across North Africa, through the Middle East, India and Indonesia and as far as the Philippines

In 661AD, the ruler of Syria challenged the fourth caliph, Ali. Ali was assassinated in the ensuing struggle. The Muslims of Arabia continued to follow Mohammed and are known as Sunni Muslims. The Persians and others split into a different sect that followed Ali. These were Shiites. The Sunnis consider themselves to be the true believers and, as such, superior to other Muslims.

There is another reason the Saudis think they are better than other Muslims; they are the official Custodians of the Two Holy Places. These are the cities of Mecca and Medina, two of the three holiest places in Islam. The third is in Jerusalem, where Muslims believe Mohammed was transported in a vision. A winged horse stood there to transport him to heaven. On this site now stands the mosque al-Aqsa. Nearby is the Wailing Wall, where Jews come from around the world to pray. This is one source of the conflict between Muslims and Jews. There are others.

When the Sudanese flight engineer mentioned the winged horse carrying Mohammed to heaven, Harry raised an eyebrow in question.

"Yes," the engineer said, "flying to heaven. Just like your Jesus."

Harry had never thought of it in that way and had no answer.

Non-Muslims are forbidden to enter either Mecca or Medina. A mosque in Medina holds the tomb of Mohammed. Mecca is his birthplace and it also holds the Kaaba, an enormous man-made stone structure at the heart of Islam.

The present Kaaba, built around the time of Mohammed, is thought to be the tenth such structure. According to doctrine, the first was built by angels at the dawn of earth, the second by Adam, the third by Adam's son, and the fourth by Abraham who is believed to be the father of all Muslims. Embedded in one corner of the Kaaba is the sacred Black Stone that is an object of veneration. Its origin is said to be a meteorite sent from heaven by Abraham.

Christians, Muslims, and Jews recognize Abraham. The dispute between Muslims and Jews stems from the differences in the promise made by God to his descendants. The seeds of this ancient dispute were sown by the different interpretations of the way God's word was passed down from Abraham's children. To Muslims, the covenant passed down by God was with Ishmael; to Jews, it was with Isaac.

It was easy to tell the difference between Sunnis and Shiites. Almost all of the Saudis were of the Sunni sect. They wore thobes; white, loose-fitting ground length robes, and a headdress of white cloth held in place by a black band known to ex-pats as a fan belt. The Shiites wore the red-and-white checkered headscarf such as that worn by Yasser Arafat. The Arabs from outside of Saudi Arabia wore a variety of clothes depending on their origin. None was ready for the cover of *Gentlemen's Quarterly*.

Harry remembered a conversation with the Sudanese flight engineer. Harry had been surprised to learn that leading persons in the Bible were also present in the Koran. The engineer had later mentioned a pronouncement from the angel Gabriel.

"Gabriel?" queried Harry. "Gabriel is in the Koran?"

The engineer smiled indulgently. "Yes, of course. And Jesus, too. He was a prophet, not the Son of God. The Christians have got that wrong."

Harry did not respond, but thought, "Could they both be wrong?" Why, he wondered, were persons from Biblical times also prominent in the Koran? Could the Bible have influenced Mohammed? Unless you believed in divine revelation, Mohammed had to have knowledge of the teachings of both Jews and Christians. There are, he learned, some similarities between the tenets of Muslims and Jews.

Sunnis were not to be seen in the local restaurants near the hotel. The fare was plain, usually chicken in one form or another. Eggs cooked in various ways were also common.

"How could they ever survive without chickens?" George asked one evening as they ordered yet another chicken dish for dinner.

Vegetables were abundant. Harry especially enjoyed eating a dish called homus. It was crushed garbanzo beans with olive oil and pine nuts on top. All food was served with Arabic bread. It was round, flat, soft, and tasted good with everything. When wrapped around meat carved from a large vertical cylinder of grilled lamb, beef, or chicken, it was called a schwarma. They were sold from sidewalk cafes, and Harry ate them often.

By then, they had met several Saudis in management and a few of the line pilots. They had spent a few minutes drinking tea with their Chief Pilot, who held the title of Equipment Manager. There was one for each fleet of aircraft. His name was Mustapha, and he seemed to have a permanent scowl fixed on his face. He was short and wide and if he had been just a little thicker, he would have resembled a cube. Like most Saudis, he wore a moustache. He looked mean but, Harry told himself hopefully, appearances can be deceiving.

Harry and George discussed Mustapha over a chicken dinner that night. "So what do you think?" George asked.

"About what?" he asked back.

"Mustapha. These Saudis. What do you think? If you could describe them in one word, what would it be?" Harry pondered for a long moment.

"Difficult," he said. "Very difficult."

George smiled. "That's two words, three if you count one of them twice."

"Okay," said Harry, "there's no extra charge for that. What do you think?"

George was drinking a glass of non-alcoholic Schlitz beer. He put down his glass, looked serious, and said, "I couldn't have put it better myself. What have we gotten ourselves into?"

It took several days of walking through the streets near the hotel before either Harry or George realized that something was missing - - women. They never saw any. Harry knew that Arab countries were male-dominant, but no women on the streets? He knew they were not allowed to drive cars, but not allowed to leave home? They did see a few one evening when they visited the cornishe, a promenade along the shore of the Red Sea. It happened to be a Thursday evening and, for the Muslims, it was the beginning of their weekend. They could not be absolutely sure they were looking at women because they were wrapped from head to toe in black chadors and they wore a scarf around their heads that also covered their faces. Harry gave them the benefit of the doubt and assumed there were women beneath all that black cloth.

One woman was seen in the sea, chador and all. This daring lady was sitting on a wooden chair in knee-deep water, enjoying the gentle surf as it drenched her chador. The other women were with families, enjoying the sunset while resting on carpets and blankets, drinking tea and eating sweets. Some of those carpets were handmade and looked to Harry, an amateur carpet expert, to be expensive. The people seemed friendly. Some of them smiled and waved, and a few offered food.

"You know," Harry remarked, as they walked along the sea, "when you think about it, we've seen almost no women anywhere. Even in the Saudia offices, all the clerks and secretaries are men, Pakistanis usually. The shops, the restaurants; they are all staffed by men. What do the women do all day?"

George shrugged. "Damned if I know, but it sounds to me like a pretty good deal." He laughed. "Did I really say that?" he asked. "Would I want my wife to stay home all day, every day? Is there any way I could make her do it? Hell, no. But here, they probably don't know any better."

89
THE LITTLE PRINCE

After completing his training and while flying the line, Harry would have occasional brief conversations about the role of women in Saudi Arabia. In a diplomatic way, he asked why their women were treated differently than men. For their own protection, was the answer. And if they did not want to be protected, what about their right to be free? They are not qualified to decide that, was the usual response.

In an enlightening conversation with a Saudi first officer named Faisal, Harry heard an interesting side of life in The Kingdom. Faisal wanted to marry an Egyptian girl, but the government discouraged marriage to foreigners. He had persisted for an entire year and had gotten nowhere. Allah stepped in when Faisal attended the opening of an uncle's new business. There were some four-thousand princes in Saudi Arabia and one was there that night. In conversation with the prince, Faisal had mentioned his bureaucratic impasse. The prince was interested. Would you like me to help, he asked. If you would be so kind, Faisal answered. The prince wrote down a telephone number and handed it to Faisal, telling him to call in the morning. He did and happily heard that his request was now approved. The prince, Faisal told Harry, was twelve years old. Wow, thought Harry, that is some kind of influence, especially for a twelve-year-old.

Another first officer told Harry about his engagement. His aunt arranged a meeting with a cousin. They met and drank tea for one hour under the close supervision of the aunt. He was then asked whether he agreed to marry the girl, or, as he put it, did he give a green light or a red one. He liked the girl and agreed to the marriage. They spoke on the telephone many times after that meeting, but he did not see her again until the day of their wedding, one year later. It would never sell in Milwaukee, Harry thought.

Another told Harry that his wife would allow sexual intercourse only when both were fully-clothed. Difficult, thought Harry, but not impossible. Harry wondered why anyone would talk about such an intimate part of his life. He decided that the first officer had to tell someone, and Harry happened to be sitting right there next to him. He never pressed for such information, and he tried his best to avoid it; but it came out anyway. He got along well with the Saudis and perhaps that was the reason. And maybe they had no one else to talk to.

Harry would fly his final line check with a handsome young Saudi captain who qualified as a non-Arab Arab. He had attended a university in the U.S. and he had very much enjoyed living there. He did not have a moustache, and that was unusual. Harry hoped that was a good sign. The flight was to Casablanca, where they spent three days. During breakfast one morning with the captain, the subject of marriage came up.

"Ah," he said, "how I envy you westerners your freedom."

Unsure what he meant, Harry had asked him to explain.

"I am twenty-eight," he said, "and I should have married long ago. Always, there is pressure from my family to marry, and within one year, or perhaps two, I will marry a woman they will choose for me. How I would like to be free to choose my own wife; but in Saudi Arabia, that is not possible. So I envy your freedom."

He said this in a wistful, longing way that made Harry feel somewhat sorry for him. For most Saudis, it was normal to have a wife chosen for him, but not for this one.

90
AMMAN

With George's help, Harry sailed through the ground school. Next on the program were sessions in the cockpit procedures trainer, a mock-up of the cockpit that was used for very basic training, such as learning procedures and checklists. It was known as the CPT. Then the group was sent off to Amman, where Saudia used the simulators of Alia, the Jordanian airline. The simulator looked like a real airplane cockpit. Unlike the CPT, everything worked as it did in the airplane. The sim actually moved, and the feel of the flight controls was authentic. It had graphics, too, and approaches could be flown to any of dozens of airports in its data bank. The visual presentation of the selected airport looked just like the real one, including prominent buildings and local automobile traffic. Weather conditions could be set as desired, from clear weather to fog with zero visibility. Even turbulence could be added to the program. It was so realistic that the crew actually felt the wheels bump over the cracks in the taxiways during taxi. It was about ninety per cent of the real thing. It was, in many ways, better for training than the airplane itself. Along with selective weather conditions, a range of problems could be presented for the crews to deal with. Exercises could be stopped and started by flicking a switch. It was a superb training device at a fraction of the cost of using an airplane.

Harry and George flew together, one as first officer and the other as captain. There were four sessions of four hours each, with the pilots exchanging seats midway through each session. It was the pilot in the left seat who was undergoing the training, and the final two hours was a check "flight." They worked well together and that can be important. If Harry forgot to call for a checklist when appropriate, for example, George might ask "Ready for the engine fire checklist?" Both flew well, and the instructor, a Dutchman, seemed pleased with their work. They had spent their evenings reviewing checklists and various procedures and it had shown in their performances.

The crew had not much time to explore Amman but from what little Harry saw, the city seemed very different from Jeddah. Women were seen in the streets with uncovered faces. The Jordanians were friendlier, more open. The city was not flat, like Jeddah, but had hills within it and mountains could be seen in the distance. He would return to Amman for future simulator sessions and then he would bring Irene. Together, they would see more of the country, including the famous Petra, with its ancient caves carved into the red cliffs of southern Jordan.

91
JEDDAH UP CLOSE

After the first weeks in the Sheraton, Harry and George expanded their investigation of Jeddah. They visited the gold souk, a warren of tiny shops that dealt only in gold in all its various forms. Here, there were Saudi women buying gold, so they heard, as insurance against divorce. That was easily done and all that was needed was for the husband to say, three times, "I divorce you." Gold jewelry was sold by weight alone and the design did not matter. The business there, as everywhere they had been, was done only in cash. When Harry bought a new car after completing his training, he paid cash, as did all other car buyers. Checks and credit cards did not exist in the Jeddah economy. Money was kept openly in boxes and drawers, usually in plain sight. There was no fear of theft because the penalties were severe. For example, a thief lost his hand if caught a third time, so not many took the risk. They saw a Saudi a businessman receiving a large bundle of money that he stuffed openly into a large briefcase bulging with more cash. No one took any notice.

Paydays neared as the moon grew full. They took place on the day of the full moon. The paychecks were handed out at flight operations. Most of these checks were, that same night, taken to a local moneychanger near Saudi City. Al Radji looked like a small "mom-and-pop" shop but without the "mom." It was a small, bare room staffed by Pakistani men and, on payday, it was the most popular place in town. Some checks were changed into cash using machines that counted banknotes in a blur. Most of the money was sent around the world from that nondescript, one-room financial center. Harry was often part of the hectic crowd there, and he marveled at how efficiently this seemingly haphazard system worked. As far as he knew, the money always reached its destination; but he wondered how it got there. The money transfers had to overcome the bedlam that reigned there every payday. Well, he told himself, somehow it works. It worked despite the crowds, the confusion, and the frequent arguments. Some of the disagreements were with clerks, but a few were with Saudis pushing themselves to the head of the queue.

The mayor of Jeddah, they were told, had used his substantial influence to persuade foreign contractors to "donate" monuments across the city. Many of these were placed in the centers of the city's numerous traffic circles. They saw many, and some were impressive. But the Saudis, more used to driving

395

camels than cars, would now and then try to drive across a traffic circle, instead of going around it. They saw one or two cars impaled on them.

"Well," said Harry, "they probably thought that if a camel can do it, so can a car."

Camels were not far in their past. They were often seen in the outskirts of the city. Only twenty years before, humans were bought and sold in the market places of Jeddah. Saudi Arabia had rushed headlong into the twentieth century before it was ready. The catalyst was oil and the mountains of money it generated.

The traffic in Jeddah was catastrophic. They saw accidents every day, many serious. The Saudis bought, in large numbers, new Mercedes and BMWs but they did not seem to know much about driving them. One evening, they saw a Saudi replacing a wheel unaware that he had broken his axle. He thought he had a flat tire. He had broken his axle by driving up one of the high curbstones that were supposed to prevent cars from swerving off the road and onto the sidewalk. Some cars were abandoned when a malfunction occurred. It was easier to buy a new one than to rescue one that had broken down. And, indeed, they did spot some apparently abandoned cars as they went about the city. An almost-new Mercedes, they were told, had been abandoned simply because it ran out of gas.

One evening, leaving a restaurant, they heard the sound of screeching brakes emanating from a parallel street. Looking between two buildings, they saw an airborne car fly across that space, then heard it crash with the awful sound of tearing metal. How a car could become airborne for some twenty or thirty feet was a question they could not answer, even using their imaginations.

One day, driving through central Jeddah with a friend, Harry witnessed a vehicular argument between two cars just ahead. One was a new, gleaming white BMW driven by a Saudi wearing a thobe. The other was what the British call a banger: a battered and crumpled old car driven by a non-Saudi Arab. The BMW was annoying the banger by blasting its horn and coming dangerously close in an effort to pass where there was no space to pass. Finally, the banger had enough. As the BMW drew alongside, the banger turned hard into it, broad-siding it with the entire length of the car. It bounced off, then careened back into it once more. The BMW quickly sped away, its side badly mangled.

Near the airport, and not far from the hotel was a group of apartment buildings that, though unoccupied, were famous. Harry counted them. There were eight buildings, each with ten floors. They were unoccupied because they had been built without separate elevators for women. No proper Saudi would live in such a building; so they just sat there and became a landmark. Gender separation was serious business. Even on the buses, the few women riders sat in the rear of the bus behind a partition. They entered and left by a separate door. Damn, thought Harry when he heard about it. That gives new meaning to riding in the back of the bus.

92
SAUDI CITY

They visited Saudi City several times. Harry knew one or two pilots there, as did George. On their first visit, they had spent a pleasant few hours at the apartment of George's friend, an ex-Air Force pilot named Dan Grogan. It was a two-bedroom apartment and its basics were fine. As Dan described life in Saudi City, he brought out a bottle of his "best vintage" homemade wine. The bottle had once contained the grape juice used to make the wine, and now it held the finished product.

"We don't mark the year," he said as he poured, "only the month. I made this one four months ago, so you're drinking the house's finest. This batch tastes almost like real wine; but you never know how it'll turn out. Sometimes you have to cut it with juice or soda, sometimes you just have to pour it down the drain. Well, okay, welcome to Saudi City," he said as he raised his glass.

Harry took a tentative taste. "Not bad," he said as he put down his glass. "You'll have to give me the recipe."

Dan, short and wiry with a crew cut and bright blue eyes, smiled affably and nodded. "The house accepts your compliment, but no complaints about any hangovers, please. This stuff bites back."

It was easy to make, he told them. Add water to yeast in a glass, let it ferment overnight, then put it in a container with grape juice, sugar, and water.

"We use plastic five-gallon jerry cans. It starts to bubble after a few days and you need to be sure to use a check valve cap to let the pressure out. Otherwise, the stuff will explode. That actually happened to me on my first try because no one told me about that check valve. I came home one night to find fermented grape juice all over the walls and ceiling of my bathroom."

Almost everyone made wine, he told them, and a few made beer. A very few made pure alcohol, known as sidiki, or sid. Using various additives, it could be made to taste exactly like Scotch, bourbon or whatever else was fancied; but that was asking for trouble.

He talked about another way to make wine, but said, "I don't recommend it." Howard Weissman was the winemaker. He was from New York, and he was Jewish. No one knew how he had managed to penetrate Saudi Arabian Airlines. He was something of a legend, Dan told them, because he drove around in a jeep without a windshield in what was probably the only car in

Saudi City without air conditioning. In midsummer the heat and humidity were such that windshield wipers were sometimes needed on clear days.

That was because the water in the outside air condensed as it struck the cold windshield. Howard did not have this problem.

But he did have a back problem, so he flew with a back pad. He carried the pad in a plastic bag bearing the logo of El Cortez, a large department store in Madrid. You could always make out Howard from a distance, Dan said, because he always had that plastic bag tucked under his arm. He was also famous for his shirts. Unmarried, he did his own laundry, but never ironed his uniform shirts. That was another way to identify Howard from a distance: wrinkled shirts. Howard had his own way to make wine, or so the legend went. Red wine or white, he asked his guests before dinner one night. He then poured red or white grape juice into glasses, added sugar and yeast, stirred vigorously for a minute or two, then served the concoction. The reviews for Howard's instant wine were not favorable.

The Saudis knew about the wine and beer, but they overlooked it as long as it was done with discretion. But sidiki was another story. That was not tolerated and although fortunes were made from selling sidiki, it was certainly not worth the risk, which was jail.

"You do not want to go to jail here," Dan said, "you might never be heard from again."

He related an incident involving a friend who had unknowingly parked illegally, and left his friend in the car while he went into a shop for a few minutes. When he returned, his car and his passenger were no longer there. The police had removed the car and taken his friend to jail. The missing friend was a first officer with Saudia and it took three days just to find him, then another few days to get him out.

"I won't tell you all the horror stories he talked about," said Dan as he poured more wine, "but believe me, you do not want to go there. Keep your nose clean around here."

Dan was married but had left his wife and family behind, as many did. Living alone, he did not bother to make his apartment attractive. The ceiling bulbs were bare, newspapers were pasted over the windows, and there was nothing hung on any wall. It looked more like a jail cell than an apartment, thought Harry, as he glanced around. But with a little effort, it could be a cozy place. Dan noticed Harry examining his apartment.

"I know, I know. This place looks like a monastery; but I figured why go to all that trouble to fix it up? Here, you just never know when your number is up, especially in the beginning, so I still buy my eggs two at a time. And I keep my bags packed."

"Come on," said George, "it can't be that bad."

Dan frowned. "It can," he said, "if you're not lucky. By that, I mean if you cross the wrong Saudi, you can pack your bags. There are some good ones, some who've lived abroad and been around; but most see life differently than we do. For them, up is down and black is white. That sounds hard to believe, but it's not far from the mark. There are two sets of rules, one for them and one for us."

He told them of a Norwegian friend who was a training captain in the Tri-Star simulator. Haakon Hellner had been told not to fail any Saudi pilot.

"Told how?" Harry asked.

"Just like that," Dan said. "You will not fail any Saudi pilot."

Harry made a soft whistle as he exhaled. "Jesus!" was all he could say.

"The double standard is normal here, so you better get used to it now."

"You mean let the horseshit bounce off?" Harry asked, recalling the advice he had been given in the Park Lane Hotel.

Dan smiled. "That's exactly what I mean. If you take all the horseshit seriously, you won't last long here. Some guys become alcoholic and others get seriously depressed. Sometimes both. I know a few who start drinking early in the morning and don't stop; but there are some things to enjoy here, unbelievable as that might sound right now."

"Like what?" asked George. "I have yet to hear anything positive about this place."

Dan opened another bottle of his finest. The bottles had a hinged top and they were, he said, perfect for making wine. "Life here in the ghetto is great, socially. There are some fine folks here and the ties between us are strong, even with people we hardly know. We're all in this together. Women are not allowed to drive here, so if a guy is off on a trip and his wife needs a ride, there will be plenty of volunteers. There're some strong bonds here.

"The social life is basically dinner parties and we almost never leave the reservation unless we have to. Like going to work. Just up the coast is a place called the Cabin, where we often go to spend a day windsurfing and swimming. There's a reef a hundred yards or so offshore where the bottom drops sharply down about thirty feet. You can spend hours out there paddling around with flippers and a snorkel, looking at the marine life. I had never seen anything like that and it's really something. We get a group together, pack a lunch and a few bottles of wine, and off we go. We rent the cabin there. Well, we call it a cabin but, as a Belgian friend says, 'Here we call it a seaside cabin. In Belgium, we would use it to keep the pigs in.' Definitely not Miami Beach, but at least there's shade and running water. And a toilet. I've had some great times out there. We even roasted marshmallows one night. We had a great Christmas Eve party there last Christmas. We roasted chestnuts from I don't know where, and we sang Christmas carols, believe it or not. One of the best Christmases I ever had," he said with a laugh. "Imagine that. A great Christmas right here in the middle of all these Arabs!"

Dan told another Christmas story, one that took place the day before the Christmas beach party. All ex-pats were given a block of six days off each month. They were also given free travel on Saudia flights, provided they traveled in uniform; but it wasn't easy. Papers had to be signed and clerks had to be stroked. A London-bound Tri-Star was only half full when a clutch of British ex-pats boarded for their trip home for Christmas. After the doors were closed, the forward door re-opened and a Saudi in a thobe appeared and ordered all ex-pats to leave the airplane. There was an embargo on crew travel, he said. The captain, a Saudi, refused to intervene, despite written travel authorizations signed by the General Manager of Flight Operations.

One of the Brits was a crusty old flight engineer and, as he passed the Saudi grinch who was stealing his Christmas, he looked straight into his eyes and said, "You are an asshole." The next morning, which was Christmas Eve morning, the engineer was ordered to report to his boss's office. There, he was asked if had said those words. He had, he confirmed. He was then informed that his off-days were cancelled for the next six months. His unspoken answer was to reach across the desk separating them, tear from a pad a sheet of paper, and write his resignation. Without speaking another word, he arose, left the office, and within three days, was back home in England and looking for a job.

Another bottle of "grape juice" appeared and Dan, after searching his cupboards, found enough food to make tuna salad sandwiches. Apparently he had already eaten his two-egg supply and tuna was all he could find.

"Dan," said Harry after testing the new bottle, "this one is even better than the last one. My compliments to the winemaker. Where can I put in my order?"

Dan nodded and grinned. "It's pure luck" he said, "but thanks. It wouldn't taste so good next to the real stuff; but it's for sure better than nothing."

It was a pleasant afternoon and informative, too. Harry and George learned a good deal about life in Saudi City and when Harry put it all together, he decided that he and Irene could manage to build a decent life there. That night he called Irene and he told her what he had found that day.

"Well," she said after a pause, "it does not sound like the center of Antwerp, but I think we can make it work. What about your training?"

He had told her some of the Five O'clock Follies horror stories and she was concerned.

"If it was only the flying, I would not be worried. But some of these Saudis sound like first-class jerks." That was an American word Irene liked to use. "It's perfect for some people," she once said.

"So far, so good," he answered. "I still have my line training ahead, and they seem to lose a few there. I'll do my best, but I think you ought to come down here and have a look at all this. You might decide this place won't work for you. How is our son, by the way?" Harry had already decided that their child would be a boy.

There was another pause. "Yes, I would like to come and see for myself. See what you can do. And our son is fine. So far, no problems for me. Yes, the more I think about it, the more I think I must come. And the sooner, the better."

Harry agreed to start the paperwork the next day. That would not be easy. The Saudis liked paperwork.

Harry had, of course, heard much about life in Saudi City. Many views were conflicted; so he had been unsure what to expect and he had many questions. He was grateful to Dan Grogan for providing some answers. Its basics looked fine to Harry. It was about a mile-and-a half square, surrounded by a high wall, and housed about eight thousand people. Most were American or European, but many were from other countries. There was lush greenery throughout, growing right there in the desert. Water can produce miracles, even in deserts. The accommodations varied substantially, so there was strong competition for those that were larger and more attractive. Harry and George had been placed on a waiting list and now they had an idea of what kind of quarters they could expect.

The houses and apartments were categorized according to the number of bedrooms, which, of course, depended upon the size of the family. Much subterfuge took place when dependents were invented on paper to justify a larger house. Honest people became liars and forgers so that they could qualify for an accommodation that was more desirable. Men were mindful of their wives and families who were not there to view them when the quarters were assigned. Harry and George talked with the man in charge, an American, and he told them of the conniving lengths some would go to so they could get the quarters they wanted. Fake documents proving the existence of wives and children, he said, were not uncommon. Only wives qualified for visas, so some girlfriends, using forged wedding certificates, became wives on paper so they could come to Saudi Arabia. Harry, with Irene by his side, would one day undergo a nerve-wracking encounter with the American's Saudi superior when trying, honestly, to change their assigned quarters.

The complex was neat and clean, with many tennis courts and swimming pools. These seemed to be the focal points of the social life in Saudi City. Those who did not play tennis or enjoy the poolside life had little to do. Luckily, both Irene and Harry liked swimming and tennis. There was a small shopping mall that included an American-style donut shop. Harry was surprised to see a movie theater in the center of the city. He was surprised because he had not seen any cinemas anywhere in Jeddah. This one was an open-air theater and it had an artistic look about it. That was surprising, too; but the hope that one night soon, he might be viewing movies under the desert stars was punctured when he was told that, for legal reasons the theater had never opened. It had something to do with a law preventing the gathering of crowds. Well, thought Harry, it might not show films, but at least it looks good. From first glance, life in Saudi City looked more promising than Harry had expected. It was life outside the city, such as going to work, that looked to be troublesome.

93
COINCIDENCES

A coincidence is hard to define, but you know when one happens. Two persons start out in different places at different times, follow different paths that might zig and zag by plan or by whim, and see those paths eventually cross at the same moment. If one of the persons had zigged instead of zagged at any point along the way, the coincidence would not have happened. There must be, Harry sometimes thought, many such non-coincidences.

The most extraordinary coincidence in Harry's life took place in the middle of the South China Sea. An officer from the plane guard destroyer would visit Harry's carrier, the USS Ranger, for the day. Would anyone like to spend a day on the destroyer? The mechanism for the transfer was already in place. That was a Bosun's Chair, which was a cage-like apparatus drawn from one ship to another on a line suspended between the two ships which were "flying" formation. Why not, thought Harry, and he volunteered to visit the destroyer. It was a fine day, and being hauled across the water between two ships cutting through the sea was exhilarating. Arriving at the destroyer, the chair was taken in hand by an officer and several crewmen. As they helped Harry out of his seat, Harry was astounded to see that the officer was a fraternity brother from his university days. Imagine, said Harry later, all the twists and turns each of our lives had to take for our paths to cross here in the South China Sea. That seemed more like an act of God than a coincidence.

At first, Harry had enjoyed being on board the destroyer. He was given a red carpet welcome, and having Tom show him around was, if not interesting, different. Then the weather began to change and the destroyer began to move. The Ranger almost never moved and, when she did, it was barely noticeable, just enough to remind you that you were at sea. The destroyer never stopped moving. Never stable, she pitched and rolled continuously. As the sea became heavier, the small ship moved in ways that made Harry wonder if she would stay upright. He spent a few minutes on the bridge with Tom, and by then, the inclinometer there showed a roll of forty-five degrees. To Harry, it seemed more like eighty-five degrees, with the sea so close he could reach out and put his hand in it. Solid green water crashed against the bridge as the bow plunged into the sea, coming back up with tons of seawater cascading from its bow. It was, in a way, frightening, and if not for Tom's calm demeanor, Harry might have thought the ship was in trouble.

In this sea, there was no way for Harry to return to the Ranger. He became nauseous and he regretted his visit to this small ship thrashing about in an awful sea. He was given a bunk on the main deck in the aft section of the ship. The space had a hatch open to the weather, but by now Harry was too seasick to close it properly. He removed his shoes, and tumbled into the bunk, too ill to even undress. He was reminded of the comment of a friend describing a hangover. At first, he had said, I was afraid I would die. Then I was afraid I wouldn't die. Harry felt like that now. The hatch came open and the sea water came in, thoroughly soaking his bunk. Several inches of seawater sloshed about the deck. The bunk was a foot or so above the deck with a space between the bunk and the bulkhead. When the ship rolled one way, the water flowed away from Harry. When it rolled back, it hit the bulkhead beneath his bunk, flew up and over Harry in his bunk. His shoes were thrown from one side to the other, making loud thumping sounds as they hit different parts of the space. Harry was soon drenched, but he was too miserable to care.

Harry spent the worst three days of his life on that destroyer. Unable to return to the Ranger, he caught up with her in Yokosuka, where both ships would spend a few days. Harry's spirits began to rise as soon as one foot touched solid ground. He made his way to the Ranger's berth, where the ship was just arriving. He boarded gratefully and found his way to his Ready Room. There, someone who knew Harry was an avid fan of the Milwaukee Braves, had written on the chalkboard in large letters: Harry Has Not Been This Sick Since The Braves Lost The World Series. Despite his washed-out feeling, he laughed out loud when he read it.

94
LARS

Meeting Lars Johnson at one of the Five O'clock Follies that Harry occasionally attended was just an ordinary coincidence. They had met in the early days of Trans Polar and became friends. They had not seen each other since Harry left Oslo for Brussels. Now their paths crossed again in the Sheraton Hotel in Jeddah, Saudi Arabia. Lars had already completed his training and was flying the line. He was living in Saudi City and he had stopped by to visit a friend. He met Harry instead. They embraced warmly, pleased to find each other. Of course, Harry had many questions for Lars and he asked them all, searching for some positive information to counterbalance all the negative news he had heard since his arrival.

"Don't hold your breath," was Lars' advice. "It gets better once you are on your own, but not much."

Lars was Swedish; tall and heavyset with an iron-gray crew cut and a moustache to match. Like all Scandinavians Harry had met, Lars was honest and straightforward. He had a pleasant demeanor and if he was not smiling, he seemed about to. His bright blue eyes seemed always amused. He loved to tell jokes and he did it well, with a special talent for affecting accents and adding expression to the characters in his stories. Harry loved to hear him tell them. Lars always said what was on his mind, and Harry asked how that worked in Saudia.

"Well," he said thoughtfully, as he gnawed his ever-present pipe, "there have been some problems. These Saudi guys see the world in a different way from us. For them, black is white and the other way, too. The problem is, they are always right, even when they are not right. It's not easy and you must give some ground even when you are right. But only so much. Then you must stand fast and sometimes that works."

Lars was not smiling when he related a recent experience that made Harry's skin crawl. Lars had been home in Sweden during one of the six-day breaks all ex-pats were given each month. He was scheduled for a thirty-day leave period following his break, but an absurd regulation required him to return to Jeddah before he started his leave. Then his father died and Lars sent a telex requesting that he be allowed to stay in Sweden for his father's funeral, and not return to Jeddah first. He was surprised and grateful when he received a reply authorizing him to start his leave in Sweden.

Returning to Jeddah after his leave, he was summoned by his equipment manager. Why had he not returned to begin his leave? The manager was a rude and arrogant young man about half Lars' age. He wanted to show who was boss; but Lars was ready. First, he showed the telex authorizing him to start his leave in Sweden. That was examined closely and dismissed contemptuously. The man who sent it was not authorized to do so, he said. Lars then produced a copy of his father's death certificate. The manager picked it up between thumb and forefinger, as if it carried the plague. He glanced at it briefly and dropped it disdainfully onto his desk.

"This is in Swedish. How do I know what is written here?"

Lars was ready for that, too. He'd had the document translated into English at his embassy. Outmaneuvered, the manager glowered and, without a word, waved Lars out of his office; but he was not yet finished with Lars and his dead father.

That night, Lars received a call from Crew Scheduling to inform him that he would, the next morning, fly an unscheduled route check with his manager. Lars considered his options. This check flight was "my manager's revenge," as he put it, and there was no way he would get through this check. He decided to become sick, something he had never before done; but his survival in the company was on the line. A doctor's confirmation was needed, but this was easily obtained with an "extra" payment. It was not discovered until later, but one of Saudia's doctors turned out to be a veterinarian. He could easily, for a "contribution," be persuaded to sign almost anything. Lars' incident faded away, probably because his manager's superior learned of it; but it spoke volumes. To use the death of a father to demean a captain and to demonstrate authority said much about the Saudi mentality.

Lars did smile, and widely, when he told Harry of an incident that took place in the flight operations parking area. Although there was ample parking space, the Saudis often parked helter-skelter near the entrance to avoid a long walk. This sometimes prevented other parked cars from moving. One Saudi made the mistake of blocking Lars' old car with his new Mercedes. Lars had just returned from a long all-night flight and was not in his usual pleasant mood. He backed slowly out of his space, placed his rear bumper squarely against the side of the Mercedes and pushed it sideways, carving a huge dent in its side as he did. He drove off "feeling damn good."

"Not even a Saudi has the right to block my car," said Lars with obvious delight, "and you can be sure he will not park in such a way again."

With a laugh, Harry agreed. "No, probably not."

He was not sure he would have done what Lars had done, but he, too, felt "damn good" that Lars had done it.

Harry had heard about Lars at the Five O'clock Follies. He had achieved celebrity throughout Saudia for two in-flight incidents. One was precipitated by a spilled cup of coffee. It had splashed across his lap, thoroughly dousing his shirt, his trousers "and," he said later, "even my underwear was soaking wet. I had to do something." So he had removed his shirt and trousers and hung them over the back of the navigator's seat to dry. But the cockpit door had been left unlocked, and a confused gray-haired woman, searching for the toilet, had blundered into the cockpit by mistake. She took one look at the captain sitting in his underwear and smoking a pipe, threw up her hands to block her view, and stammered, "Oh dear, this does not look like the ladies' room. Have I made a wrong turn?"

"Yes, madam," Lars calmly replied. "This is the men's room. Yours is that way," and he pointed back to the cabin with his pipe. "First turn on your right."

The cockpit door caught him another time. On his way to visit the cabin, he had stopped before the door to tuck his shirt into his trousers. To do that, he had unbuckled his belt and his trousers had slipped to the deck as he adjusted his shirt. At that moment a flight attendant opened the door to reveal to the entire first-class section their captain, standing with his pants down around his ankles. He casually lifted his pants around his neatly tucked shirt, buckled his belt, and entered the cabin. A woman in the first row applauded as he did.

"Nice legs, Captain," she said with a smile.

Lars was genuinely pleased to hear that Harry had found a "woman." That was how Swedes referred to a wife. He offered enthusiastic congratulations and asked when he would meet her in Jeddah.

"Funny you should mention that," said Harry, and he told Lars that Irene would come soon. He asked Lars about that. "How does it work?"

"It is complicated," Lars said, frowning, "so give yourself enough time." He told Harry how to start the paperwork, and added, "Good luck."

Irene needed a reason to visit Saudi Arabia, and a visa. Tourists were not invited. Irene would need an entry visa and only Harry could sign her application. Not only that, said Lars, but only Harry could sign her exit visa application. She could come and go only if Harry approved. That carried male-dominance to a new level.

Lars' wife, he told Harry, was a strong-willed Norwegian lady who "did not fit in here." On her first visit, he said, she had, on her arrival, run into a problem with the customs agent. For unknown reasons, but probably because he enjoyed harassing women, he refused to give back Inger's passport after he stamped it. After a long and useless discussion, she had finally had enough.

"You can send it to me in Saudi City," she said angrily, as she turned and strode purposefully towards the exit. The agent realized his mistake and thoughts of awful consequences must have quickly crossed his mind. He ran, actually ran, after Inger to hand over her passport and to apologize.

A similar incident had happened to the wife of Lars' friend, who was traveling with her child of about eight. When customs complications arose, which seemed endless, she told her daughter, in Swedish, to begin crying hysterically. After a few seconds of wailing, she and her daughter were instantly cleared. Saudi men were used to dealing with Saudi women who were compliant. They were unsure what to do with independent women such as Inger and the wife of Lars' friend. Harry tucked these stories into a corner of his mind. They might be useful one day.

Often, one coincidence led to another coincidence. Harry called these sub-coincidences. One happened now, when Lars told him that he would soon return to Sweden for his block of off-days.

"You are welcome to stay in my apartment, you and your wife, while I am away. Much better than a hotel and she will see how well she will fit in Saudi City. Some wives, they cannot do it. Better to know now, not later."

Two days later Harry packed a bag and moved into Lars' apartment in Saudi City. Lars also let Harry use his car. That would give Irene a preview of life in "The Ghetto" as she would come to call it. It was good to have friends, Harry thought. Staying in Lars' place might make a great difference in Irene's perception of Saudi City.

In the morning, he began the process of obtaining Irene's entry visa. That task required four signatures and took an entire morning. It was a formality, but a very tedious one. The Saudis thrived on paperwork and the stamps that went with it. Each signer had his own personal stamp that was printed over his signature with a loud thump. Saudi Arabia, someone had told him, would collapse without those stamps. The visa request was eventually approved and he called Irene that night with the news. A few days later, he met her at the airport and took her to their temporary home.

She liked Lars' apartment, which was new, but she was not impressed with Saudi City. She was even less impressed with the quarters Harry had been assigned the day before she arrived. It was a two-bedroom apartment in a large building that had just been completed. The road passing in front of it was not yet finished, so dust and sand were everywhere. Other empty apartments were nearby, one faced a swimming pool, and Irene wondered if they might have that one. Harry was not optimistic, but it was worth a try. The American in charge of housing could not help, but perhaps if they saw his boss? He wished them good luck. "You'll need it," he said as they left his office.

His boss was a middle aged Saudi with a stone face. He was in a foul mood because the Ramadan had started. Harry immediately sensed unpleasant vibrations. Why did they want to change their quarters, he asked irritably. Harry explained they had found others in the same category, also vacant and unassigned, which they liked better. They would be happy there. The Saudi exploded.

"Happy?" he thundered. "Did anyone promise that you would be happy here? Do you think I am happy? I have had nothing to eat or drink all day and now I have to listen to you complain about not being happy."

There was more but Irene interrupted in mid-tirade. She stood up abruptly and calmly said, "Harry, pack your bags and let's get out of this place. We cannot reason with such people."

The Saudi was stunned into open-mouthed sputtering. He was unused to talking to women who talked back. Irene turned sharply and left the office. Harry was close behind. As he left, he wondered vaguely what the consequences of this prickly meeting might be, but there were none.

As often happens in life, this disappointment was a blessing in disguise. Their assigned quarters, once completed and decorated, became a happy home for their years in Saudi City. Irene at first disliked the compound, but came to like it more and more as time passed, and fine people from around the world moved into their lives; but that was still ahead. For now, Harry's life was focused on the next hurdle in his Saudia career: line training

95
LINE TRAINING

His name was Tim Webb and he was British right down to the ground, as they themselves liked to say. He had been assigned as Harry's Instructor Pilot for his line training. Short, thin and gregarious, Tim gave off friendly vibrations when he and Harry met before their first flight. He laid down the ground rules for Harry's line training. It would be, he said, familiarization of the routes flown by the 707s in Saudia.

"You," he said, pointing at Harry for emphasis, "will do all the flying and I will help in getting you to know the routes and airports. Nothing to it."

Tim seemed to be a gentleman and a reasonable man. That was on the ground. In the air, he became someone else.

First, he flew every other sector himself, sitting in the left seat while Harry flew as First Officer. Harry did not like that, but what could he say? But more than that, Tim became as close to a tyrant as an instructor can be, sometimes losing his temper in the process. First, adopting Saudi techniques, he made large issues of small details, once loudly berating Harry for switching navigation radios between two stations in an "unprofessional way." Instead of tuning in the station ahead at the precise midway point, he had done it a few miles sooner. It was a "windshield wiper" technique, and their relationship went downhill from there.

Harry withstood all the abuse without complaint for a few weeks, until flying an approach into Dhahran in the middle of the night. Despite clear weather and no other traffic, Tim asked Harry to fly a complete instrument procedure. No problem there, and Harry was halfway through the approach when Tim suddenly erupted with a curse and threw his kneeboard -- he was the only airline pilot Harry had ever seen use a military type kneeboard -- towards the rear of the cockpit with some force where it struck the cockpit door with a loud crash. Until that moment, there had been complete silence in the cockpit for several minutes, not even a radio transmission, and Harry had been flying a precise approach. Tim's explosion shattered the quiet and Harry's first thought was: engine failure! But a quick scan of the instruments showed nothing amiss and Harry quickly realized that Tim was upset with his flying. But why? The approach had been on the mark; or so he thought.

Tim began to scream. Harry held up his palm towards Tim.

"Tim," he said evenly with a tone of irritation, "now goddammit, let me get this thing on the ground and then we'll discuss your problem."

The problem, it turned out, was that Harry had flown the profile in a way that, although legal, was not the way Tim would have flown it. The weeks of verbal abuse finally caught up with Harry and he let it out, sitting in the cockpit in the middle of the night on the ramp at the airport in Dhahran. At the end of Harry's explosion, he was surprised to see Tim smile.

"Well," he said, "I have finally gotten to you. I know I have been hard on you at times, "but that's the way they did it to me, so that's the way I do it to you. It's the Saudia way."

Harry could not believe his ears and he said so. "Tim, that is an awful reason to treat me like a dog. Just for the record, I don't agree and I don't like it. Not only that, you scared the shit out of me up there just now. I thought we'd had an engine failure."

Their relationship went more smoothly after that, but, even so, Harry relished what happened on their final flight together. It took place as they returned from an all-nighter to Nairobi in Kenya. Tim decided to fly the homebound sector and they neared Jeddah in mid-morning. Tim had an eye for the girls and as the flight approached the descent point, he was paying more attention to a pretty Turkish stewardess than he was to the airplane. Should I alert him, Harry asked himself. Nah, he decided, he deserves this. Harry allowed the plane to pass the descent point by some thirty miles, then casually began to fasten his shoulder straps. That caught Tim's attention. After a quick glance, first at Harry, then at the instruments, he told Harry with a note of urgency to "Call for descent!" as he hastily fastened his own shoulder straps.

The clearance took a couple of minutes as more miles passed, and Tim began to perspire. Of course, if the descent got out of hand, Tim could request a 360-degree turn to lose altitude; but how would such airmanship look in the eyes of the student he had been criticizing for weeks for trivial mistakes? No, Tim would not ask for a 360, no matter what, Harry thought. Too embarrassing. As it became clear that the airplane would not descend in time to land, Tim put out the speed brakes, large panels that extended from their stowed position on the upper surfaces of the wings. They create drag and slow the airplane, increasing the airplane's rate of descent. Tim badly needed more descent. Their use causes buffeting and was regarded as a last resort to salvage poor judgment.

There was another complication. A few days earlier, Jeddah had opened its new airport. It was just a few miles north of the old one and its runway layout was identical. From the air, they looked the same. Arriving from the south, the old one came into view first. To give himself more flexibility, Tim asked Harry to tell the air controller they would continue visually; he had the airport in sight. The problem was that it was the wrong airport.

With the speed brakes and early extension of the flaps and the landing gear, Tim finally managed to put the airplane in a position to land at the closed airport. Harry enjoyed immensely Tim's discomfiture; but at some point he had to break the news to Tim that he was about to land at the wrong airport. But at what point?

He waited until Tim was on final approach at 1,000 feet, then nonchalantly asked, "Tim, you're not going to land at the old airport, are you?"

Without a word, Tim advanced the throttles, flew in level flight for a few miles with the gear and flaps down, then landed at the new airport. Air Traffic Control never realized the mistake and the secret was in Harry's hands. After shutting down the engines and completing the checklist, Harry expected Tim to say something, anything, about what could only be considered a major screw-up. Not one word, ever.

The German in Harry's ground school class was Helmut Radke, and he was having line training problems of his own. Harry knew him to be a typically industrious and efficient German. He and Harry crossed paths now and then in the flight operations area and he complained bitterly about his Instructor Pilot. He was a Saudi and he was "a dumbkopft pain in the ass." Along with the standard harassment, "windshield wiper" questions were many and frequent. Helmut managed to struggle through his final check flight, which his instructor said was "okay," but he might want to see one more instrument approach.

Helmut was disappointed but resigned to more training. Two days later he received a call from crew scheduling, assigning him to operate a series of flights within The Kingdom.

"Who is the captain in command?" he asked.

"You are," he was told. Helmut, unsure, called the chief of crew schedule to confirm that he had been "released" to fly in command. He was assured that he was.

Helmut flew six sectors over two days, pleased that his line-training ordeal was finally over. The morning after his return, his equipment manager called him in.

"Why did you fly in command before you were released?" he was asked, as though he was a child who had misbehaved.

He explained the situation, but was told that because he had flown in command without official clearance, he was "terminated." Helmut tried to argue his case and mentioned the name of the chief crew scheduler who had sent him out.

"Talk to him," Helmut urged, somewhat desperately. But his manager refused. That might have cast blame on another Saudi. There was only one side to a discussion with a Saudi. Within a week, Helmut was on his way home to Germany.

Harry's final check flight was to Casablanca with a Saudi check captain named Amir Mahoud. The flight made a transit stop in Tripoli and Harry made an awful landing there. Every now and then, after a good approach, the 707 would decide to land a few seconds before the pilot expected it. That had happened now and it was a "very firm" touchdown, as the Saudi later described the landing. To Harry, it felt like a carrier landing. It was not a good start. The sector to Casablanca went well and Harry began to feel better. Amir was a handsome and intelligent young man of about twenty-eight. He was one of the few reasonable Saudis Harry would meet. They spent several days together in Casa, as it was known, and it was there, during breakfast one morning, that he told Harry how he envied him his freedom to choose his own wife.

Harry was pleased and surprised to find that Casablanca was more European than African. French was commonly spoken and Harry used the few words he had picked up in Brussels. They were usually met with pleasant smiles. Most women wore European clothes, and outdoor cafes were everywhere. Alcohol was freely available and the food, with its French influence, was delicious -- a very different world compared to Jeddah, and Harry enjoyed their layover.

A unique experience there was a round of golf on a course in a curious location. Nine holes had been laid out in the center of a race track and Harry had actually played a round of golf as horses raced around the track. There were only a few golfers and none seemed to think playing golf in the middle of a horse race was unusual. Luckily, none of Harry's errant shots flew onto the race course during the races. Even the losing horses were lucky that day. Hitting a horse with a golf ball was not easy, but the way Harry sometimes played, it was surely possible.

Leaving the hotel the next day, there was a near disaster when Harry could not find the key to the hotel safe where he had left his passport. After searching frantically, he enlisted the help of a desk clerk who found the key in the elevator. At the airport, there was another serious problem. During the pre-flight check, the autopilot was found to be inoperative. According to the manual, the autopilot was required for long flights such as the one from Tripoli to Jeddah. Harry sensed Amir's disappointment. He was in command and the decision was his. To make it easier, Harry suggested that it would be no problem for him if Amir chose to hand-fly the airplane back to Jeddah. That would be tedious but not unsafe. And it would be Harry, not Amir, doing the hard work of flying a long sector without the help of the autopilot. Amir pondered the situation for a minute, then said, "Okay, let's go," and they were soon off for Tripoli. This time Harry made a perfect landing.

Now came the hard part. Flying the 707 without an autopilot for several hours was demanding. Amir did not offer to help, not even with the radio position reports. Was this part of his test? More likely, it was because of the lovely Dutch girl who was in charge of the cabin. Amir spent most of the flight chatting with her while, now and then, glancing at the instruments to ensure himself that the airplane was in the right place. Despite his fatigue after almost five hours of hand flying, Harry made a good approach and landing at Jeddah. Amir had turned off the aircraft's instrument landing system so that Harry had to fly a visual approach. To do this, he used a system of lights placed alongside the runway. They provided glide slope information. They were not as precise as those on the carrier but they did not need to be. For Harry, with his carrier background, the approach was an easy one and he ended it with a textbook landing.

Amir was pleased and his debrief was routine. Harry was relieved to be at last released to fly in command. It was delicious to look forward to a flight without Tim Webb sitting beside him. Although their arrival had been in the middle of the night, the flight engineer, an American named Joe Long, insisted on celebrating Harry's status as "Saudia's newest captain." He invited Harry to his home in Saudi City, roused his wife out of her bed, and opened several bottles of home-brewed beer. Joe was tall and thin with a large drooping moustache and was almost never without a cigarette between his lips. The beer had a strong taste of yeast but it was the real stuff and it was the right touch at the right moment. It was only after the second beer that Harry felt the tension fall away and he began to enjoy his successful rite of passage through the ordeal that was line-training in Saudi Arabian Airlines. Sometimes, it was hard to realize fully how difficult an endeavor was until it was over. This was one of those times.

96
SAUDI CITY UP CLOSE

Within the next few weeks, in between Harry's flights, Irene returned to Jeddah and moved into Harry's assigned quarters. Determined not to live in a jail cell like some apartments she had visited, Irene had shipped paintings and carpets from Belgium, some from her apartment and some from Harry's. Harry was pleased to be reunited with a few of his favorite carpets, some of which were returning to the country where Harry had bought them. They had come home. The quarters were furnished and soon Irene had the place cozy and pleasant. The price was right; There was no rent and Saudia paid for the utilities.

"Hard not to save money," Lars told them, "when all you have to buy is food, fuel for your car, and grape juice."

Finding friends was easy. They were everywhere, and soon they fell into a social cycle of tennis, swimming and dinner parties. Every few weeks, they joined a group for a day at the Cabin.

One of their first "Arab" experiences came early when Harry and Irene, along with Lars and his wife Inger, visited the Red Sea near Saudi City. The beach was hard sand and they drove right up to the water's edge, about a hundred yards from the coastal road. They had donned swimming suits -- "swim costumes," Lars called them, using the British term -- at home. The women wore bikinis. As soon as their car was parked, they took off their outer garments and began to remove from the car a few beach chairs and a cooler with soft drinks and food. The beach was deserted, but not for long. Within minutes, a car diverted from the road and positioned itself facing them just a few yards away, its Saudi driver staring directly at the bikini-clad women. A few more minutes brought a few more cars. Within ten minutes, a semi-circle of some five or six cars and a motorcycle, all pointed straight at them and all holding Arab men intently staring at the women. Only the sea kept them from being surrounded.

"Let's go into the water," Harry suggested, "and maybe they'll leave."

But it soon became clear that they had no intention of leaving, that this sight was too good to be true. The swimmers soon gave up, returned to the car, dressed and drove off. As they did, not one car moved and a newcomer joined the gallery. They never swam there again.

That experience convinced Harry to take Dan Grogan's advice and he bought a share in the Cabin. It was on a remote stretch of beach twenty-five miles up the coast. The cabin was not only an escape from Arab eyes; it was a visit to another world. A group gathered there about once each month for a joyous day of snorkeling, wind-surfing, eating and drinking. The Cabin was primitive, but it provided shade and a toilet, the basic necessities of life on a Red Sea beach. It was, for both Harry and Irene, a first look at spectacular tropical marine life. It was on display some one hundred yards out where the seabed fell off sharply at the reef. Fins and a snorkel were all that were needed to enjoy the vivid colors of the many varieties of fish in the crystal clear water there. A day on the water generated thirst. To quench it, most brought home-brewed wine, and tasting contests were held to determine the best "grape juice." The day sometimes ended with a campfire at sundown The orange-red sun setting far across the Red Sea was often exquisite, and a fine ending to a great day.

After some reluctance, Harry had finally persuaded himself to become a dessert vintner. First, he had to buy the ingredients, so he visited the Safeway supermarket near Saudi City. He was surprised to find that the visit made him nervous. In the back of his mind, was the image of being stopped by the police with his car full of sacks of sugar and cases of grape juice.

Harry knew there were two police forces in Jeddah, one to thwart crime and one to enforce religion. The religious police made sure that shops and offices closed during the prayer hours five times daily. Not only must they be closed, the workers had to be formed in groups and led in prayer by one of their colleagues. The prayer hours were loudly announced by the wails of the mezuzah over loudspeakers. They were everywhere and they soon became a major nuisance to the non-Muslims. Another annoyance was that the prayer times changed with the phases of the moon; so it was hard to know when a shop or office was closed and, with Harry's luck, he always seemed to arrive just as they were closing. That meant a wait of twenty minutes or so while the staff prayed. The prayer was not voluntary and one mission of the religious police was to ensure that the people prayed, like it or not.

Harry was not the only one buying the stuff to make wine. There were two other shopping carts loaded with the makings: bags of sugar piled atop cases of grape juice. That made him feel easier. Still, once provisioned and on the way home, he stopped several times just to be sure there was no police car behind him. He felt like a fugitive.

He remembered how delicious the wine was that he had drunk with Dan Grogan, so he called Dan for instructions. He gave them cheerfully but warned him, "not to expect it to taste like mine. They never come out the same. You got a lucky batch." Dan wished him luck and Harry was soon listening to the pleasant gurgle of grape juice turning into wine. Weeks later, after pouring it back into the grape juice bottles, he stowed one bottle in a corner of a closet. That one would be opened when they left Jeddah. One thing was sure: Harry would not retire in Saudi Arabia.

Without Tim at his side, the flying was pleasant. One aspect that made it so was the routine briefing of the cabin crew before each flight. Most were young girls from Europe, but many were from Thailand and the Philippines. Harry thought they had been hired by someone who appreciated pretty girls, as most were very attractive. They did not like to fly with Saudi captains, so there were smiles of relief when Harry entered the briefing room. One of them told Harry about a Saudi captain who had sent back his cup of tea seven times because it was not to his taste. He would hear many such stories.

Many of the first officers were European or American and, with them, there was never a problem. But, now and then, a Saudi made life difficult. On one of his first flights, Harry was paired with a Saudi who was on his very first flight after his training. Farid was a slight, dark-complexioned youth of about twenty with a moustache and a scrawny beard. Reminiscent of Rio, there were many shades of skin color among the Saudis. Farid was as black as they came. As in Rio, the shade of a man's skin seemed to make no difference to the Saudis.

It was a morning flight to Medina, about forty-five minutes away. This city held the tomb of Mohammed and was, of course, an important and popular destination. The flight went smoothly until their return to Jeddah. Then, something unusual happened. As Harry and his first officer alit from the crew bus and entered the arrival area, a distraught crew scheduler met them. Harry naturally suspected he had done something wrong; but the scheduler went straight to Farid, explaining that he was desperately needed for a second flight to Medina. The scheduled first officer had not shown up, the passengers had already been boarded and the aircraft was awaiting his arrival so it could depart.

Farid, without a moment's pause, said simply, "No."

Harry could not believe his ears and neither could the scheduler. Puzzled, eyebrows furrowed, the scheduler repeated his request, this time with some urgency. Farid had set down his flight bag. Now he reached down and picked it up.

"Did you not hear me?" he asked sharply. "I said, no."

With that, he turned and strode quickly out the door. Ah, thought Harry, the Saudi work ethic on display.

That ethic showed up regularly when Saudis failed to report for flights they considered undesirable. High on that list was the nightly trip to Tabuk in the north of Saudi Arabia. What made it unpopular was its timing. The three-hour round trip left at midnight. Whenever Harry was assigned stand-by duty, he checked the schedule to see whether a Saudi captain was operating the flight. If so, he could count on his telephone ringing ten minutes after the report time. "Captain, we need you" were the words that told him the scheduled captain had not checked in. Usually, they did not bother to call to say they would not come.

The ethic made an unexpected appearance on a charter night flight to London. Harry was scheduled for an off day and had just returned in early evening from a tiring three hours on the tennis court when he found a messenger waiting with a note asking him to call crew schedules immediately. The word "immediately" was underlined. Trapped, Harry called. Captain, he was told, we need you for a flight to London tonight. The departure was set for 2000, which meant an all-nighter. Harry took a deep breath.

"I am very sorry," he said with as much courtesy as he could muster, "but I have just been working out for three hours and I am unfit to do this flight. Sorry."

That "sorry" was met by silence, then a renewed attempt to pressure Harry to change his mind. He stood firm. Finally, the scheduler accepted his refusal. Five minutes later the phone rang and this time it was Harry's Assistant Equipment Manager applying the pressure. He was a disagreeable Lebanese captain named Rajah. The airplane was needed in London, he told Harry, and there would be no passengers. Along with a first officer, a second captain was assigned to the flight. That meant Harry could sleep en route, he said, and no other captain was available. Harry read the handwriting on the wall, and, with his back against it, agreed to do the flight.

Oh, oh, Harry thought as he checked in and saw the other captain was a Saudi. He was short and plump with an enormous moustache, enormous even by Saudi standards.

After shaking hands, his first words were "Captain, would you mind to operate the first half of the flight? I have had no sleep today and I am very tired indeed. I will do the second part of the flight."

That had been Harry's plan and he grimaced as he replied. "Sure, go ahead. I'll do the first half. No problem."

He would not admit that he, too, had no sleep and felt more than tired. He was exhausted.

Ali sat in the jump seat as Harry made the takeoff and began climbing to cruise altitude.

Passing 5,000 feet he said, "Captain, I will now go to the cabin and sleep. I will return after three hours."

Three hours, then four hours, passed and Ali did not return to the cockpit. The flight engineer was an American and he was aware of the situation.

"Harry," he asked, "you want me to go back and get that guy?"

Harry pondered the problem and decided he would rather continue working than to ask Ali to take his seat. And, anyway, he would not be able to sleep in this situation. The London weather had deteriorated and he was not sure he trusted Ali to make an approach in bad weather; so he pressed on and Ali continued sleeping.

Just as the airplane passed the French coast and began its descent into the London area, the cockpit door opened and Ali entered. No longer in uniform, he was wearing pajamas. And not just pajamas; they were silk pajamas, with an Armani logo on one breast. He took his place in the jump seat behind Harry, took out a pipe, filled it, and began smoking.

"How is the weather?" he asked nonchalantly.

Harry glanced back and frowned. He briefed him about the weather, wondering if Ali would finally offer to take over the airplane, but he puffed on his pipe and said nothing. Harry would be damned if he would ask him to fly the approach.

As in landing at night on a carrier, landing the 707 at night in bad weather started Harry's adrenalin flowing. Despite his earlier fatigue, he was quickly alert and ready. The airport was now reporting a ceiling at 200 feet, with visibility of 600 meters. Those numbers were the minimum for which a 707 was legally permitted to start an approach. Once past a certain point, the captain could continue the approach, even if the weather went lower. Harry hoped that would not happen

Harry decided to fly a coupled approach, one in which the autopilot is connected to the runway's instrument landing system. Harry flew approaches well, but the autopilot flew them better. As the airplane neared the runway, the first officer called out, in increments of one hundred, the number of feet above the decision height. If the runway was not in sight at that height, a missed approach had to be initiated. As the first officer called out "One hundred feet above," Harry curled his fingers around the throttles, ready to throw them forward. "Decision height," was called, and no runway was in sight. Just as Harry raised the nose slightly and began to push the throttles forward, the runway lights became visible through the mist. A moment or two later, Harry saw the runway, quickly took off the power he had just added, lined up on the runway centerline, broke his rate of descent by gently raising the airplane's nose, then slowly pulled the throttles back to idle and landed.

"Good job," said Ali with his pipe still between his teeth.

Without looking back Harry said, "Thanks. And thanks for all your help." He said it with exaggerated courtesy. He hoped Ali got the message.

One night, on a flight to Riyadh Harry ran into rare bad weather. The thunderstorms were small and scattered, but they were enough to put the fear of Allah into Harry's Saudi first officer. He later told Harry that he had never before seen a thunderstorm and he was frightened; so frightened that he began to weep as they circumvented a storm cell with lightening flashing all around. Harry had seen worse, much worse, but, to Samir, it was frightful, and he was sure he was about to die.

That reaction was due to inexperience, something that was in short supply among young Saudi pilots. One of them, on a flight to Amman in clear weather with isolated cumulus clouds well below them along the way, asked Harry whether he thought returning to Jeddah was too risky, in view of the weather. Harry was astonished. The weather did not get much better than this, he explained, and the risk was zero. They would return to Jeddah, he told his disappointed co-pilot.

Experience is an important aspect of the judgment that is essential to good airmanship. Mechanically, some of these young Saudis flew well, as long as everything worked the way it was supposed to, especially the autopilot. They had the reactions of youth that contribute much to basic flying; but they had, in Harry's view, major shortfalls. One was that few could hand-fly the airplane. They had been taught to manage the airplane instead of to fly it. That led to another deficiency: almost none could make a visual approach, one without electronic guidance. Now and then, Harry would turn off the ILS and ask his first officer to land visually. The result was usually disastrous because they had been trained to fly with the autopilot engaged while they "supervised the airplane." Harry sometimes wondered whether one of them could get the airplane back on the ground if he himself suffered a heart attack and the ILS was not working. Supervising an airplane on autopilot makes sense, Harry thought, but only if the back-up ability to hand-fly the airplane is in good working order.

It was when something went wrong that experience showed its value. One young Saudi captain, recently released to fly on his own, caused a near catastrophe because of panic and the poor judgment that resulted. His Saudi first officer was also inexperienced, flying only his fourth flight since his release. This was a combination asking for trouble. Returning from Riyadh one afternoon, the flight was greeted by a rare, small thunderstorm over the Jeddah airport. The captain began his descent and flew into rain.

"I am returning to Riyadh," he immediately announced and, without clearance, turned around and headed back there. He was advised that the storm had already passed and the Jeddah weather was basically clear with very light rain and good visibility; but panic had already set in. He turned back to Jeddah as ordered but, in his anxiety, he did some remarkable flying, all of it bad.

He started by not once using any checklist. He did not lower any flaps, came over the end of the runway 300 feet above it, landed halfway down it, did not use speed brakes or thrust reversers, and left the far end of the runway at high speed, narrowly missing the Instrument Landing System installation for the opposite runway. The airplane finally came to a crunching stop in the dessert, enveloped in a cloud of dust and sand.

Throughout the approach and landing, the only words heard later on the cockpit voice recorder were, "windshield wipers." Whether those two words were meant to turn them on or off could not be determined. How ironic, thought Harry, recalling the many "windshield wiper" questions he had been asked during his training. As soon as the airplane came to a stop, both the captain and the first officer, using emergency ropes stowed above their seats, left the cockpit through its side windows and sprinted to the terminal. Later, when the captain was asked why he abandoned the passengers and ran to the terminal, he replied, "Because it was raining." Miraculously, no one was injured. Allah was smiling that day.

Allah was not in such a good mood when a fatal accident took place at the old airport in Riyadh before Harry joined Saudia. Inexperience could not be blamed this time, but poor judgment was clearly responsible. That judgment was by the captain, who was a Pakistani with extensive experience. The flight was a fully-loaded L1011 Tri-Star flying from Riyadh to Jeddah. Although Saudia never released the accident report, a BBC documentary told the story, and Harry had seen it. Included was the verbatim record of the cockpit voice recorder. Halfway to Jeddah, the cabin chief, who was a European girl, entered the cockpit to inform the captain that there was smoke in the cabin. After some seconds of silence, the captain ordered the girl to "return to your duties."

She came back a second time with the same result. On her third visit, the captain instructed the flight engineer to inspect the cabin. He returned to report there was, indeed, smoke in the cabin and it was rapidly becoming thick. After some deliberation, the captain decided to return to Riyadh. He landed on the main runway, but instead of coming to an immediate stop and evacuating the airplane, he taxied slowly to the end and turned off.

By then, flames had broken out in the cabin, and the passengers were in high panic. Because the flight engineer, also in panic, had failed to depressurize the aircraft, the cabin doors could not be opened. Initially, they open inward and the cabin pressure prevented their movement. Many passengers tried desperately to get out through the cockpit. More than fifty dead bodies were later found squeezed into the cockpit, including that of the captain, who was crushed beneath the rudder pedals. The fire had started in a cargo hold, and the aircraft burned right down to its main deck. All of its passengers and crew perished. Its burned-out hulk stood on display for years as a monument to bad judgment. Harry flew to Riyadh often, and every time he saw the remnants of the airplane, he shook his head and wondered how such an accident could happen.

97
A GOLDEN AIRPLANE

Most of Harry's flights were routine and within The Kingdom. Except for charter flights, Casablanca and Madrid were the only destinations where 707 crews could enjoy a layover outside Saudi Arabia. Harry spent many nights in Dhahran and Riyadh but that was almost like staying home. Now and then, a non-routine Kingdom flight came along. One such flight started for Harry when he received a call from crew scheduling on an off day.

That often happened, and to circumvent being available for such calls, most crew members used telephone answering machines to screen calls. After Saudia caught on to this game, it sometimes sent out a messenger to catch people at home who did not answer their telephones. The messenger was an elderly Saudi wearing a gray robe. He was known as "Casper the Ghost." During one such visit from Casper, Harry and Irene had actually hidden from view in their own apartment to avoid his prying eyes. Without ringing their bell, Casper had peered into their living room window to "catch" them at home.

On this morning, Harry had carelessly picked up his phone and was officially caught at home. In another company, he might have avoided the flight by claiming he had been drinking alcohol. That would not work in Saudia. The caller spoke urgently the dreaded words: "Captain, we need you immediately." This time, he added a few more: Do not take time to put on your uniform, do not even shave, just come immediately. Harry did not shave, but he did take a few minutes to don his uniform.

A scheduler met Harry as he entered the flight operations area. Follow me, he was told. Harry was led to a waiting crew bus and taken straight to his airplane. It was standing on the tarmac before the Royal Terminal, used only for flights by the royal family. The aircraft stood directly behind the King's personal B747 and Harry could not miss the red carpet leading from the terminal to its stairs. Behind Harry's airplane was a B737. The three airplanes made up a royal entourage, the King in one and his luggage and spear-carriers in the other two.

As Harry settled into his seat in the cockpit, he had no idea where he was going. The first officer was a Saudi. He informed Harry, that, "Everything is ready, Captain, even the checklists are done."

Hmm, thought Harry, that is readiness of a new level. "Well, thanks, but I hope you won't mind if we go through the checklists again, just to be sure."

Harry asked where they were going and whether the King had boarded his airplane.

"Dhahran, Captain, and the King will arrive at any moment. Please be ready."

A few minutes passed and the King was not yet in sight. By now, Harry was catching up with himself. "What about the weather, what about our flight plan, when should we start our engines?"

The first officer had been through this before. The weather was fine, he said. It would be unusual for the weather not to be fine, Harry thought, as sometimes months passed in Saudi Arabia without a single cloud in view. When the door closes on the King's airplane, the first officer told Harry, close ours. When the King's airplane starts its engines, start ours. When the King's airplane begins to taxi, just follow him and take off after he does. It was a simple case of Follow-the-Leader. A few more minutes passed and still no King. Harry was, by now, ready, and he called Ground Control to confirm all this for himself. Yes, he was told, you are cleared to start, taxi and takeoff at your discretion. You will have priority over all other aircraft. You are cleared direct Riyadh, direct Dhahran and your altitude will be assigned after takeoff. Easy, thought Harry.

By now, some thirty minutes had passed and the King was nowhere in sight. The minutes became hours and finally a long limousine pulled up to the far end of the red carpet and the King emerged. Down the carpet and up the stairs he went, leading a large retinue into his airplane. His door closed and Harry closed his. He and his first officer watched intently for the King's engines to turn, ready to start their own, external starting air pressure in place; but the King's engines did not turn and, after a few minutes, his door opened and out came the King. Down the steps he went, out the red carpet and back into his limo. Stairs were pushed into position on Harry's airplane and the door was opened. An aide appeared to tell Harry the exciting news that the King had decided to return to the palace for lunch. Departure would be delayed until his return. No one knew when that might be. Harry sighed and wished he had shaved. It looked like a long day ahead.

By the time the King returned Harry had been sitting in the cockpit for some five hours. So much for being needed immediately, he thought. This time, the King's airplane started its engines, taxied and took off, with Harry in close pursuit and the 737 right behind him. The flight was routine and, after arrival in Dhahran, Harry was directed to park next to the King's airplane. How long would the King be in Dhahran? No one knew.

Harry had heard about the opulence of the King's airplane. He called the airplane on the Ground Control frequency and a Saudi captain answered. Might Harry be allowed to visit the airplane? Most welcome, Captain; please come and be our guest.

Harry walked the few yards between them and was met at the top of the stairs by the captain, who was friendly, and eager to show Harry his airplane. And what an airplane it was! The tour started in the cockpit that was, of course, state of the art. Instead of two inertial navigation systems, there were three, and a computer used the average of the three to determine the airplane's position. Just aft of the cockpit had been carved out a large communications center which appeared to hold every radio ever invented.

"We can communicate with the entire world without ever leaving our airplane," the captain said proudly. "Flight plans, weather, everything."

Behind the cockpit was a complete surgical operating room with a television hookup to the Cleveland Medical Center. The King had heart problems and although he traveled with two doctors, who were surgeons, any medical procedure could be directed and monitored via live television. Moving aft, Harry was taken into a plush conference room that held a long rosewood table with some twenty chairs. And that was just the upper deck of the airplane.

Harry could not believe his eyes when the Saudi captain guided him to an elevator. If you count the cargo hold, there are three decks on the B747. On this airplane, the captain explained, the forward cargo section had been turned into a luxurious lounge. Harry was reminded of a comment by a Pan Am captain who flew the very first operational flight of the 747. Hijacking had just begun the age of terrorism then and he was asked for his response to a would-be hijacker on board.

"Well," he said, "we hope he would end up on the wrong floor."

The lift, as the Saudi captain called it, was needed because of the King's heart condition, and it descended to the crew lounge in the belly with a stop at the main deck. From the crew lounge, a small escalator could be flipped down to the tarmac so the King could avoid using stairs.

They exited the lift on the main deck that held a section of about forty passenger seats. To Arabs, it probably seemed luxurious but Harry would have called it garish. The Arabs seemed to prefer bright and gaudy to soft and discrete. Aft of the passenger seats were the King's quarters, and they were opulent indeed, with hand-made oriental carpets on the decks throughout. The walls appeared to be covered with velvet. To Harry, it was overwhelming, although a few of the carpets caught his eye. There were several bedrooms, each with a full bathroom fitted with faucets and taps made of solid gold. Overkill, if I've ever seen it, thought Harry. He wanted to ask what the toilet seats were made of but decided against it.

Making their way back to the lift, they passed a small compartment containing about a dozen television screens. These monitored the airplane from various external viewpoints for security purposes. A man in a military uniform sat drinking tea and smoking cigarettes as he looked at the screens. Other devices, the man explained, monitored various doors and access panels around the airplane. He would know the moment one was opened.

Back at their starting point, the captain invited Harry to join him and the crew for lunch. Harry hesitated.

"I can guarantee you will enjoy it," said the captain, as he noticed Harry's indecision; but Harry decided to return to his own airplane. He never knew what was happening on his airplane when he wasn't there. And, anyway, the King might suddenly appear and Harry had to be ready when he did. He thanked the captain for the hospitality that Harry had found was a trait of the Arab character, one in which they seemed to take great pride. He need not have hurried back to his airplane as it was six hours before the King showed up for the trip home. Yes, a long day, indeed, and Harry's unshaven face reflected it.

98
PARIS

The next time Harry was called for a charter flight, it took him to Paris with Captain Baaroum as first officer. They had flown together several times and got along well. This time, they were sent with an empty airplane to Hail, a small town in central Saudi Arabia. This would be a royal flight, they were told, and, as such, was no ordinary charter flight. The first twenty rows of passenger seats had been removed, and the deck was covered, wall-to-wall, with Persian carpets. Large, brightly-colored pillows were strewn about the area. There was enough catering for an Army and what catering it was! There was, of course, no wine; but everything else that makes up a five-star restaurant was on board, and it was the best that Europe offered. Most of it, except for a few packages of Brie cheese rescued by Harry just in time, would be thrown out in Paris.

Arriving in Hail at sundown, they waited several hours for their passengers, who turned out to be a royal princess and her retinue of about thirty, including several children. When Baaroum was told the name of the princess, his eyes lit and he turned to Harry and smiled broadly. They could expect a "very generous tip," Baaroum said, with a wide smile. The trip went well and they arrived at Charles DeGaulle airport, known as Charlie DeGaulle to most American pilots, about two in the morning. Most things made in France seemed, to Harry, to be unnecessarily complicated, and this airport was no exception. Its arrival procedure, for example, required an altitude at certain points that changed according to the altimeter setting of the moment. Now, that, thought Harry, was noise control above and beyond the call of duty. Its departure procedure was even worse.

Lars had told Harry about a Swedish friend who, on his final line check, had flown with a Saudi captain to London, with a night stop in Paris. Because he had made a minor mistake in reading the approach chart during their arrival, the Saudi sternly told the Swede to memorize not only the departure for the next morning, but also the entire route to Heathrow airport, including the arrival there. That was not only absurd, but unsafe as well. Still, the Swede stayed up the entire night, committing the route to memory and managed to survive the check flight, worn and weary and with airport numbers rattling around his head for days to come. How not to conduct a check flight, thought Harry, when he heard the story, and far beyond mere windshield wiper questions.

After the last royal passenger had left the airplane, Harry turned to Baaroum. "Okay," he asked lightly, "so where is our tip?"

Baaroum scowled. "That cheap son of a bitch," was all he said but he said it with some bitterness. This was not the Saudi way.

Late the next morning, Harry answered the telephone in his hotel room. On the other end was an American voice, calling, he said, for the princess. She was too tired last night to express her appreciation for a safe flight and she had asked him to bring a "small gift" for the crew. How many were there, he asked, and would it be convenient to come this morning?

"Ten," answered Harry, "I'll be in my room when you get here."

Forty-five minutes later Harry opened his door to a soft knock. Standing there was an elegantly-dressed man carrying a briefcase. Entering the room, he declined Harry's offer of coffee and did not even sit down. He set his briefcase down, then dipped a hand inside and withdrew a thick stack of one-hundred-dollar bills. Harry accepted the money and asked the man to thank the princess for him. They shook hands and the man was gone. He had been in the room for only three minutes, but they were very rewarding minutes. The stack of bills held ten-thousand dollars, one thousand for each of the crew.

That night, Baaroum and Harry met in the hotel bar to have a drink before dinner. Baaroum was already flying high when Harry got there. Harry heard his name called out loudly as he left the elevator. The lobby was large and open and the call came from the bar at the far end. Even before Harry sat down, Baaroum had summoned the bartender to take Harry's request for a drink.

"Scotch and soda," said Harry, as he got up on a barstool.

"No, not Scotch and soda," interrupted Baaroum. "Chivas Regal and soda, a double. And quickly."

The bartender, whom Harry knew from previous visits, shrugged and went to bring a drink.

Before long, Harry had three or four drinks lined up in front of him, all doubles and all ordered by Baaroum. He beckoned to the bartender, who leaned over to hear Harry above the chatter.

"Listen," said Harry, quietly, "the next round is on me. Just put it on my bill."

He showed the bartender his room key. The bartender was Lebanese and he knew about Saudis. He raised his eyebrows to question Harry's order.

"Look," he said, "he's a Saudi. Take the drinks."

Harry nodded, thought for a moment, then said "You're right. Cancel my order."

The bar was circular and was, by now, full. Baaroum began admiring two very attractive women across the bar.

"What we need," he said, "is girls. What about those two over there?" He gestured with his drink towards the two women. Without waiting for a reply, he walked around the bar and spoke to the women. A few minutes later, he was back, the women with him. Harry sensed they were working girls. There were introductions and more drinks were ordered. Baaroum, wasting no time, asked one of the girls to accompany him to his room. The girl replied in fluent English with a strong French accent.

"We have just met," she said with a fetching smile, "and already you want me to go to your room? First, we will have a drink, then we will discuss it."

The discussion did not last long. After a few minutes, Baaroum and his new friend left the bar. Harry dined alone and did not see Baaroum again until the next morning as they were checking out. Baaroum was smiling broadly. He had called down to the bar and asked the second woman to join them. Both women had spent the night in his room.

"And what a night!" he exclaimed. "You should have been there."

Harry could not resist asking: "Baaroum, what does your wife think about all this?"

Baaroum shook his head sadly. "She tells me to do as I please, just to leave her alone. She is not a typical Saudi wife."

And you, Harry thought, but did not say, are not a typical Saudi husband.

Although not typical, there were many Saudi men who behaved as Baaroum did. Most were bachelors aching to taste life outside The Kingdom. Their favorite destinations were Bangkok, Manila, and Casablanca. The reason was the easy availability of women in these places. Casablanca had the added advantage of being in an Arabic-speaking country. The Saudis, too, had off-day blocks and some used them to satisfy their hunger for life in the outside world. A few, risking discipline, brought alcohol on liquor-free Saudia flights, getting a head start on their holidays. One Saudi captain, on duty, had shown up at the Bangkok airport very drunk. He was high up in the Saudi pecking order and was disciplined with a one-month suspension with pay, a very light slap on the wrist.

Some Saudi women, too, underwent a metamorphosis after leaving The Kingdom. Most kept their chadors, and it was strange to see them eat by lifting the veils that covered their faces, then lowering it after each bite. Others were more daring. As soon as the seat belt sign was turned off, they hurried to the toilet and changed into western dress. They were like butterflies emerging from their cocoons, and some were beautiful.

A Dutch first officer told Harry about an incident in a Bangkok bar. A drunk Saudi pilot was seriously harassing a bar girl, and an American patron had objected. The ensuing argument ended when the American said, "You are not in your country now," and punched him in the mouth. Arrogance does not play well outside of Saudi Arabia.

That same first officer had died while scuba diving in a sunken ship in the Red Sea. When his body was returned to Holland, Harry heard, all the vital organs had been removed. There was no way to confirm this, but Harry could easily believe it. Islamic teachings that the body cannot be violated apparently do not apply to non-Muslims.

Harry once met Baaroum on the tarmac in Casablanca as Harry was leaving his airplane. Baaroum wanted to be sure that he would not miss Harry. That was an unusual place to meet, but Baaroum was desperate. He had been enjoying the good life in Casa for six days and had not only run out of money; he had run up a huge bill at his hotel.

"Can you let me have a few dollars?" he asked, as they shook hands.

"Of course," said Harry, as he reached for his billfold. "How much do you need?"

"Twelve-thousand dollars. Do you have it?"

Harry put his billfold back in his pocket and shook his head. "Sorry, Baaroum, but you're asking the wrong man."

Baaroum never explained how it was possible to spend twelve thousand dollars in just six days. Using his imagination, Harry figured it out for himself. Baaroum was a high roller, even for a Saudi.

99
DINNER WITH TARIK

Tarik al Masri was another first officer with whom Harry flew often. Like Baaroum, Tarik was one of the non-Arab Arabs, and he and Harry got along well. He was bright, pleasant and friendly, with a high sense of humor. During a flight to Dhahran, where they would spend the night, Tarik announced that Harry and the flight engineer, an American, were invited to dinner with Tarik's family, who lived there. Harry looked forward to an evening with a Saudi family. It would be the only time that Harry would visit a Saudi home.

They were met at the airport by Tarik's brother, who drove them to the house. There, they were greeted by Tarik's father. He was elderly, tall, and courtly, with a white beard to go with his moustache. He spoke English well, and had once visited the U.S. He did that, he said, for the unusual reason of wanting to taste American dates.

"Tasty," he said, "but very costly."

Like all Saudis, he was courteous and hospitable.

"My home is your home," he said, and Harry saw that he meant it. The kindness in his face was plain to see. Hospitality was a hallmark of the Saudi character. It had its beginnings, Tarik had told him, when the Saudis were nomads, living in tents, and hospitality was sometimes essential to survival.

They were seated in a sparsely decorated room. Bare by our taste, thought Harry, as he glanced about. Persian carpets and wooden chairs with high backs, a few potted plants, and nothing hanging on any wall. They chatted as a male servant poured mint tea. Mint grew abundantly around Medina, and Harry brought some home whenever he flew there. He and Irene had come to like it very much.

After a pleasant half-hour the servant whispered into the father's ear.

"Shall we go into the dining room?" suggested the father, gesturing towards the door. Except for a large carpet, this room was bare, too, not even chairs. They had removed their shoes upon entering the house and now they sat on pillows arranged around an exquisite carpet. Harry knew that Tarik had three sisters and wondered when they would appear; and they had not yet met his mother. After a few moments, a woman servant appeared, carrying a large tray piled high with lamb and rice, steaming, and with a delicious aroma. Two more women servants quickly followed, each with trays heaped with food. The trays were placed in the center of the carpet.

Tarik had explained that they would eat in the Arab way, sitting on the floor and using their hands instead of forks.

It was more than a dinner; it was a feast, with enough food for a dozen hungry people. There was no way to eat it all, and finally Harry had eaten enough, more than enough. He turned to Tarik, who was sitting next to him.

"Tarik," he said, "this was certainly a wonderful meal, one of the best I've ever eaten."

Tarik smiled, pleased.

"Yes," he said, "my mother and my sisters have been working for three days to prepare this food."

"I can believe it. Where are they? I'd like to thank them."

Tarik stopped smiling. "Oh, no," he said. "It would not be allowed for you to see them, but I will tell them that you enjoyed their food. They will be very pleased to hear this."

Not only did the Saudi women ride in the back of the bus, they were not permitted to meet house guests. Harry had once heard someone say that, in Saudi Arabia, camels have more interesting lives than do some women. He was beginning to believe it.

100
MOGADISHU

Mogadishu was a third-world airport in a third world country. Somalia, judging by its airport, was probably not advanced enough to qualify as a third-world country; but the flight there was one of Harry's favorites. It was a leisurely mid-morning departure, which made it a gentleman's round trip of about eight hours, all in daylight. Passing over other third-world countries on the way, radio communications were difficult. Most were over the high-frequency radio, which was sometimes unreadable because of static. The unusual accents did not help.

The airport had only one runway, and one low-frequency radio beacon. There was no published approach procedure, so a visual approach and landing, which took them over the heart of the city, was the only option. That suited Harry. He enjoyed making seat-of-the-pants approaches to a runway which ran parallel to the coast and was just a few meters away from the sea. Sometimes, if the wind was right, the airplane actually passed through sea spray during its landing and takeoff runs.

There was never any other traffic, so the taxi was easy. That was fortunate because Harry learned that the taxi director, a thin, wizened old-timer, was the same man who operated the radios.

"So," Harry asked during one transit, "you wear three hats: airways control, tower control, and taxi marshal. I hope you get triple salary for all this."

The old man grinned a toothless grin and shook his head. "Oh, how I wish, Captain, how I wish. But alas, no, one salary only, and a very small one."

Harry noticed that he wore a cap with "Taxi Man" written on it. Pointing to the cap, Harry asked "Do you have a different cap to wear when you're talking on the radio?"

"Yes, Captain," he said with his toothless smile. He explained that he had two other caps, one for airways control and another for tower control. One problem, he said, was that these two radios were on different floors. Changing radios meant not only changing caps, but changing floors, as well. That explained the gaps Harry had noticed when changing frequencies.

After the engines were shut down, the old man always met Harry at the bottom of the stairs and shook his hand.

"Anything today, Captain?" He was asking if Harry wanted to buy some shrimp or mangoes. They were cheap and plentiful and Harry always hauled a box of one or the other back to Jeddah. Irene was always happy to see them. They were not only cheap, they were delicious. Food always tasted better when it came from far-off places.

Harry made many trips to Mogadishu, but never left the airport. Then, an unusual event took place and Harry had one of those rare, unforgettable experiences. It was a series of events, and it began when the President of Somalia was involved in an auto accident on a rural road. "Rural," in Somalia meant jungle, and Harry would see the exact place where the accident happened.

The President was flown to Jeddah for hospital treatment. When he was released, Harry was tapped for a special flight to carry him home. It was just another flight to Mogadishu until after the airplane was parked by the Taxi Man. When the door was opened, a dignified, casually-dressed man, stepped into the cockpit and identified himself as the Information Minister for Somalia.

"Captain," he said, as he entered, "the President has asked me to show his appreciation. He invites you and your crew to be his guests for lunch. This is an urgent request directly from the President."

The word "urgent" meant, to Harry, that the request was an order, not a request. Harry thanked the minister and explained that the airplane was scheduled to return to Jeddah after disembarking the President.

"Yes, yes, but this is an urgent request from the President himself. Do what you must, but, please, join us for lunch. The President insists."

Harry nodded and began thinking quickly. It would not be diplomatic to refuse, but, to accept, he would need permission from Jeddah. He turned to his Saudi first officer. "Call flight ops on the HF radio and tell them that the President of Somalia has invited us for lunch and that we request to delay our return for three hours. Be sure to say that the President himself has invited us."

The co-pilot, speaking in Arabic, quickly got through to Jeddah. HF radios sometimes worked better over long distances. The first officer signed off and turned to Harry with a grin.

"They say to stay as long as we like."

Harry smiled and turned to the minister.

"We're okay to stay for lunch. Please lead the way."

Now the minister smiled. "Follow me, please. He left the cockpit and descended the stairs. A bus was waiting at their foot. Harry picked up the mike and told the cabin crew about their surprise invitation to lunch.

After the crew boarded the bus, which was old and worn, the minister gestured to a seat and turned to Harry.

"Please sit here," he said.

He took the seat next to Harry and would not leave his side for the next few hours. The bus slowly made its way off the tarmac and onto a two-lane road leading along the coast and passing along a stretch of sandy coast leading into a heavily-forested area. After a few minutes, the bus slowed as it passed through an area of road construction. Harry noted that for some fifty yards, the road was being widened to four lanes. Why only fifty yards, Harry wondered. As if he heard Harry's thoughts, the minister leaned towards Harry and spoke softly in his ear.

"It was here," he whispered, "that our President had his accident. Now the road is being made safe."

Sure, thought Harry, for fifty yards.

After half an hour, the bus turned into the forest, which, by now, was beginning to look like a jungle. Was there a road? Harry was not sure. There was one, he saw, made of dirt and sand. After a few hundred yards, the bus came to a stop in a small clearing.

The minister smiled. "We have arrived at our destination," he said. "Please disembark now."

Disembark? Here in the middle of a jungle? Harry got up and walked to the front of the bus. There, he could see the welcoming committee, which was an old man standing next to what appeared to be small cart with large wheels. It stood next to a red carpet, which led into the jungle. Harry hesitated.

"Please," said the minister, "leave the bus and follow the carpet."

Harry followed instructions and, as he stepped down from the bus, he was handed a half coconut filled with an unknown liquid. A straw protruded from the coconut. Ah, thought Harry, a pre-lunch cocktail. He accepted the drink and, with the minister at his side, began to walk along the carpet, at one point bending low to avoid foliage in his path. As he straightened up, he saw, with surprise, that he was now standing in the middle of a large clearing with the sky obscured by the umbrella of the jungle overhead. Several Persian carpets lay in the center of the clearing. The minister guided Harry to the edge of one, and pointed to one of many large pillows surrounding the carpets.

"Please, Captain, sit here. And your crew."

Harry sat down with the minister on one side and one of the stewardesses on the other. She was a tall and lovely Swedish girl named Elise. She had beautiful, long blonde hair, perhaps never before seen by some of these men.

"Others will soon join us," the minister told Harry.

And they did. Many others and, judging by the deference with which they were received, they were Very Important Others, about twenty in all. Most were in military uniforms, some wore civilian coats with ties. Plainly, these men were the heart of the government of Somalia. As they filed in, they shook hands with the minister, who introduced them to Harry. Each took a place around the carpets. None could take his eyes off Elise. Missing was their host, the President.

"He is in need of rest," explained the minister, "but he has asked me to offer you the full hospitality of our country."

The next surprise was music. A three-piece band emerged from the jungle and began to play primitive stringed instruments and a flute. Two female dancers were next on the program, and they gyrated in an unusual way to the unusual music. This, thought Harry, is a long way from Milwaukee. Still, he enjoyed it and told the minister so. The minister smiled happily.

"Yes, lovely," he said, "our native music. I am pleased you like it. Is it not better than your Rolling Stones?"

Harry suppressed a chuckle and nodded. "Yes," he agreed, "much better." And he meant it.

Next to appear from the bountiful jungle around them was lunch. That came on large trays carried, with extraordinary ease and balance, on the heads of very young serving girls. The trays were set on the carpets in front of the minister.

"Goat," he explained, as he tore a large handful from the carcass on the tray and put it on one of the plates before them. He then gestured to the girl to present the tray to Harry, and, with a circular motion of his arm, to the other guests. The following trays were passed along in the same way. Before long, all the diners were sampling food which Harry had never before seen, let alone tasted. He saw that the VIPs, although eating enthusiastically, never stopped looking at Elise. To them, thought Harry, she might have been a goddess from another planet.

One of the serving girls appeared with a large pitcher carved from wood.

"What is it?" Harry asked the girl. She smiled and looked at the minister, who replied for her.

"It is the milk of the camel. Delicious."

Harry politely declined.

Elise, apparently a risk-taker, said, "I would like to try this. Is it fresh?"

"Oh, no," said the minister. "If it is fresh, it produces diarrhea. It must be at least four days old."

Elise quickly withdrew her extended cup. "Perhaps later," she said with embarrassment, deciding this was a risk not worth taking.

The band, which had disappeared into the jungle during lunch, now reappeared. The minister leaned towards Harry.

"Now, it is the time for dancing," he said. Dancing? With whom? That question was answered when a man in uniform stood up, walked across the carpets, and spoke to Harry in the local language. Of course, Harry did not understand. He turned to the minister, who said, "He is asking for your permission to dance with your lady." He nodded towards Elise.

Harry looked at Elise, eyebrows raised, questioning. She smiled and nodded. Harry turned back to the minister and said, "If the gentleman wants to dance with her, he should ask her, not me."

When this was translated, the man seemed puzzled. A woman who could make her own decisions? He recovered quickly and, with a broad smile, extended his hand to Elise. She took it, stood, and began dancing in a stiff and formal way. There were three other girls in the crew and they, too, were soon dancing. Some of the men began dancing with other men, loosely, not touching. It was not easy to dance on carpets spread across a jungle clearing, but they managed with pleasure and enthusiasm.

The jungle's next surprise was a man carrying a video camera. To a loud cheer, he began recording the dancing. Well, thought Harry, this jungle is full of surprises. I wonder what other miracles it has in store for us. That answer came some twenty minutes later when a large television with a video recorder was trundled into the clearing and, within minutes, all the dancers were watching themselves on the television set. Gasps and shouts filled the air as they did. Now, thought Harry, I have seen everything.

Harry did not want to wear out the minister's hospitality and he suggested that it might be time to return to the airport.

The minister nodded in agreement and said, "Yes, but first a few words of thanks from our President." He signaled a uniformed guest, who stood and spoke in Arabic. He spoke with obvious feeling. Harry, of course, understood not one word, but it was easy to grasp the meaning and he was somehow touched. He turned to the first officer, seated nearby, and asked him to respond. He did, and was rewarded with loud and prolonged applause. A few minutes later, the minister led the crew back along the red carpet towards the bus. The guests had gone before and lined one side of the carpet. As Harry and the crew passed the dignitaries, each shook the hand of every crew member. This, thought Harry, as he shook all those hands, was one helluva lunch, even without the camel milk.

101
OUAGADOUGOU

During Harry's early days in Trans Polar, Harry had stayed for a couple of weeks with Tomas Wilman, who was to become the Chief Pilot. Whenever the telephone rang, Wilman would say, "If that's for me, I'm in Ouagadougou." Harry had assumed that this was some imaginary place Tomas used to avoid taking calls; so it was with great surprise when, one day in Jeddah, he was called by crew scheduling and told that he would, the next day, operate a flight there. It was not until the following morning that he learned that Ouagadougou was not only a real city, but that it was in the country of Burkina-Faso. Harry had never heard of Burkina-Faso, but a glance at his charts showed that it was in the horn of Africa just below Mali. Harry had never heard of Mali either.

Harry's passengers were pilgrims who had overstayed their welcome in Jeddah after the Haj, been rounded up, and were being sent home. This happened regularly, Harry was told by his Saudi first officer, and the airplane was full. The cabin crew was all male. That was because some of the pilgrims were known to be reluctant to leave the airplane upon arrival and had to be disembarked forcibly. Also on board was an English ground engineer to deal with any mechanical problems that might arise in Ouagadougou.

The flight would pass over unfamiliar territory with the usual communication problems of third-world countries. Guided by the Inertial Navigation System, Harry would fly across half of Africa to Ouagadougou. That system was, to Harry, a miracle. It used extremely sensitive gyroscopes to detect changes in direction. These changes were translated into airspeed, wind, ground speed and the position of the airplane. The INS displayed both the latitude and longitude, and the time and distance to the next waypoint. Great care was needed to insert the correct waypoints as the autopilot simply took the airplane from one point to the next. Nine waypoints could be inserted and, after passing number nine, the autopilot took the airplane to number one; so the points had to be updated as the flight progressed. One airliner had crash-landed far off track when the crew had neglected to do that; so when the airplane passed waypoint number nine, it turned back to the original waypoint number one. As often in life, the right buttons had to be pushed at the right time.

At flight operations in Jeddah, Harry had been handed a flight plan cranked out by a computer. That sheet of paper was all that Harry needed to fly from Jeddah to Ouagadougou. It listed all the points over which the plane would pass, along with their geographic coordinates. It also listed the magnetic heading, the distance, and time of flight to each point. These points were inserted into the INS computer on the airplane. After departure, the INS was connected to the autopilot, and it flew the airplane from one point to the next, hands off all the way.

The INS found Ouagadougou, and Harry landed routinely in clear weather. They would spend the night there, but Harry was uncharacteristically unenthusiastic about exploring the city. That changed when his telephone rang a few minutes after he entered his room. Calling with an interesting proposal was the Saudi cabin chief.

"Captain," he said, "I have spoken with the concierge here and he has provided a list of places for us to visit this evening. A night tour of Ouagadougou. Very lively, he says. We are going and we would like you to join us. What do you think?"

Harry did not think long. This sounded too interesting to miss and he agreed to meet the crew in the hotel lobby early in the evening.

The enterprising cabin chief had arranged taxis, and off they went in a gaggle of three ancient cars for an evening of excitement in the great city of Ouagadougou. Their first stop became their last and they spent the entire evening in the same bar. "Bar" was using the word loosely, thought Harry, as he entered the dark and gloomy room. With a cement floor and cinder-block walls, it looked more like a garage than a bar. The only person there was an exceedingly dark man behind the bar. He was polishing it with great vigor and it was almost as bright as his beautiful teeth when he smiled to welcome them. How was it, Harry had often wondered, that these third-world people always had such perfect teeth?

The barman, speaking English, asked, "How can I help these good gentlemen? What can I get for them?"

Glancing about the room, Harry got up on a bar stool. "What can you suggest?" he asked. "How's the local beer here?"

The dazzling smile reappeared as he answered. "Oh, our beer is famous, sir, and I am sure you will enjoy drinking it. Please try one bottle. If you do not like it, no need to pay."

Harry smiled back. "You talked me into it. One bottle of beer, please. No glass." Drinking from the bottle was always safer in places like this one.

Everyone ordered beer or Coke and the barman served them with cordiality, smiling throughout. Then he turned, picked up a telephone behind him, spoke urgently for a minute or two, then turned back to Harry.

"And how do you find our beer, sir? Tasteful, is it not?"

Harry had to admit that it was indeed "tasteful" and wondered how such beer could be made in such a place. He inspected the label, which told him only that Tasty Beer was made in Ouagadougou by the Tasty Beer Company. Good enough, thought Harry, as he took another drink. There was no need to be confused by the list of ingredients in the beer.

Before he had drunk his first beer, a shaft of sunlight penetrated the darkness -- it was still broad daylight outside -- as the door opened and a pretty girl came into the room. Ah, thought Harry, the telephone call. Within minutes several more girls appeared, almost like magic, and began talking with the crew. All spoke English, in one form or another. The first girl went straight to Harry and offered her hand. She was lighter complexioned than the barman, but her teeth were just as perfect and she displayed them in a stunning smile. Although black, she did not have Negroid features. She reminded Harry of Lena Horne.

"Sir, hello, my name is . . . ." She spoke a name which Harry was unable to repeat, despite several tries.

"Never mind," she said with a musical laugh, "it means 'flower', so you can call me that. Would you like to buy a drink for me? I am very friendly company and the drinks here are not dear." Still smiling, she perched herself on the stool next to Harry.

"Sure," said Harry, "have one on me."

She smiled that smile and spoke to the barman in the local language. The barman looked at Harry, questioning. Harry nodded.

"Yes, please give Flower a drink, whatever she wants."

A minute later, a tall drink was placed before her. She raised it towards Harry, said "Thank you, sir," and took a sip. After the first few minutes, Harry forgot that she was black. She was charming and pleasant and she had what Jack Rooney used to call "a dynamite body." It was covered in a gown-like dress, brightly-colored, and although it fitted loosely, it was plain to see that it curved in and out in all the right places when she moved.

Harry looked around and saw that the bar was suddenly full of girls. Just then, the door opened again and several young men sauntered into the bar. They were musicians, Harry saw, and each carried an instrument. One wore a New York Yankees' baseball cap. Ah, thought Harry, the entertainment has arrived. The band took up a place in one corner of the room, smiling and laughing. Harry noticed they all had perfect teeth. Without bothering to tune up, they broke into a local version of "Come Fly with Me," an old Frank

Sinatra favorite of Harry's. Tasteful beer, pretty girls, and now Frank Sinatra. Their night on the town of Ouagadougou was off to a promising start.

After the song was over, Harry went up to the band and spoke to the man wearing the baseball cap.

"You a Yankee fan?" he asked. He was answered with a blank stare. "Your cap," Harry said, pointing to it, "where did you get it?"

Not in Yankee Stadium, that was for sure. The man's face was split by a wide grin displaying more perfect teeth. Miraculous, thought Harry, how a smile could change a face.

"Ah, sir, this cap," he said, and he pointed to it, too. "It was given to me by an American man long ago. He told me to guard it with my life. No idea the meaning of the letters," he said, still smiling. Harry smiled back.

"Just as well," said Harry. "There are some people who don't like the New York Yankees. I, myself, am one of them."

The grin disappeared and was replaced by the blank stare.

"Sir? Is it not a good cap?"

"It's a good cap," Harry assured him, and he felt foolish for bringing it up.

The door was opening and closing often now as other patrons began to fill the room. They were spectators more than patrons, thought Harry, and although each ordered a drink, it was clear they had come to see the foreigners, not the band. Now the cabin chief, who was a Saudi, stood, led a girl to the center of the room and began to dance. Harry was surprised to see a Saudi dancing. Soon, others joined in, and over the next few minutes, the place took on a festive air. Here we are in the middle of Africa, thought Harry, and this place is beginning to look like New Year's Eve; and outside it was still broad daylight!

Obviously, thought Harry, not all Muslim countries followed the same rules; or perhaps they followed the same rules in different ways. In either case, some Muslim countries seemed to be more Muslim than others. Alcohol and dancing were not allowed in Jeddah; but here they were apparently normal. And the girls who had appeared so quickly were plainly looking for business. That also was not allowed in Jeddah. Women were almost never seen in public there. The Saudis in the crew lost no time in taking advantage of the differences in the rules. Even Muslims had to strike when the iron was hot. Well, thought Harry, who could blame them? Here, in a dark bar in the middle of nowhere, they could enjoy the fruit that was forbidden at home.

"Sir," Flower asked, as she placed her hand on his arm, "would you like to dance with me?"

By now, Harry had drunk two bottles of Tasty beer, and dancing seemed like a fine idea, even though he was not good at it. The tempo of the music had increased and they danced without touching. Flower moved with easy grace and rhythm, smiling with pleasure as she did.

"Sir," she said after a minute or two, "you must relax and listen to the music. Listen, then let your body and your feet follow."

There was no way Harry could do that, even after two beers. He did his best, and he enjoyed watching Flower, who seemed taken over by the music, which was now unfamiliar to Harry.

The Saudi cabin chief had gotten, from the concierge, the names of several restaurants, but it was beginning to look like dinner would be a casualty of the festivities. They were all getting hungry, but no one wanted to leave. The cabin chief spoke to the barman and, ten minutes later, several platters of fried chicken were carried into the room, along with heaps of fried potatoes. They tasted delicious and went well with the Tasty Beer.

Before long, the food, the beer, and the dancing took their toll and it was hard for Harry keep his eyes open. The curtain, as he liked to say, was coming down. It had been a long day and now he was feeling every minute of it. He noticed that several of the crew, including the ground engineer, had left with girls, and he decided it was time to go back to the hotel. Flower seemed genuinely disappointed when he told her he was leaving.

"Sir, I was hoping we might have the night together, perhaps in your hotel. I am pleasant company in the bed, too. You will not be disappointed. Do I not please you?"

Harry thought of the sensuous way she danced. In earlier years he might have considered taking her to his hotel. But those days were over.

"Yes," he said, "I'm sure you're good company in bed. And I've been very pleased to be with you. But now it's time for me to go."

He slipped a hand into his pocket and withdrew several folded banknotes he had obtained before leaving the hotel. He separated a large one -- they came in different sizes -- and pressed it into her hand. As he did, he bent over and kissed her lightly on her cheek. She smiled a disappointed smile and tucked the bill into her bodice.

"Thank you, sir, and please visit Flower the next time you come to our city. The barman, he will know where to find me."

Harry was unsure if she was disappointed because he was leaving or because she had missed an opportunity to earn some money. Some of each, he hoped. It would probably be a long time before Harry returned to Ouagadougou, but he promised to call Flower if he did.

On his way out, Harry asked the barman for his bill.

"All paid, sir. Your companion paid the entire amount, including yours."

Which companion, Harry wanted to know. The barman described the Saudi cabin chief who had, by now, left with one of the girls. This was the traditional Saudi hospitality, even in a far-off bar. Harry smiled and made a mental note to thank his cabin chief in the morning. Then, he took from his pocket a card printed with the name of his hotel and handed it to one of the taxi drivers waiting outside. He had not seen much of Ouagadougou, he mused as he rode back to his hotel, but it was most certainly not an imaginary place.

102
N'DJAMENA

Chad was another one of those African countries Harry had never heard of. Chad sat squarely in the center of the northern part of the continent. It was below Algeria, with Niger on one side and Sudan on the other. Like many of the others, Chad sent pilgrims to Jeddah every year. And, like other pilgrims, many were not eager to return home.

By now, Harry was used to picking up his telephone to be sent to unexpected places; but he was surprised when he was told that his flight to Chad the next morning would be an unscheduled route check with his Assistant Equipment Manager. Captain Rajah was a Lebanese Muslim, and he was one of the few Arabs that Harry could not seem to get along with. He was an unpleasant man, but Harry had dealt with such men before. There was no reason he could put a finger on; it was just one of those relationships that did not work. Had he said something in an unguarded moment about Rajah that had found its way back to him? He didn't know, but he sensed some hostility.

Rajah was an intense man with an unkempt beard and dark, deep-set eyes. To Harry, he had a look of evil. Harry had flown with him in the simulator, and they did not get along well. Rajah was a Muslim who took his religion more seriously than most. He was known to carry his prayer carpet on all flights and to never miss a prayer call, even in flight. Some thought it was more for reasons of ambition than spirit. Could he be trying to impress his superiors? It was hard to know.

There had to be a reason for an unscheduled check flight. Could it have been his resistance to accept that flight to London with Ali? Harry could only guess, but the signals were unsettling. His foreboding grew when they met at flight operations in the morning.

"Have you ever been to N'djamena?" he asked, even before he said hello.

When Harry shook his head, Rajah smiled thinly and said, "Good, very good." This, thought Harry, is not a good omen.

The airplane was packed with reluctant pilgrims who had overstayed the Haj. The flight went normally, or so Harry thought, until the descent point. There, to simulate an arrival in bad weather, Rajah placed a passenger pillow against the windshield in front of Harry. The actual weather was clear.

Harry knew airline policy forbid this practice. Should he mention that? No, he decided, that might make it worse.

"What kind of approach should I expect?" Harry asked during the descent.

"You shall make a standard VOR-DME approach," he answered, with a hard edge in his voice.

VOR was a type of radio beacon that provided bearing information to a pilot. DME meant that it also had a distance-measuring feature, which provides a pilot with continuous distance from the radio he has tuned in. Before leaving Jeddah, Harry had checked the NOTAMS. These are Notices to Airmen, and they list current information about facilities along airways and at airports. Those for N'djamena told Harry that the DME part of the radio was out of service. That meant that although the radio was working, the distance feature was not.

This time Harry spoke up. "Captain," he said, with courtesy he did not mean, "I am not legally allowed to make a VOR-DME approach with the DME unserviceable."

Rajah simply nodded. "Do your best," was all he said. Harry thought hard. He did not mind getting Rajah into trouble but he did not want to put himself in jeopardy. That was a possibility here. Should he refuse to make an illegal approach using an illegal practice? He knew that Rajah had a reputation for being vindictive. No, better not press him on this.

The runway ran east-west, and wind dictated landing to the east. That helped. To begin the approach, Harry flew over the radio and zeroed his Inertial Navigation System as he did. He could then use its distance read-outs in place of those of the radio. The INS is accurate enough to be used in such a way, even though it was not legal. Following the procedure on the approach chart, Harry flew outbound from the radio and made the depicted turn back to the airport. The chart designated, in miles, the point to begin final descent to the airport. When he reached that point, Harry pulled back the throttles, only to have Rajah push them back up. Harry looked sharply at Rajah, who was in the observer's seat behind Harry.

"You shall descend when I tell you to descend." A minute or two later he took away the pillow and said, "Now land the airplane."

The extra seconds at the higher altitude had brought Harry closer to the airport and too high to follow a normal glide path.

He ordered full flaps and pulled the throttles to idle. He pushed the nose down to gain airspeed. He would need the extra speed when he put the power back up. For now, it was more important to lose altitude. When the glide path looked right, Harry raised the nose slightly and pushed the throttles forward. The engines slowly accelerated as the speed bled off. With a combination of luck and airmanship, Harry came over the end of the runway at just the right height and right on his target airspeed. He made a normal landing 1,000 feet from the end, right where he was supposed to land. He congratulated himself mentally.

Rajah was not impressed. The positive side of their trip was that they would not remain overnight. The negative side was that Rajah used almost the entire flight home to debrief Harry. Leaving the first officer to monitor the airplane, he asked Harry to move to the cabin, now empty except for the flight attendants. There he brought out his list of comments about Harry's check flight. There were thirty-eight items on the list. After the first one, Harry did not need to hear more.

Number one concerned the time of the pushback from their parking slot. As the airplane began to move, the flight engineer had called out, "Blocks off at 0838, Captain?" Harry confirmed the time. Rajah's comment was: "You allowed the flight engineer to call the blocks-off time, Captain." Now he spoke with scorn. "This is very poor command technique."

It went downhill from there, each item more meaningless than the one before. Finally he came to the landing in N'djamena. Harry thought he had saved a bad situation brought on by Rajah placing the airplane in a precarious position. Rajah did not agree.

"Captain," he asked caustically, "what was your airspeed as you touched down?"

Harry's brow furrowed. "I don't know," he answered "but we were right on speed crossing the threshold. Touchdown speed is not in the manual."

Every pilot in Saudia knew these kinds of numbers, meaningful or not. Rajah replied that it is in the manual, the Boeing manual.

"And," he went on, "you touched down three knots above that speed."

Harry did not bother to inform Rajah that the Saudia manual, and not that of Boeing, was their only authority. You cannot reason with such a person, he told himself. Rajah simply enjoyed being mean.

Rajah did not tell Harry whether he had failed his check flight and Harry would be damned if he would ask. So late the next day, he called crew scheduling and asked if he was still programmed to fly to Riyadh the following morning. He was, and that was all he had to know. Rajah be damned!

There was a post-log to this story and Harry was delighted to hear it. A few weeks later, Harry flew with Joe Long, the American flight engineer. He told Joe about his check flight with Rajah. When Joe heard the part about the three knots, he exploded.

"That sonofabitch!" he said with great sarcasm. "I was with him last week in Dhahran on a clear day when he landed twenty knots fast halfway down the goddamn runway. He used full brakes and max reverse thrust, and we still almost went off the other end. In fact, our nose wheel was on the overrun. We couldn't turn around and they had to send a tug out to push us back onto the runway."

Harry knew he should not feel good hearing about this near disaster, but he positively beamed. "Joe," he said with a grin, "you have just made my day."

103
RAMADAN

Those Muslims who could afford it were very strongly encouraged by the principles of Islam to make, before they died, the pilgrimage to the Holy Land. The journey would cleanse their souls and prepare them for the afterlife. Before the modern era, this voyage was a Herculean effort. They came from across the Islamic world, some from as far away as Indonesia, and they came by boat, camel, and even by foot. It was the voyage of a lifetime and it might take years. Many who left home never returned. Some who set out never reached Mecca. This motivation marked the devotion of the followers of Islam. The age of aviation changed greatly the access to the Haj.

In TEA, Harry had carried pilgrims from Nigeria and Algeria. At the start of the Haj, airliners landed in Jeddah at a rate of one every minute. They brought worshippers who had never imagined they would one day walk around the Kaaba in Mecca. Some were so taken with the Holy Places that they decided not to go back home.

Pilgrims who were reluctant to return were only one of the unusual aspects of the religious period known as Ramadan. It turned life upside down in many ways. First, fasting from sunrise to sunset translated into not only hunger and thirst, it also changed personalities. Many fasters became irritable and some became difficult. Some who were difficult became unbearable. Fasting provided a built-in excuse to act obnoxiously, and many took advantage of it. The daily fast built up the great hunger that was one of its objectives. That led to gorging, with great quantities of food, the moment the sun went down. That, in turn, led to eating binges that sometimes lasted throughout the night.

Saudia provided a venue for such binging in the crew hotel in Riyadh. The company had taken over an entire Marriott Hotel there and used it only for crew layovers. At any one time, dozens, sometimes hundreds, of flight crewmembers were there waiting to operate a flight. All of these crews were based in Jeddah, so they had to be flown to Riyadh to crew the many Saudia flights that left from there. Harry had once carried sixty-seven crewmembers from Jeddah to Riyadh. These passengers were known as "deadheads," and they took up about half the seats in Harry's 707.

"That's nothing," Lars told him one day. "My record in a Tri-Star is 189."

The hotel had one unique feature. It was staffed with armed guards to prevent those on the men's floors from visiting the women's rooms that were on the higher floors. Harry had heard about an American pilot who was ignorant of this restriction. Somehow, he found his way to the room of a Turkish female flight attendant in the forbidden section where he was "apprehended" while drinking tea in the middle of the afternoon. He was on his way out of the country within twenty-four hours.

"He was lucky he was not shot," said the pilot who told Harry the story, only half joking.

During Ramadan, the company set aside several rooms where the fasts could be broken in style, with mountains of food served long into the night. It was more than a breakfast; it was a celebration. Harry had often heard the sounds of the music and the laughter as he passed through that part of the hotel. And he had smelled the cigarettes that were forbidden during the fast. Of course, no one was fit for work the next day, and few Saudis did. So day became night as they slept through most of it. It was normal for Saudis not to report for flights during Ramadan. Usually, they did not bother to call; they simply failed to show up. It was more or less expected.

During one Ramadan, Harry was awakened early one morning at the Marriott by a call from the crew scheduler. Instead of flying back to Jeddah as a deadhead, he would operate a flight to London. Fine, said Harry, who enjoyed visiting London. As the crew was driven to the airport, the Saudi first officer fell fast asleep. He had obviously been awake all night breaking his fast. Once airborne, he soon fell asleep in the cockpit. As it was a ferry flight with no passengers, Harry gently shook his shoulder to awaken him and told him to go back and sleep in the cabin. He was useless in the cockpit, anyway. Some six hours later, and approaching Boulogne on the French coast, the first officer had not yet returned to the cockpit; so Harry sent the flight engineer to bring him up front for the descent and landing. Still half asleep, he was able to operate the radios and read the checklists.

That flight was, in a way, a microcosm of life in Saudi Arabia during Ramadan. No one and nothing worked as it was supposed to. Many Saudis, including flight crews, slept during the day, every day. You got used to that after the first few days but it seemed, to Harry, to negate the purpose of the fast. It was supposed to be a hardship, not a party, as it was for many. Anyway, he thought, it makes a great excuse for avoiding work, and many took advantage of it. Harry had been told that the Koran allowed postponing a fast day to a non-work day, but he had never seen anyone do this. Fasting provided a good reason to stay home and a good excuse to be disagreeable.

It was during Ramadan that Irene and Harry underwent an unusual experience, probably related to the frustration caused by fasting. Most winter evenings in Jeddah were beautiful, but one was especially so. Harry suggested a drive along the nearby cornische, a promenade that followed the Red Sea shoreline. It was just before sundown, and Irene brought her camera, hoping to catch one of the spectacular sunsets there. The first sight they saw was a Saudi woman, covered from head to toe in her black chador, swinging slowly in a child's swing in a play area.

"Stop the car," said Irene excitedly, as she took her camera out of its case. "This is too good to miss."

A chador-clad woman in a swing would be a rare photo.

Harry stopped briefly, Irene quickly took a photo, and they continued along the shore. After a minute or so, Harry was irked by the car behind him blowing his horn nonstop. Harry slowed and then stopped, thinking perhaps the horn blower wanted to point out a problem with his car. There was a problem, but not about Harry's car. A tall Saudi in a thobe left his car and was quickly at Harry's window.

"Give me your camera," he demanded gruffly.

"What's that? Who are you?" asked Harry.

"I am a Saudi citizen and I saw you take a photograph of one of our women. Please, give me your camera."

Almost before Harry could reply, a police car pulled up alongside Harry's car. Within minutes, a second police car appeared. Harry sensed trouble but said only, "This is my camera. Why should I give it to you?" By now, a policeman was at Harry's window, talking in Arabic to the Saudi who had stopped them. He wore a fierce expression and spoke no English. He reached inside the car and snatched the key out of the ignition.

Harry's alarm rose quickly and he saw this was an argument he could not win. Taking the camera from Irene, he handed it to the policeman, who opened it and removed the film. He unrolled it and held it up to the light, not to view it, but to ruin it. To be sure, he then threw the film to the road and stomped vigorously on it for a minute or two, then handed the camera back to Harry.

"My keys, please," said Harry hopefully, extending his palm. Discretion was clearly the better part of valor here. Better to get elsewhere as soon as possible. He was somewhat surprised and very grateful when his keys were handed back to him. Smiling his thanks, he started his engine and drove off slowly, very slowly.

104
VAN

He came into the world in Irene's hometown of Antwerp. They named him Van, taken from van Doren, Irene's family name. Harry managed to be there for the birth and actually played a small role by holding Irene's shoulders as Van was born. There are only a few moments of true exhilaration during a man's life and this, for Harry, was one of them. There was no way, then or later, that Harry could put into words the emotions that overcame him during those moments of Van's birth.

Irene endured the ordeal without a sound, and, when Van was held up to her, she asked only, "Is the baby normal?"

The nurse smiled and nodded enthusiastically. "Yes," she said. "Normal."

Harry's thrill of Van's birth lasted long into the evening as he sat, alone, in Irene's apartment. As he drank a glass of Scotch in celebration, he slowly came back to earth. Harry had never thought about being a father except in a vague sort of way. Now he was one and he was joyous and serious, both at the same time.

As Van's birth had neared, one of Harry's friends had remarked, "I hope you're aware of what an anchor you're throwing out here."

As he sipped, he thought about that anchor. Yes, he ruminated, there would be much responsibility, but he was ready. He vowed to be a good father. As a child grew and developed going through life, it was one step at a time; but viewed as a whole, the path seemed formidable. There was much to learn, much to undergo. Harry would do his best to help Van along the path called life.

105
LOVE NOTES

There was a large bank of mailboxes in a room next to flight operations. Each crewmember had his own. Along with mail from abroad, the boxes sometimes held notices and directives from the company. One such notice, known as a love note, read simply, "See your Equipment Manager." These notes were dreaded because the recipient never knew the reason for the summons. One day, after returning from an early flight to Medina, Harry found a love note in his mailbox. *Damn*, he thought as he read it, what have I done now? Might as well get it over with, he decided, so went upstairs to talk to Captain Mustapha, not knowing what to expect, but braced for bad news. A love note usually preceded terminations. Harry did not expect that, but you never knew.

Harry spoke briefly with Mustapha's secretary, a Pakistani youth with a friendly manner.

"Please, Captain, have some tea. I will tell Captain Mustapha you are here."

He pressed a button that would summon another Pakistani, whose job it was to provide tea.

Before the tea arrived, the secretary came out of the inner office and said, "Please, Captain, you can go in. Captain Mustapha will see you now."

Mustapha looked up from a paper he was reading as Harry entered. He smiled and Harry relaxed somewhat. That smile probably meant the news was not bad. He arose and shook Harry's hand. That was another good sign.

"Please sit, Captain. Your tea will arrive shortly. I have some information for you, and I hope you will be pleased."

Harry returned the smile. "I hope so, too" he said.

"You are seconded to Saudia." Mustapha began. That was a British term which meant Harry was sub-contracted from another company.

"Yes, Trans Polar," said Harry. "Don't tell me my company has gone belly up."

Mustapha's eyebrows went up. "Belly up? What does it mean, belly up?"

"It means," said Harry, "going out of business for one reason or another. What is the news?"

"Belly up," mused Mustapha, "like a dead fish. Yes, very descriptive. Like many American expressions. Yes, I am afraid Trans Polar has gone out of business and that makes their contract void. You were expecting this?"

Harry sucked in his breath, wondering what was coming next. "Let's just say I'm not surprised," he answered. "There have been rumors. So what does this mean for me?"

Saudis enjoyed those moments when they could play the role of Allah and determine the fate of others. This appeared to be one of those moments and Harry could see that Mustapha relished it.

He smiled and pushed a sheaf of papers across the desk.

"Not much, really. We have decided to continue your employment under our standard contract. It is for three Hegira years, and your salary will remain unchanged. I have already prepared the papers."

He felt relieved. He picked up the contract and glanced at it briefly.

"This is a standard contract?" he asked.

"Yes, standard, like all the others." Harry knew that Saudis often saw life very differently than did westerners. But within their own view of the world they lived honorably and, as far as Harry knew, they were truthful.

Harry took a pen from his shirt pocket and asked, "Where do I sign?"

Mustapha appeared surprised. "You may take it home and read it. There is no need to sign today."

By now, Harry had found the place for his signature. Without replying, he signed his name and handed the papers back to Mustapha.

"I trust you," he said "and my wife and I like living here. We will be pleased to continue."

That was a stretch, but it was mostly true. They did enjoy the living; it was the working that was sometimes hard to endure.

"Anything else?" he asked.

"No, no," was Mustapha's quick answer. "Nothing more. Thank you, Captain, for your cooperation. You will find a copy in your mailbox during the next few days."

Harry rose, shook Mustapha's hand, turned and left the office. He hurried home to tell Irene the good news.

The news was good news because the rumors about Trans Polar had already turned into fact. Harry knew the company had gone bankrupt. He had even spoken about it with Lars, who, by coincidence, had been at its "Belly Up" party in Oslo. Chief Pilot Tomas Wilman had catered the event. He did that by visiting the airport and ordering a supply of food and drink as though they were for a Trans Polar flight. And, in a way, it was; the last one.

Before he signed the order, Wilman casually said to the catering agent, "You should know the company is about to be bankrupt."

The agent simply smiled and said, "I did not hear that."

He was quickly invited and took part in the company's last hurrah. It was, said Lars, a grand success.

"Happy to be in Saudia now?" Lars asked, after he told Harry the news.

Harry was indeed happy to be in Saudia. Any job was better than no job; and he and Irene had settled nicely into the social life in Saudi City. He actually looked forward to staying in Saudi Arabia.

106
ANYONE FOR BEIRUT?

Harry did not find another love note in his mail box until well into his second contract. He was not sure if that was because he had become inured to the horseshit or because he had become adept at avoiding situations which might have provoked it. After a rocky start, Irene came to like the "ghetto," even though she left it only to shop at the supermarket or to spend a day at the beach. Their social life revolved around tennis, swimming pools, and dinner parties. There was a wide cross-section of international people living in Saudi City, with cultures from around the world. Most were pleasant and interesting. Among them were many Belgians and Dutch. The Dutch speak Flemish with a different accent so she had plenty of opportunity to converse in her native language.

Van was a happy child and Harry found himself enjoying fatherhood far more than he had expected. Irene was an excellent cook and now she had plenty of time to burnish her skills. Her dinners were regarded as the best in the complex. Did she miss working in the bank?

"Oh, now and then," she said, "but this is a new world for me and I am enjoying it."

She had plenty of time to devote to Van's care and she did it with great love. There were many potential baby-sitters who were pleased to care for Van when the need arose. Taking care of friends' children was common, and Irene and Harry had done their share; so there were many volunteers when Harry and Irene took advantage of their six days off each month and visited other places in the region. They traveled to Athens, Istanbul, and Cairo. These were places where Harry had seen the airport, but not much more. They had never made his list of cities he wanted to visit, but they were fascinating.

In Istanbul they were impressed by the Blue Mosque and they took a boat trip on the Bosphorus, the body of water which separates Europe from Asia. Harry had been cheated and embarrassed by a moneychanger on a main street in Istanbul. The man had twice counted out the notes as Harry, suspicious, watched very intently as each note was placed in his palm. That slight-of-hand magic cost them $100.

In Cairo they saw the Pyramids, the Sphinx, and the bust of Tutankhamen, which was exquisite. In Athens, they saw the Parthenon and other famous landmarks.

In a men's room one afternoon during a tour there, Harry was relieving himself when a fellow American entered in haste, took the urinal next to Harry's, and, after some fumbling with his trousers, began to urinate like a race horse.

"Ah," he exhaled with obvious relief, "they charged me a nickel to come in here but it's worth a quarter."

Harry nodded and smiled.

"Sometimes," he said "even more."

A poignant trip was to Juan les Pins on the French Riviera. During a lunch on an outdoor terrace, they fell into conversation with an American couple at a nearby table. They were pleased to find an American to talk with, and they invited Harry and Irene to their table for coffee. They were from Oklahoma and had set out to see the Mediterranean by boat. They were plainly people of quality. Jimmy was tall with a ruddy complexion and what remained of his thinning white hair was closely cropped. He was personable and engaging and did most of the talking for both of them. Betty was attractive and was once, Harry thought, a beautiful woman. She was quiet and reserved and Harry thought he saw sadness in her eyes.

When she left to visit the ladies room, Jimmy explained her sadness. Their only child, a beloved son, had been killed in Vietnam. She had never gotten over that, he said, and she never would. This trip was an attempt to salvage the rest of her life. They had seen much of the Mediterranean and were about to set off across the Atlantic for South America.

"Wow!" said Harry, impressed. "That's some trip! I admire your courage. What kind of boat?"

"Come and see it," Jimmy said. "It's just a few minutes from here. We'll have a coffee, maybe a drink."

The boat was not large, only about thirty-five feet, and that made their Atlantic crossing even more adventurous. The coffee and a few glasses of Cointreau stretched out into an entire afternoon. Betty joined the conversation now and then, but never the laughter.

"Well, I'll be damned," said Jimmy when Harry told them he lived in Saudi Arabia. "We lived there for a couple of years long ago." Not only that, Jimmy was a retired pilot.

"Some coincidence." said Harry. "What did you do there?"

Jimmy had been hired to map Saudi Arabia from an old B17, a bomber used during World War II.

"Well," said Harry, "easy these days, but maybe not so easy back then. How did you go about it?"

Jimmy had improvised a basic technique. He had simply tied one end of a piece of string to several washers. He tied the other end to a point on the overhead panel between the forward windshields. The string stayed vertical even when the wings of the airplane were not level. Using it as a guide, he was somehow able to line up a prominent point on the horizon and crisscross the entire country without overlapping the strips he overflew.

"And that worked?" asked Harry with surprise.

"Believe it or not, it did. And very well. But the entire time we mapped the place, we never saw a cloud and that's what made it work."

They had worked for a prince, lived in Riyadh, and were paid "more money than I ever imagined."

When they parted, Harry and Irene wished them "Bon Voyage." As they walked back to their hotel, Irene said, with great feeling, "My heart hurts for her." There was a catch in her voice and tears filled her eyes. "To lose a son! I cannot even begin to imagine how that must feel. I hope, with all my heart, that our Van never has to go to war."

Harry did not respond. What could he say?

They had enjoyed skiing holidays in the French Alps. They stayed in a small, cozy, family-run hotel in the picture-postcard village of Bourg St. Maurice nestled at the foot of the slopes. The rooms were tiny but the food was French cuisine at its best. And at the end of a long day on the slopes, no one cared about the size of the room, only about dining well and falling into bed.

Skiing was a new experience for Harry and he learned the basics from a French instructor whose principal advice was, "Do not fall down." Then, when Harry did, sternly admonished, "I told you, do not fall down." Harry learned quickly and, after a few days, was safe for solo. Irene was an excellent skier. Harry had experienced many unique moments since he had left Milwaukee. Among the best was the glow he felt standing high in the mountains on a clear, beautiful day, about to begin a long downhill run. The splendor of the peaks etched against a bright blue sky, along with the anticipation of exhilaration, gave him a rush almost like that he sometimes felt in an airplane when a view of surpassing beauty presented itself.

Saudia flew twice weekly to Madrid and, a few times, Harry had taken Irene along when he operated a flight there. Several days in this beautiful city, staying in a two-room suite, and being paid per diem to do it, was as good as life can be for an airline pilot. He recalled a friend saying the job was not only better than working, it was better than *not* working. These visits to Madrid made the point. This great city is not on the regular tourist route but, for Harry, it was one of Europe's finest. It boasted broad, tree lined boulevards and impressive old buildings. Parks and monuments seemed to be everywhere. One unusual feature Harry had not seen in other cities was that many buildings had bushes and trees, real trees, growing on their roofs. And, of course, there was the Spanish life style he had first enjoyed in Palma de Majorca. Irene's knowledge of Spanish, learned in night school in Antwerp, helped them to enjoy it. Madrid would become Harry's favorite European city.

One layover there coincided with a concert by Julio Iglesias, one of the top singers in Europe and the world. Harry attended, and he experienced a truly memorable evening. The concert was held in a football stadium, one which had once hosted the World Cup championship game. Harry had been surprised to learn that this great sports event, held every four years, was comparable to the Super Bowl in terms of popularity and media interest. It was soccer in America; but the rest of the world called it football.

The enormous stadium was filled with many thousands of wildly cheering Iglesias fans. His hold on them was clear. The first few notes of each song were met with thunderous shouts and applause. At one point, the stadium lights were put out and everyone there lit a candle while Julio sang. It was an overwhelming experience and Harry enjoyed it immensely. He regretted that Irene had missed it.

Not all problems confronting a captain come up on the airplane. Harry had such an experience during a layover in Madrid when his telephone rang just as he was about to leave his room for the crew pick-up. Calling, was his Swedish first officer to tell Harry that he was ill and would not be able to operate the flight. He said he was ill, but he sounded drunk. Harry quickly went to his room and, sure enough, Per Neilson was unable to stand when he got out of bed as Harry entered the room. The odor of alcohol was pervasive. Unsure of what to do, he was sure of one thing: Per could not fly in this condition. Harry immediately picked up the phone, called Saudia flight operations at the airport and told them that the first officer was sick and a four-hour delay was needed. That would provide some time to figure out his next step.

Next, he called his flight engineer. He was the American who had worked Harry's final check flight after his line training. Joe Long had afterwards provided the celebratory home-brewed beer. Harry explained the situation and asked Joe to come to Per's room. There was a pause.

"Harry," Joe said evenly, "I do not want to be a part of this. If you want my advice, here it is. Four hours will not help. Tell flight ops you need a replacement. Let them sort it out; but do not let him get in the airplane if he's drunk or even close."

That made good sense to Harry. Why take a risk to shield someone who did not deserve it?

He informed flight operations that Per would be unable to do the flight. Harry would remain in the hotel awaiting instructions.

"But there is no one," a plaintive voice said. "Can we not wait another few hours?"

Impossible, Harry replied, the first officer was too ill to fly. He knew there was only one solution and that was to provide minimum crew rest to the incoming first officer, then send him back to Jeddah. By this time the inbound crew was in the hotel. Harry found the room number of the first officer. He was Howard Weissman, the famous Saudi City winemaker. Harry had flown with him often and he knew Howard loved Madrid.

He called his room, explained the situation, then added, "Howard, this is unofficial, but for sure they will give you minimum rest and send you back."

Harry did not say it, but his meaning was clear. If Howard left his room before he was officially assigned, he could not be blamed for being unavailable. Ten minutes later, a telephone call from flight operations made it official; Howard would operate the flight back after minimum crew rest. This time, Harry went to Howard's room and knocked. There was no answer but Harry heard movement in the room.

"Howard," he called out, "I know you're in there. Now, it's official, and you'll work the flight back. You have ten hours of crew rest, starting now. Open the door, please."

Howard was a New Yorker in every way, especially his accent. He was thin with sad eyes, a marked face and a thin moustache. He had a reputation for being different. It was not only his wrinkled shirts, his instant wine, and his jeep without a windshield. He had other habits which marked him as unusual. Now, he opened the door with a sour expression and a furious frown. He said nothing, just nodded and closed the door.

The final act in this little drama took place at 33,000 feet somewhere over Egypt. One of Howard's unusual traits was that he was averse to air conditioning. He and Harry had once had a disagreement in a crew van in Dhahran when Howard told the driver to turn off the air conditioning. It was hot and humid and Harry told the driver to turn it back on. To show his disapproval, Howard rode to the hotel with his head stuck out a side window of the van. He had the same aversion to cockpit air during high-altitude flight. It was a strange aversion for an airline pilot.

Because of it, he often covered himself, head and all, with a blanket while flying. He had disappeared under his blanket soon after leaving Madrid. Obviously upset, he emerged only to make position reports and order cups of hot water for the tea bags he always carried. Eschewing airline food, he brought his own food, as well. He had said not one word to Harry and Joe since their departure.

Finally, Joe had enough.

"Goddammit, Howard," he said sarcastically, "you gonna join the human race or you gonna sit there like an asshole under that blanket all the way to Jeddah?"

After a pause Howard came out from under his blanket, still wearing his frown.

"Welcome back to the real world, Howard," said Harry. "Thanks for joining us. Sorry you missed your Madrid layover, but it wasn't our fault. Now lighten up."

Howard was not a typical airline pilot.

These excursions to Madrid and other places were, for Harry and Irene, an important part of their life, and they helped to make the isolation of Saudi City less artificial, more natural.

"It is," said Irene at times, "a crazy place. But I like crazy places."

Occasional trips abroad went a long way towards making it less crazy.

Now, love note in hand and on his way up the stairs to see Captain Mustapha, Harry ruminated on the life they had made in Saudi City. In some ways, it had become a piece of the U.S. They had made a home there, so it was with some misgiving that Harry responded to his love note. He did not expect a problem, but the prospect of termination was always there, lurking in the back of his mind. He mentally reviewed the past few weeks for something he had said or done that might have caused a problem. He could think of only one possibility.

A few weeks ago Harry, Irene, and Van had been at a barbecue in the Saudi City home of a Belgian friend. Among the ex-pats was one Saudi, attired in his white thobe. Harry saw the Saudi scowl as he spoke with Van. Concerned, Harry approached them and joined the conversation, asking the Saudi what had caused the frown. He smiled pleasantly. "Nothing, really. He is a bright lad."

Harry forgot to ask Van what he had said and now he wished he had.

By this time, Harry had come to know Captain Mustapha and they got along well. Still, Van's words were in Harry's mind as he entered his office. In any other company, it would be absurd to think they could cause a serious problem; but this was Saudia and anything was possible. Mustapha welcomed him with a handshake and buzzed for tea. Harry relaxed somewhat as Mustapha engaged in a few pleasantries. The Saudis never went directly to the point, but they got there sooner or later.

This time it was sooner.

"Captain," he said, as their tea arrived, "I have an opportunity for you, and I am sure you will agree with me that it is a wonderful opportunity."

Opportunity? In Saudia? Harry fidgeted in his chair.

"Aha," he said, "and what might this wonderful opportunity be?"

Mustapha put down his tea and smoothed his thobe with his palms. "We must send a captain to Trans Mediterranean Airlines in Beirut for a few months. I am sure you know that TMA is a cargo company. Your name has come up and we are pleased to offer this opportunity to you. It would be just a few months and I am sure you will enjoy it there. It's a wonderful city, much different than here. What do you think?"

Harry had started thinking before Mustapha finished his first sentence.

"Yes, it is a wonderful city. I've spent a couple of weeks there, so I know. But from the news reports it seems to be somewhat" -- he searched for the right word -- "unsettled right now, isn't it?"

Mustapha winced almost imperceptibly. "Oh, nothing unusual. It has been unsettled there for years, so nothing unusual. And you would not be in Beirut very often, just to pass through now and then. They fly around the world, as you probably know, so you would not be there very much."

"First," said Harry, "how many months are we talking about? And second, do I have a choice here?"

Mustapha smiled. "Three or four months. And, of course, we would much prefer that you went voluntarily. But if you choose not to volunteer . . . ."

He did not finish the sentence and he did not need to. The handwriting on the wall was clear.

"In that case," he replied "I'd like to volunteer to go to Beirut for a few months. What about my family? Are they invited?"

Mustapha frowned. "Of course, if you choose to take them, we would not object. But perhaps you might want to examine this possibility after you are in Beirut."

That made sense. "Of course," said Harry, "and I need to discuss this with my wife."

Mustapha stood to indicate the meeting was over.

"We will provide the details within the next few days. I am sure you will be very pleased that you have so kindly offered to go to Beirut for us. There is much to enjoy there."

"I hope so," replied Harry as they shook hands, "but just to be sure, I'll take my bulletproof vest."

He said that with a smile so Mustapha would not take it seriously.

"You will not need the vest," he said returning the smile. "I do not expect any trouble."

107
BEIRUT

The trouble that Mustapha did not expect began the very night Harry arrived in Beirut. He had traveled in the cockpit of a TMA airplane which had brought cargo to Jeddah and was returning empty. During the flight, Harry had a long conversation with the crew. Yes, there could be trouble, they told him, and the situation was tense. They arrived at midnight in clear weather. Harry expected to be met by someone, anyone, who would provide some direction. The crew was gone within minutes and Harry stood alone on the top of the stairs waiting for his welcoming committee. None came.

He queried one of the mechanics.

"No problem, sir. The flight operations center is near." He gave directions which seemed simple enough. As they were speaking, Harry heard muffled explosions in the distance. He asked the mechanic what was happening.

"There has been shooting since early evening," he said. "Take care."

Harry passed through the terminal and saw there were no taxis on the other side. That was unusual. Only two-hundred meters, the man had said, so Harry decided to walk, carrying his bags. The two-hundred meters became a half mile and, as he trudged along the road, he noticed there was no traffic. None. That was even more unusual. His apprehension grew.

Just as the lights of the operations building came into view, Harry was startled to hear, among the explosions, a strange *whooshing* sound. Looking up, he saw several rockets streak directly over his head, their exhausts inscribing bright arcs in the night sky. Before he reached the building, the rockets had become a barrage. Their target was beyond the airport, and Harry heard clearly the detonations as they struck the ground. He was starting to feel nervous. This was not part of the agreement. He did not own a bulletproof vest, but, at this moment, he wished he did.

He entered the building and found a bare and brightly-lit empty room. This was flight operations? He called out, then thumped the counter a few times with his fist. After a few minutes, a man emerged from the adjacent room, sleepy, and rubbing his eyes.

"Yes, what is it?" he asked wearily.

Harry explained who he was.

"Yes," the tired face replied, "we are expecting you."

The sound of the rockets overhead became louder.

"What the hell is going on here? he asked.

"It's nothing," the man said, "this will all be over in two or three days. But it is not possible for you to go to a hotel now. You will need to wait until morning. For tonight, you must sleep here. There," he pointed to the door leading to the room he had just left, "are some mattresses and blankets. Just for tonight."

This, thought Harry, was worse than Vietnam. There, he had a clean bed and no sounds of war when he was in it. Still, there seemed no choice. He made up a bed, which was a blanket thrown over a mattress, and tried to sleep; but between the sounds of the rockets exploding, the snores of another "guest," and his great apprehension, sleep was impossible.

Calm came with the dawn and Harry was grateful.

"Bonjour, Captain. I hope you slept well," said his mattress-mate. His name was Marcel, he said, and he looked as though he had been living in the operations center for months. Short and plump, shaggy and unshaven, his rumpled clothes gave him the appearance of a refugee.

"It's okay now, Captain. Our crew transport will take you to your hotel. It's the Coral Beach Hotel, just on the sea and near the city. You will enjoy it there."

Harry doubted that, but said, "Thanks. As soon as possible, please. You can send my bill there," Harry said with a smile. Marcel's dour face broke into a grin. "No charge for the accommodation, Captain. I hope you enjoyed your stay with us."

Their car passed through two checkpoints on the way to the hotel. These were military check-points, manned by armed men in uniforms. Harry would later meet an English captain who told him that his driver had one night, inexplicably, driven through a checkpoint without stopping. His car had been fired upon, and one round had come through the rear of the car, passing within inches of his backside. He had resigned the very next day "to save my ass," he said.

Riding to the hotel, Harry thought; I think I liked Beirut better the first time I came. He had made some wonderful memories here; they crossed his mind as he looked out the window. He rarely thought of Astrid anymore, but her image flashed through his mind now; they had shared a great adventure here. He had enjoyed Beirut then. It seemed unlikely he would enjoy it now.

The hotel was shaped like a horseshoe with the open end towards the sea. Harry was given a room in the middle of the shoe and on the second floor. It overlooked the swimming pool and the sea beyond. In another direction he had a fine view of the surrounding hills.

He ate breakfast, which was a plate of fruit, goat cheese and Arabic bread, then decided to sit on his balcony for a few minutes before going to bed. It was early morning, but he needed to catch up on the sleep he had missed he night before. There were a few people in swimsuits enjoying the morning sun. As he admired an especially well-fitting swimsuit worn by an attractive young lady, he was shocked to hear a volley of shots ring out, and to see the impact of the bullets on the cement near the sunbathers. With loud screams, they dispersed quickly and Harry, just as quickly, dove into his room. What had he gotten himself into? What he had gotten himself into, he later learned, was the beginning of a civil war which would last for years and which would tear Lebanon apart.

The Chief Pilot was an American named Bob Anthony. He called in mid-afternoon to say that a car was being sent to bring Harry to the airport to discuss his plans for him. Lebanon looked much less intimidating in the daylight, although the armed checkpoints were still in place. Scary, thought Harry; he sure as hell did not want to bring Irene and Van to this place.

Anthony was a craggy old timer with chiseled features and thick gray hair, and he was smoking, with obvious pleasure, a very big cigar.

"Cuban," he said as he offered one to Harry. "We can get them here."

Harry held up a palm. "No thanks, I never did learn how to smoke those things without getting sick. Does the CIA know you smoke Cuban cigars?"

Anthony smiled. "No," he answered, "and I hope you're not going tell them." He was a retired Air Force pilot. Harry wondered what turns of destiny had brought him to Beirut. Well, what the hell, he thought as they shook hands, think of all the twists and turns that brought me here.

"So," he said, as he gestured towards a chair, "how are you enjoying the good life in Beirut so far? I heard you had an exciting arrival. Been shot at yet?"

Harry had to smile. "Not yet. Not me, anyway," and he told Anthony about the shooting incident at the hotel. Damn, he thought, was that only this morning?

"Yes, those things are happening more and more these days. Believe it or not, I was kidnapped a few weeks ago. But it was some kind of mistake and they let me go right away. I see dark clouds ahead, but I could be wrong. I hope so. This was a great place to live before all this shooting started.

"Okay, today we'll move you to the Mayflower Hotel. Safer, and right near the Hamra. That's the main street. It's right around the corner from the Pickwick. That's an English pub where the TMA ex-pats hang out. An ex-

RAF pilot runs it. You need to get a validation on your U.S. license before you can start flying. So tomorrow morning, you'll take a written test on Lebanese air law. Don't panic," he added, when he saw Harry scowl. "Here's the test with the answers filled in. Study it tonight. In the afternoon, you'll be interviewed by the DCA. That's the FAA here, but most of them don't know squat about flying. Just a formality."

"Now," he said, as a pretty girl brought in a tray of coffee and sweets, "here's the plan." He interrupted himself to offer the sweets to Harry. "I'm not sure what these things are, but you'll never eat better pastry. Try one."

Harry did and agreed they were delicious, soft and flaky, with nuts and a taste of honey. "You'll fly a base check day after tomorrow, then a couple of line flights to the Gulf with one of our check captains. After that, we plan to send you to Bangkok. You'll operate from there to Tokyo, Hong Kong, and Taipei. Been to those places?" he asked hopefully.

"Damn," said Harry with a frown "that sounds like a full schedule. Yes, I've been to Hong Kong, not the others. Any problem?"

Anthony smiled. "No," he said "if you can handle Hong Kong, you can handle the others. They're straightforward. Normally, we would give you a few line training flights out there, but things are so screwed up right now, we just can't do it. We need someone out there ASAP. What did you fly in the Navy?"

The abrupt change of subject surprised Harry. It must be on his record from Saudia.

"A4s," he said. "How about you?"

Anthony shook his head. "I flew big ones. A4s? Carriers?"

Harry nodded. "Yes, several. Kitty Hawk was my last one."

"What I wouldn't give," said Anthony somewhat wistfully, "to make just one landing on an aircraft carrier. Maybe in my next life."

That, thought Harry, probably sums up the feeling of most Air Force pilots. Their envy was sometimes palpable.

Anthony nodded. "Vietnam?" he asked simply.

Harry briefly told him about his time in the Tonkin Gulf. "From what I've seen so far, it was safer there than it is here."

Anthony chuckled. "You get used to it. What about your wife? Wouldn't be smart to bring her here, but she could join you in Bangkok. She'd have to stay in the crew hotel, though. Any kids? No pictures, just tell me how many."

Harry smiled. "Okay, no pictures. One son, almost four. My wife would never leave him behind. That feasible?"

"Sure," he answered, "as long as he stays in the crew hotel. Can they get out of Jeddah without you? I hear they make life difficult for wives to travel."

With foresight, Harry had arranged an exit visa for Irene and Van before he left Jeddah.

"Yeah, she needs my permission to leave, believe it or not; but I've already done the paperwork. What about transport?"

Anthony was ready for that one. "We'll provide commercial transport. I'll point you in the right direction to get it started. Now, any questions?"

"Only one. Where," asked Harry, "can I get more of these great pastries?"

Anthony smiled. "Almost anywhere," he replied. "Aren't they great?"

Having the answers in advance can go a long way towards doing well in a test, and Harry did very well indeed. No one seemed surprised that he did not miss a single question. The interview was more farce than real when it quickly became apparent that the questioners were not pilots. One question said much about their expertise.

"What," asked one, "do you consider the greatest technical advance in commercial aviation in recent years?" Harry mentioned a few, none of which seemed to satisfy the interviewer. Finally, he answered his own question. "What about the afterburner?" he asked. "Was that not a great advance?" Harry did not mention that afterburners were used on military airplanes, not civilian ones. "Yes," he agreed tactfully, "that was certainly a significant development."

The base check consisted of three normal landings with Bob Anthony and lasted only twenty minutes. Next was a turn-around trip to Dubai with a tall and courtly check captain named John Wigley. The flight was an all-nighter and it was unique. After a pause during the day, the shelling had resumed and a few of the shells fell near the airport. So Harry and Wigley, an Englishman, boarded their airplane in the hangar, started the engines, then taxied to the takeoff position without airplane lights and via unlit taxi-ways. Harry would have had a hard time getting there, but Wigley, of course, knew the airport well.

"No need for concern," he said lightly, "I can get there blindfolded. Which, come to think of it, is more or less what I'm doing now."

It was still dark when they returned to Beirut. Approaching the airport, Harry saw flashes of gunfire twinkling around the area surrounding Beirut.

They turned off their navigation lights and did not use their landing lights. That had been normal in the Navy and Harry made a good landing, then followed Wigley's directions to the hangar without the aid of taxi-way lights.

"You won't need to do this in Bangkok," said Wigley, as they entered the hangar. "There's no need for another flight," he said, after the shut-down checklist was done. "I'm going to sign you off. You are officially on your own. Good luck."

Harry shook his hand and asked if there were any pearls of aeronautical wisdom he might pass along about flying with TMA.

"Only one," he said. "These Lebanese are smart and proficient. They can do the job, but sometimes they need a kick in the ass" -- he pronounced it 'ahss' -- "to get them moving. Don't let them run the show."

Harry nodded his thanks. "See you in Bangkok?"

"Well," he replied, "it's off my usual route, but you never know. Give my regards to Patpong Road."

The Mayflower Hotel seemed safer than his airport "accommodation" although Harry suffered a near heart attack as he returned there from lunch the next day. The restaurant had been recommended the night before by a TMA captain he had met at the Pickwick Inn, around the corner from the hotel. The pub was run by ex-RAF pilot, Johnny Manning, a grizzled old pilot who was short and thin with an enormous walrus moustache. Johnny had flown in the Battle of Britain and the TMA captain cautioned Harry, "Don't ask him about it unless you want to spend the rest of the night listening to war stories."

Harry would like to hear them one day, but not just then. He had a pleasant evening at the pub, which was like a tiny corner of England transplanted to Beirut.

A few years later Harry would read in an English newspaper that gunmen had entered the Pickwick, destroyed the pub with automatic weapons fire, and took Johnny with them when they left. He was held prisoner for some weeks and was finally released unharmed. It was front page news throughout the episode.

The restaurant was nearby and he had eaten well: a large salad, along with chicken roasted on a spit and a plate of homus, a paste made of chickpeas with sliced pine nuts and olive oil spread on top. It was eaten using, as a scoop, pieces torn from Arabic bread, which was flat and round. Harry was surprised to learn than Lebanon grew excellent fruit and vegetables. He was more surprised when he tasted the local white wine. It was excellent.

His near-coronary took place as he neared the hotel on his way back there. Just ahead, in the middle of the street, was a group of three or four male youths. One was in uniform and looked to be about fifteen years old. He was holding a weapon which the others were examining. Harry had already seen that guns were commonplace on the streets of Beirut, so he was not alarmed. But suddenly, the young man holding the gun raised it and fired a burst into the air. By then, Harry was within ten feet of the group and the explosions sounded like cannon fire. Instinctively, Harry dove into the nearest doorway, his heart pounding.

The soldier who had just fired his weapon saw Harry's reaction and laughed; but Harry was not laughing, he was terrified. I've had enough of Beirut, was his first thought. His second thought was to call Anthony and ask when he could expect to leave. He called from the hotel and, after some difficulty, heard him on the other end.

"I was just about to call you," he said, and went on to tell Harry that he would leave the following evening as a passenger on a TMA flight to Bangkok. There would be a crew change in Dubai, but Harry would stay on the airplane.

"I'm ready to leave," said Harry, "and the sooner the better."

He briefly described the gunshots. He heard Anthony laugh.

"You're not going to miss Beirut?" he asked. Still chuckling, he said "Okay, have a nice time in Bangkok. Let me know if you need anything. The tickets for your wife and son have already been telexed to Jeddah."

108
BANGKOK

The flight from Beirut had been a long one. It was tiring because the cargo airplane had no passenger seats, only those in the cockpit. Harry had served as a flight attendant, heating the meals and bringing coffee for the crew.

"You are not as pretty as a stewardess," said the captain, smiling as he accepted a cup of coffee, "but you make good coffee. Thanks."

They were friendly and engaging and appeared to know how to operate a 707. Harry broached the subject of the unrest in Beirut. How bad is it likely to get, he wanted to know. Opinions varied, but none were sanguine. Each foresaw serious problems ahead, just different degrees and time frames. They briefed him about the flights he would operate from Bangkok. He looked forward to seeing Hong Kong again. The Tokyo and Taipei airports would be new experiences.

After checking into his room, Harry had been unable to sleep. That was probably from a combination of fatigue and jet lag. He decided to investigate Bangkok. Might as well check out my new neighborhood, he thought. So he hauled himself out of bed and went out into the streets of Bangkok, hoping to stay up late enough to re-set his body clock on local time. That was never easy.

Harry did not have to go far to deliver Wigley's regards to Patpong Road. That stretch of glitz and glitter was a short walk from the Sheraton Hotel. It ran just a few blocks, and it was lined on both sides with bars, clubs, and massage parlors. To get there, Harry had to contend with two problems he saw immediately were endemic to the city of Bangkok. One was air pollution and the other was traffic. It was hard to say which was worse. The traffic was often gridlocked and that made the air foul. Much of the pollution belched from two-cylindered, three-wheeled vehicles which resembled the carts used on golf courses, and which were used as taxis. A cloud of black smoke followed each of them through the crowded streets. They were called putt-putts. Fresh air, Harry saw, would be hard to find.

It was late morning when he turned into Patpong Road. It was already going strong, even at that hour. All the bars and clubs featured pretty young girls in their doorways trying to entice passersby to sample their pleasures. The bodies of Thai women are not designed for topless dancing, thought Harry as he glimpsed a few through the open doors as he passed along the street. They performed the usual gymnastics around the usual vertical pole. Did men never tire of watching girls twist themselves around a pole?

What was remarkable about Patpong Road, even in the morning, was its energy. Neon lights blazed, girls were everywhere, and young boys on the streets tried enthusiastically to sell a wide variety of products, including more girls. It reminded Harry of Olongapo. There, you had to enter a bar or club to view its wares. Here, they spilled out onto the street.

There was a second Patpong Road. It was parallel to the first and was called, appropriately, Patpong II. There, Harry ate breakfast at Cheap Charlie's, recommended by the crew he had flown with to Bangkok. It was a local restaurant which catered to ex-pats. Not fancy, but with great-tasting food, he was told. It was bare but clean, with travel posters stuck on its tiled walls. The waitress wore only a long tee shirt and flip-flop sandals. Her long, straight hair fell below her waist, which looked thin enough for Harry to put his hands around. She smiled and giggled as she took Harry's order. The menu was extensive, with food from several different countries, including, surprisingly, Mexico. He settled on a large omelette and it was delicious.

The bars of Patpong Road did not appeal to him just then, but on Patpong II, an attractive massage parlor caught his eye. Now, that was inviting, and he paused. A massage! He remembered those in Japan and his body cried out for one now. He decided he needed a massage. He entered into a dimly-lit room and was immediately greeted warmly by a well-dressed, middle-aged Thai woman who spoke fluent English. She wore a loose-fitting dress made of Thai silk, and her hair was pulled back and tied in a knot. Large golden rings dangled from her ears. She bowed and put her two palms together in a prayer-like gesture that Harry would see often in Bangkok.

"Sawadeecup," she said pleasantly. "Welcome, sir. I am most pleased to see you here. Your first visit, I think. My name is Suzie. You have chosen the best massage house in Bangkok. We have many beautiful girls who know how to please you. Would you like to see them?"

This enterprising lady did not waste time, and even as she spoke, she took his arm and guided him to a plush lounge area where two Oriental men were drinking beer and watching sex films on television. A large panel of glass divided the room into two sections. Behind the glass were a dozen lovely young Thai girls, each with a numbered pin. They wore only a bra and panties, which suggested they might provide more than a massage. A few looked as young as fifteen. They looked bored until they saw Harry, then began to move about, smiling invitingly as they did.

"Choose anyone you like," said Suzie.

"Look," said Harry as he viewed the girls, "I want only a simple massage, an ordinary massage. Nothing more. Can I get that here?"

Suzie nodded and smiled a knowing smile which said, "Oh, how many times have I heard this?" Aloud, she said, "Yes, of course. We have many kinds of massages. You can choose. The price is different for different massages. But if you like only a massage, that can, of course, be arranged. And if you change your mind during your massage, that can be arranged, too. Which girl do you like?"

Choosing from a roomful of girls, some of them childlike, disheartened him. It was like selecting a puppy in a pet shop. In Japan, the hotsy baths had offered serious massages without sex. There, the girls wore white smocks. Here, it appeared the massage, if there really was one, would be an afterthought As much as a massage appealed to him, this would not do. He took a deep breath and turned to Suzie.

"I like them all," he said. "But, I think I made a mistake coming here. Your girls are beautiful, and you are beautiful, too. But I'll come back another time. Sorry to bother you."

Suzie frowned slightly, sensing she was about to lose a customer. Then she smiled and again took his arm.

"Are you sure you would not like a massage from one of these pretty girls? They are wonderful, I can promise. They will make you feel very wonderful indeed. Let me introduce one of my girls, then decide."

Harry hesitated for only a second and shook his head.

"No, I'm sure. Thanks, anyway."

Suzie nodded and bowed very slightly, once again placing her palms together.

"Sir, thank you for coming to our massage house. Until the next time?" She offered her hand.

Harry returned her bow and took her hand. "Until the next time," he answered, then turned and left.

He was briefly stunned to find himself suddenly in the bright sunlight. He stood and squinted, his eyes adjusting. Who needs a massage, he asked himself. Now, he began to feel the curtain of sleep coming over him. He made his way back to the hotel through the gauntlet of bars, clubs, and putt-putts. This time, he fell asleep easily.

109
TOKYO

Two days later, Harry worked a flight to Tokyo with a stop in Hong Kong. The transit time was only an hour, so he had not much time to reminisce about Nancy Wong and his first visit to this exciting city. It was a fine, sunny day and he walked about the ramp near the airplane, viewing Hong Kong across the water, remembering. The appeal of this magical city was still there and Harry could feel it gently pulling at him.

Last night, Harry had called the two crewmen who would fly with him. What about dinner, he suggested. Both were amenable, and Kamal and Jacques took him to the nearby Carlton Hotel at the far end of Patpong II. They were one Muslim and one Christian with Harry, who was nothing, in between. Live music and fine food came together to make a pleasant evening. They talked mostly about the situation in Beirut, which had worsened in the past few days. There was talk of relocating the company's operations to Cypress. The future was looking uncertain, they agreed, and they were expecting the worst.

This flight was part of TMA's world service. From Tokyo, the plane would fly to Anchorage, New York, one of several airports in Europe and finally, back to Beirut. Harry would like to fly all the way around the globe one day. Not many had ever done it.

The route to Tokyo took them along the southern coast of Japan's main islands, where they were pushed along by the strongest tail wind Harry had ever experienced -- more than 200 knots of wind brought their ground speed up to almost 700 knots, more than 800 miles per hour! Somewhere along the way they spotted an active volcano. Harry had a good feeling about returning to Japan. He had enjoyed himself there during his Navy days, and he looked forward to returning there now. On the way, Jacques briefed Harry about Haneda airport, and their arrival and landing were routine.

They stayed at the Hilton Hotel in the center of Tokyo. The first thing Harry noticed about his return to Japan was that the driver of their car wore not only a chauffeur's cap, but also white gloves. He held open the door when the crew got in the car. When they departed two days later, he noticed that the flight plan had been typed, not written, as was every other flight plan he had ever seen. He received regular calls at the hotel updating the progress of the inbound flight. One call was to ask his choice of food for the return to

Bangkok. The menu was long and the food, he would find, was exceptional. In Japan, they did things right.

Jacques and Kamal knew Tokyo. They knew the best bars and restaurants, and Harry saw several, enough to see that Tokyo was a city of entertainment. He had never before seen such an array of giant neon signs. It was not cheap, but his guides knew value. They knew value in other ways as well. When Harry mentioned that he might buy a new camera, both of them quickly advised Harry the best place to buy, based on price and currency exchange rates.

One extraordinary bar was the Queen Bee. It was a plush nightclub with prices that matched the décor and the girls on display there. Its bar was circular and it rotated in a round room with a wall close to the bar, following its contour. The wall was lined with gorgeous women in long gowns who, Harry thought, were the Japanese version of delicious. Without speaking, and using only body language and provocative smiles, the girls tried to entice the three men to invite them to a table in the adjacent night club.

"Don't even think about it," Jacques said, as he noticed Harry eyeing the girls. "You don't have enough money. We know other places."

Harry smiled. "Even if I had the money, those days are over for me. But there's no charge for looking, is there?"

Jacques chuckled. "No, no charge. Looking is free, thank God."

Harry was surprised to learn that the center of Tokyo was a place where people worked and played but did not reside. Not many lived there. The price of the land was astronomic, he was told, and that was most likely the reason. Another great place to visit, Harry thought, but he wouldn't like to live there.

The flight back to Bangkok was nonstop. They arrived during rush hour and it took them almost as long to taxi to the hotel as it did to fly from Tokyo. It seemed so anyway, as the traffic was stop-and-go all the way. On checking in, Harry was handed a telex which told him that Irene and Van would arrive in a few days. He smiled as he read it. They would be a welcome sight.

As he entered the elevator, a pretty young Thai girl walked in, too. There was no one else in the car and, as the doors closed, the girl turned to Harry and smiled. It was a warm and inviting smile. Obviously unable to speak more than a few words of English, she made a circle with a thumb and a finger of one hand, inserted into it the straightened index finger of her other hand, then made an in-and-motion. Its meaning was hard to miss. She raised her eyebrows in an expectant expression that asked, "Are you ready?"

Before Harry could speak, she said, "Cheap, sir. One fuck, five dollars, two fucks, ten dollars. Okay?"

Her English was wanting, but there was nothing wrong with her arithmetic. Harry politely declined, but he admired her ingenuity.

Harry had a few days until Irene and Van arrived and he used them to investigate Bangkok further. The Club 99 was one of the places he researched. This club was modeled on those in the U.S. and, for the first few moments, he thought he was back in California. It was small and intimate, and the bartender's name was Joe. A three-piece band played popular American music. The singer was excellent, and when Harry asked her if she knew "Leaving on a Jet Plane," she smiled and nodded. "The next song," she said. From then on, that became the next song played whenever Harry entered the club.

There was a curfew in Bangkok and all the bars closed at midnight. When the clock struck twelve at the Club 99, the door was locked, but those inside could stay all night if they chose. During the closed-door session on Harry's first visit, he met an Australian pilot who flew for Quantas. They found common ground because Sam Dodson had read about the Norwegian Ram Runners and even remembered Harry's picture in the Sydney Morning Herald.

"Good on you, mate," he said. "Let me buy a beer for the bloke who stuck his thumb up Robert Hawke's nose."

Sam was Australian right down to his toes. He was tall, with long sandy hair that flowed over his ears, bright blue eyes, rugged good looks, and a passion for drinking beer.

"Tell you what, mate," he said, after they had drunk a few together, "come with me back to the Sheraton. We have a crew room there. You can meet some of our blokes and have a pint or two."

Although it was well past midnight, the Quantas crew room was crowded and the Aussies were in a party mode. The first thing Harry noticed as they entered was a game involving the flipping of coins. The players sat crosslegged in a circle on the floor and watched intently as one of them threw into the air two coins which had been placed on a paddle-like stick. Their eyes followed the coins as they reached the top of their flight and dropped to the floor. Excited cries followed each toss.

"What is it?" asked Harry.

"A stupid Aussie game," Sam replied. "It's called Two Up. They bet on whether the coins will land even or odd."

As he spoke, two coins landed, and shouts of glee and groans of despair ensued. As they did, one of the players suddenly pitched forward into the playing arena and lay there motionless. No one moved to help him.

Concerned, Harry asked "Shouldn't someone do something?"

Sam frowned. "No way," he said with disdain. "If he can't handle the drink, then he shouldn't drink it. He'll be fine in the morning."

The game continued around the fallen player as if he were not there. The Aussies, Harry thought, are a tough bunch.

Harry met Irene and Van at the airport. They had been apart only a few weeks, but it seemed longer.

"Any problems?" Harry asked, as they rode to the hotel. A woman traveling alone in Saudi Arabia could expect problems. Surprisingly there were none.

"And what about here?" Irene asked.

"So far, so good," Harry said, "the hotel is okay and they've given us a corner room which is larger than the others. There is a fridge and a small grill. Just like home. Van will sleep on a mattress on the floor."

Irene seemed pleased when Harry told her the Sheraton was in the center of the action. "Just like the Groenplaats," he joked, referring to the plaza in the center of Antwerp which Irene loved to visit.

They settled in easily. That evening, Harry led his family through Patpong Road to the Carlton Hotel for dinner. Van was a sensation. At the age of four, he was chubby with clear blue eyes and blonde curly hair. The Thais had never seen anything like him. One woman, passing them on the street, stopped and swept Van into her arms as she planted a big kiss on his cheek.

"Beautiful!" she exclaimed, as she put him down.

The girls in the doorways of the bars could not believe their eyes. They called the other girls to see this delightful vision of a blue-eyed boy with blonde, curly hair. One invited them inside where Van was placed on the bar and offered a Coke, as a gaggle of bar girls made motherly sounds in Thai. Days later, when Irene asked Van what he had seen there, he pulled up his shirt and wiggled like a dancer. Harry was pleased.

"A fast learner," he told Irene.

Most of Harry's flights were to Tokyo, via Taipei or Hong Kong. Now and then, he flew from Singapore. Those flights meant he had to travel there as a passenger with Singapore Airlines or Thai Airlines, and stay overnight. That brought back memories of Astrid. I don't want to live in the past, he

477

told himself, but neither do I want to lose it. Those memories would always be precious. But, as often happens in life, the disaster of Astrid's rejection had led to something better. Strange how life works its magic, thought Harry, as he drank an Anchor beer while dining at Fatty's one night. Incredibly, the waiter there remembered him. And not only him, but what he and Astrid had eaten that night. The Chinese were amazing people.

There were times when he operated the other way. That was from Bangkok to Dubai, with a layover there. Dubai was one of the United Arab Emirates, a confederation of sheikdoms huddled around the peninsula jutting into the Persian Gulf. Dubai was still a Third-World country then, and Harry enjoyed it there. It was on one of these flights over the Bay of Bengal that Harry had set his personal off-course record of 135 miles to avoid the most menacing weather he had ever seen.

Although Muslim, Dubai was very different from Saudi Arabia. Life was much freer, and a man could buy a beer there. Harry usually drank his at the Intercontinental Hotel, which was the only major hotel in town. He became friendly with the manager and he sometimes took Harry spearfishing in the creek. That was the water that lay between Dubai and the emirate to the north. The few fish they managed to spear were prepared by the hotel chef and provided dinner.

The emirate to the north was Sharjah, and it held the airport which TMA used. Harry learned that the sheik there, embarrassed because Dubai had an airport and he did not, built one bigger and better. It did not matter to him that his airport was just a few miles from the one in Dubai. After all, his prestige was at stake. But business was slow, and Harry's flight was usually the only one listed on the departure board in the terminal. You had to be desperate, thought Harry, to list a cargo flight on your departure board.

Except for the pervasive pollution, Irene enjoyed Bangkok. She was, after all, a city girl, and now she was in the heart of one of the great cities of the east. The shopping was almost inebriating for a woman who loved to shop. Fabrics, gems, paintings and eastern antiques were enough for any shopper, however dedicated. Harry and Irene bought some of each. The paintings, especially, were a bargain. Beautiful oil paintings were inexpensive and painted in the traditional style. They bought a few, and enjoyed them for years afterwards.

They spent a few days in Pataya, the beach south of Bangkok on the Bay of Bengal. On that beach one day, Harry was approached by a man selling gems. No expert, Harry firmly said "no" many times. The more he said it, the cheaper the stones became. Finally, down to $20 from $500, Harry took a chance and bought one. Examined in Bangkok a few days later, he was offered less than one dollar. Irene had the stone mounted in silver. To Harry, it looked like $500, and who knew the difference? Van enjoyed the beach and had a ride one morning on a baby elephant. Because of its rough hide, he did not like it, but it made a great photo. They enjoyed the sea and the fresh air and it was with reluctance that they returned to the crowded streets and foul air of Bangkok.

Harry had not needed one, but Irene had entered Thailand with a visa of three months. That visa expired when Harry's posting was extended a few weeks. The next thing Irene knew, she was standing in a Thai courtroom with a Thai lawyer and not understanding one single word. She replied to the judge in English when prompted by her lawyer. Say "yes," he would say and Irene would say, "yes." It was just a formality, but her fingerprints were taken and placed in the record. At future parties, she sometimes bragged that she was the only one there with a criminal record in Thailand.

Soon after Irene's courtroom incident, Harry was handed a telex as he reported for a flight. It was time to go home to Jeddah. Harry was surprised to find himself thinking of Jeddah as home, but he'd had enough of hotel life and he was ready to leave Bangkok. He and Irene had been treated as part of the family by the hotel staff. Everyone, guests, as well as staff, loved Van. He learned to dive at the hotel pool and Harry would long remember his exasperation at teaching him how to do it. How could something so easy seem so hard to learn? A loud cheer erupted from the poolside onlookers when he finally did it.

Irene and Van flew back to Jeddah with Saudia. Harry did it the hard way. He operated a flight to Dubai, the next day to Beirut. There was a respite from the war, and the city was calm. He was grateful for that. Before he left, he stopped to say farewell to Captain Anthony.

"Good luck, Captain," he said. "I think you're going to need it."

Anthony nodded. "Thanks for your help. Sure you're not going to miss Beirut? I might be able to arrange another combat tour."

Harry grinned. "No thanks, once is enough. I almost enjoyed it. Almost. But Bangkok was fine. We liked it there."

They shook hands and a car took Harry to the Mayflower Hotel for his last night in Beirut. He would leave in the morning as a passenger on a TMA cargo flight to Jeddah. He looked forward to drinking one last beer in The Pickwick and talking once again to Johnny Mann. Tonight, perhaps, he would listen to his tales of the Battle of Britain.

Harry had just entered his hotel room when the telephone rang. Surprised, he picked up the receiver and heard Captain Anthony say, "Harry, good I caught you. We have a problem and we hope you can help us."

Uh, oh, thought Harry; that sounds like bad news. Aloud, he said, "Problem? What kind of problem?"

There was a pause and he visualized Anthony drawing on his cigar, then heard him exhale.

"We need a captain for a flight tomorrow night. It's an easy one and I was hoping you might delay your return to Jeddah for a day or so. It would pull us out of a bind. What do you think?"

All the flights were easy when someone else was doing them.

"Easy?" asked Harry. "How easy? My wife expects me home tomorrow."

There was another pause. "Just up the road to Damascus, a quick stop in Khartoum, then back here. We need you. What do you think?"

Stupidly, Harry asked, "Is there no one else?" He knew what the answer would be even if there was someone else.

"No, this one came out of the blue. We'll send you back commercial the next day. Promise."

Harry had always been a team player and now he found it hard to say "no." And anyway, Anthony had been fair with him. So, although he agreed mentally, he had reservations.

"I've never been to either place," he said. "That a problem?"

Now Anthony knew he had him. "No, no problem at all. Easy airports and we'll send along a first officer who knows the way. Okay?"

Harry sighed. Why was he always so easy? "Okay, but this is the last one." He could almost see Anthony smile.

"Guaranteed," he said, "and thanks."

They landed in Damascus in the middle of the night and were directed to a remote area of the airport. Stacks of crates were standing there, ready to be loaded. They were put on board very quickly, as though someone was in a big hurry to get them out of Damascus. The time of night and the urgency aroused his suspicions.

"What's in the boxes?" he asked one of the Arabs supervising the loading.

He shrugged and replied that they were filled with arms. Rifles, he thought.

"I am traveling with you, Captain, to be sure they reach their destination."

Harry smiled. "You don't trust me?"

The Arab smiled back. "Not you, Captain, but the next part of their journey."

Harry became interested. "And where might that be?" he asked, in what he hoped was a light tone. "Is there a revolution somewhere?"

The Arab did not smile this time. "A kind of revolution. These guns are going to Eritrea and I am going with them. And these men also." He gestured towards two very mean-looking characters near him. Faces covered with hair, wearing headdresses, and swaddled in robes, they looked like they had stepped right out of an "Indiana Jones" movie. Only their eyes were visible and they did not look friendly. Harry had heard of the problems in Eritrea, which was struggling to free itself from Sudan.

"What will you do with them?" he asked. What a stupid question, he berated himself.

"They will be used, and we hope, with success. Captain, I believe we are ready to go."

After becoming airborne an airways controller asked, as they often did, for their point of departure and their destination.

"We are from Damascus to Khartoum," said Harry. Could that really be Harry Ferguson of Milwaukee saying that? It sounded like a passage from "The Arabian Nights!"

The Khartoum airport also stuck them in a far-off corner where the area swarmed with armed soldiers. Someone was taking this cargo very seriously. The crates were quickly unloaded onto trucks and sent on their way.

"Thank you, Captain, and Allah be with you," said the Arab, as he shook Harry's hand and left.

Just then another voice, this one from behind him, said, "Captain, your cargo is at hand and ready for boarding. Do you need fuel?"

Harry turned and found himself looking at a well-dressed Arab man in a western suit, clean-shaven, hair well trimmed, and wearing rimless spectacles.

"Cargo?" asked Harry. "What cargo? I was not told about any cargo. We're going back to Beirut."

The man extended his hand and Harry took it. "I am Rashied and I have rented your airplane to take my camels to Beirut, then on to Dubai where they will participate in the camel races there next week. You did not know?"

In his few months with TMA, Harry had hauled horses, monkeys, pigs, and even deer. The deer had been an interesting story. They would be used to start a herd of deer in Taiwan.

"Why would anyone want a herd of deer in Taiwan?" Harry had asked the deer's escort.

"Ah," he answered "for their horns, of course. These are ground up and used by the Chinese as an aphrodisiac. Very costly."

Harry did not ask if they worked. The escorts of the deer and the horses carried special pistols which could be used to kill any animal which began to react violently during flight. He had not before carried camels; but there was always a first time. Anthony had probably not mentioned the camels in case Harry might object to carrying them. It would not have mattered. Camels, horses, deer, pigs, whatever. It made no difference to Harry. They were all easier than the sheep he had once carried out of Australia.

The camels were quickly on board and on their way to Taiwan; first stop: Beirut. They seemed to enjoy the flight, and the pistol was not needed. The sun was just blinking over the mountains east of the city as he came to a stop in his parking slot in front of the TMA hangar. This, thought Harry, has been an unusual night, even for TMA.

Keeping his word, Anthony sent Harry to Jeddah the next day as a passenger on Middle Eastern Airlines. Almost before he knew it, he was back in Saudi City, drinking home-brewed wine, playing tennis and enjoying the social life. Of course, he still had to go to the airport now and then but, by now, he knew the territory. It had taken some time, but he had finally learned to let the horseshit bounce off.

110
HELLO, MALTA?

1986

The winds of change began sweeping through Saudi Arabia in 1986. These were financial winds. They began early in the year and they reached gale force as the year wore on. They were driven by the price of oil, which fell below ten dollars per barrel. The country's income, which had before seemed infinite, was now shrinking rapidly. Even when the income levels were in the stratosphere, the country was spending more than the oil was bringing in. Saudi Arabia had been on a buying spree for many years. Roads, hospitals, and schools were built throughout the country. The Royal family took its share of the money and, some thought, spent it frivolously. Harry had heard that the king had an estate in southern Spain which employed several hundred. Tales were frequent of enormous gambling losses in Monte Carlo by princes. An entire airline had been bought for cash. A year or two earlier, the General Manager of Flight Operations had been presented with ten new B747s that he neither needed nor wanted. That made no sense to Harry until Irene pointed out that the Royals might want them for an escape valve should it be necessary to leave the country quickly. Harry had heard rumors of discontent from the Saudis he flew with. There was even talk of armed rebellion to bring the country back to its Islamic roots.

It was certainly true that the country had strayed far from those roots. Alcohol, for example, was freely available on the black market. Pornographic video films were also there for those who wanted them. An American captain whom Harry knew had piled up a fortune smuggling those films from Turkey. A flight engineer made an even larger fortune distilling the pure alcohol known as sidiki. Most of their customers were Saudis.

The nose-dive in its income generated an air of panic and the country began massive spending cutbacks. Some of the panic overflowed into Saudi Arabian Airlines and cutbacks were made there, too. One day, Harry found in his mailbox a love note that did not even bother to direct him to see his Equipment Manager. It simply informed him that his contract would not be renewed. He was one of scores who had the bad luck to hold a contract that would expire within the next six months.

Driving home to take the bad news to Irene, Harry pondered his future. This was a setback but he had been there before. Life in Saudi City had changed substantially since he had first come. Many friends had come and gone. Now it was his turn.

He would miss some parts of the life there. Saudi City had, in some ways, become a piece of the U.S. The school was American. Little league baseball had sprung up, and some of Harry's most pleasant memories would be teaching Van to play, and then watching the games. Van had not grown up with baseball and had to be taught the basics. Simply throwing a baseball took days to learn; hitting it with a bat even longer. Harry coached the team part-time and saw every game when he was not away. For Harry, these games would be the most enjoyable he would ever watch in any sport, at any level.

An enterprising American mechanic had strung cables across the rooftops of Saudi City in a makeshift television network. From his apartment, he broadcast videotapes of American programs. He distributed mimeographed schedules. The Saudis could have censored his system but did not. This touch of home made life in Saudi City better for everyone.

There were parts of Saudi City he could live without. Life there was like living in a cocoon. It had an artificial feel to it. Another important ingredient was that Van's school, run by an American organization, went through only the eighth grade. That was only two years off. After that, he would need to attend school in another country. Harry did not like to think about that. In any case, there was nothing he could do about it. An unknown future stretched ahead. He wondered what it held.

The next morning Lars Johnson came to Harry's apartment, bringing with him a copy of *Flight International*. This was a weekly magazine read by most in the aviation world. Pilots read it from back to front because the ads for flying jobs were listed in the last few pages. Pilots, like most people, were always looking for a better job, one with more money, a better airplane, or a better place to live. The news of the cutbacks had spread quickly, and Lars was aware of Harry's predicament. Finding a job while in Saudi Arabia would not be easy.

"Have you seen this?" he asked, as he accepted a glass of Harry's best home- brewed wine. Harry and Irene had once spent a few days with Lars and Inger in Sweden. The morning after they arrived, they had been surprised to see Inger take a bottle of aquavit from the refrigerator and place it on the breakfast table. Tiny frosted glasses were already there, waiting. The Swedes often started their day with a glass of this clear white alcoholic drink, she explained, as she raised her glass in a toast. What a great idea, thought Harry.

Since then, he offered wine to Lars whenever he visited, regardless of the time of day.

Lars had the magazine folded open to the pages listing job openings. His finger pointed to one from Air Malta that had "immediate positions for qualified B707 Captains." Malta? Surely, thought Harry, that had to be some kind of omen. He told Lars about his brief visit there when he had lost an engine. He remembered that he had always wanted to take Irene to see the time warp on this tiny island in the middle of the Mediterranean Sea.

"And think about the seafood," said Lars, trying to bolster Harry's morale. "There should be plenty good seafood there." Lars loved seafood. "And real wine!" he added enthusiastically. "Think about that!"

"Air Malta," mused Harry. "What do we know about Air Malta? What do they fly?"

Lars knew everything about every airline in the world. "Mixed fleet," he said, as he sipped his morning glass of wine. "A couple of 707s, some 737s. You might have a chance for the 737. You know, Harry, the 707 is about to go out of business. Extinct. Is that what you say?" Harry nodded.

"Yes," he said, "extinct. Too expensive now. I would surely like to fly the 737."

The B737 was the most popular airliner ever flown. It was used worldwide and more 737s had been built than any other passenger airplane.

"I'll send a letter tomorrow," said Harry. Of course, he still had to get the job, but his spirits rose just thinking about living in Malta.

"No letter," said Lars firmly. "Call now. There is a telephone number."

Yes, the sooner, the better. Harry picked up the phone and dialed the number. One of Saudi Arabia's investments had been in its telephone system. It was as good as any in the world.

"Hello, Malta?" he asked, as a pleasant female voice answered the telephone. "I'm calling from Saudi Arabia."

Her name was Carmen, she said, and she sounded very friendly. Harry remembered that in Malta it seemed that everyone spoke English. Harry explained who he was and why he was calling.

"Captain Meyer is busy now," she said, "but I can tell you that interviews will be held in London in a few weeks. The position is for eight months. And, of course, Captain Meyer will need to see some documentation of your experience and qualifications. I advise you to send them as soon as possible. Send the basic information by telegram and the rest later. You are the second to call from Saudi Arabia today. What is happening there?"

Harry grimaced. Someone was already ahead of him.

"I'll tell you when I see you," he said. Then he added, *"If* I see you. Anyway, please put my name on the list."

She promised to do that and said, "I look forward to seeing you in Malta."

Harry smiled as he thought of his brief visit there. "Well," he said, "I *hope* you see me there, and thanks very much."

111
THE INTERVIEW

The interview was held in a small hotel in central London. After a brief wait, he was shown into a room with three men sitting behind a large oak table. The three men held copies of Harry's resume. After a few pleasantries, one of the interviewers, a slight, disheveled Maltese man wearing glasses, identified himself as the Manager of Air Malta's Human Resources Department.

"What do you think of the salary we are offering?" Harry had been expecting this one, and he handled it easily.

"The money is not important" he said. "I'm more interested in the working conditions and the living conditions."

That was true. In Saudia, his salary was far lower than that of a comparable position in a major airline in the U.S, but his expenses were low, too. Accommodations, utilities, medical care, and schooling: all were paid by the company. The only expenses were $3.00 to buy a tank of gas for his car, food, and grape juice to make wine. It was hard not to save money, and they had saved plenty.

"I make 300 pounds per month," the Resources man went on, "and I live very well."

Harry thought quickly. The salary would not make or break his decision, but it was important. He had figured out that his own salary of 1,000 Maltese pounds worked out to about $3,000, a substantial decrease, but certainly adequate, especially if a department head lived well on one-third as much. He seemed satisfied with Harry's answer.

The next question came from the Chief Engineer. He was English, and he looked English. He had a ruddy complexion, unruly hair, and teeth that needed attention. The question was technical, one involving starting B707 engines. Harry was ready for that one, too. He had reviewed the operating manual before coming to London. He did not want to be embarrassed by being unable to answer, for example, the memory items related to an in-flight emergency.

The third interviewer was the General Manager of Flight Operations. He was Captain Meyer and he was a stern-looking man who spoke near perfect English with a trace of a German accent. He asked a few personal questions and then ended the interview by saying, "Captain, we do thank you for your interest in Air Malta, and we will inform you shortly of our decision."

And that was it. The entire interview had lasted less than ten minutes. Harry had brought his flight logbook with him. He was not asked to show it. Was that a good sign? He did not know.

112
HELLO, MALTA

Harry squinted into the bright afternoon sunshine as he left the airplane at Luqua airport in Malta. In his pocket was a telegram from someone named Grasso. It told Harry that he had been hired by Air Malta and instructed him how to proceed from London to Malta. Saudia would pay for the ticket to London. Irene and Van left Jeddah a week before Harry. They would wait in Antwerp to see how Malta worked out.

Schools for children often controlled the lives of their parents. Irene had been able to place Van in a local school that, of course, taught in Flemish. Van and Irene usually spoke to each other in "Belgian," as Harry called it. He sometimes did not know what his own family was talking about, but he got used to it. Van was fluent in Flemish but he could not read or write it. That caused problems, but with many extra hours studying with his mom he managed to overcome them.

"But it's not easy, Dad" he told Harry on the telephone. Harry's heart skipped a beat whenever he heard Van call him, "Dad."

It had not been easy to leave Jeddah. It was often said that you learned why you did not like working for Saudia when you left it. The checkout form was a multi page document that required signatures from many offices, some of which he had difficulty finding. Each signature came with one of those thumping stamps the Saudis seemed to love. Many of the officials were either not there or found some reason why they could not sign his form that day. Interruptions for prayer hours did not help. Harry needed two weeks to collect all the signatures.

One of those signatures was that of the Saudi in charge of housing in Saudi City. An appointment was arranged for the inspection of Harry's apartment. He had heard that this inspector was particularly difficult, so he had cleaned the place thoroughly. He had hired a couple of Yemenis to help. The inspector, young, and with a condescending manner, could find no fault but he hesitated before he signed, thinking. Then he went to the living room air conditioner and said, "Please show the filter." Harry had missed that and he cleaned it while the Saudi waited, smiled, then signed the form. Harry would not miss the bureaucracy of Saudi Arabia. He hoped Malta would be kinder to common sense.

In the early evening of their last day together, Harry and Irene invited their friends for a farewell glass of wine. Feeling daring and with not much to lose, Harry had set out chairs in the small grass patch in front of their apartment. Then he brought out the first bottle of wine he had ever made. He carefully peeled back the hinged top of the grape juice bottle, sniffed its contents, and smiled.

"It smells," he announced with a grin, "like real wine."

"Wine does not smell," Lars reminded him. "It has an aroma."

"Okay," said Harry, "the aroma smells good, very good."

He filled all the glasses, then raised his own in a toast. "May good friends meet again in a better place."

He took a sip and smiled again. "This," he said with surprise, "is a great vintage. Don't ask how I did it, but I have made a great port wine here."

All agreed that it was indeed a great vintage.

"Relatively, anyway," said Lars, who often said that life was too short to drink cheap wine. "Except in Saudi Arabia," he was always careful to add.

All wished Harry and Irene well. We will keep in touch, they promised. These friends had shared with Harry and Irene the common bond of a unique life in Saudi City. They would miss them very much.

After clearing Maltese customs, Harry took a taxi to the Country Hotel, an impressive building near the airport and made of limestone blocks. That had been in the telegram too. Harry remembered those blocks from his visit a few years ago. All of Malta seemed to be made of them. This building, he would learn, was once an Officers' Club and quarters for the British Army. It was mid-February and although sunny, the day was cold. Harry would quickly learn that central heat had not yet found its way to Malta, and his hotel room was colder than the weather outside. There was a small electric heater but it made no difference at all in a room that was large, cold, and damp. This was the famous Mediterranean climate? He slept that night fully-dressed and with his jacket on top of the bedclothes.

Grasso's telephone number had been in the telegram, and the next morning Harry called it. Grasso answered and said he would send a car soon

"How soon?" asked Harry. He heard a chuckle.

"As soon as I can get a car, Captain. They are all out right now, but soon. Not more than an hour. Not more than two hours, for sure."

"Good enough," Harry said, and added that he would have breakfast while waiting.

Walking into the office an hour later, Harry heard a familiar voice cheerfully say, "Good morning, Captain Ferguson, and welcome to Malta."

Harry smiled. "You are not, by any chance, Carmen, are you?" he asked.

She smiled back pleasantly. "I am," she replied, "and do you remember that I said I would see you in Malta?"

"I do," said Harry, "I just wonder how you knew."

Carmen was middle-aged, attractive, and well-dressed. How nice, thought Harry, to deal with a real secretary instead of a Pakistani man dressed in a loose-fitting shirt and floppy trousers. George Bingham had called them Pakijamas. Harry was starting to like Air Malta already.

"Secretaries know everything. Mr. Grasso is expecting you. Just through that door," she said, as she pointed to his office.

Grasso was a burly man with white wavy hair, horn rimmed glasses, and a friendly manner. He went straight to the point.

"There are sixteen of you here for the summer, and a few others will be here as soon as cars can be found. We have arranged a medical examination and here is the address of the tailor who will provide your uniform -- walking distance from the hotel. Captain Meyer will brief you on your flying program. You will need a Maltese license, and he will talk to you about that. Your medical examination will be Thursday morning at ten o'clock at St. Luke's Hospital and we will provide transportation."

So far so good, thought Harry.

Grasso handed Harry two sheets of paper.

"Your contract," he said. "Bring it back the next time you come."

Harry's contract with Trans Polar had been handwritten on a page torn from a spiral notebook. With Saudia, it was a multi-page document, parts of which had been incomprehensible. This one looked more like a contract should look: brief, clear, and to the point.

"I'll do that," said Harry, as he took the papers and glanced at them.

Harry had never failed a medical examination in his life and he'd had many; but he failed this one. Of course, he would not know this for several days. The first sign of trouble came when he reported to the hospital for his electrocardiogram test. The lady in charge directed him to a small room the size of a large closet.

"Please remove your shirt and lie down," she ordered, as she left the room. A few minutes later, a lad of about ten entered and began applying sensors to Harry's chest. What is this, he thought, with annoyance, and he called out to the woman who was just outside the door.

"What is it?" she asked, as came back into the room, frowning.

"This boy," said Harry pointing to the youth, "what is he doing?"

The woman's frown became a smile.

"Oh, no need to worry. He is my son and he sometimes helps me. He knows how to do this."

"Look," said Harry, "if you don't mind, I would prefer you did this yourself. Just to be sure. You don't mind?"

She did not mind, she said, but her expression said that she did. She spoke in Maltese to the boy and began applying the sensors herself. "If you insist, sir."

Harry could speak only a few words of Arabic, but he had heard enough to realize that Maltese sounded much like Arabic. He would learn that there were other similarities between the two peoples. The Arabs, like many others, had held Malta for a long period. They left a strong legacy. He had already noticed, for example, that the Maltese homes made of limestone had enclosed balconies made of wood. They were much like those he had seen in Jeddah, with the difference that in Malta, they had windows. Those in Jeddah did not, Harry was told, to prevent unwanted eyes viewing Saudi women.

He underwent a series of tests that morning and then returned to the hotel. During lunch, he met several others who had come to Air Malta for the summer. Grasso had said there were sixteen, and now he met three of them. They came from disparate places and they were easy to distinguish. They came from India, Sri Lanka, and Zambia. The man from India was a flight engineer and he was a Sikh with a drooping moustache and a head-dress which was, he said, a strip of cloth measuring eighteen feet and wound around his head. The young man from Zambia was as black as black can be. He had handsome features, beautiful white teeth that looked even whiter when he smiled, and the physique of a panther. Harry's third lunch companion, from Sri Lanka, was also a captain. He was a small, brown man who lived in London. Air Malta promised to be an interesting company. Harry hoped there would be a way to extend his contract after the summer. The captain from Sri Lanka had been here before.

"They usually don't," he said, "but you never know. They are growing now and they might do so this year."

They enjoyed a pleasant lunch together, partly due to the Sikh. He very much enjoyed telling jokes and laughing at them, too.

After lunch Harry asked directions to the tailor and asked, "What about Valletta? Is it a long way? Can I walk there?"

He felt the need of a walk and fresh air to cleanse the hospital smell from his nostrils. Yes, a long walk, he learned but "the bus goes along the way so you can ride part way if you tire." Harry remembered those old buses and they did not appear to go much faster than he could walk.

The stop at the uniform shop was a long one. It included two Cisk beers pressed on him by a friendly and talkative tailor. Harry learned much about Malta as he was measured for his uniform. Shaking hands warmly, he thanked the tailor for his hospitality, left the shop and continued towards Valletta. As he did, he saw a sign announcing that he was about to pass the Royal Malta Golf Course. He smiled, as he recalled playing there with Gene. He decided to stop for a coffee.

As far as he could see, nothing had changed. The clubhouse still resembled a bomb shelter and held only one person. He was the club professional and his name was Freddie. They exchanged pleasantries and when Freddie learned Harry was an Air Malta pilot, he told him there was an Air Malta captain just about to finish a round of golf. Would Harry like to meet him?

"Wait in the bar, I will send him in. About thirty minutes."

A foursome soon came in off the course and one of the players glanced about and found Harry sipping a coffee at a table.

"You the gentleman from Air Malta?" he asked, as he approached the table. His name was Ian Lockery and he was from India but you would not know that from listening to him. He spoke the King's English. He did not look Indian, either. Close-cut silver hair, bright clear eyes, with a lean, athletic body, Ian reminded Harry of Sean Connery. Irene would later refer to him as the Indian James Bond. He offered a drink and each ordered beer.

"Look," said Ian after they shook hands, "if you play, this is the only place. You must join. Are you interested?"

Harry was interested, and Ian, a man of action, excused himself and left the room. He returned a few minutes later with a membership application in his hand.

"No need to read it," he said, as he pointed to a place on the paper, "just sign here."

Harry did, and Ian took the paper to his playing partners who were enjoying drinks in another corner of the room. Harry could not hear what was said, and Ian quickly returned to Harry with a grin.

"You are set. I, and Jack Graham over there, have just signed on as your sponsors. Let me take this back to the office and then you can buy me a beer."

"Are you saying I'm now a member?" Harry asked when Ian returned.

"No, I'm afraid it's not as easy as that," he answered. "You must first be approved by the members at what's known as a vetting -- English tradition. It's basically a cocktail reception where you will meet some of them. Just a formality. The club will contact you about the date. Now, what about another beer?"

Harry decided to return to his hotel on one of Malta's buses. It was an old Bedford bus and looked to be pre-war vintage. The driver had made his corner of the bus into a shrine, with pictures of Jesus and Mary posted on the walls and ceiling around his seat. A statue of Jesus stood on the dashboard. Harry had noticed such shrines on the streets of Malta, but was surprised to find one on a bus. Passengers sometimes made the sign of the cross as they boarded. Harry hoped this was not an omen that they placed more trust in God than in their driver -- perhaps some of each. No need to take unnecessary risks, not even on a bus.

As he stepped down from the bus, he saw, next to the bus stop, a shrine honoring the Virgin Mary. Such shrines could be seen all across Malta and they were tended with great care. People often made the sign of the cross as they passed one. Some placed flowers on them. Religion was still an important part of life in Malta.

A few days, later Harry had a call from Grasso telling him that a car would, in thirty minutes, take him and a few others to see the company doctor. About ten of the sixteen new crew were there when they arrived. It was a large, old stone house and one room was used as an office. Dr. Fibonacci called them in, one by one, to discuss their tests. Harry was the third one summoned and he was astounded to be told that he had failed his examination.

"What is the problem?" he asked, frowning. It's your heart, he was told. The readings are negative. Harry's frown grew deeper. "Doctor, could there be some mistake? My heart was checked just one month ago and it was perfect."

No, no mistake. The doctor was sorry, but there was nothing to be done.

"Nothing? Of course, there's something. I'll have another ECG. After all, this is my heart we're talking about."

493

Now, it was the doctor's turn to frown. "There is no point," he said, as he turned away and reached for another folder. "Another test will have the same result."

Something did not smell right. Harry knew there was nothing wrong with his heart. The odor became worse as Harry left the room and he heard the young man from Zambia being told he had the same problem. He stopped and turned.

"Doctor," he said, stepping back into the room. "If you won't approve another ECG, I'll have one at my own expense. I want to know what's happened to my heart in the last month. How can I arrange a re-test?"

Dr. Fibonacci was speaking to the Zambian lad. He paused, thinking. "Yes, Captain, another test will be useless, but I will take up your case with the Air Malta medical board. Perhaps it can be arranged." Realizing what was at stake, Harry had become tense. Now he exhaled.

"Thank you, Doctor. Will I hear from you?"

Fibonacci nodded, annoyed. "Yes, yes, in a few days."

When Harry returned to the Air Malta office, he was asked the result of his examination. When he mentioned his heart problem, he saw Grasso raise his eyebrows.

"You are the third one. Did you offer him any . . ." he paused, thinking, "any gratuities?"

Harry would later learn that of the sixteen new crewmembers, twelve had been failed. Only Harry and the Sikh would demand a re-test.

Harry's eyes narrowed. He remembered that the captain from Sri Lanka had brought with him a bottle of whiskey.

"You mean bribes? Is that what it takes? No, I did not." Was this another part of the legacy the Arabs had left behind, Harry wondered. Grasso frowned and said quickly "No, no, not bribes. But perhaps some . . . ," he paused again " . . . incentive? Is that the right word?"

"It's not the right word, but it'll do. No, no incentive, either," Harry said, "but the doctor told me he would take it up with the Air Malta medical board."

Grasso's eyebrows came back down, then rose again. "What medical board? He is the only one on it. Let me see what I can do. Call me in the morning."

The re-test was a major medical event. It was administered by three doctors and included a stress test on a treadmill. Tennis and swimming in Saudi City had kept Harry fit and he felt no discomfort.

"So," he asked, as he stepped down, "how does it look?"

The doctor holding the clipboard replied, without looking up from his board, that "Dr Fibonacci has asked me not to reveal to you the result of the test. Sorry."

Harry could not believe his ears. "Doctor," he said, with a rising tone of anger, "we're talking about my heart. If there is a problem, I want to know."

The doctor looked up and smiled faintly. "Of course. And if you had a problem, I would tell you. But I am not telling you. That is to keep Dr. Fibonacci satisfied. Do you understand?"

Harry understood. He no longer had a heart problem.

That afternoon, Harry met with Captain Meyer, who was much friendlier than he appeared during Harry's interview. The accent was Austrian, not German, he said. Next on the schedule was a test of Maltese air law. He handed Harry a sheaf of papers.

"The questions will come from these. Sorry, but you will need to learn them all. After the test, please write down any new questions you can remember. For our file," he added, with a smile.

Well-armed, the exam went well. Harry returned to Captain Meyer's office with several questions and his list included this one: On what date does Malta change to summertime? "I knew this one already," said Harry as he pointed it out, "but I wonder why it's in an air law exam."

Captain Meyer chuckled. "Who knows? But thanks. We will add it to our file."

Next was a base check with several others in an Air Malta 707.

"Basically," Captain Meyer said, "we just want to be satisfied that you can land the airplane. Every now and then, we get someone who has never flown one, only in his log book."

Then there would be a few days in the simulator near London's Gatwick airport. Captain Meyer himself would be the instructor. Harry had last flown just a few weeks ago and did not expect any problems. Before going to London, Harry and an Austrian first officer spent a couple of nights at the hotel reviewing the manual, especially the emergency items which required action by memory. The Austrian, Klaus Mueller, did not seem experienced. Along with the checklists, Harry went over some of the techniques he used in flying the simulator. Harry began to suspect that Klaus was one of those whose 707 flight time was only in his log book.

Harry flew in the sim with another captain; this one was English. His name was Tony Downs, and he and Harry got along well from the start. There were two sessions of four hours. In both sessions, each captain spent two hours in the left seat. That was plenty of time for the instructor to introduce various problems to the flight. It's important in the sim to have a first officer who helps in different ways, but he had to take care to let the captain make the decisions. Tony did it well. That was helpful when everything was going wrong at once, as was often the case in the sim. Harry returned the favor when he flew as Tony's first officer. The flight checks went well and Captain Meyer seemed satisfied.

While at the simulator, the flight crews stayed at a hotel in the nearby town of Crawley. It was a delightful English town, one that Harry imagined an English town should look like. Harry wished Irene could see it. Perhaps one day, she would. He had long thought, in the back of his mind, that he would like to take her to Malta. Now, that seemed about to happen. Harry looked forward to it. There was just one more hurdle, and that was a line check on one of Air Malta's regular routes. That was scheduled for the day after Harry's return to Malta.

Ian Lockery had not mentioned that he was a check captain and now they met again for Harry's final line check flight. He had flown one training flight to Gatwick Airport near London and it had gone normally. Today, the flight was to Heathrow Airport, west of London, and the first officer was Klaus Mueller, who was also being checked. Ian sat in the observer's seat behind Harry. Harry flew to Heathrow, and Klaus flew back to Malta. Harry noticed that Klaus was very unsure of himself and, several times, Harry had to direct him to do things he should have done without being told. There had been a long delay as they waited at the end of the runway for takeoff in London. The departure procedure was complicated and seeing that Klaus was not reviewing it, Harry suggested that he do so now, while he had a few minutes. During the departure, Harry had to remind him to make the direction or altitude changes depicted on the chart.

That was bad enough, but it got worse during the arrival at Malta. Air Traffic Control sometimes controls an aircraft's point of descent. Usually, however, it's up to the pilot to request descent at a point he has pre-planned. The 707 had a commonly-used descent profile. It was, in miles, three times the airplane's altitude in thousands of feet. An aircraft at 35,000 feet would normally begin to descend at 105 miles. This distance was modified by factors such as altitude of the airport, effect of the wind on ground speed, and whether a circling or straight-in approach was expected. This profile could be monitored during the descent. Passing through 20,000 feet, for example, the plane should be at 60 miles.

Harry had quickly figured out that their descent should begin a few minutes after passing Palermo on the island of Sicily. Klaus seemed unaware that he should start going down until Harry asked, "Klaus, what about the descent check list?"

With a late start, Klaus made a mess of his descent, then allowed himself to become high and fast during his approach. Harry was undecided. Had he been on his own, he would have taken control; but with Klaus also being checked, he was uncertain how far to allow him to go. Ian was the captain-in-command and, technically, it was his decision. Harry was anxious as they closed with the runway in a situation rapidly worsening. He could wait only a few more seconds before taking control. At that moment, Harry heard Ian whisper urgently, "Take over, Harry."

Harry did so instantly. "I have it," he said brusquely and, in one movement, knocked Klaus's hand away, grabbed the throttles and pulled them quickly to idle as he made a last-second line-up correction and landed the airplane.

It's not critical for a first officer to be a good airman. The captain is always there to monitor and to take control, if necessary. Air Malta needed Mueller and after an extra flight, he was cleared to fly the line. Harry flew with him now and then and he did not improve.

He was not stupid, just unfocused. His mind always seemed to be elsewhere. You had to "mind the shop" in the cockpit and Mueller often did not. Being a pilot was not difficult, but it required certain basic traits that Mueller seemed to lack. Harry kept a close watch on him when they flew together.

Harry's first flight in command was to Fumicino Airport in Rome. The flights came quickly after that as the summer season approached. Flying in Air Malta was a night-and-day difference compared with flying in Saudia. The people he worked with were pleasant and friendly. The flights were all turn-arounds to Europe. A few went to Tripoli and Cairo in North Africa. Most of the European trips were to the United Kingdom, but many went to other major cities, such as Brussels, Amsterdam, Paris and Frankfort. Harry found himself in places he had never expected to visit. He enjoyed his tour of European airports.

The cabin crews were all Maltese; but in the cockpit, Air Malta still needed foreigners. Harry flew with crewmen from Pakistan, India, Portugal, Austria, and even far-off Brazil. The Brazilians were pleased when Harry told them of his visit to Rio de Janeiro. Harry was pleased to recall it.

The flying was interesting, but physically demanding. That was because the airplanes worked around the clock and although rest hours were scheduled, sleep did not always come easily. Sleep cycles did not always fit rest periods. After an all-night flight, he might sleep until early afternoon, then try to sleep again before a late night departure. That was difficult. The biorhythms of a pilot's life were seldom normal. Jet lag, for example, was for Harry a problem without a solution. In Air Malta, although Harry's sleep schedule was often disrupted, there were no time zone changes. That was one reason he liked flying there; his body was always on the same clock.

It was time to buy a car. Cars in Malta were old, battered, and expensive; so Harry had arranged a few days off and flew to Frankfort to buy one there. The trip became an adventure. He spent one night in Frankfort and, the next morning, bought a 1979 Mercedes from a used car dealer. He had always wanted to own one. They were strong cars and would be able to cope with Malta's potholed roads. He struck out for Malta early in the morning.

On the way back, he stayed at a small hotel in Bolsano, in central Italy. He had paid as he checked in so he could leave early in the morning without the bother of checking out. But when he tried to leave at dawn, he discovered he was locked out of the reception area and there was no other way out. A large woman was mopping the floor. Harry knocked on the glass door and signaled that he wanted to leave. The woman signaled back that she had no key. Harry shrugged and went up to a second floor hallway, looking for a way out. Spying an escape route, he went out a window onto a flat roof covering the lobby, threw his bag onto the street, then climbed down a drain pipe after it.

He drove to Naples, where he boarded a ferry to Malta. The boat was Italian, the food was delicious and, except for his plank-like bed, the voyage was pleasant. His one complaint was that the dining room opened for lunch more than an hour late. He had missed breakfast and he was hungry, but it was, after all, an Italian boat. He especially enjoyed sitting on deck in the bright sunlight as the profile of Mount Etna slowly came into view and just as slowly disappeared as the ship steamed south. The arrival in Malta was at night and he stood at the rail as the ship rounded the tip of Valletta, the lights of the city ablaze, and came alongside the jetty in Grand Harbor.

But the adventure of the Mercedes did not end when he drove off the ferry. In 1987, Malta was still in the grip of a long-time socialist government with all its attendant bureaucracy. Before Harry was legally allowed to drive his car, he had to endure registering it. That required fifteen different trips

-- Harry called them missions -- to several different offices to complete the import formalities. This was bureaucracy at its exasperating worst. Some months afterwards, in a noisy election with a turnout of more than 95 percent, the socialists were thrown out of office. In Malta, everybody voted. Even those living abroad were supplied with tickets home so they could vote. Harry hoped the new government would make life easier for car importers of the future.

Finally, he had a car. Now, Harry needed a place to live. He rented a large apartment overlooking Balluta Bay in the town of St. Julians. He brought Irene and Van there for the summer. They liked Malta, but not the summer heat. In his earlier visit, Harry had seen Malta as charming and quaint. That view changed as he became a resident. The country still had third-world aspects about it. Its roads, power, water and telephone systems were far behind the rest of Europe. The roads especially were abysmal and the sidewalks were not far behind. In the U.S., they would, thought Harry, be a civil attorney's dream. Power cuts were frequent, as were wrong numbers when using the telephone. Air-conditioning was nonexistent and that made Harry's summer a hard one. Record temperatures reached highs of 107 degrees. In the midst of this searing heat wave, Harry's apartment suffered eight days without water.

That brought back memories of water hours on the carrier. Ships made their own water, and that made it precious. When supplies were low, restrictions were put in place. One was that showers could be taken only when water hours were not in place. That would have been fine had the ship followed its own guidelines and turned the water back on when water hours ended. The ship did not always do that. Sometimes, when Harry padded down the passageway to the community shower, he found no water when he turned the handle. That was exasperating but at least the water hours did not apply to the toilets. Without water in their Malta apartment, the toilets could not be used.

There is always a way. The Royal Malta Golf Club had, by now, accepted Harry. The committee chairman had called twice to invite Harry to a vetting but he had been scheduled to fly on those nights. When it happened a third time he said, "Never mind, we are waiving the vetting. You are officially a member."

That gave Harry access to the swimming pool, the showers, and, most important, the toilets. After they swam in the sea, which was a short walk down the hill to the bay, they rinsed with bottled water. A nearby cafe allowed them the use of its toilets. The lack of water was a major inconvenience, but, compared to living on a ship, life in Malta was pleasant.

Water in Malta was pumped up pipes to rooftop tanks and from there, by gravity, to the taps. These tanks could be seen all across Malta. When the water stopped flowing, as it did that summer, and the tanks were empty, a back-up system of water trucks was used. Of course, everyone wanted the trucks at the same time and the archaic telephone system made it difficult to ask for a truck. After several days of dialing, Harry had finally gotten through and he was there when the truck arrived.

He lived in a three-story building. How, the truck driver wanted to know, was he supposed to get his hose up to the roof? Harry thought fast. He did not want to lose this truck. Do you have a rope, he asked. He did. Harry took the rope to the roof and dropped one end over the edge, then hollered down for the driver to tie the line to the hose. When he did, Harry hauled it up, and then asked the driver to turn on the water. He filled all the rooftop tanks. His own tank was only half-full when the truck ran out of water. So much for being a nice guy, he muttered to himself.

Crises always pass, and this one did, too. The power cuts were routine and they learned to live with them. The frustration of using the telephones never ended. Still, he kept reminding himself, it was better than living on an aircraft carrier. In his heart, he did, at times, miss living on a ship but he would never admit it, not even to Irene. Life at sea was hard in many ways but it came with great rewards. Living and working together in close quarters forged strong bonds. You got to know people on a ship, and shipboard friendships lasted a lifetime. Those friendships were hard to find in an airline.

The problems of Malta's infrastructure tarnished its charms but did not materially change them. They were, in a way, a part of Malta's character and flavor. They usually evoked a shrug that said, "Well, that's Malta." The island still held, for Harry, the look and the feel of Milwaukee when he was a boy. Valletta was still a fascinating place to spend a morning. Upper Barrakka Garden still offered a stunning view of the Grand Harbor. Medina, known as the Silent City, still dominated the skyline of the island. Merchants in trucks still stopped in Harry's neighborhood to sell vegetables and bread. The problems were problems they could live with.

The flying picked up as the summer approached, and soon Harry was flying 90 to 100 hours each month. That might seem an easy month but those were flight hours, logged from "blocks off"' to "blocks on." That meant from the time the blocks were removed from the airplane's wheels at the beginning of a flight, until they were put in place at its end. It did not include ground time, which was at times substantial. The crew had to report one hour before the flight. Ground time at destination airports often included long delays due to the summer traffic. Delays in London were especially long, at times up to four hours, and sometimes, even longer.

When they put it all together, Harry and Irene decided they liked Malta. So, one day, Harry drove his Mercedes to the airport to talk to Captain Meyer. Is there any chance of a permanent position, he asked. Meyer explained the situation. The 707s would be phased out after next year. B737s were being augmented. Would Harry be willing to pay for his training to transition to the 737? He would.

"We might be able to work something out, Harry, and if I can arrange it, Air Malta will pay for the training. It will depend on where it's done. I will know more in a month or so. Check back then."

Irene was pleased, and Van, too. He did not like his school in Antwerp. He did not like the Belgian weather, either. He liked the sun and the sea of Malta.

"Dad, I vote to stay in Malta," he told Harry one day when they were swimming in the bay. But it was Captain Meyer's vote that counted.

Verdalla was an American-run school for children of ex-patriots. It was in Pembroke and, like the clubhouse at the golf course, it resembled a bomb shelter. In this case, it was like several bomb shelters, as it was at one time a large complex for the British forces. It was made, of course, of limestone blocks. Betting on the come, Harry went there one day to investigate enrolling Van. From all he could learn, Van would fit in well. The school went through high school and the students were a mixture of many nationalities. It was expensive, but Air Malta would pay the tuition. Now he needed a new contract, a long-term contract. That was in the hands of Captain Meyer.

113
ANNAPOLIS

May 1997

Malta seemed far away as Harry and Irene sat with a few friends in the stands at the football stadium of the U.S. Naval Academy on a glorious spring morning. They could not have ordered a finer day. It was sunny, clear, blue and bright. They were awaiting, with great anticipation, a fly-by of the Navy's famous Blue Angels flight team. That spectacle would, in a few minutes, begin the day's ceremonies. Today would mark the culmination of an entire week of such ceremonies. Harry and Irene had thoroughly enjoyed them all. The rousing sounds of a Navy band rang out across the field. Harry loved those sounds. "Anchors Aweigh" never failed to stir his blood. It came right after "The Star-Spangled Banner" on his favorite list of such songs. Gathered across the stadium floor were 939 Midshipmen in dress white uniforms about to become Ensigns in the United States Navy. One was their son.

The path Van had traveled from the Verdalla School in Malta to a place on the field below had been a long one. Many hurdles had been surmounted just to get in. Recalling those difficult months, Van once wrote to his dad, "It was hard getting into this place and it's even harder getting out. It's not easy here."

Perseverance had been rewarded with the prize he was about to receive: A commission in the United States Navy. "Proud" was not a strong enough word to describe how Harry felt at that moment.

As he waited, he enjoyed the glow of that feeling. He marveled at the chain of events had brought them to this place on this day. In a way, one of the links of that chain was put in place at the Verdalla School one morning when a new library was dedicated in an old bomb shelter. Doing the honors was the new U.S. Ambassador to Malta. Coffee and cakes were served outside the building after her remarks. Harry and Irene were talking with the wife of one of the U.S. Marines attached to the embassy. As they chatted, the ambassador walked by.

"Hey, there goes our ambassador," said the marine's wife. "Have you met her yet?"

When Harry replied that they had not, she cried out loudly. "Hey, Sally, these people would like to meet you."

Irene often said that a main difference between Americans and Europeans was the degree of formality. They were at opposite ends of that scale. Americans called you by your first name at the introduction; Europeans sometimes never did. Harry saw Irene wince when she heard that cry of "Hey, Sally." Later Irene shook her head and said, "I cannot imagine that happening in Belgium."

The ambassador didn't seem to mind. Hearing her name, she stopped, turned and walked towards them with a smile, extending her hand as she did.

"I'm Sally," she said pleasantly, "and I'm glad to meet you."

They became friends. Later, when Van was applying to the Naval Academy, he needed three letters of recommendation. Harry thought of Sally. Would she be willing to write such a letter?

"I can do better than that," she said, "you write it and I'll sign it."

He got a second letter from close friend and former squadron-mate Dick Ehr. Dick was also from Milwaukee. After losing touch when Dick left the squadron, they found it again when they met by chance in the air terminal at Chicago's O'Hare Airport. It was another of Harry's remarkable coincidences. Incredibly, Dick was flying the airplane Harry was taking to New York that day.

If you say "Dick Ehr" quickly, it comes out Digger and that had been his nickname as long as Harry had known him. Dick was a retired Navy captain and had recently retired as a captain with American Airlines. He was as true and as fine as a friend can be. He had a quick wit and he was smart, as smart as anyone Harry knew, and he had a phenomenal memory. A rabid golfer, he could recall from years past the golf courses and some of the memorable shots he had made on them. He kept track of the courses themselves. He had, by then, played on some 500 different golf courses.

"That could be a world record," Harry told him one day, "have you checked the *Guinness Book of Records*?"

One day, on one of those courses, he watched as Harry hit his tee shot into a water hazard. He stepped up to Harry and held out his hand.

"Congratulations," he said seriously.

"For what?" asked Harry. "Hitting a ball in the water?"

Digger smiled. "Until you lost that one," he said, "you played 114 holes without losing a golf ball."

Harry was astonished. First, because he usually lost balls at a much faster rate, and second, "How in the hell could you know that?" he asked.

Dick grinned. "I just notice those things," he said. "A bad habit."

On a visit to Milwaukee from Saudi Arabia, Harry had made the mistake of asking Dick how the Notre Dame football season had gone. To say that Dick was an ardent fan of his alma mater would be to belittle the word "ardent." Harry heard a detailed report, including a play-by-play description of the entire fourth quarter of a key game against arch rival Southern California.

Dick knew Van well. He wrote an exceptional letter on Van's behalf and handed it to Harry with the words, "Go ahead and change it any way you like." Harry had not changed one single word. Harry believed that these two letters had been key in winning Van a place at the Academy. A third letter, written by the school's headmaster, was icing on the cake.

Of course, his achievements had much to do with it. His scholastic record was excellent. To facilitate entry into a university, Harry and Irene decided to send Van to a school in the U.S. for his senior year. That came after Van himself made it known that he wanted to attend a "real" school for his final year.

"I shouldn't say this," said the Verdalla advisor one day in answer to Harry's question, "but if you can afford it, Van should go to a school with higher standards. He is the only serious student here."

That was enough for Harry.

He investigated several schools and settled on Wayland Academy. By good luck, it was in Beaver Dam, just an hour's drive from Milwaukee. The school looked like one Mickey Rooney might have attended in an "Andy Hardy" film. The campus was right out of a Hollywood movie set. The first clue that the school was serious came after he brought Van for an interview. After waiting in the reception for some thirty minutes, a dignified, elderly man appeared and said, "We are ready now for the interview."

As Harry stood, the man said, "Oh, no, sir. Not you. It's your son we want to talk to."

As Harry waited for Van to return, a well-dressed man with gray hair, wearing a tweed jacket came in, spoke a few words to the receptionist, then turned to Harry, his hand extended.

"My name is Ellis and I'm the Headmaster. I understand you're enrolling your son?" Harry stood and took his hand.

"Yes, trying to. He's in there right now," he answered, nodding towards the door Van had gone through.

"So I'm told. He will be given a short exam, as well as an interview. I have seen his record and it's impressive."

"Yes," said Harry "he's a lot smarter than I am."

Ellis smiled. "They are getting smarter all the time. Well, I wish you good luck. Your son will like it here."

Harry took that last comment as a good omen. He had already decided that this was the right school for Van.

Van did well in the interview and even better in the academics, finishing second in his class. He won a personal letter from President Clinton naming him to the President's Council of Academic Fitness. He won four other awards at his graduation and each time he stepped forward to receive one, the entire student body chanted his name.

"You have to be indulgent," said the Headmaster. "Van has been unofficially appointed the 'King' of his class."

After the interview, the next time Harry saw the Headmaster was the following Fall at a football game in which the badly undermanned Wayland team was being massacred by a team from a military school. The situation was hopeless and, to end the slaughter, Harry, in the middle of the third quarter, overheard the Headmaster send word to the officials "not to stop the clock for any reason until the game ends." That made sense to Harry and he approved the decision with a smile and a "thumbs up." Common sense was not always common.

As salutatorian, Van had given an address. A few days earlier Harry had offered to help. What's your theme, Harry wanted to know.

Van said seriously, "I'm going to reveal who shot JFK."

He never told Harry what he knew about that assassination, but the audience loudly applauded a speech that compared the integration of the varied nationalities at Wayland to a similar goal among nations.

One month later, Harry and Irene brought Van to Annapolis. They had stood together in the queue leading into the induction center on the Academy grounds. Van had not slept one minute, he told them. It's normal, Harry reassured him, to be nervous and excited before such an important day. That was his adrenalin at work. They embraced and waved goodbye as he disappeared into the building, then went to the cafeteria in Dahlgren Hall for coffee and breakfast.

As they sat down and glanced up at one of several television screens there, Irene cried out in surprise. "Look! It's Van."

Sure enough, the screen showed the barbershop where each new midshipman was getting his first Navy haircut. As Van stepped up to the chair, Harry saw him say a few words to the barber, who smiled.

"Just take a little off the top," he later said he had told the barber. He took almost all of it off.

Harry and Irene spent the day touring the Academy grounds. They are known as The Yard and they are remarkable, especially to a Navy man such as Harry. It was his first visit and he felt an emotion he had not felt in a long time. They walked along the Severn River, toured the chapel where John Paul Jones is interred, and viewed its impressive buildings. Monuments of famous Naval heroes were scattered along the walkways crisscrossing its beautiful grounds. One monument was a Skyhawk, the airplane Harry had once flown from the deck of the USS Kitty Hawk. Irene spotted it before Harry saw it.

"Didn't you fly that one?" she asked, as she pointed to the airplane, its wheels up and perched on a thin, round pillar. Overcome by memories, Harry could only nod. U.S. Navy history was all around them. The Academy had begun molding Naval officers in 1845, so it had a wealth of its past to display.

Late that afternoon, Harry and Irene joined other parents in bleachers overlooking the square before Bancroft Hall. This enormous gray building housed the entire brigade of 4,500 midshipmen. The plebes, as first-year midshipmen are called, arrived in military formation and filed smartly into rows of chairs. Harry was impressed. Had they learned that in just one day? They watched emotionally as Van raised his hand and was sworn into the Navy. Soon afterwards, they met with him at the statue of Tecumseh, an Indian chief during the French and Indian Wars. It was a popular meeting point in the Yard. Harry was never able to find out why the statue of that Indian stood there.

Van looked wan and worn. A more forlorn young man, Harry had never seen. His heart went out to him but he knew Van would do well. He was where he had always wanted to be. Since before Van could remember, he had wanted to be a Navy pilot. He had drawn pictures of airplanes by the hundreds, built models by the dozen. He had even built in his room a replica of a B737 cockpit using training panels Harry had gotten from Air Malta. His voyage would start here. They would not see him again until the end of his plebe summer, six weeks away. That would be a summer to remember.

"Yes," agreed Van six weeks later, "one to remember. I would rather forget it, but I don't think I can, not ever."

Their first visit had been just long enough to see Van into the Academy. When they came back six weeks later, they stayed a few days. They took a bed-and-breakfast room in an elegant old mansion in the heart of Annapolis.

It was run by a retired Army officer who, himself, prepared their hearty breakfast each morning.

"You need to start the day the Army way," he told them, "and I'm just the man to help you do that." Asked what was on the menu, he replied "Everything." Denny's could not have done it better.

Annapolis might have been a town uprooted and transplanted from England. Harry had seen a few English towns and Annapolis was a close copy. It is the oldest state capital in the country, they were told, and its dome-shaped capitol building dominated the city. Its main street ran from the dome down to the harbor. The shops and cafes lined the main street, then split and followed the harbor, which was crammed with yachts and sailboats. On the terrace of the Meridian Hotel, overlooking the bay, they had their first meeting with Van. He had lost weight and he looked exhausted. They listened raptly as he described his experiences during plebe summer.

There were many, but one stood above the rest. Among many useless rules, plebes were required to walk only on centerlines of sidewalks. One day, walking along a sidewalk centerline in the Yard, Van met a lieutenant, who was one of his instructors. Van stopped, braced, and saluted, saying, "Good afternoon, sir," as he did.

The lieutenant frowned. "Sir?" he queried. "You don't know my name?" Strain as he might, Van could not recall the name.

By now, a second plebe had arrived behind Van on the sidewalk centerline. Not allowed to leave the line, he came to attention behind Van.

"Perhaps," the officer said to Van sarcastically, "your classmate can help you remember my name."

Van made an "about face" and asked the plebe behind him if he knew the officer's name. He did, and spoke it. Van did another "about face." In the few seconds that took, along with the pressure of the moment, he forgot the name.

The officer was growing angry. He spewed saliva as he spoke. As his anger rose, so did his flow rate of saliva. Van caught most, but some flew over his shoulders and into the face of the second plebe. Unconsciously, he wiped it off. The officer's eyes widened in disbelief.

"What are you doing?" he asked sharply.

"Wiping your spit off my face, sir," the plebe replied.

The officer exploded. "Did I authorize you to wipe my spit off your face? Did I?"

Picturing the spitting incident in their mind's eye, Harry and Irene howled with laughter. Even Van joined in.

"It's a lot funnier now than it was then," he said. "I had no idea what to do. And neither did the guy behind me."

This, he told them, was one very small sample of a day in the life of a plebe.

"Van," said Irene, "you look tired. Why don't you have a nap before you go back?"

Van nodded. "A great idea," he said.

They took him to their room and put him into their bed. He fell asleep instantly. Life at the Naval Academy would never be easy, thought Harry, as he watched Van sleep, but one major hurdle was now behind him.

Malta had been good to them, mused Harry, as he leaned back and scanned the sky for the Blue Angels. Captain Meyer had called Harry one day with the good news that Air Malta would offer him a three-year contract on the B737. The training would be held in Malta for Harry and two other captains. Transitioning to a new airplane is an arduous and comprehensive ordeal. The flying was easy, especially for an experienced pilot. Learning the airplane was the hard part. There were various systems, checklists, emergency procedures, simulator sessions, and more. There was much to learn.

The 737 was a delight to fly. Much smaller and lighter than the 707, and with power boosted controls, it could be flown with two fingers. The 707, on the other hand, in certain flight regimes, needed brute strength to force the airplane do what the pilot wanted it to do. It had never given Harry a hernia but, at times, that seemed to be its goal. It was not unusual to hear a pilot grunt as he maneuvered the 707 for a two-engine landing in the simulator. Another big difference was that the 737 was much easier to land in a crosswind than was the 707. The more Harry flew the 737, the more he liked it. He looked forward to the years ahead.

About one year after Harry completed his checkout on the 737, he answered a knock on his door to find the owner of his apartment standing there. Roger was short, thin, and nervous. He and Harry had gone through several unpleasant disagreements about who was responsible for what. What was wrong now, Harry wondered.

"Do you have a few minutes?" he asked, as Harry waved him inside.

"Of course," said Harry. "How about a coffee?"

Over the second cup of coffee, he told Harry that he wanted to sell the flat. Was Harry interested? Harry had not thought about buying property in Malta because of his uncertain future; but the idea captured his imagination.

He had two years of his contract still ahead with a strong chance of renewal. They liked the place and owning the apartment would mean they could make renovations they had often spoken of. Why wasn't this window bigger? Why was there not a window in the middle of the wall facing the bay? They had other ideas, such as knocking down part of the wall between the kitchen and the living room and installing an arch with a counter. The owner's offer seemed an important omen. Two weeks later, after much discussion and modest negotiations, they bought the apartment.

Two weeks after that, Harry bought a boat. It was a simple dinghy, 12-feet long and with two sails. His only experience on a sailboat had been during a two-week holiday in a 35-footer along the French and Italian Riviera. Harry and Irene had loved it. They and a Belgian couple had rented the boat in Juan les Pins near Cannes and headed east. By noon that first day, they had reached Monte Carlo. They stopped a half-mile offshore for a swim. Then they spread out the food they had bought earlier, opened a bottle of red wine, and enjoyed a pleasant lunch. Harry would always remember that scene: eating sandwiches made with crisp French bread, sipping good French wine, and gently bobbing about as they viewed world-famous Monte Carlo. It was a splendid view and at that moment, Harry decided he would one day own a boat. After buying the apartment, buying a boat seemed a logical next step, especially when he recalled their sailing holiday.

An incident that occured during that holiday stayed with him always. Harry's friend was not the sailing expert he had claimed to be. Arriving in Ville Franche one day, with strong, gusty winds, he was unable to guide their boat into its assigned berth. Afer a long struggle, he was about to give up, when Harry had an idea. He donned a life jacket, tied the boat's anchor to it, then jumped into the water. He swam to their assigned berth, and cut the anchor loose, allowing them to pull their boat to the right spot. A few minutes later, a similar boat arrived. The skipper of this boat was an elderly man with a crew of one girl, of about ten, and a dog. Serenely puffing on his pipe, and without help from his crew, he quickly and easily placed his boat in its berth. There is, thought Harry, no substitute for experience.

Van loved their dinghy and often took his binoculars to the terrace to scan the sea stretching out below their apartment. Was the sea state high enough to warrant a sail? If so, he was ready to go. He and Harry had many adventures sailing up and down the coast along the shores of Malta. Now and then, they ventured into Grand Harbor, where the view from the boat was much different than that from the Upper Barrakka in Valletta. It was stunning in another way because it offered a full view of Valletta and some of its bastions. Harry found being on the sea in a small boat relaxed him in a way no other pastime did.

Now, a loud stirring of the crowd in the Naval Academy stadium broke Harry's recollections. He heard its buzz. He peered intently at the sky, searching for the Blue Angels he knew were coming. And here they came. Sweeping low over the field in perfect formation, they were gone almost before the crowd realized they were there. The thrill of seeing the Blues, even for these few seconds, quickened Harry's pulse. The Blues always did that. He turned to Irene and smiled.

For those few moments Harry let himself wonder whether Van might one day be a Blue Angel. As he sat on the field below, he had in hand orders to flight training in Pensacola. He would be following in the footsteps Harry had put down there forty-one years before. Anything was possible in life, and he and Irene had taught Van to aim high. Becoming a Blue Angel one day was not out of the question, he decided, depending on how events fell. Harry knew Van had the right stuff, but luck was always the unknown ingredient.

Harry had once asked Van if he would like to be an astronaut. Van had pondered that for a few seconds, then replied, "Nah, I'd rather be a Blue Angel." Well, damn, thought Harry, who wouldn't? For a Navy pilot, that was the top of the ladder.

His attention was now drawn to the ceremonies beginning on the dais below the goal posts at one end of the field. A few speeches, more music by the Navy band, and soon the commissions were presented. Vice President Al Gore handed out the first one-hundred. Van, ranked 47th in his class, was among those. After accepting his folder, Van took a few steps, then turned and looked into the stands, where he knew Harry and Irene were seated. He raised his commission and pumped it up and down enthusiastically before he left the dais. Harry, Irene and their small band of friends let out a long, loud cheer. Van could not, of course, hear them, but that did not matter.

114
HANGING UP THE GOGGLES

February 1993

Harry had retired a few months before Van entered the Academy in 1993. That was, in a way, a double blow. Not only had he reached the big six-oh, as Van called it, he had to stop flying. He was still fit, and his flying skills had not deteriorated at all; but the law said he was too old to continue flying. Was he ready for such a major change in his life? He had, of course, given it much thought as the time approached. Well, he told himself, nothing lasts forever and he'd had a good run.

On his first few flights at Whiting Field in Milton, Florida 37 years before, he had become seriously airsick. For a few weeks, it looked like his flying career would be a short one. But he overcame the problem and it had never recurred. Since those first awful flights, he had flown some 20,000 hours. He had made 439 carrier landings, many at night, and flown nearly 100 combat missions. That should be enough, he told himself.

Still, he knew he would miss it. Not all of it, but much of it.

He would not miss the all-night flights to Manchester. The fatigue following such flights took longer to overcome as he got older. He would not miss the way his flying schedule controlled his life in unexpected ways. But he did love his job and he knew he could never replace the sense of exhilaration he often felt in the left seat. Funny, he thought, on the day before his birthday, he was fit and qualified to fly an airliner. The next day, he was too old.

What was the hardest part of coming to the end? There were several. One day a few weeks before his last flight, an attractive older woman boarded the airplane in London. Harry said, "Ah, how is nice!" a phrase he had heard his Yugoslavian first officer use many years before. It had stuck in his mind and he used it often as a compliment to a pretty girl.

This time, his first officer said, "She's too young for you, Harry. Can't be more than fifty."

He said it with a smile, but his remark unexpectedly struck a nerve. Fifty years old and too young! It was true, of course, but he had not before thought of it in that way and it made a hard comment about being sixty years old. My problem, Harry told himself, is that I still feel like thirty-five.

He would miss the beauty of flight. He had, over the years, seen stunning views of the earth below and the sky above. Cloud formations, mountains, sunsets and sunrises, night skies crowded with brilliantly-winking stars: views so splendid that, at times, they filled him with wonder. He had seen the Aurora Borealis several times while airborne and it was indescribable, the most awesome sight he had ever seen. It was, at such times, that he asked himself how such beauty could exist without a creator of some kind. Despite being a non-believer, he was, at times, overwhelmed by the wonder of it all. Long ago, he had read somewhere a collection of quotations from young children. The one that stayed with him was, "Don't forget to look at the wonder." It was sometimes hard to do during the confusion of life, but he always tried.

There were other times, times of dark nights and awful weather. Turbulence sometimes tossed his airplane about like a wind-blown chip of wood. Severe turbulence could cause loose objects to fly about the cockpit. There were times of massive thunderstorms and lightning that did not stop. Weather could cause problems on the ground, too, making takeoffs and, especially landings, very difficult. Airport weather might change unexpectedly, compounding these problems. Such difficulties had never frightened him but the years had made him cautious. He used to welcome such challenges; now he tried to avoid them.

One of his last flights with Air Malta turned out to be one of his worst. It was an early afternoon departure on Christmas Eve. He would take a charter flight to Bristol, a small airport in southern England. He expected to be home for most of Christmas Eve.

The first hint of trouble was the late arrival of his inbound aircraft. That was annoying, but not unusual. Checking the weather, he saw that the destination was below allowed minimums and forecast to remain so. That was more than annoying and it changed everything. He could not legally fly to an airport with such weather. He discussed the situation with the Flight Dispatcher and a solution was worked out. The flight would be sent to a nearby airport from where the passengers would be bused to the original airport. Those waiting to fly to Malta would be bused the other way. If they got lucky, the weather at the first destination might improve and they could land there as planned.

Then Murphy stuck his nose into their plan. During the descent, Harry was nonchalantly informed by air traffic control that the airport had just been closed because the crew that operated the crash truck had decided to go home early to celebrate Christmas.

"Can they do that?" Harry asked incredulously.

"I'm afraid they have already done it," was the reply.

By now the airplane was passing 10,000 feet and he was faced with a dilemma. As he turned it over in his mind, a thought occurred, and he asked for the current weather at his original destination. It was barely above minimums and with blowing snow, he was told. He asked for radar vectors to its Instrument Landing System and then added, "We request no more weather information." The first officer started to object, but then understood. Harry did not want a new weather report that might preclude an approach. The last weather received made his approach legal. A new report might change that.

The runway was short, the ceiling was low, and the visibility was poor. Harry broke out of the clouds well lined up with the runway, then brought the throttles sharply back to idle as he came over its end. No need for a "greaser" this time. He made what is generously called a firm landing and brought the airplane to a stop a few hundred yards before the end of the runway. I am, he thought, as he taxied to the ramp through the swirling snow, too old for all this.

Their old friend Murphy was not yet done with them. As they went through the shutdown checklist, the cockpit door opened and a voice said, "Captain, congratulations. You are the only airplane to land here tonight. But I'm afraid I have bad news."

Bad news? How much worse can it get? He turned to glance over his shoulder at the ramp agent.

"So? What is it? What else can go wrong?"

The agent grimaced. "Your Malta passengers have been sent by bus to Gatwick. We did not think you could get in here tonight. You will need to collect them there. That's from Air Malta at Gatwick. I have just spoken to them."

Harry actually laughed out loud. "Wonderful," he said. "Now we can fly to Gatwick and wait for them. We can celebrate Christmas there! How long is the bus ride?"

The agent grimaced once more. "Three hours, give or take, depending on the roads. Bad weather tonight."

Harry laughed again. "Yes," he agreed, "we noticed that, too."

The weather at Gatwick was better, the agent told him.

Christmas Eve at the Gatwick Airport was certainly different. The first officer found Christmas music on the local radio and played it for the cabin. A stewardess had brought herbal tea and brewed some for the crew. Air Malta came through with first-class meals for all of them. Their busloads of passengers finally showed up in surprisingly good spirits and they were soon on their way to Malta.

"At least," Harry announced to the passengers, after they were finally airborne, "you won't have snow and ice for Christmas this year. There will be no snow in Malta today. There is some nice, warm weather waiting for you there, and the drinks tonight are on the house."

He heard their cheers through the closed cockpit door. Harry was supposed to be home on Christmas Eve. He got there as the Maltese were on their way to mass on Christmas morning.

That flight, and a few others like it, made retirement seem less foreboding. For the last few years leading to the end of his flying career, he had been readjusting his outlook on life. Where to live? That was the first question. During a visit to Milwaukee, he had stumbled onto a housing bargain. Sometimes life worked that way. He had not been looking for a house when one fell into his lap. With retirement in mind, they bought the house and rented it to one of Harry's relatives, waiting. If nothing else turned up, Milwaukee would be a good fallback position.

When Harry bought something substantial, he bought with a view to selling. This house would be easy to sell. It was a small Cape Cod home on a cul-de-sac. That left the apartment in Malta. They had long planned to sell it when Harry retired; but their thinking slowly changed as that time neared. The apartment had two advantages. One was that Malta had no property taxes. Their housing was free. Another was that it was almost burglar-proof while they were away, even for long periods. The more they thought, the more they agreed. Why sell it when it could be used as a winter home? Instead of going to Florida when winter struck Milwaukee, they could return to Malta. They would be long-range snowbirds, but heading east instead of south for the winter had one other advantage. It allowed them to visit Antwerp on the way. Sometimes decisions make themselves. Keeping their apartment in Malta was one of those.

Harry's final flight was to London's Heathrow airport. The first officer flew there and Harry flew back. He wanted to make his last landing in Malta. He did not expect champagne, a band, or newspaper reporters. He did expect someone from the company, perhaps Captain Meyer, to meet the flight and say something appropriate. A photo or two would have been enough. It was, after all, the end of a long and interesting career. There was no one. As the shutdown checklist was completed, the first officer put out his hand and said, "Congratulations, Harry, have a great retirement."

Harry picked up the mike to say a few words to the men in the control tower. He had never met them, but he had been working with them for six years. When he pressed the mike button and opened his mouth to express his thanks, no words came out. He was suddenly and unexpectedly overcome by emotion and, for a minute or two, could not speak. When he finally did, his voice trembled slightly.

"It has been our pleasure to work with you, Captain, and we wish you all the best for the future," one of them answered with sincerity.

It was not a news item in *The Times of Malta*, thought Harry, but better than nothing, and Harry was touched.

115
MILWAUKEE

1993

There are many great differences between Malta and Milwaukee. One was trees. Harry loved trees. They do grow in Malta but they are scarce enough that trees newly planted on the golf course were often stolen the same night. In Milwaukee, on the other hand, large, beautiful trees were everywhere. Harry's back yard held three maple trees reaching fifty feet or higher. Wisconsin in the summer was bright green and held vast areas of rolling hills covered with forests and thousands of lakes, some an easy drive from Milwaukee. During the summertime, Milwaukee had much to offer. Spring showed a glimpse of the summer ahead and that made it promising, despite its changeable weather. Autumn was Harry's favorite season. He liked watching the warm days of September turn cool and brisk in October, changing green trees into splashes of vivid color. But those winters! They turned brilliant colors into white and gray and they could be brutal. Their apartment in Malta solved the problem of Milwaukee's frigid winters.

After Harry's last flight, he decided to test retirement for one year. Then, he reasoned, "If I feel the urge to go back to work, I'll start looking." There were positions in aviation for retirees with Harry's credentials. But Harry enjoyed retirement and, as he sometimes said, "Until I stopped flying, I never realized how time-consuming a job could be." The urge to go back to work never came into his head. There was plenty to do, places to see, friends to visit. He liked the extra time and he especially liked following his own schedule. Going to bed when he felt sleepy and not because he needed to rest for an early-morning flight; that was pure pleasure. Late on some nights in Malta, when the wind was right, he heard the distant takeoff roar of a B737, leaving on an all-night flight to Manchester. Harry smiled to himself, pleased he was not in that cockpit.

And, of course there were regular visits to see Van in Annapolis. They traveled by car and Harry saw parts of America he had never seen before. They crisscrossed Virginia several times, once while autumn was in full, spectacular color. Its beauty awed Harry and Irene. Harry had never known Virginia was so beautiful.

During one of those visits, they attended a football game in the stadium where Van would one day receive his commission. These games were colorful for many reasons. One was an Academy tradition that required plebes, after each Navy score, to race from the stands to the end zone on the field. There, en masse, they performed a number of pushups equal to the total Navy score. The game was against a weak team from Rutgers and the score was lopsided. After each score, there went the brigade of plebes down into the end zone to do its duty. Near the game's end, with the Navy push-ups reaching thirty-seven, Rutgers finally scored a field goal. From the stands on their side of the field, three students dashed into their end zone, flopped down on the turf and did three pushups. The crowd loved it.

Van returned their visits by traveling to Malta for the Christmas holidays. That became harder after he left the Academy but, by then, he was living in places that Harry and Irene could easily visit. The first was Pensacola, where Van was learning to fly. That was memory lane for Harry. They followed him to other bases and, finally, Harry had the great pleasure of pinning Navy wings of gold on Van's breast. That was one proud moment among many for Harry and Irene.

After becoming a Naval aviator, Van was sent to a squadron in Virginia Beach, where he learned to fly the F14 Tomcat. Harry flew the simulator there and was amazed by what this airplane could do. Standing at his side, Van put Harry's Tomcat on the runway at the Oceana Naval Air Station.

"This," Van said, with a professional tone, "will be an afterburner takeoff. Easy. Get airborne on my command but do not climb. Raise the gear and stay on the deck, then call the end of the runway."

I can do that, thought Harry, and he did, starting the clock's timer as he began his takeoff roll.

"Okay, end of runway," he said, as he passed it.

"Check your airspeed," was Van's next order. Harry glanced down at his airspeed and was astonished to read 450 knots, about 520 miles per hour. He had achieved that speed after just two miles of runway!

Now, Van told Harry, "Raise your nose to seventy degrees nose-up and hold it. Call 250 knots."

Harry took his eyes off the flight instruments long enough to glance at Van.

"Seventy degrees nose-up?" he questioned. That would have been unthinkable in Harry's Skyhawk.

Van nodded. "Just do it."

Harry did and was astounded to watch the altimeter wind rapidly around the dial. "Okay," he said, "250 knots."

Van told Harry, "Assume level flight attitude."

Harry did that by rolling inverted, pulling his nose down to level flight, and then rolling upright.

"Check your altitude," were Van's next words.

Harry did and read 34,000 feet! He glanced at his clock to see that less than two minutes had elapsed since he had released his brakes!

Van moved the sim to an aircraft carrier off the coast of Virginia.

"Want to try a couple?" he asked.

Harry grinned. "Sure. Why not? It's only been thirty-five years since my last one."

Harry made three approaches, crashing into the ship's fantail on the first attempt. The next two were on the flight deck but forward of the arresting gear cables. Bolters, but at least they were daytime bolters. It could have been worse.

116
A SEPTEMBER MORNING

2001

Harry awoke in Milwaukee early on a bright, golden morning in mid-September. As he usually did, he did not arise upon waking, but instead, remained in bed for a few minutes looking forward to the day ahead. He would later play golf with Dick Ehr and two other former squadron-mates who lived in the vicinity. They had flown in their first squadron together. The four golfers played together once or twice each month. Bob Schulze and Don Carr lived near each other, just north of Chicago. They would meet at a golf course midway between there and Milwaukee. Although they had served together more than forty years before, their friendship was as strong now as then. It was remarkable, Harry often thought, that such bonds could last so long; but flying together in a Navy squadron forged relationships that lasted forever.

Early in his flying life, Harry had met a retired Navy pilot in a bar somewhere. Around their third drink, the pilot brought up the subject of those bonds. He told Harry to write down the names of all those Navy friends dear to him.

"Write down those names and fold up that paper and put it away," he said. "If you look at it forty years from now, those are the people you will still be close to. It will be those people you'll keep in touch with and send Christmas cards to. You'll go to the graduations of their children, go to their birthday parties; their funerals, too. They'll be friends for life. The Navy does that."

Harry had not written those names down; but, more than forty years later, he had to agree.

A fifth member of that first squadron lived in LaCrosse, on the Mississippi River. Every year or two, Don Gilbert hosted the Lacrosse Open at his beautiful home there. The five former Spad Drivers, comprising the entire field of contestants, would spend a few days playing golf during the day and eating, drinking, and reminiscing in the evening. These grand reunions were highlighted by Anne Gilbert's famous "sticky buns," the featured item on each morning's menu. The golf was mediocre, but the camaraderie was without equal.

Harry threw back the sheets and rose out of bed to meet the day. He slipped into his golf outfit, shorts and a golf shirt, and made his way into the kitchen. Sipping coffee at the table, Irene was glancing through the morning newspaper. Harry leaned down, kissed her lightly on the cheek and said, "Good morning and what's new today?"

Before she looked up to reply Harry picked up the remote control and turned on the television. Just as the screen came into focus, Harry saw a jetliner crash into a tall building. A movie commercial? What the hell is this, he asked himself. He turned up the volume and now Irene was watching, too. In those first few seconds, neither realized the scope of the disaster that had just happened right before their eyes.

They had just seen, on live television, a second attack on the World Trade Center. The first had been only minutes before. As they watched, mesmerized, replays were shown again and again. At times, news is so stunning that it cannot at first be taken in. It was only after the first numbing shock wore off, that Harry could begin to absorb what he had just seen. Then he slowly realized that America had just been struck in a modern-day Pearl Harbor. Was there more to come? A chilling glimpse of what might lie ahead was a scene showing crowds of jubilant Palestinians dancing in the streets, wildly cheering the deaths of 3,000 innocent people.

Harry recalled watching a recent documentary about the Palestinian people. The scene he remembered most vividly, one that he would never forget, was that of a girl of about eight, standing with her arms folded and her eyes burning with hatred.

"I live," she said in a voice charged with passion, "only to kill Jews."

Her face was the face of terrorism; her voice was the voice of terrorism, speaking out in its war against America.

It took some time for Irene to find her voice. "Harry," she said now with anguish, "that is the World Trade Center. We have been there, right up at the top, just a few years ago. Look what they have done to it!"

There were tears on her cheeks as she spoke. Harry remembered the pride he felt when he and Irene had sped to the top of this soaring building in an elevator that made the ascent in only a minute or two.

"Americans," she had said when they reached the top, "can do miracles."

Now, before their eyes, these two splendid towers were brought crashing down in minutes. What was happening?

As they sat riveted to the television, Harry began to ponder where this might lead and what role Van might eventually play. His first thought was to place the blame on Islamic terrorists. There had been many such attacks over the last few decades. They had begun with the hijacking of U.S. airliners in the

Middle East in the early 1970s. The American embassy in Teheran had been seized in 1979 and hostages had been held for longer than a year. In 1983, a barracks in Beirut had been destroyed by a suicide bomber, killing some 240 Marines. In 1986, an American airliner was seized in Beirut and a Navy Seal had been brutally murdered and thrown onto the tarmac. In 1993, in a first attempt, Muslims bombed the World Trade Center. That was a near catastrophe. U.S. military units were twice bombed in their quarters in Saudi Arabia, with great loss of life. Two U.S. embassies in Africa were bombed. Then, in the most brazen attack of all, the USS Cole had been ripped apart and nearly sunk in the port of Aden by a band of Muslim terrorists on a small boat.

Harry believed that the seminal link in this chain of terrorism was the seizure of the U.S. Embassy in 1979. Embassies, by international law, stand on the sovereign soil of their governments. To invade and occupy an embassy was no different from seizing a government building in the home country itself. This was an act of war. If ever a line called out to be drawn in the sand, this was the place. President Carter had an array of options to answer this challenge: diplomatic, economic, financial, and, as a last resort, military. He chose to do almost nothing, mounting with several helicopters a hapless rescue effort that was fated to fail. An unequivocal stand in Teheran would have sent a hard, strong message to terrorists. "Do not play with my balls," is a Flemish expression Harry had heard in Antwerp in such situations. The unspoken part of this message was, "or be prepared to lose your own." That was the time to deliver such a message.

Confronted by his rendezvous with history, Carter turned away. With a firm stand, he might have blunted or turned back the onrush of terrorism. Instead, he showed the world that mighty America was indeed a paper tiger. The lesson for terrorists was clear: America would not fight back. Carter's feckless refusal to take strong action, Harry believed, had led inevitably to the destruction of the World Trade Center he had just seen on television.

This perception of American weakness was reinforced in Somalia in 1993. There, a large American force was sent earlier by President Bush as part of a U.N. force to put down insurrection, violence, and mass murder. Confronted by a war lord named Aidid, the U.S. military met strong resistance. Eighteen Americans were killed; one was seen on world-wide television being dragged through the streets of Mogadishu. Newly-elected President Bill Clinton caved in to media pressure and withdrew his forces.

This lesson was not lost on Osama bin Laden, who had several times declared war on the U.S. He had proudly claimed credit for the destruction of the World Trade Center. His own words, following the American withdrawal from Somalia, were instructive:

"Where was this false courage of yours when the explosion in Beirut took place in 1983? And where was this courage of yours when two explosions made you leave Aden in less than twenty-four hours! But your most disgraceful case was in Somalia; where -- after vigorous propaganda about the power of the United States and its post-cold war leadership of the new world order -- you moved tens of thousands of an international force, including 28,000 American soldiers, into Somalia. However, when tens of your soldiers were killed in minor battles and one American pilot was dragged in the streets of Mogadishu you left the area carrying disappointment, humiliation, defeat and your dead with you....You have been disgraced by Allah and you withdrew. The extent of your impotence and weakness became very clear."

Osama Bin Laden obviously saw the United States as a "paper tiger." Having defeated superpower Russia in Afghanistan, he was now encouraged to take on superpower America. He had good reason to believe he could win. Not militarily, of course, but perhaps on the battlefield of American public opinion.

The United States had retaliated in a meaningful way after only one of the attacks against it. In 1986, President Reagan had struck back at Libya's Kadaffi after his terrorists had killed American soldiers in a German nightclub. He sent bombers after Kadaffi in his homeland. The colonel disappeared from the world stage after that strike. Harry believed that failure to respond to the other attacks had emboldened the terrorists to escalate their war. Would there be a response this time?

President Clinton had clearly lacked the resolve to strike back when he had good reason to do so. He had refused to even take custody of Osama when it was offered by Sudan, his base at that time. Harry had once read that someone -- perhaps Mao Tse Tung -- had written: When meeting the enemy, retreat if you hit steel; advance if you find mush. In Clinton, the terrorists had found mush. How would President Bush respond? Harry believed Bush was made of stronger stuff and would not let this attack go unanswered. But, he wondered, what would his answer be?

Harry recalled the words of Margaret Thatcher some years earlier. When asked the central lesson of the twentieth century, she said; do not appease aggressors if you value the lives of innocent people.

Osama Bin Laden had proudly claimed credit for the horrific acts that murdered 3,000 innocent people. Thank God, thought Harry, that Osama did not have nuclear bombs. He would surely have used them, had he been able, and the rubble of Manhattan would now lie under a mushroom-shaped cloud. Harry believed that Bush must answer this attack in a meaningful way. At some point in this chain of terror, a stand had to be taken; the terrorists must meet steel. Would Bush take preemptive action? Would such action be justified? Would the American people support it? These important questions would be answered in the coming months.

The Islamic terrorists had often proclaimed their intention to destroy the West. Not only would they destroy the West, they would destroy all who stood in their way, including their brother Muslims. In Algeria, for example, news reports had for years described the tens of thousands of Muslims, including innocent women and children, who were murdered because of differences over which Muslims would rule. Such brother-against-brother terrorism was not unusual in that part of the world. The West pretended not to notice.

The mood in Milwaukee was hard to describe. Harry had never before seen such unity of purpose and resolve as he now saw all around him. It was not only grief; it was determination; it was outrage; it was patriotism. A heart-wrenching scene Harry witnessed a few days after 9/11 underscored all these emotions and more.

In no mood to cook, Irene had suggested a take-out dinner from a neighborhood restaurant. As Harry prepared to leave the house, he listened to the television. He heard a voice propose a show of the unity Harry had noticed everywhere during the few days since the attack. Let everyone stand outside his home at the curb holding a lighted candle, the voice said, and let those who did this awful act know that we stand together. Some fifteen minutes later, as Harry drove to the restaurant, he was astonished to see a broken line of people standing curbside, holding lighted candles. Harry felt a rush of emotion as he drove between the gathering lines of candles.

The restaurant was entered through its bar. The kitchen opened to the dining area. Harry had been there many times and he knew how it worked. Standing at the open door leading to the kitchen, he was met by one of the waitresses.

"Take-out?" she asked. Harry nodded and gave his order. "Ten minutes," she said, as she relayed his order to the kitchen.

Harry noticed that although the dining area was full, it was quiet. The mood was somber. Missing were the conversation, the laughs. Even the clinking of knives and forks seemed subdued. Then, in the quiet, a young woman arose and went to stand before the salad bar. She removed from a vase there a single flower. Holding that flower over her heart, she began softly singing, "God Bless America." Another voice joined, then another. Within minutes, every person there, including Harry, was standing and singing from the heart. Harry, like some others he noticed, had difficulty singing. He had never experienced anything like this and his voice was choked with emotion.

117
IRAQ FROM MALTA

March 2003

As events marched along after the disaster of the World Trade Center, it became obvious to Harry that President Bush would, one way or another, lead the country into an invasion of Iraq. Where Clinton failed to act, Bush rolled up his sleeves and confronted the terrorist. First, he neutralized Afghanistan, home of the Taliban and Osama Bin Laden, who had taken credit for the carnage of 9/11. Osama had many times proclaimed his intention to destroy the United States. No one had taken him seriously.

Bush would next take on Iraq. He would do this with the cooperation of the United Nations, if possible, without it if necessary. Despite his efforts to rally the U.N., that body was proving reluctant to act against Iraq, even though its many resolutions over many years stated it would do so. The U.N. believed in diplomacy, not force. It failed to understand that diplomacy without the credible threat of force is ineffective.

The United Nations was established in 1945 to foster world peace. It is ironic, Harry thought, that this entity for peace, can, in large measure, be held accountable for the conundrum that Iraq had become. That was because of its Oil for Food Program, or, as more accurately labeled by General Tommy Franks, The Oil for Palaces Program. This program, initiated and administered by the U.N., allowed Saddam to sell oil. The enormous earnings from the sales were intended to buy food for the people of Iraq. Instead of food, Saddam bought, not only palaces -- 78 of them, to the tune of $2 billion -- but also great amounts of military equipment. With Iraq, and Saddam, on the brink of disaster -- economic, financial, and political -- the U.N. came to the rescue. It allowed Saddam to use these vast funds -- as much as twenty billion dollars, even more by some estimates -- to pick and choose those he would deal with. In exchange for military equipment, selected companies overflowed with rivers of U.N. money, while the Iraqis went without food. All this happened under the direct supervision of the U.N. This was blatant corruption on an unprecedented scale.

The result was that recipients of this largess -- including the U.N., which took for itself 2.2 per cent of every transaction -- accumulated huge profits. Especially profiting were France, Russia, and China. They were chosen by Saddam because each held a veto power in the U.N. Security Council, and could prevent a U.N. resolution of war against Iraq. They did this, and, in the end, President Bush went to war without the official sanction of the United Nations, as did President Clinton in the war in Kosovo, a few years earlier. It can be argued that the United Nations, by allowing Iraq to rearm, was in large part responsible for creating the crisis which ended in the invasion of Iraq. By not only looking the other way, but by actually taking part in these corrupt wrong-doings, the U.N. was key in enabling Saddam to re-build his forces, allowing selected companies to accrue vast profits in the process. The list of those countries which had companies supplying military equipment to Iraq, is long. At its top is France.

Had the U.N., led by France, Russia, and China, had its way, Saddam would still be torturing and murdering his own people; he would still be re-arming; he would still be developing weapons of mass destruction; he would still be invading his neighbors; and he would still be planning to strike his Satans: Israel and America. And France, Russia, and China, would still be piling up mountains of Oil for Food dollars. Despite their best efforts to forestall the invasion, the invasion of Iraq put an end to this money pot. It was not surprising, Harry mused, that they preferred the status quo, and made such strong efforts to preserve it.

At that time, much of the world was convinced that Saddam had weapons of mass destruction. There was an abundance of evidence, much of it from Iraq itself, that it held such weapons. Saddam was, after all, a man who had used poison gas for the first time since WWI, at times against his own people. He had invaded two countries, and sent missiles into Kuwait, Saudi Arabia and Israel. He had tortured, raped and murdered Iraqis by the hundreds of thousands. Mass graves numbering more than 300,000 would one day be uncovered.

He had ravaged our planet by torching hundreds of oil wells in Kuwait. He was, by all measures, a brutal and ruthless despot, one who would do anything, however horrific, to have his way.

Harry believed there was sound reason to remove Saddam. He saw it as a dirty job that needed to be done. He was gratified to read that the U.S. Congress agreed with him and President Bush. An October 2002 bipartisan resolution authorizing military force in Iraq was approved by 77 senators and 296 representatives. Weapons of mass destruction were only one of sixteen reasons listed for using force. Many of those voting in favor of this resolution changed their minds when the going got tough during the aftermath of the invasion. War is not for the fainthearted.

Along with his biological and chemical weapons, there was strong evidence that Saddam was developing a nuclear bomb. There was convincing information that he was allied with Osama in an effort to destroy Israel and the west. The two attacks on the World Trade Center and against other U.S. assets over many years told Harry that a stand had to be taken, sooner or later. If not, the attacks would continue and very probably increase. With solid evidence pointing towards awful weapons in the hands of desperate men, Harry believed America was at grave risk. Invasion carried enormous risk, too. But, thought Harry, there are times when risks have to be faced. This was one of those times. He supported President Bush's decision, knowing that Van would very likely be involved.

Over the years, Harry had often thought about Vietnam and his role there. He had read several books about it, trying to understand what it was all about. He concluded that the interests of the United States were not at risk there. The Vietnamese were not trying to bring down America. Iraq was different. There, forces were gathering to kill Americans and destroy America. The events of 9/11 were, perhaps, only a beginning.

As the invasion neared, Van was flying F14 Tomcats from the USS Constellation. The "Connie" had arrived in the Persian Gulf in December. There was little doubt that he would fly missions over Iraq as part of Operation Iraqi Freedom. Harry would not learn the details of those missions until much later. Now, in his living room in Malta, Harry followed closely the events in the Persian Gulf. The Internet provided much information, and he spent hours at his computer. The graphic scenes on live television were mesmerizing. The concept of embedded reporters contributed much to public understanding of events in Iraq as they were unfolding. Harry saw the war through their lens, not the filters of press releases.

Satellite television had finally come to Malta and, every day, Harry sat glued to his set; watching, thinking. The news usually included strikes by the Tomcats Van was flying there. Every evening, around bedtime in Malta, the television announcer said, "And now we take you to our correspondent on the flight deck of the USS Constellation, somewhere in the Persian Gulf."

It was nighttime in the Gulf and Harry would learn that Van's squadron flew only at night. The reporter usually stood abeam the ship's island and faced aft. As he spoke, visible over his shoulders were Tomcats being catapulted into the night sky of the Gulf. Harry and Irene would never know for sure, but it was probable that one of those Tomcats was flown by Van. It was an anxious time for Harry and Irene.

E-mail helped. They received regular mail from Van on their computer. Harry would never stop marveling at the wonder of email. It was changing the way the world worked. Of course, Van was not allowed to send any information of a military nature and Harry, despite his intense interest, did not ask. Well, he could wait.

The wait would be not as long as expected. One of Van's emails told them about the Navy's Tiger Cruise program. This policy allowed parents of a ship's crew to join the ship for the final sector of its homeward voyage. For Harry and Irene, that meant boarding the Connie in Pearl Harbor and sailing with the ship to San Diego. As passengers, they would be known as Tigers. Would they be interested? Harry was instantly excited and, without telling Irene, told Van to put their names on the list; but Irene needed coaxing. "Living on a ship? With 5,000 people? For six days? I have to think about it."

It took a few days, but Harry finally convinced her that this was the opportunity of a lifetime. He started by reminding her of a day long ago on board the USS John F. Kennedy in Palma de Majorca.

"I remember your exact words," said Harry. "You said, 'I would love to make a voyage on your beautiful ship one day.'"

Irene nodded, her eyes misty. "Yes, that was a beautiful day on your beautiful ship. And I do remember saying that. But I never expected to have the chance to do it."

Harry put his hand on his wife's shoulder, looked into her eyes and said; "Now you have the chance. Don't miss it. You would regret it forever."

Yes, she agreed, there might never be another chance like this one. That Harry would go even without her helped to change her mind. Slowly, over the next few days, she, too, became excited "to make a voyage on your beautiful ship."

They talked of little else for days, and Harry began planning their trip to Hawaii. Then came a bombshell email from Van. There were more candidates than sleeping spaces, he wrote, and some of the names had been removed from the list. Two were theirs. Harry was disconsolate. Irene, who had, by now, become enthusiastic, was disappointed. Could nothing be done? Did you tell them that your dad is a former A4 pilot who flew in Vietnam?

"Dad," Van wrote, "that's the first thing I told them. But it's some kind of lottery system and your number did not come up. I tried everything I could think of, but it looks like you are out of luck."

Harry searched for a way around this setback. By now, he had the ship's schedule, and the Connie would be in Pearl Harbor for five days.

"Irene," Harry asked at dinner, "how would you like to go to Hawaii and see your son come down from the ship. We'll have five days with Van and a Hawaiian holiday at the same time."

This time Irene did not have to think about it. "Wonderful!" she said. "When do we leave?"

527

118
YOUR SIGNAL IS CHARLEY

May 2003

Harry and Irene stood in the port catwalk near the bow as the Connie slowly made her way out of Pearl Harbor on a brilliantly blue and sunny morning. A few minutes earlier, they had been on the flight deck and watched as the USS Arizona Memorial slipped out of view. Now, off to the east, they saw the skyline of the Waikiki Beach hotels and, just beyond, the famous outline of Diamond Head was coming into view. It was a glorious day to be alive and on the way to San Diego, courtesy of the U.S. Navy.

A small miracle had brought them here. That miracle had been performed by Chief Petty Officer Smith, who was in charge of registering Tigers as they boarded the ship for the cruise to San Diego. After their emotional reunion with Van on the pier, he had brought them onto the hangar deck to wait while he tended to his duties. The Tigers were already pouring on board, bags in hand. Harry was more than envious; he was jealous, upset and disappointed. Life was not fair, but this was absurd. Here he was, a former Naval aviator with a combat record, and he had been displaced by one of these Tigers because of a lottery draw.

Harry noticed that after each of the Tigers checked in, he was handed a small bag with "USS Constellation" printed on it. Below, in smaller letters, was, "Tiger Cruise 2003." Could Harry have one of those bags? It never hurt to ask. He went up to a tall, handsome, black man with a flashing smile, who looked very much like Michael Jordan.

"Chief," Harry began, unsure how to phrase his request, "we were supposed to be on this cruise but we didn't make the cut." He went on to tell Chief Petty Officer Smith about Van and about his own carrier past. "Could we have one of those bags for a souvenir? My wife would like to have one and I will be happy to pay for it."

Irene had not asked and he knew he would not need to pay, but it sounded better this way.

Chief Smith listened attentively and said not one word until Harry had finished. Then he spoke. "Sir, let me see if I have this right. You flew A4s on the Kitty Hawk in Vietnam. Your son is a Tomcat pilot on the Connie, and you're not on the list?"

Harry nodded. "That's it," he said.

Chief Smith put a hand on Harry's arm. "Sir," he said after a pause, "please come with me."

He steered Harry to an officer standing near the check-in table and spoke to him in a low voice. Harry could not hear the conversation.

Just then, Van came up from below decks and joined Harry and Irene. Chief Smith returned a moment later. Smith spoke first to Van. "Sir," he said, "I understand your folks are not on the list. If you don't mind, I'll see what I can do to fix this problem."

Van shook his head. "Chief," he said, "I appreciate your interest but I've done everything I can. Nothing worked. Just bad luck."

Chief Smith smiled his gleaming smile. "Sir, you're talking to a problem-solver and I'm going to solve this problem. This is just not right. Where can I find you a couple of hours from now?"

Van guided his parents through a labyrinth of ladders and passageways to his squadron Ready Room. They would wait there. The wait would be long, more than four hours; but Harry did not mind. The place was filled with Van's squadron-mates and their parents and the mood was jovial. The parents, especially, seemed ebullient. And why not, thought Harry. They are setting out on the adventure of a lifetime. Irene, always outgoing and friendly, was soon talking to everyone there. They were impressed to meet a woman from Belgium, even though most had no idea where Belgium was. They had heard of it; they knew it was somewhere in Europe, and that was good enough.

Harry talked with several of the pilots and, before long, had answers to many of the questions he had wanted to ask Van via email. What were the missions like? How long did they last? What kind of ordnance did they carry? How accurate were they? What resistance had they met? He found answers to all these and more. They knew from Van that Harry had flown in Vietnam, and they had many questions of their own.

There were great differences between flying in Vietnam and Iraq. Van's colleagues were astonished when Harry told them that he never flew above 5,000 feet. That was to enable him to roll inverted and pull down towards the ground to get below the arming altitude of the SAMs when a missile alert was sounded.

"Damn," said one pilot. "Over Iraq, we were never below 20,000 feet. The SAMs couldn't get up that high."

He went on to say that on some missions, he had seen scores, perhaps hundreds, of missiles shot up at them and fall short of their airplanes. They were fired without radar guidance because the Iraqis knew that any radar emission would be instantly registered and targeted by a specially-designed missile. In a way, Harry thought, it was how the North Vietnamese had filled their airspace with shrapnel, hoping an airplane would fly into it.

The lengths of the missions were much different. In Vietnam, Harry's normal mission was an hour-and-forty-five minutes. Some missions over Iraq, Harry was told, could last up to seven hours and required in-flight refueling at least once, sometimes two or three times. Although Iraq was a short flight from the ship, there were problems of coordination and traffic. Each flight had to wait its turn. Too many airplanes, he was told, not enough air space. Harry told them about waiting in line to drop bombs on a river crossing in Cambodia. They did not waste bombs on such targets, they told him.

The difference in bombing tactics was night and day. They were incredulous when Harry told them that in Vietnam, he bombed with the "eyeball" system, using only a sight mounted above the instrument panel. These pilots used "smart" bombs that were guided to their targets in several ways. The Tomcat carried equipment that enabled it to bounce a laser beam from a target, then drop a bomb which followed the beam. A Forward Air Controller, on the ground or in a low-flying airplane could reflect the laser beam off a target. Harry knew about FACs. The bombs could also be programmed to hit a target by following signals from satellites. Each bomb carried a backup system using inertial guidance. It was used if the primary system failed. Because they were smart, they were expensive, and any unreleased bombs could be brought back to the ship. That was unlike the Tonkin Gulf, where unexpended bombs had to be dropped into the sea.

"I know they're smart," said Harry, "but just how smart are they? How accurate?"

One pilot smiled. "Oh, within a couple of meters. Close enough for government work."

They could not believe that Harry had, in North Vietnam, seen bombs hit as far as a quarter mile from their targets.

"It's not easy," he said, "when you're down there near the ground and stuff is coming up all around you. And if the weather was bad, well, it was just that much harder. Even finding the target was hard, especially in bad weather. We map-navigated and if you couldn't see the ground, you were out of luck."

"Sir," said one of the Tomcat pilots, extending a hand. "Let me shake your hand. There is no way I could have done that. That was seat-of-the-pants flying, real flying. We do it all with computers. All we need is one good finger. And we have a guy in the back seat to help. You did it all alone."

Harry nodded and said, "You got used to it." He told him that he had flown the Tomcat simulator and, "believe me, what you guys do is for sure a lot harder. I had a helluva time keeping up with the airplane."

The pilot laughed. "So do I. But you'd pick it up in a hurry. I'm not sure I could ever learn to fly the way you guys did."

Just then, Chief Smith entered with a wide smile and a handful of papers.

"Sir," he said, as he handed them to Van, "your parents need to fill these in. Their cruise is approved, but it took some talking."

Smith himself, with approval of his superiors, had taken Harry's case to the top. He went on to say that the delay was because Irene was not an American. The captain of the ship did not have authority to sign the request of a foreigner. That required approval by the Commander-in-Chief of the Pacific Fleet and he, incredibly, could not be found. Eventually, after two hours of searching, Chief Smith had said "Captain, someone needs to make a decision right here. I hope it's the right one."

The captain had shrugged and picked up a pen. "Give me those damned papers," is how the chief quoted the captain.

Once under way, Harry and Irene had looked up Chief Smith, to thank him properly.

"Hey," he said, "it's the least I could do for one of our Navy family. You deserved to be on that list."

Chief Smith was indeed a problem-solver. It was often said in the fleet that Chief Petty Officers ran the Navy. Here was a good example.

Now, the Connie cleared the harbor and turned east into the open sea. Climbing up onto the flight deck for a better look, Harry and Irene watched Diamond Head and Waikiki Beach fade into the horizon. They liked the bracing feel of the salt air sweeping across the gently-rolling deck. Hawaii had been good to the Fergusons. Before leaving Malta, Harry had booked, on the Internet, a room in a hotel near Waikiki Beach. Van had reserved a room while the ship was in Perth, Australia, on her way to Hawaii. In an extraordinary coincidence, their hotels were just two blocks apart.

Waikiki Beach has a special ambiance. Without knowing why, people there feel good. Good feelings were in the air, there for the taking. The beach itself is not special. Harry remembered the superb beach he had once seen in Nha Trang in Vietnam. Waikiki could not compare with it. But it had something Nha Trang lacked and that was a spirit, a feeling, camaraderie, even among strangers. Harry had found it nowhere else.

The beach held the charm of Hawaii: the music, the dances, the culture itself. It also had shops, hotels, terraces, and restaurants. These aspects of a good life would not be seen in Nha Trang for decades, and perhaps never. You could not step off the beach of Nha Trang into an open-air bar, sit down under a palm tree growing between the tables, and sip a Lava Flow. When the Fergusons did that, Harry felt the magic of Waikiki Beach.

Much of the magic came from being with Van once again. It was a pleasure for Harry just to rest his eyes on him, to touch him, to hear him speak. Irene could hardly take her eyes from him. The three spent much of their time together. Harry rented a car and they toured the island. On a visit to the ship, they met Don Ho in Van's Ready Room. This famous Hawaiian singer was warm and gracious. The previous evening, he had hosted Van's entire squadron at his club on the beach. Harry and Irene had, that evening, gone on a dinner cruise, and that was more magic, dining with the lights of Waikiki in view, then watching a delightful show by the youngsters who had just served dinner. Marvelous!

The Connie's crew numbered some 5,500 men and women. Women on a ship were new to Harry, but he soon got used to seeing them moving about the carrier. Eight-hundred Tigers had been added to the ship's complement and accommodations were tight. Irene was berthed in a two-person room, fitted with extra cots, with three other women. She saw it as an adventure.

"It's not the Queen Mary," she said, with a laugh, "but I like it. It's exciting. I'm so glad I came."

To visit the ladies' room she had to pass along a corridor, called a passageway, and go through watertight doors called hatches. The bottom of the hatch opening was about one foot above the deck and bruised knees often resulted from stepping over them. They were called knee-knockers, and Irene had to pass over six of them to reach the restroom. Going to the toilet became a test of courage.

Harry was the third man in a two-man room. He slept on a cot squeezed behind two bunk beds and along the base of two writing desks. Their fold-down tops had to be raised for him to get into bed. His toilet was near, so there were no knee-knockers to contend with. Close spaces sometimes make close friends and by the time the Connie reached San Diego, Harry felt he had known his roomies for years.

The food could not match the haute cuisine served on the Queen Mary, but it was solid and tasty fare. The meals were served buffet style and there was plenty of variety. Simple arithmetic told Harry that the ship was serving about 19,000 meals each day! That number could not compete with McDonald's, but it was done on a regular basis in the middle of Pacific Ocean. That was a formidable achievement.

Other aspects of the Tiger cruise were different from sailing on the Queen Mary. One was an air show on the second day underway. It was thrilling to watch the sleek jets flung into the sky, join together in formations out of view of the ship, then sweep across the sea at flight deck-level. One Tomcat dipped below the flight deck and broke the sound barrier with a deafening roar that rattled dentures and battered eardrums. Harry watched in awe as the pilots wheeled and spun about the ship, doing things he had not even dreamed in his own Navy flying days.

For these shows, Harry and Irene stood on a weather deck above the flight deck. This time, instead of watching anxiously over the shoulder of a newsman on television, they watched in person as Tomcats were fired into the air. The deck was jammed with Tigers jostling to find a place at the rail, one with a view of the flight deck below. Harry was not adept at such maneuvers, but Irene was an expert. Slowly, she wriggled her way through the throng, pulling Harry behind her, as she gently pushed and coaxed her way to the rail. There, the view of the jets being launched was exhilarating. Harry, like all Navy pilots, never tired of watching airplanes operate from the carrier. For Irene, it was the thrill of a lifetime.

There were tours of the ship, and Harry found himself in places he had never before seen. One was the station beneath the flight deck where the arresting gear cables operated. Entering the space with a small group, Harry and Irene were pleased and surprised to see that the man in charge of this vital part of bringing jets aboard the ship was Chief Smith. He welcomed them with a broad grin.

"Good to see you again," he said. "How are you enjoying your cruise?"

Harry and Irene grinned back. "Fabulous," said Irene, "and all thanks to you."

Chief Smith nodded, still smiling. "Happy to help," he said, and then went on to explain to the group how the arresting gear cables worked.

Afterwards, Harry went to Smith and said, "Chief, I've landed on these ships 439 times and, until now, I never knew how I did it. Thanks for the tour. And thanks again for our cruise."

Smith once again smiled his dazzling smile. "My pleasure, sir."

One night, there was an amateur hour on the hangar deck, and a Steel Beach Picnic was held one fine afternoon on the flight deck. The airplanes were rearranged to make space, and it was filled with charcoal grills and the familiar aroma of hot dogs and hamburgers being barbecued. There were mountains of potato salad. Chocolate brownies and ice cream topped the menu. A band near the island blasted out popular music and Harry understood not one word of the lyrics. The captain had turned the ship downwind and, at just the right speed, there was no wind across the deck. Footballs were thrown across the wide expanse of the landing area. This festive beach party, moving slowly through the Pacific Ocean towards San Diego lacked only warm sand and cold beer.

When the Connie was some 400 miles from California, the ship's aircraft were sent home. Van flew one of those airplanes, and Harry and Irene watched the pre-flight briefing in the Ready Room, then climbed up the superstructure to view the launch. They watched as Van manned his plane and was, in his turn, catapulted from the ship. He banked his airplane towards San Diego, the first stop on the way to his home base in Virginia Beach. That was an emotional moment and a very proud one. The airplanes would land in about one hour. It would take the Connie another two days to get there. Without its flock of airplanes, the ship looked barren. The empty flight deck appeared even vaster than before, and the hangar deck became a gigantic cavern. Harry could not recall being on an aircraft carrier without its aircraft and it was an unusual sensation.

Before leaving Hawaii, Harry bought a cellular telephone. To open an account, he had to give personal data to a young lady with a friendly and pleasant voice. One item she needed was a personal codeword that could be used to identify him. Like what, asked Harry.

"Oh," she answered, "your favorite color, or your favorite singer. Whatever."

"Ah," said Harry. "That's easy. My favorite singer is Frank Sinatra." There was a pause.

"Could you spell that, please?" she asked. Harry chuckled into the telephone. "Frank Sinatra. You don't know Frank Sinatra?"

Another pause. "Sorry," she said, "but I've never heard of him."

Harry spelled the name then added, "You should listen to him sometime. You can actually understand what he is singing."

Her comment made Harry realize how far from his past he had come.

Before leaving their hotel, Harry had picked up his new phone and called two numbers in California. The first was to George Parker, a squadron-mate from Harry's first squadron at Miramar Naval Air Station in San Diego. As Executive Officer, George was second in command. Harry had learned much from George Parker. He had learned about being a fine Naval officer, as well as a sound pilot. His nickname was Shorty, and someone had once posted a group photo of the squadron's pilots with a caption above each pilot's head. The one above George, who was standing behind a row of kneeling pilots, read, "I finally made the back row with the big guys." George Parker's low body altitude had not stopped him from being one of the best pilots Harry had flown with.

During the Korean War, George had found a special niche in the lore of Naval Aviation. On a mission from the USS Princeton, a pilot had been hit in the canopy of his aircraft, and shards of plexi-glass had struck his face. Blood flowed into his eyes in a way that he was unable to see. Using verbal instructions, his wingman managed to guide him back to ship. There, two LSOs, one on the platform and the other in Pri-Fly, somehow talked the blinded pilot safely down onto the flight deck. One of those LSOs was George Parker. This near-miracle was featured in the film, "Men of the Fighting Lady."

Harry and George had kept in touch through the years. George had eventually retired in San Diego and now Harry called him. They were arriving on the Connie; would he like to meet for dinner and a drink, perhaps two?

"I'll meet you at the pier," he said, without a moment's hesitation, "and the dinner will be on me."

George invited Harry and Irene to stay with him and his lovely wife, Alice, "for as long as you are in town." Ah, thought Harry, how good friends can make a good life.

His second call was to Jeanne. They had not kept in touch until a few years ago when, one day in Malta, Harry found in his mailbox a postcard from San Diego. It was from Jeanne. She had gotten Harry's address from a mutual friend and decided to write. How are you doing, she wondered. They communicated now and then, first by mail, then on the Internet. There were long gaps between their letters.

Harry could not believe he was nervous about phoning her. He felt like he was back in high school and calling for a date. Her answer was warm. She would love to see him again and could he call when the ship arrived? They would arrange a meeting. Her voice sounded exactly as he remembered and Harry felt a tiny thrill when he heard it. He had not expected that.

"How long has it been?" she asked. "I've lost track."

Harry had not lost track. "Would you believe thirty-eight years?" he responded, trying to keep his voice light. There was a pause.

"Wow, imagine, thirty-eight years! Well, you should have a lot to tell me. Do you still drink martinis?"

Harry smiled into the telephone, remembering. "Yes, believe it or not, I do. But not as often as I used to. How about you?"

She chuckled softly. "Only on special occasions. I think this might qualify. What do you think?"

He could almost see the smile in her voice.

Harry thought for just a moment. "If this doesn't qualify, then nothing ever will."

"Call me," she said before she hung up.

At 1000, the ship would come alongside the pier at the North Island Naval Air Station. The Kitty Hawk had left for the Tonkin Gulf from that same pier a lifetime ago. Now, the wheel of life had brought Harry back to the place he'd started. Harry's experiences on the Kitty Hawk had defined his life. He thought about that life now as he stood on the flight deck, peering off into the early morning mist, searching for the first sight of land. The mist, he knew, would slowly dissipate as the sun rose higher. The ship would not berth for another hour, but Harry was eager to see California again.

A man makes countless decisions as he travels through life, and some of those decisions were in Harry's mind now. The funny thing about decisions was that you knew only the road taken, not the one bypassed. Unlike a fork in the road, a man cannot go back to a decision point and start over. A man had to live with his decisions. It did not help to speculate on what might have been had he taken the other road. That led to regrets. They could be devastating, and Harry tried to avoid them.

The greatest decision in his life was his resignation from the Navy. He thought about that decision often, even many years later. Had he done the right thing? Did he have those awful regrets? Sometimes late at night, mulling over that decision with a drink in his hand, he wondered if he had lost his nerve. At the time he made it, he was thoroughly convinced he had not. It was a simple protest of the way the war was fought. He was willing to give his life for his country, but not like this. He did not believe the war, fought in a way that could not be won, was worth his life. Still, many comrades had gone to the Tonkin Gulf two, even three times. Some did not come home. Who knows, he would tell himself, whether you might now be part of a hillside in North Vietnam had you not resigned. No, he usually decided, you did your duty as you saw it and there was no dishonor in that. But late at night, every now and then, he had his doubts.

There had been another option. Naval aviation was voluntary. He could have surrendered his wings, avoided being part of the war, and stayed in the Navy as a ground officer. He had not thought about that possibility until a friend brought it up one night at the Flying Spinnaker. He did not consider it longer than a few minutes. Not only did his wings represent an arduous eighteen months of learning to fly "a nickel at a time," they made him a member of a truly extraordinary brotherhood. He valued that beyond words. No, there was no way he could give up his wings of gold. They meant too much.

Harry had taken a month to reach his decision to resign. Two other important decisions, taken a few miles from where he now stood, had been taken in moments. That was the night on Mount Soledad when he had decided not to propose to Jeanne and asked her not to visit the Kitty Hawk the next morning, before he left for Vietnam. It was hard not to have regrets about that night. He convinced himself over the years that it was not meant to be. Still, he sometimes mused, handled differently, it might have been.

He would never know what might have been. He did know what was. That was a life doing what he loved to do, seeing much of the world, working with interesting people in interesting places and above all, Irene and Van: the treasures of his life. There were no regrets when he thought about them.

Almost as if he had called her name, Irene appeared on the catwalk, shielded her eyes from the sun, and looked about the flight deck, searching for Harry. She spotted him, waved, climbed the few steps leading onto the deck, and walked quickly towards him, smiling. Any regrets lingering in Harry's mind vanished at that moment. Her eyes were bright with excitement.

"Isn't this wonderful?" she asked with her usual enthusiasm. "Almost there! And just when I was beginning to know my way around the ship."

They slept in different parts of the ship but usually had breakfast together. This morning, Harry had climbed out of his cot early. He wanted to be on the flight deck when the ship sighted land. And he wanted to call George Parker.

She kissed his cheek, then noticed his cell phone. "I see you have your mobile," she said, using the European term. "Are you calling your friend?"

Harry squinted into the mist, still straining to see land. "Trying. No luck so far. Too far out." Irene looked too.

"No land in sight, is there?" she asked. "Which friend are you calling? Your pilot friend or the other one?"

By the "other one," she meant Jeanne. Harry had told her about Jeanne and she had only smiled and said, "What happened before me, happened, and it has nothing to do with me. Or us. At least, I hope so."

Harry said, "I'm calling George. I'll call Jeanne tomorrow. I know how eager you are to meet her," he teased. She only smiled. Harry put his arm around her shoulders and turned her to the east. "Look!" he said with a trace of excitement. "California!" Its dim outline was just becoming visible through the thinning mist.

California had always held magic for Harry. He had loved living there and he had long planned to return one day, permanently. But the winds of life had other plans. They had blown him across the world. Over the years, California somehow faded from his future. Life has a way of changing plans; but he loved visiting there and now he was excited to see it again.

By now the flight deck was becoming crowded with Tigers, all with cell phones, all trying to call the United States from several miles offshore. Finally, George answered.

"Harry," he said, "I'm on the way. I'll be there when you pull in. Call again after you're alongside and I'll tell you where I am. I'll look for you on the forward catwalk. If we don't connect, I'll meet you at the bottom of the brow. Alice is making a nice lunch for us. She says, 'Hello'."

Harry had not seen George Parker in many years, but he was sure that when they met, it would be as if those years apart had never happened. Friendship can do that, and George was a friend.

"Irene and I are looking forward to seeing you. Alice, too. We'll see you at the pier. Drive safe. We don't want to miss that lunch."

George laughed and said, "See you soon."

San Diego is a Navy town. As the ship slowly closed with the shore, and with Point Loma now clearly in view across the water, signs of the town's affection for the Navy began to appear around the ship. First came the large motor yachts, then sailboats joined the welcoming committee. The air was festive and the boats were filled with people celebrating the return of the USS Constellation, home from the war. Many boats carried hand-lettered signs of welcome. "Well Done, Connie," read one.

Now several tug boats took charge of the ship. Gently, they nudged the giant carrier into position alongside the quay. Harry and Irene watched from the catwalk as the crowds gathered below. There were thousands, and many of them carried signs, too; most of them personal, directed to someone in the crew. One such sign was a message to a sailor standing next to Irene. It was held high by his brother. His mother and his sister were there, too. The excited sailor nearly fell overboard when he saw it, jumping, waving and screaming hoarsely, at the top of his voice. Two bands blared out music for all of San Diego. One was a military band and the other played mariachi music. Both seemed appropriate. Harry noticed two television crews on the pier, and Alice Parker later told Harry that she had seen him on CNN.

A fireboat passed back and forth throwing streams of high-pressure water in high arcs across the harbor. Several helicopters buzzed around the ship. Cars on the far side of the water blew their horns as they passed. All of San Diego seemed to take part in this grand welcome for this great ship.

Harry had seen these celebrations before, both from the ship and from the shore. Very likely, this would be his last. As he looked across the scene before him, he felt an emotion well up from deep within. He realized, as never before, that the Navy would always be in his heart. His bond with Naval aviation had not ended when he left; it simply moved to a different viewpoint. His Navy friends would always be there, and so would his feeling for this great service. His memories from his years as a Navy pilot, the good ones, along with those not so good, would be a part of him forever. It was right that his last cruise, his Tiger Cruise, had ended in San Diego, where it had all begun. San Diego and the memories he had made here would always be a vital part of him.

At that moment, his cell phone rang. He barely heard it above the tumult. He clicked it on and pressed it closely to his ear.

"Hey, Harry, I see you up there," said George Parker. "Your signal is Charley, and welcome home."

*Girls of
the
Orient.*

The Author as a "Nugget" in VA 145. 1957

The Author, left, with George Shattuck and Don Gilbert. The cigars celebrate their 100th landings on the U.S.S. Oriskany in 1960. This ship was the carrier used in the film, "The Bridges of Toko Ri."

This photo, taken by the author; shows Skyraiders from the USS Ranger flying over Corrigidor in Manila Bay in 1959: These aircraft were from Attack Squadron 145, the author's first squadron. Aircraft 501 is flown by squadron skipper, Cdr. Bill Alexander

This drawing of a T2 Buckeye is by Van Rypel. As a student, he flew this airplane in 1999. Thirty-seven years earlier, author Ron Rypel flew the Buckeye at the same base as a flight instructor.

Future and former Navy pilots in the cockpit of an Air Malta airplane.

The author climbs into a Buckeye in 1963.

Belgian Tour Guide.

With bright blue eyes and blonde hair, Van was the delight of the Thais in Bangkok. At times he was swept off the sidewalk and kissed by women who found him irresistible.

Another woman who found Van irresistible was the lovely Jennifer Stone of Annapolis. They married there in July 2003.

Irene with newly commissioned Ensign son, Van, in Annapolis. 1997

Van tries captain's hat and shoes. 1975

Delaney Anne joined the Rypel family in February 2006.

The Rypels, with popular entertainer Don Ho, in Van's squadron Ready Room on board the USS Constellation. The ship was in Pearl Harbor after returning from Operation Iraqi Freedom in May 2003.

At the Key West Naval Air Station, Van Rypel becomes the U.S. Navy's newest Lieutenant Commander in March 2007. Looking on are Jen and Delaney Anne Rypel.

An F5 Freedom Fighter stands with the Rypels at the Key West Naval Air Station in May 2006. Van flew this aircraft as an aggressor pilot, training fleet pilots in air combat tactics.